The Fool's Progress

The Fool's Progress

du honest

(a novel)
^

EDWARD ABBEY

Henry Holt and Company • New York

The Fool's Progress is a work of fiction. Although
based, as any earnest novel must be, upon the author's
experience, understanding, and vision of human life,
he has made no attempt to portray actual persons or to
depict actual events; each and all are totally imaginary,
any resemblances accidental, any likeness a coincidence.

Copyright © 1988 by Edward Abbey
All rights reserved, including the right to reproduce this
book or portions thereof in any form.
Published by Henry Holt and Company, Inc.,
115 West 18th Street, New York, New York 10011.
Published in Canada by Fitzhenry & Whiteside Limited,
195 Allstate Parkway, Markham, Ontario L3R 4T8.

Library of Congress Cataloging-in-Publication Data
Abbey, Edward, 1927-
The fool's progress.
I. Title.
PS3551.B2F6   1988   813'.54   88-4677
ISBN 0-8050-0921-3

First Edition

Designed by Jeffrey L. Ward
Printed in the United States of America
10 9 8 7 6 5 4 3 2 1

Parts of this novel first appeared, in different form, in *City Magazine, New
Times, Confessions of a Barbarian* (Capra Press), and *Slumgullion Stew: A
Reader* (E. P. Dutton).

SIR SAMP: Has he not a rogue's face?
Speak, brother, you understand
physiognomy; a hanging look to me.
He has a damn'd Tyburn-face, without
the benefit o' the clergy.

FORE: Hum—truly I don't care to
discourage a young man. He has a
violent death in his face; but I
hope, no danger of hanging.

From William Congreve's *Love For Love* (1698)

The Fool's Progress

A Prelude

Henry . . . ?

Hen-reeeeee! Henry Lightcap!

The teacher stood in the open doorway of the one-room school-house, looking out. A woman in her fifties, thin, anxious, exasperated. She wore a cotton print dress that came down to her ankles, a light sweater; her pale hair was drawn tightly to a bun on the top of her head. In one hand she held a brass bell with iron tongue, the wooden handle of the bell polished by years—by decades—of use.

She advanced to the doorstep of the building, stopped and looked up and down the dirt road before her. To the east a quarter mile away the road passed between the house and barn of the nearest farm; westward the road wound through a second-growth forest of hardwoods, disappearing into deep shade. On either side of the schoolhouse lay open fields of grass, beaten down by the running feet of children, intersected with pathways still muddy from recent rain. Both fields and roadway were empty of any human form.

The teacher stared intently into the woods of the hillside above the road—a scrubby growth of sapling trees barely beginning to leaf out, tangled jungles of sumac and laurel, dogwood and wild grape, the rotting remnants of a split-rail fence. Nobody there? The shadows of afternoon clouds folded slowly across the hill. Impatiently, angrily, she shook the heavy bell. The jangle of brass rippled outward through the soft and humid air. Nobody answered.

Shading her eyes with her free hand, the teacher peered far off into the shadows, toward the blue ridges of the Allegheny Mountains rising steeply into a hazy smoke-colored sky.

1

Hen-reeeeeee! the woman shouted, into the silence the trees the distance. No reply. She paused, took another deep breath, chest expanding. You, Henry Lightcap! she yelled—You . . . get . . . in . . . here. . . .

She waited.

No response but the whispering of the leaves, the insects in the brush, a breath of air in motion—and from the farm up the road the rattle of team and wagon coming off the barn ramp.

The teacher waited. From behind the window near the door a cluster of hovering children stared out through the glass. Large-eyed faces, freckle-skinned and towheaded—solemn little girls with bright hair and ribbons, smirking little boys in bib overalls and blue chambray shirts buttoned formally to the throat.

For one last time, as she had often done before, the teacher hollered up at the woods on the hill, pitching her voice toward the paired ears she thought were up there somewhere, toward that boy she imagined hidden under the laurels, hugging himself in mingled fear and delight. Henry! she cried—and her voice, trained by the years, carried well, carried all the way to the top of the hill—You there, Henry Lightcap! . . .

And one last time she jangled the bell.

But there was no answer from the green and vernal, the deep and haunted, the dark transpiring forests of the Appalachian hills.

1

IN MEDIAS RES, ARIZONA

I

. . . slamming the door behind her. Slams it so hard the replastered wall around the doorframe shivers into a network of fine reticulations, revealing the hand of a nonunion craftsman.

I listen to her booted feet stomping over the graveled driveway, into the carport. (The "car-port"!) Then the vicious brittle *clunk!* of car door likewise slammed. God but that woman has a temper. Shocking. Now the thunderous roar of four-cylinder Nipponese motor starting up, the squeal of burning rubber, the yelp of a startled dog as she skids around the broomplant, past the dead saguaro and down the lane toward the street. Past the mailbox and fading away, out of my life again forever, into the dim inane of Tucson, Arizona.

I see police helicopters circling—blinking red like diabolical fireflies—above our doomed damned beleaguered city. Red alert. Elaine is on the loose.

Woman. Wo-man. Womb-man. Woe-man.

Easy come, easy go. My first and no doubt false reaction is one of relief. An immense and overwhelming sensation of blessedness. There never was a good war or a bad peace, as Abe Lincoln or Ben Franklin said. (We had similar troubles.) I sink slowly into my easy chair, hers actually, but it's all mine now. For the moment.

Gloating, I look around "our" living room. Our "living" room. All those books jammed in their shelves—all that B. Traven and R. Burton and M. Montaigne and James M. Cain & Co., all them Sibelius Stravinsky Shostakovich Schubert records etc., Waylon & Willie & Hank Senior, that stereo, that 1922 Starcke upright grand, the Franklin stove and the leatherbound basket chairs from Mexico, that big solid blond slab table of California sugar pine, a master-piece of the joiner's art, nothing but dowel pegs and butterfly joints, not a nail or screw or touch of glue in the whole thing—wealth. I am rich, rich at least for the next few days or until her attorneys get to work on me.

And so forth. When I hear the word "settlement" I reach for my checkbook.

The power of property. I will sell everything in this house in the next twenty-four hours, everything not bolted down; convert our goods into something better, cash, and buy a cheap houseboat on Lake of the Ozarks. No, Lake Tahoe. I have always wanted to live on a houseboat. No rent, no mortgage payments, no gas, sewage, garbage, phone or electric bills, live on catfish and bluegill, grow a hydroponic garden of my favorite vegetables—the carrot, the po-tato, the bean, the turnip.

Henry indulges himself in a favored fantasy. I shall live the clean hard cold rigors of an ascetic philosopher. A dive into the icy lake at dawn. Two quick laps around the shore. A frugal breakfast of cool water and unsalted watercress, followed by an hour of medi-tation. And then—then what? What then? Then I'll row my house-boat ashore, jump into my rebuilt restored 1956 Lincoln Continental four-door convertible and speed away to the nearest legal whore-house for some quick fun & frolick before lunch.

The GM Frigidaire in the kitchen, that giant and neurotic ma-chine, starts revving its engine. Sounds like a Boeing 747 warm-ing up for takeoff. I've never known a refrigerator that works so hard at keeping cool. For two years I've been living in the same house with this monster and I'm still not accustomed to it. I never will be.

The noise increases. An ugly hatred grasps possession of my soul. I march to the bedroom, take the revolver from under my pillow, enter the kitchen, confront the machine. Vibrating, roaring, the Frigidaire presents to me its bland broad bronze-colored front. On the door panel a bunch of magnetic letters say, "Go to Hell Henry." I raise the revolver—a .357 Magnum—cock the hammer, fire. Point-blank, right through its smug face. A black round hole appears in the center of the door, the letters slide down a few inches but main-tain rough syntactical order:

GO TO HELL HENRY

Losing cool through its new nostril, the Frigidaire roars louder than before. Or am I hallucinating? Going down on one knee, taking no chances, I fire into the base—once, twice—through the grille into the motor into the bowels the guts the living quivering glands of the machine. The cogs whimper to a halt, shutting down the condenser and compressor; strands of black smoke and the smell of Freon issue from beneath. I've hit some vital parts. But now I hear the buzzing of a stalled electric motor. Sure, I could simply pull the plug, cut off the Frigidaire's life support system. Would be the merciful thing to do. But I want to *destroy* this mad molecular motherfucker, fix it so it never breathes again, never again grates on the tranquillity of a contemplative mind. I poke the muzzle of my piece through the shattered grille, into the furry dust and black-widow cobwebs of its underparts, and point toward the motor. Pull trigger—BLAM!—and there's the screech of lead slug, hollow-pointed and dilate, smashing through a clutch of copper coils.

Silence.

My ears ring but I've settled this bastard's hash. I rise to my feet and tuck the revolver into my belt. Peace. Stillness. A beauteous calm reigns in my kitchen, except for the usual background noise, from the city, of a diesel freight train clattering down the rails, of the endless caravan of forty-ton Peterbilts, Kenworths, Macks, Whites, grinding along the Interstate, of air-force jets screeching through the air a hundred feet above the campus of the University of Arizona, reminding those pointy-headed professors and idle scheming students who—or rather, What—is really Boss around here. I close the kitchen windows, the better to enjoy my freedom. The refrigerator takes off again.

The noise this time comes from the top of the machine, from the fan and defrosting mechanism, thermostatically activated, in the rear of the freezer compartment. A separate motor? Evidently. There are two rounds left in my handy handgun; I open the freezer door, shove aside the frozen chicken and frozen boxes of Lean Cui-

sine (Elaine's) and blast two holes through the fan vent behind the
ice trays in the back wall. The little fan scratches to a final stop. I
dig a handful of ice cubes from the tray and fix myself a drink. My
hands are shaking. But not from this trivial shooting.

Sit down.

How can she do this to me? Damn her anyway, how can she be
so cruel, so heartless, so—violent? At such a time, with total disaster
weighing on my heart? You picked a fine time to leave me, Elaine.
How could she know about that? You had a month to tell her and
you never quite got around to it. But ignorance is no excuse. Goddamn her, how could she be so cold and bitter and full of hate?

Familiar emotions. I've been through this ordeal before, a number of times. I know the sequence. First the abrupt departure and
my immediate sense of liberation. That passes quickly. Next comes
the anger, the rage, of which our defenseless Frigidaire has been
first victim. (I look around for other targets. That electric range
with its console like the dashboard of an airplane? That electric
water heater in the closet with no exterior temperature controls?
The air-conditioning unit on the roof? How about the telephone on
the wall, unplugged at the moment but always a threat?)

Relief followed by outrage. Those are the first two stages.
The third stage is the worst and it will come soon enough, about
three o'clock in the morning: The Fear. The Terror. The Panic—
awakening in the dark to find myself, as I had dreamed and dreaded,
alone. Again.

That will come. Meanwhile we've got a half quart of the Wild
Turkey to see us safely past midnight. And if that fails? I draw the
revolver from my belt and look it in the eye. I tilt the muzzle toward
my face and try to see down into the black infinity of the rifled
bore. Like this:

Absolution. The thought of suicide, as Nietzsche says, has got me
through many a bad night.

I put my tranquilizer away. Some other time, perhaps. In fact,
knowing what I know, knowing what I have been told and shown,

there's no perhaps about it. The natural right of self-slaughter. Always a viable option, a good working alternative. No other animal on earth enjoys so free a choice. No one has a right to complain about life because no one is compelled to endure it. Who said that? I'm hearing voices already.

I look around the silent kitchen. Nobody here but me and in the freezer, beginning to thaw, the frozen chicken. Life is hard? Compared to what? Anxiety got you down? Try fear.

She's not coming back this time. Ahead lies another long dark night of the soul. Her parting gift: despair. And so on, that much is clear.

Time for palliatives, ameliorants, placebos. I rise from my chair, feeling numb and wooden, and choose a record album from the shelf. Wolfgang Mozart, Gustav Mahler or Willie Nelson? Ernie Tubb or Giovanni Palestrina—old pal of mine. I feel the need for something gruesome but hearty. Soul music. I stack the spindle with the *Resurrection* Symphony, flip switch, turn volume up to nosebleed capacity and retire hurriedly to the shelter of the kitchen. The first great magnificent chords blast through the walls and rumble up my backbone at the rate of 33⅓ revelations per minute. Good man, Gustav. . . .

Yanking down the bourbon bottle, I pull the cap and take a quick preliminary suck, like a calf at cow, before filling my glass. Easy on the ice. A dash of the branch from the tap, good old Tucson City Water, rich in trichloroethylene and other industrial solvents. My hand is shaking. Remember your glands. Easy, easy, got to taper off on this stuff, all things in moderation, there's less than half a bottle left. Courage: God will provide. Paracelsus called it the elixir of life. Like him I'll get shitfaced fallingdown snotflying toilet-hugging drunk. Reality management.

Mahler. Bourbon whiskey. What else is available? Music begins where words leave off but even music is sometimes not enough. Trapped in my own soap opera, I yearn toward grandeur. (But not grand opera. Not those screaming sopranos, those tensile tenors, that athletic howling of the damned: musical entertainment for people who hate music.) What I want is a quiet decorous classical tragedy with a few belly laughs thrown in for fun. A farce with funeral.

What else is available? The telephone. The telephone hangs there

7

on the wall in mute black Bakelite. Lifeline. Hope. Reach out and grab somebody with a drowning embrace, a stranglehold of want. Goddamn their eyes. I plug the thing in and open my book of numbers. It's Will I'd like to call, of course, but pride forbids. He ain't heavy but he's my brother. Maybe later. What you really need, when the horse throws you—

The phone rings. At once, out of habit, I unplug it. When I want electronic communication I'll initiate it myself. I'm in no mood for taking calls from unidentified parties. The ideal telephone is the one-way telephone. Don't call me I'll call you. Maybe.

I find the number I'm looking for and replug the phone in. It's ringing. Still ringing. God Almighty—maybe it's Elaine, smitten by remorse.

"Lightcap here."

"Good God Henry I've been trying to get you for ten minutes. Your phone's always busy. Are you okay?"

"Who's this?"

"It's me—Joe." (My next-door neighbor, McReynolds.) "I thought I heard gunfire."

"I heard it too, Joe, off in the brush out back. Some gun nut."

"Did you call the police?"

"What good would that do? I went out and ran him off myself. Sicced the dog on him. Excuse me, Joe, I've got to hang up on you now." I close the connection for a moment, lift the receiver and dial a number. Her phone rings. Rings again. Phone ringing in an empty room. Melanie, you tricky little fox, where are you when I want you? No answer.

Hang up, unplug phone. Think. I could call this lawyer I know. His estranged wife is picking his bones, he's as angry and helpless as I am. Henry, he said, I'll murder your wife if you'll murder mine. We'd both have perfect alibis. Be a hundred miles away in a public gathering when the crime takes place. And not even a crime in this case, except in the narrow, legalistic sense of the word, but a public service. At least if Elaine were defunct, suddenly murdered or run over by a cement mixer, I'd not have to suffer so much from guilt. My sense of loss would be mollified with little injury to pride.

Contemptible sentiments. Ashamed of myself, I open the bottle, pour. Whom should I call?

8

Mahler plunges into his second movement, the angels appear above a thunderous barrage from the kettledrums: the march macabre in bass viols of the *Dies Irae* booms through the house. We'll have no resurrection yet, not until sides three and four. Another fifteen minutes of burial alive.

If only good sweet Kathleen was here. A reliable rainy-day woman. She could cure my blues anytime. She'd pull off my shirt and jam my head in her kitchen sink, shampoo the scruff from my scalp and soul, then drag me down to the rattan mat on the floor and knead my neck, back, shoulders, lash my bare body up and down with her mane of wet heavy maple-golden hair. When my hard-on became so enormous it was jacking me up from the floor I'd roll over, clutch her in my tentacles, force entry into the handiest orifice. Take you home again, Kathleen?

I notice that the oven light is on. That Elaine, she's left the oven turned on again, no wonder it's so bloody hot in this bloody stinking kitchen. But the little red bulb gives me an idea. I'll bake a loaf of bread. My wife has left, our dog is dying, my job hangs by a hair, God and Nature have betrayed me, there's no Kathy here to shampoo my head, no Melanie to floss my teeth, I'll fool them all and bake another loaf of bread. That always helps, not much but some, and right now I need whatever help I can find.

I get out bowls, wooden spoons, measuring cups, yeast, milk, butter, salt, sugar, flour. Real flour: Hungarian stone-ground whole wheat. Old Will, naturally, that proud pompous sonofabitch, grinds his flour in his own little hand mill, mounted to a five-hundred-pound butcher's block. Sometime tonight I'll write the letter:

> Will. Dear Will. Listen, farmer, I'm in trouble again. Need some help. Would you mind if I dropped in for a month or two or three or four? . . .

I mix the yeast in water, stir, set aside for a moment. Mix warm milk and melted butter, add the foamy yeast, add salt, sugar, stir again. Sift and sprinkle in the good nut-brown flour, the crunchy wheat berries, and mix with a wooden spoon in the big wooden bowl. Thinking of the green green grass of home. Of Brother Will. Of our tough sweet beautiful mother in her seventies, quietly but indomitably vigorous, walking the hills, doing her work, leading that geriatric choir at church every Sunday morning.

Home is where when you have to go there you probably shouldn't.

Knead your dough. Sprinkle flour on the board, fold the fat warm living dough into its own center and mash it down firmly but gently—don't bruise the living yeast cells—over and over, working the outside through the inside until everything is satiny smooth as a baby's bottom.

I grease another bowl with butter, flop my glob of pale brown breathing dough into it, cover with damp dish towel and set on top of fridge, over the hot-air vent, under the ceiling. Now let it rise, double in volume, a genuine resurrection, an authentic miracle. Which was the worthier technological achievement, the moon landing or the invention of bread? The bake oven or the nuclear reactor? Only a fool would hesitate to answer.

My Frigidaire is strangely quiet and generating no hot air. Stone dead—for a moment I'd forgotten. I contemplate its fatal wounds with pleasure. Nothing more satisfying than a gut-shot refrigerator. Down with General Motors. If Will can do it I can do it. Cut the lines. Break loose. Blast free.

Mahler winds down, fading into reverie. Time to invert those disks. Refilling my drink—long night ahead—I advance to the stereo, turn the records and retreat quickly to the kitchen before the twin speakers catch me in their convergent blast. But this is the fourth movement (out of five), not a great baying of horns but a gentle female wave of choral voices *pianissimo*. . . .

In music lies the ideal world, the closest we'll ever get to immortality. Whether it's Mahler or Louis Armstrong, Gregorian chants or Japanese bamboo flutes or some grog-rotten Celt on yonder bonnie ridge braying like a jackass through his bagpipes loud enough to raise the dead—it's resurrection. Temporary but true, like life itself. Weeping in my whiskey, I plug in the phone and dial Andrew Harrington, M.D. My friend, always on call.

"Andy, I need a recipe. An antidote for pain."

"Try agony."

"I tried that. This is worse. Can't sleep, Andy."

"Well, read a book. Read some—Balzac. Or George Eliot or Anthony Trollope or Thomas Hardy. One of those analgesic Victorian novels."

"I'm baking bread."

"Ah-hah! So she's left you again."

"Again? Andy, I hear the wings of death flapping over the roof."

"I see. Keep talking."

"She's moved in with Whatshisname. That computer science professor."

"Sounds indicative." A pause. "Well, Henry, you had fair notice."

"A computer science professor!"

"Yes, I know." Another pause. "But she tried to tell you. Anyone could see it." No answer. "Come on over, Henry, I'll sit up with you. I can't sleep either as a matter of fact."

"Can't, Andy, my dough is rising." I looked; indeed it was. Doubled in size.

"Well," he says, "don't do anything weird. Get rid of those damn guns. Call one of your old girlfriends. Bake your bread, take some aspirins and go to bed. That'll be thirty-five dollars please."

"Listen, Harrington, I don't need good advice, I need some pills. Real potent pills. I feel lower than whale shit."

"What're you drinking?"

"The same old stuff."

"No pills tonight. Dangerous. Turn your tube on, they're showing *Treasure of Sierra Madre* on channel nine, best movie ever made. Turn your tube on, keep drinking, take three aspirins, fall on the floor and get some sleep. Have lunch with me tomorrow."

"Sure, Andy."

"Call me in the morning. Or I'll call you. Don't disconnect on me." Pause. "You hear me?" Pause. "Henry? You still there?"

"Still here."

"All right. Be careful."

I hang up. At once the phone begins to ring. I unplug it and take down the bread, the warm sweet dough, and lay it on the board. I punch the air out, rolling it over and over, shaping it into a nice fat oblate blob, and place it in my greased baking pan. Back to the refrigerator top, warmest spot in the kitchen. Let her breathe and swell for another thirty minutes, O staff of life.

The whiskey and ice percolate through my kidneys; time to relieve some pressure. I stumble to the bathroom, flicking switches as I go. Conserve power. Keep the utilities in trouble. Unzipping, I piss into the washbasin. Perfectly sanitary, much tidier than pissing into the toilet bowl from the male position, splashing hot piss over the rim and floor and rug and shower curtains. Could've pissed in the kitchen sink but the sink is full of dirty dishes again. What a slob that woman is. Was. Well now, with her gone, we'll have some *Ordnung* around here, some "ordered liberty," as our neofascists like to say. What's worse than a knee-jerk liberal? A kneepad conservative, that's what, forever groveling before the rich and powerful. Anyhow, we'll have stability now, control, discipline, centralized administration.

The face in the mirror grins at me. Little squinty eyes with veins of gaudy red, like Christmas tree baubles. Jaw bristling with whisker—needs a shave. Hair greasy as a groundhog. Need a shit, shave, shower, shampoo—probably a shoeshine. But still don't look as bad as I feel. Nor feel as bad as I look.

I shake and squeeze it, trying to expel that final drop. Fail, as always. The last jewel trickles down my thigh when I pack the thing back in its nest. Sign of middle age, perhaps. The dotage of the dong. The Grim Raper falters. What of it. For forty years, ever since boyhood, I've been bound in servitude to this cursed thing with a mind of its own—but no conscience—leading me about like a dog straining on a leash. Nothing but trouble. Down with romance.

Check the bread. Almost ready for the oven. A few more minutes. Now what? Shall I call Ingrid in Denver? Lynell in Santa Barbara? Becky in Seattle? Nancy in Phoenix? One o'clock by the clock—better not. The bitching hour. They wouldn't understand. What would Brother Will do? What would Tolstoy do? Montaigne? J. Prometheus Birdsong, all my other heroes dead and gone?

Alas, there is no remedy. No shampoo by Kathleen, no gluteusmaximus vibrato by sweet Melanie, what's a man to do?

Nothing but bourbon. And on solo flute, the dark secret bird of night. And my loaf of bread. Shall I call the boys—Lacey? Ferrigan? Arriaga? No, leave them in peace.

Even the bars will be closing soon. Too late now for a heart-to-heart chat with Cindy and her swelling bosoms. (They're big, she says, but they're not very practical.) Or with golden-haired Sunshine and the tattooed butterfly on her thigh. Or Laura with the wicked and perjuring smile, and Whatshername and so on, they'll all be bolting off soon on the buddy seats of Harley choppers, each

12

with one hand hooked in the waistband of the greasy blue jeans of her dope-dealing gun-smuggling child-molesting black-bearded beer-swilling pool-shooting ugly dirty evil old man. Bores and whores, all of them, but—fascinating. The smell of sin. That cock-eyed coke-sniffing glister in the eyes. The smell of lust and money. The smell of salt, sweat, Listerine and sweet papaya juice. . . .

My bread has risen. Check the oven: 375°F. I pop in the loaf and close the oven door, refill my glass and retreat to the easy chair in the living room, followed soon by the fragrance of baking bread. Even the smell makes me feel better.

Mahler explodes into his grand finale, vast heavenly choruses arching across the sky. An outburst of joy, clouds of exaltation piled on exaltation and then—a fierce short coda followed by silence. That golden stillness. "Silence always sounds good," said Arnold Schön-berg, explaining the odd pauses in *Pierrot Lunaire*. How true. Es-pecially in the tortured agonized manacled music of Arnold Schönberg.

But my wife—?

Plainly, she is not coming back. I can tell by the pattern of the cracks in the plaster. There's a code there, a message. Like the secret message in the final bars of Shostakovich's fifteenth and last sym-phony. Faint cryptic signals, like the clicking of a telegraph key, against the remote and sustained monotone of the violins—a song from outer space. What was he trying to tell us?

But Elaine, how can she do this to me?

She has her reasons.

II

Are you listening to me?

I looked up from this book: Jaynes or somebody on the origin of consciousness or something. What?

Are you listening to me?

Yes. Sure, Elaine. Of course.

What did I say?

What?

What did I say? Glaring at me.

Well . . . Trying to restore the unity of my broken-down bicameral mind, I stammered, Well, honey, you said—what you always say.

You never listen. Off in a world of your own. What lousy company.

I like it.

It's all you know. She shook her light brown hair from her eyes— those fine Liz Taylor eyes, smoldering with anger. Couldn't blame her one bit. Turned her eyes away, giving me the model's profile: the classic Nordic symmetry of vertical forehead, dark arched eyebrows, charcoal lashes emphasized with mascara, a short straight middle-class nose barely *retroussé*—but why go on with this tedious inventory? Everyone knows the formula. Who cares?

Well now, we do care, don't we. Men care and women care because the men care. We're trapped in our biology, why not enjoy it? She was a trim little WASP—white-Anglo-sexy-Protestant—not a perfect beauty, a bit thick in the thigh and short in the leg, but more or less the type the whole world adores. Thanks to our planetary communications system, magazines, movies, TV, videocassettes. Blond hair, rosy skin, slender figure—why is it that men everywhere, from Fairbanks to Tierra del Fuego, from Oslo to Capetown, from Lisbon to Calcutta, yearn to clutch this creature in their arms? Two and a half billion men on the planet—and every one, apparently, prefers a blonde. Including me. Why?

Who knows? Envy of the power and prestige of Europe and America? Some strange racial longing for the glow of the golden North, a hidden evolutionary drive toward this particular archetype? Are the angels, as we once imagined, really honey-colored honkies? The thought is too cruel to be borne. And very much taboo. But who can doubt it? Artificial female blondes swarm the streets of every nation—but where can you find girls naturally fair dying their tresses black, wearing brown contact lenses, trying to widen their hips or shorten their legs?

It's not fair. Life is unfair and it's not fair that life is unfair. Is there no justice in the world? And no mercy neither? No wonder they hate us—and hate us so much—down there in the lower hemisphere.

She turned away from me, my fair Elaine. Finally. Finally gave up. No more argument, no more debate. I heard her packing a bag in the bedroom. A small one—she'd already moved most of her personal things to her boyfriend's place, Professor Schmuck, cyber-netician. Seymour S. "Shithead" Schmuck. (Tomorrow I'll kill that guy. Tonight I'm baking bread.) Minutes later she was gone, slamming the door.

Was it all my fault?

I love you, Henry, she'd say.

You'll get over it, Elaine, I'd say, always kidding. And she did.

You say you love me, she'd say, but you don't show it. She was young, too young, only eighteen when I first clapped eyes—and then my hands—upon her. You don't show it.

What do you mean? I said. I'm crazy about you and you know it. Look at this thing.

I don't mean that.

Well what do you mean? I mean, Jesus Christ, I mean what do you want me to do? I mean what do you *mean?*

I can't tell you. If you don't understand there's no way I can tell you. I mean if I have to tell you you'll never understand.

I see. My heart sank like lead beneath the weight of her incomprehensible phrases. I'd turn away and she'd turn away and I'd pick up a book or put on an Anton Bruckner or Tom T. Hall record or go for a ten-mile walk in the moonlight or she would leave, slamming the door. Much to my immediate relief. I always loved the sound of my wife walking out the door, starting her Jap automobile, vanishing into the filthy city. To visit a friend? A relative? A relative friend? She was gone to visit her lover. And I never guessed or cared enough to guess. As long as she returned before morning I was content. I was a fool but happy.

Longing for my Elaine, I plug in and telephone Melanie. Lovely Melanie. Lovely aroma of fresh bread in the kitchen. But who wants to break bread alone?

Yeah? She sounds sleepy. Melanie, it's me. It's late, Henry. I know sweetheart, but I was thinking of you. I'll bet. I miss you. You're drunk again. I love you, Melanie, desperately. Yeah, when you're desperate you love me. Melanie, I want to tell you something. It's almost two, Henry; some of us have to go to work in the morning, you know. Tomorrow night? Maybe; maybe later. You still love me? I adore you. That's not what I asked. Have to go now, Henry. Wait a minute. Good night, Henry. . . .

Click, followed by the electronic whine, as of cosmic mosquitoes or background radiation, of the dial tone coursing through the circuits. Transistor static. I detest that noise. Music is natural, static cultural. I unplug the phone, just as it starts ringing, and open the oven door. My bread is ready, waiting for me. I grope for hot pads, pull out the pan, empty the loaf from pan onto tabletop. Perfection. A hot firm shapely loaf, golden brown, sweet as a virgin's haunch.

Breaking off the heel of the loaf, the best part, holding the warm and crusty chunk in my hand, I reach for the bottle of Wild Turkey, now almost empty, and slide down the wall to the kitchen floor. A bite of bread, a swallow of bourbon—God's on the job.

Nothing really helps. I should go for a long walk into the desert, take my agave stick, my pistol, our doomed dog, my jug of Gallo's Hearty Burgundy, fall in the gulch, finish the wine, shoot the dog, take a piss, vomit. That would help. Go to sleep on the cool sand while tarantulas creep on their eight dainty hairy feet across my face, pausing to stare with sixteen compound eyes into the cavity of my ear. Then moving on, twitching a leg, to pastures new.

Courage. I crawl from the kitchen into darkened living room, feeling along the wall for light switches, remove Mahler from the phonograph and install my hero the great American Charles Ives. An insurance executive, like Wallace Stevens, and our best composer yet. Symphony no. 4. At top volume, certainly: let the walls rock, the cinder blocks cringe, every nostril in the neighborhood bleed. I crawl for safety back to the kitchen under the terrific crashing chords of the opening—dual pianos in a black rage, followed suddenly, quietly, by strange cloudy fantasies of mingled New England village bands, a fireman's parade, a churchly hymn, the ghost effects and haunted cemeteries full of Union dead. Nearer my God to thee, the chorus sings, sort of. I think of Mother's choir. I think of family, of clan.

My great-great-uncle John Lightcap, half-starved POW, escaped from Richmond's Libby Prison in 1863, spent two weeks sneaking homeward through Confederate territory living on goober peas, chanterelle mushrooms, dandelion greens, arrived in Stump Crick, West Virginia, in time to learn that his son Elroy was dead, killed only a week before by bayonet at the Battle of Gettysburg, 150 miles to the east. Pickett's last charge. Roy Lightcap's last stand. Uncle

John's last war. Hain't fightin' no more in Lincoln's dirty war, he said, resigning the captain's commission to which his men had elected him two years earlier. He's so powerful strong on stompin' down the South and keepin' the Union big, let that cold-blooded murderous sonofabitch go down there and fight his rotten war his own self. And take his coward son with him. . . .

Maybe I should see a psychiatrist. Two I've noted in the phone-book: Doctors Glasscock and Evilsizer. Or some kind of analyst: a barium enema, a proctoscopic probe. All-Bran and psyllium pow-der. The enema within. Join a Kundalini therapy group and take part in mystic Oriental orgiastic rites. Write a book. Call it— *Cluster-Fuck: A Presbyterian Looks at Group Sex.* I may be the only redneck intellectual in America who's not yet been analyzed, psychoanalyzed, rolfed, TMized, estered, sensory-deprived, re-born, spinologized and had my colon irrigated. Never did get to know those spiritual amphibia crawling in and out of Esalen hot tubs.

Once as a matter of fact I did let Elaine bully me into attending a group encounter session. She believed in it (that season) and felt I needed the treatment. And why? What's my problem? Well, I have this queer thing about pretty girls: I like them. And this weird thing about steady jobs: I don't like them. I don't believe in doing work I don't want to do in order to live the way I don't want to live.

And so she paid twenty-five dollars to get me in a group. I snuck out after ten minutes of holistic gender blending, having enjoyed about as much as I could stand. All those warm fuzzies and fearless feelies massaging one another's emotional pudenda:

Who are you? says this man I never saw before, staring at me with the pale eyes of a codfish. We sat on the floor facing each other, paired off like the others, knotted up in the lotus posture. (No chairs in the room.) Okay for bandy-legged little Asiatics but hard on a native American. All but me, I saw at a glance, were veterans of these rituals, self-absorbed and comfortable. Another Lost Gen-eration. We should've told them to stay lost.

Who are you? he says again.

Well, the name's Lightcap. Henry H. Lightcap.

Who are you?

What?

Who are you? He stared at me.

I get it. It's a game. Okay, who am I?

Who are you?

I looked around: the other pairs were doing the same, one asking Who are you? over and over, the other responding in therapeutic manner. Only the session leader, a little hairy man from Topanga Canyon, California, was not taking direct part in the game. He lounged in a corner of the room supervising, a warm loving smile on his terribly sun-baked face. Too many years spent staring into the sun, I suppose, trying to dissolve the old subject-object dichotomy that Descartes (they say) imposed on us. It's a "personal universe"; every window really a mirror. (They say.) We are a bunch of windowless monads—nomads?—groping for return to the womb of total nullity. But let's be open-minded about this.

Near the leader, leaning on the wall, was a bundle of foam-rubber bats; later these people would pound one another with foam rubber, venging their frustrations in harmless futility. What good is that? Impotence breeds fury.

But the leader looked pleased. Since there were eighteen customers (patients? clients? acolytes?) in the group, he'd just pocketed eighteen times $25—$450 in legal tender. Not bad for one evening's work. Enough to pay for his first skin-cancer treatment. Bald-headed bushy-bearded fat-bellied little guru, no wonder he looked upon us with such warm regard. WE ARE ALL ONE, his T-shirt said. That's a filthy lie, I thought, an insult to human potential.

Who are you? my partner kept chanting.

Why? I said. (He was getting annoyed. My answers were wrong. I saw tension at the corners of his mouth.) Why who?

Who are you?

Who! I hooted like an owl. Who, who!

Who— (A tic in his left eyelid.)

Who who who!

Fisheyes hesitated. He blinked several times. Who, he began again—

The group leader interrupted. Okay people, time to switch. Now let your partner ask the Big Question. He checked his watch.

My opposite number relaxed. This part he liked. Hang loose, his manner said, keep cool and floppy-necked like a quiche eater in a Naropa fern bar.

Okay, I says, so who are *you?*

He sighed, closing his large moist eyes. Who am I, he began, announcing not a question but an overture. I am a mote in a sunlit pool, he said. I am a photon of conscious light waltzing with electrons in the blue of the ether. He smiled.

That's a lie, I said. Who are you?

Eyes closed, head tilted back, smiling with euphoria, he went on. I am a neutron in a cloud chamber, twinkling from quantum to quantum. I am a dancing Wu Li master floating through the Universal Mind.

I waited. His mouth opened then closed as I said, You're lying. You're a fish-faced grouper faking his way through a group encounter ripoff. You've been robbed of twenty-five dollars.

The itchy little tic reappeared in his left eyelid. Who am I, he sighed again, working hard to keep his cool lukewarm. I am a molecule of organic energy on the ocean of eternity, finite but unbounded.

There's a piece of shit on your lower lip.

He frowned, reaching toward his mouth. Then stopped. Who am I, he chanted. I'm an attorney named Willis Butz—I mean, no, I'm, I'm nothing and I am everything, I am you and you are we and we are all one.

One what?

What?

One what?

He stopped. He opened his eyes. He glared at me. Who the hell *are* you, you bastard, and how'd you get in here?

I left. But not before recovering Elaine's twenty-five dollars from the Head Fuzzy-Wuzzy. Give me my money back, I muttered in his ear, while the others were flailing backsides with their soft limp bats, or I'll make an ugly scene. The guru frowned, mumbling something about no refunds. I'll tear this place apart, I said. He glanced around, smiling and nodding at the lambs who were watching us, then invited me to step outside. Expecting a karate attack, I followed cautiously. In the hallway he said, Now what's your problem?

Just give me back my twenty-five dollars.

You're a sick man, he said gently. You need help.

Give back that money, I said, or you'll need help. I mean medical help. I was bluffing, of course, but stood eight inches taller and outweighed him by forty pounds. In the actual world, as opposed to the world of dancing Wu Li masters, bulk is important. You're running a nasty little racket here, I added, and you better watch out. This is Tucson, Arizona. We got high ethical standards here.

I do a lot for these people, he said sweetly. That's why they keep coming back.

If you really helped them they wouldn't have to come back. They're a bunch of aging adolescents and you're keeping them that way.

He looked up at me with soft empathic eyes, that cooked-brown, fried and refried face. Do you realize that you are going through a midlife crisis?

The whole world is going through a midlife crisis. I held out my hand. The twenty-five.

The world is an illusion.

I know. But it's the only one we got. The money, please.

He returned my money. You shit, he said over his shoulder as he walked away.

I didn't argue. Let every man be his own guru, every lady her own gurette. Such is the latest holy word from Swami-Roshi-Yogi-Rambanana Bung.

Laughing all the way to the Dirty Shame Saloon where I found myself among friends—Lacey, Arriaga and Harrington. I want to buy a drink, I said, for every man in the house, if any. When Elaine's twenty-five dollars was gone I drove home at a slow, safe, sedated pace, unnoticed by the "authorities," parked under the carport, threw up in the driveway, crept into the house on hands and knees as a brain-retreaded pilgrim should and fumbled around for the light switch. I knew it was somewhere on the wall. But where was the wall?

The lights blazed on.

She glared at me. Her turn now. You bastard! she said. (That word again.) And started to cry. It took half an hour of my wormiest cajolery before I could wrap her in my lawful loving conjugal arms, thirty minutes more until we became one flesh.

But what sweet succulent soothing flesh.

Elaine.

20

III

Actually I'm thinking of Melanie again. And the monogamy problem. When I stepped from her shower, toweling my wet head, dripping over her bathroom rug, she was waiting for me on the toilet seat, head high to my groin. At once she took my flaccid tool in her mouth and sucked on it thoughtfully, like a child with lollipop. Melanie, wait a minute— But she knew what she was doing, she knew the way to a man's heart. I did not love her, as such sentiments are commonly understood, but I sure was fond of her. And growing fonder by the moment. I've never met a nymphomaniac I didn't like.

She drew back her head and gazed with pride at what she had done. Swollen, upright, proud. I stepped on the bathroom scale. We looked at the pointer. My God Melanie I just gained five pounds.

We will now have a brief intromission.

IV

I gnaw my crust, inhale the fumes from an empty bottle. She loved me, did she not? Elaine, I mean. Nearly three years together, through the better and the worse. It seemed much longer. And now, suddenly, she is gone. I feel her absence as a tangible, living, palpable presence. But when I look—she is not here. Where she was is nothing. The void. The intense inane. A psychic amputation.

Henry raises his dark head, sees himself reflected in the black night glass of the window. Deux Henris! A homely man with coarse black oily hair, buzzard's beak, jaw like a two-by-four. He grins his evil wolfish grin. Nobody so wicked in appearance could feel such pain, right? Stands to reason. But the face fades out, obliterated by ennui, leaving the empty moronic grin which fades in turn.

He howls softly like a dog and beats his forepaws on the floor. That helps a little. Not really. There is no remedy. O Death thou comest when I had thee least in mind. Winter in the heart. Antarctica in my soul.

He senses within his head an avalanche of whiskey-sodden brain cells losing their purchase on stability, sliding like a mudbank into the landfill of his cerebellum. Whole tiers and galleries of corrupted gray matter fall with a CRASH! into the sinkhole of his spirit.

He thinks of the cheap paneling above the urinal in a bikers' bar on Speedway. On that wall where graffiti are inscribed with knife blades, some condemned soul in the fraternity of the damned had written

> *No chance*
> > *No hope*
> > > *No escape*

So what. What of it. Keep sliding, let it fall, somewhere down in here we'll hit bottom, reach bedrock and bottom out. And then, like this honest loaf in my hand, we'll rise again. Villon says,

Mort, j'appelle de ta rigueur . . .

Death, I challenge you to do your worst, you who ravished my mistress, stole her from me and will not be satisfied until you have me too in your clutches. I challenge you to do your worst. You're called. Let's see your hand.

According to the latest microbe biologists my body is *really nothing but* a megalopolis of unicellular organisms. According to the theories of the chief witch doctors of the new physics (now about eighty-five years old) we and our sweethearts, our women, our children, our friends, our pet dogs, are "really" nothing "but" a whirligig of swarming subatomic events, ephemeral as mayflies on a breezy day in spring.

Is that so. You don't say.

Ignore them. They haven't got Henry Lightcap in a circuitron or under their electron microscopes yet—and they never will. The world is bigger than those metaphysical black-hole sphincters will ever understand. One man—with a woman in his arms—outweighs their whole slimy universe of nuclear ectoplasm, graph-paper abstractions and Day-Glo polka-dot electric Kool-Aid scientific pointillism.

That's what I think and my name is Henry Lightcap. Henry H. Lightcap. Henry Holyoak Lightcap, by Christ and by damn.

Jesus, this bottle is empty. My bread is cold. There is no woman in my arms. Take another piece of bread, Henry, and think of something. Of what? Of something. Think of—

Alicia. Melody. Gertrude. The prettiest girl I ever knew was named Gertrude Dieffendeffer. The second prettiest was Eleanor Barff. Or how about—Caroline? Lola? Birgit? Candace? Demerol? Percodan? One thinks of heavy sedation at a time like this. .357? A .44 Magnum? Should go gunning for Dr. and Mrs. Schmuck. Load the old twelve-gauge, one barrel for each. A crime of passion. No decent jury would convict. They'd be weeping throughout the public defender's summation. Manslaughter, at worst. Maybe negligent homicide. Get my picture in the papers. Be a hero, swamped with hand-penned letters from lovesick females. Phone ringing like a burglar alarm with calls from ladies sick for love.

It's no help. Think, Henry, think.

He grins the grin. Keels forward on his face, thinking: I've got to see Will. Got to get to Will's. There just hain't no alternative. But God—three fucking thousand five hundred fucking miles east of the Santa Cruz River. Too far. So late.

Will, why ain't you here.

V

Where am I now? (Panic.)

Black in here as a witch's womb.

He rises to hands and knees, feels along wall for light switch. Click. No light. (Terror.) Maybe I'm dead. Dark as a tomb in here. Try switch again. Still no light. That's right, the bulb, never did change that bulb. My God for a minute I thought I'd gone blind. Or died. But where am I anyway? Which bulb? Last time I looked I was in the kitchen eating bread by the light of the oven, remembering Melanie, recalling Kathleen, missing Elaine.

He listens. The house seems strangely quiet. Then remembers—the Frigidaire is dead. Shot in the bowels and left for junk. He gropes forward, feels the picture-window draperies in his hands and pulls, hauling himself to his feet. The drapes come down and he falls with them, stumbling over one of Elaine's footstools, end tables, table lamps, coffee tables, piano benches, some goddamned thing. On his knees again.

Good sweet Christ, he prays.

But has succeeded at least in admitting light to the room. Through the window he sees a multitude of lights—a city—and over the eastern mountains the eerie red glow of one more cloudless dawn. A false dawn? Perhaps. But where? What city? What world is this?

"Elaine," I call. No answer. "Elaine?"

At once the sick despair rises in my veins like an injection of some lethal drug. Like an overdose of lithium. To hell with that. I'll not yield this time. It's a new day a-dawning. It's the new Henry Lightcap here on hands and knees, tongue hanging out like a Technicolored necktie and we're fighting it this time, boy, I tell you boy no little woman is a-gonna keep Henry Lightcap down for long. Not Henry *H.* Lightcap.

Lightcap rising with the morn. I hear a cactus wren chatter outside in the cholla thickets, the sharp clear whistle of a curvebill thrasher, the lonesome peep of a phainopepla, the true song of a cardinal or maybe it's a mockingbird. And my name is Ivan Ilyich, by God, and I'm crawling up from the dead. Lazarus returns. This here is Lightcap speaking, men, and it takes more than a woman, more than half a quart of Wild Turkey, more than another routine marital disaster, more than one more standard moral catastrophe, to keep old Henry down.

I stand up on my two feet like a man.

Something cold hangs from my open fly, limp, long, lonely as a snake. I tuck it in and zip up. Let us have—music! Coffee! Sausage and eggs! Time for the quick emotional lift, then the caffeine, then the basic American grease fix.

A gray light fills the room, dim but good enough to see by. Music first. I sit on the shaky bench before our old-time cabinet grand and stare at the keys. Eighty-eight keys that open the door to a nicer world than this. I lift my hands, straighten my back, and hammer out—*fortissimo*—five great six-digit Lightcapian chords: C minor, F-sharp minor, G major, C major, E-flat major! Resurrection! Bare foot heavy on the pedal, I recapitulate, then launch into wild improvisation. A splendid massive cloud of sound rises from the piano. I learned this technique from Charles Ives, nobody else. Keep that right foot on the pedal and when the cacophony seems unendurable pour on more coal, more power, more glory.

Crashing up and down the keyboard like a lion crushing cane, like a stallion trampling Fritos, like an elephant in bamboo, like a bull stomping crockery, like a turkey through the corn—Dubarry done gone again!—I modulate suddenly, with wrenching force, into

24

the finale of Schubert's *Unfinished* Symphony, then Beethoven's Fifth, then Bruckner's Fifth, Mahler's Fifth, Tchaikovsky's Fifth, the Sibelius Fifth, Carl Nielsen's Fifth, the Prokofiev Fifth (a mad socialist industrial machine running amok), the Shostakovich Fifth and finally, naturally, old Johannes Brahms, his Fifth.

Leaving the ducal grand salon, his cigar smoking like a chimney, Brahms said in farewell to the assembled lords and ladies, "If there's anyone here I've failed to insult—I apologize." Good man. A born-again atheist in more ways than one.

Brahms never wrote a fifth symphony, the nitpickers will object. Nor Schubert a finale to his Eighth. Well they have now. I wrote it for them and it may well be their finest work. It's a fact, curious but true, that most symphonists reach apogee, produce their liveliest most vigorous most dramatic work (not necessarily their best), in their fifth effort.

Enough of this esoterica: time for the coffee and the grease. I put a Schütz motet and a Merle Haggard song cycle on the music machine and head for the kitchen, followed by the golden vapor of Schütz's angelic choral harmonics. Set kettle on burner, stick filter in Pyrex jug, pat sausage into patties and put skillet on stove. Smell them nitrates sizzle—good!

I take four eggs from the silent, bullet-stricken refrigerator—warm and damp in there—and look about for a clean bowl. Sink crowded with dirty dishes, pots, pans, wineglasses, tumblers, bowls, garbage. But there's Elaine's wok—walk? woke?—hanging on the wall. That will do. I crack the eggs, dump in a can of El Pato's diced green chilis, and stir the steaming mess with a wooden spoon, creating out of chaos a rational, systemic paradigm of order.

The miracle of eggs. In the beginning was the egg. The chicken was an afterthought, a mere transmission mechanism for the production of further eggs. The world itself is egglike. Those astrophotos of galaxies, spiral nebulae—do they not resemble fresh eggs broken in the pan? The universe itself may be no more than one gigantic cosmic egg. And the function of mind? To fertilize that egg. Creating—who knows what grotesque and Godlike monster. Best not think about it.

Stirring my eggs in her wok, I recall Elaine's artistic cooking period. She was a fad follower, like most of us, straining to keep up with the latest fashion, always a shade behind. Est and Arica, group encounter therapy, aerobic dancing, jogging, haute cuisine, cuisine minceur, primal screaming, Zen, John Anderson, Gloria Steinem, fat-tire bicycles, punk rock, acid rock, acid rain, Elton John, Bob Marley and the Wailers, Back to the Bible, soap opera, home computers, Bucky Fuller and geodesic domes, *Whole Earth Catalogs* and space colonies, whatever the thing of the week, the trend of the month, the rage of the season, she was onto it like a leech, into it like a chigger. And so for a time—maybe a month—early in our marriage, she turned her fine passion, insecure temperament and incoherent energies toward the high art of *cuisine française.*

How can I forget the day she served me *oeuf poché en aspic.* Surely one of the most repellent inventions in all of human history. Only a Frog could have thought of such a thing. Frogs and viscosity. France, said Henry de Montherlant (a good Frenchman), is the woman of Europe. That was when our troubles began, was it not?

What's this?

Poached egg in aspic, she said. There was a blush of pride on her sweet rosy Saxon face. Her violet eyes glowed like sapphires.

Aspic? It looks like—like . . . Like something out of a horse's hoof, I thought but did not say aloud.

It's a tomato sauce gel, she said. A kind of gelatin. She was watching me closely, already nervous. It's good, Henry. She ate a spoonful; I watched in horror. Please Henry. It's very good. Really. She probed deeper with her silver spoon (a gift from her Grandmaw) and broke the soft egg inside. A yellowish fetus-amoeba spread within the menstrual-colored jelly. To me it resembled something out of a nightmare by Poe. The facts in the case of V. Waldemar.

Under Elaine's watchful eye, I took my spoon and touched the thing on my plate. It quivered as if still alive. Elaine, I said, you're my darling and I love you urgently more than life itself and I know this must have taken great time and effort . . .

She stared at me. I knew she was going to cry.

. . . and I really appreciate this, honey, but doggone it sweetheart I was outside all day in the cold and wind [I'd been out bow hunting with Lacey] and you know I'm kind of really hungry. I mean *hungry.* Can't we—do you think maybe—I mean, could I maybe *fry* this hideous thing?

She rose from the table.

I didn't mean that, I said at once, didn't mean that, only kidding, darling, look, watch, I'm going to eat it. Watch. Too late. She groped toward the bedroom, blind with tears. Me and my big loose mouth. Honey, I shouted, you know I'm only kidding, honey. I got up from my chair. Elaine! I roared as the bedroom door slammed in my face.

She was a master—a mistress—at slamming doors. One of her favorite gestures. Every doorframe in the house is outlined with ornamental traceries of cracked plaster. I could hear her sobbing inside. I tried the door but she had turned the key in the lock.

Useless for me to hammer on the door or to attempt, prematurely, the first necessary signals toward reconciliation. I returned to our "dining nook" in the kitchen, in this tract-style travesty of a house, and looked again at the blob of inedible pink matter on my plate. That glob of misery and mystery. I set it on the floor in front of Fred the cat. He sniffed cautiously, not quite touching it, and backed off. I took the plate outside and offered the thing to Solstice our dog. (Born on June 22.) She didn't want it either. So I flung it, plate and all, into the branches of the chinaberry tree in our front yard. The living glop oozed down from twig to twig in mucoid hockers, like snot from a sick calf, and dropped onto the defenseless pads of a prickly pear. There it gathered itself together again, coagulating on the spines, and continued its slimy progress toward the center of the earth. . . .

That was near the end of the honeymoon, the typical ninety days of passion before the grim reality of domestic bliss begins to sink into the mutual consciousness of man and wife. It was only the first of many such incidents. One evening when I came home from work she greeted me at the door wearing a brocaded kimono.

Beautiful, I said. She smiled, bowed, led me inside. Supper was ready. But it was on the floor—or more precisely, laid out upon this foot-high end table. I sat down, Elaine pulled off my boots, washed my hands with warm rosewater in a porcelain bowl. She knelt on a cushion at one side of the low table, I knelt on a cushion opposite. But this position was uncomfortable for me. I changed to a sitting posture but there was no room for my legs—I'm six foot four inches—either in front of, beside or beneath that damnable toy table. Nor did I have anything to lean back against. I placed my cushion so that I could recline against the front of the sofa. But then

I could not reach the table. I pulled the end table closer, across the carpet, and toppled a slender vase filled with fresh live—chrysanthemums? Oh damn! I'm sorry, Elaine.

She smiled and said nothing, sopped up the water with a napkin, replaced the flowers. Smiling graciously, she poured the tea, an authentic brew called soochang bing—or bong, I believe. The kind that smells like old straw soaked for six months in a horse trough. Delicious, I said, closing my eyes the better to savor its rare bouquet.

She smiled, eyes lowered, removed the lid from a porcelain pot and with matching ladle served a dark thick purple soup into tiny porcelain bowls. A tincture of iodine hovered on the air. We picked up miniature matching ceramic spoons, too short to sup from at the side, too thick and awkwardly curved to allow insertion into the mouth. The idea, evidently, is to bend the head far back and pour contents of spoon into mouth, as if feeding an infant.

I worked on it and got a few mouthfuls down. Best boiled sewage effluent I ever tasted, I thought, while Elaine observed my every move, each response, with hopeful eyes. Well? she asked, as I paused for reflection. Good, I said, good, mighty good, what is it? It's a sort of Japanese bouillabaisse, she said, called maru tamayaki. If I heard her correctly. Really good, I said, wondering what kind of marine life was hidden in the soup.

I dipped the scoop deeper into my little bowl and came up with something dead white, a languid soft invertebrate substance. Testicles of octopus? Placenta of jellyfish? What's this? I said. Tofu, she said; soybean curd. Soybean curd? Come on, Henry, you've heard of tofu, you'll like it. She swallowed a spoonful of the stuff and watched me.

I smiled at my wife and placed the wet tofu in my mouth, swallowing quickly before I lost courage. It went down easily enough, I guess, although I felt a queasy tremor of protest from my stomach. Delicious! I exclaimed.

I knew you'd like it.

Tofu, eh? Those Japs sure are clever little fuckers. I groped for another lucky dip, feeling about for some sort of solid matter. Soybean mash, I was thinking—in America we make cattle eat it. No wonder there's so many short people on this planet. I groped in the beet-dark soup and fished up maybe a dying squid—limp strands of purple pseudoflesh dangling like tentacles from my spoon. I looked at Elaine; she was watching.

Kelp, she explained.

You mean—seaweed?

Yes. The tears (goddamnit) already welling to the surface of those marvelous eyes. Don't be so suspicious, Henry. I'm not trying to poison you or anything, you know.

Honey, really, it looks good. Real good. I was just curious, honest. Just never saw anything like this crawling in my soup. Before.

She stiffened.

So it's kelp? I went on hastily, kelp, eh? Well I'll be damned. I stared at the thing hanging from my spoon, not quite brave enough to bring it to my lips. Like the innocent North Dakota virgin who married a Frenchman and wondered, after five years of steady sex, why she never got pregnant, I could not quite bring myself to swallow the stuff.

Those little Nips are an ingenious people, I said. Sony, Datsun, Toyota, Kawasaki, Honda, kamikaze, hari-kari, seppuku, Pearl Harbor, the creeping kudzu vine—how can we ever thank them? And now kelp, seaweed in my soup, what do you know about that. Wonderful. Well, with a hundred million of the little mothers crammed onto a few islands barely big enough for one half million actual humans, no wonder they eat seaweed. And soybean curd, whales, krill, birds' nests, labels off beer bottles.

Bird's nest soup is a Chinese dish.

One billion of *them*. Eat more beef, I say.

Now she was getting angry. Her High Church blood was flowing. If we Americans didn't feed so much grain to cattle and hogs we could support more millions of people. Billions. Africa, Asia, Latin America, we could feed them all.

There's too many short people in the world already.

It ever occur to you maybe you're not as smart as you think you are?

Nobody could be that smart.

You're talking like an idiot. You don't really believe that height makes you superior. A pause. Do you?

I shrugged. Put it this way: if those billions of short people are as good as us, how come they have such tiny heads?

You're sick. You and Hitler should get together. You'd love South

Africa. Why don't you join the KKK? Silence. She watched me still looking at the Oriental weed hanging from my spoon. Well—are you going to eat it or not?

Elaine . . . I looked at her. Her eyes were wet with tears. Lower lip a-tremble. Elaine, sweetheart, I was born and bred on a sidehill farm in Appalachia. Actually bred first, then born. Ain't we got no pokeweed greens? turnips? smoked ham? red-eye gravy? sweet corn? sowbelly? venison sausage? even beans? And I mean beans, not bean sprouts.

You were born in a barn. More likely a pigsty.

Our Lord & Savior was born in a barn, I reminded her. I recited my favorite Christian poem:

> There was an old bugger named God
> Who put a young virgin in prod
> This amazing behavior
> Gave us Jesus our Savior
> Who died on a cross, the poor slob.

Elaine put down bowl and spoon. False rhyme, she said. Daintily she dabbed her lips with napkin. She was making a patient effort to control herself, her rage, her anguish. Gracefully she started to rise—

I gulped down the mass of soggy kelp. Half choking I croaked, Good, honey, goddamn it's good. Damn good. Delectable. My Christ but it's good. I mean quite fucking superb.

But I was late, too late with too little. Tears streaming down her pink and glossy cheeks, she bolted for the bedroom.

Elaine! I howled. Too late again. The door slammed shut. The lock snapped to. The dreadful racked weeping sounded through the hallway.

Too late the phalarope. Grabbing the bottle of sake, which tastes no worse than Gallo's hearty chablis, I got up, got out, drove to Ferrigan's Bar & Grill, ordered a hot turkey sandwich with mashed potatoes, gravy, cranberry sauce, Green Giant corn niblets. And a bottle of beer. (The waiter brought the bottle itself for my inspection, as customary in a high-class place, showed me the label— Coors—and with due ceremony and graceful flourishes opened the bottle right there, at the table, in my presence, as tradition requires.) I topped off the meal with a Dutch Masters cigar, Walgreen's best. Satisfied, I asked myself a question: Lightcap, How can you be so rotten? How can you be such a rotten obnoxious swine? After a moment's thought I answered, It ain't easy.

It took me only a couple of months to cure Elaine of gourmet cookery. We went back to basic American fare—the pig and the egg for breakfast, the cheese and crackers and tuna for lunch, the cow and chicken and lamb for supper. With mashed potatoes and gravy, with turnips and blackeye peas, with beer and red wine. A good diet for me, I was working outside in the open air in those days, helping Harrington build his house, but poor Elaine began to put on weight at thigh and hip. That did not trouble me; I liked her plump, well rounded; but she, like millions of other females here and abroad, had been trained to believe she must have the flanks of a whippet, the buttocks of a boy. Hated androgyny again! She trimmed her diet down to salads and yoghurts while her husband carved his protein and chomped on carbohydrates. She became a jogger.

She bought the uniform: the Nike shoes, the flimsy erotic Adidas track shorts, the heavy-duty reinforced breast sling, the long-billed sunshade, the AM/FM Walkman radio headset, and commenced to laboring up and down the streets with Eric Clapton and James Taylor bawling in her ears, the jogger's look of smug pain and spiritual fortitude on her face. Favoring her sore foot, she gulped the dust and grime and noxious gases of the passing motor traffic.

Conserve energy, I pleaded. Running is wasteful. All joggers should be chained to treadmills and compelled, under whiplash, to generate electricity.

Bug off.

I'll buy you a new ax. A maul. Wedges. A sledgehammer. We need more firewood. More rocks for the garden wall.

Drop dead.

I dropped the subject.

The euphoria of running wore off after she'd dropped five pounds and gained a shin splint and two bulging calf muscles.

Next move? I braced myself.

Feminism reared its fearsome head, a fright wig crawling with serpents, eyes to paralyze Achilles, the grievance of a million years of servitude glaring from the dark recesses of the female mind.

She came under evil influence at the University, as I should have anticipated. Led astray by bad companions, she began reading Woolf, Greer, Steinem, Firestone, Millet, Schulman, Hite, Brownmiller, Rich and other restless Hebraic natives from the rubyfruit jungle. Virginia Woolf had suddenly become—that very year—one of the world's great writers. But not Jane Austen: Austen condones marriage, even urges its pursuit as a legitimate option for upwardly mobile bourgeois-type girls. Furthermore Austen had refused to be born Jewish and who but the Semites, from Moses and Jesus and Paul and Mahomet to Freud and Dr. Brothers and the Ayatollah Khomeini, have succeeded in making of sex so gruesome a rack of torture? Five hundred million decapitated foreskins. Half a billion vaginas dentata. Who's afraid of Virginia Woolf? Me—I am.

Combat in the erogenous zone.

VI

I was dozing off to sleep one night, deplete and satisfied after a brisk little bout in bed with Elaine, when she muttered these curious words in my ear:

We're going to change that old format.

Pardon?

Change that old format.

Sure, honey. . . . My heavy lids dropped down again. I was a happy man, ready for the blissful dreams that follow spendthrift sperm. What's this post-coitus regret bullshit? In the sweet hiatus after sexual love I tend to hear little thrushes calling from magnolia trees in Paradise. ("Paradise"—another word for man's original garden, the preagricultural wilderness.) After making love I feel not sadness but serenity, hear bluebirds in an alpine meadow, dream mystical daydreams in the out-of-doors.

But I was attacked by an unkindness of ravens. Not a dissimulation of birds or exaltation of larks but a gaggle of geese, a murder of crows, a school of hagfish, a coven of witches:

Did you hear me, Henry?

What?

Did you hear me?

Sure, honey, you bet.

What did I say?

I struggled against my drowsiness, sensing danger. You said, Did I hear you.

Yes. And what did I say?

I thought. Thought hard, mastering my irritation. Irritation? Homicidal outrage: there's nothing I hate more than being disturbed during those exquisitely languorous moments when drifting into slumber. And I have a bad temper, though I'm fighting it. I said, You said, Did you hear me.

She gritted her fine sharp teeth. In an icy voice, teeth like icicles, she said, I said we're going to change that old format.

What old format?

Foreplay, penetration, ejaculation, sleep, she recited, as if it were a formula.

What's wrong with it?

It's no good. It's obsolete.

Ominous word. I tried to be helpful. We could skip the foreplay.

I'm serious.

Save the foreplay for later.

Henry, a woman has needs too, you know. We're serious.

We? Another ominous word. We? Who's we, white woman?

You know what I mean. She was tense, frigid with anger, at the same time slightly fearful. This was a new sensation for her, baiting her man.

No, I don't know what *we* mean. (Temper, temper.) I mean what you mean. What do you mean? You're talking about coming? going? unloading rocks? the big round O? the holy tortilla?

She started to rise from bed. I'm leaving.

I grabbed her. Why are you always threatening to leave? Is that the only way you can carry on a discussion? (Here's your hat, there's the door, what's your hurry?) You mean you didn't come this time, is that what you're mad about?

You know.

Know what?

What you said. Yes, I did not—come. As you so crudely put it.

Oh? Crude? (And I thought I'd put it very nicely, tactfully, as I always put it.) Really? You didn't come?

Henry—I never come.

Pause. Silence. The words sink.

Oh God, I said. (I'm going to write a book someday: *The Joy of*

Jerking Off. At least you don't have to talk afterwards.) What the hell do you mean you never come. Never? Hardly ever?

I mean never, Henry. You know what never means.

Forever?

Never. Not yet.

I can't believe this, Elaine. What the hell do you mean? Now I was getting irked, rising to my elbows, another good night's sleep ruined, nothing for it now but aspirin, Wild Turkey, hours of Gibbon or Burton or Shakespeare under the reading lamp and that feeling by dawn of total moral and mortal exhaustion. I said, We've been officially married for two years, Elaine. Sleeping together, fucking together, fighting together for over three years and now you claim you never come. Never came? Never? Not once?

Fight and fuck, she said, fuck and fight, that's all we ever do.

What's wrong with that? That's love. Pause. Not even once? In three whole years?

Not once.

You've been faking all this time? All that groaning and gasping and clasping and wiggling, that was a fake?

You're the fake.

My God, Elaine. I can't believe this.

It's true.

Oh, God . . . (I was in trouble.) Is it my fault? (Silence. Pregnant silence.) What about—other men?

She hesitated in what I interpreted as a coy and calculating silence. Well—there were only two others. Before you. College boys.

What about them? Could they make you come?

Again the cruel silence. Finally she said, All men are the same.

I see. (All men are brothers.)

Most men. Some are different . . . or so I've heard. Pause. Besides a man doesn't *make* a woman come, as you call it. He works with her.

I see. He works with her. (Works!) I thought of my last Chinese fortune cookie, the one I got at the Old Peking Restaurant on Speedway after I'd eaten my favorite Chinese dinner, Combination Plate #2. The joker's cookie. All men are the same, my little slip of paper said, they only think of one thing: Luckily every woman has one. Why do girls have vaginas? So the boys will talk to them. I thought of the female sexual organ in its outward manifestation. Vulva, inner and outer labia, clitoris, etc. Never did envy the gynecologist. All those business hours spent peering into that bearded oysterlike aperture. Not that a man's dangling apparatus is half so pretty. A nude woman, if attractive, is a pleasure to look at, but a naked man is merely a man with his pants off—ridiculous.

I thought about these things while Elaine stared wanly into space, and I said—but what could I say? I was shocked. Appalled. Devastated. Bored. I said, I'm sorry, Elaine, good Christ. What about jacking off? Can you come that way?

Don't be crude. Girls don't—women don't—do that.

Oh no?

Women masturbate.

And you can come that way?

We don't "come." We orgasm.

You what?

We orgasm. That's the proper word, since you don't seem to know.

Orgasm is not a verb. No. My anger was stirred again; this really roused me. Not a verb. Never was, never will be, not once.

It is now. *Orgasming* is a verb.

God's curse on such a verb. You can't do that to our noble American language. You shall not verbalize nouns. I hate that bastard jargon: She "orgasmed" all over the croutons. Mr. & Mrs. Turkeyballs "parented" three kids from birth to the Juvenile Detention Center. The critics "savaged" his latest masterpiece. You can't do that. I hate it hate it hate it.

You're going to have to change your ways and attitudes, Henry. Join the modern world. You're thirty years behind the times.

That's too close.

Screwing her courage to the sticking point, she stuck it to me. I hate to say this, Henry, but—you know, you're not a good lover. You're lousy, in fact. You've got to learn some technique.

Ah, I thought, technique, technique—another ominous and chilling word. And when they say I hate to say this you know they love it.

Nevertheless: I tried. I was a dutiful husband, in my humble fashion, and I wanted to be a good husband. A modern American hubby. So we worked at it. For an hour that night. And for hours and hours every night for weeks, for months. Refining the old technique. I worked hard, tinkering with her delicate and complicated genitalia, especially the *kleitoris* (Gr.), key to a woman's heart. Studied the cliterature. Learned to eyeball the labia minor at close range without blinking. And as we know but few will confess, the female sexual organism—and I do mean organism—is not in itself, considered apart from context, what you might consider a thing of beauty. A thing of beauty is a joy *forever.*

We worked hard at sex. And when you have to work at it it's hard work. Every time I pulled off my jeans I felt I should be punching a time clock.

The Joy of Sex!—Elaine brought home that dreary tract one day, those tidings of comfort and joy by some Californicated Englishman, and we studied the ghastly pictures, the two hundred different positions. What a joyless book. That poor fucker the instructor-model, performing his gymnastic routines over and over, with slight variations, for three hundred pages, each and every time upon the same woman. No wonder he has that look on his soft hairy degenerate face of a bored he-dog hooked up on the street with an exhausted bitch, longing to leave but unable to extricate himself from what breeders call a "tie." The woman in the book looks only slightly happier; somebody out of mercy should have emptied a bucket of ice water on the miserable couple. Technique, technique, technical engineering, curse of the modern world, debasing what should be a wild, free, spontaneous act of violent delight into an industrial procedure. Comfort's treatise is a training manual, a workbook which might better have been entitled *The* Job *of Sex.*

Christ, Elaine, *Playboy*'s better than this.

Playboy is a sexist magazine.

I know, it exploits men, three dollars a copy now. But at least there's a faintly erotic aspect to the pictures. At least there's some dim humor in the cartoons.

Sex is not a laughing matter.

How true. Yes, she actually said that, I heard it. That's what those dreadful women and those insidious books had done to my good sweet innocent young Elaine. The seduction of ideas. But even she grew weary of it.

We haven't tried this one yet. Number 149.

I don't want to, she said.

Why not?

It's too humiliating.

This book is humiliating. A sick commercial insult to the human soul. And I flung it—flang it!—against the bedroom wall. As I would an obnoxious cat. To hell with that garbage, Elaine, let's just fuck for the fun of it. No more contortions. No more pretzels. No more Hindu-Hebrew-California masochism. Fucking can be fun, honey, honest. Let's throw this Levantine garbage away and make a baby.

That shook her. A baby? With you?

Why not?

I'm too young. I have my career ahead of me. (Which career is that, I wondered.) I refuse to be forced into woman's traditional role. Would you help?

Help what?

Change diapers? Bathe it? Feed it?

Feed it? You're the one with the tits, how could I feed it? That's your job. Would I feed it, of course not; I'll keep you fed though, that's my job, I'll bring home the pigmeat, keep a roof above our heads in wintertime; I won't change diapers but I'll buy the damn things.

Thinking, What would my friend George Santayana say to this? He said, It takes patience to appreciate domestic bliss. My friend Nietzsche? He said, The married philosopher is a figure out of a stage farce. And Montaigne? He said—but I forget. No I don't. He said, Marriage is like a gilded birdcage: the birds on the outside want in, those on the inside want out. Aloud I said, You know how an Eskimo woman cleans her baby? up there in the frozen North?

I hate know-it-alls.

I know it. Do you know?

No. And I don't care.

With her tongue, that's how. In the winter, when there's nothing else available. But that was before ski planes, snow machines, Prudhoe Bay, Pampers, welfare checks and progress. Did you come this time?

You mean did I orgasm? No.

Poor Elaine. I cuddled her close, kissed and caressed her, murmured sweet lies into her ear—and dozed off. Dimly as in a dream I felt her slip from our bed, sobbing, and creep on bare feet into the bathroom. I cried too and fell asleep. I did not hear her return.

All that hard work and nothing gained. Love in the Western world. High cuisine and gourmet sex, nothing worked. Disaster loomed above us like the ninth wave at Massacre Beach. Sure, I loved her as much or more than ever but love alone is not enough for anybody. Some poet said, We must love one another or die. (Auden—that queer creepy fellow.) But we're going to die anyway—he forgot about that.

Elaine needed something more than mere love, whether romantic, matrimonial, conjugal or sexual. She needed something that neither I nor any man, alone or unaided, could give her. What is it? I have my theories. She needed what humans need: a sense of community. Interesting, dignified and essential work to do. (Like finding food or raising a baby.) She needed connection with the past and future of family, clan, kinfolk and tribe. And most of all she needed ownership of a piece of earth, possession of enough land to guarantee the pride and dignity and freedom that only economic independence can bestow. Without that, what are we? Dependents, that's what. Employees. Personnel. Peasants. Serfs. Slaves. Less than men, less than women. Subhumans. But this need is so deep and ancient that most people have lost even the consciousness of it. Only the instinct remains. What's the first thing the nouveaux riches do with their money? They buy a big place in the country with barns, pastures, horses, whitewashed fences, fields. And rightly so.

Meantime her feminism hardened, becoming militant and embittered. She not only read but thrust into my hands those awful books by that maddened horde of scribbling women. Fascinated, I learned that ever since the end of the mythical Golden Age of Matriarchy, human society has been operated solely and exclusively for the benefit of men, that men have conspired for twenty thousand years to enslave our own wives, mothers, grandmothers, sisters, daughters, granddaughters, nieces, sweethearts, lovers, mistresses and female friends.

A fascinating and fantastical tale. An intellectual neurosis for which our psychiatric technicians have yet to devise a name. But as always, the more preposterous the doctrine the more fanatic its adherents. There is no animal so spooky as the true believer. We argued, in and out of bed, for hours, days, weeks.

Certainly, I agreed, males dominate females. In every known human (and mammalian) society this is the case. The explanation however is so obvious it escapes the observation of feminist intellectuals: men are bigger, stronger, more aggressive. Intelligence, morality, justice have little to do with it. The rule of law means the rule of those who make the law, interpret it, enforce it. Bulk counts. Might does not make right but it sure makes what is. As Georg Wilhelm Friedrich Hegel pointed out, in his twenty-six-volume footnote to Plato, Vat effer iss, iss right.

But, Elaine said—

I ranted on: Women the victims, men the victors? Tell it to the Marines. Tell it to those grunts, all boys, who sweated, fought, suffered and died in the green hell of Vietnam while their majors and colonels circled above in helicopters, observing, chewing cigars, barking insane irrational incomprehensible commands. Tell it to the serfs of merrie olde England who plowed, sowed, reaped, and saw the fruits of their labor stolen from them by the lords—and ladies— who claimed ownership of the land. A claim enforced by sword lance club mace the noose the rack the wheel the fire. Tell it to Faulkner and the slaves of the Deep South ("God shat upon the earth and He called it—Mississippi"). Tell it to the indentured bondsmen of colonial Pennsylvania. Of Old Virginia. Tell it to Big Bill Haywood, Joe Hill, Wesley Everest and the ghosts of the IWW. Tell it to Jack Cade, Wat Tyler, Ned Ludd, Nat Turner, John Brown. Tell it to Diogenes and H. Thoreau. Tell it to those who died in the Colosseum, to Spartacus and the twenty thousand slaves, all men, who were crucified with him by the victorious Romans. Tell it to the slaves—men, women, children—who built the Pyramids, the Great Wall of China, the Parthenon, the Appian viaducts, the walls of Toledo and Burgos, the Taj Mahal, the city of Machu Picchu, the cannibal temples of Mexico, the lost and forgotten horrors of imperial Africa. Tell it to the people who pick our bananas, our coffee beans, our tea leaves, our tomatoes strawberries grapes and lettuce. Tell it to Aleksandr I. Solzhenitsyn and the surviving *zeks* of the Gulag and the KGB. Tell it to Lech Walesa. Tell it to the ghosts of Eugene Debs, Norman Thomas, John L. Lewis. Tell it to the coal miners, the steel puddlers, the chemical workers, the uranium miners, the schoolteachers. Tell it to Jean Valjean. Tell it to Leo Tolstoy, Peter Kropotkin, Michael Bakunin, Nestor Makhno, Taras Bulba, Enrico Malatesta, Ramón Sender, Pablo Barruti, Pancho Villa, Emiliano Zapata and B. Traven.

But, Elaine began again—

Yes, I agreed, most women have been victims, right alongside their husbands, sons and brothers, ever since the invention of agriculture and the urban conglomeration (two dreadful setbacks for humanity). Most women, like their men, have been peons and cotton pickers, factory hands and office clerks, service workers and wage slaves—subjects. Yes. But—

But, Elaine insisted—

—but, I agreed, not all women, not all men. For the women of the rich and powerful, life is different. Do you think the lady of the manor would change places with a male field hand? Would Princess Diana give up her role for the part of a dock worker tramping home to his kennel in the slums? Huh? The great division in the social pyramid is not between the sexes but between the classes. The gulf is horizontal not vertical. Sixty percent of the wealth of the USA belongs to 2 percent of American families. When the manly galley slaves of imperial Egypt toiled so desperately at the oars of the great trireme, who was that long-haired dark and comely personage being towed behind on water skis? Antony? No ma'am, it was Cleopatra. When Adam delved and Eve span, who was then the gentleman?

Adam? she suggested.

Shut up! I explained.

But what I'm trying to tell you—

Please. Let me finish. The debate dragged on for another hour, another month, then collapsed without warning when she abruptly gave up feminism for aerobic dancing. Every evening. Feminism was bad for her figure. First things first. Me, neglected husband, I retreated into celibacy. For a week. Then resumed slipping around on the sly, sneaky as a tomcat, subtle as a rooster.

Leading to further controversy. She screamed, I shouted, she quoted, I sneered, she cried I bellowed she slammed the door. Our house crumbled. I won the argument, I think, but lost my third and final wife.

And I never could make her come. Instead of coming she went.

VII

He eats his eggs and sausage, drinks his coffee, gnaws his crust of bread. April sunlight, bright, cruel, heartbreaking, pours into the kitchen through the morning window. The music of McKinley Morganfield, better known as Muddy Waters, pours from the stereophonic speakers. Good man, old Waters.

Henry eats his breakfast, bleak and lonely, and makes his plans. Plug in phone, call welfare office, tell them he's taking another leave without pay, they won't mind. Visit bank, empty checking account, pick up needed cash. Load up the old Dodge with camping gear, essential firearms, spare parts, a certain few books. Write a farewell letter to Elaine. Shoot the dog. Get in truck and point its battered nose eastward, toward the world of the rising sun and Stump Creek, West Virginia. Home.

Only three thousand five hundred miles to go. Brother Will, I say to my shattered heart, my private little secret, here I come.

Prepare thyself.

2

1927-37:

STUMP CREEK, WEST VIRGINIA

I

Lorraine my mother lay in bed in the antique gothic farmhouse, in the little bedroom on the second floor where the child was conceived. She was breathing the fumes from an ether-soaked bandana held under her nose by Joe Lightcap her husband, while bald wrinkled Doc Wynkoop pulled the baby gently, fairly easily, from the exit of the womb.

According to the father, a minute before actual birth the baby's head had emerged from the natal aperture, opened its eyes, took one quick look around—saw the light of the kerosene lamp glimmering on the floral wallpaper, saw Joe's dark anxious aboriginal face, the red face and bloodshot eyes of the doctor, the ancestral portraits of old Lightcaps, Shawnees, Gatlins and Holyoaks hung on the walls, saw the double-barreled twelve-gauge, loaded, which stood in the corner near the head of the bed, saw the Bible on the night table, Mother's cedar chest, the wardrobe closet, the lace curtains, etc.—took everything in and then retreated, withdrew, slid right back into the dark radiant chamber of conception.

No thanks. Thanks but no thanks.

At that point Doc Wynkoop grasped the baby firmly by the ears and head, rotating the body forty-five degrees, and drew it forth. *Drew me forth*, protesting mightily—no need here for a whack on the rump—and tied off the cord, knotting the umbilicus in a knot that's held to this very day. He swabbed away the silvery caul, that shining suit of lights, like the garb of a traveler from outer space, smeared the tender parts with unguent oil, and laid the child on his

42

mother's breast. She took him to suck at once, silencing for a time the howls of indignation. She named the boy Henry.

The doctor passed the afterbirth to Joe, who probably fed it to the hogs. Grandmother Gatlin arrived soon afterward, a little late. Joe passed a five-dollar bill to the doctor and the promise to deliver, within a week, five bushel of potatoes and a home-cured ham.

Doc Wynkoop climbed into his black Model A Ford and drove down the rutted red-dog road through night and falling curtains of snow toward the highway and the town of Shawnee, ten miles south. We had no doctor in Stump Creek. Not since the death of Doctor Jim fifty years before—and Doctor Jim was an Indian, a shaman Shawnee medicine man, not an M.D.

Henry Holyoak Lightcap was the second child. My brother William, about two years older, complained loudly from his crib in the adjoining room, beneath the sloping ceiling of the east roof, under the impression that he'd been temporarily forgotten. Correct.

Winter nights. In frozen February the child lay snug in his mother's arms. Outside, beyond frost-covered windows, the ice-shagged pines stood under the Appalachian moon, mute with suffering. Frost glittered on crusty waves of snow that covered the pasture, the frozen brook, the stubble of the cornfields. The moonlight tinted the snow with the pale blue tones of skim milk. Through the stillness came the sound of an old oak cracking in the woods, branch split by freezing sap. Then came the wail of the iron locomotive on the C&O line, burning coal as it chugged up grade toward Trimble's crossing a mile away, pulling fifty-five gondola cars of bituminous coal to the coke ovens of Morgantown and Wheeling and Pittsburgh.

Desolation of the iron cry—Song of the Old 97—loneliness of the silent hills, silvered furl of black smoke and white steam rising toward the moon.

The moon shone down on rigid ice floes in Crooked Creek, on Stump Creek, Rocky Glen and Cherry Run, on the nameless streamlet that drained the wooded hillsides of Lightcap Hollow. The moonlight glanced and glinted on the ice-filled ruts of the road, lay on the granite and sandstone monuments of the Jefferson Church graveyard where tiny American flags hung stiff in the gelid air above brass stars bearing the initials GAR—Grand Army of the Republic. The winter moon was so bright, so clear, you could read the names on the stone, the names of our buried neighbors: Ginter, Gatlin, Hinton, Hankerson, Fetterman, Finley, Rayne, Risheberger, Holyoak, Mears, Lightcap, Clymer, Trumbull, Trimble, Stuart, Stewart, Stitler, Prothrow, Groft, Bennett, Duncan, Dalton . . . to name but the oldtimers, kinsmen and neighbors, enemies and strangers.

Economists would have called it a "depressed area." A land of marginal and submarginal farms, small coal-mine operations, thirdgrowth timber cutting, crossroad market towns like Shawnee, seat of Shawnee County. Haunted country—haunted by the ghosts of the Indians who gave the place its title, who left little but their name when they were driven out late in the eighteenth century by a Colonel George Rogers Clark who burned their villages, torched their cornfields and ruined the survivors with smallpox, alcohol and tuberculosis.

II

Inconsolable memories:

Pump and pump handle sheathed in ice on winter mornings; my first chore of the day, recalled Henry, was taking a hot kettle from the kitchen stove to thaw and prime that pump and fill the kitchen water buckets.

Herding in the milk cows on frosty mornings, I'd stand where the cows had lain to keep my bare feet warm.

With a green willow stick, whipping a crab apple halfway across the valley, I aimed at my big brother, Will, or at little brother, Paul, or at our baby sister, Marcie.

The smell of the flowering dogwood in April.

Summer: heat lightning. Thunder above the hayfield. Fireflies and lightning bugs. The June bug game. The leap from crossbeam into haymow twenty feet above the floor, high in the dusty air of the barn.

Dumping wood ashes into the two-hole privy below the house— another of my childhood chores. Will had graduated to harnessing our team of horses to the plow, the spring-tooth harrow, the manure spreader, the seed drill, the cultivator, the mower, the wagon. But Will was a precocious boy, big for his age; he always worked hard. He liked it.

Splitting kindling wood for the kitchen stove, after I'd pumped two buckets of water. Hewer of wood and drawer of water—that was my role for years, until Paul grew big enough to do it in his turn.

Our half-Shawnee grandmother—Milly Cornflower Lightcap— was the daughter of a medicine man known to the whites as Doctor Jim (a condescending honorific) because of his healing arts and herbal lore. Doctor Jim never revealed his secret tribal name, not to any kin of ours; there was dangerous power in the name, easily lost. He lived alone in a one-room cabin in the woods, last of the Shawnee full bloods, and survived for eighty years by trapping, hunting, poaching, by odd jobs, charity and scavenging, and by his medical skills, much in demand locally. When he died he died alone, chanting (we presume) his personal death song, and lamenting the destruction and exile of his people. Never did go to Oklahoma. Never did join the cash nexus. Never did get baptized.

Grandmother Cornflower was half white by ancestry, *her* mother an indentured servant named Tillie Ostrander who'd run away from a family of Pennsylvania Dutch (Germans) in Lancaster County, Pennsylvania. Tillie crossed over the mountains and allowed herself to become the third or fourth wife (he outlived them all) of Doctor Jim. It was tolerable then for a white man to take an Indian girl as wife—not honorable but tolerable—but for an all-white girl to bed down with an Indian, a buck savage, a male aborigine, a witch doctor, and to love him, stay with him, refuse to leave him even when her brothers came looking for her all the way from beyond the Allegheny Mountains—that was a shameful thing. A thing to be spoken of in whispers. A disgrace near as low—not quite—as Negro blood.

There was talk in Shawnee of lynching Doctor Jim, or at least running him out of the territory, packing him off to Oklahoma with the rest of his drunken, trashy, idle, defeated tribe—those shattered remnants from the Trail of Tears.

Nothing came of it. Doctor Jim defied his enemies, making it clear he would die fighting before he'd leave his homeland. The runaway girl stood with him, beside him, bore him a girl-child and died in the process. My grandfather Jacob Lightcap married the shaman's daughter, the half-breed girl Cornflower. She was dark-skinned, with rich thick hair of mahogany brown. Her eyes were a bright gray-green, strange to see in the broad face with its high Mongolian cheekbones.

Grandmother Lightcap: Cornflower: I remember you from childhood: short, heavy-bodied, mother of six, your face wrinkled as a dried apple, your easy smile and the dazzling white false teeth you were so proud of, the round little granny glasses you wore about forty years before they became a brief fashion. Grandmaw, I remember your sweet and gentle voice, that voice so soft we had to *really listen* when you talked or we'd miss the tail on the fable, the moral pinned to the hinder end of your thousand and one stories. How the rabbit got his cottontail. How the toad got his warts. How the bear got his claws and the loon his necklace and the panther his scream and the owl his huge eyes . . .

She showed us, me and brother Will, her oaken chest full of treasures. The cream-colored doeskin dress, fringed and beaded, with high-top moccasins to match. The bearskin robe old Doctor Jim had dressed and cured and worn for thirty years. Her father's calumet or ceremonial pipe, the bowl made of clay, the stem of wild cane. The shaman's deerskin medicine pouch in which he carried his important herbal powders and such sacred objects as a set of bear claws, an eagle feather, a mountain lion's tooth, the corn pollen, the native tobacco, a witch's toe, three tiny copper bells and a copper medallion inlaid with turquoise and garnet—objects which had come from central Mexico centuries before, passed and bartered on from hand to hand, tribe to tribe, until finally reaching some Shawnee ancestor in the Appalachian hills, long ago.

Grandmaw gave the pouch to Will, since he was the older of us, obviously the more responsible. To be guarded with his life, she said, and passed on. I was seven years old when she died and so remember her only dimly but sweetly, an ancient gray-haired woman with the sweetest most beguiling voice, the most rich delightful laugh of any woman, any human, I've ever known.

She died; our father buried her beside her father, Doctor Jim, on the hillside at the edge of the red oaks near the spring and sunken ruins of the old man's cabin. Cornflower was a Baptist Christian but only formally. Not spiritually. Like Doctor Jim she was buried where she wanted to be, in a corner of the earth that had sustained her woodland people for maybe—who knows?—one thousand, ten thousand, twenty thousand years.

Our father too always said he wanted to be planted there, among those moldering Indian bones, with a red oak for his monument. Unlike other members of the Lightcap clan he claimed pride, honor, glory in his redskin genesis. Even boasted of it sometimes, even in public, which embarrassed our aunts and uncles. They preferred to stress the Saxon side—that antique strain of hillbillies, bowmen, thieves, peasants, woodcutters and deer poachers stretching back into the murk and misery of medieval England. Those merry times of overlord and gibbet, of peasant and serfdom, of the rack and the wheel which followed the massacre of the English forests. When the trees were gone freedom disappeared. Soon after the time of the death of Robin Hood, betrayed—like Che Guevara—by a nun.

We come from lowly lineage, us Lightcaps, from the worst of a bad lot, escaped bondsmen and indenture-jumping servants, the scum of Europe, the riffraff and ruffians of the Old World. But we have learned to live with our heritage. "Your criticism is greatly appreciated," says my Uncle Jack's business card, "but fuck you all the same." He deals in fertilizer.

Our mother was a Presbyterian. She'd be buried, if she ever consented to die, among her Holyoaks and Gatlins in the official compost pile, the rich good consecrated ground, of Jefferson Church. Her church. Hers—who else kept it going as much as she? Who else played the organ, supervised the children's Sunday school and conducted the cracked old voices of her geriatric choir week after week, year after year? "You sound good," I told her once, after she'd apologized for a performance, "you sound downright angelic." "Well we should," she said, "we're all pretty near halfway to Heaven already."

III

On cloudy October afternoons the boys followed their father down the furrows of the potato patch. Joe turned up the spuds with a plow hitched to a single bay mare, the old nag we called Bessie. Our father sang as he tramped over the clods, gripping the plow handles, the reins (seldom used) draped over his neck. He guided the horse mainly by cluck and call. "Haw!" for a turn to the left, "Gee!" for the right. And "Whoa . . . whoa there . . ." as he paused near the end of the row to look back at Will and Henry and Little Paul.

The boys stooped low above the sandy loam, dragging gunny-sacks, resurrecting the potatoes—les pommes de terre, apples of the earth—rich brown solid nuggets of pleasure and nutrition, raw, fried, boiled or baked.

"Don't miss any, boys," says Joe, "dig down there. Get 'em out. That means you too, Henry. Mind now, every one you miss costs you a nickel." The father watches for a minute, dark gaunt face half amused, half serious, then turns back to his plow, clucks at the horse. She steps ahead on ponderous shaggy feet, iron shoes crushing the weeds at field's edge, turning right—Gee!—as Joe Lightcap turns the plow on its side to ease it around for the return row. The horse clomps into the dried-out drab-green potato plants straggling over the ground. Joe sets the plow, the share digs in, the moldboard rolls the damp earth elegantly up and aside. The buried tubers reveal themselves, ready to be gathered, stored, cooked, eaten.

The boys are well paid for their work, by 1930s values: ten cents a bushel. Every Saturday night, payday, after supper, by the light of a kerosene lamp hanging over the dining room table, Joe will teach his boys the finer points of poker—stud, draw, lowball, ana-conda, Montana Gouge—and win back most of the wages that he's paid them. Not all; he's a kindly, generous man.

Our mother did not approve of this weekly ceremony. Darning socks, she watched with scornful eyes as Joe raked in another pot. The washtub simmered on the cookstove: almost time for the boys' weekly bath. She was eager to break up the game before Henry, the most careless player, lost everything he'd earned. Sunday school to-morrow morning. The game continued for another half hour before Lorraine interrupted. Joe had reduced Will's earnings for the week to two dollars, Henry's to fifty cents, Paul's to one dollar.

"Joe," says Lorraine much later, as they nestled together in bed, "you shouldn't do that to the boys."

"Why not?" he says, grinning in the dark. "Them boys got to learn to hang on to their pay. Besides, they love the game."

"Poor little Henry. You took all his wages but fifty cents. That was mean."

"He's got to learn. Got to learn to stop trying to bluff too much, stop trying to fill inside straights, learn when to raise and when to fold. Anyhow he'd waste the money on soda pop and Little Big Books."

"They worked hard for that money."

"Will did. Will worked hard." Joe listened to the sound of the old hemlock tree thrashing in the night wind, brushing against the clapboard siding under the eaves. "Henry don't. Henry never worked hard in his life. That limb is still worryin' the corner. Got to cut that thing off."

Lorraine turned a little away from Joe. "In his life? Henry is ten years old. He's a bright boy. Mrs. Lingenfelter says Henry's I.Q. is one hundred ten. She says Henry's the brightest pupil she's ever had.

"You mean he ain't dumb enough to be a farmer, Lorrie? Is that what you're saying?" No answer. "I don't believe in that I.Q. business anyway. I.Q.—what the hell does that mean? I quit? I'm queer? I think it's a lot of happy horseshit, that I.Q. business."

"Joe, don't talk like that." But now *she* was smiling in the dark. "If he studies hard and does well in high school, Mrs. Lingenfelter says Henry might go on to State Teachers' College in Shawnee."

"He's so smart why can't he play poker?"

"Joe, Joe . . . he's still a little boy. He's only a child."

"Yeah? Well Will's only twelve and he can do the work of a grown man." The limb of the hemlock, seized by the wind, thumped against the outside wall. "Maybe I ought to saw down that whole tree before it comes through the attic roof some night."

"They're both good boys. But they're different."

"You mean Will's a Lightcap and Henry's a Holyoak. Ain't that what you mean?"

"They're both good boys. And yes, you're right—Will is more like your family. And please don't cut down our old tree. That tree is . . . part of the family. That tree looks like I feel, sometimes."

"It's old, Lorrie. Bark's full of beetles. It's fallin' apart. It's a danger. One of them widow-makers falls on a kid someday, then you'll be sorry. Ain't I right? What's more there's near as much brains in my side of the family as ever there was in yours. Just because we hain't throwed off any bank clerks or schoolteachers yet don't mean the Lightcaps ain't as smart as anybody. Smarter'n most.

Like my Daddy used to say, one man's as good as the next—if not a damn sight better."

"All right, Joe, all right. They're both good boys. All I meant was Henry is—quicker."

"You mean smarter. Maybe he is. But Will is doggeder. I mean that Will is a dogged son of a gun. I like that in a boy, that doggone doggedness. He lends a hand, grabs a root and hangs on. Like a badger. I sure do like that in a boy."

"All right, Joe, you're right. They're both ours."

"You mean shut up and go to sleep."

"That's not what I meant."

"Goddamnit, Lorrie—" Joe felt his black temper rise, instantly. He choked it off, changed the subject. "Should cut that tree down." The autumn wind brushed the shoulders of the farmhouse, prying at the clapboards, lifting at the eaves, trying the asphalt shingling on the roof; the wind pushed the big limb of the hemlock back and forth, bumping on the outer wall.

"I love that tree," she said. "I love the sound of it touching the house. Please don't cut it down."

"Okay, honey. Just that big limb. I'll leave the tree stand." His huge rough hand caressed her bare shoulder. "Just for you, Lorrie."

"Joe, please . . ." For he was turning upon her now, his powerful arms pinning her down, one hard thigh sprawled across her legs. "I'm not ready . . ." she said.

"We never was," he said.

IV

I can see her, my five-foot four-inch one-hundred-pound mother, walking up the road under the autumn arcade of flaming sugar maple trees. She walks fast, briskly, with big strides for so small a body, head high and eyes up as she watches the blaze of October colors. She carries a light willow stick and swings it like a boy. She wears an old sweater, darned and patched, a man's sweater that comes below her hips, an ankle-length homemade dress, a red bandana tied around her head.

She was a beautiful woman despite four babies and two miscarriages in the space of ten years (those ravished years of her youth); she had fine flaxen hair that fell to the small of her back when she let it down; we loved to watch as she washed her hair. She had bright hazel eyes, widely spaced—sign of intelligence—a thin fragile-looking little hen's beak of a nose and a narrow but expressive mouth trembling most of the time on the verge of laughter. Or of grief.

She was about thirty years old then, a young woman. Fierce with energy, forever busy, always working at something, cleaning up, nursing a child, feeding chickens and gathering eggs, chopping at weeds in her garden with abrupt, harsh, angry strokes of the hoe. Each Monday she did the family wash (down in the cellar in winter, outside under the walkway in summer) with the sputtering gasoline-powered Maytag that the old man had found for her, somewhere, years before. One by one she guided each soaked garment through the hard rubber rollers of the wringer into the rinsing tub and back again into a basket. Paul and I would help her hang the damp things on the line.

In the evening after dark after she's tucked us all in bed, our father out in the barn seeing to the stock one last time or down in the cellar fixing harness, sharpening tools, whittling another stretch board for the pelts of fox, muskrat, skunk, then—why then and then only—our mother, free at last for a little while to live a private life, would sit at her piano and play. Lying in our double-decker bunks under the sloping ceiling, half asleep but listening, trying to stay awake, we heard the soothing, lyric sound of nocturnes and sonatas by Chopin and Debussy, or perhaps a few tunes from the hymnbook, something not too rousing, appropriate for bedtime—What a Friend We Have in Jesus, The Old Rugged Cross, He Walked with Me, Take My Life and Let It Be, Amazing Grace, or Leaning on the Everlasting Arms . . .

Striding through the October wind. Women don't stride, not small skinny frail-looking overworked overworried Appalachian farm women like Lorraine Holyoak-Lightcap. But our mother did. She strode over the reddish dirt of the road, the burned slag from the coke ovens of Deerlick, Blacklick, the coal-mining towns. She walked rapidly in the windwashed afternoon, switching her stick. She gazed at the red-gold leaves of oak, beech, elm, maple and poplar and hickory—chlorophyll withdrawn for the freezing times ahead, leaving behind in each veined leaf the flame-colored chemistry of fall—and stared up at the streamlined clouds in the silver blue of the sky.

What she longed for, I suppose, was something far away from the ramshackle farmhouse, the unpainted barn, the pigpen chickencoop outhouse toolshed springhouse wagonshed of Lightcap Hollow. Lorraine was the daughter of a professional schoolteacher; her brother was a cashier in a bank; her sisters lived in town in houses with hardwood floors, electricity, hot and cold running water, centralized heating, even refrigerators.

V

Inconsolable memories. Appalachian autumn. Rustle of wind through the dry corn, rattle of dead leaves beneath our feet, the frosty breath of morning, the sleepy stasis of Indian summer.

Mornings and at night we walked our trapline with flashlight and .22 rifle. Hoping for fox, silver fox (wealth!), but catching mostly only skunk and muskrat. Sometimes in early dawn we'd find a muskrat dead in our trap, half frozen into the ice. Or now and then, not often, one small furry foot with chewed-off stump clutched in the steel jaws. A cruel business, our mother kept reminding us. Will shrugged, I was embarrassed, the old man scoffed.

"Look, Lorrie," Paw would growl, "they don't hurt much. The trap grabs and holds 'em, that's all. Those poor critters are gonna die anyhow, out there in the cold and dark. We're just harvestin' the surplus."

"You don't *harvest* living creatures," Mother said. "What a disgusting word. You're killing them for personal profit."

"All right, all right. But we need the money and you know it."

One evening Paw brought one of our Victor single-spring varmint traps up from the cellar. He was going to settle the cruelty argument with Mother once and for all. Carefully, while Mother watched, knitting, our old man squeezed the spring and spread the trap flat on the dinner table. He latched the bait pan to the release trigger and drew back. The trap was ready. "Okay, Lorrie, now watch this." Paw clenched his big right hand into a fist and smashed it down on the pan. The trap sprang shut. Grinning, he held up his caught right hand and the trap, its tether chain dangling. "See?" he said. "See that, goddamnit? I told you, Lorrie, it hardly hurts a-tall. I hardly feel it. See?" Triumphantly he looked at me, at Will, at Paul. "Ain't this what I been telling you boys all along?"

Impressed, we looked at Mother to see what she would say. Smiling her ironic smile, needles clicking in her fingers, she said, "You're not finished, Joe."

"What's that mean?"

She paused. "Now we want to see you gnaw your hand off."

VI

The field corn ripened, the silk at the tip of each ear turned rusty brown. We picked the dried silk and rolled it with pages from the Monkey Ward mail-order catalog into enormous, evil, sickening stogies. We sat high in the shadowy barn, on the square ax-hewn crossbeams above the granary, lit up and smoked ourselves sick. We were hiding from the old man in a bad place to hide: if he ever caught us smoking in the barn there'd be trouble. We heard him too, hollering for Will and me.

"Will!" he hollered. "Henry! You rascals in there?"

We grinned at each other, holding our breath. Quietly, Will crushed out his cornsilk stogie with his thumb and forefinger.

"Will!" Paw bellowed again. "We got corn to cut."

Choking back laughter, we froze in silence as he stomped across the planking of the barn floor, heard him swear as he whacked a heavy blade into a post. The corn knife, like a sword, like a machete, swished through the air when he swung it. We heard Paw go out through the hinged door set in the sliding main door and from there down the earthen ramp to the workshop. Then came the rumble of the grindstone gaining speed as he treadled it with one foot, the screech of steel against stone. Sparks would be flying under the drip of water from the cooling can.

Will stirred uneasily, unable to relax while near a man working. Such a sober serious conscientious fellow, he felt what I seldom felt—the urge to help out. To lend a hand. To grab ahold. "Guess we better go." He made no move to relight his cigar. "Guess we better go, Henry."

"You go, I'm a-stayin' right here."

Will made a threatening gesture, I shrank back, he laughed, stood up and nonchalantly walked the twelve-inch beam to the corner post, dropped down the pegged ladderway to the floor, disappeared. Uncomfortably I watched him leave. I knew I'd be in trouble if I didn't follow. Not that Will would ever tell on me, any more than he'd tell on anybody. But the old man would growl at him, badger him. Anyhow I needed the wages. Another tough poker game coming up Saturday night.

They were halfway to the cornfield when I ran to catch up. Paw carried the twelve-gauge and two fresh-sharpened corncutters—one for me. The beagle hounds ranged ahead, quartering left and right, reading the ground. The sun was noon high but low in the south, obscured by a gray scud of overcast. A raw wind blew in from the northwest. I turned down the earflaps on my brand-new corduroy hunting cap. Proud of that cap. The field corn was ripe but the leaves and stalks appeared a rusty green; that's why we were cutting and stacking it now, husking later.

The old man wore his usual autumn outfit: the billed cap, the tan canvas hunting coat with last year's hunting license in celluloid case pinned between the shoulders. Under the coat he wore bib overalls, felt boots buckled tight around the pantlegs.

We attacked the standing corn. Paw took the outside row next to the rail fence, Will the next, me the third. When we each had an armful Paw took our loads in his big hands, holding the bundle vertical, and mashed it down onto the sharp stubble. The bundle stood upright on its own to become the center of a shock, a tepee, a wigwam of corn.

Paw set a hard pace. Will kept up with him but I had trouble. My back seemed to hurt; I lacked motivation. Will was big, strong for his age and enjoyed the work—actually thought it important.

We reached the end of the field, or they did, where the big woods comes down the hill from Frank Gatlin's place. Paw and Will started their return, passing me going in the opposite direction. My corncutter clashed against Will's—a flash of sparks—and for a moment we struggled hand to hand, sword against sword, like Errol Flynn and Basil Rathbone in *Captain Blood*.

"Cut that out," growls the old man, "afore one of you gets hurt."

The beagles burst into yelps of discovery, off and running. They'd jumped a rabbit. Paw set his machete down carefully, didn't want to nick that fine-honed edge, and picked up the shotgun. He broke it open, loaded two shells into the breech, snapped it shut. Thumb on the safety, he watched the dogs.

They were coursing up the slope of the field by the edge of the woods. Fifty feet before them ran the rabbit, white tail bobbing through the weeds, the auburn grass, the copper-colored blackberry vines. The rabbit veered to the right, traversing the brown hayfield above the corn. The circle was beginning. None of us moved a step. Soon the rabbit would turn right again and come bounding through the corn toward us, followed by the eager hounds. Would be a tough shot, though, in the standing corn, unless the rabbit was stupid enough to cross the wide swath of six-inch stubble before us.

"Lemme get it, Paw," begged Will quietly.

Joe hesitated, then said, "Come here."

Will stepped beside him. Joe placed the heavy, double-barreled gun in Will's hands. Will hefted it to ready position, leaning way back.

"Hey," I whined, "when's it my turn? Will—"

"Shush!" growled the old man. "Don't scare that bunny. He's a-coming." To Will he said, "Push the safety." The beagles were racing down the hill, baying as they crashed through the corn. The rabbit was somewhere close in front of them, running silently for its life. Will raised the shotgun to his shoulder, legs spread wide, leaning back from the waist under the weight.

"Push hard against your shoulder," Paw whispered. "It'll buck. Don't forget the second trigger." He stared into the corn toward the cry of the hounds. "Here it comes. Lead him by a foot."

Will peered down the sightline between the barrels, cheek pressed against the stock. The rabbit leaped from the thicket of corn fifty feet away and raced across the lane of stubble. Will fired—a violent blast—and seemed to miss.

"Shoot again."

Barrels swinging as he led the rabbit, Will pulled the second trigger. The cottontail somersaulted through the air, thumped backside first against the bottom rail of the fence and came to rest.

"Good shot," says the old man.

"Lucky shot," I said. "You missed the first time."

"Maybe," Paw said. "Maybe he missed and then again maybe that rabbit was runnin' so fast he couldn't stop even though he was already dead. Stop at that speed he'd be wearin' his asshole for a collar."

The beagles began to worry the dead rabbit. "Git!" shouted Paw and they backed off, whimpering, eyes shifting uneasily from Joe to the rabbit and back. "All right Will, you shot your rabbit now clean it. Got your knife?"

Will nodded, pulled the jackknife from its pocket on the side of his high-top leather boot, flipped the blade out, picked the rabbit up by the ears and opened it with one quick slit from sternum to anus. He pulled out the steaming guts—entrails, stomach, liver and lungs—and tossed them to the dogs. He wiped his knifeblade on the soft fur of his kill and handed the rabbit to Paw. Paw stuffed it into the game pocket inside the back of his coat. "Okay boys, we got our meat, now let's get this goddamn corn patch cut and shocked."

He kept us going into twilight. The old man was doubling on me now, doing two rows to every one of mine—even Will could hardly keep up with him. I longed for the sound of Mother rapping on the bell by the kitchen door: for suppertime.

The full moon of November—following close upon the setting sun—is the longest moon of the year: the harvest moon, the hunter's moon. We saw it rising round as a banjo through the mists above the eastern hills when finally we heard the bell.

"Suppertime!" I cried, dropping my machete in the dirt. My back ached, my hands ached. I jammed my armful of corn into the final shock and bolted for the house.

"Henry!" yelled the old man. "You come back here. Pick up your corncutter, don't leave it on the ground to get all rusty from the dew, Jesus jumping blue Christ."

Okay, I thought, *okay*. Minutes later I was in the kitchen. The warm and comforting kitchen: red coals glowed through cracks in the cast-iron cookstove. My mother stood by the stove under the amber glow of a lamp bracketed to the wall. She was stirring a pot of stew. She looked tired. The two kids and the baby sat at the oilcloth-covered table, rosy faces smeared with food. I smelled potato soup, stew meat, gravy. I started to wash my hands in the tin basin of soapy water on the stand beside the door.

"Henry," says Mother, "where's Will and your father?"

"They're a-comin'. Got one more row to cut."

"Bring us a pail of water before you wash up?"

I took the bucket from the nail on the wall, stepped outside to the pump. There was a coffee can on the planks, full of water and drowned insects. I hung the bucket on the lip of the spout, primed the pump and cranked the handle, long as a baseball bat, up and down. The pump gasped and croaked, leather suckers four years old. A column of water rose by imperfect suction to the spout and gushed into my bucket.

One shoulder sagging, I lugged the water into the kitchen and hoisted it to the washstand.

Paw and Will came in. Will displayed the dead rabbit to Mother and the kids. They seemed impressed. Will hung the rabbit outside in the cold air, under the porch roof, out of reach of the dogs.

Sitting at the table finally, we watched as Mother bowed her head and clasped hands together prayerwise. "Dear God . . . bless this house and all who dwell in it. Bless this food we are about to receive, for which we thank thee. For thy many gifts we are humbly grateful, Lord. Amen."

Grace would normally be said by the head of the household. But our father would not pray to anybody.

Mother raised her head and little Paul, age six, blurted out, "Pass the taters, pass the meat, thank the Lord and let's eat."

Mother looked at him. Paul blushed and lowered his face. Paw smiled. After a brief silence, Mother dished out thick potato soup, filling first Paw's bowl, then Will's, then mine and her own. The children had already eaten. Paw sliced four chunks from the round loaf of homemade bread in the middle of the table. We ate fast, Will and me.

"Take your time, boys," Mother said. "Elbows off the table, please."

"Goin' to Houser's," I said between gulps. We played basketball in Ernie's barn; he lived in Stump Creek and had electric lights in the barn. Four miles by bicycle.

Paw looked at Will. "You too?"

"I figured on it. You settin' out more traps tonight?"

Paw pulled the watch from the bib pocket of his overalls, studied it. "Coal train's comin' up the grade in about fifty-five minutes."

"Joe," Mother said, "you're not going down there tonight? Not with the boys. Please."

Paw buttered another hunk of bread. "We need the coal, Lorrie. It's gonna be a long winter."

"We could buy it for once."

"How?" said our father.

She was silent for a moment. "You could dig some more out of the old mine on the hill. Like you used to."

"You looked in that hole lately? Props are rotten. Roof's gonna cave in most anytime."

"Then you should seal it."

"I been meanin' to do that for a year." He scooped more stew onto his plate. "But tonight we got to get coal. Full moon's up, it's a good night for it."

"The brakemen will see you."

"You think they care? Good Christ, Lorrie—" Mother hated swearing, especially at table. "God, Lorrie, there's ten million men out of work these days. Why do you think Roosevelt's fixin' to get us into another war?" Angrily he broke his bread. "Ten million!"

"Joe, promise me this," Mother said. "Don't let Will climb on the train."

"Oh, Maw," Will said. "I can do that easy."

"Promise me," she repeated.

"Sure," Paw muttered.

We walked down the road under the maple trees. Paw wore his miner's helmet with the carbide lamp attached to the front. We each carried a bundle of sooty burlap sacks. The moon sailed high; silver light lay on the dirt road before our feet.

"But why not, Paw?"

"Not this time, Will, I promised her."

"You could load twice as much."

"I know it, son. Don't I know it? Next time."

Will stopped complaining. He knew when it was useless to argue with our old man. We heard a screech owl in the pine trees. A fox barked far up the hill, followed by the howls of our beagles behind us, brokenhearted, tied up under the front porch.

We came to the railway trestle. We climbed the concrete abutment and walked two hundred yards down the tracks—I walked on a rail—to where the grade began. We could hear the steam locomotive a mile away, whistle wailing as it approached Groft's crossing. I felt vibrations in the steel rail. Paw strode ahead between the tracks, big boots treading on every other crosstie, his shadow hard-edged in the moonlight.

We waited near the start of the mile-long hill. Paw took our sacks and draped them over his shoulder. He carried a bunch of short tie strings—binder twine—in his pocket, ends dangling. He repeated the usual instructions:

"I'll load and tie and drop the sacks off along the tracks. You boys drag the coal to the bottom. I'll be with you soon as I can. If either one of you tries to climb aboard this train I'll tan your hide good."

The beam of a headlamp swung across the trees; the engine appeared around the bend, rocking slightly from side to side, belching smoke and sparks from the stack. We backed into the elderberry bushes. The locomotive roared past in thunder, making a race for the grade. We saw the engineer with a pipe in his teeth leaning out his window, studying the tracks ahead, old hogger's steady hand on the throttle lever. A red glow lit up the interior of the cab as the fireman opened the firebox hatch and shoveled in coal. Then they were gone, followed by the tender with its steel sentry box for a brakeman, followed by the chain of iron gondola cars heaped with blue-black bituminous coal.

Paw stepped onto the shoulder of the roadbed. The train was slowing. He winked at me and Will, grinned, trotted along beside a gondola, caught the ladder, swung aboard and climbed to the top. As he moved away we saw him pull a sack from his shoulder and commence to stuffing it with coal. He faded into the moonlight.

The train was moving slower and slower. Will and I looked at each other. "Dare you," I said. I knew if he did I could. He knew it too. Paw was out of sight. We heard a faint thump ahead as the first sack of coal fell to the cinderbank.

Will hesitated for about two seconds. "Okay," he said. "Watch me close. Run with the train. Don't forget to lean forward when you jump off. Land a-runnin'." He glanced both ways. The train kept rattling around the curve, car after car. "We'll get off as soon as we cross the bridge."

He turned and jogged, grasped a steel rung and lifted himself from the ground, standing with one foot on the bottom step. I reached for the ladder of the next car, grabbed and hung on. The train jerked me forward but I got my feet on the ladder. I watched Will holding on with one hand, showing off, leaning far out to see ahead to the trestle crossing.

The train rumbled slowly on. Will's gondola crossed the bridge;

he jumped off and ran forward a few steps, easily keeping his balance. Paw's first sack of coal, neatly tied, lay on the cinders beside the track. Many more beyond. Will looked up at me as I glided past. "Okay, Henry, jump off." I grinned and clung to the ladder. "Henry!" he shouted, "you get off there." I thumbed my nose at him and rode on.

I was enjoying the ride. Just a little bit farther, I thought, then I'll jump. Looking back I saw Will drag a sack of coal to the edge of the embankment and roll it down toward the wagon lane in the woods. That reminded me how angry Paw would get if he found out I hadn't helped.

I'll ride to the top of the grade, I thought, then jump off, sneak around the old man and rejoin Will at the lower end. I looked ahead but could not see the engine; it was already in the big cut at the top of the hill.

A man walked toward me down the shoulder of the railway. It was Paw. I shrank against the dark side of the gondola, trying to make myself invisible. He stooped over a loaded sack, checking the tie and pushing it off the bank. He never noticed me.

Now, I thought, better get off this here train before I get in trouble. I looked down at the cinders and crossties beneath my feet. They were passing faster than before. I braced my nerves to let go, make the jump. But hesitated.

You got to jump, I told myself. But it was too late; I sensed it in the rattle of the wheels over the joints in the rails, the scream of the whistle, the locomotive highballing down the far grade. An icy wind streamed past my ears. Wait for the next hill, I thought. I crawled into the space under the sloping bulkhead of the car and found protection from the wind. Not much. I pulled down the earflaps of my cap, buttoned the collar of my coat, sat tight and waited.

The scattered lamps of Stump Creek flashed by. I was already four miles by road from home. We raced through the village of Pine Run—five miles. The next little town would be Sawmill—seven. Close to Sawmill the train slowed suddenly, air brakes hissing. I cracked my frozen limbs into action, found the ladder and jumped to the cinders before the train stopped. Men with lanterns hurried toward me. They seemed to be yelling my name. Railroad bulls, I said to myself. They're gonna put me in jail. I stumbled across a ditch, climbed a fence and ran into the dark.

A long train ride but it was a longer walk home. Took me half the night. I followed the highway as far as Stump Creek, dodging into the bushes whenever I saw the lights of a car approaching. This side of the village I took the shortcut over the hill. The moon was low and the Big Dipper heeled over on its handle when I limped up Lightcap Hollow under the tunnel of trees. Two lamps glowed in the windows at our house. I was hoping to sneak in through the cellar door and crawl in bed before anyone knew I was home, but the hounds started yapping. When they recognized my scent it was too late.

Mother was glad to see me. She cried as she hugged me. Paw looked solemn. He must have caught hell from Mother and that meant I was in trouble with him. Will wasn't around: in hiding, maybe, or maybe in bed. He would be looking for me too, come morning.

Paw led me out to the barn, where Mother wouldn't hear, and gave me ten whops across the rear with his belt. Not too hard. It didn't hurt much. I had a copy of the *West Virginia Farmer* folded inside my pants. The old man said he'd given Will twelve licks because Will was two years older and should've known better than to let me climb on that train.

Will got me on the way to school next morning, down by the macadam road where we waited for the bus. Little Paul watched and tried to pull Will off my back but that was a waste of time. When the bus finally came Will let me up. I picked the gravel out of my face, staunched my bleeding nose with my bandana and climbed aboard after Will and Paul. Duane Bishop, the driver, looked at my face but didn't say a word. He knew better than to question Will.

But I didn't care. I was a hero for nearly a week.

What's more we got in the coal the next night, all of it, by team and wagon in the moonlight. Thirty bushels of good lump coal— about a ton and a half, Paw said. Enough to keep our house warm for the next four months, along with a few cords of oak and beech from the woodlot. The wood was free. Like the coal.

One night in bed, after my train ride, our mother said to her husband, "He hung on to that train all the way to Sawmill. Seven miles in freezing cold. Then got off and walked home. At night. A ten-year-old boy. Who would you say is dogged now, Joe?"

Joe Lightcap stared through the moonlit gloom at the ceiling and thought about it. After a while he said, "Lorrie, there's dogged and there's stupid. Will is dogged."

"I see."

Joe lay back and thought some more. "Henry ain't stupid though. That's what worries me. He's in for a life of lots of complicated complications."

My mother smiled to herself. "At least it won't be a dull life."

A pause. "Just what do you mean by that, Lorrie?"

Another pause. "Only what I said."

3

HENRY BEGINS HIS RETREAT

A little time slippage here. I seem to have passed out, or on, so to speak, down to the kitchen floor. The clock on the wall says ten-thirty and sunbeams slant through the east window at an acutely discouraging angle. Well then, and what's that puddle of stinking Freon under the refrigerator? Oh yes. A long night.

There's an awful shuddering noise driving toward the house from the southeast. Like giant blenders in the sky. Those heavy-duty military gunships again, trying to intimidate me. Twice a week they fly this route, directly over my roof. The walls vibrate, the windows rattle, the birds fall silent, the dog whines. Should load up the old carbine, sight it in on those evil motherfuckers. They pass over, rotors thumping, and fade.

Time to get moving. All those miles to go. I rouse myself, rise to my feet, head throbbing with life and pain, and stagger into the bedroom. Pack what clean clothes I can find. Not many.

Might as well leave the laundry for Elaine one more time. She can always give my underwear to her boyfriend, Dr. Schmuck. I stuff the sleeping bag and raincoat into a duffel bag, lug everything out and throw it into the back of the truck.

Solstice the dog comes shambling up, eyes bleary and leaking, black coat dull, skin full of ticks, tail wagging with feeble hope. She's dying of the valley fever. Lung fungus, a common and prevalent ailment in the hot dusty smoggy air of southern Arizona. Dogs or humans, everybody who lives here gets it; some die. I stroke her black head, pluck a couple of bloated gray ticks from her ear. "Didn't get your Nizoral last night, eh?"

Back in the kitchen I wad a pill inside a piece of cheese and take it to the dog. She gulps it down. The drug won't cure her, it merely slows the progress of the disease, providing her with a longer lingering more-satisfactory death. But what else can a man do? Anyway she's Elaine's dog, let Elaine come and get her. Of course, being female, she prefers me. The dog I mean.

Which reminds me, might as well give my dental hygienist one more chance. Surely she didn't mean those harsh cruel things she said last night. Though I can't remember exactly what they were, I recall the gist of the message: go away.

I plug in the telephone and dial a familiar number—the tooth-and-mouth clinic where she works. After the usual delays and circumlocutions—I've introduced myself as Dr. O. Vincent Amore—the receptionist (that dense suspicious bitch) finally buzzes Melanie's little cell. She is undoubtedly at work on a patient and there is no reason whatsoever why she should interrupt her work to answer the lunatic telephone—but she does. I've noticed that reflex everywhere now: people are trained, they are *conditioned* to jump when the telephone calls, always, anywhere. Everybody going around with trembling hands, the push-button smile, the forty-mile video stare in the eyeballs.

"Hello," she says, bless her sweet heart.

"Hey, how's my oral masseuse today?"

"Oh. It's you is it. Sorry, Henry, I'm busy right now." And indeed I can hear at her elbow the gurgling of a human mouth wedged open with plastic shoehorns. "Goodbye—" she starts to say.

"*Don't* hang up. This is important, Melanie. Just give me thirty seconds."

"I'm watching the clock."

"How about lunch with me today. At the regular place. Shrimp cocktails, frozen daiquiris, Coors beer, whatever you want."

"I don't think so."

"Melanie, you haven't cleaned my teeth for three months." Gland calling out to gland for love, for unity.

"Henry, I can't."

"What do you mean you can't?"

"I mean I can't. I'm going with somebody else now, Henry."

"Melanie!"

"Well Henry, I didn't hear from you in weeks. Months, really. Life goes on you know. I mean you can't expect people to just keep waiting for you, you know, week after week. I mean—you know."

"Sweet Melanie."

"I'm sorry, Henry. But I'm not really sorry. You've got your stockpile. Call Gloria. Call Alice. Call Annie. Call Pamela. Call Heather. Call Whatshername. You'll make out, you always do."

"Melanie . . ."

"Got to go now, Henry."

"What about my teeth? Who's gonna floss my teeth?"

"Put them in a glass of Lysol."

"Melanie—!"

"Stick your head in too and soak for thirty minutes—goodbye."

Crash.

The silent hum of eternity comes across the line. Dial tone. I hate that noise. I unplug the phone and resume packing the half-ton Dodge Carryall. A 1962—best truck Detroit ever made. A panel truck, solid, ugly, honest. Most of my camping gear is already on board: five-gallon water jug, fuel, Primus cookstove for rainy weather, foam-rubber pad, tarp, grub box full of canned goods and potatoes and jerky and salami, the iron grill, skillet, Dutch oven, ancient pots and pans black as sin from a thousand campfires. Rifle and shotgun mounted in the rack, unloaded but functional. Old greasy Navy wool blanket, a saddle blanket, even a bridle: souvenirs of a previous job. Just the sight of that familiar well-used honest practical equipment makes me feel better, eases the crablike pinch of pain somewhere behind the biliary ducts, near the liver and the pancreative gland where a man measures out, hour by hour, the number of his days.

I mean our days on Planet Earth, best damned planet in the whole queer cosmos. Why I wouldn't trade one morning in the Black Rock Desert of Nevada or the Allegheny Mountains of Appalachia for a complete eternity in Yeats's gold-plated Byzantium, Dante's polyurethane Paradiso or T. S. Eliot's Ivy League Heaven.

Got to get back to Will and the farm. Go home for a while. Back to the hills and the woods and the crick and the dogs. Get my hands on something hefty again. Like an ax handle. Get out of this foul city and don't never come back. Return to the myth-infested hills of ancient Appalachia.

The dog keeps watching me as I trek in and out of the house, carrying my few and portable possessions. She knows I'm leaving. I lean down and give her a pat on the dry muzzle, the lean bony head. "Sorry, old girl."

I'm leaving the house with books and papers when the military helicopters come a-thundering toward my roof again, not more than a hundred feet above. Once again (temper temper) Henry loses his temper. I rush to kitchen, plug in phone, dial another well-known number.

The sweet simpering voice of an Airperson, Technician Fifth Grade, responds: "Corporal Drew Information Office Davis-Monthan Air Base Arizona National Guard may I help you?"

"Major Fleming."

"Sir?"

"Wanta talk to Major Fleming."

"May I ask who's calling please?"

"General Henry Holyoak, Special Project Consultant, SAC."

"Yes sir. Just a moment sir." Sound of busy signal. "Could you hold the line for just a moment sir, Major Fleming is on another line."

"Yes, I could hold the line for a moment, but"—the three gunships bashing through my air space, rattling the crockery in the cupboard shelves—"I prefer not to. Get me Major Fleming, Corporal, this instant, at once, or your sweet ass is hamburger."

"Yes sir."

Another delay. Then the familiar sandpaper voice. "Major Fleming speaking."

"Major Fleming?"

"Yes sir." A pause. "Is that you again, Lightcap?"

"That's right, Fleming, this is Henry Lightcap speaking to you through the miracle of the telephone and you know why. Your dirty stinking helicopters are flying right over my house again, Fleming, making one hell of a racket, and I want it to cease and desist. Immediately."

"You're talking to a major in the Arizona National Guard, Mr. Lightcap."

"Yes? So? Well you're talking to a private first class retired in the United States Infantry and I'll have to insist on the usual courtesies here. Get your goddamned helicopters out of my backyard. The noise is driving me and my dog insane."

"That's the sound of freedom, Mr. Lightcap."

"No, it's the sound of tyranny, Major Fleming. The same noise you hear in Russia, Poland, Afghanistan. Tyranny, I say."

"They sound different over there, Mr. Lightcap."

"Tyranny is tyranny."

"Over there they sound like Communism."

"Yeah? Well here they sound like hell. Like bats out of hell, Major Fleming, and I'm sick of it and if they come over one more time I'm getting out the old M-16 and shooting them down."

"You do that, Lightcap, and we'll napalm your house."

"You do that, Fleming, and I'll collect the insurance and sell the lot for a 500 percent capital gain. I'll be a modestly wealthy man."

"I'm taping this conversation, Lightcap."

"So's the FBI, Fleming. You're in trouble."

"Maybe. We'll see. The CIA's on my side."

"Well now that you and your boys got run out of Vit-nam by a bunch of raggedy-ass rice farmers in black pajamas, what little country you gonna jump on next, Fleming? Can't you find something tinier than Vit-nam? Why not Easter Island, Fleming? Or how about Tobago? Trinidad?"

"This is very entertaining, Lightcap, as always, but I do have work to do. Goodbye." He hangs up on me. The helicopters are gone now, anyway. Peace has returned, except for the usual permanent background rumble of truck traffic on the Interstate, freight trains on the Southern Pacific, fighter jets screaming over the University of Arizona.

Work to do? Yes, I still have to call Cardamone and the welfare office. I'm already two hours late.

"Lou, I can't make it today. Got the flu or something."

There's a long silence on the other end. He says, "That's all right, Henry."

"In fact I need a four-week leave. With or without pay, I don't care. Make it six months."

Another long pause. I hear Lou's labored breathing. He takes a deep breath. "Henry—do you really want to be a public welfare administrator?"

"Lou, that's a tough question. Can you give me some time to think it over? About six months, maybe?"

A brief pause this time. "That's what we thought, Henry. Your final paycheck will be in the mail Friday."

"Shove it up your ass."

"We're phasing you out, Henry. You know you've been late or absent thirty-two times in the last three months. We're going to have to let you go, Henry."

"Take your job and shove it."

"Have to do it, Henry."

I unplug the phone.

Now what? What now? I gulp down four aspirins in a slug of cold coffee. How to burn out your stomach, quick. But I have no choice, this hangover is murderous. And not a drop of booze left in the house; I think I even emptied the last of Elaine's cough syrup a couple nights ago. Anyhow truck's loaded, we're ready to go. First to the bank to clear out checking account, then to the Dirty Shame Saloon for a fast lunch, then—then on to the winding asphalt trail for Everyman's Journey to the East.

I dash off a brief warning note to Will.

Dear Will,

Will you potbellied baldheaded bastard I'm coming home. Leaving today. It'll take me a week or two because I'm visiting some friends on the way but I'll be there. So dont say I didnt warn you. And why am I coming home? I am coming home to rescue you, old brother, from that museum display of 19th Century Americana you're making a fool of yourself in. Before the Pittsburgh suburbs overrun you completely. You & your comical draft horses & yr organic horseshit & yr bugriddled potato patch & screwworm milk goats & corn-borer cornfield and all those cute little Foxfire hippie Mother Earth nature nixies pitching their tents in yr barnyard. Well, anyhow, I'm coming home for a while. Help you guard the place. Lightcap's Last Stand. We got to draw the line somewhere Will and maybe Stump Crick is the place. If it aint already too late.

Fraternally, Henry.

PS: I'll be coming alone, as you might expect. Just me and my fleas. Give my love to Marian and to Mother and tell them not to worry about me, I'm alright, it's the world that's dysfunctioning and I mean that literally.

I stick the letter in an envelope, the envelope in my shirt pocket. Wanhope—melancholia—*of Cerberus and blackest midnight born*—clutches me in its venomous grip. But only for a minute. I pull on my best cowboy shoes, the pair with the pointy toes for kicking snakes and the undershot heels caked with old horseshit, and that makes me feel better. What I always really wanted to be, like most American boys, was a free-lance cowboy. Not a real working cowboy, of course, not one of those red-nosed leaky-eyed runty little half-breeds with the two-digit I.Q.s that actually do the actual tedious chores on a cattle ranch, but a movie-type cowboy driving a white Lincoln convertible from rodeo to rodeo.

But that's not true either. What I really want to be when I grow up (if I live that long) is a hunter. I mean a *hunter*. Not a recreational shootist, for godsake, but an honest-to-God *hunter* in a small band of buddies pursuing the sacred game across the desert-plain and into the forest while our tough loyal women wait for us in wigwams back at the home camp under the red cliffs of—of where? Southwest Africa? Utah? The Wind River? Mount Olga and Ayers Rock? Most anywhere will do but here—where we are.

Desperate phrases. How can I even think such things?

Seeking guidance, I raise my eyes to the Jesus calendar by the fridge, relic of a visit to El Rapido Tortilla Factory in oldtown Tucson. Some mocker named Lightcap has tacked it on the wall next to a replica of one of Modigliani's reclining nudes—rosy nipples, flat belly, dark eyes, neat little tuft of pubic hair nestled between the thighs and a savory trace of sweat under the upraised arms. The calendar, rather different, bears on its cover a representation of an effeminate Aryan blond-haired blue-eyed soft-featured Jesus Christ—Christ as the Bearded Lady—revealing with one hand his bleeding heart (like a narcotics agent showing his badge) while the forefinger and index finger of his other hand, the right, point directly upward. One Way. To the ceiling, the cracks in the plaster, the bowl of the light fixture black with fried insects, and beyond. Toward the eternal.

Truck is loaded, ready to go. What about Fred the cat? Fred is gone, hunting songbirds. What about the goldfish? I dump them in the birdbath outside. They'll have at least a sporting chance until Fred finds them or the curvebill thrashers or the sparrow hawks or the saguaro elf owls. A fighting chance: what more does anyone have?

Time to go. I sit down and write my farewell address to Elaine:

Darling Elaine,

I dont blame you one bit for walking out on me. I deserved it and so did you, after putting up with my antics for—what is it?—three long years. I was unfaithful to you but never in my heart, sweetheart, only down below. How often? I didnt count. Who with? Nobody you ever knew. But no matter what I was doing I was always thinking of you. And why did I do it? Well— one million years of primate biology is kind of hard for one man to repeal, on his own. Thus the lies, the sneaking around, the deception, thinking you'd never know. But of course the woman always knows, sooner or later. "They can smell it on you," as Harrington warned. Yes, I know, there's something wrong with me. Is there no cure? Surgery: whip it out and whack it off. Or maybe old age and debility, though you can't count on that. "He old but he aint dead," as Chuang-tzu said of Lao-tzu. And even if I'd been faithful as a dog there was that other question: *How to live? How?* Ever since your father made the down payment on this house I've felt like a rat in a maze. Trapped in the old cash nexus. He made the down payment—but I had to meet the monthly. You know I couldn't do it, Elaine. Couldn't keep it up or even get it up anymore. We must simplify our lives, my darling—simplify! simplify! like Jesus said. Write to me c/o Will, RFD, Stump Creek, W.Va., Zip Unknown.

So long,
Henry

PS:When you sell this shabby little shoebox of a house, as no doubt you will, remember me. The equity ain't much (about $20–25,000 now?) but whatever you get I could sure use my share of it. Whatever you think is fair. My debts are many, I have nothing, the rest I leave to the poor. Goodbye.

The babble of an idiot. I seal the letter in an envelope and leave it for Elaine on the kitchen table. She'll be here as soon as she knows I'm gone.

Now what? Now we are ready, I to depart—I stroke the dog on her bony skull—you to remain. Which is the better only God knows.

Poor Sollie looks unhappy. She fears and dreads these ominous departures, has sensed by now that I'm leaving for good. I scratch her neck, pick another engorged tick from behind her ear. (God in his wisdom gave us the bloodsucking tick. The theologians have been trying to figure that one out for three thousand years.) What a miserable specimen of dog she is. I check her food dish and water bucket: both full. I reenter house, make that last essential phone call to Professor Schmuck's secretary at Computer Science, leave message for Elaine about Sollie, turn on a couple of lights and the radio for burglar protection, lock the doors, hide the key under the rubber rattlesnake in the carport shed, stumble into my truck, start motor, engage the slipping clutch. Driving down the lane with its center line of bur sage and sore-eye poppies. Past the mailbox and into the dirt street.

Stepping hard on the gas, I stir up a plume of dust—farewell, Tucson. I glance once into the mirror to see if our flag is still flying. Yes it is, flapping from the pole on the roof, our sun-bleached rainbow flag, symbol of peace, brotherhood, happiness, the freedom of the open seas. Tom Paine designed that flag in 1789. A good man, that Thomas Paine.

And then—oh no—I notice something else appearing through my trail of dust, a dark animate object, dog-shaped, loping after me on arthritic legs. Please, not that. But it is.

I stop the truck, open door on passenger side, wait. Presently she comes, heaves herself with great effort up and onto seat, sits there panting, tongue hanging out like a wino's necktie. Assuming a confident nonchalance she cannot feel, the dog stares through the cracked windshield at the road ahead, ready to go. I slam the door and drive on, lurching forward, sick of the dog already and ashamed of myself for being such a chickenhearted fool. Slowing for the STOP sign on Silverbell Road, I consider—but only for a moment—returning to the house for Sollie's food dish, her water bucket, her sleeping rug, her leash, flea powder, Nizoral pills. No, I'm a busy man, I've dallied far too long, it's nearly noon. Anyhow it would be impossible for me to return to that empty haunted silent reproachful house. My heart could not bear it.

Impossible. Can't be done. But I do it. I turn the truck 180 degrees, drive back to house, pick up Sollie's things. The dog remains in her place on the passenger's side of the bench seat, not watching me, pretending these are routine procedures, hoping I'll not notice that she's there. Off we go.

We're not yet clear of Tucson. Next stop the bank. I'll take the four hundred or so left in our joint checking account—vulgar necessities of material contingency—before heading north and northeast onto the open road, the asphalt trail leading homeward. Where is home? Home is where you shall find your happiness. Whatever that may be.

Heavy traffic on my route. Forty-ton dump trucks loaded with gravel obstruct my passage. Move it, damn it, or get it the hell off the road. Chuckholes here and there, everywhere. A sticker on the tailgate of the truck in front of me says, "This Truck Pays $7,500 a Year in Road Taxes." Not nearly enough, you road-hogging pavement-busting traffic-jamming swine.

I work around the truck only to find my way blocked by a black old bomb of a Chevy sedan riding one inch above the asphalt, a row of six dark small heads barely showing above the dashboard. The driver apparently watches the road through a periscope. *La Raza* moving in, one must be understanding, they don't want to live in Mexico either and who can blame them? Life is better in Newark, N.J.

Be fair, you bigot, I say to myself, think of the cultural riches the Mexicans have added to the decadent materialism of the gringo. Tacos for instance. Nachos. Burritos. Salsa music. Spray-paint art. *Patrón*-style politics. Plastic Madonnas on acrylic-plush dashboards and other intellectual, scientific and artistic treasures I'm sure I could think of if I really set my mind to it.

I slip around the low rider and find myself behind a high rider, a sunglassed T-shirted neckless urban redneck wearing one of those funny hats like cowboys wear and operating this four-by-four GMC road tank with six KC Lites on the roof of the cab, chrome-plated roll bars in the tiny bed and something like tractor tires with raised white lettering—DIRT DIGGER—mounted on each oversize wheel. His left bumper sticker reads YOU DON'T LIKE THE WAY I DRIVE, STAY OFF THE SIDEWALK. His right-hand sticker says HAVE YOU HUGGED YOUR TOILET BOWL TODAY? Bad manners everywhere. The truck's headers rumble like machine-gun fire as the driver gears down for a red light.

Big noise, tiny balls.

We stop, we roar, we proceed. Henry pulls around the giant toy truck and past a little Honda Seppuku sedan, racing for the next intersection through a broken field. Too late, too late, he is jammed by a red light. I brake and wait, drumming my fingers on the wheel. Something about urban driving makes me testy, impatient, a touch irritable. Me and a hundred million others. But a wise man does not yield his equanimity to such trivial things.

A girl on foot picks her way cautiously through the crosswalk, between the ranks of muttering panting steel beasts. A fine specimen of young American female, well developed in every essential respect. Pretty face, breasts, buttocks—the eternal verities. Contemplating this restorative picture, I am startled to hear a metallic squealing noise at my immediate rear. I glance up at the traffic light to see, at this moment, the light change from red to green. The son of a bitch behind me has hit his horn in rheostatic anticipation of the green light, as if his head itself were wired to the controlling terminals.

This sort of thing exasperates Henry Lightcap. Instead of driving on he sets the parking brake and gets out of his truck to have a few words with the fellow behind. Yes, it's the man in the Seppuku. He gapes at Henry in astonishment as Lightcap leans down to speak to him through the open window, face-to-face. Like a gentleman.

"You blew your horn at me," says Henry.

Amazed, the man stares at Henry. He is large, well dressed but limp, shoulders sloping as if deboned, his eyes unable to focus on any particular object. A man in the grip of abstractions. Hands trembling. Nerves haywire.

"I hate horn blowers," Henry says, leaning closer.

Sensing danger, the man starts to roll up his window. Lightcap checks it with a heavy hand on the glass. The man glances at his rearview mirror, shifts into reverse and begins to back up. Henry opens the lightweight soybean door and slams it hard against the front fender of the car, springing the hinges. Bent, warped, out of reach, the door stays jammed in its open position as the driver backs off to a safe distance. He pauses a moment, gears crunching, then swerves forward to the right-hand lane and dives into the mainstream of traffic beyond. The man's passing scream of trite obscenities ("asshole; cocksucker; motherfucker") is lost in an uproar of brawling auto horns.

Henry walks to his vehicle, climbs in beside his patient dog and waits calmly for the return of the green. He feels better now, like any boiler that's popped its safety valve. Jap crap, he thinks. Rice rockets. Niki-Tiki sewing machines. Hondas, Toyotas, Sonys, Kawasakis. Tofu metallics, noodle-soup plastic. Vile cheap imported garbage: to think that we Americans, in our blindness and stupidity, should throw our own people out of work, shut down our great mills, let the Forest Service clear-cut our forests and the BLM stripmine our hills and the beef industry gnaw down our rangelands to the bone in order to produce raw materials to trade to those Nipponese ant people in exchange for their bright cheap slick robot-manufactured electro-mechanical junk, none of which, not one single item of which, we actually need.

Now now. Temper temper. I mutter my prayer: "Oh Lord, please help me to become like the others—gentle, kind, tranquil . . . soon."

On to the bank. As always, fresh difficulties appear. We find good parking space at the front door, thanks to double-wide slots reserved for our physically handicapped friends, but there is a long queue of folk inside standing within corridors of velvet rope. A few geriatrics and quite a few official minorities, clutching their government checks, impede my progress toward a teller, cash and liberty.

Inching forward with the human centipede, gradually but slowly making progress, I hear the old geezers in front of me, lisping through their dentures, say, "Remember them good old days when you could just walk into a goldanged blankety-blank bank and get your check cashed?" "That was before they got them son-of-bitchin' computers," says the other; "now everything is automatic, that's why it takes so long." "Course we didn't have much money in them days neither," the first says. "That's true, Luther, but we didn't need much: you could buy a new suit for $19.95 in them days."

Mumbling, grumbling, we crawl along. The first old man says, "Now they claim pretty soon the computers will do everything: you won't have to go to no bank at all, never even leave your room, just sit there in front of a display screen, push buttons, food'll come out of a slot by your elbow like shit out of a tube." "You ever been to one of them automated hog farms? That's the way they take care of hogs already." "We're next," somebody says up ahead. "You know what *my* computer tells me?" says another veteran; "my computer tells me in fifty years there won't be no computers." A short silence follows this amazing statement.

"Next!" yells a teller.

I find myself at a window facing a solemn young woman of the Afro-American preference. I've already scribbled out a check to "Cash" for $385, the amount remaining in our account, according to my check register. I present this document to the clerk, along with my bank I.D. card with its color photo of Henry H. Lightcap, number 1331-0323-0287, authorized signature on reverse side. Never looking at me, saying not a word, the clerk frowns at my check and card, punches some buttons on her computer terminal, waits a moment and announces the result:

"You have one dollar left in your account." With a smile of satisfaction she raises her black irises to my face, interested in my reaction.

Calm, very calm, cool as a Christian with aces wired, I say, "Run that through again, please." But my mind, sick and disorderly instrument though it is, has grasped at once the bitter truth: Elaine got here first. It was, after all—madness—a joint account. Decent of her, though, to leave me that one symbolic dollar, keeping our account joined, together, alive.

"One dollar," the teller says.

"Exactly one dollar?"

"Yes."

"I'll take it."

"There's a five-dollar service charge for closing the account."

"I see. Suppose I withdraw ninety-nine cents?"

"We don't accept accounts of less than one dollar." She stares at me with insolent pleasure, aware of the waiting queue of human types behind me, the file's passive acceptance of delay, confusion, indignity, humiliation—the New Age.

Henry considers creating a scene. But reconsiders. Any act of rebellion, even mere verbal abuse—and why pour his spleen on this poor dependent employee?—will be met with force. Official violence. That broad fellow over there in the blue suit, with club and revolver, is not here merely to watch us creepers crawl. He means force. If I should object to force I will be arrested. If I object to arrest I will be clubbed. If I defend myself against clubbing I will be shot. These procedures are known as The Rule of Law.

Anyhow I have other resources. I open my wallet and present the teller with my credit card, a MasterCard® in my case, Valley National Bank Arizona number 5288-6766-3314-9855, 1192 VNB AZ valid thru 07/80, Henry H. Lightcap, by Gawd. My genuine authorized signature on the backside.

"Okay, Miss," I say. "I'll use this. Give me a credit form."

I slip her my MasterCard®, she slips me the slip of paper, I fill it in for $499 while she fingers the clitoral buttons of her dream machine. As I slide the form toward her she reads the numbers on the screen. "Mr. Lightcap, you've already gone three hundred dollars over your credit line."

"What does that mean?"

"That means you can't borrow any more money on this card until you pay your bill."

"You mean the minimum payment due?"

Again she taps buttons, waits, gives me the news. "No, it means your payment is six weeks overdue so now you have to pay the whole bill, which is"—button, button—"which is $1,352.55."

"I'll speak to the manager. What's your name, young lady?"

She points to the nameplate on her counter. AMITY. "Next!" she cries to the file of forgers, murmuring but resigned, in my rear.

The manager is out. Only the assistant manager is available and he does not rise at my approach. Deep in his black padded leather armchair, shuffling a sheaf of papers, he does not even glance at me as I seat myself in the hard chair beside his desk. The supplicant's chair. According to the brass nameplate I'm dealing with a Larry

Klick. I toss my bank card and credit card onto the glossy surface of his desk.

"My name's Lightcap," I say. "I'm here on business." No answer. "Henry Lightcap," I explain. That should rouse him. It does not.

Finally, though, he condescends to glance at my cards, then at my face, then at my cards again. Both cards are smudged, I'll admit, blurry, as they have been ever since Elaine ran my pants through the washer with my wallet in the hip pocket. Got my money laundered, my cards obscured.

"Yes, Henry, what can I do for you?"

He called me Henry. A bad start. This banker type is at least fifteen years younger than I, a sleek plump blondish commercial lout with a twenty-five-dollar razorcut blowdried unisex coiffure, the dry, fluffy, styled and layered look. Each hair is fixed in place with an invisible net of wax from a spray can. Even the dandruff on his shoulders wears a metallic sheen. He's dressed in what might be a Bill Blass suit, I suppose, desert tan, with a fake old-school tie (Eton? Harrow? Tucson High? Boystown?) strapped around his fat neck. Vest buttoned up with cute wooden buttons matching the four wooden buttons on the ends of his coat sleeves. Square gold monogrammed cuff links, immaculate white French cuffs. Soft contact lenses, I suspect, on his milky eyes. Tassels on his shoes. Eyes like fisheye tapioca. *And tassels on his shoes.*

"What can I do for you, Henry?" he says again.

"I want to check out four hundred dollars on my MasterCard®." I think of the loaded .357 Magnum in my truck. What I should've brought in here is my MasterGun®. No waiting. Instant recognition. Honored everywhere. No finance charges, no fees, no paperwork.

"Sorry but your credit line is used up."

My heart sinks. My face falls. My gorge rises. "How do you know that, Larry?"

"Saw you talking with the teller."

"Is that your job, Larry? Watching the tellers? How could you hear what we were saying?"

He smiles. "We have our little systems. My guard is watching you right this minute. You look like the nuisance type. You'd better leave."

I squint at the ceiling. "I read in the papers you've got an asbestos fiber problem in this little branch bank, Larry. Not only here but in every VNB branch in Arizona."

He looks at me directly. There's a gleam of life—even anger—in those piscine eyes. "That's a lie. That's false. Chrysolite asbestos is absolutely safe. We've got sworn affidavits from independent testing laboratories."

"Cashiers dropping dead from mesothelioma. Asbestosis. Cankers like death's-head toadstools in your clerks' lungs. Deadly nightshade in their gallbladders."

He hesitates. "What do you want?"

"Money."

"You've come to the wrong place."

Once more I survey the interior—the tellers' cages, the safe-deposit vault, the video cameras mounted in the corners, the imitation Navajo sand paintings mounted on the wall, the shiny flecks of something toxic in the low fiberboard ceiling, the uniformed guard standing at parade rest near the main entrance, pretending not to be watching me. "Wrong place? This looks like a bank to me."

"It's the wrong place for you."

He's trying to insult me. I rise from the chair. You can't insult a Lightcap. We're above that. I take my cards. "When I want money from swine like you I'll take it by force." (MasterGun®.)

"You better leave, Lightcap."

He's making notes on a pad. I replace the cards in my wallet. "You ought to get out of here yourself, Larry. How do you feel these days? Feel a funny ticklish sensation in your throat?"

"Goodbye."

"See you in the obituaries, Larry."

"Get out."

"I'll come back to piss on your grave. You like chablis, I suppose? Rosé? Perrier?"

"I'm calling the cops, man, if you're not out of here in thirty seconds." He glances at the pink quartz digital chronometer on his wrist. Made in Japan. "You've got thirty seconds."

I leave, letting him have the last word. As I did the guru years before. You can't strip an assistant branch-bank manager of *all* his pride. He'd become an animal. Besides, he does have the local constabulary on his side and we've discussed what The Rule of Law boils down to: violence, gunfire, sudden death.

But we are short on cash. I count the change in my pocket: $34.56. Three thousand five hundred miles to go. About one dollar per hundred miles. And a bankrupt credit card. I see that we shall soon be suffering from that familiar disease called lack of money, a leading cause of poverty everywhere.

Ah well—I still have my wits. And my bulk. Though inside I'm scared, outside I look big, dark, bulky, ugly, dangerous. I'm aware of that and take full advantage every chance I get. Furthermore I've got more interesting problems than poverty. Sartre wrote that Hell is other people. But Dante was right: Hell is existence without love.

Got to go home for a while.

Nor am I above an act of petty vengeance. Speaking of love. Love of fun. I see the blue Porsche convertible parked in a slot "Reserved for Ass't Mgr." I open the back of my truck, lift the lid of the grub box, take out a large Idaho potato and force it into the tailpipe of the Porsche. I jam it in deep, out of sight, pushing with my thumbs. That should pop his fucking valves. Or at least give his muffler a hernia.

Back to the controls of my Dodge SuperHeap where Sollie the dog waits patiently, sitting in her place, gazing at the pink police ticket under the windshield wiper. Now what? I read the ticket. "Parking in space reserved for handicapped." Thirty-five-dollar fine. Anger surges through my veins. Handicapped? Who are these so-called "handicapped"? Am I not handicapped? An emotional spastic, a psychic quadriplegic, a moral basket case? Are we not all handicapped in our various fatal pitiful ways? Why should they, that minority in wheelchairs (another major minority!), have special privileges merely because they're cripples? If they can't walk let them creep. If they can't creep let them crawl. Are their arms only painted on? Time to fight back, I say. Time to launch our long-awaited countermovement, Henry H. Lightcap's Christian Crusade Against Crybaby Communist Crips, and if they don't like it we'll pull their plugs.

I tear up the ticket—rip it asunder (I love that word)—and drop the pieces in a handy trash can. HELP KEEP OUR CITY KLEEN. Climb

into truck, back out and head for the Dirty Shame Saloon. Got to
have one drink, only one, before I hit the open road.

Crossing the bar. Read the welcoming sign above the Dirty
Shame's elk-antlered doorway: GET DRUNK, BE SOMEBODY. The comforts of alienation. A dark ill-lighted unclean place, stinking of stale
beer and moldy floorboards, bourbon whiskey and archaeological
vomit. I love this joint. The buxom lass behind the bar brings me a
schooner of draft beer and my shooter of Wild Turkey. And a char-
grilled Polish sausage for Solidarity. The basics. Keep that liver
working, active, on its toes. Keep that pancreas slightly anxious. It's
true that man is the only animal that poisons himself with alcohol.
It's also true that man outlives every other animal on earth except
elephants, tortoises and crocodiles. And women.

I order another Polish sausage with onions and sauerkraut. Another beer. Solidarity Forever. Read the placards on the wall: MADD:
MOTHERS AGAINST DRUNK DRIVERS, and next to it, DAMM: DRUNKS
AGAINST MAD MOTHERS. There is a kind of order in the natural world.
The laws of compensation continue to function. For every action a
reaction, for every blow, a counterblow, for every torn leaf a fresh
bud, for every death a new life. The pulse of the springs of life
cannot be suppressed. No matter how much iron and cement and
asphalt and Astroturf and Du Pont fiberglass and driller's mud and
Hereford cowpies they pour upon the earth, the grass will overcome. Will come and *over*-come!

But it may take a while.

Should I phone Harrington? Arriaga? Lacey? Have one last round
of drinks with my old cronies before ricocheting off, like shit off a
shovel, into the pilgrim's final journey, my Journey East?

To rescue Brother Will.

No, I guess I won't. Would be too merry to endure. My heart
could not bear it. Too much like a wake. I don't even have the heart
to say goodbye. Imagine instead that we're coming back.

Lurching into the men's room for a final piss before departure, I
read again, as I always do, the fresh new writing on the wall, *vox
populi*, the voice of the people:

When did the Irish learn to walk on their hind legs? When
the English invented the wheelbarrow.

Fuck the Queen.

What's the happiest five years of a Chicano's life? Third grade.

Gobachos eat shit.

What do you get if you mate an African with a gorilla? A retarded gorilla.

Honkies eat shit.

Smells bad in here. I leave.

Now what? Well, another beer, another shot, another sausage cannot hurt. Then I must go. Yes, I am living a pig's life. This is not the way to live. But what then, as Tolstoy put it, is a man to do? What is, really, the good life? We'll see. Back in the hills maybe I'll figure it out. Got enough cash left for cheese and crackers, the siphon hose for gasoline, my arsenal for self-defense, my dying dog for companionship. How much wealth does a man need? The less the better if he's a free man. Yes: our liberties we prize. Our rights we will maintain. Don't tread on me. Liberty or Damnitall. Live free or die.

A few strange faces drift in and out—carpenters, plasterers, operating engineers—but nobody I know or want to know. I pay the barmaid—her name is Carlita—and stagger outside into the dazzling glare of April Arizona. Into the truck, onto the street, past a new billboard—

> ## Ya' Know, God Really Cares

—and north toward the highway.

I sing an old song:

> Jesus loves me, that I know,
> 'Cause the billboards tell me so.

Headed for Will's place, old Fort Llatikcuf as our Shawnee ancestors called it. Emphasis on final syllable. Three thousand four hundred ninety miles to go. About a thousand and two hundred leagues. (Big leagues.) Be of good cheer. Though it's over the hill to the poorhouse, as Rilke wrote, we been there before.

Henry lays back his head, both hands on the wheel, closes his eyes for a moment and howls for the hell of it, howls like a hound dog, like a coyote, like a wolf, as the wind screams past the open window at his side. His dog joins in, they howl together forlorn and furious, *basso profundo molto doloroso*, they put everything in and get everything out in one final farewell vulpine duet of defeat, despair, damnation, dejection, doom, death, dust, defiance—fraternity of the damned, the proud prolonged and primal hullabaloo of bottom dogs. Fat automobiles rush past on either side, their occupants staring at Henry and the dog. Neither cares.

Henry rolls up his window and lights a cigar. He pulls a bottle of beer from the sixpack on the floor, twists off cap and takes a hearty swig. Sets bottle in bottle holder on dashboard, close to hand. Beyond the city limits he reaches the secondary highway that winds northeast over the mountains toward Oracle, Winkelman, Globe, Show Low, Gallup, Albuquerque, Santa Fe and points beyond. He smokes the cigar, drinks the beer and thinks, as the wind whistles through the rusty cracks in the floorboards, of comfort. Of joy. Of Comfort (built for speed) and Joy (built for comfort). And the Raunch House Bar. Now there was a pair. And a place.

Solstice the dog, dying but content, stares straight ahead at the blue-gray road, the hot and lonesome asphalt trail. The gleam of hope shines in her leaky elderly stoic eyes.

I stroke her lean backbone. "We'll make it, Sollie. We'll get there, never fear."

We roll ahead past Oracle Junction, then pause for a moment, pulling off the pavement. The rented beer is trickling through me, building up pressure. I walk away from the road through the thicket of broomplant lining the ditch, step over a sagging fence and take shelter from the sun in the shade of a mesquite tree. The tree is bright, brilliant, joyous with fresh green leaves. Joy of April. An old dirt road runs nearby, paralleling the highway. Garbage scattered about as usual. I unbutton my fly, pull out The Thing and am about to piss when I notice the baseball glove in the grass at my feet. A boy's fielding glove, worn out, thrown away. I cannot resist the urge to pick it up, feel it, smell it. Long unoiled, dried out by the desert air, the leather is cracked, stiff, in poor condition. But not completely dead.

Slipping it on my hand, smacking the palm, holding it under my nose, it still feels like horsehide and smells like a baseball glove. Like April and mud. Like West Virginia in the spring. Like the Allegheny Mountains. Like the game. Like baseball, and girls, and the heartbreaking joy of a new season.

4

April 1942:
THE RITES OF SPRING

I

The war? What war? Henry Lightcap, fifteen years old and lean as a willow sapling, had deeper things in mind. Henry loved the chant of the spring peepers, ten thousand tiny titillated frogs chanting in chorus from the pasture, down in the marshy bottoms by the crick, that music of moonlight and fearful desire, that plainsong, that Te Deum Laudamus, that Missa Solemnis deep as creation that filled the twilight evenings with a song as old (at least) as the carboniferous coal beds beneath his homeland. (Grandfather Lightcap had signed a broadform deed to the mineral rights in 1892 but nothing ever came of it. Or ever would, thought Paw.)

Henry detested high school with a hatred keen as his knifeblade but loved getting on the bus behind Wilma Fetterman, watching as she climbed the high steps, her skirt riding high, his eyes fixed on the tendons behind her knees, the sweet virgin untouchable gloss of her forever inaccessible thighs. Henry, virgin himself, thought that he understood the mechanical principle of the human sexual connection but also believed, with the hopeless sorrow of youth, that he himself would never, never be capable of the act because—well, because his penis, when excited and erect, rose hard and rigid as bone against his belly button. There was no room in there, no space whatsoever, for a female of his own species. The thing could not be forced down to a horizontal approach, as he assumed was necessary, without breaking off like the joint of a cornstalk. He told no one of his deformity. Not even his mother. But though it was hopeless, he continued to love watching Wilma Fetterman climb the school-bus steps.

He loved the lament of the mourning doves, echoing his own heartache, when they returned each spring from wherever they went in winter. He loved the soft green of the linwood trees, the bright green of the Osage orange against the morning sun. He loved the red-dog dirt road that meandered through the smoky hills beside the sulfur-colored creek, into and through the covered bridge and up the hollow that led, beyond the last split-rail fence, toward the barn, the forge, the pigpen, the wagon shed, the icehouse, the springhouse and the gray good gothic two-story clapboard farmhouse that remained, after a century, still the Lightcap family home.

He loved his Berkshire pigs. He loved the beagle hounds that ran to meet him each evening. He loved—but intuitively not consciously—the sight of the family wash hanging from the line, the sound of his father's ax in the woodyard as the old man split kindling for the kitchen stove. He even loved the arrogant whistling of his older brother, Will—hated rival—as Will brought the horses up from the half-plowed cornfield, the team harnessed but unhitched, traces dragging, chains jingling, over the stony lane to the barn.

But most of all and above all and always in April Henry loved the sound of a hardball smacking into leather. The WHACK! of a fat bat connecting with ball. And better yet, when he was pitching, he loved the swish of air and grunt of batter lunging for and cleanly missing Henry's fast one, low and outside, after he's brushed the hitter back with two consecutive speedballs to the ear.

He loved his brand-new Joe "Ducky" Medwick glove, personally autographed (at the Spalding factory) by Joe himself. He loved the feel and heft and fine-grained integrity of his sole uncracked Louisville Slugger, autographed by baseball's one and only active .400 hitter, the great and immortal Ted Williams.

Brother Will liked the game too, in his calm complacent way, but never lay awake at night dreaming about it, never dawdled away hours composing elaborate box scores of imaginary games in a fantasy league that existed only in the mind of Henry Lightcap.

Henry had his reasons. He had a real team also. And real opponents. The Blacklick team was coming to Stump Creek for the first contest of the season.

Henry and Will picked their lineup, writing names down on a ruled paper tablet. Henry would take over the mound, Will, as usual, handle the catching. Their little brother Paul could play right field where he'd be mostly out of the way, not in a position to do much harm. Their best player and one genuine athlete, the sharp-eyed clean-cut Eagle Scout Chuck Tait, would sparkplug the team at shortstop or take over first or relieve the pitcher, wherever needed. That made four players, the solid core of the Stump Creek nine. But where to find the other five? Stump Creek, West Virginia, population 120 (counting dogs and girls), clumped in a lump beside County Road 14, did not offer much talent.

They brooded over the problem and decided the best they could do was have the Adams brothers, Clarence thirteen and Sonny twelve, play second and third base, and let the Fetterman boys, Junior (his baptized, Christian name) age thirteen and Elman age eleven, play the outfield. That Elman, says Will, he couldn't hit a cow's ass with a snow shovel. But we need him.

We're still one player short, Henry pointed out; we need somebody at first base. They thought about that for a while. Finally Will mentioned the name of Ginter.

No, said Henry. Who else? Not Red Ginter. Who else we got? But Red, said Henry, Red's seventeen. Yeah but he's still in fourth grade. That was three years ago. Well that's where he was last time he went to school. Blacklick would have a fit. We promised no players over sixteen. Besides . . . Besides what? Red won't play. Ask him. Who else we got? He can't play, says Henry. He's big but he won't move, he won't run.

He'll catch the ball if you throw it to him. He'll do for first base.

Can't hit the ball. Undercuts—swings his bat like it's a golf club. Strikes out every time.

Yeah but he takes a mighty powerful cut at the ball. Will smiled, his dark eyes musing. I saw him hit a ball four hundred feet on a line drive one time.

I saw that. A fluke hit and anyway it went foul.

He's the only one we have left, Henry.

Henry thought about it. What about Red's little brother? Leroy? Maybe he could play.

Christ, muttered Will, making a rotating motion with his forefinger close by his right ear. Leroy's crazy as a moon-eyed calf. We don't even want him around.

They were silent for a minute, sitting there in the kitchen at the oilcloth-covered table, under the amber glow of the kerosene lamp, staring at their paper lineup of eight ball players, five of them children. Then it has to be Red, says Henry.

II

Swinging out from the school bus late in the afternoon, Henry and Will walked half a mile homeward up the red-dog road, under the trees, then cut off over the hill through the Big Woods toward the next cove on the south. Once called Crabapple Hollow, it became known as Hardscrabble when the Ginter family, coming from no one knew where, made it their family seat in the late 1800s, soon after the end of the War Between the States.

They tramped through the ruins of Brent's sawmill, abandoned half a century before, and struck a footpath leading down the steep side of the ridge toward the corn patches and pastures of Ginter's farm. Halfway down they passed the tailings pile of a small coal mine, unworked for years. A dribble of sulfurous water leaked from the portal; decayed locust props, warped by the overburden, shored up the roof of the tunnel. There were many such workings in the area; in one of these old Jefferson Davis Ginter kept his distilling equipment.

The farm buildings came in view, ramshackle structures with sagging roofbeams. The main house was a one-story slab shack with rusted tin roof; built by Ginter, it leaned for support against a much older but far steadier pine-log cabin. Ginter's coon hounds, smelling the Lightcap brothers from afar, began to bay, tugging at their chains.

The path to the back porch of the house—their goal—was wide enough for two but Henry let Will walk before him. Will was both bigger and older, a dark stolid solid fellow, broad at the shoulders and thick in the arms, built—as everyone agreed—like a brick shithouse. Even as a freshman he had played first-string tackle on the varsity football team at Shawnee High School.

The back door stood wide open to the mellow April afternoon, revealing a dark interior. There was no screendoor. Ginter chickens wandered in and out of the house, pausing to shit on the doorstep, pecking at cockroaches, ticks, ants, June bugs, dead flies, fallen shirt buttons, crumbs of tobacco, whatever looked edible. A string of blue smoke from the kitchen stovepipe rose straight up in the still air.

The four dogs chained beneath the porch barked with hoarse and passionate intensity as Will and Henry approached the house. From inside came voices—angry, outraged.

They're fightin' again, says Henry. Maybe we should come back later.

They're always fightin', Will says. Come on. He marched firmly forward. Then stopped at the sound of a shriek.

There was an explosion of hens from the open doorway followed by a stub-tailed yellow dog, airborne, as if propelled by a mighty kick. The dog cleared the porch without touching the planks, landed running on the bare dirt of the yard—something pale and soft clamped in its jaws—and scuttled like a wounded rat toward the nearest outbuilding.

Will hesitated; Henry stopped behind him.

Old Jeff Ginter appeared in the doorway holding a pint Mason jar in one hand. He roared after the dog: You ever come back in here again you docktail misbegotten yellowback mutt I'll fill your hinder end with birdshot so goldamn stiff you'll be shittin' B-Bs through your teeth for a month.

And then the old man saw Will and Henry, two schoolboys in bright sport shirts and fresh blue jeans staring at him from fifty feet away across the beaten grassless dung-spotted yard. Ginter wore bib overalls, frayed at the knee, unpatched and unwashed; instead of a shirt he wore a long-sleeved union suit buttoned to the neck, once white but aged to a grayish blend of sweat, dust, woodsmoke and ashes. He was barefoot. He squinted at the boys through bloodshot eyes. What're you two a-doin' here?

Will gazed calmly at Ginter, waiting for Henry to speak. Henry was pitcher, scorekeeper, self-appointed manager of the Stump Creek baseball team.

Henry swallowed and said, We're lookin' for Red.

What you want him for?

We need him for the ball team, Mr. Ginter. We got a game with Blacklick Saturday.

The old man swayed a little on the porch, took a languid sip from his pint, raised the jar to the light and checked the bead. He glowered at Henry. When's this here game a-gonna be?

Saturday, Henry said.

Hain't the Sunday?

No sir, Saturday.

Any child of mine plays that baseball game on Sunday I'll peel the hide off his back with a drawknife, hang him by the ears to yon ole snag. Ginter gestured toward the dead butternut tree in the yard. Like I would a blacksnake. Till he stops wigglin'. Ain't Christian to play games on the Sunday.

No sir, it's Saturday.

Old Jeff relented. They're out at the pigpen sloppin' the sow, him and Leroy. Leroy's name suggested an afterthought. Now you mind and let Leroy play too or by God Red don't play.

Will and Henry glanced at each other. Will shrugged. They had no choice.

Yes sir, Henry said.

Behind the barn they found Red Ginter leaning on the pigpen fence, watching his little brother Leroy. Red was six feet six inches tall, weighed 240 pounds, had a small red-haired skull that tapered to a point between his ears. Like his father he wore bib overalls, long-sleeved gray underwear, no shoes.

Henry said hello. Red ignored him, ignored Will who said nothing but stood close by, ready for trouble. Will never did talk much— but then like Red Ginter he didn't have to. They stared at young Leroy.

Leroy, crouched on hands and knees inside the pen, was creeping over the muck toward a three-hundred-pound sow. The sow lay on her side, eyes closed, giving suck to a litter of eight. Leroy, twelve years old, was playing piglet. Ernk, ernk, he grunted, lowering his belly to the ground, wriggling forward, ernk, ernk, mumma. . . . Leroy's pink harelip formed what he understood as an ingratiating, shoatlike appeal.

Red encouraged him. Keep a-goin', Leroy. No sign of malice in Red's pale, dull eyes. And don't settle for hind tit neither.

Leroy squirmed closer. Ernk, ernk, mumma, gimme suck too. He was barefoot; his ragged bleached-out overalls seemed two sizes too small. The reddish hair on his head was thin, fine, short, giving him a half-bald look. Ernk, mumma, he crooned in begging tones, ernk, ernk. . . .

The great sow, lying peacefully in the April sun, at ease in the cool mud, opened one tiny red eye and saw Leroy inching toward her and her children. She grunted.

Leroy hesitated. Ernk . . . ? He raised his head.

The sow grunted again and scrambled to her feet. Leroy rose to his hands and knees. The sow squealed with outrage and charged. Her brood hung swinging from her tough teats, unwilling to let go. Leroy jumped up, turned. Nom nam nun of a nitch! he yelled, I gotta get the nom nam outa here! He leaped for the fence and rolled over, falling to the ground outside. The sow crashed into the planks and stopped, backed off and shook her head. She glared at Leroy.

Red Ginter, bland-eyed and unmoved, turned his face to Will and Henry. Henry explained the purpose of the visit.

I play first or nothin', Red says.

That's okay, Red.

Bat first too.

Will and Henry looked at each other. No options.

Leroy bats second, Red went on.

What? says Henry. Not Leroy!

You heard me, Red says. He picked up a wooden bucket full of skim milk, potato peelings, turnip greens, muskrat entrails, chicken heads, eggshells, bacon rinds. He emptied the bucket into the wooden trough inside the fence. The sow shuffled to the trough, snorted, plunged her snout into the swill. Red thumped the bucket on her head, clearing the bottom. The sow twitched her ears and kept on feeding. The piglets hung from her udders, still suckling.

III

Henry and Will tramped homeward over the ridge, into the Big Woods, past the forgotten sawmill, through the gloom of the trees. A hoot owl hooted from the darkness of a hollow sycamore, calling for its mate. Another answered from a faraway pine.

You hear that, Henry? says Will, as they paused before the split-rail fence that marked the Lightcap frontier.

Henry listened carefully. The owls called again, first one, then after a few moments of thought, the second.

Will grinned at his little brother; the bright teeth shone in his brown honest face. Will said, They're a boy owl and a girl owl.

Baloney. How do you know?

Because the first owl says, Hoo hoo, wanna screw? And the second owl she says, Hoo hoo, not with you.

Bull-loney.

They went down the hill into Lightcap's Hollow. While poor Henry, nursing in silence the secret of his desolate, hopeless incapacity, thought of Wilma Fetterman climbing into the school bus, of Betsy Kennedy draping her splendid cashmere-sweatered breasts over the back of her chair as she turned to tease him, of Donna Shoemaker turning cartwheels in her cheerleader uniform at the pregame pep rally. A pang of agony coursed upward through Henry's aching core, from the misaligned piston rod of his groin to the undifferentiated longing in his heart. Never, never with a girl.

The owls hooted softly after him through the soft green cruelty of April, down the hills of the Allegheny. The ghosts of Shawnee warriors watched from the shadows of the red oaks.

IV

A light rain fell Saturday morning, leaving pools of water on the base paths, but the sun appeared on time at noon. Henry and Will and little Paul filled burlap sacks with sand and paced off the bases. Chuck Tait came soon after with a bag of lime to mark the batter's boxes, the base lines, the coaching positions. They built up the pitcher's mound, chased Prothrow's cows into deep left field and shoveled the fresh cow patties off the infield. They filled in the pools with dry dirt, creating deceptive mudholes which only the home team need know about. They patched the backstop with chicken wire and scrap lumber. The Fetterman boys came with their gloves and a new bat, then the Adams brothers with gloves and two fractured, taped bats. (Both were cross-handed hitters.) No sign of the Ginters. There was time for a little practice; Will batted hot grounders to Chuck and the Adams boys, high-flying fungos to Paul and Elman and Junior in the outfield.

Henry felt he was ready; he'd spent an hour every day for six months throwing a tennis ball at a strike zone painted on the barn door, scooping up the ball one-handed as it bounced down the entrance ramp. Precision control, that was his secret. He only had three pitches: an overhand fastball, not very fast; a sidearm curve that sometimes broke and sometimes didn't; and his newly developed Rip Sewell blooper, a high floating change of pace which he lofted forward with the palm of his hand, a tempting mushball of a pitch that rose high in the air and drifted toward the plate like a sinking balloon. Weak pitches—but he had control. He could hit the center of Will's mitt whenever Will called for it.

The Blacklick team arrived an hour late, Tony Kovalchick the captain driving his father's twelve-cylinder 1928 Packard sedan. The three smallest boys sat in the trunk holding up the lid with a bat. The Blacklick players fingered rosaries; they wore sacred medals. Stump Creek surrendered the field to the visitors for a ten-minute warm-up.

Tony and Henry compared scorecards.

Your guys are too old, Henry complained. Those are all senior high school guys.

That's our team, Tony says. You wanta play baseball or you wanta go home and cry?

Carci, Watta, Jock Spivak—those are football players.

You got Will and Chuck, they're varsity. And who's this Red Ginter? Ain't he the one nearly killed some coal miner in the fight at Rocky Glen Tavern Saturday night?

Not Red, you got him mixed up with somebody else. Henry pointed to the Packard. A pale little fellow with strabismic eyes sat on the running board. Who's he? He's not in your lineup.

That's Joe Glemp. He's our umpire.

Umpire? He's cross-eyed!

Yeah, don't make fun of him. He's kind of sensitive. He can't play ball worth a shit. But he's a good ump.

You're crazy. He can't see anything but his own nose. Anyhow Mr. Prothrow's gonna be umpire. Henry looked around; old Frank Prothrow was nowhere in sight.

The visiting team always brings the umpire, Tony said complacently. You know that, Lightcap.

You're nuts.

It's in the rule book. Black and white.

Not in any rule book I ever saw. Let's see this rule book.

Let's see this Mr. Prothrow.

Henry looked again. No Prothrow in view. But there came the Ginters, Red and Leroy, tramping up the dirt road, Red carrying his ax-hewn homemade hickory bat on his shoulder. The one with the square shaft, like a tapered four-by-four. Henry appointed little Paul the field umpire. The Stump Creek nine took the field, Red Ginter on first nonchalantly catching Chuck Tait's rifle-shot throws from short, Henry on the mound, the children at second, third and scattered across the outfield among the grazing milk cows.

Play ball! hollered little Joe Glemp with harsh authority, masked and armored, crouching behind the broad back of Will Lightcap hunkered down at home plate. Tony Kovalchick, batting right-handed, stepped into the box, tapped mud from his cleated shoes, made the sign of the cross and dug in for the first pitch.

Henry, glove in armpit, rubbed the sweet new Spalding between moist palms and surveyed his team. All were in place except Leroy in deep right yelling obscenities at a cow.

Henry faced the batter, noticing at once that Tony choked his bat by three inches. Will gave Henry the sign, fastball wide and low. Henry wound up and threw exactly where Will wanted it, cutting the outside corner. Tony let it go by.

Ball one! shouted the umpire.

Will held the ball for a few moments to indicate contempt for the call, then without rising tossed it back to Henry. Tony crowded the plate a little more. Will asked for another fastball, high and inside. Ball—began the umpire as Tony tipped it foul. One ball, one strike, little Joe Glemp conceded.

He can't see but he can hear pretty good, thought Henry, rubbing the ball like a pro. Will called for the sidearm curve, low and outside. Backing off slightly (weakness!), Tony swung and tipped the pitch off the end of the bat. Two strikes. He scowled at the pitcher. Now we got him, Henry thought, he's getting mad. Will called for the floater, mixing them up, and Tony waited, watching the ball sail in a high arc toward him, and lost patience and swung furiously much too soon, nearly breaking his spine. He picked himself up, brushing mud from his knees, and stormed back to the visitors' bench.

A fat Italian boy named Frank Carci now stood in the box, anxious, tense, well away from the plate. A second-string center, he was better known as Snotrag: both on and off the field, the entire football team used the tail of Carci's jersey for noseblowing. Henry and Will struck out Snotrag with three fastballs high and inside, the batter drawing away from the plate as he swung, each time missing the ball by a foot.

Big Stan Watta came to bat. Stan was big but the next batter, Jock Spivak, fullback, was bigger. After a brief conference Henry and Will agreed to pitch to Watta and then, if necessary, walk Jock. Will called for the sidearm slider, low and outside. Henry threw it, the ball failed to slide, Watta trotted into second base with a stand-up double.

Jock Spivak took his stance deep in the batter's box, measuring the plate with his slugger's bat. Will and Henry stuck with their plan: a free pass to first for the big man. On deck was the easy third out Mike Spivak, Jock's kid brother, a weak hitter.

Henry checked the runner at second, then threw the pitchout high and outside into Will's guiding mitt. Ball one. Watta returned to second. Henry repeated the pitch, Will standing away from the plate to catch it. Ball two. Quickly now, impatient to get at the easy batter, Henry threw ball three. Jock Spivak spat on the plate, moved forward a step and grinned like a tiger.

Henry threw the ball neck high and a foot outside. Laughing, Jock stepped across the plate—Ball four! shouted Glemp—and smacked the pitch true, hard and high into far right field. Leroy Ginter dreamed out there, wiggling bare toes in a fresh cowpie. The Stump Creek team hollered for attention. Leroy wiped the drool from his chin and ran three steps to the left, four to the right, slipped in another pile of cowshit and fell to his knees. Nom nam nun of a nitch! he screamed, throwing his glove at the ball. Missed. The ball bounced into the weeds along the fence. Leroy made no move to retrieve it. Stan Watta crossed home plate. Laughing all the way, Jock Spivak jogged toward third. Junior Fetterman found the ball and pegged it to Chuck Tait at short, who relayed it to Sonny Adams at third. Sonny dropped the ball. Half sick with laughter, Spivak headed for home. Sonny threw the ball to Will, trapping Spivak between home plate and third. Spivak stopped but couldn't stop laughing. Will ran him down and tagged him out.

Backlick 1, Stump Creek 0, bottom of the first. The home team came to bat.

Red Ginter slouched into the batter's box with the squared-off log on his shoulder. He took a few underhand practice swings, like a golfer at the tee, spat on the ground and waited for the pitch. He wore the same greasy bib overalls, the same grime-gray flannel underwear he'd been wearing all winter and would not remove till May. Like his old man, Red knew only two seasons, winter and summer. Let the weather change, not him. He waited, cheek bulging, peering at the pitcher from beneath his dangling, reddish forelock, a sloping, pale and freckled brow. His small eyes, set close together, betrayed no gleam of human light.

The pitcher, Tony Kovalchick, raised both arms above his head and began an elaborate windup.

Ginter waited, legs far apart, rotating the bulk of his club in slow ominous circles behind his shoulder. The first pitch sped in like a bullet straight down the middle. Ginter reared back and took an awkward but vicious cut at the ball, swinging eighteen inches beneath it. His bat scraped a groove through the dirt behind the plate.

Sta-rike! yells Glemp, jabbing the air with his thumb.

The Blacklick catcher—squat square massive Dominic Del Poggio—chuckled as he flipped the ball to Tony. The pitcher allowed himself a smile. Both could see already that this game was going to be such a laugher they might not make it through the fifth inning.

Untroubled, Red awaited the second pitch. It came: a repeat of the first. He let it go by. No balls, two strikes.

Teasing the batter this time—anything for a laugh—Tony threw a careless slider inside and too low, almost on the ground. Red swung down and up, digging another furrow through the dirt, and golfed the ball foul in a drive of flat trajectory toward deep left, where it struck a cow on the head and caromed into the weeds. The cow sank to its knees, then fell on its side, where it lay comatose for half an hour. The count at the plate remained the same: no balls, two strikes.

Red Ginter waited, pale eyes bland and empty. The pitcher and catcher—after brief talk—played the next pitch safe: a fastball chest-high across the center of the plate. The long-ball hitter's dream pitch. Red watched it go by. Three strikes and out. Leroy Ginter, second batter, took his place.

As Red shuffled back to the bench Chuck Tait rose to meet him. Look, Red, Chuck says, you're swinging way under the ball. He imitated Red's underhand swing. Now watch: you have to level your stroke. Watch. He demonstrated a swift beautifully smooth perfectly level swing, in the manner of Williams and DiMaggio. See? Like that. He gave a second demonstration, pure grace, sweet perfection.

Chewing on his plug of Red Man, leaning on his four-by-four, Red stared down at Chuck from ten superior inches, some eighty extra pounds, and spat a jet of tobacco juice onto Chuck's shoe. You bat your way, baby face, he says, and I'll bat mine. He tramped past Chuck and sat on the bench.

Chuck stared at the dirty splotch on his clean new sneakers and said nothing. But to Henry and Will, later, he grumbled, No team spirit. None of your guys have the real team spirit.

Clowning at the plate, Leroy struck out in three wild swings, two from the left side and one from the right. He slammed his taped bat on the plate—Nom nam nun of a nitch!—broke it again, and ran off toward the elderberry bushes beside the creek, where two heifers browsed on the shrubbery.

Chuck Tait stepped up and cracked the first pitch between first and second, a clean single. He danced back and forth on the base path as Will came to bat. Will let the first pitch go by and Chuck stole second. Will waited out a second pitch, then doubled Chuck home with a drive over third base. Henry Lightcap came to bat, anxious and eager, aware of Wilma Fetterman and the other girls watching from the sidelines. Trying hard to be a hero, he popped out to second base.

Blacklick 1, Stump Creek 1, top of the second. Hating himself, Henry took his place on the mound, threw a few warmup pitches and checked his fielders. Nobody in right field. Leroy had disappeared. Thank God. He signaled little Paul to take Leroy's place and faced the batter, Mike Spivak. Henry pitched carefully, following Will's instructions; Mike hit an easy grounder to second. But

Clarence Adams bobbled the ball and Mike slid safely into first base. He always slid into first; nobody knew why.

Now the dangerous Dominic Del Poggio waited at the plate, ready for the pitch. Will, keeping one eye on Spivak edging off first base, called for an outside pitch. Henry threw it, Spivak ran for second, Will hurled the ball precisely to Chuck, covering the base, for what should have been an easy out. But Clarence, thinking the throw was meant for him, leaped for the ball and got run over by the base runner, piling them both in the mud. Chuck tagged the runner out. A discussion followed.

Joe Glemp, peering sternly at his own nose, declared the runner safe on grounds of interference; furthermore he penalized the home team by awarding Mike Spivak free passage to third base. The decision led to more discussion, bitter, prolonged, hectic. But the umpire stood firm. Dominic waited, grinning.

Concentrating on the batter, Henry threw two strikes low and inside, then jammed him with an inside curveball. Dominic swung and hit the ball with the handle of his bat, an easy slow roller toward Red Ginter at first base. Red waited for it, waited and waited, one foot on the bag; the runner got there before the ball.

Blacklick scored another five runs. The cow hoisted herself erect and staggered into center field. The game, like the cow, lurched into the shadows of the afternoon. The visiting team led, inning after inning, but not by much: Chuck Tait, Will Lightcap and Henry (after the first inning) managed to single, double or triple each time they came to bat, for Kovalchick's pitching turned out to be steady and predictable: nothing but fastballs down the middle. By the end of the fifth inning every player on the Stump Creek team had got on base at least once. Even Elman. Even Paul, the baby.

Everyone but Red Ginter. Never lifting his bat from his shoulder, he waited for the pitch he wanted. Which never came. Red went down on called strikes every time, spat in the dirt and said nothing.

At the end of the fifth inning the score stood 14 to 12, Blacklick leading. The sun hovered close to the roof of Prothrow's barn on the hill to the west. Henry and Tony agreed to end the game after seven innings.

In the sixth inning each team batted around the order, scoring on fumbled grounders, dropped fly balls, wild throws, doubles by Stan

Watta, Jock Spivak, Tony Kovalchick, Chuck Tait, Will Lightcap and Henry. As he waited on second, wiping his brow with the felt of his cap, Henry thought for a moment he saw Wilma smiling at him. But he couldn't be certain, she sat so far away in the encroaching twilight among a cluster of other girls, all of them smiling, laughing, talking. Laughing at me? he wondered—the pride in his two-base hit sank before the pain in his lonely heart.

Red Ginter struck out again, letting three fat pitches float past through the center of the strike zone.

Blacklick scored five runs in the top of the seventh, taking advantage of fly balls to the Fetterman boys, bouncing grounders to the Adams brothers, a throw to first a little wide that Red would not reach for, and an intentional walk to the left-handed Dominic Del Poggio, who replayed Jock Spivak's stunt by stepping across the plate to hit the pitch-out into far left field.

Nobody on either team hit a true bona fide home run. The pasture fence stood four hundred feet away at the nearest point. Beyond the fence and a row of trees ran the creek and beyond the creek lay Prothrow's cornfield, twenty-five acres of stubble and weeds.

In gathering darkness and deepening gloom, Blacklick ahead 21 to 16, the home team came to bat. Last of the seventh. Last chance. Chuck Tait, leading off, intense and eager as always, hit the first pitch inside first and down the foul line for a triple. His fifth hit of the game. Tony Kovalchick, still pitching, sighed wearily and faced Will Lightcap. Will doubled again, scoring Chuck, and Henry singled, scoring Will. He took second then third on wild throws by Panatelli in left and Carci at second. Blacklick 21, Stump Creek 18, man on third and nobody out. Sonny Adams walked. Clarence popped to second. Junior Fetterman popped to the pitcher for the second out, Henry holding on third. The end was near: Elman Fetterman, Stump Creek's last and poorest hitter, the final hope, stood limp at the plate. But Elman tried, he went down swinging, and the catcher—massive nerveless impassive Dominic—let the third strike get past him. He groped for the ball while Stump Creek hollered at Elman:

Run Elman run!

Elman ran. Dominic found the ball, whipped it toward first and hit Elman on the rump, spurring the child facedown into the base. Henry raced home, Sonny took second and Elman stood up on first smiling happily with his second big hit of the day. Two runners on base, two outs and the score now 21 to 19.

Top of the order, Red Ginter. Hope—stifled by reality. Henry had to call him in from far left field, where he'd been hunting for Leroy. Red slouched toward the batter's box, holding his private bat by its rough-cut, heavy end. He spat in the dirt, inverted the bat, took his stance. Feet far apart, shoulders hunched, towering like an impotent Goliath over the plate, Red stared blank as a zombie at Kovalchick and waited for the first pitch, the inevitable but slowing fastball down the middle.

Will rose from his squatting position beyond third, where he was coaching the runners, and contemplated the tiring, exasperated pitcher. Henry, watching from the bench, saw Tony Kovalchick touch the silver medal at his neck—St. Anthony—make the sign of the cross and begin his final windup. Red stopped chewing.

Kovalchick leaned back, one leg high in the air, about to rock forward and lob the pitch—

Fuck the Pope! shouted Will, loud and clear.

—released the pitch, awkwardly, his body rigid, off-balance, and threw weakly into the dirt halfway between the pitcher's mound and home plate. The ball dribbled crookedly toward the batter in little rabbity bounces.

Ball one! yelped the umpire as Red stepped forward this time, confidently, and swung down like Sam Snead with a driving iron and caught the ball with his slashing club as it made its last pathetic hop toward the plate. A flurry of dirt rose in the air, as if Red had dug too deep and missed, but every ear present heard the sharp *crack!* of hickory meeting hardball with magnum impact.

There is a certain special unmistakable sound that ballplayer and fan recognize instantly, as if engraved on memory and soul among those clouds of glory on the other side of birth, beyond the womb, long ago before conception when even God Himself was only a gleam in a witch doctor's eye.

The sound of the long ball.

All faces turned toward the sky, toward the far-flung splendor of an Appalachian sunset, and saw Red's departing pellet of thread, cork, rubber and frazzled leather rise like a star into the last high beams of the sun, saw it ascending high, higher and still higher over Jock Spivak's outstretched despairing arms in the remotest part of center field, far above the fence, over the trees and beyond the creek, where it sank at last into twilight and disappeared (for two weeks) in the tangled fodder of Mr. Prothrow's cornfield.

Sonny Adams followed by Elman Fetterman came trotting across home plate, dancing in delight. Blacklick 21, Stump Creek 20, Stump Creek 21. The home team swarmed with joy around the runners, waiting for the last and winning run.

But where exactly was it? that winning run? Where was Red? Red was nowhere. Red was everywhere. Red stood in front of home plate leaning on his bat, watching his first hit of the game vanish into immortality somewhere southwest of Stump Crick. Run? he said. What the hell you mean, run? Hit's a *home* run, hain't it? What the hell I gotta run round them goldamn bases fer? He spat a filthy gob of tobacco juice into the trenched soil at his feet, shouldered his bat in disgust and strode down the red-dog road, headed for Ginter's hollow.

Blacklick claimed a tie, 21-21. Stump Creek claimed a victory *de jure*, 22 to 21. The discussion never was settled to the satisfaction of anybody except maybe Red Ginter. And Leroy, who didn't care one way or the other. Old man Prothrow found Leroy that night bedded down in a stall on cowshit and straw, between two heifers, when he checked his cow barn before turning in.

The fight between Will Lightcap and Tony Kovalchick, Stan Watta and Jock Spivak also ended, more or less, in a draw. Called on account of darkness.

V

No team spirit, Chuck Tait complained. I don't think I'll play with you guys anymore. You hillbillies just don't have the right team spirit. Chuck was a town boy; he lived in the heart of Stump Creek in a brick house with coal furnace, plumbing and electricity. His father was village postmaster, owned the general store, drove a new Buick. Chuck joined the Army Air Corps in 1943, learned to fly a Mustang P-51, and would return from the Pacific Theater with captain's bars and a chest covered with ribbons. He started an insurance business and later evaporated, forever, into the state legislature. Red Ginter joined the U.S. Army and rose to the rank of master sergeant for life. Leroy joined the Salvation Army and became a major general.

And Henry? Henry Lightcap fell in love. He fell in love that year with Wilma, with Betsy, with Donna and eleven other girls. He knew his cause was hopeless but he tried. Though it was not Wilma or Betsy or Donna or the others but Mary, Tony Kovalchick's little sister, who provided the needed succor. One rainy night in May, in the backseat of Will's 1935 Hudson Terraplane, Mary Kovalchick showed Henry Lightcap a thing or two. Henry joined Mary. She conjoined him. For a number of times. He never again went back, after that, to throwing tennis balls at barn doors or baseballs at Roman Catholics.

Will Lightcap, he stayed with the farm.

So it was and so it all really happened down there in that Shawnee County, in the Allegheny Mountains of West Virginia, about five thousand years ago.

5

THE DOG RETURNS

Me and Solstice the dog and another soggy sixpack, bound for the high country. The old Dodge rumbles on, my horse, my love, my Rosinante—truck chassis, oversize tires, granny gear for rocky roads, the convenient floorboard ventilation system. Elaine's Toyota was—is—new and I paid for it but that's all right, I like this thing better anyhow. For the long haul. For gypsy living.

We stop to give a lift to a White Mountain Apache on the edge of the town of Globe. Fat, moonfaced, hungover and redeyed, stinking of whiskey, he climbs in, sags half dead against the door and utters not a word all the way to Cibecue. Forty miles. Suits me; that's the kind of conversation I prefer on a bright and golden Arizona afternoon. We climb two thousand feet from the desert onto a high plateau creased with narrow little canyons where sycamores grow among dry rocks, limbs flung out in crazy, electrified abandon. No leaves yet: still winter at this elevation. One bat-eared microwave relay tower stands on a ridge, insulting the uplands, passing its stream of oily lies through the innocent air. But that can be ignored; I ignore it; gaze instead across the cold clear classic gray-green integrity of the landscape.

The altimeter on the dash reads 6400. Good. A good height from which to contemplate the misery of the lowlands. But it ain't that easy; I've dragged the misery with me. It's still creeping like strontium through my bones, weighing on my heart like lead poisoning. I know, I know, only an idiot has no grief—but I am bored with grief.

A flashy new pickup truck with cherry-bomb tailpipe brays past me on the upgrade, cutting the double yellow line. Two humanoids sit in the cab wearing the bright well-pressed cowboy shirts and immaculate white hats, with high crowns and rolled brims, of Marlboro men. (That awful laundry bill.) A shotgun and a rifle rest in the gun rack. Two saddles in the bed. No detail has been overlooked: a sticker on the rear bumper reads COWBOYS DO IT BETTER.

By God that's true, I think. Ask any cow. How would *you* like to spend your working hours six months a year sitting on the middle of a horse contemplating the hind end of a cow? Imagine the effect on the simple tabula rasas of our grandsons of the pioneers. The Cowboy and His Cow: The Tragic Truth Behind the Myth.

Onward, through the scrubby woods and past a solitary wintershaggy horse in a huge and lonely field. The field looks lonely, not the horse. Why is that?

We descend into Salt River Canyon, leaving the Tonto Forest behind, perhaps forever, I don't know. Tonto means "fool" in Spanish. Fool Forest and the Lone Ranger's batman.

The Apache at the far end of my front seat appears to have passed out, but when I approach the branch road to the village of Cibecue he comes half alive and makes clear through gestures that he wants out. I drop him off. Without a word he staggers away, weaving down the centerline of the road north. Will probably make it home by nightfall and if he don't he'll sleep off his drunk in a grassy comfortable ditch. Voluntary simplicity.

I pop the top from another Coors, drive on for a mile or two and stop again. This weak green watery beer races through a man like a diuretic. Standing among the jackpines of the Apache-Sitgreaves National Forest, I shower the pine needles with a gentle acid rain, training my golden stream on a large black ant that I've caught in the open, bombarding his armored head with golden droplets the size—from his perspective—of volleyballs. Angered and dangerous the ant scampers about trying to find the source of this deluge. I back off, button up, satisfied and relieved. Every man has his phobia: my pet phobe is the ant, the anthill, the formic way of life.

I fill the dog's water dish and watch her drink. She's thirsty, dehydrated by the long drive through the cactus country south of Globe. Her ribs stick out through her dull black coat, her eyes are sad and lusterless, her muzzle dry. Not long for this world. She'll soon be out of it, lucky dog.

I gaze into the depths of the forest. A thousand Ponderosa pines straight and tall, conscious of my alien presence, wait patiently for my words, for my decision, for my departure. A sweet dark stillness broods in there, yes and black bear too, mule deer, wapiti, Merriam turkey and oblivion. Once again I ask myself the simple obvious question: Why not? Why suffer anymore? You've lived over a half a century now, you've had your share—the love of a number of beautiful women, the friendship of enough good men, the test of blood, muscle, nerve and skill in some lovely, dangerous and very strange places. What do you want? Why not go for one last walk in the woods, in the spirit of undying adventure, never to return.

My dog watches me. She looks concerned, sympathetic but not alarmed. She knows me better than I do.

We climb back in the truck, roll onward. Into the town of Show Low, named for the turn of a card that cost one partner his half of a cattle ranch. I think of Will and Marian clinging like oak burls, clinched like nails to their 120 acres back home in Shawnee County. I lower my beer out of sight and coast into town, admiring the familiar highlights of Show Low, Arizona:

LOG CABIN MOTEL, GAS: DIESEL MECHANIC ON DUTY, BEST WESTERN— VACANCY, PINK PONY STEAK HOUSE, FIRST CHURCH OF CHRIST JESUS, CENTURY 21 REALTY, PANAVISION TV, CHURCH OF JESUS CHRIST OF LAT- TER-DAY SAINTS, A&W ROOT BEER, SAFEWAY, YELLOW FRONT, TRU-VALU HARDWARE, AZTEC REALTY, 40-ACRE PARCELS $295 PER ACRE, GALLENO'S MEXICAN FOOD, SWEET THINGS BAKERY, TAYLOR'S EQPT RENTAL, and forty-four more of the same.

This here child needs hot coffee if we're gonna get into Gallup by midnight tonight. I pull over at Mom's Café and belly up to the salad bar. There is no salad bar in Mom's Café, there never is. I hunker down on a stool at the counter, order coffee and doughnuts.

"Ain't got no doughnuts," the little blue-haired waitress says. She looks older than my mother. I say, "Make it pie." "What kinda pie?" "What kind you got?" "Coconut cream." "Forget it—just bring me coffee." She brings the coffee, weak as tea but boiling hot, in an undersize mug with false bottom. She looks tired, she looks downright weary, she's old enough to be my grandmother, any- body's grandmother, and she should be home in front of the Tee Vee right now, crocheting mittens for her great-granddaughter.

She starts to go. "Are you Mom?" I ask her. "Yes but I ain't your mom, mister." "I mean are you the Mom that owns this café?" She points. "That's Mom over there, readin' that *Penthouse* magazine." She means the slender little man behind the cash register at the entrance, the Asiatic type who looks like the latest refugee from Ho Chi Minh City. They're here, they're everywhere, our many chickens coming home to roost.

"Where are you from?" I ask her. "Oh I ain't no native either," she says, "I was born in Springerville, that's about thirty-five miles down the road." We both pause for a moment, thinking about things; I sip my hot thin coffee. "Well," I say softly, as if to mollify the resigned anger I sense behind her eyes, "like we say, it's a free country." "Yep, it's free," she replies, "free of charge."

I drink a second cup of coffee, leave Grandmother an overgenerous tip (spoiling the natives) and pay the tab at the cash register. The little man with the sculptured features, skin drawn tight as a mask over his Vietnamese skull, puts down his magazine and gives me a quick grimace of a smile. He too looks tired, melancholy, lonely—from Saigon to Show Low is a longer journey than any I ever made—and I can imagine, too easily, the images of fire and torture and loss and unappeasable hatred that must torment his sleepless nights. Human, the poor devil, like the rest of us, too human for his own good.

Out of here.

Into the sweet air and the smell of yellow pine, into the grasslands among the ancient cinder cones, into the freedom of the open range. Good God but it's a relief to escape, if only for an hour, the squalid anthills, big or little, Show Low or Shanghai, of twentieth-century man. A world without open country would be a universal jail.

The old Dodge races onward, wind roaring at my ear. My dog sprawls on the seat, nose toward the window. A few horses graze on their thousand-acre paddocks. A good life for a horse. On the western ridge a windmill spins in the breeze, silhouetted against a sunset that spreads from horizon to horizon. Far to the north, sixty miles away and a thousand feet below, I see the rosy barrancas of the Painted Desert and a few purple volcanic buttes on the skyline. Those are Hopi lands, enclosed within the much bigger reservation of the Navajos. Nobody envies the Hopi.

A car approaches and passes with headlights blazing—it's getting dark. I'll never make it to Gallup tonight. I watch for a side road and when it appears drive for five miles eastward on a dirt track through no-man's-land, public land, cow country. Bats, grasshoppers, nighthawks flicker through the air. I pull off the road and park among junipers. Sweet smell of cedar on the air, the music of space and stillness in the sky. There are no lights visible anywhere except above: Cassiopeia, the Pleiades, the Big Dipper, the North Star, great Orion.

We go for a walk, my dog and I, watching the sunset die by slow degrees on the western sky. We walk for miles on the dirt road, see nothing man-made but a corral and loading chute and windmill. My belly hurts; we return to the truck. I fill the dog's water bowl, pour a ration of Purina Hi-Pro Krunchies into her feed dish and give her another Nizoral tablet, encased in a lump of cheese, for the fungus in her lungs.

I know, when a man's best friend is his dog that man needs help—professional help. I understand that and I acknowledge it and I say to hell with it. I eat my supper, a fat warmed-over cheese burrito spiced with hot salsa, drink one more beer, and go to bed in the back of my truck, wrapped inside the familiar greasy comfort of my Peace Surplus mummybag. (Korean conflict: Truman's War.) Sollie beds down on her old saddle blanket on the ground, under the rear bumper. I think of the sad little man at Mom's Café: thank God us Lightcaps skipped the Johnson-Nixon War.

6

1943-45:
WILL'S WAR

I

Diaspora of the Lightcaps.

Two of us—the old man and little Paul—already in the ground, under the hemlocks at Jefferson Church graveyard. Sister Marcie teaching high school in Santa Cruz, California, and our baby brother Jim a logger in British Columbia. Exiled. Even our mother has left the home place, living in a little apartment in Shawnee close to her friends and the Holyoak family. Only Will, everybody's ideal older brother, stayed home on the farm.

How did this happen? How could we ever have allowed such a thing to happen to us?

It's hard to understand. But it seemed to begin, for my family, along about 1943. We'd survived George Washington's War (1775–83), Andrew Jackson's War (1812), Polk's War (against Mexico, 1848) and even "Honest Abe" (sounds like a used-car dealer) Lincoln's War (1861–65), although we lost a great-great-uncle at Antietam and another barely escaped starvation in Libby Prison, and we stuck together through McKinley's War (1898) and Wilson's War (1917–18), but when Roosevelt's War (1941–45) came along—things began to fall apart. The whole country began to come apart. And then we'd lose little Paul in Truman's War (1949–52). And would almost lose Jim and two cousins in the Johnson-Nixon War (1964–75). But the trouble really commenced, for us Lightcaps, one evening in late May, 1943, right after supper.

(And we were a peace-loving people.)

The fireflies were blinking outside the windows. Marcie and

Jimmy were running around under the sugar maple tree and across the yard, catching those luminous bugs in Mason jars. Silent heat lightning flickered over the eastern hills.

"You what?" Paw roared.

"Signed up," said Will quietly. Not proud or smug or defiant but with his usual resolute manner. Will didn't talk much but when he said something you believed him. When he did something he did it. Did it right. Did it so it stayed done.

"When'd this happen?" Paw roars again.

"It didn't happen. I volunteered."

"When?"

"A week ago."

"For Christ's sake why didn't you tell us?"

"I'm telling you now."

"Not the Army?"

"Yeah."

"Not that goddamn Roosevelt's Army?"

"That's right, Paw."

Mother shut her eyes, shuddering. We stared at Will in silence, in twilight, over the supper table. The yellow light from the kerosene lamps played on the shiny oilcloth. I was impressed, envious—once again Will had beaten me into the spotlight. Mother looked shocked, frightened, almost stunned. But the old man was simply enraged.

"You're gonna go git your head blowed off for that damned old windbag Winston Churchill?"

Will said nothing.

"For that scheming old sneaky son of a bitch Roosevelt?"

Will remained silent.

"For that bloody old communist tyrant Joe Stalin?"

Will did not reply.

"I'm disgusted," Paw said. "Absolutely disgusted. That any son of mine would go fight in that rich man's war. Would risk his neck for"—he put on his fake Groton-Harvard accent—"foah thu bull-luddy"—rolling the *r*'s—"Buh-ritish . . . Empah!" He glared at Will from beneath his shaggy, twitching eyebrows. "I'm ashamed. I am sick with shame. My own son. . . ."

Will sat motionless and silent, staring at his plate, swabbed clean with bread, waiting for Paw to calm down. Of course Will had

108

anticipated this reaction from our old man. He did not seem much disturbed by it. What he dreaded was Mother's question. And she was a Holyoak—pro-English.

She spoke. "Will—you know you could get deferred. We need you here. Houser's boy got a deferment." She meant farm work—producing food for the War Effort.

Will permitted himself a small smile. "Henry can handle my place."

Little Paul whispered, "Will's joined the Army? He's gonna be a serviceman?"

Paw picked up the word. "Serviceman," he sneered. "My son Will the serviceman. Gonna go serve Churchill, Stalin and Roosevelt."

I saw Will's hands tighten then, his face flush a little. Looking up at the tin-plated ceiling, he muttered, "Soldier. Not serviceman."

"You think there's any difference?" Paw bellowed.

Mother intervened, trying to head off trouble. "You still have a year of high school, Will. You should finish."

Will relaxed a bit. He'd been expecting this objection. "War'll be over soon. I can finish school then." If I feel like it, I imagined him thinking. I knew that he despised high school; if it weren't for shop and industrial arts and football he'd have dropped out a year ago. "We'll be back in about a year, I expect."

"We?" said the old man. "We? Who's this 'we'? Who talked you into this foolishness anyhow?"

Will said nothing. So I blurted out the truth, despite Will's warning frown. I'd heard about it days ago. Everybody at Shawnee High knew. "They all signed up together," I said. "The whole varsity team. Him and Chuck Tait and Homer Bishop and Charlie Kromko and the Spivak brothers and Floyd Hendrickson and Bill Gatlin and Dick Holyoak—the whole first string. They all went up to Morgantown together and signed up."

Paw's look of disgust became even deeper. "Bunch of damned fools," he snarled. "And I know why you done it too, it's because of that eager-beaver Bible-kissing short-pants Eagle Scout Tait kid too, hain't that right?" Will did not reply. "Because of him, hain't that so?"

Will leveled his brown, dark eyes at the old man. "Don't yell at me, Paw," he said softly.

Father and son stared coldly at each other for a few long silent moments. Paw wasn't about to tangle with Will and he knew it and we knew it.

Will looked away. "Guess I'll go feed the horses."

"Wait a minute," Mother said. A pause. Then she asked the question that she knew Will would never answer from the old man. "Will . . . why'd you do it?"

Will hesitated, not meeting her eyes.

"I can't believe it," Paw mumbled. "After all I tried to teach these boys. Just can't believe it."

Brother Will was not stupid. He was thick but he wasn't stupid. Embarrassed by the necessity to answer, by his inability to please, by his obligation to personal honesty, he looked out the nearest window and mumbled, "Well, they all wanted to go." And stopped.

"Yes?" says Mother.

"They wanted to go. Not just Chuck. Charlie and the others. All of them." Chuck Tait was the quarterback. But Will was the team captain. Chuck was the star but nobody liked him; Will was slow, stolid, dependable—everybody trusted him. "So, well, I had to go too."

As if that explained everything. Or anything.

"What are you?" Paw thundered. "They go, you have to go? Are you a man or a sheep?"

Will froze again, staring at Paw.

"Joe," Mother says. "Please." She looked back at Will, a haunted yearning in her tired eyes, sorrow on her thin and weary face. "Go on, Will. Tell me."

"Well," he says, embarrassed, "that's it. You know, those guys, they're not very—somebody has to look after them. Make sure they get back alive. In one piece." He laughed awkwardly. "They're all town boys except Homer and Bill. Great guys," he hastened to add, "good football players, but . . ." He lapsed toward silence. ". . . you know, not too bright."

Quite a speech for Will.

"Look who's talking," Paw said. "William the Brain. D-minus Willy. Christ," he went on, "what makes you think they'll even let you stay together? The Army couldn't care less what happens to you and your buddies, once they throw you into Roosevelt's meat grinder."

"The recruiter promised we'd stay together," Will says. "He swore it."

"They signed up for the paratroops," I said, horning in again where I knew I was not wanted, eager to see how Paw would respond. Again Will gave me a dirty look.

Paw did not disappoint me. "Paratroops!" he bellowed. "Suicide, you mean, you joined the suicide troops. I knew that football was no good for your brains. All that banging heads together." And yet, watching him, I thought he was secretly pleased. Our old man always did admire the daring, the foolish, the reckless.

"Paratroops?" said Mother, puzzled.

"They jump out of airplanes," I explained, "and float down to the ground in parachutes. If the parachute opens. While the Germans down on the ground are shooting at them."

Mother closed her eyes.

"We got no quarrel with the Germans," Paw muttered. "Nor with the damn Japs neither."

Mother could find nothing more to say. Too confused and shocked to protest, too brave and frightened to weep, she got up quickly, gave Will a sudden hug and kiss, put her shawl around her neck and went out. Off on another of her long walks; we knew she wouldn't be back for an hour.

The rest of us sat at the table gaping at the dirty dishes. Little Paul, age twelve, says, "How about another poker game, Paw?" Henry, age sixteen, says, "Soon as you and Marcie clean off the table, shrimp." Will says nothing. And our Paw, age forty-three—a man of the century—pulls out his old Barlow pocketknife, flips the blade open with one hand and whittles himself a toothpick from a kitchen match. Scowling, outraged, proud.

II

We were plowing up the last of the potatoes that day, that Sunday afternoon in December, when old Clarence Nesbit came banging down our road in his loose-bolted loose-shackled fourth-hand Model A sedan. The one that once got four instant flat tires when the front bumper fell off at forty miles an hour. Clarence braked suddenly when he saw us in the field, jumped out of the car without shutting off the engine and hollered over the rail fence.

"Joe! you hear the news?"

Our old man stopped the horse, lines draped around his neck, and turned his dark bony face toward Clarence. Will and Henry, watching, recognized the sarcastic smirk on Paw's face, knowing without a word what Paw thought of Clarence—an elder of the Church—and waited for the smart remark. The stub of a hand-rolled cigarette was stuck to Paw's lower lip. A wisp of smoke rose past his squinted eyes. "How's that, Clarence?" he says. "Your pigs get the janders again?"

Old Clarence was too excited to notice Paw's sneer or catch his words. "It's war, Joe," he shouts, "war! The Japs bombed Pearl Harbor. Bombed the heck out of it."

"Surprise," says Paw.

Old Clarence was so upset his pale blue eyes were bulging, so excited that a string of drool hung from the corner of his prim, tiny mouth. "I heard it on the radio, Joe, not fifteen minutes ago, them Japs they bombed Pearl Harbor."

Paw sucked on his stub of a cigarette, drew it from his lips and flicked it away. "Well, Clarence . . ."

"What do you think we oughta do, Joe?"

Paw smiled. Behind Clarence's back he saw the old Ford, untended, motor vibrating, starting to inch forward down the grade. "Well, Clarence," he said, "if I was you—I'd climb in that tin lizzie of yours before it rolls away without you."

"Oh my, oh my goodness gracious," yelped Clarence, running to his car. He gave us a wave and drove away.

The old man stood behind the plow, watching the departing dust, then fetched out papers and tobacco tin from a shirt pocket and rolled another cigarette. "That Roosevelt," he muttered, half-smiling in admiration, "I knew he'd get us into that rotten war somehow."

Meanwhile, up on high where things matter, all over America, the *officers* were getting busy. And they were happy. They were very happy. All of our leaders getting ready to push. Getting ready to lead, as they always do, from behind.

So Will disappeared in early June 1943, with his friends. Shot hell out of the Stump Creek baseball team that summer. We had to let Sonny Adams play catcher, with sister Marcie in right field, Leroy Ginter in center (Red was already in the South Pacific), and Baby Jim at second base. Henry drove Will's Hudson Terraplane over the hills—in reverse, the power gear, after the camshaft burned out—from Stump Creek to Boone City to Kellysburg to Gatlinville to Marion Center. Without a license, taking the back roads. Siphoning gasoline, when needed, from farm tractors here and there. We won four and lost eleven that summer. Henry's batting average rose to .440—but he was scorekeeper.

Now and then Mother received a note from Will, down in Fort McClellan, Alabama:

Dear Mother we did the 20 mile march last night with full field pack. They put salt tablets in our canteens. It is very hot here. The chiggers bite a lot send some nail polish and calamine lotion. I qualified as Expert Rifleman. I scored 295 out of 300 possible. Maybe that will make Paw happy. All the sergeants are Johnny Rebs. They can't talk English very good. Everybody talks boll-weevil English down here. But they sure can holler loud. Charlie Kromko is going to OCS but he promised to get back with us when we go to CENSORED Chuck got into the Army Air Corpse. Tell Henry to try to get in the Air Corpse or the Navy or the Merchant Marine. He wont like the US Army. One boy from Maine CENSORED himself on a pine tree last night. We all felt sorry for him. The officers are a bunch of CENSORED I love you. Give Marcie a kiss for me. Tell Paul and Baby Jim to wipe their nose. Tell Henry to check the oil in my car when he drives it or I will ring his neck.

Will.

Late in the summer came communiqués from Fort Benning, Georgia:

Dear Mother we all qualified for Jump School except Homer & Ernie. Homer was two inches too tall and has flat feet. They said Ernie was too fat and too short. He's in a heavy weapons platoon. He likes mortars and bazookas and .50 cal machine guns. It is nice in a parachute. It's easy to do. You hook your chute to a cable in the airplane and when the Sergeant says Jump you Jump. If you don't jump he pushes you. Easy. The hard part is when you hit the ground. The officers say we are going to ship out in CENSORED for CENSORED but we get a two week furlough first. So I'll see you in September I guess. Tell Paw not to cut down the red oaks by the spring above the cornfield. How are old Ned and Bess and Ellie and Bones? I even miss the chickens some. Tell Henry to keep his hands off my 30.06 or I will kill him. Tell him he can use my .22 if he cleans it every time he shoots it. Otherwise I will have to kill him. How is the corn doing?

> Love from Your Will.

Paw scowled over those letters, snorted, swore, but must have been secretly pleased. We heard him boasting about Will every chance he got, telling Charlie Carci and Hoyt McElhoes and the others at the Labor Day shooting match what a terror his boy would be when he got to Europe. Or "Yerp," as everyone called that remote and chancre-ridden continent. "Now you fellas know I ain't got no quarrel with the Germans. They're just a bunch of damn fools like us, only better organized, and if they had any goddamned sense they'd shoot that son of a bitch Hitler theirselves, save us the trouble. But I sure do feel sorry for them when the Army turns my boy Will loose over there. I wouldn't be surprised, when the word gets around, if them Germans don't surrender about the time they hear Will is getting off the boat." This was said, of course, with a wink and a grin—but we knew that the old man half believed his own words. And the more he talked the more he believed them.

Our Paw set great store by a man's ability with a rifle. "The rifle," he'd say, "is the weapon of democracy. It was free men like us that invented the Pennsylvania long rifle. Only cowards like that windbag Churchill or bloody dictators like that Traitor-to-the-Revolution Joe Stalin need tanks and airplanes." Paw himself was an expert small-bore rifleman. Three years in a row—1931 to 1934— he'd been a member of the West Virginia state rifle team, which simply meant he was among the twelve best shots in the state. He had a sashful of medals in his treasure chest, that old steel-bound trunk where he kept his pearl-handled .44 Colt revolver, and the Stetson hat with the rattlesnake hatband, and the triangular-bladed trench knife that Uncle Paul brought back from France in 1919 and the photographs of him and his IWW buddies swarming over a sawmill in Eugene, Oregon. Paw once shook hands and talked with Big Bill Haywood; he heard Eugene Debs give his last speech before the Government locked him up for opposing Wilson's War.

"But"—Paw would continue, ruining the effect, spoiling his case with his patient neighbors—"Will and those boys should be going to Wall Street, New York, and that Washington, D.C., not to Europe. That's where our real enemies are."

Uncle Jeffrey, our mother's older brother, another damned Holyoak, overheard some of this talk. *"Sprachen sie Deutsch?"* he said to our father. All of the Holyoaks hated Joe Lightcap and with good reason: because a Holyoak girl named Lorraine had long ago and once upon a time, somehow, mysteriously, outrageously, allowed herself to be seduced into marriage with a hillbilly, a low-class deer-poaching redneck. . . .

"I'll sprachen-sie any damn thing I feel like," Paw says. "This is still a free country, Jeff, and I'm freeborn, white and mean as a gut-shot bear, and if you don't like it you bow-tied bank clerk you can go back to merry old England where you belong and kiss the Queen Mother's royal asshole."

Yes, our uncle Jeff worked in the First National Bank in Shawnee. He was rumored to make over two hundred dollars a month. And he did wear a bow tie.

Uncle Jeffrey flushed with anger but made no move. Like all the Holyoaks he was familiar with Paw's hot temper and a mite afraid of him. "Well," he said sullenly, suppressing his rage, "at least there aren't any Germans in our family."

Paw took that up at once. "The Ostranders was Dutch." Referring to his mother's ancestry—Grandmaw Cornflower's mother. "Dutch," he repeated.

"Really, Joe? I thought they were Pennsylvania Dutch." By which Uncle Jeffrey meant what was the fact—that they were Germans.

Paw never blinked. "As a matter of fact they were Huns. Huns,

Jeff." He grinned his dangerous grin. "You have any other notions about my family, Jeff? Speak your mind, such as it is. You have anything to say about a Shawnee medicine man, for instance?"

"Guess I'll be going," says Uncle Jeff, retreating to his polished, immaculate, like-new Plymouth sedan. Only a bank clerk would drive a car like that. But he was actually a nice man. Unlike most of the Holyoaks, he enjoyed rabbit hunting and a good target shoot now and then. He was always good to me and Will and the kids. Felt sorry for us.

Paw smiled, having routed the enemy, and went on bragging about Will to Charlie Carci. I knew he'd been sucking on a bottle of Ginter's moonshine, him and Carci both. They were pitching horseshoes after the shoot, and I could tell by the way Paw threw each shoe—hard and low and flat, one ringer after another. Whiskey did that for him.

IV

In late summer, in the stifling heat of September, when the goldenrod and sunflowers were in full bloom, Will came home for his two-week furlough before shipping overseas.

Big dark broad and stout as a bear, he showed up one day in his U.S. Army dress uniform, his Expert Rifleman's medal on the left breast of his tunic, the Expert Infantryman's blue and silver badge on the right and the little silver wings of a parachute above the Expert medal. On each sleeve he wore the handsome stripe of a Private First Class. An overseas cap with the blue piping of an infantryman was perched rakishly on his square, close-cropped head. On his feet he wore the blunt-toed, square-laced boots of a paratrooper, polished to the gleam of glass. The boots made a terrific racket when he walked across the floor; he clattered like a tank.

Will hugged Mother, who cried a lot as she kissed him. He shook hands with me and Paul, hugged Marcie, tossed Baby Jim in the air. He nodded to Paw, who nodded back and left the house, growling that somebody in this goddamn overgrown underdone family had to see after the animals. Will took the .22 rifle off the wall and showed us how to do the manual of arms. Paul was impressed. Will removed his tunic and let the kids feel the medals and badges, then clomped upstairs and into the boys' bedroom. Will had to bend his head to get under the lintel of the doorway. He sat on one of the double-decker bunks that the old man had built for us about fifteen years earlier and took off the soldier suit—the plain light brown tie (tucked into the shirt), the olive drab shirt and trousers. He hung the uniform on hangers in the closet. Even his underwear was brown. He took off his dog tags: name, blood type, serial number. He put on a clean flannel shirt and the clean Osh-kosh overalls which Mother had put away for him in the drawer beneath his bunk. He pulled on his old leather hunting boots, laced them up and asked me about the car.

I was afraid of that. Reluctantly I told him about the uphill problem, the lack of power, the need for using reverse a lot. He nodded calmly, not surprised. "Camshaft again," he said. "How many times you change the oil, Henry?"

"All the time, Will. We're gettin' about fifty miles to a quart."

"Uh-huh. . . . What about the leak in the radiator?"

"Not bad. We just pour in some rolled oats now and then, like you said. Sawdust works good too."

"And it still runs?"

"Sort of. Something wrong with the generator but we always park on a hill."

Will put on his cap and walked around the boundaries of the farm. We followed—Paul, Jim and me; Marcie was helping Mother fix a big dinner. The old man stayed out of sight. First thing Will did was visit the spring on the hillside in the woods. "Soon as I get back I'm buildin' a cabin here, Henry. Don't let Paw log these oaks."

Near the top of the hill he paused at the two graves, side by side, of our great-grandfather Doctor Jim and Grandmaw Ostrander—"Cornflower." The graves were sunken now, after so many years, overgrown with creepers, ivy, briars, but the two thin slabs of chestnut were standing yet, though leaning a little. The names and dates were weathered but still readable. Will straightened them, tamped the sod with his bootheels and marched on. He stopped on the open ridge to inspect our sixty acres on the north side, our best hayfield. The hay rake and mower stood where Paw had left them in August, after the last cutting. Weeds were growing through the spokes of the wheels; the perforated steel seats were sprinkled with bird droppings; the wooden tongues lay half hidden in the timothy.

"Why ain't those machines in the shed?" Will asked.

"Paw's figuring on one more cut in October."

"That's no reason to let 'em get rusty."

Paul and I looked at each other. I said, "What the hell, Will, that old iron junk's obsolete anyhow. Paw says as soon as the war's over he's gonna plant this whole hill in Christmas trees. You know— Scotch pine. There's gonna be good money in Christmas trees now, Paw says."

"The stock can't eat Christmas trees."

"Paw says he's getting rid of the stock. Paw says he's getting sick and tired of feeding these goddamned animals that only work half the year but eat all year round. That's what Paw says."

Will scowled. He stared across the fields, across the Big Woods and Honey Hollow toward the farther hills, the Allegheny Mountains, the blue haze of distance. "Don't sell the horses," he said.

"What?"

"You heard me." He marched on. We tramped after him, whispering to each other. What'd he say? He said don't sell the horses. Why not? He didn't say why not, you deaf or something?

Will didn't like the looks of the field corn either. The stalks stood shoulder high, tall enough for the season, but the ears were small, Will said—too many nubbins. "You manure this field, Henry?" Who, me? "Did Paw?" No. "Why not?" Manure spreader's broke down. "Fix it." I'm no damn mechanic. "Why didn't Paw fix it?" Said he didn't have time. Said he'll get a new one when the war's over. Said he has better things to do. "Like what?" Well, I said, Paw says he can make more money now in the woods. "Doing what?" He's cutting pit props mostly. "Pit props?" Locust posts— for the coal mines. Lots of money in locust posts right now with the mines going full time for the War Effort.

Will hurried ahead, making no comment but looking displeased. He stopped now and then to pick up the fence rails that lay on the ground, put them back in place. That Army's sure done something to Will, I thought; he acts like he owns this place. Thinks he's the boss. Thinks he's a sergeant already. Next time he jumps out of an airplane I hope he breaks his neck. Talking to myself, of course, and I crossed my fingers when I said it.

We headed back toward the house. We crossed the run in the middle of the pasture, stepping from rock to rock, and angled up among the cow patties toward the barn. Will stopped off in the barn to argue some with Paw but the old man wasn't there. Probably hiding down in the basement, oiling the traps, or maybe off with his ax and his wedges and his one-man crosscut saw. He never minded working in the woods alone, though he knew as good as anybody it was dangerous.

Will marched up to the Hudson Terraplane, where I'd parked it on the ramp of the barn. He lifted the hood, inspected the battery connections, checked the radiator, pulled the dipstick and looked at the oil level. He poured a bucket of water and added a quart of oil, closed the hood, got into the car and let it roll off the ramp and down the road. Paul and Jim ran along behind to see. When the car was moving pretty fast Will let out the clutch and got the motor started. Then he stopped, put her in neutral and got half out of the car, one foot on the road and one foot on the gas pedal, and he raced the engine and watched the black smoke pouring out of the tailpipe. He backed the car up the ramp again and shut her down. I went into the house and helped Marcie set the table.

Will came in and made some telephone calls, cranking hard on the handle. He didn't look at me. Paw showed up just as supper was ready and we all sat down at the table.

Baby Jim said grace, as everybody bowed their heads, except Paw. (And me.) Jim said, "God is great God is good let us thank him for this food," as Mother had taught him, more or less, except he made "food" rhyme with "good," which was wrong according to the Holyoaks. As the dishes started to move Paul the wise guy added, "For this food we're about to eat praise the Lord now pass the meat." Mother did not bother to say anything about that either. She had mostly given up on us, I guess.

We ate Will's favorite Sunday dinner though it wasn't Sunday: baked chicken, dumplings, mashed potatoes, gravy, string beans, peas, sweet corn, and hot apple pie—all you could eat. Will drank two glasses of buttermilk sprinkled with pepper. Everything but the sugar, salt and pepper came from the premises.

Right after supper Will took off. He let me go with him. We got the car started and drove into Stump Creek, taking a powerful race to mount the hill to Roy Stitler's garage without having to turn around and back up. I had to admit to myself I probably couldn't have done it. Will parked the car over the grease pit. Old Roy was waiting for us with a new used camshaft and the other parts Will figured he'd need. Roy hooked his electric worklight on the frame and Will crouched down in the pit and for the next two hours they worked on that Hudson motor from the bottom up. They talked about the Army and the war and women, with Roy doing most of the talking and Will doing most of the laughing. My job was to wash the greasy parts in a bucket of gasoline on the floor and to hand them the tools they needed when they hollered for them. I spent half the time leafing through the grease-smeared magazines on Stitler's workbench: *Outdoor Life, Field and Stream, Real Detective, Ace Detective*—and a pulpy number called *Snappy Stories* with a colored illustration on the cover that gave me a hard-on I could've used for a pry bar if I had a good enough fulcrum.

"Hey Henry," yells Roy, "let go of your pecker for a minute and hand me the cam stretcher."

I poked around on the bench in the jumbled mess of socket wrenches, crescent wrenches, spark plugs, head gaskets, distributor caps, fanbelts, piston rings, hoses, battery cables, copper wire . . . "Bullshit," I said, "there's no such thing as a cam stretcher." They laughed some more. "Go to hell," I said.

"That there Henry," says Roy, "he's about as much help as tits on a motor."

"Go to hell."

"Just gimme that mallet, Henry," says Will, gently enough. His hand and bare arm, stained with oil, was stretched out from beneath the car. His fingers wiggled. "The wooden hammer, Henry, the big one." I placed the mallet in his hand; both disappeared. The sound of hearty banging came from the pit. Like country mechanics anywhere, both Will and Roy depended on hammers for the fine alignment of parts.

By nine o'clock everything was in place, including the new camshaft, a new used generator and battery, new points, new plugs, new secondhand starter assembly. The ring job and the basic overhaul would have to wait, for the duration. The motor ticked over like a Hamilton watch as Roy and Will listened carefully under the upraised hood. Roy accepted payment for the parts but refused to take anything for his labor or the use of his shop and tools. "Shit no Will you don't owe me nothing for that you keep your soldier pay and no sir no sir I will not and you take this here piece of iron in to Shawnee tonight and you have a good goddamn time or I'll never play poker with you and your old man again. Screw a couple of girls for me when you get 'em in the backseat. If I ever have to look at this sorry bucket of bolts again I want to see footprints on the dashboard—upside down."

By nine-thirty we were back at the farm and Will was taking a bath in the washtub in the kitchen while the rest of us listened to Fibber McGee and Molly on the Philco radio. I went upstairs to put on a clean shirt and heard Marcie coaching Baby Jim at his prayers. "Now I lay me down to sleep I pray the Lord my soul to keep if I should die before I wake I pray the Lord my soul to take."

"Wait a minute," little Jimmy says, "I'm not gonna die tonight. Am I, Marcie?"

"How should I know?" says Marcie. "It's what you're supposed to say when you go to bed." The kid started to cry. "Oh for heaven's sake, you don't have to if you don't want to."

Will came up wrapped in a towel. He put on his splendid uniform and the shining boots. As I combed my hair by the light of the lamp I asked where we were going. "We?" said Will. "It ain't we, Henry, it's me. You better stay home and squeeze your pimples."

Very late that night Will returned. I heard the Terraplane grinding up the road, heard Will come in the front door and stumble against something in the entryway, heard him padding as softly as he could up the narrow stairs. Heard Paw meet him in the hall.

"It's pretty late, Will." "Yes sir." "Around three o'clock." "Yes sir." "You been drinkin', Will?" "Had a few beers, Paw."

I imagined them staring at each other in the gloom, no light but that of the stars filtered through the curtains in the front window. Will was nearly as tall as the old man, a good ten pounds heavier and twenty-six years younger.

"Good night, Will."

"Good night, Paw."

The next evening after supper Will again scrubbed himself, shaved ("Never seen a boy of mine wash up every day without halfin' to be told every time," Paw mused in wonder; but Mother looked disappointed at seeing him leave so early) and buttoned on his glittering uniform. William G. Lightcap, Pfc. Meeting his buddies in town, he explained—for most of his teammates were home too—gonna shoot some pool, hit the bowling alleys, maybe go roller-skating, who knows. Paw smiled skeptically. Mother looked worried. And off he roared again into Shawnee (pop. 9,500), named, as the town limit signs explained, FOR THE FORMER PREVALENCE OF RED MEN IN THIS VALLEY.

Will came home late almost every night. He worked hard all day—patched fence, shoveled cowshit from the stalls, hoed the tomato patch, repaired and oiled the cultivator, the seed drill, the manure spreader, and even cleaned out the chicken coop one morning, which was supposed to be one of my chores—but off he went every night into Shawnee, leaving a plume of oily smoke behind.

Most of the time our old man stayed out of sight, off in the Big Woods cutting trees, but one night him and Will got into an argument about something. Will stayed away for three days and nights the second week of his furlough. Mother cried a lot, secretly, when she thought no one could see or hear. She took long walks in the evenings. Paul and Marcie and me had to clean up and wash the dishes. I looked forward to getting into the Army: no more washing goddamned dishes; no more Mom's home cooking.

Two days before he was scheduled to leave for Norfolk, Virginia, there to board a troopship for MTO, Will brought a girl home to have supper with us. She was short, dark-haired, thick in the legs with a behind about one ax handle wide. She had a pretty face though, I guess, if you liked plucked eyebrows and bright red lipstick on the mouth. Marcie thought she was pretty and Marcie was an expert. This girl wore saddle shoes, bobby sox, a long full skirt and a pink sweater. She was quiet, very polite. Her name, Will said, was Marian—Marian Gresak. He spelled the name out slowly and carefully for Paw's benefit. Paw looked doubtful. She wore a necklace with a little oval-shaped silver medal attached; pinned to her sweater were Will's silver wings. We're engaged, Will announced. Quietly but firmly. Mother and Marcie, delighted, hugged her and kissed her—like women would. I knew Marian all right. She was one of the cheerleaders at Shawnee High. She was not one of the pretty ones, not compared to Donna or Betsy or Lou Ann Risheberger. I had to corner Will on this question. "Why her?" I asked when I got him alone for a minute outside.

"Why who?"

"You know what I'm talking about. Why her?"

"Oh, you mean Marian. Well, you see, it's like this, Henry: I like her." He grabbed my shoulder and squeezed, hard. "You'll like her too. Won't you, Henry?"

I wriggled loose. "I suppose. But why her?"

Will thought for a minute. He grinned. "Because she likes animals. She wants to live on a farm."

Our old man maintained a civil surface, on the surface, but I overheard him later mumbling about Polacks, Catholics, ring kissers, genuflectors, Pope lovers, mackerel snappers. But not where Will could hear him.

On the last day Will drove to the bus station in town. We saw him off, along with Homer Bishop, Ernie Houser, the Spivak brothers, Bill Gatlin and the rest of Will's gang, except for Chuck Tait and Charlie Kromko who were already in different worlds—one an air cadet trainee, the other an officer candidate.

There was no band this time. The women hugged their sons and wept quietly, the fathers shook hands firmly, smiled grimly, made what jokes they could. "Looky here, Will," Paw says in farewell, "you take care of them sons of bitches Adolf and Benito and get yourself back here inside of six weeks or I'm going over there myself to finish it. Then we'll go get them warmongers down in Washington, D.C., and them war profiteers up in Wall Street, New York. Don't you forget."

"I'll be back, Paw. Don't sell the horses. Don't log off the oaks. Don't plant Christmas trees and don't sell any of the land."

"You do your job, boy, I'll do mine."

"Don't you forget." Gratefully, Will turned to Marian, embraced and kissed her for a full minute right in front of the whole crowd. The other boys were getting into the bus. Quickly Will shook hands with me, hugged Marcie, little Paul, Baby Jim. Finally, the difficult part, he said goodbye as best he could to Mother. That was hard to watch.

October 1943. The Appalachian hills were aflame in 449 different colors of autumn. None of us would see Will again for nearly two years.

The letters from Will trickled home in V-mail by way of an APO address in New York through the winter of 1943–44, from Bizerte, Palermo, Napoli, Mignano. He and his little squad of West Virginia farmboys and high school football players, after weeks at a replacement depot in Naples, were funneled intact into a rifle company of the Thirty-sixth Infantry Division, General Fred L. Walker (an Ohio farmboy) commanding. By this time Will was an actual not acting squad leader, a real buck sergeant. He never rose above that rank—and never wanted to. Will and his squad of eight arrived too late for the landing at Salerno but well in time for the attempt to cross the Rapido River north of Naples and Mignano. Their first battle took place under the heights of a mountain of shattered rock and an ancient stone-walled monastery known as Monte Cassino.

The story, as Will eventually told it, sounded like this:

The Rapido River is a fast river. *Molto rapido.* In January 1944 it was in flood, sixty feet wide, ten feet deep and icy cold. The Germans were bunkered down in hills on the north side of the river with machine guns, mortars and artillery. On the night of January 20 that shithead back in Fifth Army Headquarters, General Mark Clark, ordered our whole division to paddle across this river in M-2s—little plywood boats about the size of your living room sofa—and attack the Krauts on the other side, head-on.

The first problem was to get the boats to the river. That meant we had to carry them by hand about three miles at night across the fields to the south bank of the river. The damn little things weighed about half a ton each. We had to carry them because the ground was too muddy for trucks—a truck would sink to the axles in that old Dago muck. Also the ground was full of mines. And I mean those wooden box mines, hard to detect. The engineers had tried to clear safe paths for us through the minefields but in the dark it was mighty difficult to find the paths. We practically had to feel our way by the tape markers and the marline cord. And of course as we stumbled through the mud hauling those damn boats the Krauts were firing at us with their big guns, the 88s and that godawful thing they called the Nebelwerfer that fired six shells at once. Those shells had holes in the side that made a kind of whooping noise when they flew through the air. Just the sound was enough to make a man shit in his britches. We called them the Screaming Mimis. So by the time we even got to the river half the men in our battalion were dead or wounded or lost or hiding in shell holes. Our platoon leader, a young guy from Waco, Texas, was killed right away, and half the platoon was gone. Our captain was gone. Half the company was gone. We couldn't see a damn thing. We had no radio or phone contact with anybody. But me and Floyd and Homer and Dick Holyoak and the Spivak brothers and Ernie got to the bank without a scratch on us. The only one missing was Bill Gatlin and he was safe and warm in a V.D. ward in the base hospital in Naples. He always was smarter than the rest of us. Real exciting, except for the Screaming Mimis and the machine-gun bullets flying over our heads. And we still had our boat and we still had our orders: cross that river and start killing Germans. No officers in sight, though you couldn't see much anyhow. So we set the boat down on the bank of the river and I looked at my squad and they looked at me and I said, Well, boys, what do you think we should do? Nobody said anything at first, then a couple of shells exploded about fifty yards behind us and old Homer, he said, goddamn it, Will, it can't be as bad on the other side as it is here, let's cross. So we lowered the boat as best we could down off this six-foot mudbank and into the water and climbed in and started to paddle toward the other side. It was pitch-black dark except for the flares here and there but we could tell where the Germans were because that's where all the bullets were coming from. We'd gone about ten feet across and about twenty feet downstream when I felt the water inside the boat getting up to my knees and rising fast. The damned boat was full of holes and water spurting in like a high-pressure spigot. Okay, boys, I said, let's do a one-eighty: this here M-2 is sinking. We were all loaded down with our rifles, steel helmets, hand grenades, extra bandoliers of ammo, trenching tools, bayonets, combat packs and our shoes full of water. We almost didn't make it back but got there somehow and climbed up that mudbank and let the boat sink and then we started digging in. We dug real deep, you can bet your bottom dollar on that, and there we stayed for the rest of the night. And oh but it was a long cold wet January night but we didn't mind too much because we figured come daylight things would get even worse. We couldn't see anything but we could hear plenty. The artillery fired all night, on both sides, and now and then when there was a pause you could hear the wounded fellas crying for help. Then the daylight came and there was that great big old Monte Cassino fort on top of the mountain looking right down on us. It was the ugliest evilest building I ever saw in my life and we knew the German observers were up there somewhere with binoculars studying our positions and pretty soon the artillery fire got worse for sure. A few of our boys had made it across the river in the night and were dug into the mud on the other side. We couldn't see them but we could hear their M-1s and a couple of guys with the BARs. After a while we couldn't hear very many. And then after a while we couldn't hear none at all. We saw three men try to swim back across the Rapido. None of them got halfway across. We wanted to give them covering fire but we couldn't even see where the Germans were, they were fortified deep in the rocks on the side of the hill or maybe up in that Monte Cassino monastery, we didn't know. And besides—and don't think we didn't think about it—if we fired and gave away our position why inside two minutes we'd have six Screaming Mimis coming right down on top of us in one neat compact bunch. There wasn't anything we could do except hunker down in our holes and wait. I mean wait until somebody got a good idea. Like how to get out of there. By noon the air was full of smoke from the smudge pots that was supposed to conceal our troops and then about three in the afternoon this fresh young second lieutenant showed up through the smoke waving a carbine and yelling. We'd none of us ever seen him before. He had a crazy gleam in his eyes and even though it was cold and foggy he was sweating. Or maybe it was just the oil from the smoke screens. He looked awful. He ordered us out of our holes. Attack! he screamed, we're going to attack! Shells and bullets flying all around. Lieutenant, I said, we got no boat. Our boat is sunk. And you better get down in this hole right quick. Sergeant, he says, get your men out of there and follow me. Sir, I says, we don't have any goddamned boat. Sergeant, he says, don't argue with me, the engineers are building a pontoon bridge up the river. Now come on out of there. I looked at the boys; they looked at me; we knew how long that bridge would last, if the engineers even got it finished. Which they didn't. About five minutes, that's how long. The Krauts had every crossing point sighted in with heavy artillery. I saw the Spivak brothers looking at their knuckles and Dick and Ernie shaking their heads No. Sir, I said to the looey, they don't want to go. Now why don't you get down in this hole before you give away our position? Across the river we could hear the Nebelwerfers howling: *whoop! whoop! whoop! whoop! whoop! whoop!* Six fat shells rising into the air. The lieutenant pointed his carbine at me. Sergeant, he said, I am ordering you and your squad to come with me. That's an order. But Ernie and Homer and Dick had their rifles pointed straight at him. Lieutenant, I says, I guess we're not going to go right now. And I thought I could see his finger tighten up on the trigger. He was dead if he pulled it. But he hesitated. We heard the Screaming Mimis coming our way. Get down! I hollered, get down! He was staring up into the smoke. The six shells hit about ten yards away. Things like black broken dinner plates whipped over my head. Made a noise like a buzz saw cutting into nails. There was no sound from the lieutenant. When I looked up a second later he was still standing there like before except his head was gone. Whole thing: face, helmet, ears, brains, skull, most of the neck. Blood shooting up like a fountain. And then what was left took a couple of steps back and sort of telescoped down into the mud.

At this point in the story Will stopped to finish his beer. He only told me about it once. Then continued:

The dog tags were still there. His name was Burkett. He came from a little town in Pennsylvania called Coal Run. A ninety-day wonder fresh out of OCS. God, it could have been Charlie Kromko if Charlie hadn't lucked out and been sent to England instead. No brains but lots of nerve. He'd been a student at Penn State. Majored in history. Didn't have time to learn much though. Poor bastard trying to do his duty. His mission, as he saw it, was to get us across that river and get us all killed, wounded, or captured. Homer and Ernie and Floyd and them they had a different view: their mission as they saw it was to stay alive. And me—well my mission was kind of intermediary between the squad and the officers. I had to please the officers somehow, make them think we were doing what we were told. But I had different orders from the boys. Their orders to me was to get them home in one piece. I thought about it carefully during those two days and nights on the Rapido and decided I'd take my orders from my men. I led where they agreed they wanted to go. We spent 85 percent of the war hiding in holes. That's how we won.

That's how we won when we spent that month in the rocks on the east side of Monte Cassino. There's not much dirt on that mountain. Nothing but broken stone. We couldn't hardly dig in anywhere so we built little stone walls and hid behind them. Stone chips flying through the air all the time. Lots of eye wounds in our outfit— needed more eye doctors than surgeons in the field hospital. Rained on us all through February. We like to froze to death. That's where Floyd got his million-dollar wound—sliver of granite in the left eye. But it took him back to Naples and then back home and he's got a 33 percent disability pension for life. He didn't complain at the time. And then we got sent to Anzio and spent two months there, holed up twenty-foot deep behind sandbags. The Germans was so close once we could hear the burp guns stuttering—those machine pistols they had. And they had that big railroad gun about fifteen miles up the coast—what they called the Anzio Express. Then came the breakthrough past Velletri and the march into Rome on June the fourth—two days before the Allies landed at Normandy. In Rome we marched in a circle because of a traffic jam—the general didn't trust his Italian guides and got lost for an hour—and had time for a few bottles of *grappa* and a few kisses from the signorinas before they herded us right though the city after the goddamned Krauts. As usual the infantry won the battle and the headquarters staff enjoyed the victory. And then by God just one mile north of Rome our whole column was stopped dead by seven Germans in a stone farmhouse. Seven young soldiers with one machine gun and a self-propelled antitank gun and no place to retreat and they held up the whole Thirty-sixth Division for two hours. And damned if our platoon leader—our third in three months—didn't volunteer us to kill them, and we snuck around through the woods, just like we used to do along Stump Crick playing Indian, and outflanked them and shot them when they wasn't looking. The dead Germans lay in a trench under some orange trees. The trees were in bloom (said Will), this was late springtime in Italy, and the one thing I remember and will never forget is the sweet smell of those orange blossoms over the smell of cordite and the sound of bees mixed in with the buzzing of flies closing in for lunch. We searched the bodies and found a letter in the German lieutenant's pocket which ended, ". . . *In perpetuum, frater, ave atque vale.*" He was a schoolteacher, that crazy Kraut, his name was Kretschmer, and he came from a town in Bavaria called Augsburg. I kept the letter and delivered it myself to what was left of his family—no more brothers—about a year later. No, I didn't tell his parents that I was the guy who killed their son. It was a lucky shot anyhow.

The Thirty-sixth marched on, Will and his squad in the recon column. The Thirty-sixth Division would have no rest. With victory in Italy assured, Mussolini and his mistress soon to be hanging by their heels at a gas station near Milan, Will's outfit was transferred in August to southern France. They took part in the swift advance up the Rhine. Then came the miserable winter of 1944-45, when they fought in rain and snow in the Vosges Mountains. Will's battalion was cut off, surrounded, nearly destroyed. Temperatures close to zero. Still alive, Will and his squad found shelter in snow-covered ruins near the town of Colmar. Homer Bishop lost three toes to frostbite—another lucky wound—and was sent home. The snows melted again and Will Lightcap, still a buck sergeant, followed his squad into the flooded valley of the Rhine. White flags hung from every house and the young frauleins—"furlines"—were there to greet them, eager to trade virtue and honor for cigarettes and C rations. Fair enough. Ernie Houser caught the clap, as Bill Gatlin had done in Mignano, and became the squad's fourth casualty. In jeeps and weapons carriers Will and his three remaining teammates—Dick Holyoak and the Spivak brothers—rode through Bavaria, through the Black Forest, and on to Kitzbühel and V-E Day. Will saw Von Rundstedt and Hermann Goering brought as prisoners to division headquarters. He saw some other things as well—the death camps full of stacks of dead Jews, Slavs and gypsies—and thought that perhaps there was a meaning, after all, to Churchill's War.

But what Will cared most about was his private victory: every member of his original squad would return alive and mostly intact to Shawnee County, West Virginia, in the Appalachian region of the United States of America. That, he'd admit with pride, was the real reason he wore a Bronze Star among his ribbons. The official citation mentioned "gallantry in action while under constant machine-gun and mortar fire." Actually, explained Will, the officer he dragged back to safety, there among the rocks under Monte Cassino, was only drunk, not wounded, and making so much noise Will's squad was afraid he'd bring down the Screaming Mimis. That was

Captain Fred H. Sprankle of Chambers, Pennsylvania, a mortician by trade. The captain, falling-down drunk, was bellowing the song about Angelina, the waitress at the pizzeria (the one with the gonorrhea), when Will went out to get him. The captain was awarded a Silver Star for leading a charge that nobody followed. "Anyhow," says Will, "he was a friend of mine, that Sprankle: I won forty dollars from him in a poker game."

Nor was Will the only one to return with a medal. There were three Purple Hearts in the squad: Floyd Hendrickson for his eye wound, Homer Bishop for his lost toes and Bill Gatlin for his case of Angelinitis.

Old Bill was a-layin' on his bed in the Army hospital in Naples when this tall hawk-nosed three-star general came striding in followed by an aide with a briefcase full of Purple Hearts, followed by two Army photographers, three reporters from *The Stars & Stripes* and about sixteen colonels. (As Bill told it.) This was a week after the glorious disaster at Rapido River and the Fifth Army commander was real busy that afternoon a-passing out the Purple Hearts mainly for the consolation of the folks back home and for whatever passed for a Christian conscience in his cold and calculating brain. Making a gesture. In a big hurry, thinking about more important things, the general made a wrong turn in a corridor and charged into the venereal disease ward. Before anyone in his retinue could muster up the courage to whisper a word in his ear, Mark Clark reached for the hand of the first casualty he came to, shook the hand, and said, "What's your name, soldier?"

"The name's Bill Gatlin, General, and I'm mighty glad to meet you." (Our Cousin Bill.)

"Pleasure's all mine, soldier." Photographers taking pictures; flashbulbs flashing. "Where you from?"

"Stump Crick, West Virginny, sir, and mighty proud of it."

"That's good country, soldier. Good country. Where'd you get wounded?"

Old Bill was wearing hospital pajamas and a blue corduroy robe. He placed his right hand on his groin, closed his eyes and groaned a little bit. "Right here, General."

The general made a face of deep sympathy. "Ah, that's a tough one, soldier, a tough one. But I mean, where'd it happen? Which battle?"

"Well sir," says Bill, "it was up yonder by that Mignano town. Me and Homer Bishop was havin' a smoke in this old stone barn when we found this Ginzo signorina and her young pig hidin' under a pile of straw in the corner of the stable just about the time them Screamin' Mimis a-started comin' down agin, and I says to Homer, Homer I says, I don't care—"

The general was already pinning the Purple Heart to Bill's chest and looking ahead to the next wounded man.

"—don't care if it's agin all regulations, this might be the last chance I'll ever have to slip the old bone to a good piece of foreign pussy and by God I think I better do it now before them Nebelwerfers blows my ass clean over the whole MTO so I give this girl my last pack of Lucky Strikes and I says to her I says how about you and me honey have a little that there you know fucky-wucky okay? and she says—"

General Clark shook hands again with Bill, not hearing a word he was saying, wasn't even listening to him, and says, "Carry on, soldier. It's men like you who make our victory certain," backs off the regulation three paces, salutes and hustles on to the next bed.

Private Gatlin, sitting up, returned the salute, and kept gabbing away:

"—she says hokay Joe presto presto prestissimo so I crawled in with her and her young pig she's a holdin' all the time and unloaded my rocks presto presto and pulled up my pants and I says to Homer, he's standin' guard at the window, I says all right Homer your turn, go ahead and top her off and, wait a minute, General, I hain't even got to the interesting part yet—" He winks at the reporters.

But the general was already five beds down the aisle passing out his Purple Hearts. So Bill finished the story for the benefit of the reporters, all three of them grinning these shit-eating grins.

"—So that ol' Homer he dives into that heap of straw on top of that signorina and her shoat and just about the time he's set to hide the old baloney why down come six of them Screamin' Mimis right outside the barn and I hear the pig squeal bloody murder and some stones fall out of the wall and when the dust clears I see old Homer with his teeth gritted and his eyes shut a-humpin' the holy hell out of that poor little innocent pig and the pig a-squealin' and the signorina watchin' and in a second Homer fires his wad and opens his eyes and here's this pig in his arms and Homer shuts his eyes agin thinkin' hit's all a bad dream but now the signorina is a screechin' at him and she wants two packs of cigarettes not one because she claims that shoat was cherry and she is mad and Homer he's sore as a boil but he got to pay up because sure enough that poor little virgin thing is bleedin' some and there's witnesses but I reckon maybe Homer got the best of the deal anyhow because six days later I got this dose of the blue munge and all he got was the crabs. All the same me and the boys figured Homer should of done the right thing by that pig and married it anyhow. . . ."

General Clark was now striding out of the V.D. ward, his face red with rage, followed by his platoon of chicken colonels. One of them gave Bill a cold evil dirty look as he went by and Bill he gave the colonel a grin and another salute from the sitting position. Some captain came back in a minute and reclaimed the Purple Hearts but he didn't get Bill Gatlin's. No sir. The reporters were still there, talking with Bill, and Bill refused to surrender his medal. The captain went away mad but he went away. Bill gave his Purple Heart to a reporter for safekeeping, in case the captain came back with a couple of MPs. They kept the story out of the papers but every G.I. in Italy heard about it inside of a week. Ruined Mark Clark's career—he got that fourth star, made full general, but never got to be a hero in anybody's mind but his own. If there, even. And nobody felt sorry for Clark. The Thirty-sixth Division—T for Texas—had lost 1,681 men, within forty-eight hours, at the Battle of the Rapido.

"As was anticipated," wrote Mark Clark about it, "heavy resistance was encountered in the Thirty-sixth Division's crossing of the Rapido River."

"The frontal attack across the Rapido River," wrote the German commander in Italy, Generalfeldmarschall Albert Kesselring, "should never have been made."

General Fred Walker, division commander, wrote in his diary, "The great losses of fine young men during the attempt to cross the Rapido to no purpose and in violation of good infantry tactics are . . . chargeable to the stupidity of the higher command."

What higher command? Which? Walker blamed Clark. Clark blamed General Harold Rupert Leofric George Alexander, the MTO commander. Alexander attributed the idea of an Italian campaign, an attack against "the soft underbelly of Europe," to Winston

Churchill who, in connivance with his crony Roosevelt, was able to test his pet theory, as he had done at Gallipoli in April 1915, by means of the lives of others. Churchill never visited the Italian battlefront. Not once. He never visited any battlefront. Neither did FDR. Neither did Stalin. Neither did Hitler.

After his rescue of Captain Sprankle, Will was offered a battlefield commission as second lieutenant—there was always a need for fresh platoon leaders. Company C had already lost three of them, together with most of three platoons, under mysterious circumstances: folks they'd never met personally or even seen or even heard of kept shooting at them. Will declined the honor of a commission, preferring to remain a squad leader. His reasoning was as follows: There's only about eight, nine men in a squad; I could keep my eye on that many. But there's forty in a platoon; I was afraid I'd lose some.

He came home in October 1945 still a buck sergeant. Three stripes on each arm. No rockers. No little brass bars. Only a buck. He was proud of that too.

VI

"What you Lightcaps so proud of all the time? You ain't rich. You ain't famous. You ain't important. You ain't even good-lookin'. What you got to be proud about anyhow?" That was old Raymond Houser (Ernie's uncle) talking.

Well—that's true. That's the simple truth, Raymond. The only thing the Lightcaps had to be proud about is that they were—and still are—and always will be!—Lightcaps. That's all we got.

7

ON TO GALLUP

In the morning. Thank God for morning, an end to endless night. The dog and I walk for a while toward an opaline sky, the topaz sunrise. I splash my head in the cold water of an algae-coated stock tank, return to camp and make breakfast—water and Hi-Pro for Sollie, cold cheese burrito and another can of Coors for me. How could I have failed to pick up some Mexican beer, real beer, back in Tucson? At least three things the Mexicans are good at: murals, manslaughter and beer. Which is more than you can say for most of the nations of the Peace Corps world.

Onward again, northeast, Merle Haggard unreeling in my cassette player as he sings a Hank Williams number: "I don't worry 'cause it makes no difference now." How true, how true—give me another ten days, Merle, or maybe six weeks, and I'll sing along with you, old buddy. After Merle, with Tom T. Hall on deck, how about some classical chicken fat, some high-class schmaltz? Why not Mozart and his Sinfonia Concertante smiling through the tears, happy ending guaranteed? No matter how deep the sorrow in the middle, Mozart always gives us a sprightly, gay and sparkling finish. If art can't make you feel better—after first making you feel worse— what good is it?

The pink outliers of the Painted Desert rise across my northern horizon. Suddenly we're in sight of Sanders and former Highway 66, Main Street of America—Get your kicks on Route 66—now U.S. Superstate Interstate 40. This is Indian Country, the Navajo Nation, Home of *Diné*—the people. The term implies not arrogance but only the native simplicity of original and aboriginal tribes anywhere. All who aren't Greeks are barbarians.

Turning eastward on the four-lane superhighway, I run a forty-mile gauntlet of red-and-yellow billboards, a near-continuous wall of urgent exhortation from the village of Sanders to the small city of Gallup, New Mexico:

SALE! INDIAN JEWELRY ONE MILE AHEAD! LARGEST COLLECTION IN ARIZONA SNACK BAR ORTEGA'S INDIAN CENTER STOP RELAX SHOP ICE CREAM SHOP ORTEGA'S INDIAN RUINS FINE JEWELRY WHOLESALE RETAIL SNACK BAR MALTS SHAKES BURGERS RUGS BEADED BELTS MOCCASINS TOMAHAWKS BOWS & ARROWS POTTERY KACHINA DOLLS NAVAJO RUGS 33½% OFF! SAND PAINTINGS 40% OFF! INDIAN CENTER 50% OFF! NECKLACES TURN HERE EASY OFF EASY ON NEXT EXIT THIS EXIT LAST EXIT (TURN AROUND!) INDIAN SOUVENIRS 55% OFF! EXXON INDIAN CITY NEXT EXIT GULF TEXACO SHELL MOBIL NAVAJO ASSEMBLY YOUTH CHURCH WELCOME TO NEW MEXICO LAND OF ENCHANTMENT (GATEWAY TO TEXAS) FORT COURAGE BREAKFAST 99¢ COFFEE & GIFT SHOP CHEE'S INDIAN STORE (one-room tar-paper huts among the billboards, swarms of children, rack-ribbed unbranded unclaimed horses browsing on the roadside weeds, herds of sheep grazing on dust and stubble, the Rio Puerco carrying its radioactive waters down an ever-deepening channel of erosion and pollution, frame & stucco shacks, abandoned hogans of log and mud, more horses, more kids, more strings of bright laundry fluttering on clothesline, horse-trampled cornfields, dusty pastures of cropped alfalfa, acres of tumbleweed and sagebrush, dead junipers hacked down to stumps, living junipers mutilated with ax and hatchet, firewood getting scarce in this region, solitary men shuffling along the highway toward Gallup, nothing else to do, stuccoed hogans with green shingle roofs, shingles held down against wind by worn-out auto tires, plywood wigwams, cement tepees, a flock of sheep escorted by a single child in a field that glitters with metal and broken glass, the bright desert sun shining down meanwhile with unlimited and impartial benevolence upon the dust, the animal dung, the human excrement, the acres of cardboard, wrapping paper, bottles, tin cans, junked cars, burned mattresses, smashed bottles, broken chairs, the sleeping drunks, the short heavy wide-hipped women (most of them pregnant) hunting for something—a child?—in a sagebrush flat, and children, more children, children everywhere. . . .

Feeling oddly tired for so early in the day, I stop at a gas station to fill my twenty-two-gallon tank with regular. Check the oil: quart and a half low; I add a quart from the supply of Yellow Front oil burner's special I carry in the back. Check the radiator: low again; really should repair that leak. I fill the radiator and head for the men's room to tap a kidney. Reading as always the writing on the wall, *vox populi clamantis in deserto*:

Q: What's the difference between the Navajo Nation and a bowl of yoghurt?
A: Yoghurt is a living culture.

HONKIES EAT SHIT

Q: Why dont the Navajo Nation declare war on the US Govt?
A: Because theyre afraid the US Govt would cut off their welfare checks.

HONKIES EAT SHIT OUT OF PLASTIC HATS

I find something heartwarming in this frank, informal, business-like exchange of views between the races. But am glad to move on to the seclusion of Don Williams's gun shop, book shop and general trading post—where I have business—well off the main line of Gallup's cultural life. Stopping at a liquor store en route, for my friend Don likes his beer. He's that type. And I ain't *flat* broke yet.

Two Navajo gentlemen approach me as I leave the store. They are barely able to stand. Give us some money, man. I give them each a dollar bill. (Spend it wisely, fellows.) Leaning on each other, they shamble inside the store, vague eyes seeking the sweet-wine shelves for something cheap, fortified, time-tested. Thunderbird wine, for example. Or Twister. Or Easy Days and Mellow Nights. A sound choice from the standpoint of strict cost/benefit analysis.

Don looks up from his workbench—loading rifle shells—as I enter, raises his glasses, smiles and gets to his feet. "Is that you, Henry?" The light is behind me.

"It's me," says I, "in the flesh."

He comes toward me, takes my hand. "You call that flesh?" He looks me over. "Old Henry, you're thin as a bean pole. You lost some weight. What's happened to you?"

"Nothing much. Routine troubles." I offer him the sixpack of Dos Equis.

Don looks sad and rubs his sagging paunch. "I have my troubles too, Henry."

"What're yours?"

"What's yours?"

"Domestic. What's yours?" Should I share my little secret with Don? No, not today. Maybe someday, when I get back this way. If I ever get back this way. I open two bottles of the Mexican beer.

Don locks the front door of his store and turns to me. Big and burly, gray-bearded but ten years younger than I, he looks genuinely aggrieved. "Henry," he says, "what's the most horrible thing that could happen to a man?"

"I don't know. A night in bed with Margaret Thatcher?"

"Come on, I'm serious."

A customer taps gently on the window of the door. Without looking around, Don reverses the sign that hangs inside the glass. Now it reads OPEN on the inside, CLOSED COME AGAIN on the outside. The stranger goes away.

I keep guessing. "Germaine Greer? Fritz Mondale? Henry Kissinger?"

"No, really."

"Well what? Tell me."

"My doctor tells me I can't drink anymore."

"Find a better doctor."

"He says I've got something he calls an irritable colon, for godsake. No more beer, no animal fats, no fry bread, tacos, salsa, and especially no more booze." I start to withdraw the bottle I've been holding toward him; he removes it from my hand. "One beer can't hurt me."

His problem puts mine in clearer perspective. I'm sorry I mentioned it. But after a while he fishes part of my story out of me. "There's only one cure, Henry. Get yourself another woman." I know that, I tell him, but my heart's not in it now; I'm going home instead. "Home?" he says, "where's that? You're home already, the West is your home, people like you can't even get across the Mississippi River without a passport." I tell him my heart longs for the Smoky Mountains of Appalachia, the green spring woods of home. "What bullshit. You can't go back there, Henry." I tell him I want to see my brother again, my old gray-haired mother, Paul's grave, the old man's grave, the grave of Cornflower. "But you *are* coming back?" Maybe, probably, who knows.

Giving up on the question for the time being, Don shows me recent additions to his stock. He's acquired new rugs, more books, new firearms, including a couple of muzzle-loaders. Against the wall stand racks of rifles and shotguns, a cabinet full of handguns, piles of Navajo rugs, buffalo robes, sheepskins. Kachina dolls fill several shelves. But his main stock is books, especially the rare and out-of-print in the field of Western Americana. There are no billboards showing the way to Don Williams's trading post and every time I stop here his inventory seems larger; it would appear that he buys more than he sells. How does he make a living? He smiles. "I'm a dealer; I wheel, I deal."

"How do you define a rare book, Don?"

"A good book is a rare book. But not all rare books are good books. Have something to trade? Something to show me?"

"I've got an old carbine that might interest you. A .25–.35."

"We'll have a look at it." But he's in no hurry. "Let's eat first." We go up the inside stairs and into the apartment above the store. His wife, Jenny, is in the kitchen mixing pancake batter. Juniper burns in the cookstove. April can be winter in Gallup, N.M., here at sixty-five hundred feet above sea level; the kitchen stove helps keep the apartment warm.

Jenny seems glad to see me. She puts down her mixing bowl and gives me a strong embrace. She's a good tough sweet well-rounded woman and it's disturbing to feel her in my arms. Half Anglo, half Navajo, she has the round Mongolian face, high cheekbones and long rich mahogany-colored hair of an Indian woman, the light eyes and slender figure of a European. She's a beauty. The face and eyes remind me of Grandmother Lightcap.

Jenny has never borne a child but there's a four-year-old Indian girl toddling about in the kitchen. The child is too small for her age, poorly coordinated, wearing a black patch taped over one eye. She grabs the calf of my leg as I sit down and rides back and forth on my foot. Another case of fetal alcoholism. The poor kid was a drunk before she was born, an alcoholic fetus taking its nourishment from a placenta marinated in booze. A common story on the reservation.

Don and Jenny had found the baby, only a few hours old,

wrapped in a newspaper and deposited in their alleyway garbage can. No one would ever know, most likely, who the mother was. But nevertheless they still dread the possibility, slight but real, that the mother might be alive, may remember the location of that garbage can, may come back someday demanding the return of her baby. There is no love so fierce as mother love. Also, in the state of New Mexico, a child is worth eighty-five dollars a month in AFDC—welfare payments—until the age of eighteen.

Jenny and Don had named her Celestina: gift from the sky.

Don makes coffee, Jenny stacks blueberry pancakes on a platter on the hot stove. We eat the pancakes and drink too much strong coffee and talk once again, one more time, about the American Indians and their never-ending problems. You think you've got troubles, consider the Navajo. Don and Jenny know the tribe well; they'd taught school for a combined total of twenty-two years in the heart of the Navajo reservation at Shonto, Chinle and Window Rock. Now they live in Gallup, drunk-tank capital of the American Southwest, chiefly in order to remain near their favorite people.

"Indians," says Don, passing me a cigar and unwrapping one for himself, "*los indios*, as Columbus named them, old Cristóbal Colón himself. You know why?"

Sure, he thought he was in the East Indies. Fourteen ninety-two, the ocean blue, and all that.

"Not so. Columbus knew he was nowhere near India. He knew what East Indians, Oriental Indians, looked like. Colón knew he'd found a new people, a new world. He was so charmed by the natives he found in the Caribbean—a people so sweet, generous, happy, so *blessed*, he thought, that he called them *los gentes in Dios*—the people in God."

We light our cigars, blow the smoke above Jenny's head. The child still rides my leg, clinging like a limpet, giggling.

"*Los gentes in Dios*," Don repeats. "And that's what Columbus wrote in a letter to Ferdinand and Isabella. In the next paragraph he offered to bring their majesties a shipload of '*inDios*' as servants and playthings. 'They have few and simple weapons,' he wrote, 'and conduct warfare only as a game.' With a handful of men, he said, meaning Spaniards not *inDios*, he could easily enslave the whole population of the Caribbean and put them to useful work, like mining gold and silver."

Jenny says, "I always wondered if that name Colón doesn't have a close connection to asshole."

I mention the *favelas* that I've seen along the highway; the garbage dumps and shantytowns seem twice as large as only a few years before.

"You want to know what the Indians' problem is?" says Don. "The Indians' problem is so basic and simple that nobody will mention it. It's an unmentionable. Taboo. When Kit Carson rounded up the Navajos in 1864 he counted 11,000 of them. In 1868 the Navajos got their territory back, a reservation of sixteen million acres, most of it good range for deer, antelope, sheep, cattle. There was timber in the mountains and a permanent stream in every canyon, everything they needed for a good life in the traditional way. But in the census of 1890 the tribe had grown to 15,000. In 1920 there were 20,000. In 1940, 40,000; in 1960, 80,000; now there's 160,000. At least. See the pattern? The population doubles every twenty years. By the year 2000 we'll have 320,000 of them trapped on a piece of land that could once have supported about 10,000 in health and dignity. Look at them now. Look at the land now: a dust bowl."

"You think that explains a highway slum?"

"That's no mere slum, that's the Third World." Having drunk all the coffee, Don opens our last two bottles of Dos Equis. His fingers tremble. Too much coffee? No, the truth is that Don still loves the Navajo, that's his trouble. "We've got our own banana republic out there. We control the police, we supply the funds and equipment, the energy corporations extract the oil and coal and uranium, the tribal bosses get paid off, the rest of the people get babies, the monthly welfare check, the food stamps, the Head Start program. A lot of nothing."

"Maybe the young bloods are right," I say. "Maybe revolution is the answer."

"That's your solution for everything."

"Revolution makes the world go round. As Abe Lincoln said, 'There never was a good war or a bad revolution.' "

"He never said that."

"Revolution plus birth control. Bayonets and bazookas for every working mother, condoms for the boys."

"You had a good time in the Army, didn't you, Lightcap?"

"I liked it. But I didn't reenlist. And I don't keep two hundred guns in my house like some folks I know."

"Is it still your house?"

Pause. Now that's a good question. Don't really care to be reminded that I've lost my home, my wife and my job in the last forty-eight hours. It's my turn to stare out the window. I drink my beer in silence. I talk too much.

"Sorry," Don says gently. Another pause. "Let's go have a look at that piece of yours."

Downstairs, in the gloom of his dusty cluttered shop, among rugs and saddles and silverfish, rare books, Kachina dolls and high-altitude cockroaches—only the weapons are kept perfectly cleaned, lightly oiled, in their locked gun racks—he holds my near-antique .25–.35 Winchester by its balance point, puts on his glasses and peers at the markings on the receiver. No bluing left, the surface wears a silvery sheen. Someone long ago had engraved the image of a pony on the steel. Don opens the breech and holds the carbine up to the light, taking a good look into the barrel. "Clean bore. No pits. Lands look good."

"I never fired it much. It's an oddball caliber, hard to find ammo for it."

"Load your own."

"I'm too lazy for that."

He works the action: loose but smooth. "This is a rare artifact, Henry. I could get five to six hundred for it in Dallas. Maybe a thousand."

"I won't take a penny over two hundred dollars. I don't want any handouts from you, Williams."

"You always said you were part Indian."

"My grandmother was half Shawnee. We're a proud, independent and self-reliant people. I'll take three hundred dollars."

"Done." He reaches high on a shelf and brings down a thick square leatherbound book. He blows the dust off the top, opens the book and removes two C-notes.

I look them over, count again: one, two. "Seem to be a bit short here, Don."

He puts *Log of a Cowboy* back in its place and pulls out a first-edition copy of *Commerce of the Prairies*, Vol. I, by an early nineteenth-century bore named Josiah Gregg. He opens the book,

141

leafs through it. Nothing there. He scratches his gnarly chin whiskers and studies his library for a minute, replaces Gregg and takes down Parkman, *The Oregon Trail*, withdrawing two fifties from pages 50–51.

I tuck the welcome bills into my pocket. Into my front pocket, not in the wallet in my hip pocket where thieves do tend to break in and steal. "You always do your banking in books?"

"It's the safest place to hide money I know. Especially in Gallup. I don't trust the banks and I'm not real intimate with the IRS. I could pay you off with a side of beef or a couple of rugs or how about a good book?"

"The money will do."

He says, "I hope you're not headed east without arms." I reassure him, mention the revolver, the shotgun, etc., the two-shot Derringer in the ashtray. "Good," he says; "hard to feel sympathy with any man goes around without a weapon these days. Especially on the road. What kind of handgun did you say?" It's a .357 Magnum, I tell him, double action and so on. "That's okay," he says, "but the .41 is best. Better range and more knockdown power than the .357, less recoil and more accuracy than the .44 or a .45. The .41 is the optimum personal antipersonnel weapon. I recommend it."

"I'll try to remember that." Now that I have his money I am itching to be off.

"In fact I've got three of them on hand. Maybe we could cut another deal. What else do you have in that truck of yours? And what year is that truck?"

"Maybe next time." The mad sick restlessness is seeping into my nerves again, rising by capillary action up my limbs, through my groin, into my entrails, toward my heart. A fatal embolism of the soul. Indian Country depresses me. But in my condition everything depresses. How to leave here gracefully, how to begin . . . ? "Don," I say.

"Hold your horses," he says. "Keep your shirt on. Jenny's fixing you a snack for the road."

I leave soon after, scot-free, with three huge elk-steak sandwiches—no mayonnaise, please—in a paper sack, and the cool three hundred dollars in cash in my pocket. Mayonnaise, I explain to Jenny, like hollandaise, was invented by the French to cover up the flavor of spoiled flesh, stale vegetables, rotten fish. Beware the sauce!

Where food comes beslobbered with an elegant slime you may well suspect the integrity of the basic ingredients.

What a pig, she says, and gives me a kiss. Don and I embrace. Come home soon, compañero; you'll die of claustrophobia back there in the East. I was born among those hills, Don, I can take it; if you can live in the East you can live anywhere. But if you can live anywhere, says Don, why live in the East?

How true. If only I could make that point clear to Brother Will.

Alone with my elk-steak sandwiches, my money and my renewed flow of tears—oh the sweet luxury of private weeping—I grope through the Gallup streets toward the Interstate. I stop at a telephone booth to warn Van Hoss in Santa Fe that I'm headed his way. Calling collect, of course. Any party who won't take a collect call is not worth talking to. Furthermore Van Hoss is rich, the swine, he can afford it. But instead of old Van himself I hear the voice of a suavely seductive young female prerecorded on his filthy answering machine:

Helloooo. You have reached the studios of Willem van Hoss, New Mexico's foremost painter of Western American landscapes, Native American horsemen and All-American exotic nudes. This month's special, *Valerie Emerging from the Bath*, is priced at only $14,495. At the sound of the tone you will have thirty seconds in which to leave a message. Valerie speaking, thank you.

Beep.

The operator, a little slow, wakes up and says, "I theenk ees no wan there, Robert Raidford sir, weel you please place your call later please?"

"Thank you, operator." Just as well. I refuse to talk to answering machines. A man's got to draw the line somewhere. I'll try again when I reach Albuquerque and if he still doesn't answer I'll be forced to drop in unannounced. Santa Fe is only sixty miles north of Albuquerque. Van Hoss won't mind, he'll be glad to see me, the scum.

"Ain't that right, Sollie?" I rub the dog's head as we swing forth onto the Interstate to join the roaring race of iron into the Mystic East. We're running full and fairly cool, 2,875 miles to go, on a four-lane superhighway gashed by violence through a sandstone hogback five hundred feet high. The speedometer reads 65 mph, tachometer 3300 rpm, ammeter dead center, oil pressure gauge 35 psi, the compass ESE as we bear toward Church Rock, Thoreau and Albuquerque. Altimeter says 7600 feet and rising as we climb toward the Continental Divide.

On the wind, with the odor of burning juniper, the fragrance of sagebrush, the smell of mud and horses, comes the image of my enchanted youth. . . .

8

1945-46:
HENRY'S WAR

I

During the summer of '44 when Will and his squad were fooling around in northern Italy, Henry took his thumb and a small canvas satchel and hitchhiked around the USA. From Stump Creek to Chicago to Seattle, from Seattle down the coast to L.A. and from there back home through the desert Southwest to Stump Creek again. A simple three-month grand tour. But the damage was done; that boy was lost: it was love at first sight with the slabs of the sunburned West. Never again could he be content, he thought, with the little blue fuzzy hills of Appalachia. So he thought.

His motive for doing the trip was simple. If I'm supposed to fight for my country, he told himself, wading ashore on Honshu Island in a year or two, then maybe I ought to at least see the homeland before I risk my neck for it. Make sure it's a legitimate proposition.

"Paw," he says, "I think I'll run away from home this summer. See the country. Maybe come back around Labor Day."

"Here's twenty dollars," the old man says, digging out a wad of worn and greasy greenbacks. He stuffed the roll into the bib pocket of Henry's overalls. ("Overhauls," we called them.) "That should get you to Minnesota." Grinning, he handed the boy his straw hat. "Here's your hat. There's the door. What's your hurry?" Henry looked hurt. "Hey now, I'm only kidding. You got your bindle ready?" The boy nodded. "Good. Now here's my advice: Don't let any man take you for a punk. Never eat at a place called Mom's. Don't play cards with strangers. And if you do, watch out for the cross-lift and them second-card mechanics. Listen for a swishy sound. And if anybody named Doc you don't know deals you a pat hand in straight draw, play it cautious. One of them other strangers will likely be holdin' four of a kind. You got that?" Henry nodded. "Now go say goodbye to your mother."

Yes, the old man was glad to see him go. With Will in Italy, that gave Joe Lightcap a good excuse to practically give up farming that year. He never did much like farming anyhow. He was a logger, he liked to say, and a sawyer, not a damned serf. With money he earned from part-time work in the coal mines, he was already paying off a little one-man sawmill near the Big Woods. That's what Paw wanted, a one-man business. He no more liked being an employer than an employee. Both, he'd say, were forms of slavery. He'd rather do everything himself: cruise the timber, fell it, buck it, skid it to the wagon, haul it to the mill, fire up the engine, saw the logs, even stack the slabs—all by his lone self.

Mother and the kids could handle the chores on the farm. Only one milk cow left now (Paw had sold the other a week after Will went overseas), and the pigs, chickens, ducks, garden, potato patch, cornfield, hayfield, easy enough for a woman and three kids to manage. The old man even sold one of the pair of draft horses, keeping the other for snaking logs out of the woods. Unwise to break up a good team like that: Will would be unhappy when he heard about it.

"Will would?" The old man rolls another Bugler. "What's Will got to do with it?"

The old man drove Henry to the highway at dawn one morning in late May. Henry's plan was to hitchhike from Shawnee to Wheeling and from there through Ohio toward Chicago. Paw did not approve of hitchhiking; to him it seemed like a form of begging. But Mother had exacted a promise from Henry that he would not hop a freight, ride the rails, become a hobo. The idea terrified her.

A cool and misty morning, sun barely up. Robins twittering in the sumac, one mourning dove cooing in the woods, a rooster crowing from the roof of somebody's hen coop. No traffic on the road yet. Waiting at the junction, the old man and Henry took their breakfast from Paw's big metal oval-shaped coal miner's lunch bucket: fried-egg sandwiches, deep-fried doughnuts, lukewarm coffee from a jar. A dog barked from somewhere beyond the fence rows.

"Your mother's upset, ain't she?"

"Yes sir."

146

"Cried a lot?"

"Yeah."

"She'll get over it, Henry. She'll be all right. She knows you got to do this. I did it myself, run off from home. About twenty-seven years ago. Only I stayed away two years. You'll be back in September, that right?"

"Got one more year of school, Paw. Then the Army."

The old man rolled another cigarette. He was forty-four that spring, in his prime, a tall strong broad-shouldered man with the black hair and dark eyes of an Indian, a nose like an eagle's beak. He cocked one leg, struck a match on the seat of his britches and lit the cigarette. "All right," he said, "guess I'll be going." They heard a car coming west on the road. "Here comes your ride. You got that twenty I loaned you?"

"Yes sir."

"You remember everything I told you about?"

"Sure, Paw."

"Okay. Shake hands." They shook. The old man squeezed the boy's skinny shoulder. "You're on your own now, Henry. Now get out there, stop that car and see the West."

The car was coming over the hill, advancing rapidly. Henry grabbed his bundle, his little canvas satchel, and stepped to the edge of the pavement, thumb outstretched. The car shot by without even slowing down. A four-door Buick sedan with Pennsylvania license plates. No one but the driver inside, either.

Paw shook his fist after the departing automobile. "You come back here and give my son a lift, you cheap Republican dog turd." That didn't do any good. The car kept going. The old man looked at Henry. "Maybe I scared him off. Maybe he thought I wanted a ride too." Father and son avoided each other's eyes, both made awkward by the necessity for saying goodbye all over again.

They were saved by the approach of another vehicle, an antique Ford truck with two farmers in the cab and an empty bed in back. Henry stuck out his thumb. The truck stopped, slowly, with much creaking of brakes, directly abreast of Henry. The old men inside stared at the boy. Both were gray of whisker and leaky-eyed, each with a thread of brown tobacco juice dribbling down the chin. They looked like twin brothers. The nearer one said to Henry, "How far you a-goin', boy?"

Henry gulped. "Pacific Ocean, sir."

The old geezer took that in and considered for a while. "We hain't a-goin' that fer. But we'll take you as fer as we're a-goin'. Throw your traps in the bed and climb on."

Paw had retreated to the door of his 1933 Willys-Overland coupe. Now, as Henry bent to pick up his gear, the old man stepped quickly forward and peered into the cab of the truck. "This is my boy Henry," he says, placing a hand on Henry's shoulder. "And he's a damn good boy, not very handy but bright as a bug. Where you fellas headed for?"

The old men looked at each other, then at Paw. They chewed their chaws. The one on the near side spoke again. "We'uns is bound for that Stump Crick. We're lookin' fer a fella name of Joe Lightcap."

"I'm Joe Lightcap and you passed Stump Creek turnoff three miles back."

That startled them into silence for another minute. Henry fidgeted with his baggage; he thought he heard another car coming. "You Joe Lightcap?" says the first old man.

"That's right."

"You the fella has them beech logs fer sale?"

"That's right, boys."

They stared at each other, then suspiciously at Paw. "Iffin you're Joe Lightcap, how come you hain't in Stump Crick?"

Lightcap grinned. "If you ain't been there yet how do you know I ain't?"

Another pause for thought. In the silence Henry heard, then saw, the next car racing over the eastern hill, bearing down on them. He moved onto the blacktop, thrust out his arm and waved his thumb up and down like a semaphore.

The car roared past in a rush of wind, moving so fast he barely identified it as a 1937 La Salle with Virginia plates, barely glimpsed two uniformed men in the front seat. Soldiers. He watched the car fly on, then weave suddenly from side to side with agonized screech of brake drums. The driver made a hasty stop.

"Goodbye, Paw," Henry shouted. He started to run after the car but it was now backing up at full throttle, engine howling. Henry halted. The car came roaring backward with savage torque, jerked to a violent stop beside him, bouncing on its springs. A foxtail fluttered on the radio antenna. The two men inside looked at the boy.

Holding the wheel was a master sergeant, at his side a captain; both had an array of hash marks on their sleeves and rows of pretty ribbons above the left breast pocket. They looked flushed in the face, excited, happy—the fumes of whiskey poured from the open windows. The driver grinned at Henry. The captain stuck his face out in the morning air—a big man with a brave mustache curled at the ends, shaggy black eyebrows bunched above the imperial red nose of a hero—and shouted at Henry:

"Son! We're drunk as owls and we're crazy as pelicans but we ain't queer—can you drive?"

So long, Paw.

Twenty-four hours later Henry stood on the southwest outskirts of Madison, Wisconsin, thumb out and forty dollars in his pocket, bound for the Rocky Mountains. Two weeks later and he stood on a sand dune in Oregon, looking at the Pacific. Captain Meriwether Lewis said it for him in the summer of 1805: *Ocian in view O joy!*

II

The President of the United States

To: Henry Holyoak Lightcap
R.F.D. #2
Stump Creek, West Virginia

SSS board #114
Shawnee County
West Virginia

Selective Service No.
000 033 912 465

(Local Board Stamp)
May 19, 1945

G R E E T I N G :
  You are hereby ordered for induction into the Armed Forces of the United States, and to report at Shawnee Co. Courthouse Shawnee, W. Va., on June 20, 1945 at 0800 hours
· ·
(Place of reporting)   (Date)   (Hour)

for forwarding to an Armed Forces Induction Station.

J. Wilbur Fisher
· · · · · · · · · · · · · · · · · · · ·
(Member, Secretary, or Clerk of
Local Board)

IMPORTANT NOTICE

"No."

"What else, Paw? What else can I do?"

"No!" he says. And "No!" he roars. "You're not gonna fight in their rotten war. Hitler's whipped. What do they need you for? They already got Will."

"We still got Japan to lick."

"Japan is whipped. Churchill's got his empire back. MacArthur's got his Philippines back. Roosevelt owns the Pacific. What more do they want?"

"Japan still ain't surrendered."

"But they're whipped. They got nothin' left."

"We still have to invade the home islands."

"Why?"

"Because—" He had me there. "I don't know. Because that's the plan. Unconditional surrender."

"Unconditional bullshit. You stay away from those home islands. Them Japs'll fight like badgers if we invade their home islands."

"What am I supposed to do, Paw?"

"Hide in the woods."

Henry looked at Mother. She was bent over her sewing, crying silently, saying nothing. The kids watched in awe: Paul, Marcie, Jim—big eyes, gaping mouths. "Paw," Henry said, "I have to go too."

"Why?"

"Because the rest are going. Everybody I know—Junior Fetterman, Ken Wolfe, Tommy Marlin, the McGee boys. Even Leroy Ginter, they're drafting him. Right down to the bottom of the barrel."

"That's not the bottom of the barrel, that's under the barrel. They must be losing their goddamn war."

"I'm going, Paw."

"Everything is going to Hell," the old man said. But he was the only one who said it and not to any strangers either. Joe Lightcap thought he was the only Wobbly east of the Mississippi River. The only freethinker in West Virginia. The only isolationist left in Shawnee County—a Republican county at that. Nobody paid him any attention and he knew it and the knowledge made him angry and lonely and sick in his heart. Joe Lightcap was not a philosopher; he took ideas seriously.

"Ideas can hurt people," he would say. "Ideas are dangerous. I'd rather have a man come at me with an ax than a Big Idea."

Most people avoided Lightcap when they saw him in a thinking mood. But not Jeffrey Holyoak the bank clerk. Uncle Jeff had graduated from high school, even gone to college for a year, and had some ideas about things himself. He was not afraid to stand up to the old man when they faced each other over a tub of iced beer and soda pop at the family Labor Day picnic in 1944.

"How's Will, Joe?" A dangerous question and Uncle Jeff knew it.

"Will? He's in France now. Still fighting Winnie's war."

Uncle Jeff smiled. "It's our war, Joe. I'm proud of Will and I'm proud of all of them. They're fighting in a good cause, Joe."

"What cause is that?"

"The good cause. They're fighting for democracy and peace."

"Fighting—for peace? That's a good one, Holyoak. I like that. That's pretty damn good."

"They're fighting for the Four Freedoms. Against an evil dictatorship."

"You mean Roosevelt's Four Freedoms. I thought you were a goddamn Republican, Jeff."

"Yes sir I am. But this is not a Democrat war, not a Republican war, it's an American war. An All-American war." Uncle Jeff was getting a bit steamy himself. Other men stood nearby, listening. And some of the boys, like Henry. The women turned their backs and moved away. "But maybe that word American doesn't mean much to you, Joe."

Now it was our father's turn to smile. The smile revealed that he'd been hurt. He lowered his bottle of Iron City Pilsener and said, "What are those Four Freedoms, Holyoak? Can't seem to recollect them myself."

"Well . . . freedom of speech. Freedom of religion. Freedom from hunger . . ."

"Yeah? What's the other one, Jeff?"

Uncle Jeff hesitated, turning red. "Fear," somebody murmured in the background. "Freedom from fear," Uncle Jeff said.

"Pretty good. Just a little coaching and you done good. Real good. Now what's this evil dictatorship we're supposed to be fighting? You mean Joe Stalin?"

"I mean Hitler and Tojo and you know what I mean."

"What about Stalin? You know how many million people he murdered, Holyoak?"

"We'll take care of him later."

"Oh we will, huh? Another war, huh? Right after this one, you reckon?"

Uncle Jeff was silent for a moment. "In good time. When we have to."

Paw said, "Tell me more about this democracy we're a-fighting for, Holyoak. What's your notion of democracy anyhow?"

"Government for the people, by the people and of the people."

"We got plenty of government *of* the people all right. But I hain't seen no government *by* the people yet. Name the Bill of Rights, Holyoak."

"What?"

"The Bill of Rights. You believe so much in democracy, name me the first ten amendments to the Constitution of these here U.S. of A."

"You know so much, you name them."

He should not have said that. Our old man had the Bill of Rights down pat and he began rattling them off like a genuflector reciting his catechism. Uncle Jeff cut him short after Article III. "Okay, Joe, okay okay. We believe you." He took a deep slug from his bottle of Nehi orange crush. "You should've been a schoolboy, Joe." He recited two lines of his own: "She was the girl in calico, He was her bashful barefoot Joe." Laughing, he glanced at the men around him.

The old man squeezed his bottle of beer so tightly I thought he'd break the neck off. Quietly, so that everyone had to strain to hear, he said, "Tell me just one thing, Jeff. Just one thing and then I'm gonna go home. Just tell me this: This is such a noble holy goddamn war, how come the draft?"

"What?"

"Conscription, Jeff, conscription. How come the government has to force men to fight in this holy noble bloody English war of yours?"

Uncle Jeff hesitated for only a second. "My son volunteered. Nobody had to draft Dick. And they didn't draft your boy either, Joe."

Our old man waved this qualification aside. "Two out of ten million. They knowed they'd be drafted anyhow. Answer my question,

Holyoak, How come the draft? Why does Roosevelt have to con-
script teenage boys, under penalty of prison or worse, to fight in
this here noble war?"

Silence. Uncle Jeff thought about it. "Well," he finally said, "to
be fair. That's why. So that some boys wouldn't have to go off and
fight while the slackers stayed home. That's why."

It was my father's turn to laugh—and it was a scornful, bitter
laugh. "The government was afraid there'd be too many slackers
and not enough fighters, ain't that right, Holyoak?"

"Maybe. The draft law was approved by Congress. Congress was
elected by the people. Congress spoke for the majority."

"You think so? It certainly didn't speak for the majority of the
boys who'd have to go and do the dying, did it? Why the draft,
Holyoak? If this is such a good and holy war, why do we need the
draft?"

Again Uncle Jeff hesitated. I felt sorry for him, up against a crazy
anarchist like my father.

"Well . . . I think I gave you a good answer, Joe."

"No, it's no damn good a-tall. The majority of Americans never
wanted to get into this rotten war. And when Roosevelt maneuvered
us into it, even after Pearl Harbor, the majority still never wanted
to go overseas to fight. That's why the government needs the draft,
Holyoak. Because there was no other way they could get our boys
into it. They have to force them to fight."

Uncle Jeff was still trying to be reasonable. "Joe, we have to have
some confidence in our government. Otherwise—"

"You think the government knows what's best for us? You think
the government knows better than the people?"

We could see the thought "Yes, sometimes it does" forming in
Uncle Jeff's puzzled, thoughtful, kindly eyes. But he was surrounded
by Appalachians. Mountaineers. Country men. "I didn't say that,
Joe."

"Do you think American men are cowards, Holyoak?"

"Never. Never." His face turning red again.

"You think they have to be *forced* into a war they believe in? You
think we wouldn't all be fighting, Holyoak, every damn man here,
if we seen it had to be done?" The old man's voice remained low,
deep, intense, deadly—his fighting voice. "Free men don't have to
be pushed into war, Holyoak." Silence. And while Uncle Jeff groped

153

for the right answer, our father turned away, turned his back on all the Holyoaks and Gatlins and their kin—his by marriage—and walked away by himself, alone, alone again, across the baseball diamond where the kids were picking up teams for a game of mush-ball. There was little Jim and Cousin Sonny alternating hands on a bat to see who'd get first pick. I saw Jim forking the top end of the handle with his fingers; he'd better pick me, Henry thought. And Paw crossed the outfield pasture, where three of Prothrow's cows followed him for a piece, and he lifted his long legs over the fence and disappeared into the woods. He always did like it best in the woods. He felt he belonged there. He'd probably walk the whole way home, three miles, cross-country.

There was a silence as the men watched him go. The women, in their separate group, resumed their talk of pie socials, the next blood-donation drive, the latest marriage. Only Henry's mother remained silent, her head lowered. Among the men, only Uncle Harold could not keep his mouth shut. "Somebody ought to report that crank to the FBI."

The Gatlins looked at Harold. Grandfather Holyoak said, "Don't talk like a fool, Harry."

"Well, dang, all I meant was he shouldn't talk like that. Not in front of these boys. He—" And then he became aware of Henry and Paul, watching him. He flushed a little, stopped.

Henry's heart was beating so loud, so hard, as he tried to speak, that he thought he'd drop dead. But he got it out. "Our paw . . ." he stammered, "our paw . . . he's the bravest man in all Shawnee County." He touched Paul on the shoulder. "Come on. Let's get in that game." Henry stalked off, Paul trotting beside him.

III

Henry reported for induction, as ordered. What choice did he have? The draft was like a well-organized cattle drive, with this difference: most cattle have brains enough to attempt to resist, to escape. But not humans. It's not that we lacked the courage or intelligence to resist; we lacked the means to resist. And the will. We were solitary, frightened, unorganized teenagers caught in the moving parts of a gigantic subhuman social machine. We were barely given time to kiss our mothers goodbye. No bands played and the cheerleaders were busy elsewhere.

Slow train to the Deep South. Soot and smoke from the coal-burning engine poured into the open windows of the filthy carriages. But the dirt was better than suffocation from the heat. The boys read their comic books, played cards, smoked cigarettes, gathered in clumps here and there with guitars, harmonicas, banjos, Jew's harps, and made music of the only kind they knew: hillbilly, country, bluegrass. They talked about their girlfriends, their mothers, their dreams of the future—after the war. Nobody talked about the war. Roosevelt was dead, somebody named Truman was the president, and none of them cared. The war was a great blank abyss on the edge of their lives, a black hole of nothingness.

The locomotive whistled far ahead, a wail of despair that drifted back, with sulfur and ashes, over the sleeping heads of a thousand teenagers dressed in khaki. The train rumbled through the valleys of western Tennessee, rocked and rattled, rollicked and rolled toward the southern dawn. Fireflies shimmered in galaxies above dark humid fields of hay, tobacco, cotton. Frogs clanked in the swamps, dogs barked from isolated farms, dim lights glowed in little one-store villages and from the woods came the chant of the whippoorwill, American bird of the night.

IV

They were greeted at Fort McClellan by the training cadre, stern hard aggrieved men with sullen faces, who barked yelled howled screamed sputtered and roared at them in voices bitter with contempt. Mostly Southerners, the cadre spoke what Henry and his friends called "chigger English" or "boll-weevil American."

"Mah nay-em," says one, "is Coprol Hay-in-ton." (My name is Corporal Hinton.) "Ow-ah fust layah-sun t'day we-ell be eeh-in mi-lah-tay-ree cut-ass-see." (Our first lesson today will be in military courtesy.) "Now-ah . . ."

"Corporal?"

"Y'all wee-el address non-coh-missioned uffishahs bah tattle and last nay-em only."

"Corporal Hinton, sir?"

"Only uffisahs ah addressed as suh."

"Sorry, Corporal Hinton. My question is—"

"The dee-skushion comes latah. Nowah: whut is the fust an' mos' im-potent doodee of the soljah?" The corporal stared at the silent platoon. One boy raised a hand. "Yay-uss, Pravvit?"

"To kill Japs, Corporal Hinton."

"Wrong." The corporal studied his reluctant draftees, his eyes a smoldering brown under black effeminate eyelashes. No one offered a second answer to his question. The corporal singled out a dark lanky boy with wandering eyes, straying attention. "You theah. Lat-cap. Whut is the fust an' mos' im-potent doodee of the soljah?"

Henry thought about it. "To salute?"

A pause. "No," said Corporal Hinton. "Wrong. We'll dee-skuss the salute latah. No. The fust an' mos' im-potent doodee of the soljah is—obee-jence. Obee-jence, Lat-cap. The soljah mus' lunn t' obey strickly, an' execute prumply, the lawful o-dahs of his suhpee-yuhs." Another pause for reflection. "Pravvit Lat-cap!"

"Yes, Corporal Hinton."

"Whut is the mos' im-potent doodee of the soljah?"

"Obey orders, Corporal Hinton. To obey orders strictly, promptly, obediently, without even *thinking* about them."

A pause. The corporal considered. "Raht ansuh, Pravvit Lat-cap, but wrong attitude. You spoze to obey o-dahs strickly, prumply, without not even *thankin'* about thankin' about them. Gimme twentah-fahv."

"Twenty-five, Corporal Hinton?"

"Pushups, Pravvit Lat-cap."

V

Loved those parades. Henry always loved a parade. He enjoyed the battalion review, marching past the stand, rifle on his shoulder, pack on his back, the steady tromp tromp tromp of booted feet around him, and the order "Eyes . . . right!" ("When I order 'Eyes right!' " the drill sergeant said, "I wanta hear them eyeballs click.")

He loved the long march back to camp at night, the freedom of the rout step, the soldiers' chorus:

> Oh we're evil sonsabitches
> and we're raiders of the night,

we're ugly horny bastards
who would rather fuck than fight.

There was an official infantry song, something about "Kings of the Highway," but none of the boys would learn it, like it, sing it. We knew bullshit when we saw it. Smelled it. Stepped in it. Dog soldiers, foot soldiers were not kings of anything, they were the peons of war. Instead, tramping home to barracks, we sang our own song:

So, heidy-deidy christ almighty
who the hell are we?
Wham! bam! thank you, ma'am!
We're the infantry.

But best of all Henry loved the combat training, the art of the bayonet, the science of the rifle, the fine techniques of killing men. He knew such training would come in handy when the war was over.

Loved that bayonet drill. Fix—bayonets! On guard! Lunge! Thrust! Butt stroke! Slash! Lunge and thrust again!

"Put your guts into it, Lightcap," growled Sergeant Bell. "That ain't no stuffed dummy, that's a live living Jap there. He hates you. He wants to kill you. So yell when you stick it in him. Holler. Stick it in and twist it. Make the dirty little yellow slant-eyed bastard scream—real vigorous-like."

Henry nodded, grinned, sweated, stabbed, thrust and slashed, grunting like a butcher.

"You ain't yelling loud, Lightcap. When you club his teeth with the butt stroke, yell. You got to hate, Lightcap."

The cadre hated everyone. They hated Japs, Germans, Jews, Dagos, Frogs, Limeys, Commies, Wops, Indians, Meskins and of course Niggers and of course and especially Yankees. In the eyes of Alabama anyone from north of Kentucky was a Yankee. Weren't too keen on women neither. But loved dogs, okra, guns and Coca-Cola. Things balance out.

Henry loved Kitchen Police. He enjoyed being a kitchen policeman, peeling spuds, scrubbing boilers, plucking chickens, mopping cool floors in the shade of the mess hall when the rest of the com-

157

pany was out in the hot stinking sun, in July, digging straddle trenches in the red clay of Alabama.

Henry even loved the cooks, especially the first cook, everybody's favorite, Sergeant Twee Twipes. Everybody loved Sergeant Twipes, a touchy hot-tempered hair-triggered little man about five foot five inches high, a rigorous perfectionist with a fondness for detail, whether the task at hand was the cleaning of what he called the "coffee urinals" (semantic confusion in the sergeant's mind) or in the meticulous preparation of his pièce de résistance, a dish known variously as *La Merde sur le Bardeau* (literally, "Zee Sheet on zee Shin-gale," as explained by Private Herbert Waxler, the company intellectual) or simply as SOS in the relaxed terminology of the rank and file. Creamed beef on toast might not be everyone's favorite but Henry could eat it. Grim as army food might be, Henry liked to say, at least it beat Mom's home cooking. Any day! But best of all in the old mess hall he loved Sergeant Twee Twipes, even when the sergeant lost his temper, as he did every ten minutes, and began screaming again, pointing at the chevrons on his sleeve: "Look!" he screamed at Henry; "twee twipes! Twee, Lightcap!" (Not one. Not two. Twee.) Sergeant Twipes suffered from a speech impairment that became conspicuous when his spirit was inflamed; he'd worked hard for his three stripes. "I worked hard for these twee twipes, Lightcap," he'd explain, many times, dancing up and down on his tippytoes and plucking at his badge of rank, "and you'd better weethpect them! Or I'll have your ath in a thling!"

Respect them? Henry loved them.

Henry loved Field Police. He enjoyed policing the company area, he with his buddies picking up cigarette butts under the sharp eyes of his friend and mentor Corporal Hinton. "Aw-raht, may-in," Corporal Hinton would chant, "less *poh*-lees the ar-ya na-ow. Don' wanna see nothin' but a-ess-holes an' ail-bows"

Henry loved mail call and the weekly letter from Mother:

Your father spends more and more time working in the woods. I wish he wouldn't work alone but he does—he insists on it. I worry about him, he comes home late so often. He's been spend-ing 10-12 hours a day out there with his ax and saw and cant-hooks and the old horse Fred. Someday he's going to have an accident and who will help him? He seems to be happy, tho' he worries a lot about you and Will. But he says the war will end soon. Says the Japanese are making peace "overtures" through the Russians and the Swedish legation in Washington. Or so he reads in that IWW newspaper of his. But says Truman does not want the Japanese to surrender *too soon*. We had a short note from Will last week. He's stationed in Austria now at a place called Kitzbuhl. Says he has seen some terrible things in Germany but didn't say exactly what. Very glad, he says, that the war is over in Europe. All the boys in his squad came through alive. He asks about the farm and I don't know what to tell him. The coal company has begun stripping those 60 acres on the east side of the hill that your father leased many years ago. How can I tell Will about that? I dread it. His heart will break. Paul and Marcie and Jim and I are raising a big garden this summer—our "Victory Garden." Did you know that little Paul has become very good at the piano? You never paid much attention to your little brother but he's a fine, sensitive, talented boy. He admires you, Henry. Thinks you are the "smartest" Lightcap. I tell him that intelligence is valuable only when combined with a generous heart and a kindly nature. You and I know that "brains" aren't everything, don't we, Henry? Marcie and Jimmy are doing fine. All is well here. We miss you very much. I pray for you every night. Love and a hug from your Mother.

Henry's mate on latrine duty, a boy named Johnny Pearce from Latrobe, Pennsylvania, looked morose as he scanned his latest letter. He was staring at a small sheet of pink stationery with a floral fringe. What's wrong, Johnny? says Henry.

This letter.

Yeah? What's wrong?

She says she don't love me no more, Henry.

Who does?

My girlfriend. Louise.

You sure? What's it say? Read it.

It's kind of personal.

Don't read it.

I don't mind. Maybe you can tell me what she really means, ex-

actly. I'll read it. Pearce cleared his throat. She says, Dear John . . .
He paused, gulped, stopped.

Henry waited.

Pearce started again. She says, Dear John: This is going to be a
very difficult letter for me to write. I wish I did not have to write
it. But I think it would be unfair of me not to tell you. John, I am
in love with Ronnie Coulson. He is a 4-F but I love him very much.
I plan to marry him very soon. As a matter of fact we are getting
married tonight. I made up my mind last night. When you get this
letter we will be man and wife. Don't write to me anymore. I know
that you will be very happy without me and I wish you every possible success and happiness in the years to come.

Silence. Henry said, That's all?

Yours sincerely, Louise Rapp.

And that's it?

Well, that's all she wrote. What do you think, Henry? You think
she still loves me?

Henry considered, leaning on his mop handle and staring out the
open window at the drill field. He thought of Wilma Fetterman.
He thought of Mary Kovalchick. He thought of Lou Ann and Rose-
mary and Donna and Betsy and Mary Jane McElhoes. Johnny, he
said, you been screwed, blued and double-tattooed.

Henry loved guard duty. He loved the General Orders: (1) To
take charge of this post and all other government property I can get
away with; (2) To walk my post in a military manner; and (3) To
take no shit from the company commander.

He loved the V.D. movies.

He loved the Saturday morning inspection: loved to display his full-
field equipment for Captain Kotzwinkle. Rifle on the right (from the
captain's point of view); then the handsome new gas mask on its case,
then the six cans of C rations, then the Iron Pisspot (or helmet), then
(above) his articles de toilette—cake of unused soap (Palmolive in olive
drab wrapper), the comb (bristles pointing down), toothbrush (bristles
to the right, pointing down), the razor blades, the safety razor (head
to right), toothpaste tube (full, unsqueezed), the shaving brush (centered), the tiny canister of salt tablets, the open haversack, the bayonet
(uncased), the canteen (open), the canteen cup, the mess gear (fork in
middle, tines forward and up), the cartridge belt with canteen cover
(attached), the first-aid packet (sealed) and, top row, his neatly folded

shelter half (half a pup tent), his raincoat, his extra underwear, his tent cord (coiled), his entrenching tool and his five little tent pegs all in a row (points forward).

Henry loved rifle inspection. Loved it when the captain stood before him, followed by the platoon leader, and Henry snapped open the bolt of his rifle, jerked his head for a glance into receiver and chamber, thrust the rifle out and the captain snatched it with a rattle of metal and wood, peered into bore (lovingly cleaned and polished by Henry), thrust it back at him, murmured "Good work, soldier" and moved on. Henry tingled with pride. He loved the captain, that grave gray-eyed gray-haired man hedged about with the untouchable sanctity of an officer. (An enlisted man must never, *never*, NEVER touch an officer, instructed Sergeant Bell. Why not, Sergeant Bell? Because if you do, Private Lightcap, God will strike you dead. And if He don't I will.)

Yes, Henry loved his rifle. He loved his bayonet—the firm heft of it in his hand, the carbon steel blade, the sleek blood groove—but best of all he loved his rifle, the U.S. Cal. .30, M-1 (Garand), a gas-operated clip-fed self-loading shoulder weapon.

Men, said Sergeant Bell, this here wee-pon is called the M-1. This is a good wee-pon and the purpose of this here wee-pon is to kill folks with. You all remember that. Now how do you go about killing folks with this wee-pon? Pay attention. . . .

He loved the target range.

Ready on the right. Ready on the left. Ready on the firing line. (Pause.) Commence firing.

Henry lay in prone position, loop sling tightened, body at forty-five degrees to line of aim, legs well apart, cheek against stock, eye close to rear sight. Right forefinger inside trigger guard, he aligned his smoke-blackened sights with the base of the bull's-eye five hundred yards away, exhaled slightly for steadiness and squeezed the trigger. Slowly, gently. Shooting for record. The butt plate jolted against his shoulder.

Call your shot, said his coach, Lieutenant Kelly.

Bull's-eye, three o'clock. Sir.

They watched the target sink into the pit, vanish, then rise. The white disk marker came up and hovered for a moment before the black disk of the bull's-eye, the spotter a touch off-center, to the left. A five at nine o'clock.

161

Very good, Lightcap. But check your windage. See the flag? We've got a nine to ten mile-an-hour wind coming from the right.

Henry turned his windage knob one point to the right—four clicks. His next shot was centered. Zero. And the next. And the next. After nine shots he had a perfect score: 45. One more to go. Pleased, the lieutenant fed him another cartridge. You're doing good, Lightcap. Damn good. One more in the bull's-eye and we'll wrap this up.

Henry wanted that Expert's medal so bad he could taste it. If Will could do it he could do it. He grinned at the boy on his right, Herbert Waxler. A flinch shooter, involuntarily closing his eyes and jerking the trigger when he fired, Waxler was missing most of his shots. Waxler hated Germans; but he feared guns. A paradoxical, self-contradictory position. Waxler would not qualify and Henry gloated because Henry did not like Waxler; nobody liked a pompous young man who used the word *feces* when he meant *shit*. He saw Waxler staring with resignation at the red danger flag—Maggie's drawers—waving once again across his target. Another clean miss.

How you doing, Herbie?

Lieutenant Kelly spoke quietly but sharply in Henry's ear. Mind your own business, Lightcap. Concentrate on your target.

Yes sir. Henry chambered his final round, closed the bolt, took a deep breath, exhaled partially and centered his sights on the target. The target in his sights.

Now, the lieutenant whispered, squeeze . . . that . . . trigger.

Slowly, with love and care, Henry squeezed his trigger. Whump! went the rifle. He did not flinch.

Waxler fired at the same moment.

Call your shot, Lieutenant Kelly said.

Dead center, Henry said.

Happily, coach and student watched Henry's target being lowered into the pit, then saw it reappear. Much too quickly. The red flag fluttered across the target. A total miss. They gaped in surprise.

You didn't blink, did you Lightcap?

No sir. *No* sir.

They heard a cry of joy on their right. The white disk marker was centered on the bull's-eye of Waxler's target. Waxler's first, last and only perfect shot.

Lightcap, said Lieutenant Kelly, you fired at Waxler's target.

Henry, his rifle still in aiming position, looked across his sights. God, Lieutenant—you're right. That's what I did.

Excessive pride, Lightcap. Hubris. See what it cost you? The lieutenant glanced quickly up and down the firing line, then slipped Henry an extra cartridge. Cheating a bit. Here you go. Quick, shoot, before they lower your target.

Henry loaded, aimed, fired. Too quickly. His target went down, came up. The red disk spotter rose with it, indicating a four at six o'clock.

The range commander shouted through the P.A. system: Cease firing. Clear rifles.

Henry had missed a perfect score at five hundred yards by one point. Lieutenant Kelly was disappointed; Henry was angry. He stayed angry through the remaining trials, through the kneeling, sitting, offhand and rapid-fire shooting, and ended his afternoon on the range three points short of qualifying as an Expert. He had to be content with the Sharpshooter's rating. Once again Brother Will had beaten him.

But Henry loved the Army, all the same. He loved the night patrols. He loved crawling through barbed wire under a low ceiling of live machine-gun fire. He enjoyed the twenty-mile march with full field pack, the bivouac in the rain among the chiggers, mosquitoes, water moccasins and rattlesnakes, the tactical training on the surprise-target range where cardboard Japs with bucktooth grins popped suddenly from foxholes and Henry blazed away, shooting from the hip as he and his platoon marched forward in ragged skirmish line.

Henry failed to love only one course in his basic training. That was the weekly information and education class—the I&E. Henry did not love First Lieutenant Manning, from regimental headquarters, who warned Henry and his comrades, week after week, that life was serious, that the military was in earnest, that someday soon he and his buddies would be loaded aboard a troopship for the Far Pacific and launched with a nation's official blessing into the mad adventure of their first and terminal amphibious assault. Into the red mouth of the Setting Sun.

In late July, at the last meeting of the class, Lieutenant Manning concluded his lecture and asked for questions from "the men." Nobody spoke. Even Herbert Waxler had nothing to say. A troubled silence lay upon the one hundred teenage boys of Dog Company. The lieutenant was about to leave when Henry rose from his bench in the bleacher seats and dared to ask the one question that had been uppermost in his mind for seventeen weeks. Standing at attention, as required, and framing his thought *pro forma*, Henry said, Lieutenant Manning, sir?

The lieutenant paused. Yes?

Henry swallowed, palms sweating, and said, Why?

Why what?

A second pause. Well sir, you tell us the Japs have lost nearly all their empire, their navy is destroyed, their air force is gone, the home islands are under blockade and the people are starving. Looks like they lost the war.

Almost. What's the question, Private?

So—why? Why do we have to invade Honshu? Sir.

Final pause. Lieutenant Manning said, Remember Pearl Harbor, soldier? As we did the Alamo? We are going to invade Japan because—the lieutenant's voice rose suddenly in pitch, becoming harsh, strident—Why? Because we must invade Japan in order to achieve complete final absolute and unconditional victory. He glared at Henry Lightcap. That's why, soldier.

Silence. For a moment.

But sir, thought Henry—but the words came out aloud—that's insane. We'll get killed.

Silence again. The lieutenant stared at Henry as if Henry were a strange, repulsive, unidentifiable insect crawling from the lieutenant's soup. Then he turned to First Sergeant Bell. Take that man's name, Sergeant. See that he gets some special information and education this evening.

Yes sir. With pleasure, sir.

Henry spent three hours that evening, after regular duty, at close-order drill (solo) under the personal supervision of Corporal Hinton. Henry carried his rifle and wore his steel helmet, cartridge belt, canteen, gas mask and full field pack. Fifty pounds.

Halt. Ry-aht . . . face! Awh-dah . . . harms! Henry stood at rigid attention, facing Corporal Hinton. Sweat poured in rivulets, in streams, down the boy's despairing exalted martyr's face. He stank with sweat. His heavy green fatigue suit was black with sweat.

164

While Corporal Hinton, cool and comfortable in starched pressed bleached-out khaki, an overseas cap perched jauntily on his potlike head, faced Henry with pleasure and conviction.

Pravvit Lat-cap: what is the fust an' mos' imPOtent doodee of the sol-jah?

Obedience, Corporal Hinton.

Thass raht. An' when may a soljah question an odah, Pravvit Lat-cap?

Absolutely never, Corporal Hinton.

Thass raht. Now: when you-all is odahed t' march t' shore on that Honshu Owl-lan' whut will y'all do?

I will march ashore on Honshu Island, Corporal Hinton.

An' will y'all question that odah?

Never, Corporal Hinton.

Nevah?

Absolutely never, Corporal Hinton.

Corporal Hinton looked at his wristwatch. The time was 2130 hours. The sweet stinking Alabama twilight stretched about them like a patient etherized upon a table. Fireflies drifted from point to point in discontinuous noncontiguous flight, like neutrinos, through the dark corridors among the trainee hutments. Mad crazed kamikaze June bugs smashed themselves with joy against the lighted windows. From Hutment B, Henry's squad room, came the fluttering sound of playing cards. Poker. Corporal Hinton checked his watch again and contemplated, with satisfaction, the glaze-eyed and trembling Henry Lightcap. He drew himself up for the final order: Pravvit Lat-cap . . . dee-ass-missed!

Beaten on the outside, defiant on the inside, Henry staggered back to kennel. He'd learned his lesson. Never give information to the enemy, directly or indirectly. He and Ken Wolfe agreed privately, as privates, that they would never invade the home islands of Japan. Not personally. When ordered to the Pacific theater they would go AWOL. Hide out in the Smoky Mountains, build a cabin high in the forest, live off bear meat and poke greens. Or maybe better, tag along with the troops as far as Seattle, then sneak off into British Columbia, Alaska, the Yukon, marry Eskimo squaws, never come back. Never come home. The penalty for desertion—if caught— might be death. But the penalty for obedience was definitely death and in that respect they were already caught. They told no one else of the secret war plan, not even their close friends Earl Kinter and Johnny Pearce. Two was enough. Three was dangerous.

The secret Lightcap–Wolfe agreement was reached late at night during latrine duty, on the same day that Truman-Stalin-Atlee at Potsdam repeated the Allied ultimatum to Japan: unconditional surrender or total destruction. This message our leaders called "an appeal for peace."

When the news of Hiroshima reached Alabama, Henry's first reaction was a thrill of joy, followed by an immediate sense of relief. But he and the others were at once reminded by the officers that the war must go on. Henry felt depressed. On August 9, Nagasaki Day, things looked up again. But again they were reminded that Japan had not yet surrendered. His spirits sank. Again. On August 10, with the Soviets invading Manchuria, Japan offered to surrender. Henry felt better. But their officers pointed out that Japan was not yet actually occupied by American forces nor the treaty of peace signed. Henry worried. (The officers were worried too—peace looming over them.) On September 2 the armistice was formalized in Tokyo Bay. Henry felt better. The Japanese had been allowed to keep their filthy emperor after all, which had been, as we later learned, the only sticking point for months. On September 3 American forces occupied Tokyo and fanned out over Honshu Island, meeting no resistance anywhere. The emperor had spoken: Shit, he snarled, and sixty million sheep squatted and strained. Henry felt he could relax. But then the officers began talking about the deadly menace of Communist Russia; evidently the war, in one form or another, was meant to continue. Henry worried again. Perhaps the war would go on forever. And after Russia, what? Who then would be the enemy? China? But China was ours. But there was still Yugoslavia to worry about. And Bulgaria. And Albania. Henry felt sad. He was becoming a worrier.

In early September, after a two-week furlough at home, things took a turn for the better. Henry and friends were shipped not to the Pacific but to Italy on a converted Italian liner called *La Mariposa*—the butterfly. In Naples, Italy, as a member of the Army of Occupation (the chief occupation being a wild black market in cigarettes, C rations, peeps, jeeps and nylon hosiery), Henry acquired a mistress, learned to ride a motorcycle, discovered pizza pie and grand opera and finally began to enjoy the endless war. Why not? Might as well. All governments need enemies.

Only one thing would bother him a little in the years to come. Whenever he remembered the early days of August 1945 and his conspiracy with Ken Wolfe to desert the Army of the United States, he felt a sense of shame. A sense of shame that faded gradually with the decades but never left his memory. Shame about what?

That thrill of joy on August 6?

That was half of it. But the other half was the same old trap: how could he even have considered letting those other guys—his friends, his buddies, his mates—invade Honshu Island without him? Without Henry? He could not have done it. Never. Not that they needed him; they'd have managed to die without Henry's help. But maybe *he* needed *them*.

That's how they get you.

A man by himself hasn't got a fucking chance.

9

INTO THE PAST

Eastward, eastward, at seventy miles per hour, engine loping, keeping my eyes peeled, my eyeballs skinned, for the highway patrol. Remembering that my operator's license expired six months ago, I lift my heavy boot off the gas pedal at the top of the grade, shift into Mexican overdrive—neutral—and let the old truck coast down the east side of the continental divide. She rocks and rattles over the patches in the asphalt, wheezing, clanking, slowing to sixty, fifty, forty, surrendering (as we all must) to friction and entropy.

Should avoid these main highways. Must remember not to forget. Stick to the secondary roads from Albuquerque on. Yes sir.

My "irritable colon" is acting up. You might call it that. I take the first exit east of Prewitt, turn again up a dirt lane across a cattle-guard into a bunch of junipers. Stop. The midget forest. My dog roams about, sniffing rabbit sign. I dig a cathole on the south side of a happy juniper and squat among the sun-dried cow pies. All forms of excretion are pleasant, said James Joyce. Not always true. I inspect my stool for signs of mortality: it's loose, structurally weak. Unsound. Much too dark.

Too much fear and panic in my viscera. The cold chilblains on my heart. How can one little wo-man, one little *wif-mann*, do this to me? Me, Henry Lightcap, six feet four inches of bone, hair, hide, gristle and nerve and it all turns to jelly when a girl barely old enough to wipe her nose walks out on me.

I cover the hole. Still squatting, I discover I've forgotten to bring any paper with me. I reach up, break off some bunchy handfuls of juniper and wipe myself clean in the ancient Navajo manner. Rough but adequate. Scratchy but—curiously refreshing.

Blue lupine, purple owl clover and golden desert marigold bloom at the side of the road. Such lush splendor. Such abundant faith. Such suchness. Next time use flowers.

The wind rushes through the wing windows as Solstice and I race through the badlands, the coal-black lava fields, toward the town of Grants, New Mexico. WELCOME TO THE URANIUM CAPITAL OF AMERICA says a billboard on the outskirts. We'll see about that. Looks more like a fanbelt capital to me. I stop at the first Serve-Ur-Self station for gasoline and a seven-course lunch: pack of beef jerky and a sixpack of beer. God is great, God is good/let us thank him for our food.

I top off my tank, making sure to drain the hose by holding it high above the pump. Approaching the sullen high school dropout in the cashier's glass box, I pull the MasterCard® from my wallet. Might as well use that discredited credit card as long as I can get away with it. Although I've now got cash in my britches I am well aware that penury and hardship loom in the future. And thirty-one hundred miles to go—a thousand leagues. "Poverty," said Samuel Johnson, "is the enemy of happiness. . . ."

The kid in the box notes the number on my plastic shim, then checks it against his list of stolen credit cards. I find no need to tell him the account is overdrawn. Valley National Bank will get the word around soon enough.

"That's a good card," I tell him. "Don't expire till August." He grunts. I show him my backup I.D., the business card that identifies me as "Henry H. Lightcap, Special Project Consultant." He is not impressed. I turn it over, show him the formal printed notation on the back: "Your criticism is greatly appreciated. But fuck you all the same." He doesn't even smile.

The boy runs my card through his imprinting machine and hands it back to me along with the sales slip. "Sign there," he says, his dirty finger on the red X.

I take up the ball-point pen on the windowsill but before signing I point to the refrigerated display case inside the cubicle. "I also want a sixpack of Michelob," I tell him, "and a package of that jerky." Like many of these new-style gas stations, the place offers food and drink for sale. Plastic food, industrial drink.

He hands me the beer and jerky. "Four eighty-five."

I push the credit slip back to him. "Charge it."

"You can't buy beer with a credit card."

"No? Then I won't sign the slip."

"You got to, you bought eleven point four gallons of gas."

"You can take the gas back."

"It's already in your truck."

"It's in the tank. Get a hose and suck it out."

He stares at me, his acne-studded face suddenly inflamed.

"I'll even lend you the hose." (My leetle robber hose, José. My good old Chicano credit card.)

"Jesus . . ." the kid mutters. "Meet more nuts on this job." He repeats procedures, adding the beer and jerky to the bill, and again shoves the credit slip under my chin. "Sign there," he says as before.

Pen in hand, I look him in the eye. "Sign there, *please.*"

"Sign there, please."

"Please, sir."

"Please sir for Christ's sake."

"That's better."

No manners anywhere anymore. Time to bring back the horsewhip. The epée. The duel. The garrote and the rack.

I give a stick of jerky to my dog and drive on into the radioactive slum of Grants, New Mexico. Kerr-McGee country. Maybe I'd better have a couple of cups of coffee before resuming my steady transfusion of beer. Still seventy miles to Albuquerque then another sixty to Santa Fe. Entering a little Mexican café, I pick up a disheveled copy of the Albuquerque *Daily Journal* on the counter beside the cash register—disregarding the cold stare from the red-beaked matron perched behind it—and take my place in a window booth. Where I can keep my truck and dog under surveillance. The knife slashes in the vinyl upholstery of my booth have been bandaged with silver-gray duct tape—a homey touch. I open the newspaper. The waitress comes shuffling forward, followed by a few of her favorite flies. She is an Indian girl brown as a bun, fat as a burrito, pretty as a sopapilla. Her name tag says "Gloria."

"Gloria," says I, "bring me coffee, por favor, and a bowl of chili stew with blue-corn tortillas like they make in El Rapido Tortilla Factory in Tucson, Arizona."

She grins bashfully. "We only got the white flour kind."

"Okay, honey, whatever." I open the newspaper. Routine front-

170

page stuff: the perpetual Mideast crisis, some movie actor running for the U.S. presidency, more murder and massacre in Afghanistan, Guatemala, Cambodia, Chile, El Salvador, etc.—same old ancient news. I turn to the inside pages, the human interest material: "Man Knifed on South Bean St." . . . "Mother Convicted of Drowning Deformed Baby; Right-to-Lifers Demand Death Penalty" . . . "Man Riddles Giant Saguaro with Shotgun Blast, Is Fatally Injured When 5-Ton Cactus Falls on Him" . . .

There is a God.

I read on. "Chief Engineer on Dam Project Killed by Lightning; Same Storm Washes Out Coffer Dam" . . .

And a Just God he is.

And here's a blurry Telephoto of a solemn little Hispanic couple standing beside what appears to be a bell jar or *cloche*; inside the bell jar is a flat round pallid wrinkled object. The caption explains: "AP Photo—Rubio Martinez and wife Maria of Las Cruces New Mexico stand beside a shrine encasing a tortilla Mrs. Martinez was frying when a pattern of skillet marks formed an image that she says looks like the face of Jesus Christ. More than 10,000 people have visited their home since October 1977 to view the miraculous tortilla. . . ."

(Support Your Border Patrol.)

Tortillas. I am lapping up my chile stew when I notice a pair of beaded and hairy turistas at a nearby table. They look like dope dealers. One has unfolded his huge pale tortilla, staring at it in mock amazement. The thing is big as a cowpoke's bandana, so thin it's nearly translucent. He gets an idea, grins at his buddy, wipes his mouth and blows his nose on the tortilla. Sniggering, he refolds the tortilla with care, just as it was, and replaces it on its saucer. In this humble little eatery the tortilla will undoubtedly be warmed up and served again to a later customer.

Back to the paper. After Reston, Buckley, Royko, Safire, I turn to my favorite girls' column, "Ask Beth":

Dear Beth:

Every guy I start dating wants to jump in bed with me. My girlfriends have the same problem. Girls want to build strong relationships but guys seem to have just one thing on their minds. How can we deal with this? —N.D.

171

Dear N.D.:

Puberty causes both boys and girls to have sex on their minds a lot, but boys seem to have a more specific and insistent interest. Also our culture teaches boys to be more aggressive than girls. Accept that boys feel this way but remember that it does not mean that sexual activity is required of them or of you. It's your right to say "No thanks!"

Some things never change. One million years ago the Pleistocene cave women were telling their nubile daughters the same story, both as bewildered then as their descendants are today.

It all reads so familiar, from front page to back. What can be older than the news? I refold the paper. And note the date. This here Albuquerque *Journal* is three weeks old. I've been conned and swindled once again.

I leave the waitress a good 25 percent tip—I can't afford it but I'm in love with her, that soft brown body, that ivory smile; I envy the man who sleeps with her tonight—and pay my bill at the cash register near the door. The red-beaked hatchet-faced henna-haired witch on the stool never looks at me as she reads the check and rings up the charge. I lay the refolded newspaper on the counter at her elbow. "That paper," I say, "is three weeks old."

Lips moving, she makes no reply until she has counted out my change. Then says, still not looking up, "Today's papers are in those vendor boxes outside."

"Then why'd you leave this old paper on your counter?"

I see the hint of a malicious smile on her thin lips. "New paper costs twenty-five cents. Some people don't like to pay the twenty-five cents. So we save this old paper for people like them."

For chiselers and cheapskates like me. Temper temper. Watch it, Henry, don't do anything violent. Calmly I say, "What's that awful smell in the air?"

Alarm on her face. "What awful smell?"

"The awful smell in the air."

She sniffs. "I don't smell anything."

"Smells like some kind of poison gas. Hydrogen sulfide, maybe. Or sulfur dioxide. Is there a uranium mill in this town, ma'am?"

"This is the Uranium Capital of America, mister. We're proud of that smell. That smell means money."

"You like the smell of money?"

She scowls. "I'm busy," she says, tapping on the glass of the counter. Fingernails like claws. The prim concave mouth clamped tight as a suture.

"Sorry," I say. "Just one more question."

"Yes?" She stares out the window.

"How much of a commission do you get on the sale of those newspapers in the vending machines?"

"We get five cents a copy."

I look at the coins in my hand. I take a nickel and slap it hard on the counter. The sudden noise makes her jump. "Radioactive nickel," I say. "Stick that in your dentures and suck on it."

She reaches for the telephone. "I'm calling the police."

My heart sinks. Three thousand miles to go. At least thirty more coffee shops. Running the gauntlet of merchant America: can I take it? "Listen, you old buzzard," I mutter, "if the local cops got their sphincters as puckered up as yours they'll never get their asses out of compound low." I leave peacefully but not before blowing a kiss toward the waitress. "Venga, Señorita Gloria, vamos a Santa Fe." She smiles shyly, shaking her head. I hope she pockets my tip before the witch spots it.

Back to the truck. Solstice the dog is glad to see me. Somebody loves me. We clear out of Grants, ugliest town in New Mexico, a town with no socially redeeming features whatsoever. It's not even obscene. The Brain Damage Capital of the Southwest. All that radon gas. I pop the top from a can of Michelob and step on the pedal. DANGEROUS CROSSWINDS, says a highway sign. Jamming good old Merle into the tape deck. "I don't worry," he sings, " 'cause it makes no difference now. . . ." Quite so. Far out over the red mesas veils of rain hang halfway to earth, evaporating in the winds and arid air, tantalizing the range cows, the dry grass, the dust that wishes to become mud.

We pass the village of Acoma: neat little stucco houses with blue (good luck) window frames, each with a garland of ripe red chili peppers hanging on a wall, each with its woodpile and ax driven into chopping block. Saddle horses beneath the cottonwoods. Junked autos upside down give the town that contemporary high-tech look.

We top a ridge and real mountains reveal themselves on the eastern horizon, towering beyond red mesas and purple buttes and blue plateaus—country so beautiful it makes a grown man weep. Weeping, I pull off at an exit called Scenic Overlook; time to liberate some beer. As others have done before me; I can smell the urine deposits from half a mile away, crystallizing on the litter and garbage that always form an integral part of official Scenic Overlooks.

Onward, on the road again. I flip Merle Haggard over and he starts singing about his own troubles, always a consolation to hear. Don't just lie there, he says, like cold granite stone; we're too close to be alone. . . .

Albuquerque, forty miles. Thirty miles. Bat-eared microwave relay towers—grotesque aliens from another world—stand on the higher ridgetops to survey our land, the scouts and sentinels of an invading army.

A giant ore truck thunders past at 85 mph, mud flaps flapping, twin stacks belching diesel smoke, streaking the clear air with a plume of sooty hydrocarbons. Scum. Swine. If only I had a pair of heat-seeking rockets mounted on each front fender of my Dodge and a red button on the gearshift knob—! I long for the day when I shall never again have to read the name *Fruehauf* on the asphalt trail before me.

Never mind.

Across the high plains of tawny, lion-colored grass, sweet and serene in the golden light. Under the splendid silent sun. Down to the valley of another Rio Puerco.

Albuquerque twenty miles.

Pinto ponies lounge along the fence, grazing on cheatgrass and green tumbleweed. A pillar of dust leans in the middle distance, whirling like a toy tornado. I pass Stuckey's Pecan Shoppe: GENUINE MEXICAN ONYX $2.98. HOTDOG 89¢. BREAKFAST $1.98. We seem to be nearing Western Civilization.

Albuquerque ten miles. We top another ridge. Below lies the valley of the Rio Grande and the vast flat dirty gray gridiron of the city. On my left, a few miles to the north, stand the wartlike craters of three volcanic but dormant cinder cones where once upon a time and long ago, in the largest crater, a pair of college boys set fire to a truckload of used auto tires, sending a broccoli-shaped tower of black smoke four hundred feet into the sky, creating an hour of panic in the streets of Albuquerque.

Good old Van Hoss and me, we done it. On Bastille Day, 1952.

And got clean away too, before the police arrived, and the fire department, and the university volcanologists. Most satisfying celebration I ever had a hand in, for sure, until the great night of my masterpiece, my housewarming party at Hacienda Lightcap in El Culito de San Pedro Mártir in Chingadero County, old New Mexico.

Now that was a party. . . .

10

March 1956:

THE HOUSEWARMING PARTY

I

Village plaza, El Culito. Founded by the sons of Coronado in the sixteenth century, the town is four hundred years old and looks it. There is one street, unpaved, lined by a row of mud huts and cottonwood trees. The houses are made of adobe bricks baked hard by the sun, eroded by the rains. Chains of red chili peppers hang by each blue doorway, geraniums bloom on deep windowsills, green and fuzzy hollyhocks stand along the brown walls.

On the west side of the broad dusty plaza stands an adobe church—San Pedro Mártir—with wooden bell towers, each tower surmounted by a gilded cross. Snuggled against the crosses are lightning rods. Two nuns in black habit walk briskly toward the doors; a hum of busy prayer resonates from within.

East of the plaza, facing the church, is a long rambling structure of mud and wood and sheet-metal roofing, a house with many doorways, many rooms. But the windows are boarded up, the doors padlocked. Attached to the house at its southern end is what appears to be a country store, also closed. Sheets of plywood, hastily tacked in place, guard the plate-glass window of the store's business side. A message on the plywood says,

FOR SALE OR LEASE
CALL MATHER REALTY
327-4459
ALBUQUERQUE, N.M.

The afternoon sun glares down from the bold bare New Mexican sky. A couple of ravens flap across the blue void. The open plaza remains empty, lifeless, forgotten. No traffic appears on the dirt roadway. Or not yet. But one mile north, beyond the flat-roof town, beyond the apricot orchards, alfalfa fields, irrigated pastures and corn patches, a rooster tail of fine dust ascends the air, catching the sunlight, coming closer moment by moment.

Despite the bright sun, the air is cold with a chill wind from the north. Mid-January. A crust of frozen snow glares like frosting on the cakelike strata of the Manzano Mountains, ten miles eastward and a mile high across the golden desert.

Action. Two empty beer cans clatter into the plaza before the stiff wind, followed by an old, once-red, sun-bleached pickup truck. The pickup swerves to avoid a panicked chicken, curves at unsafe speed around the vacant plaza and stops with a sliding flourish, a four-wheel drift, to face the rambling adobe house with its attached general store.

Switched off, the pickup motor dies. Something drops from beneath the engine, hitting the hard ground with a metallic clank. In sudden silence the two inside the cab of the truck—a young woman and a youngish man—sit and stare at the eroded mud walls of the house, the blank boarded windows, the sagging false front of the store.

"Well?" says Henry. Smug smile on his face, he looks from the corners of his eyes toward the handsome, large-eyed but frowning woman at his side. Tentatively, cautiously, he slides his right arm across her shoulders. "What do you think?"

"I wish you wouldn't drive that way."

"I know. Sorry. But what do you think about this place?"

"What *is* this?"

He lets his gaze rest with satisfaction on the deep fissured brown walls, the dilapidated storefront. "This? This is it, honey."

"Impossible."

"Our new home, Myra."

"You've got to be kidding."

He pulls two keys with tag from his jacket pocket. "Come on, I'll show it to you."

"Take me back to the train station."

"Myra. . . ."

"I'm going home."

"Honey. . . ." He tugs her close, browses with his lips on the sweet fragrance of her neck, the dense dark curls of her hair, the delicate and vulnerable ears. "Honey lamb, honey pie, honey baby, this is home. Forget New Rochelle for a minute."

"I don't mean New Rochelle. I mean New York."

"Same thing. Come on now, Myra, please."

"I heard something fall out of the motor."

"Just a bolt. Mounts are loose."

"Sounded a lot bigger than a bolt."

"Maybe the battery. Or the muffler. Clamps are rusted."

She pulls herself away from him, readjusts the fur collar of her coat. "Henry, if this truck won't run. . . ."

"Don't worry, I'll fix it." He gestures toward the street, some parked and dismembered automobiles, a few swarthy natives who have emerged from their adobe huts to stare. "This place is full of Chevrolet experts, tools, spare parts." Happily he waves at the silent bystanders, the yapping curs. Nobody waves back. "Chili peppers, friendly faces, an ancient community rich in deep Christian traditions."

"Like the stake, maybe? Maybe thumbscrews and racks?" She looks over her shoulder at the shadowed church looming before the sun, cutting off the light, and shudders. "Henry, I don't like it here. We don't know anybody here. We're too far from the city. It's cold and it's bleak and that house is a ruin."

"It's a hacienda. We're only twenty miles from town. Wait'll you see the inside. Come on." He opens his door, gets out, the dogs back off. He takes a quick look under the truck, then opens the door on Myra's side, takes her hand and gallantly helps her out. "Really, sweetheart, you'll love it. The walls are two feet thick." He tugs her gently but firmly toward the wooden veranda; she totters beside him on high heels, half hobbled by a tight sheath skirt that comes below her knees; her legs are encased in nylon stockings.

"I can walk, you don't have to pull me."

"You'll love the old store," he says. "One huge room. Will make a great studio for your work. A fine gallery. We'll have every collector in the country dropping in here before you know it. Myra Mishkin's atelier, you'll be as famous as O'Keeffe inside two years."

"I like Tenth Street better." She looks back at the dogs, now pissing on the wheels of Henry's pickup, taking territorial possession.
"Red Hook is friendlier than this."

"But first," he goes on, "you must see our living quarters." They
climb three steps to the porch. Avoiding the gaps in the veranda
floor, he leads her to the main entrance, tries both keys, undoes the
padlock, pushes at the massive pinewood door. Jammed in its off-
plumb frame, the door will not budge. Henry leans his shoulder
against it, shoves manfully, and the door yields, grating inward
with a groan, retracing a groove in the earthen floor.

Dark in there.

"Well . . . ?"

"It's all right, just a minute." Henry steps aside, rips the boarding
from the nearest window frame, revealing the depth of the great
wall, the broken panes of glass.

"It's broken."

"We'll fix it."

"Today? Sunday? How?"

"Don't worry. Tonight we'll hang a blanket over it. Tomorrow. . . . Come on, Myra, step inside." Proud but anxious, Henry
stands at the entrance.

Doubtfully she looks inside. "You first. I smell spiders."

"Not in January, honey." But he goes in first. She follows. They
halt inside the doorway. Myra looks at the room. Henry looks at
Myra, his eyes shining with pleasure. And hope.

Molecules of dust float on the shaft of sunlight slanting through
the window. The light falls on a double bed in the center of the
room. Henry's bed—he made it: an inch-thick slab of plywood resting on cinder blocks, on the plywood a mattress, on the mattress
two worn humble sleeping bags zipped together as one.

"You brought the bed down here."

"Of course."

"Oh no. . . ." She looks further. Beside the bed is an apple box
standing on end, on top of the box a candle planted in the neck of
a wax-coated wine bottle. (Chianti, '51.) Inside the box are books:
the Kama Sutra, the I Ching, *The Prophet*, *3000 Years of Hebrew
Wit and Wisdom*, collected poems of Emily Dickinson, Elinor Wy-
lie, Muriel Rukeyser and Edna St. Vincent Millay, *The Golden
Bough*, *The Interpretation of Dreams*, *The Dream of the Red*

Chamber, the *Bhagavad-Gita*, the *Journals of Delacroix*, *Psyche and Symbol*, et cetera.

"My old books," she says in wonder.

"Mine are over there." Henry points into the shadows along the wall where stacks of apple boxes, mounted on bricks, bear the philosophy student's basic library, from Heraclitus's *Fragments* to Diogenes Laërtius to *Zorba the Greek* and *L'Homme Révolté*.

"You surely didn't bring everything."

"Look at the fireplace, honey." He indicates the dome-shaped adobe fireplace in one corner of the room. "Look. You ever see anything so goddamn picturesque." The fire is laid: crumpled paper for tinder, topped with kindling, pinyon and juniper logs.

"That's supposed to keep us warm?" She looks around. "There's not even a stove in here? Not even a gas heater? Good God, Henry. . . ."

"This is New Mexico, Myra. I'll put some kind of space heater in if we need it. Maybe we can run a stovepipe up the fireplace chimney. There's a big potbellied stove in your studio."

"My studio?"

"The store, honey. You'll see in a minute. But first—" Smiling slyly, Henry pulls a bulging paper sack from his pocket, then a corkscrew.

"Where's the kitchen?"

"The kitchen? Well, you won't much like the kitchen. But we'll get it fixed up."

"Where's the bathroom?"

Henry has drawn a bottle from the paper sack; he sinks the corkscrew into the cork. "And now I think a little celebration is in order. For your return. For our first night together in El Culito."

"Where's the bathroom, Henry?"

He shrugs, twisting the screw. "Outside." He sits on the bed, pats a place for her at his side. "Come here, honey. Rest that sweet bottom on Daddy's bed."

"What do you mean, outside?"

"The wineglasses are in that box by the door. Grab us a couple." He pops the cork, sticks one nostril then the other into the opening of the bottle, sniffing vigorously. "Not bad. Not half bad. Them Gallo boys will get the knack of it yet. The glasses are in the box, Myra."

"God I wish you wouldn't do that."

"Do what?" He holds the Hearty Burgundy up to the light. "Good legs too."

"Stick your nose in the wine."

Henry runs a finger under the business end of his large bent hawk's beak. "My nose is clean. Glasses, please."

"What you mean is there *is* no bathroom in this dungeon, right? This mud tomb. That's what you mean, isn't it, Henry? You bastard. You get me all the way out here, three thousand miles, to live in a mud icebox in the middle of a Mexican slum."

"They're good people." Tired of waiting, Henry takes a swig straight from the bottle. "They have deep rich Latino traditions." He takes a second drink. "They understand life."

"Poverty, you mean. This is one of your economy moves, isn't it."

"Voluntary simplicity, Myra. Many professors of philosophy but no philosophers. I want to be a philosopher, goddamnit, a fucking goddamn bona fide *philosophe*. There's two ways to be rich: (1) sweat and scheme and grovel for money and never get it anyhow; or (2) live the simple life. Sit down."

"No."

"Lie down."

"No."

"Then shut up." Henry rises from the bed, goes to the cardboard box by the door, fishes among the plates, cups, tumblers wrapped in newspaper and finds two dusty wineglasses. He wipes them out with his hip-pocket bandana, returns to the bed (there are no chairs in the room), fills both glasses, offers one to Myra. Still standing, rigid with anger, wrapped tightly in coat, skirt, stockings and her folded arms, she shakes her head. Henry drinks, empties his glass, refills it. "Please Myra. Come here. Sit down and relax."

"Take me back to the station."

"Can't. Muffler fell off the exhaust."

"Fix it."

"I will, first thing in the morning. Honest. We'll need some wire, tin snips . . ."

"Oh God, if you'd get a job like other men—"

He grins at her, the vulpine grin beneath the raptor's nose, and strokes the bulging fly of his pants. "I've got a job for you, honeysuckle."

"Don't be gross. We could have a decent car, not that junkyard truck. We could live in a real house with a real bathroom yet. A kitchen. Windows with glass. We could go to Europe."

"Yeah, the cold puddle of Europe. As somebody said. Lawrence? I've been there twice. Once was enough." He rises again, walks wide-legged to the fireplace, takes a kitchen match from the box on the mantel and strikes it with his thumbnail. He touches the burning match to the crumpled Albuquerque *Journal* under the sticks. A cheery yellow flame stands up. He lights the candle, slips an arm around his wife's waist. "It's been a grim month, honey." He nuzzles her delicious neck. "A month of celibate agony."

"I'll bet. I know you better than that."

"Nothing but anguish and an aching throbbing palpitate longing deep in the heart of me."

"I know where your heart is." The first tears leave snail trails down her cheeks. But on her lips appears the faint glimmer of a smile. "Palpitate?"

"Feel for yourself." He embraces her with both arms now, drawing her close, one hand on the back of her neck, the other on the small of her back, creeping south. He kisses her. She resists but without energy. He kisses her again and her mouth opens slightly, her eyes close, her tongue seeks his. They try to exchange tongues. That doesn't work but they always try. He leads her to the bed, sits her down, puts her wineglass in her hand. His woman. His first and final wife.

"You could at least shut the door."

He does that, pushing and kicking it back in place, and lowers the wooden bar. A twilight darkness fills the room but the candle glows, the pinewood kindling sparks and crackles in the fireplace, the pinyon logs begin to flame. A trace of woodsmoke graces the air. The room is cold but looks warm. Sitting close beside her, forgetting his wine, he encircles her waist with one arm, permits his free hand to rest on her knee.

"You didn't really rent this place, Henry?"

He grins through the gloom. "Rent? Me? On a T.A.'s wages?" His grin grows broader, revealing a mouthful of strong wholesome omnivorous teeth. "We're the caretakers, honeypot."

"The what? You what?"

He takes the wineglass from her hand and gently firmly eases her down upon the bed. Her coat falls open, the narrow skirt rucked high. He unbuttons her blouse down to and below the Star of David nestled between her ample Russian mammaries. Slavic breasts, nut-brown Semite nipples, with cute little hairs in the corolla. Hesitates—which one to kiss first? Always such a tender touching teasing dilemma. Nosing between her breasts, back and forth like a hungry child, he insinuates a hand between her knees, between her thighs, into the warm nude flesh above the stocking tops. Meanwhile slipping the panties down to her shins.

The fire snaps and pops in its smoking den; a fragment of brick falls down the flue, crashing into the fire. A chunk of burning wood rolls onto the adobe hearth. They look at it, then at each other. Henry smiles down at his woman, his wife, an easy friendly smile, but the gleam in his eyes reflects the urgency of the fire. That yearning burning every-which-way-turning, all-consuming need.

She unbuttons his jeans. "Why don't you ever wear any underwear?"

"Forgot. . . ." Grateful as a dog, he drags his slavering tongue down from her lips to the base of her throat, through the deep channel between her breasts, down to the nicely rounded stomach, fruitful as a sheaf of wheat.

"Forgot? Forgot where you left your underwear? I'll bet. I'll bet you forgot." Fingers tangled in his tumbled hair, she clutches his head to her groin. "Keep going," she orders.

He whines in delirium, one eager hound dog you bet your life, and sinks chin-first through the musky thicket of her pubic curls, down like a diver to the little sea-salt slot below and finds her key, *kleitoris* to a woman's heartland, *Kyrie eleison!* His mind's screen whirls with visions: a girl's rose-pink lace-trimmed panties flying like a pennant from the aerial of his pickup truck; wind in the willows; D'Indy's *Symphony on a French Mountain Air;* crosshatched ripples in a rippling brook; a rose with dewy petals; his nostrils deep in the fine bouquet of a good rare rosé . . .

She utters her little modulated scream, *Kyrie!* oh Lord have mercy, like the cry of a baby redtail at morning. He lunges up and forward, pinning her knees to her armpits, and rams his bolt into the snug hot clasp of the firing chamber, all the way for Harry and

St. George. Takes a bead on the left ovary. Hesitates. Turns to the right. Hesitates again. Impaled, impatient now, she rakes his spine with sharp fingernails and squeezes once, twice, three times, with everything she's got—and trips Henry's trigger.

He comes like a smoking load of rocks tumbling under the tailgate of a forty-ton dump truck, and so forth.

Closing her eyes, fading into sleep, she says, "So there really is no bathroom in this house?"

"Out back," he says, "like I told you. A clean airy old one-holer near the well."

"How do we bathe?"

"We'll find a big washtub, heat water on the kitchen stove, clean up like us country folk always done, steeped in tradition."

"Oh God. . . ." She opens her heavy blue eyelids one last time, murmurs, "Who's that looking in the window?"

"You'll love it here."

"You think so?"

"Yes."

"I don't think so. Please, Henry, there's someone at the window."

Henry gets off the bed, pulls on his jeans, removes a blanket from the trunk by the bed and goes to the window. The two little boys look in with round brown solemn *mestizo* faces. "You wanna buy some chili pepper, meester?" says the older boy.

Henry hangs the blanket to spikes in the lintel of the window and goes back to bed. The candle flickers, the fire hums nicely in its fireplace flue, sucking the warm air out of the room, drawing it through ceiling and loft and sheet-metal roof to the winter evening of El Culito de San Pedro Mártir, Nuevo Mexico, USA.

Myra is asleep. He eases off her coat, blouse and stockings but leaves the skirt where it is, bunched in a roll around her waist. On second thought he lowers the hem to a modest point not far below the junction of her thighs.

Henry, like many sexual maniacs, has a fetish for skirts. The word itself—*skirt!*—excites him instantly. There's something about that airy garment, he feels, that delectable ambiguity of concealment and accessibility that makes it, of all feminine accessories, the most maddening device for torturing men ever invented.

He gazes with fond pleasure on his sleeping wife, notices the goose bumps on her skin and slowly, reluctantly, while the firelight flickers around them, covers her to the neck with the flannel-lined folds of the zipped-together sleeping bags. He adds more wood to the fire, takes a slug of wine from the bottle, blows out the candle and slips himself in behind Myra, hands on her haunches, cradling her warm bottom in the husbandly comfort of his lap. He closes his eyes, falls half asleep. . . .

Oh damn. Not again.

"Henry," she murmurs in her dreams.

"Don't you pay us no mind, sweetheart," he mumbles in her nearest ear, "you just keep right on a-sleepin'. We'll do all the work this time . . . me and ol' Slim Jim here. . . ."

II

There was considerable work to do. In the morning after breakfast (in bed) he patched up the windows, covering the broken panes with good-quality cardboard from their many boxes of household goods. Ad hoc improviso, he assured her; we'll get a professional glazier down here as soon as I get my first paycheck. (Teaching assistant, philosophy department, he would be paid $150 a month. Plus free tuition. And the academic prestige. And other privileges pertaining, like a shared office and textbooks at discount and departmental coffee.)

You call that a paycheck?

It's all we got, honey. If I get it.

You might get a real job.

So might you.

I have my work to do.

True. He had no answer for that. They inspected the cold vacancy of the general store. There was the cast-iron stove in the center of the room, its belly cracked, damper unhinged and grate broken, but still usable, as he proved at once by building a fire. The lengthy stovepipe, meandering upward through cobwebs and darkness, suspended from the roof by strands of baling wire, leaked smoke and soot at the joints but seemed to work; the iron belly glowed a cheerful cherry red.

Myra took heart from the warmth and began dusting the many shelves, found a broom and swept the tongue-in-groove pinewood floor. She even cleaned out the meat display cases, dusty and barren except for two lengths of greenish baloney and a half loaf of long-horn cheese covered with a blue velvet mold. No other merchandise remained except a few pouches of Bill Durham tobacco under glass near the 1898 cash register—a functioning antique—and two used horse collars pegged high on the wall.

Horses wear collars? she said.

They used to. You know, Victorian dandyism. Like women in corsets.

You'd never get me in one of those, buster.

You'd prefer it if you were pulling a plow. You're not throwing out that perfectly good horsecock? Not that cheese?

I mean a corset, wisenheimer. You mean this? This garbage is a century old.

That's food, Myra. Kosher, man. Scrape off the mold, for god-sake, we'll eat it.

She threw it out. You'll be sorry. I'd rather starve. We might need it. You might—I'll be gone. She threw the relics, wrapped daintily in the Albuquerque *Daily Tribune* (a fitting envelope) onto the dump behind the store where even the village dogs disdained to touch it. Even the flies were not much interested—and these were El Culito flies. Chicano flies.

They set up her easel, set out her jars of brushes, her palette and palette knives, her fifty-five squeezed and mangled tubes of Grumbacher oils—those vivid pigments with the fervid names: cadmium red, madder orange, cobalt blue, raw umber, burnt sienna, scarlet vermillion . . .

There's no electricity in here, I suppose.

Power's off but the wiring is here somewhere. I'll sneak an extension cord across the plaza tonight. We'll tap into St. Peter Mártir.

But those refrigerators . . . ?

They run on gas. Propane, butane. There's a tank out back. I'll have it filled one of these days.

One of these days.

One of these days. Soon as I get paid or you sell a painting.

Eager to be of service, flush with good intentions, Henry helped her stretch and size a half dozen canvases though he secretly loathed the chore. He unpacked her splotched Pollockian-spattered smock— she was of course an action painter—found her a chair to relax in between attacks on the canvas and set a coffeepot on the stove.

The coffee burbled. The good aromatic smell rode the currents of the air. He found her cup, her special coffee cup. Life took on a plausible tone once again, even for Myra. He loved to see the sparkle return to her eyes, the rose to her cheeks. He admired the authority and severity of her stance before the easel. Attention: Artist at Work: DANGER. If only she could draw a picture, he thought, keeping the furtive, traitorous idea deep inside his mind. If only she could sketch a reasonable likeness of a cow, say, if only a sort of Buffet or Dubuffet parody of a cow, or delineate in recognizable terms the structure of the quaint sun-silvered shithouse in the backyard. By the well.

But although she couldn't draw she sure could paint; she hurled and stabbed and troweled the greasy muck of many colors at the defenseless canvas in a fury of ecstasy, dancing back and forth like a fencer. He loved it. She was dedicated, she was serious, she was far more serious and dedicated about her work than Henry was about his. As she often pointed out. And what was Henry's work anyhow? He didn't know. To be a philosopher? That's not work, that's life.

Myra's nonobjective push-and-pull abstract expressionism was basic *schmierkunst* in his view, lacking form, depth, subject, object, grammar; was all verb and no reference—*I am a verb!* she sometimes cried out in her sleep, or I *am* a verb!, while Henry made his adverbial entrance through the nominative case—but at least it had a frame. A purpose. With or without any symbols from the psyche, any echoes from the collective unconscious (her analyst back in Manhattan was a Dr. C. G. Young), she knew what she was doing, and why, and how. I *am* a verb!

While Henry Lightcap, where was he? Erewhon. Where was Henry when the lights went out? Reading Schopenhauer, Nietzsche, Wittgenstein and Heidegger. Down in El Culito reading *das Denkerkraut*.

He showed her the well, which she viewed with distaste. The

pump worked but you had to prime it. Always leave this coffee can full of water, he explained, after you use the pump. Why? she asked. Leaky suction valve, he explained—you know what that's like. She gave him the hard eye: That's a joke, Henry? That's some kind of maybe a joke, Lightcap?

He blushed, grinned, tugged his forelock, shuffled about and showed her the shithouse on its little hollow mound of earth among the dead sunflowers and last fall's fuzzy hollyhocks. Henry, I can't do it. Sure you can. I can't, I won't, it's impossible. You'll get used to it, look, it's clean, I scrubbed it out myself, Myra, Christ, nothing to it, and first thing tomorrow I'm going to whitewash the whole inside. It stinks. No it doesn't, look, we got a sack of lime here, see, you take this can here and fill it with lime and just. . . . pour it down the hole. After use. I never smelled anything so rotten in my life. Myra, honey, this is New Mexico, Land of Enchantment, rich multicultural heritage. It smells. This is life, sweetheart, this is art, life, the real thing, la vie bohème, the compost heap of the people, viva la raza, viva la beatniks, viva la Appalachia, what in the name of hell do you want from me? I give you my heart, my soul, my fortune, my life, my sacred honor, what more do you goddamn want?

A bathroom.

He showed her the kitchen. Impossible, she said, checking the dry faucets of the sink—there's no water. We'll carry in the water, he explained. We? I. If there's no water why are these faucets here? They came with the sink. So hook them up, Henry. That involves plumbing, Myra: pipes, fittings, insulation, trenching, a pressure tank, some kind of motorized well pump—about a two-thousand-dollar job, a major construction project and a lifetime of headaches and plumbers' bills thereafter. You could do the work yourself, she says. We don't have the tools or the money or the know-how, he says. Your brother Will could do it. To hell with Will, he's three thousand miles away. She stared at the stained and crusty sink, the gaping black drain hole. If there's no plumbing where does the water drain to? He opened the cabinet doors and showed her the bucket under the sink.

Henry, this won't do.

Simplicity, Myra, voluntary simplicity. Simplicity means freedom.

Really? This is 1956, Henry. You're living in the twentieth century, Henry.

She opened the cupboard doors. Passable, except for a couple of dead mice, which Henry had missed, and a few surviving bands of silverfish. Myra being a city girl was not troubled by the bugs. Bugs she understood. She inspected the gas refrigerator: not only filthy but nonfunctioning. Runs on propane, Henry explained; we'll get some soon. She looked over the cookstove, a combination wood and gas burner with enameled panels, a big oven with heat gauge built into the door, a water tank and warming compartments above the cooking area. A splendid kitchen stove, thought Henry.

Does it work? Sure it works. He made another little fire to prove it. Smoke rose in greasy strands around the edge of the stove lids. He opened the damper, the fire rumbled happily, the smoke went up the pipe. This is rather nice, she admitted, admiring the nickel-plated trim, the filigree and fretwork, the sculptured iron, the four steel lion's feet that supported the stove above the surface of the earthen floor.

What kind of floor is this anyway?

He looked down and stared, silent, as if seeing the dark red integument for the first time himself. He kicked at it with the toe of his boot. A few chips of dirt broke off. It's earth, he said, probably soaked with ox blood.

No.

That's what gives it the smooth finish.

Disgusting.

That's life, that's the tradition, Myra, for christsake.

He led her through the remainder of the building, a dozen further rooms each more cold, dismal, cobwebbed, dusty and decayed than the one before. Storage space, he explained, you've got to admit we have plenty of storage space.

But nothing to store, she said; take me back to the train station. Stick it out for one month, Myra, that's all I ask. One month. You'll love it. Wait'll you see those cherry trees start to bloom in March. Think of the rent we're not paying. Think of our exotic neighbors, Hispanic folkways, a new culture, we could join the Catholic Church and learn to count beads. We'll fix things up here, invite our friends down, have a party. We'll have the greatest housewarming party since—Napoleon entered Moscow.

I remember that party, she said. Unmollified but weary of argument, she groped through dark rooms back to the cold bedroom, got into her working garments—long flannel underwear, baggy dungarees, a man's wool shirt—and returned to the one part of the place she seemed to accept, her studio.

Henry built up the fire in the potbellied stove, fried some eggs for her (we'll have our own chickens here pretty soon, he reminded her, Leghorns, Rhode Island Reds, Plymouth Rocks, a couple of killer-attack roosters for home defense), stirred in the green chilies, served lunch to her on an enamel plate and rebuilt the coffee. She sat in her chair, palette knife in hand, not answering, and stared at the big white off-white canvas on the easel, as if seeking in that immaculate purity the answer to a pretty profound question in her pretty head.

Snubbed but grateful anyway, Henry slunk out front to check on his pickup. The hubcaps had vanished—both of them. We need a dog, he thought, a Doberman, no, a Rhodesian ridgeback with a sweet tooth for little boys. He looked in the bed. His jerrycan of gasoline was gone, along with tow chain, bumper jack and spare tire. The neighborhood welcoming committee. He opened the hood of the truck. The battery had fallen over, as he feared, and was dripping acid sweat. He set the battery upright and rewired it in place with a straightened clotheshanger.

Wiping his hands on a rag, he checked the oil and water. Both were low as expected, since the piston rings were about worn out and the radiator was of the self-draining type, leaky. Just as well for these freezing nights since he couldn't afford to buy antifreeze.

Mumbling to himself, Henry looked under the truck and found the muffler still on the ground, its connection to the exhaust pipe burned through, unusable. He cut the ends out of a steel beer can with his pocketknife, making a reconnecting sleeve, and restored the assembly to its proper place with more clotheshanger wire. Pleased with his work, the pride of craftsmanship, he drove the truck around the building and into the backyard close to the pump. A winter wind was blowing.

He sat for a while in the cab, staring eastward through his dead apple orchard, past the alfalfa fields and fencerows toward the high desert above the river bottom. The desert, once beautiful, was now an overgrazed, cow-burned waste, but beyond rose the delectable Manzano Mountains edged with frozen snow, rich in firewood and mule deer and wild turkey, a national forest, public property, the commons, only ten miles away by line of sight. If he could get there.

He thought of Myra slapping paint on canvas. Expensive stuff that Grumbacher. He thought of poverty. He thought of voluntary simplicity and felt that she might come around again, hoped she'd accept him and his elected mode of living this time, stay with him on the rocky but rewarding road to self-reliance, independence and liberty.

The wind whipped a column of dust over the garden, where a tangle of dead tomato plants straggled across the sun-baked alluvium. The irrigation ditches were full of sand. The fences were down. The neighbors' horses, goats, dogs wandered freely in and out. Henry noticed a plump yearling kid among the goats and thought of fiesta, a festival. The old privy creaked and groaned, door swinging back and forth on rusted hinges, loosened screws. Three black ravens watched him from their roost on the deadest apple tree. The sun glowered through the overcast from the zenith of its winter arc, deep in the southern sky.

Everything would yet be well. Had to be. Yes, there was work to do, much of it—not least of all that overdue meeting with his thesis committee, the pending French exam, the twice-postponed oral exam, the preparation of his master's thesis. Much work. Perhaps too much work. Or could it all, somehow, be absorbed—through spongy metaphysics, an absorbent attitude, porous hope?

Down with problems. Think about—the orals. *Oral exam:* the curious term recalled his favorite student of the previous academic year, a certain Bonnie Colleen McIver. (She with the ponytail, the little round warm mouth, the smoky, racy eyes.) She'd done badly in the written examinations but performed brilliantly at her orals. For Henry. And then betrayed him utterly—breaking his heart—by disappearing into Texas with some cowboy shit kicker with an ag major in screwworm management. Sacrificing a great potential in linguistic analysis for cottonseed cake, block salt, feedlots, windmills and money. Well, essence precedes existence.

He shook off the brief depression.

Work to do! Tangible, manual, concrete and practical work, the kind that invigorates the body, satisfies the soul, soothes the irritable itching of the brain: patch those bedroom windows; cut and haul firewood; find a washtub for Myra to bathe in; repair the breaks in the veranda floor before somebody breaks a leg; check out the flue in the attic; find a ladder and nail down those loose sheets of corrugated steel flapping on the peak roof; look into the local irrigation system, talk with the ditch boss, establish water rights; buy some good laying hens (Henry loved fresh warm brown eggs speckled with chickendirt, nestled in a box of clean straw like an Easter Bunny surprise); shop around for a good all-purpose horse (how could a man live in the country without a horse?); find a pot for Myra to piss in at night; buy or better yet steal a few pecks of seed corn, a sack of pinto beans, some hardy tomato plants and melon seeds—for planting time would soon be here; and best of all get things ready for the grand opening of La Galerie Myra Mishkin, for a consecration of the house, get all their friends (and enemies) down from Albuquerque, Santa Fe, Taos, throw a party like no party ever seen west of the 100th meridian since death came for the archbishop.

Good work to do! Smiling in anticipation, thinking about it, Henry relit his pipe and gazed with pride and satisfaction at the blue sky, the golden desert, the pink and frosty mountains of great good grand New Mexico, Gateway to Arizona.

III

The committee had agreed to meet in Professor Beale's office but in point of fact no one appeared on time but the examinee, Henry H. Lightcap. He sat in the hard chair as required, facing the window and the glare of the light. Professor Beale's binoculars—the professor was an avid birder with a life list 740 species long—rested on the windowsill. Outside, beyond an expanse of campus green, was the two-story girls' dorm, Papaya Hall. A number of coeds lay about on the grass or sat against the modified fake adobe wall, sunning themselves in the late beams of the afternoon. Henry reached for the field glasses. He studied the pretty bird in the skimpy plumage perched on the entrance balustrade. She wore a brief tennis skirt. Her chin rested on her kneecaps. She was reading—yes, *The*

Stranger. L'Etranger. In French. A few pale tendrils of pubic hair, escaping the confinement of her underpants, caught his attention. Also. Henry groaned. And groaned again, with deep and heartfelt passion.

Professor Fred Beale sauntered in, a dapper fellow in gray flannel slacks and blue blazer with brass buttons, tie loosely knotted under his open, unstarched collar. Hello, Lightcap, are you okay? No answer. Sorry if we've kept you waiting. The others will be along in a moment. You all right? What do you see out there?

Henry lowered the glasses. Well sir. . . . He looked again, swinging the glasses in a short arc. Her hair was long, flowing, native blond. A golden-crowned chickadee, sir.

A what? Professor Beale snatched the binoculars from Henry's hands. No such bird. Where? Where is it?

Henry pointed. There it goes, past that tree. No sir, the other way. Around the dorm. The girl was closing her book and standing up, vaguely disturbed by something. It's gone now.

Professor Beale replaced the glasses on the windowsill and sat down behind his desk. He looked cross. There's no such thing as a golden-crowned chickadee, Lightcap. All chickadees have dark caps. Perhaps you saw a kinglet or a verdin. Describe this creature.

I didn't really get a good look, sir. Kind of pink. It flew very quickly.

Like this? Professor Beale made a rapid fluttering movement with his hand, rising and falling in the air. Or like this? He illustrated with a quick swooping traverse.

Henry looked again out the window seeking ideas, inspiration, intellectual nourishment. The examination not even begun and already he was in trouble. The girl had disappeared. And he was in love.

Like this, sir. He demonstrated a straightforward spiraling motion with extended index finger.

Odd, the professor said, staring at Henry. Very odd. He ransacked the charts in his mind for some clue to proper identification. Pink, you say? Pink?

Two men entered the office, the gaunt and spectral B. Morton Ashcraft, departmental chairman, and Gunther Schoenfeld, broad, Teutonic, fundamental. Greeting Beale and then Henry, they took their places on the more comfortable chairs. In silence for a minute or so the three men meditated upon Henry Lightcap. They were his thesis committee. He was their only master's candidate. There was no other. Ill-prepared and shocked, wits scattered, Henry waited for the first question.

Well, gentlemen, said Professor Beale, Henry's personal academic adviser and committee chairman, shall we begin?

Another pause. Professor Ashcraft, existential phenomenologist, lit his pipe. The sweet rich odor of Old Sobranie began to pollute the air. Tell me, Lightcap, he said, how is your master's thesis coming along?

What thesis was that, Henry thought. Quite well, sir, he said brightly. I've got a complete outline prepared and the introductory chapter.

When can we see it?

As soon as I get it typed up. Another week or two.

Typed up? Is it written down?

Henry hesitated. I cannot tell a lie. Yes I can. Oh sure I can. Of course, sir, he said. About forty pages with notes.[1]

Herr Doktor Associate Professor Schoenfeld pondered Lightcap through the thick lenses of his academician's safety goggles—needed protection in a career devoted to the arc welding of ideas about ideas into ironclad structures of top-heavy, double-walled, unstable proportions.[2] Mr. Lightcap, he said, tell us please eggzackly vat iss subject of thesis.

Henry rattled off the first phrase to pop into his brain: The Function of Erotic Love in the Analysis of Contingent Preconditionals in Heidegger's *Sein und Zeit*. No hesitation. A quick elusion.

Doktor Schoenfeld nodded thoughtfully. Good, good. . . . The three professors turned their eyes to the east window, to the view of Papaya Hall with its nests of twittering birds beyond the grass, the forsythia, the eucalyptus and the Aleppo pines. Schoenfeld continued: Und dot iss der, so to say, *der Zeug* for *Gebrauch?*

Not entirely, sir, but that sums up the essential theme of my thesis.

1. Cindy LeClair, 325-4484; Julie Mayberry, 326-5060; Candy Barton 322-2191; etc. . . .
2. *Die Jugendgeschichte Fichtes* (Hofmann & Campe: Hamburg, 1929).

Professor Ashcraft—gray, grave, dying of something sly but irresistible—cast a quizzical glance with semismile at the face of Assistant Professor Beale. You approved that choice of topic, Fred?

It was approved four and a half years ago, Mort. When you were chairman of Lightcap's committee.

I don't think so. But Ashcraft colored slightly under his sunken features and puffed harder on his pipe. Attacking Henry: Four and a half years, Lightcap? You know, there's a statute of limitations on these projects. Henry nodded humbly, trying to read Professor Ashcraft's wristwatch upside down. Give us a definition of existentialism, Lightcap.

Organic or functional, sir?

Summary, please.

Existence precedes essence. Henry waited for response—none—smiled at them and airily added, Or is it the other way around? In either case the essence of existentialism can be summarized, in the words of Søren Kierkegaard, as that sensation of dread, fear and trembling with which we approach the dry cleaner's door when the sign in the window says PANTS PRESSED WHILE U WAIT. Angst precedes choice—and in that dreadful choice we discover the absolute potential nullity of individual being—but choice, which defines and expresses our ontological freedom, also leads, aesthetically, to a state of metaphysical despair or even to protophysical suicide unless we are prepared, ethically, to make the leap into Christian faith, a quantum jump, so to speak, which has posed severe problems for later thinkers of the Hindu, Zen, Mormon, Jewish and Muslim variety.

Henry paused; he could feel the sweat beginning to trickle from his armpits. If any one of them asks me one simple question I'm dead. The three doctors of philosophy contemplated him with fascination. He continued: As for—

Tell me, Lightcap, Professor Ashcraft interrupted, that's all very interesting but what has any of it to do with Sartre's distinction between *le pour-soi* and *l'en-soi?*

I'm dead. Fucking Frenchmen. O Mort thou comest when I had thee least in mind. He cleared his throat. We'll improvise, he thought. We'll play it by ear. Like opening a new whorehouse, we'll run it by hand till we get some girls.

Well, he began—

And another question, Lightcap: Do you really want to be a professor of philosophy?

What? He looked up sharply from his clasped hands, which were resting on his lap in an attitude of thoughtful introspection. Sir?

You heard me, Lightcap. Do you really want to be a professor of philosophy?

I certainly want to be a philosopher, sir, and live *la vie philosophique*, goddamnit.

Answer my question.

Henry reflected. A fork in his road of life had most suddenly appeared dead ahead. To the right, the right way, a broad and shining highway led upward beyond the master of arts toward the Ph.D.— the tenured leisurely life of overpaid underworked professorhood. A respectable life. Anyone who is paid much for doing little is regarded with obligatory admiration. To the left a dingy path littered with beer cans and used toilet paper led downward in darkness to a life of shame, of part-time and seasonal work and unemployment compensation, of domestic strife, jug wine, uncertainty, shady deals, naïve realism, stud poker, furtive philanderings, skeptical nominalism, pickup trucks, a gross and unalembicated nineteenth-century eight-ball materialism. He called his shot. I will not tell a lie. Looking at his three Inquisitors looking at him, he answered them collectively:

Not really, he said.

IV

You what? Got a new job. What do you mean you got a new job? I mean I got a new job. What about the old job—the assistantship? Sank it; I quit. What do you mean you quit? I mean I got fired. Fired—what do you mean? I flunked the orals. You flunked the orals? Yep. You've got to be kidding. Nope. Henry, your whole career depends on getting that M.A. this semester. Not now it don't. What do you mean—and stop talking like a peasant. I mean I got a new career. What do you *mean* you've got a new career? I mean a new career. Like what? State Highway Department. What? New Mexico State Highway Department; we're paving the road from here to Albuquerque. We? Yep, we, me and the boys. And that's your new job? Yes'm. You're going to shovel asphalt out of a truck? No, I'm gonna inspect asphalt. You'll what? I'll be workin' for the state, not the contractor; we inspect the stuff, keep them up to standards. So you're going to inspect asphalt? my husband is going to be an inspector of asphalt? Well, someday; right now I'm only an asphalt inspector trainee. Henry, I don't believe this. Sorry, Myra. I can't believe it. I know, honey, but goddamnit you should've seen those smug bastards sitting there in that office staring at me. But you've ruined your life. I know. Don't you care? I suppose. Do you really want to be an asphalt inspector? Not really. And what about our married life—suppose I'm pregnant? What kind of a life can we give our baby? I don't know. I thought you knew everything. I know. I hate know-it-alls. I know it.

V

He also filed job applications with the U.S. Forest Service and the National Park Service. What he really wanted, perhaps, was to ride a horse through the primeval forest while composing poetry—a verse in the wilderness!—or guide timid but willing young lady tourists up mountain trails toward the giddy summit of their mutual desires. He knew or had heard that such pleasant work was available on a seasonal basis from time to time, at one place or another, and that his college diploma (B.A., thirty-third percentile) made him eligible and his not dishonorable discharge from the wartime Army of the United States gave him a five-point veteran's preference over other applicants. He mailed off the official forms, with covering letter, to three different national parks and forgot about them. Meanwhile he inspected the asphalt.

Eight hours a day five days a week Henry dug circular core samples from hot asphalt paving before the steamrollers reached it, lugged his samples into the NM Hwy Dept's mobile housetrailer laboratory and subjected them to a series of tests and analyses. The procedures were simple and routine, the mathematical formulas cut, dried and preestablished, the quality standards highly adaptable, depending on the mood of the supervisor, the amount of the payoff, the political influence of the contractor.

Every day he saw the chief inspector and the construction company foreman engaged in private discussion at the far end of the trailer lab. The thundering and continual boom of the asphalt plant twenty yards up the road drowned out their words. Black smoke billowed over the trailer, infiltrated the ventilation system. He worked in a world of pitch, tar, gravel, sand, smoke, oil, bombinating uproar, blatant corruption and the rich gentlemanly smell of bitumen. He drove his pickup home in the evening with face and hands and neck blackened as a coal miner's. He might as well have been back in West Virginia.

Henry built up the fire in the kitchen stove and carried in six buckets of water, half filling the galvanized tub. When the water became hot he climbed in and scrubbed himself, using a rough brush and a cake of gray gritty Lava soap. Splashing soapy water everywhere, stove lids sizzling.

Myra stood in the doorway in her paint-smeared artist's smock, a spatter of paint on her nose and eyebrows. (Highly arched, distinguished brows, he thought, above intelligent and mocking eyes.) She watched him, her man her husband (good God!) wiping the dried sweat and smeared soot from his face upon a clean rag and said, Happy now? Satisfied?

It's okay. You're okay. I'm okay. He got out of the tub, swabbed himself vigorously with a big towel. It's them other folks are in bad shape.

Stop talking like a fool. You threw away four years of graduate study to become an asphalt inspector.

Trainee. It's only temporary. He pulled on his jeans. No underwear.

Trainee. And now look at you. How am I supposed to explain this to my family? How can I explain it to myself?

Henry smiled, putting on a clean shirt. Remember what your father said. "Sleep over with him, liff around with him but for the luff of Gott *marry* him? Him for a husband you twist the knife in my heart."

He never said any such thing.

That's what you told me.

And don't you make fun of my poor old father either. He's dying, you know.

Everybody dies. He's almost sixty years old. He makes too much fuss about it.

Her eyes grew narrow. You cruel bastard. You cruel heartless pig. He's a better man than you'll ever be. He worked all his life. He provided for his family. He never cheated on his wife. He's a good man, a good kind honest man. . . . The tears welled up in her eyes.

Henry stopped buttoning the shirt. Sorry, Myra. I'm sorry I said that. He reached for her, tried to embrace her. She struck his arms away, turned her back to him. Honest, honey, I'm sorry. That was a stupid thing to say.

How would you feel if you had to go through heart surgery over and over?

I don't know. But he thought: Men who know how to live know how to die.

Maybe you wouldn't be so brave either.

I know. Although . . . The devil whispered in his ear. I guess I wouldn't have to clip my toenails anymore.

What a bastard you are. How can you *be* such a rotten, cheap bastard.

It's hard. He embraced her from behind, spoke softly in her ear. I'm sorry. He'll be all right. They'll fix him up, it happens all the time. People live with it. They go on.

She stood sobbing in his arms, her back against him. He bent and kissed the delicate skin of her neck, the tender flesh below the ears, and murmured in her hair. Please, honey, let's not talk about it. Think about Sunday. He unbuttoned his jeans, letting them fall to his shanks.

What about Sunday?

The party, beautiful, the party. Our grand opening. Roast goat. *Cabrito.* Champagne punch, wine, Ritz crackers, four different kinds of surplus commodity cheese. (What a friend we have in cheeses.) The housewarming, honey. All your friends are gonna be here. We have forty people pledged to show up. *The* social event of the season. We might even, who knows, sell a couple of—paintings? He lifted her big globed breasts in his hands. Hey? Whatta you say? He nudged her against the kitchen table, bending her forward over the edge. He lifted the stiff smock and tugged down on her baggy dungarees.

No, she said, not now. She rolled from beneath him and stalked out of the room, hoisting her pants high around her waist.

Her husband gaped after her with outspread pleading arms— useless. Hobbled by the copper-riveted jeans around his ankles, he made no attempt to pursue. With breaking heart, his rejected aching hard-on twitching high in the air, he whined like a sick hound, Myra . . . my Myra . . . my only Myra. . . .

The sound of one door slamming.

Pause.

He looked at his good right hand. Still couldn't see, after all these years, any hairs growing out of the palm. Nor was he any crazier than before. Masturbation is a lonely art, he reflected, but there's this to be said in its favor: you do build a good relationship with yourself.

VI

Undismayed and undeterred, Henry Lightcap made his preparations. Saturday morning he bought a young he-goat from a neighbor, one Cipriano Peralta Santiago Morales; after forty-five minutes of friendly haggling he got the price down from $20 to $6.50 with a lead rope thrown in for free. He led the frisky little fella home and tethered him to a dead tree in the orchard. The goat began at once to graze on the dry stubble, the tumbleweed, the old yellowed newspapers and the bark of the tree. It was not a fat goat but big for its age; the little horns were twice the size of Henry's thumbs.

Taking his spade, Henry dug a knee-deep pit in the soft dirt of what had once been a garden. The goat watched through the slotted pupils of its eyes, perturbed by some image from its racial unconscious, then returned to feeding. Henry lined his pit with stones and filled it with well-cured applewood, stacked log-cabin style to form a well-drawing pyre. He cut and piled more dead applewood nearby. Almost noon by the sun. Henry pulled a whetstone from its sheath and began to sharpen his knife.

The goat heard, looked and bolted, breaking off the rope at the base of the tree. Henry ran, trapped it between a corner of the house and the barbed-wire fence and caught it with a diving tackle. Should hang him up first by the hind feet, he thought, alive, then slit the throat. But that wouldn't be easy now. Sitting on the goat's back, he drew his pocketknife and flipped it open, yanked the hard head up and backward—the calm yellow-green eyes stared into his. O Death, thou comest when I had thee least in mind. Henry could feel the violent beating of the animal's heart, the surging lift and fall of lungs and rib case beneath his own 180 pounds of human weight, human power, human domination, human greed. Good God, he thought, I can't do it. I can't do it. Cursing, he sliced the keen edge of the blade across the goat's throat and did it.

There was no further struggle; the beast died quietly. Henry hung it by the pasterns to a tree near the fire pit.

Feeling sick and hollow, he let the goat complete its bleeding, catching the blood in a pail, then gutted it—dropping the steaming viscera on spread-out newspapers—and skinned the animal clean. Flayed, the young goat looked pale as a dead baby. A few flies gathered but not many; the air was chill, silent clouds floating across the face of the sun. Henry lit his fire, pausing to watch the flames rise and dance.

Myra stepped out on the back porch of the store to drop rags and papers into the trash barrel. She stopped and stared. Her husband, with blood-smeared hands, forearms, face, knelt at the side of a blazing pit. Behind him, a naked child hung upside–down from a dead tree.

Henry. Good God.

He stared back, grinned: *Cabrito*, Myra. Goat. We got to feed our guests. Got to get things ready.

She stared at him, the goat, the fire. Disgusting, she muttered, but he thought he saw a sneaking admiration in her eyes. Hell, she was a carnivore too; hadn't Henry felt her sharp teeth often enough? Disgusting, she repeated, returning to her studio.

He wrapped the unwanted organs and guts in several layers of newspaper—setting aside heart, liver, kidneys—and stashed them for the time being on the roof of the tool shed, shady side, beyond reach of the village dogs. He weighted the package down with rocks. Later he'd bury it in the pit in the garden; would make good fertilizer. He stretched the hide on the same roof, tacking it down flesh-side up toward the winter sun, and scraped off the remaining tallow. Goatskin gloves, men. Handbags, ladies.

He took down the goat and laid it in a tub filled with his secret marinade: six bottles of beer plus honey, garlic, red chili and oregano. He soaked it through the afternoon and into the night, meanwhile keeping a fire going in the pit. Near midnight, Myra sleeping, Henry wrapped the goat in marinated cheesecloth and layers of wet burlap and carried it into the dark backyard.

The fire had died to a shimmering bed of red-hot coals. He shoveled most of the coals from the pit, exposing the glowing stones. He lowered his bundle into the opening, covered it with wet alfalfa, replaced the hot coals, covered the coals with dirt and tamped the dirt firm with the back of the shovel. He put his hand on the bare dirt and felt no warmth. The heat stayed buried below, doing its work.

Meantime, during the afternoon, Henry had engaged the village band for Sunday. The band consisted of old man Apodaca, accordianist; old man Vigil, guitarist; and old man Peralta, fiddler. None were under sixty-five; the young men of El Culito, busy melting down the springs of their Chevies, played only radios.

After hiring the band, five dollars per player, he drove his truck to La Cantina Contenta, Eddie Vigil, Prop., and bought the essential ingredients for a proper art-salon soiree: ten gallons of Gallo Brothers Dago Red, a keg of beer, a magnum of La Corona Superlativa champagne (hecho en Mexico), universally acknowledged to be the world's worst but cheapest champagne. Myra had insisted on champagne punch for her gallery opening. He also bought a gallon of Gallo's fine Oakland Bay Chablis to fill out the champagne.

On the way home Henry paused at Mama Vigil's little one-stop general store for a dollar's worth of gasoline—empty the hose, por favor—and a large economy bottle of Alka-Seltzer tablets.

This party was costing him a pretty peso, a full week's pay to be precise, and Myra, when she figured it out, would throw a conniption fit. But really, what else is money good for? And would there be enough to drink? Naturally he'd invited everyone in the village to come, as well as his gringo friends to the north, and if only a tenth of the locals showed up the beer and wine might drain away fast. But Henry's friends, the wiser heads among them, would bring booze of their own.

He looked forward with confidence to the consummation of his plans and hopes.

VII

Willem van Hoss, that enormous excessive fellow, arrives in the early afternoon, driving up in clouds of dust and a cold blue wind from the north. Great belly sagging over his bull rider's buckle, red beard draped over his chest, black hat clamped on his balding head, he stomps in boots across the planking of the veranda and bursts into La Galerie, shouting—

"Chinga los cosmos!" He seizes Myra in his arms and crushes her to his broad frame, kissing her sloppily on mouth and eyes. "You sullen sexy little slut, what's a girl like you doing in this slum? Let me take you away, away forever, into the romance and the wonder of Albuquerque." She submits briefly, helpless but smiling, then slips from his grasp as van Hoss spots Henry stirring the champagne punch. "Hah, there he is, the lean skulking hillbilly himself." He strides to Henry and lifts him off his feet with a bear hug, then drops him, takes the ladle from Henry's fingers and samples the punch. He makes a face.

"I know," says Henry. "Flat, ain't it." Glancing toward Myra, he sees her going to the door to greet van Hoss's latest girlfriend, still outside in the car repainting her face with the aid of a rearview mirror. Henry opens the bottle of Alka-Seltzer tablets and empties the entire contents into the punch. A jubilant fizzing begins at once in the murky depths of the bowl. He adds a chunk of dry ice. Billows of vapor rise whirling in the air.

"Lightcap, my friend, my very best friend, you're a scoundrel." Van Hoss draws a pint of bourbon from his pocket, offers the bottle. "Drink this, Henry, and let's have a look at this *palacio* of yours."

Henry drinks, returns the bottle, wiping his mouth on back of hand. "First I want to meet your new lady there."

The girl approaches the table, staring with exaggerated awe at Myra's huge paintings hung on the walls, then at the red-hot stove in the center of the gallery, then at the paintings again. She wears a fur coat, black cocktail dress, high heels; a mane of golden hair spills across her shoulders. She stares boldly at Henry and he remembers her instantly, a painful twinge of recognition. The yellow-haired chickadee. . . .

"You like Camus?" he says.

"I love him." Her eyes glow. "How did you know that?"

"We must talk."

"How did you know?"

Henry smiles wisely. "I'm a philosopher too."

Myra butts in, bringing new arrivals to the punch bowl: art students, models, dancers, a couple of young art-history professors—*her* crowd. Politely they taste the champagne, toast her new studio, before moving on to the warm red wine displayed on the table, the keg of beer in the corner.

And now more guests come crowding in as the winter sun goes down, bringing with them the smell of fresh cold air and wind-blown dust. Dodging his primary responsibilities as host, Henry takes van Hoss on a tour of the property, out the back door and into the garden.

You said her name is Melissa? That's right. And she lives in Papaya Hall? I didn't say, Henry, but that's a good guess; who'd you bury here? *El cabrito.* They kneel to touch the raw mound. Slightly warm, a little heat seeping through, the goat should be ready. She's only a sophomore, Henry, much too young and innocent for the likes of a dog like you; and besides, you're a married man. I'm married but I ain't dead. Henry, Henry, you shock me; you disappoint me; you're in for a life of trouble, young man. I like trouble. Yes you do, Henry, and you'll get it; but in the meantime—. Yeah? Willy's big paw squeezes his shoulder—You'll have to wait your turn.

They take shelter from the wind in the doorway of the farthest room, drawing out the bottle again. Van Hoss throws the cap away. They watch the yellow grit of El Culito swirl in moaning minitornados through the dead trees. Kill it. You kill it. Okay. Henry kills it, tossing the bottle away, and leads his guest back to the studio-gallery by way of the boarded-up, dungeonlike rooms of the north wing, stumbling over loose boards, old bottles, bound stacks of antique magazines—*Woman's Home Companion, Arizona Highways, Ladies' Home Journal, The New Mexico Stockman.*

They go on through floating dust into the master bedroom, where a fire smolders in the big fireplace. The high winds outside are creating a downdraft; wisps of smoke lick over the mantel. Henry adds wood to the flames and as he does so something heavy rattles down the chimney, ricocheting from side to side, and crashes into the ashes. Another fragment of brick. They stoop and attempt to peer up inside the flue but can see only soot, the turbulent smoke. Should check out that chimney, Henry. First thing in the morning, Henry says.

From beyond the door leading to the gallery comes the sound of the El Culito string band and a labored wheezing of accordion— Vigil, Peralta and Apodaca at work.

You should buy this place, Henry, it's a ruin but you should buy it. Why?—I'm the caretaker. How many acres go with it? Fifteen, I think. What's the asking price? $12,000. And how far from town? Twenty miles. Buy it, Henry; ten years from now this place will be worth a cool million; in twenty years three million. Who cares? Albuquerque's growing, my friend, this will become a ritzy suburb; that old mission church across the plaza will make this place a big draw someday—you'll have millionaire trust-funder R. C. Bohemes from Boston, Chicago, New York genuflecting to your dog for a chance to live here. Ain't got a dog, ain't got the $12,000, and anyhow I'm a fucking anti-reductionist natural empiric pancreatic philosopher not a fucking real estate developer. What's the difference, Henry? Outlook and insight, that's the difference. Insight maybe, but not much foresight; if you don't buy it I will. You're kidding, Henry says.

They rejoin the party. The dancing has begun. Myra and her friends are waltzing around the room to the creaky but jaunty strains of "La Varsuviana":

> Put your little foot
> Put your little foot
> Put your little foot right out . . .

Straight from the sixteenth-century ballrooms of Old Castile. The existential blonde, aloof and amused, stands alone by the table, so beautiful she intimidates the boys. Van Hoss and Henry bear down upon her but van Hoss gets there first and sweeps her into the ragged quadrille. Henry and old friends Morton Bildad and Jack Roggoway go into the backyard to dig up the goat: time to eat.

Another party, offshoot of the first, is under way outside. Somebody has set fire to Henry's shithouse by dropping a cigarette into the bumhole. A circle of drunken savages, encouraged by bongo drums, prances around the pillar of flames. The blazing shack subsides into its fiery cavity. The dancers leap through the flames, howling with joy. Chaos and old night descend on El Culito.

By the glare of the fire Henry and friends excavate the scapegoat, knock off the hot earth and bear the offering, too hot to touch, on a platter into the hall. They set it on the table among the half-empty wine jugs, the near-empty but still fizzing punch bowl.

Proudly, licking his burned fingers, Henry peels off the singed burlap, then the smoking cheesecloth, to unveil the sacrifice. The hard little head with its horns and blank broasted eyeballs stares at the guests. A woman screams. Only the gourmets of tongue and brain find the head appealing but elsewhere, below the neck, the flesh is a tasty light brown, like breast of turkey, and falls easily from the bones. Bildad, a vegetarian, turns away, chanting his mantra in horror.

Lacking enough flatware, Henry serves the meat buffet-style on paper picnic plates. A few of the women hesitate at first (Good God Henry did you have to leave the head on?) but not for long. He manages to get fair portions to the members of the orchestra and to some of his shyer, soberer village neighbors before the goat is reduced to skull and bones, a rack of ribs, tibia, femur, vertebrae and feet—the mute cloven lightfoot hooves of Pan.

Success. The orchestra, fed and lubricated, resumes its music, the fire rumbles in the stove, the wind fumbles and mumbles under the eaves outside, through the loft, into and out of the attic; sheet metal rattles on the roof. One of the dancers peels down to a black leotard; another leaps onto the table and strips off her dress, revealing her artist-model's figure clothed in nothing but blue and yellow body paint. Inspired, Willem van Hoss advances to the table, bellowing like a bull, unbuttons his fly and lays his great rubicund cock, semierect, upon the boards. He challenges any female in the hall to have a crack at that. Myra picks up a carving knife, van Hoss retreats. Some of the neighbors depart, crossing themselves. Henry delivers his set speech on the joys of voluntary poverty. The dance goes on, the party rages forward, upward, outward, in all directions. Everything that rises must diverge—like a fountain, like the universe, like the branches of the tree of life itself.

VIII

He dreamed, a downward dream. He dreamed of Hell. He smelled the odor of burning brains, heard the sound of falling iron. Something like a ball peen hammer kept rapping, gently tapping, on his skull. He sensed deep trouble in his entrails, smelled death on his breath.

Henry opened leaden eyelids in the gray miasma of his bedroom. A bare-shouldered woman lay across his right arm, her nose in his armpit, snoring through open mouth. Not his wife. Not Myra. Nor was it the girl with the bell of golden hair. This was a stranger, a complete stranger, someone he could swear he'd never seen before, a sad worn-out woman with bad breath, bad teeth, skinny wrinkled neck and a little purple pouch of flesh under each eye. He felt sorry for her, his heart went out to her, but he knew at once that more than anything else in the world he wanted to get out of that bed without waking her up. Had to. But how? He thought of a fox in a steel trap, patiently at work on itself: yes, he would gnaw his arm off.

Meanwhile the rapping on and in his head continued unrelenting, increasing in tempo, accompanied by what seemed to be the clapperclaw of crows. He turned to the window. The blanket had fallen. Two desperate nuns in black, with spectacles, were scratching on the broken glass, screaming at him through the fog of his bleared vision, the cataracts on his intelligence. Screaming what? He couldn't make out the words. Something like—fway-go? fway-ho? They pointed upward straight at Heaven with extended forefingers. Way to go? Yes, ma'am, the Way. The One Way.

He nodded. Yes, sister, I understand, I understand. He crossed himself, turning his sick head away, and saw a brown stain on the ceiling directly over the bed, a stain that grew and spread and darkened even as he watched. A busy noise, like a hurlyburly of rats, rustled through the attic. The stain broke open and fragments of plaster and burning wood dropped to the floor. Orange flames, bright as sprites, flickered around the edge of the opening.

Fuego.

Henry leaped up naked, pulled the woman off the bed—the nuns fled—and draped the double sleeping bag around her nudity. Groggily awake, she stared in panic at the burning hole in the ceiling.

Henry grabbed his pants, shirt, boots. A section of the roof caved in, blocking their escape through the front door.

This way. . . . He clutched her wrist and led her through the south door into the gallery, Myra's studio, the barnlike interior of the old store. Things fell, streaming with flame. Two bodies lay on the floor under the trestle table. Henry kicked them awake. They stumbled up and followed him and the woman through smoke and fire out the back door and into the clean breathable air of the yard. Some neighbors had gathered to watch. Blue woolly smoke with happy flames gushed from the roof. The whole house from end to end, throughout the attic, appeared to be on fire.

It's all right, adobe can't burn, the woman said.

Right, said Henry, yanking on his pants, his boots. He looked wildly around for assistance, saw a bucket hanging to the spout of the pump. He ran to it but the bucket was empty. Someone had kicked over the can of priming water. He jerked the pump handle up and down. Nothing came forth but the croak of dry air. He tied his bandana across nose and mouth and ran back into the studio. The smoke was so dense he could barely see.

Myra! he shouted, Myra!

No answer. Her easel stood in a corner near the empty and over-turned beer keg, her latest and half-completed painting resting on its crossarm. Embers fell on his hair, his shirtless shoulders. He seized a painting from the wall, snatched up the easel and its canvas and blundered out the narrow doorway in back, stumbling with his awkward load.

Where's Myra? he hollered. Anybody see Myra?

His friend Roggoway, the shivering girl in the body paint, the woman wrapped in the sleeping bags stared at him in wonder. Six stunned and fear-struck eyes. She left last night, the girl said. Went back to town with the others. God but its cold. She huddled in the arms of Roggoway, seeking warmth. Bildad, like van Hoss, was nowhere to be seen.

Put her in your car, Henry said. She's naked as a snake, take her home.

Can't, Roggoway said. He pointed to his Chevy convertible crouching nose-down in the weeds, both its front wheels stolen. The ragtop smoked with fire.

Yeah . . . well. . . . Henry checked his pickup truck. It too seemed incomplete. Both rear wheels were gone. They got us, he thought. *La Raza* strikes again. He unzipped the twin sleeping bags, gave one to the painted girl. There seemed nothing more to do. He and his friends backed off a piece and sat down to enjoy the fire.

Church bells rang for early mass.

The Los Lunas Fire Department arrived sometime after sunrise— around eleven o'clock—and hosed the contents of their pumper unit over the flaming store, the smoking wreckage of the house. The local population watched with interest. The water created dazzling clouds of steam but did little to discourage the fire. When their 250-gallon tank ran dry the crew turned the truck around and raced back to the Rio Grande, five miles off at the nearest access point, to refill.

There were no fire hydrants in El Culito de San Pedro Mártir. There was no public water system. The fire continued as the peaked roof and attic of the building, supporting beams burned through, collapsed with a spectacular turmoil, like a sinking ship, into the inferno within the adobe walls. A sigh of satisfaction mingled with awe and pleasure rose en masse from the spectators.

The fire department—*el cuerpo de los bomberos*—returned and again plied the conflagration with jets of water, futile but earnest, dampening but scarcely slowing the consummation of Henry Lightcap's new home. Grinning happily, the men returned the shouts of the crowd.

An insurance adjuster, investigating a claim from the Mather Realty Company, arrived at two P.M. He found Henry and Roggoway trying to mount the two remaining wheels from the Chevy convertible onto the rear of Henry's pickup.

What's your name again, young man? Henry H. Lightcap, sir. And what were you doing here? I'm the caretaker of this property; Mrs. Mather hired me herself. I see, I see—you didn't quite do the job, did you, Lightcap? I did my best, sir. Your best is none too good. Well sir, it won't happen again. No it won't—the building is a total loss, Lightcap, as any fool can plainly see. Well you see it plainer than I do, mister. I *beg* your pardon? Them walls are solid adobe brick, mister, two feet thick—they'll last for five hundred years.

But Henry was wrong about that too. With the lintels burned out above every window and doorway, ridgepole, frames, sills, rafters and crossbeams gone, no roof for shelter, the massive walls began to crumble like cookies. Within a year, vulnerable to frost and snow, wind and rain, they would be no more than eroded remnants of their former selves, silent and dwindling monuments to the vanity of human aspiration.

Henry Lightcap revised and refined his old plans, made new plans. He conceded nothing to fate.

11

THE COMFORTERS

I

Albuquerque.

I take the Central Avenue exit, the old road, the traditional thoroughfare through what was once—long ago—the heart of the city. Trying hard to work up a twinge of nostalgia. Hard work, for the city that I loved has disappeared. Like the America of my boyhood and youth it's been blasted, obliterated, buried beneath the new America of black gummy asphalt and tinted glass and brushed sleek cool aluminum. What Edmund Wilson called, with prescient despair, "The United States of Hiroshima."

Ah well. Who cares. Why fret. Where to now. When was it ever otherwise, from Egypt, Babylon, Carthage and Rome and on till here. What next.

I pass through slums, by sheet-iron shops, the Far West Nite Club, steel fences and junkyards, Jerry Unser's Complex, Truck City, the Pow Wow Country Club, the S. D. Wrecking Yard. Well, the west side always was the poor folks' sector. Wrong side of the tracks, wrong side of the river, more like Old Mexico than the New. Even the billboards come in *español:* TOMÉ BUDWEISER: LA CERVEZA POR USTED. I'll drink to that, amigo, and I do, with the last of my Michelob. One sixpack from Grants to Duke City.

Across the river and under the arc lights. The Rio Grande rolls southward in a broad silt-colored stream, fifty yards wide and a foot deep, quivering with quicksand. Beyond the bridge I enter the old central city—the dank and dingy bars, pawnshops, porn shops, basement poolrooms, skid-row hotels, newsstands, cigar stores, even a barbershop—with a male barber! and a shoeshine boy! (eighty years old) sitting on his high throne reading—yes!—*The Sporting News*. The vista cheers my heart. The best part of the city still survives. Not all has been lost, not yet.

Now come the banks, the office buildings, the blank brutal façades of steel and Plexiglas, the necrosis at the core of the spreading metastasis. Space-age sleaze. High-tech slums. Nothing new. But the streets and sidewalks are full of people, during business hours, and that too, like the poolrooms and cigar shops, is a pleasing sight. Here where the streets remain narrow (out of necessity) and the sidewalks wide, the human beings retain some rights, and I am happy to pause at the first red light (something I don't always do), to contemplate the natives. Fungible, yes, perfectly fungible people, but human all the same: young secretaries from the suburbs— slim, blond and rosy-cheeked; middle-aged laborers from the south side of town—short wide dark and oily-haired; the entire spectrum of the white, pink, brown, high yellow and mulatto beige, navy blue and Congolese black. They're all here, the beautiful and handsome, the cretinous, ugly and horrible, the deformed, the hungry, the hairy, the bald, the mad, the cunning and the idiot. Scum of the earth. Salt of the world. Glory and disgrace of the animal kingdom. (Horns blowing . . .) The beast that came down from the trees, loped across the savanna and bashed the brains out of the first kudu it could catch. The anthropoid that later gave us Socrates' speech to the Athenian assembly, the Gregorian chants, the Upanishads and the Tao, discovered the tomato and the baking of bread, invented the vacuum cleaner and the internal combustion engine, the music of Hungary and the Sublime French Revolution—!

All pleasure consists in variety, said Dr. Johnson.

Say it again, Sam.

(Horns bellowing . . .)

I drive east toward the University. Rush-hour traffic rushes by. Fewer pedestrians now. I pass the site of the former Alvarado Hotel at the railroad station. (Myra!) A first-class hotel in the old days, jewel of Albuquerque, but now reduced, like most such places, to a sterile mat of black bitumen—another parking lot. Long ago, in the summer of '52, I'd had a martini on the rocks in the bar of that grand Fred Harvey hotel, then climbed aboard the Santa Fe line's *Super Chief* for another journey east, to Chicago and New York and thence by Cunard's *Queen Mary* for the sea voyage to Southampton, London and the dank dark medieval quad of Edinburgh University.

Up the hill past the Presbyterian Hospital, past Mama Cardita's palmistry parlor, the Scientology workshop, the karate gym. Enclosing everything is the smog, stench and clamor of the motor traffic; how grateful we of the Southwest are for Sunday, when the Indians are mostly in jail, the Mexicans can't get their cars started, and the poor white trash (my kind) shut themselves up in the Holy Burning Bush Baptist Church.

Near the edge of the University campus I reach an old bar known as Okie Joe's. Nostalgia breaks upon me like a wave. I must I shall I will have one more collegiate beer. I park, water the dog, lock up and approach the door of the bar.

Which bursts open from within, emitting a pair of coeds in fuzzy sweaters and little kilts. Short skirts are back again. Thank God for all things young and sweet and round and succulent, for all that's brief and beautiful, the glory and the power of the female race. Pausing, I watch them jaywalk the street, climb the steep grassy slope toward Hodgkins Hall, flaunting their fluff, flashing a glimpse of pink thigh and rosy cheek and lacy froufrou. Jesus! Mercy! If I were forced to choose right now, this very instant, between a platter of hot-buttered sorority girls and/or saving the entire Northern Hemisphere, including a billion or so innocent Chinamen, which would I choose? It's a tough question.

And a good question.

Enough. I leave the sunshine and slip through the portal of Okie Joe's, into the smoky gloom of the interior. Frat boys, jocks and sophomore intellectuals jostle me as I force my way to the bar. Why, this place is full of nothing but kids. Half of them girls: I note a hundred squeaky voices—it's a bat cave in here—against a howling background of teenybopper jukebox noise. War chant of the Ubangi. The Jungle Bunnies' jerkoff dance. Could that be the Rolling Stones I hear? Afraid so. This used to be a man's bar; Hank Williams was our music; Bob Wills; Eddy Arnold; Marty Robbins; Bill Monroe . . .

For relief I turn to a baby-faced blonde beside me at the bar. She seems unattended. She clutches a rum-Coke in one hand and stares into the wall mirror behind the shelves of amber bottles. She looks as lonely as I feel. And some 180 degrees prettier. As the bartender brings me my shot of bourbon and bottle of beer, I catch the girl's eye in the mirror and venture a friendly remark. "Here's to you." I down the shooter and give her my winsomest grin.

She stares me straight in the eyes with a gaze as cold as a snake's: "Look, dad," she says; "how many children you got, huh man?"

Touché. I essay another smile but no more words. I crouch over my bottle of beer and consider the next move. Shoot myself? Drink the beer? But then what? Where to? (And I think of my own little girl. Ellie—she's ten years old now. And still locked up in East Virginia with that witch of a grandmother. The Snag. The Claw. Well, we'll take care of that. Soon. Maybe.)

To the pissoir, certainly. Into the rancid yellow light, the puddled floor, the pungency of ammonia, where I do my best to keep in touch, to put my finger on the pulse of Young America by reading, once again, The Writing on the Wall:

—mene mene tekel . . .
—this aint no wigwam dont beat your tomtom here
—players with short bats please stand close to plate
—dont piss on the floor; be a man, piss on the wall
—be a hero: piss on the ceiling

Where to now for godsake? Get out of here. The racket from those speakers is destroying your inner ear. Must be 140 decibels of sheer assembly-line adolescent uproar. The Rolling Clones. The Almond Brothers. The Pimples, The Mumps, The Measles. Imitation-Afro-urban-industrial-freeway culture: music to hammer out fenders by in Yokum's Paint & Body Shop. Feeling my way through the dark and the throng, checking the buttons of my fly, I grope toward the street recalling an ancient Shawnee medicine song:

> Let us see, is this real,
> Let us see, is this real,
> This life I am living?
> You gods who dwell everywhere,
> Is it real, is it real,
> This life I am living?

Of course not. I stumble up the sidewalk into evening light, the sun of April hovering close above my favorite volcano on the western horizon. There's the fragrance of blooming oleanders on the

214

springtime air and I am reminded, with a pang, of Napoli, of Amalfi, of Tucson, Arizona, of Elaine—! (My third final wife.) Of Claire . . .

Ah no, not that. Find something to eat. Grab a newspaper, find a coffee shop, eat some soup, drink some coffee, read the daily noose and drown your sorrows in laughter and pity. There is no pain, Camus said, which cannot be surmounted by scorn. How true. I turn into a fast-food franchise, one of those large airy clean well-lighted places with only a muted murmur of Muzak in the background, scrounge about for an abandoned newspaper, find one (current) and slump with pleasure into a corner booth by the window. Yes, I like to read the newspapers but I refuse to support a noxious habit by paying for the damned things. The newspaper is the book of life. But one must maintain standards.

A face I know confronts me through the glass. A man stands on the sidewalk outside, grinning at me through the window. A short stout fellow wearing a tweed cap, tweedy coat, mustache, glasses and skinny necktie. He looks like a professor. He is a professor. I know this man. But who is he? Brain damage, brain damage—I cannot recall his bloody name. I wave him inside. Followed by two of his students, a Mexican or Indian and some variety of Oriental, he joins me in the booth. Who goes here?

Smiling at me with his yellow teeth. His weary eyes in a wreath of wrinkles. The same old permanent frown marks between the eyebrows. "Henry," he says joyfully. "Henry—don't you remember me?"

It was years ago. Decades ago. Another age, a former life: 1952? 1956? College days. . . .

"Henry—we used to integrate restaurants together." Grinning at me with expectant delight.

Yes! There were four of us sitting at a table in a sleazy off-campus bistro called the Dixie Diner. Opposite me was the large well-mannered smartly dressed black man from Alabama, a professional outside agitator named—Hobson? Right. The waitress, refusing to serve him, has just asked us to leave. We refuse. Then a giant cook comes rumbling out of the kitchen, rag in hands, a sweaty red-faced bald-headed man trembling with anger. He towers over Hobson, orders him out. Politely, Hobson requests a menu. The cook grabs a bottle of ketchup from our table, breaks it over Hobson's head.

Blood and ketchup pour down the black man's face. Politely Hobson repeats his request. The cook snags Hobson by the collar, starts to drag him from his chair. Out of here, nigger. There's a scream of rage at my side and this little guy, this fat short future professor, leaps at the cook, clawing at his neck, bearing him down to the floor.

"Roggoway. . . ." We clasp hands, soul-brother style.

"That's me. How've you been, Henry."

"Roggoway the Giant Killer."

"Henry Lightcap, caretaker."

"That cook—he nearly killed you."

Roggoway's smile grows broader, deeper, sunnier. Infected by his smile, the two kids at his side, a boy and a girl, smile in tandem. "That's right, Henry," says Roggoway, "but guess what, I kept tabs on that guy: he died eleven years ago. An aneurysm. A stroke. Each year I celebrate Martin Luther King's birthday by pissing on that lousy bigot's grave."

We gabble on; food and drink, of a sort, arrive on table. Roggoway's students, downing their coffee and cake, pick up massive textbooks and leave, reluctantly. Our conversation takes on overtones of serious intent, undertones of insidious import.

I tell him my story. The breakup, the smashup, the crackup, my molehill of petty personal disasters. He gazes intently into my face as I go on. I see a chink of authentic sympathy in his black Irish eyes, the twitch of genuine co-misery on the lip. Naturally I withhold certain details. No need to burden the poor fellow with all my troubles. He ain't a priest; nor am I supplicant for absolution.

"Well," he says, when I conclude, "where to?"

"Home. See old Will, give him a hand. Help my mother—she's close to eighty now."

He keeps looking into my head. "What else?"

I break down into song:

> Gonna build me a cabin
> on the mountain so high,
> that the blackbirds cain't find me,
> nor hear my sad cry . . .

"Henry, I want you to stay with me and Helen tonight. You'll like her. She's a good woman. And then tomorrow I'm going to introduce you to another lady I know."

"What's wrong with Helen?"

"Helen's my wife. This other one's an oral surgeon named Madge. Handsome woman."

"I don't need any oral surgeon."

"Not for your gums, you fool. For your heart."

"How old is she?"

"Not as old as you are."

My attention falters. I can visualize this woman already: an equine face, faded hair, long thin arms, brisk and understanding conversationalist, nervous tics in one cheek, that desperate loneliness in the eyes. Would be like looking in a mirror. In my heart I weep for her.

"Now now, Henry, don't cry. From what I've heard, you never had any trouble finding a woman."

"Only when I needed one."

"I have other projects for you. I'll keep you busy."

"I'm headed home, Roggoway."

"We need you here."

"Nobody needs anybody anymore. There's so many humans now we're all redundant."

"I don't need that Malthusian crap, Henry. I'm talking about real work. We can use you right here in New Mexico. We need somebody who can talk, who can mingle, who can organize, who can lead."

I look to one side, then the other, then behind me.

"Yes you," he goes on. "Listen, Henry, I know you're in pain. I went through a divorce once myself, I remember what it's like. Like an amputation without anesthesia. So what you really need is to get involved. Be active. Take part in life again, get into the struggle. Like you used to do."

"Struggle struggle struggle."

"Right. Don't sneer. Look, the DOE wants to set up a nuclear waste dump down near Carlsbad. We're going to stop that. But it won't be easy. We want to get a nuclear freeze petition on the ballot. We want a comprehensive test ban treaty. We want the CIA to stop meddling in Central America, let those people have their revolutions. We want to get an underground railroad going for political refugees—a sanctuary movement. We need a stronger affirmative action program at the University; especially for Native Americans—too many of those kids are dropping out. We want—"

"Anyone born in this country is a native American. How about some affirmative action for poor white Appalachian hillbilly trash, Professor Roggoway?"

Roggoway smiles. "You too, Henry. That's exactly what I'm trying to do here. Get you on your feet."

"What's my starting salary?"

"Now you're talking sense." Roggoway pauses, signals the waitress for his fifth cup of coffee—I see ulcers, embolisms, thrombotic clots, various kinds of internal varices in his future—and turns back to me. Maybe I can get a bottle of beer in this place. But what I need is a sensible serious structuralist drink. A double shot of bourbon in a glass, with the bottle handy.

"I'm glad you asked that question," Roggoway resumes. "It shows you're paying attention. And the answer is your salary will be nominal, naturally."

"What's natural about nominal?"

I can hear the tumblers clicking in his brain as he looks at me. The do-gooder, the bleeding heart, the concerned citizen, the militant reformer: what a pain in the neck they are: always making us feel guilty about something. We admire them, we need them, we can't stand them.

"Henry," says old Rogg, "Helen and I live in a big house. The children are grown up and gone, we've got lots of room. For the time being you can stay with us, we'd love to have you. When you meet the right woman—knowing you that'll take about a week—you'll probably want to move in with her. As to salary, you'll get basic expenses, enough for meals, first aid, gasoline—you've got a car I suppose? Money for postage, correspondence, maybe some secretarial help when we get rolling, what else would you need?"

"A drink?"

"Certainly. Although to tell the truth, Henry, I've laid off the juice myself. And I don't miss it."

As I tinker with my cup and saucer, watching the waitress bounce about—I've got this weakness for girls in uniform: cocktail waitresses, cheerleaders, majorettes, go-go dancers, meter maids, ma-

218

rine gunnery sergeants, prison matrons—I am aware of Roggoway's eyes boring into the slimy catacombs of my soul.

"Henry," he says, and his voice drops a tone or two, "you have got to change your life."

"What?"

"You heard me."

I think it over. I heard him all right. I know what he means. Transcend self-obsession. Find happiness through service to a noble cause, peace for example. Justice, e.g., a clean environment, etc. Live not for thyself alone but for others. Why not? It seems simple enough. Very hard, but clear. But—how become a saint without becoming obnoxious? I don't know about Gandhi or Mother Teresa or Francis of Assisi but I can see that Henry Lightcap, with halo, would be an insufferable prick. He's bad enough as is. "Old Rogg," I reply, "I want to see my brother."

"I'm your brother. All men are brothers."

Now he's lapsing into banalities. Time to nail him to his cross. "If all men are brothers, I've got no brother. I mean Will. My *brother*."

A pause for reconsideration on all sides. "You're so damned contentious, Lightcap."

"Look who's talkin'. I'm not the one gets into fights during nonviolent civil-rights demonstrations."

He smiles. "I know. I'm not perfect either. But I try. Henry"—I can feel the final pitch coming now—"stay around anyway, for a few days. Helen hates housework, we can always use another cook and dishwasher in the house."

"I can bake a good loaf of bread."

"There you go. Wash dishes, bake the bread, give us a dose of your opinions at the dinner table. You'll earn your keep. *Mi casa es su casa*, as we Anglos say."

"I thank you, Rogg." I can feel the tears welling up behind my eyeballs. Two sentimental fools on a dead limb, out west in Limbo, New Mexico. This world, these friends, what more could a body want?

We walk to Roggoway's house; he lives only a mile from the campus. We walk and we talk. Of housewarming parties. Of Santa Fe and Duke City and Taos and New Mexico in the fifties, before the jet-set androids took over. When there was still a rough magic in

219

the smell of pinyon smoke, the sound of *ranchero* music, a garland of peppers dangling from a yellow-pine *viga* against the mudstraw texture of an adobe wall. Now there's nothing but chic boutiques staffed with androgynous jerks selling superfluous junk to trust-fund trash. Stuff that nobody needs for people with more money than anybody needs.

"Henry," says Roggoway, "what's going to become of you?"

"I don't know. Does it matter?"

"I've got politics. Helen has her Sierra Club, her whales and mountain lions, our boys are grown up and into making money, but what about you, Henry? What the devil are you doing with your life?"

"I'm not doing anything with it. Do I have to do something with it? I just live it. It lives me."

"Too easy, Henry."

I meet his wife, the plain plump placid Helen. But there's a fierce light in the eye there: that woman's a fighter. No wonder the beef ranchers and strip miners and clear-cutters and their flunky politicians fear this dumpy little, quiet little, homely little woman.

"Now you just stick around some," Helen says in her west Texas manner. "I been hearin' about you, Henry Lightcap. Seems like all my life."

Roggoway winks at me over his wife's shoulder.

The house is full of maps, charts, magazines, books, with huge inflammatory posters mounted on the walls. *Viva la causa! Viva la huelga! Viva la revolución!* We sit around a glass-topped table in the kitchen. Helen makes cocoa. To my surprise, Roggoway the reformed drunk produces a quart of cognac. I drink my cocoa, then fill the cup with Courvoisier when the telephone draws Helen away for a minute. Roggoway stares.

"God, Henry, you need all that to get to sleep?"

"No." I empty the cup, refill it. "But it helps."

We talk. About midnight Rogg shows me to a room upstairs. It's his boy's room: star charts and UNM football schedules hang on the wall; three brass tennis trophies stand on the bookshelf. I look through the kid's books—mostly how-to-do-it manuals on auto mechanics, deer hunting, body building—and find a Bible. I take it to bed with me, thinking I can always numb myself into narcosis with a few chapters from Leviticus or Deuteronomy. But first, only for fun, I let the Good Book fall open at random, seeking a sign, and this is what I read:

Enter into the rock and hide thee in the desert . . .

Oh please no. I close the book, shut my eyes, and try again:

He will cut me off with pining sickness;
From day even unto night wilt thou make an end of me . . .

No! Once more:

God setteth the solitary in families.

That's better.

He bringeth out those which are bound with chains . . .

Yes!

But [oh-oh!] *the rebellious dwell in a dry land . . .*

O my Lord, I think, unready for such words, spare me the exile of thy wrath. For I too have been rebellious. A rebel against love.

I stay with the Roggoways one night and a morning, recover my dog and my truck and sneak northward via the back roads, frontage roads and dirt roads to Santa Fe. Yes, I am Ithaca-bound. But it's never too late for one more visit, one final visit, one more final farewell visit to old Willem van Hoss.

II

Entering the city of Santa Fe, pop. 50,000, my course is obstructed by a caravan of military trucks manned by triumphant, happy Mexicans in combat suits. Is this the long-expected reconquest of the Southwest by Mexico? No, it's only the New Mexico National Guard returning from maneuvers. Troop carriers stand parked near McDonald's ("42 Billion Sold") and Burger King ("Home of the Whopper"); in front of a Taco Bell franchise an important-looking artillery piece rests on its carriage, muzzle directed at the oncoming traffic (Taco Bell's cannon); while here, there, everywhere, columns of steel-encrusted tourists coming out of nowhere converge upon the adobe heart of America's oldest city.

Waiting for the metallic impasse to loosen up, I find among my tapes an old fifteenth-century rondeau by Delahaye:

> *Mort, j'appelle de ta rigueur,*
> *Qui m'as ma mistresse ravie,*
> *Et n'est pas encore assouvie*
> *Se tu ne me tiens en languer . . .*

> (lyrics by F. Villon)

You said it, brother.

No progress ahead, despite the swelling clamor of auto horns. I shift my truck into compound low, climb the curb on my right and drive down the sidewalk into a back alley. Somebody shouts—a yell of rage. I turn the corner and cruise through the alley, reach the next side street and turn east toward Canyon Road and Camino del Monte Sol. If they don't like the way I drive they can stay off the sidewalks.

Eventually I thread the maze, emerge onto Monte Sol—old Hoss's street. He's expecting me; I finally got past the answering machine, "Valerie" and the commercial message. No place to park, of course; the street is barely wide enough for an oxcart. The ancient double wooden gate to Hoss's private driveway is padlocked. The insolence of the rich. I am forced to leave my machine in a commercial lot half a mile off: PARKING FOR CUSTOMERS ONLY; ALL OTHERS WILL BE TOWED AWAY. Santa Fe the City Different. Different from what? Well, I suppose it's different from Pittsburgh or Detroit: the burglars *habla español* and the enchiladas come in seven shades of green.

My soul is weary of my life. I will give free course to my complaint. I will speak in the bitterness of my soul. (For I am not a patient man.) What is my strength, that I should wait? What is my end, that I should be patient? Eh?

Speak up, God. Put up or shut up. Put out or get out, nobody rides for free.

The only response I get is the bleat and bray of salsa music pouring from a caravan of low riders on recon patrol in this, the white man's part of town. Larcenous hearts bent on window-shopping and who can blame them? How would we feel if our hometown was overwhelmed by an alien race with different ways, sharper eyes, a different language, longer legs, an attitude toward us of benign contempt based on means, methods, wealth and power that lend them an incomprehensible, apparently insurmountable, bland blond blasé superiority?

I come to the residence of Willem van Hoss. What you see from the street is a massive adobe wall, seven feet high, Lombardy poplars, Fremont cottonwoods, Englemann spruce standing within. I smell juniper smoke. Still chilly here, in April, at seven thousand feet above sea level, the sun buried behind clouds; of course there'd be fires burning in his many and various fireplaces. With his antique *santos* in their niches in the wall, the candles in silver candlesticks, the oxblood floors, the Navajo rugs, the Fritz Scholders paintings, the entire dreck and kitsch of smart New Mexican interiors.

I bend down to peer through the hand-carved grille in the massive hand-carved wooden gate. A stone walkway winds between birdbaths and fountains to the white portal with its hand-carved wooden columns and the even more massive, even more hand-carved mighty front door. Some slim aesthete from *The Architectural Digest* would enjoy describing this dump; I don't. I think of the Roggoways and their stucco bungalow.

I unlatch the gate, enter and rap on the front door with the attached brass gargoyle. Silence. Again I clap the door knocker. Footsteps. The door swings partly open, a dark little Mexican girl, pretty as a picture postcard, looks up at me. "You are Señor Leaky-cup?" I nod. The pronunciation of my name sounds like something van Hoss must have taught her. "Come wiss me."

She leads me through a hallway past antique armoires, several side passages with closed doors, nineteenth-century oil paintings aged to the color of gravy. The plank ceiling four feet above my head is supported by square ax-hewn beams of oak resting on walls of adobe brick that must be three feet thick. We walk on unglazed Mexican tile, each square with a unique design.

Sickening.

The maid swings open another heavy door, revealing the grassy lawn, the tiled swimming pool, the elephantine trunks of old cottonwood trees. This is an inner courtyard, enclosed on three sides by the wings of the main house and on the fourth side by an adobe wall ten feet high. The maid gestures toward an enclosure on the roof of the south wing, above the pool, accessible by an open stairway. I see the head and naked shoulders of a man looming through a cloud of steam. Tufts of wet hair stand over his ears; he looks at first glance like a great horned owl. The owl pulls a fat cigar from his lips.

"Henry!" bellows van Hoss. "Henry my friend—take your pants off and get up here." A woman's face appears at his side, smiling at me. White teeth, large eyes, dark streaming frame of hair—beautiful. Valerie? Or one of his others? They sink, disappear.

I skirt the pool, climb the weathered planks of the stairway—the railing braced by Victorian spindles—and join the couple inside the chest-high windscreen. Van Hoss and the woman, grinning at me, sit in a redwood tub up to their necks in steaming water. On a sideboard within easy reach are the wine and liquor, drinking glasses, olives, onions, a broad array of biscuits and cheeses, an insulated silver bucket full of ice.

Van Hoss rises, stands in the tub with water streaming from his mighty shoulders, his broad red-haired chest, his ample belly, and thrusts out a hand. We shake. But he wants more—*abrazo! abrazo!* he cries. We embrace. He nearly drags me into the tub. I withdraw, strip down.

"This Henry," he says to the woman, "he always did dress like a night watchman. Like a school-bus driver. Look at that flannel shirt; I'll bet his mother made it thirty years ago. Those green twill pants— part of his ranger suit, purchased with taxpayers' money back in the late fifties. And now, the underwear. Well, of course, no underwear, no underwear at all and my God, Henry, you're thin as a rake handle, what's happened to you? Get in here quick my friend, my very best friend, before you freeze yourself to death. What'd I tell you, sweetheart, the man is built like Ichabod Crane; Christ, Lightcap, when's the last time you ate a square meal?"

The woman's name is Penelope Duval-Lloyd and she looks almost as good close up as she did from a distance. Van Hoss, I learn, abducted her from a London art gallery two years earlier; now she manages a gallery of her own in the booming resort town of Taos.

Like van Hoss I too have a fondness for those English girls with their hyphenated last names. How could I ever forget Miss Virginia Rhys-Jones? Melissa Bright-Holmes? (Papaya Hall!) Valencia Smith-Davies?

I drink my first martini on the rocks and relate the latest perhaps final episodes of my tragical history. A few snowflakes drift from the clouded sky as we soak in hot water up to our chins. And then the sun, blazing forth from an opening beneath the cloud cover far on the west, creates the paradoxical spectacle of a snow flurry superimposed on a lurid southwestern sunset.

"Only in the Southwest," explains van Hoss to his lady friend. "Nowhere else. That's why we live here. Ain't that right, my friend?" He turns his pale eyes, his blond eyelashes, his white goatee, his plump rosy intricately fissured face my way. "And now you say you're leaving us? going east? for good? I can't believe that, Henry. I cannot accept that."

"Tell me your story, Hoss."

"Real estate," he says. "And cowboy art."

"In that order?"

"They go together, my good friend." He flips his cigar butt, streaming sparks, over the outer wall and into the dark alleyway below. We hear a yelp of pain, a string of Spanish curses—some innocent passerby, more likely another lurking rapist, has just caught a burning cigar down his shirt collar. We hear the hurried patter of feet, the fading sputter of receding but explicit ill wishes: fuck your mother oh son of a whore . . . (*Chinga tu madre, hijo de puta.*) When the silence is restored, van Hoss observes, "There you have it, compañeros. What is life? A shout in the street. Galloping shoes in the twilight. *Así es la vida.*"

A pause for reflection before he tells me how he bullied and bribed his way into membership in the Cowboy Artists Association a few years before, thus guaranteeing that none of his romantic but photorealistic paintings—*Stepping Across My Zebra Dun*, e.g., or *Sundown on the Brazos*, etc.—will ever again sell for less than $35,000. Each. "Why horseshit, pardner," he says, lapsing into an affected drawl, "even that ol' Scholders don't get no more'n $15,000. And he's a artist, a genu-wine fuckin' whiskey-drinkin' redskin genius."

I ask him if he actually bought that piece of property down in El Culito, the site of my housewarming party. "Just curious. . . ."

"Did I buy it, Henry? Henry my friend, my very best friend, I did not buy it I stole it. Right after you burned down the house I went to see that Mrs. Mather with cold cash in my hand and she was glad to take $5,000 for it. $5,000 for fifteen acres only twenty miles south of Albuquerque. Only twelve south of the airport. That was, when?—about 1956? 1957? So I just sat on that little parcel for ten years, let the neighbors clean it up, plow it, irrigate it, raise alfalfa on it for free. The property tax was about ten bucks a year. Then I leased an acre of it to a Circle K store for $1,500."

"$1,500?"

"Yeah, $1,500. Per month. That helped pay the property tax, which kept inching up every year, you know. You know how those little saddle-colored fellas are in the county courthouse, my friend. Always expanding their schools. Too many kids. About five years ago I leased the rest of it to something called an investment development group out of Denver by way of Mexico City, Miami and Chicago for about $22,000. They're building something they call an 'industrial park' in there, whatever that is."

"That's $22,000 a year?"

"No Henry." He smiles and passes me a cigar. "Per month." His girlfriend grins.

"That's obscene."

"Sure is."

"And they're building it right across from the old mission church?"

"The Bishop has already blessed it. The place will employ a hundred locals. It's Mexican money."

"Mexican?"

"Well, your money actually. Yours and the other taxpayers. The money comes from the World Bank and the IMF, through the Mexican government through some building contractors in Mexico City through a Miami Laundromat through—I don't know, it gets complicated, not sure I follow the whole procedure myself. Anyway, part of it ends up in my account, no-account schemer that I am, and that's what I care mainly about. When feeling blue, I contemplate my bankbook for spiritual refreshment."

"Ends up in Zurich, you mean?"

Van Hoss smiles again, lighting my cigar for me. "Lightcap, old friend, my very best old buddy, you don't understand. I'm just a little itsy-bitsy silicon neuron in this money machine. No self-respecting Swiss financial institute would bother with my bag of marbles. I keep my pennies in a piggy bank."

"Obscene."

"Ain't that the truth."

"Roggoway is right." I gaze at the lingering, forlorn flare of the sunset. More snow is falling but we three stay warm as fish in soup. "We should load our guns and shoot you bastards. The whole filthy crew."

Van Hoss stirs in the tub, probably wrapping his girlfriend's hand around his cock, under the water. Anyway he looks pleased. He lights his own cigar and like me stares at the fading western light. "So old Roggoway is still playing revolutionary? I do see his name in the papers now and then. Good for him. Good to know some of the old crowd's keeping the pinko flame alive. Maybe I'll send him a contribution. You saw him?"

"He offered me a job, Hoss. Maybe I should take it."

"I'll give you a job, Henry, if that's what you want. We'll even get you some underwear. Stick with me, young fella, and you'll be farting through silk. And frisking with the best."

Spontaneously, naively, his words make me think of the voice on the van Hoss answering machine. At once I feel a restless itching in my genital parts. *Valerie Emerging from the Bath.* . . . Pavlov's dog. For shame. Biting my tongue, I say, "Roggoway offers me honest work, Hoss. No pay but honest work."

"Life is always better in the chief's hut, Henry."

"For the chief maybe. Doing what?"

"Oh, hang around. Keep me honest. You used to like guns. Want to be a bodyguard? I can get you a pistol permit, make it legal for you to carry a concealed weapon. Or how about night watchman here—you already got the uniform. No? Want to be a real-estate broker? I can get you the license within forty-eight hours. This is New Mexico."

The bite. The bribe. The New Mexican ethic, where anything official turns out to be crooked as a dog's hind leg. The best petty bureaucrats money can buy. Patrón politics. Bilingual nepotism. Corruption not merely as a way of life but as the end of life. But look who's thinking. Henry the Rat.

"He looks so serious," says Penelope, smiling at me over her glass of what Hoss had called "a tiny little Bordeaux." "I think he's weighing your offer."

"No he's not," says old Hoss, "he's trying to come up with a crushing rejoinder. But young Lightcap here is a country intellectual, slow of wit. Though his heart's in the right place: between his legs. We'll find a way to civilize him yet."

"I'm sure you will." Penelope rises from the tub, wrapping a huge purple bath towel about herself as she does so. But not before allowing me time to admire her long smooth back, her sleek haunches in skin as pink as an English rose. No bikini shadow on her. One tiny pimple and a few strategic moles accentuate the general effect. "I'd better see how Maria and her man are coming with dinner." Barefoot, she trips away.

Van Hoss allows me a minute or two for thought, then says, "I know what you're thinking, my friend. But consider this: Christ died on the cross to save the world. And he failed. And this: we now have a life expectancy of fifteen minutes or the time it takes an ICBM to rocket from Kamchatka to Los Alamos. Home of the Fat Boy, only twenty airline miles from here. Why not enjoy those final fifteen minutes?"

Why not, I think. The image of Penelope's buttocks, each with its own sweet dimple, lies emblazoned on my retina like the afterglow of sunset.

"Not that I expect any ICBMs to come our way," the Hoss goes on. "Except maybe by accident. The people on top have too much to lose—power, prestige, profit, all the pleasures that come with it. Starlets, for example. Ballerinas. Air Force One and a private helicopter in the Rose Garden. A ranch in the West or a villa on the Black Sea. We should get down on our knees every night and thank God our leaders are such shameless hypocrites. Ideology? What is ideology? A flag. A holy book. The color of your team's jersey. There's about as much difference between their side and our side as between the Chicago Bears and the Washington Redskins. What we really have to worry about Lightcap my friend are not the Russkies but the Southerners. I mean Latin America, Asia, Africa. Those people are breeding like fruit flies. They are starving and they are desperate. Their boat is overloaded, sinking. They are already climbing into our boat by the millions. And they don't stop breeding when they get here. Soon enough, maybe by the year 2000, life in America will be degraded to the level of life in Mexico. Assuming present trends continue. And who, my friend, my very best friend, is making any effort to change those trends?"

I stare at the lingering sunset.

Van Hoss smiles and refills our drinks. "Maybe I've got the time-table wrong. Maybe we've got forty good years left instead of only twenty. But the thing is coming, old buddy. The deluge."

"I'm not sure I believe all that."

"Then you should go back to Roggoway and his little team of twelve. Only Roggoway doesn't understand what's going on either. He's still got his head buried in politics. But our troubles are not political, they are biological. Logic alone is not enough; you've got to look at the *bio-logic*."

The telephone rings on the sideboard. Van Hoss picks it up, speaks a word, listens, smiles, puts it down. Turns his beaming billy goat's face to me. "Dinner is ready, good buddy. And I have a surprise for you." He winks. "Let us descend."

There are four of us at table under the ten-foot-high beamed ceiling. Candles flickering here and there like immobilized fireflies. Pinyon pine burning in the corner fireplace. The maid Maria in a black dress and a dark young man in vest, open shirt and democratic blue jeans wait on us, taking their orders from van Hoss in his discreet, soft-spoken *español*. He sits at the head of the majestic table, looking baronial in a rich but modest blue woollen robe, fresh white pajama shirt, silk ascot folded loosely around his fat pink neck. No doubt before this evening's over he'll be standing up and laying his dong on the table for all to see, putting the big salami on display. Or perhaps he's outgrown that sort of frivolity.

Penelope, at the foot of the table, wears a skin-tight red gown—stunning. Yes indeed.

But it's the young woman across from me who turns my bowels weak with desire. Nor am I for a moment put off by the silver cross that rests, lies cuddled, between those twin mounds of French vanilla. I know a Christian whore when I see one. I believe. I can read the meaning in her smoky sullen hazel-green eyes: a cannibal docility with unappeasable appetite. I think. She barely glances at me from time to time, never smiles, opening her lips only to accept a bit of teriyaki chicken from a fortunate fork. She says nothing.

Me neither. Van Hoss with gentle resonant voice dominates the room. Let him. Talking about—wild rice? Rabelais? White burgundy? I forget.

Almighty God, I think, why hast thou done this to me again. Nerveless, numb, I force myself to eat. I'm going to need all the strength I can muster before this night is over. I hope. God supplies guidance but I must find the strength.

Mozart in the background. Where he belongs.

Her name is Valerie. Naturally. Her last name I didn't catch. Butterfingers Lightcap, don't drop the ball this time. More wine, I tell myself, and madder Mozart—but not too much. Deft hands appear and disappear before me, refilling my glass, plates and cups and saucers come and go. I find myself staring down at the two halves of a pear afloat on a thin golden sauce. Fruit, pale and female, ivory ovaries of an idealized sweetness.

Penelope has slipped from the room. I become dimly aware, through the miasma of alcohol and my dreams, that the Hoss is smiling at Valerie from an immense distance. She nods, sullen and silent. Then van Hoss is gone. The help has returned to the kitchen. Silence. Or almost—the fire crackles in the womb-shaped fireplace.

"Henry?"

"Call me Hank."

"You're kidding. Nobody calls anybody Hank anymore."

"They don't?"

"No they don't." She rises. "Come on, I'll show you where you're sleepin' tonight."

I stumble to my feet, trying not to stare as she moves before me. "Where're you from, Valerie?"

"Alabama, I guess. Come on." She leads me through the central hallway, as Maria had done before, out the back and down the pillared gallery along the inside of the north wing. Van Hoss and his plutocrat's *palacio*. Rich swine. Bloated porcine hog of a man. The riffraff scum that always rise to the top of the social stew. Good wine, though. And nice hired help.

Valerie opens a door, steps inside. Here too a fire has been laid in one of those little adobe fireplaces, ready for the match. A king-size double bed, coverlet turned down. A half-open door reveals the adjoining bath. Leatherbound books on shelves built into the wall. Recessed lights. Cowhide basket chairs from Mexico. The usual *santo* in a niche. The inevitable two-thousand-dollar Navajo rug on the floor. The banalities of the Santa Fe (Holy Faith!) rich. How I despise them—I believe. "I been poor, I been rich," said Billie Holiday (I think); "rich is better."

Valerie kneels at the fireplace, lighting a stick of Georgia pitchpine from L. L. Bean in Maine, her lovely face concealed by the fall of glossy, honey-colored hair. I smell the fragrance of *Eau de Joi.* The maroon silk dress clings to her slender waist, the swell of her hips. Speechless, I can only stand and stare.

The fire blazes up, she rises, tugging down the tight dress, and stares me back, straight in the eye. "Well . . . ?"

"Thank you," I say. And pause. "Good night."

She smiles at last—with relief, with gratitude. "You're all right, Henry," she says. "Not near as mean as you look." She gives me a quick kiss on the nose and slips away, out the door and into the dark.

Not near as mean, I think, but one hell of a lot dumber. I stare at the fire for a while, then slowly painfully undress and stumble into the bathroom. The floor tiles feel warm to my feet. Radiant heating? Of course. I bang my shanks on the toilet, an old-fashioned W.C. with watertank mounted shoulder-high on the wall. A brass chain dangles from the tank, the figurine of a well-known eighteenth-century bewigged composer attached to the end. Pull Handel to flush. Small consolation for the ache in my groin. After a while I crawl into bed, gazing up at the mirror bolted to the ceiling. Taped to a corner of the mirror is a photo, the life-size face of Willem van Hoss, framed and matted, big smile, two fingers raised in papal blessing.

Morning comes. I stagger like a man recovering from delirium into the kitchen where van Hoss waits for me, patient and smiling. He pours me coffee. Has just returned, he says, from ten laps around the pool and a brisk walk to the Plaza and back.

"How'd you like Valerie?"

"A sweet girl. She left early."

"She's like that, sweet but flighty. Like the night-blooming cereus. Tender as a Venus flytrap and absolutely unreliable. What they used to call, in years of long ago, a crazy mixed-up kid. Don't brood about it, Henry my friend. She'll be back again tonight. Be patient with her."

"She's in love with you, Hoss."

"This is her home. The only one she has. She wants me to be her father. I'm too old for the job. I'm content to be her painter. She makes a good model, if you can get her to lie still for an hour now and then. Lightcap, my friend, my very best friend, she needs a man like you, somebody strong and steady, *sic,* to take her in hand, help her grow up. Stick around, Henry."

"Sure," I say, "thank you, but it's the old Bildad I have to visit one more time. Remember Morton Bildad? Morton the Mystic?"

"Sure I do. But he's changed, Henry. India almost killed him. Amoebic dysentery. He's a ninety-eight-pound guru now, with a beard down to his navel. He floats six inches off the ground, like a hovercraft. Keeps staring at something forty-seven light-years beyond the Horsehead Nebula."

That, I think, is what I want to ask him about.

"He's a dangerous man, Henry my friend. Worse than Roggoway by far. He'll hypnotize you. He'll tinkle windbells in your ear. He'll make your umbilicus spin. He'll extrude his lower intestine and hang it around your neck like a garland of Polish sausages. Best stay away from him, Henry."

We were close friends once, I remind van Hoss. I only want to see him for an hour, touch his hand, say goodbye. Then back to Stump Creek, West Virginia. Then finally and at last I shall turn my nose to the East, bearing straight through the throbbing heart of America, home to the hills of Appalachia. Henry Lightcap, welcome back!

"Henry my friend, my very best friend, you make me want to cry."

"Don't cry, old Hoss."

"*Abrazo?*"

"*Por qué no, compañero?*"

III

Time for country musick. One hand on the wheel, one eye on the highway, I fumble through a shoebox full of tapes searching for Beethoven's *Pastoral,* for Vaughan Williams's *Pastoral.* Can't find neither. I slam Earl Scruggs & Lester Flatt into the slot: fiddle, banjo, steel guitars, that's what I want now. Life! vitality! hope!

I stroke old Sollie's hard head, slip her another Nizoral in a lump of longhorn cheese. Poor dog, she's been leading a truckbound life lately. Once we get into the open again I'll take her for a long walk through the sagebrush, under the cold sky and the frozen peaks of the Blood of Christ Mountains. She sits up at my side, staring ahead at the mesas and plateaus; a glint of interest in those solemn eyes. This high country is good for her; maybe she'll whip that valley fever yet. That Tucson fungus.

Through Española and north, toward the valley then the gorge of the Rio Grande, El Río Bravo del Norte. Paul Horgan's great river. Kit Carson country. Land of the chili pepper, the mountain man, the cutthroat trout and the land shark.

Time for my eight-course lunch: cheese, crackers, sixpack of beer. Not what the doctor ordered, precisely, but the customs of a lifetime may not lightly be discarded. "Dispose of Thoughtfully," say the printed instructions on the sixpack. Thoughtfully I drop the first empty out the window two miles beyond Española. The can bounces along on the pavement before coasting onto the shoulder of the road. Some kid with a sack will pick it up. Recycle that aluminum. Give a hoot.

On my right, twenty miles away, stand the Truchas Peaks crowned with snow. Strange medieval little villages up in there—Peñasco, Las Trampas, Vadito, Truchas, Ojo Sarco, Llano. Grim spooky beautiful places full of people named Gallegos, Vigil, Velarde, Gonzales. They've been hiding in those remote valleys breeding and inbreeding since 1598. On my left is the river, lined with cottonwood trees barely beginning to show a trace of spring green. Men on red tractors course up and down alfalfa fields, dragging disk harrows through the brown earth. Magpies fly above the pale stubble. The smoke of burning tumbleweed rises from the irrigation ditches. April. Planting time.

It was right here, along this stretch of highway, that things first went wrong between me and Myra. Myra Mishkin, artist. In the summer of—'54? '55? We were hauling a load of her giant oil paintings—vague void muddled masterworks—from her summer studio in Taos to a gallery in Santa Fe. Stretched but unframed, they were stacked in the open bed of my second pickup truck, the 1949 Chevy with the rear end that did not exactly track in line with the front end. On wet pavement the tires left a four-tread trail. But that was not the problem. The problem was that I had forgotten to rope down the canvases. One by one as we raced along the wind picked them up and out they sailed, like wings, like hang gliders, before dropping to the highway behind us. By the time we realized what was happening, stopped, reversed and recovered the paintings, most had been run over by the traffic. Didn't really hurt them much, seemed to me, they were all flat anyway, and the skid marks, I thought, actually improved the composition. But Myra never forgave me. Never forgot and never forgave.

Into the gorge. The rocky slopes rise on either side, pink as watermelon. Fishermen stand along the green rush of the river, casting for trout. A few ravens flap about overhead, going somewhere, getting nowhere, and one golden eagle—if I stopped to really look— would still be there, on its lime-spattered perch a thousand feet above, guarding the pass. As it was that day decades ago when love was young, doomed but indomitable.

I am weeping over my fourth beer when the truck tops out on the cold somber high plateau of Taos, New Mexico. Ahead stands the sacred mountain. On my left is the dark lava-rock cleft of the river's canyon. Everywhere is sagebrush, a spacious silence, and the sweet exotic smell—like myrrh—of mysticism.

Finding my old pal Morton Bildad proves to be a problem. I have no address for him, we haven't corresponded in years, and it turns out that he has no address for himself. His name does not appear in the Taos phonebook. Living on trust funds, incense and mountain air, he requires no gainful work and therefore has no place of employment, does not "hold" what the vulgar denote a "job." Never did. Nor is he expecting my arrival: this is another surprise visit. Maybe I should let him alone anyhow, he's probably got problems sufficient of his own, being a Hindu ascetic and saint and all, a guru with dysentery. But I want to see him. Once upon a time, at the University, years ago, we were nearly brothers, or closer than brothers. I owe him at least a farewell before our final parting. He to evanesce and reincarnate, I to decompose and rot, and which is the better God alone knows.

I park near the plaza, settle into a phone booth and dial a few vaguely familiar names, seeking a lead. Old Bildad, says one, sure he's around here somewhere but I can't tell you where he lives, Henry, are you on the Path? On the what? On the Path? I'm on the road. What's your sign? My what? Your sign? I was born under a chewing-tobacco sign. Mail Pouch. That's a bad sign, Henry; what color is your aura? How do you mean? What color—red, orange, yellow, what? I think it's black. Black? Black. I thought so, I can feel the vibes through the telephone, you need help, Henry. Then help me: where can I find Bildad? Read *Be Here Now*. What's that? That's a book by Baba Ram Dass. An address book? Be patient, Henry, he will find you. But he doesn't even know I'm in town. He will find you. He's not even looking for me. He does not have to look—he *sees*. I see. No, *he* sees. Who does? Baba. Baba— Baba who? Baba Ram Dass.

Time to hang up the phone. Can't waste the whole afternoon babbling about some reamed-out Baba with another hash-smoking coke-sniffing coupon-clipping half-assed half-baked candy-assed sauterne-sipping floppy-necked quiche-eating trust funder. I am not a patient man. Life is short, particularly mine. But do try to be nice, Henry. Be generous, be kind, be large. Be yourself.

On the fifth attempt I find some assistance. Pete Dubray, an old-time alcoholic piano tuner, poker player and drinking buddy, assures me that he knows how to find Bildad. Will even draw me a map.

We meet at Eddie Apodaca's Cantina Contenta, amid the blare of off-key trumpets from the jukebox playing an old favorite of mine from the Revolution, "Adiós Muchachos, Compañeros de mi Vida." Which revolution? *The* revolution. The incompleted revolution. Dubray looks terrible but so do I: we recognize each other at once, though we haven't met for twenty years. He has become fat, florid, bald, his nose like a pomegranate, red with the broken veins of rhinophymosis. We absorb the shock of mutual and reflected disaster, then order the handiest therapy available—Wild Turkey with beer on the side. The ravages of alcohol are enough to drive any man to drink. I pay for the first round, take a sip of the whiskey. Weak. This Turkey has tap water in its arteries; some things never change, not at Eddie's.

Dubray begins with the usual lamentations. Taos ain't what it was in the fifties. Once a town of bohemians, artists, real Indians, Chicano cowboys, it has now been overrun with successive waves of uninvited immigrants: hippies, flower children, rock musicians, movie stars, Orientalist mystagogues, minimalist poets, rich idle Eurotrash with notarized patents of nobility, ski-resort developers, hard-driving entrepreneurs from Texas—and all of the above, each and every single one, with only one real passion in their hearts: real estate.

But I know this. This is the old story of the American West, how the West was won. Then lost. Paying for the second round (and the third) I steer Dubray gently toward the focus of my concern. Well, you mean Morton? he says, Morton Bildad, I tell you, Henry, nobody sees him anymore, he never comes into town and that seems like a good idea all right but how to find him? you really want to see him? what for? Old friend, eh?, okay, all I can tell you is he lives in a wigwam or something out west of the gorge, out there on that sagebrush flat near old Carson, him and his disciples, I guess they're the ones keep him alive, and from what I hear, Henry, he's got to be pretty weird and some of those diaper-head types that hang around with him can even be dangerous or so I've heard, Henry. Dangerous? says I; in what way? Why well they're supposed to practice strange rites, there's talk of missing tourists, disappeared babies, cows with mutilated udders and tails tied in square knots, people see funny blue lights out there at night, although I'll tell you, Henry, I think it's a lot of bullshit myself. . . .

Conned again, but at least I've gained a clue to Bildad's approximate location. I gas up my truck, drive south of town to the turnoff for Carson, take the dirt road along the Rio Pueblo to its junction with the Rio Grande and stop in the middle of the antiquated wooden suspension bridge to contemplate the great river for a while.

Twilight fills the canyon. Stars blink at me from beyond the purple-black rimrock. The cold mountain river flows beneath the bridge, as rivers tend to do, purling with hiss and gurgle about the basalt boulders that make up the shoreline. This was once a favorite fishing spot for friends and me, twenty-five years ago, before the town fathers of an ever-growing Taos allowed untreated sewage to flow into the river. The trout survived but never tasted quite the same as before; a certain flavor of babyshit and chlorine tainted the flesh of native brown, cutthroat and rainbow alike.

The fishermen, if any remaining, have left. No pickup trucks or cars in view, nothing on the footpath but the usual litter of pop bottles, beer cans, filter tips, toilet paper. However, one hundred yards upriver, on the right bank, is the dim form of something in white crouched on a shelf of rock at the water's edge. World's biggest snowy owl? An albino mountain lion? A woman in her nightie? Hard to tell in this deepening gloom. If that apparition holds a fly rod I cannot see it. And if man or woman, how did it get here? Taos lies ten miles away and Carson is a ghost town.

For a long time I sit on the hood of my truck, in the middle of the bridge, and listen to the river, the spotted toads, the bats, and keep an eye on the figure in white. It grows dimmer, dimmer, fading out, but never makes a move.

Masses of cold air come flowing down the canyon. Shivering, I get into my machine and cross the bridge, drive up the switchback road on the west slope of the canyon and reach the open country a thousand feet above. Too dark now to search for Bildad and his retreat, refuge, ashram, monastery, whatever it may be. I find a side road and make camp for the night within a circle of scrubby pinyon pines. I feed, water and pill the dog and take her for a looping walk through the sagebrush. We jump a few jackrabbits, startle a flock of doves, rouse one sleeping nighthawk from its nest on the ground. The coyotes, bound to be present, let us pass in silence.

Back to camp. I do not build a fire. Why spoil a clear starry night with the glare of burning wood? Why attract unwanted attention? Why send thermal signals into space where who knows what vast nitrogen-cooled brains—intergalactic WASPs, perhaps—may even now be scanning our planet for signs of edible life? I sleep in the truck with my .357 Magnum close at hand; Solstice sleeps on her pad beneath the open rear.

Awake to another lurid iridescent sunrise. A huge cloud like a hawk's wing, underlit by flame, hangs above the eastern mountains from Colorado down to Little Texas. Storm front moving in from the central plains. Winter's not finished yet.

Another long walk for the dog and me—she needs the workout—and then I return to base, build a fire of twigs and sticks, brew coffee, fry potatoes and eggs, season liberally with hot salsa and a splash of beer, and break the night's fast. Despite my perpetual bellyache, my chronic melancholia, I retain an appetite for the fuels of life. You are what you eat? Only a gross billiard-ball materialist, even grosser than I, could subscribe to so reductive an absurdity. You are what you do, what you think, feel, love, hate, express and

237

communicate to others, that is what you *are*. But it's also true that in order to be you you have to eat. There's a speck of truth in even the meanest of truisms.

I climb the nearest hill and survey the countryside with binoculars. One truck two miles off loaded with steers proceeds westward over the mesa, followed by a golden roostertail of dust. Three ravens circle above my head. One pale sun glimmers through the cloud cover. But I see no cluster of tepees, no ring of wickiups, no huddle of hogans anywhere. Where are you, Morton Bildad, O seer of visions, sagebrush sage, interpreter of dreams, extruder of entrails, dealer in magic and spells?

The stone ruins of the village of Carson dance across my lenses. I see movement there, human figures emerging from a Volkswagen microbus. They walk about, inspecting the empty buildings, regroup at their vehicle and confer. Like me, apparently, they are searching for something. Somebody. After a time they drive off toward the low hills in the west, following the dust cloud of the cattle truck. I return to my gray Dodge, trailed by my black dog, and drive on to the ruins myself. I too stop, get out, look around and find an intersection, the main road going west, the others—dim tracks, rarely used—winding off to the north and south.

Bildad, where are you? I study the scene, groping for a clue. The stone huts nearby, roofless and crumbling, contain only the usual assortment of garbage, with piles of cow dung on the lee side. Nobody has lived here since Depression days, when a few hardy souls attempted to plow and dry-farm the surrounding desert. The remains of a windmill stand behind the buildings. The water tank is full of sand and tumbleweed. One lizard watches me from its sunny nook among the lava rocks. A skirl of wind carries a sun-bleached newspaper—the Santa Fe *New Mexican*—across what was once upon a time a sort of main street. A place for a showdown. A gunfighter's street. A stage where two middle-aging gurus might face each other and settle, once and for all, the fate of the world. No place for a nice Jewish boy from New York like Morton Bildad. Or for a cranky hillbilly from Stump Creek.

Far to the south a bird with ragged black wings hovers on the blue. I don't need binoculars to recognize the red-necked turkey buzzard. A little early for the season, but—there he is. I take the jeep trail going that way.

I drive three miles over the stones, among the sagebrush and dwarf pinyon pines, grinding along in low gear. The road ends at a turn-around on the rim of a deep ravine. There are pools of water in the bottom and a few leafless, stunted cottonwood trees. A footpath leads across the slope of the ravine, traversing the chamiza, rocks and prickly pear toward a series of ledges at the upper end. On the topmost ledge two city blocks away, above flood line, half concealed by a pair of juniper trees, easy to miss at first glance, is an olive drab canvas wall tent. In front of the open flaps of the tent sits a man in lotus posture, facing the morning sun, motionless. Sunlight glints from the spectacles on his nose. He seems to be grinning at me, a large friendly gap-toothed smile of welcome. I lift one hand in a tentative wave, still not certain I'm looking at Bildad. There is no response but the grin remains fixed in place. Nobody else in view. There are some queer characters in these parts but I've got my .357 with me, stuck in my belt under my coat. I believe in my fellow man. I also believe in firepower.

The footing is rough on the narrow trail but I keep my eyes on the man waiting for me. He is bareheaded, bald as an egg, wearing what appears to be a white robe, not very clean. No sign of action in his vicinity, not even a fire despite the cold chill of the morning. I pause, sniff the air, smell nothing. But hear the thin chimes of the windbell that dangles from one of the trees beside the tent. I go on. Bildad—if it is Bildad—makes no move. Grinning at the sun, he seems immobile as a statue.

I stop again, a hundred feet away. "Morton . . . is that you?" No answer. Not a twitch of recognition. He must be in a trance. Perhaps I should let him be, leave him alone. The dog at my heel stares straight at the man, growls deep in her throat. An uneasy, interrogative growl. "Quiet, Sollie." I stroke her head. We advance. Bildad always was a little strange—but not this strange.

I stop in front of him only four feet away, blocking his sunshine. If this were Diogenes he'd complain about that. But Bildad says nothing, makes not the slightest move, continues to stare through and past me with the frigid grin of a man in a state of frozen ecstasy.

"Bildad?" I say. No reply. The windbells chime. I squat before him as you would in order to talk to a child and snap my fingers in his face. "Morton?"

He grins over my shoulder at something beyond. Far beyond. I reach forward and delicately remove his thick-lensed glasses. The blank eyes, the jaundice yellow eyeballs, stare into space. The face remains stiff as parchment. I half expect to hear a husky rattle in his throat, an effort at speech, the croak of a remote and hollow voice.

"Bildad, look at me; this is Henry. Henry Lightcap for godsake. You remember me?"

He says nothing. He seems shrunken, empty, the dehydrated shell of a human being. Odorless—a husk. The face is gaunt, a mass of wrinkles. The grin displays a few crooked yellow teeth coated with plaque. The arms and legs are thin as sticks. If I touched him he would fall over. Or crumble to dust.

I pass my hand before his eyes. He does not blink. I touch the gray beard, dirty and matted, that hangs from his chin to the middle of his chest. If he has a chest. The loose robe draped from his narrow shoulders suggests a yawning concavity beneath. I tug at the beard, a gentle pull, and his head and body rock forward slightly. I release the beard; he settles back into his former position with a faint crackling noise. His face and eyes betray no hint that he is conscious of my presence.

"Come on, Bildad, wake up. This is Henry. I've come five hundred miles to see you. There's a question I want to ask you. A very simple question, Mort, the oldest question of them all. Okay?"

No answer. I stare at his grinning mouth, his long Semitic sunburned nose, the close-set eyes. I notice the hairs in his nostrils, the fringe of white hair above his ears, the peeling skin on his sun-baked and hairless dome. And something more peculiar: a neat tidy round hole, about the caliber of a .32, set in the very center, on the exact summit of that mesocephalic skull. Odder still, there is no trace of blood around the opening, no sign of violence from within or without. Nor any weapons at hand. It's as if he had popped a cork from his cranium and launched his brains, together with the cork, directly into the sky. Into space. Quite some time ago. I look up. Nothing above but the blue vaulting firmament of New Mexico, streaked with scuds of vapor, and a lonely indifferent soaring black bird.

"Bildad . . . what's the matter with you?"

No reaction.

His small, bony hands are draped over his bony knees. I grasp his wrist but feel no warmth, no pulse. I feel the carotid artery of his neck. No vital sign. Though his mouth and nostrils are open, I can detect no symptom of breathing.

"Bildad, you fool, what have you done to yourself?"

No reply. I reach out again, reluctant to believe the evidence of my senses, and give him a cautious poke on the shoulder. Not hard. But firm. He tips over like a wooden doll—the robe falling away— and lies on his back still fixed in the lotus position, folded legs and bare feet in the air, hands on knees, eyes staring at the sky, the whole body rigid as a construction of papier-mâché. Half inverted, he confronts me with his wasted thighs, his hairy and withered bottom, the puckered asshole. Not a pleasant or inspiring view. Nor is there any extrusion of intestines, neatly coiled like a boat's bowline where he's been sitting, to add a touch of the picturesque.

Curious. Leaving him on his back for the moment, I rise, step around him and check out the camp. Here is a wooden bowl, empty, and a wooden spoon. Here is a fire pit and the ashes of his last fire, cold to my touch. A battered tin bucket, half full of water and drowned ants, hangs from a nail in a tree, under the wind chimes. Inside the tent I find an open suitcase containing a few items of clothing, a sleeping bag on a Styrofoam pad, a little G.I. folding shovel with a roll of toilet paper jammed on the haft, a one-gallon glass storage jar labeled RICE and another labeled BEANS. Both empty. I see the stub of a candle on a tin plate, a few joss sticks in a balsawood box, a pair of Birkenstock sandals worn down to the threads. Nothing much else. No books, no letters, no battery-powered radio or solar-powered TV. Ascetic? Old Bildad has become pure spirit.

I glance at him from inside the tent. He remains as I left him, on his back, limbs elevated, eyes wide open, absolutely static. I return, tilt him back to the upright posture, like a bookend, and resume our conversation.

"Morton," I say, "I don't think you're dead. I think you're floating about somewhere in the neighborhood, tethered to your astral cord, waiting for me to leave. But goddamn it, Mort, remember all those nights down at the U when you did all the talking and never let me get a word in edgeways? Now by God I'm going to talk, I'm going to say something, and you are going to listen. You hear me, Bildad?"

No answer. The gap-toothed grin, the hallucinated eyes, the Levantine nose stay as they were, rigidly directed at some point far beyond my left shoulder. The Horsehead Nebula? I shift to the side to obstruct his view but that accomplishes nothing; he stares through me. I continue. "All right, Bildad, you ugly little creep, here's the story: my third wife left me for good a few days ago, my second wife is gone forever, the first never answers my letters, my only child lives with her rich grandmother in Virginia, I lost my job, I'm down to my last two hundred dollars, the inflation rate on pigmeat is 12 percent, gas is a dollar twenty a gallon, my dog is dying of lung fungus, I'm three thousand miles from home, my truck is burning oil, clutch is slipping, engine misses on the upgrades and I've got a little secret in my guts I don't have to tell you about because being a savant and Wu Li master and mystic voyeur and all that you're perfectly cognizant (you always liked that repellant Latinate fucking terminology, remember?) of my internal troubles, aren't you you supercilious grinning metaphysical bastard, and so it appears that fate has got me by the testicles with a downhill pull and what I want to know, O shriveled mahatma of human destiny, is precisely this: If the world, as you always proclaimed, is merely maya, nothing but illusion, why does it seem so bloody real? Eh? Why does it hurt so much?"

I pause to allow him to slip in a word or two. He says nothing. I go on: "I'm not complaining, you understand. I've read the *Bhagavad-Gita* too, parts of the *Ramayana*, the *Wit and Wisdom of Edgar Cayce*, *Seth Speaks*, *Lost Horizon*, *The Razor's Edge*, the *Tao Te Ching*, the *Eee Ching*, Gurdjieff, Steiner, bits of the *Rig-Veda* and even such primary sources as the classic *Please Wipe Your Mouth You Just Swallowed My Soul* by young Mr. Hugh Prather, and I quite understand the value of disinterested detachment, yogic discipline, meditation on the eternal and keeping the nasal passages clean. But even so, there are times, I tell you, when discontent descends upon me. When peace escapes me. When the cursed melancholy envelopes me in a sepia cloud of neo-Platonic squid ink. Are you listening? You follow me?"

Grinning, eyes glazed with delight, Bildad remains mute. I proceed: "You'll note I say nothing of the general state of human affairs. My current wife sleeping with a computer science professor—a computer fucking science professor!—my friends mired in mortgages and indoor jobs and medical insurance, the hellhole of Africa, the black hole of Asia, the torture rack of Latin America, the glut and gloom and gluttony of North America, the grimy *Weltschmerz* of Europe, the despair of the whales in Oceania, the ghost dance of the grizzly bears, the death march of the elephants, the Doomsday machines above our heads—I tell you, Bildad, I realize now why the universe, as the astronomers have discovered, is receding from us in all directions at near the speed of light. Why? Red shift? No! Because of fear, that's why. Fear, Bildad. The universe is afraid. We are the plague of the cosmos. The stars are not merely flying away, they are fleeing away, tripping away on little starfeet at a hundred and eighty thousand miles per second, running for their lives."

My dog whines.

Bildad grins, saying nothing.

I stand erect now, raving at the noonday sun, shaking my fist at that pallid holy wafer beyond the overcast. "My curse upon you, little star. Twinkle twinkle and to hell with you. I never want to see your light again. Go away. Expand and expire, become a red giant, a white dwarf, a supernova, what do I care." I pause, I hesitate, I glance down at Morton Bildad. "What do you say to that, Mort?"

No comment.

I squat down again, peer into his unseeing face, his rapture-blind eyes. "Want a beer, Bildad?"

Silent as a sphinx, cold as stone, dry as parchment, he says nothing but only stares beyond me, bare feet and legs interlocked, hands pressed together palm to palm, in blessing or prayer, wide mouth ajar in the grimace of a cheerful idiot.

I pat his shoulder. Rising again, I kiss the top of his bald dome, near the little aperture with the pink membrane inside. "So long, Mort. Maybe I'll come back someday. If you're still here we'll have a good talk."

No reply.

I walk away, followed by Solstice. I climb the path. I halt for a moment at the edge of the ravine to look back. Bildad has not moved. His windbell tinkles. His pale robe stirs a bit with the breeze. His tent flaps shift. But Bildad himself stays fixed, unmoved, immobile, silent. The lonely vulture circles above, black as the angel of death against the sky. I go on, get into truck, arouse engine, turn and drive away, back to the ghost town and into the shadowy gorge of the Rio Grande, across the gray and somber flats of what is called the Taos Valley, enter and leave the town without stopping and climb ENE through the pass in the mountains toward Eagle Nest, Cimarron, Maxwell, the everlasting hills of Oklahoma. I am ten miles east of Taos, popping the top from my last canister of Bud, before I remember something. Bildad's hands. His *hands*.

Sollie sleeps on the seat at my side. Dying but content. I peer into the rearview mirror to see if we are being followed, pursued, summoned. I look for ghosts. Nobody there. Not yet. What I see in the mirror is only the empty evening highway, the dark pines of Carson National Forest and the big goofy grin of one more dazzled idiot.

Rain then sleet fall toward us. The pavement glistens. I turn on lights, then the wipers, then the heater. Climbing, climbing, laboring upward, we strive, my old steel horse and I, toward the summit of the pass.

12

1957:
HOW HENRY FOUND HIS NICHE

I

What did Henry Lightcap want? He wanted everything. (What else is there?)

He wanted simplicity—a life of order, ceremony, frugality, beauty, passion and generosity. Of clean frugality, hard beauty, fierce passion and abundant—munificent—overwhelming—generosity. The GOOD LIFE.

When their new home collapsed at the great housewarming party in El Culito de San Pedro Mártir, and Professor Beale informed Henry that he had no future in professional philosophy (You have no future here, Henry; and even less of a past—no Latin, less Greek, and you flunked symbolic logic once, linguistic analysis twice, and arts & crafts three times, and I suggest, frankly, that you seek a career outside the world of Academe, in sanitation engineering, perhaps, or shoe repair) and Myra his wife went back to Tenth Street (Will I hear from you again, Myra? and she said, You'll hear from my attorney . . .), why then Henry concluded that it was time to cast about for other means of survival. On the first of April a year later—All Fools' Day—he began work as a seasonal park ranger at an obscure and very small federal park in the bleakest loneliest corner of the state once known as Deseret. He was the only ranger in the field, sole custodian of thirty-three thousand acres of stone and silence. The boss lived thirty miles off, behind a desk.

I've found my niche, thought Henry Lightcap.

"You've found your niche, Henry," the superintendent said.

Quite. He refused to work at any job for more than half the year.

If as Henry Thoreau claimed a man could get by on six weeks' work a year, then Henry Lightcap—with the occasional odd wife and maybe a kid to support—should be able to manage on six months' work a year. With a wee bit of the unemployment compensation, now and then, on the side, to help tide them over the winter months. And why not? And why the hell not? He earned it, didn't he? Was not as if he were accepting relief money.

"Of course," continued the superintendent—his name was Gibbs, Gibbs Pratt—"your job only lasts about six months. You'll be terminated in October. Depending on the funds."

"Terminated, sir?"

"Laid off. Furloughed without pay." He laughed. "Not exterminated. But if you do your job and keep your nose clean—you will have to shave every day, Henry—why we'll hire you back in the spring for another season. And so on, year by year. And then if you pass the civil-service exam you can become a full-time career man, like me, when and if an opening pops up.

Gawd forbid, thought Henry. But the old man did serve pretty good whiskey. These Park Service types were noted for their serious drinking—remote duty stations, frequent transferrals, hazardous rescue operations under extreme conditions, etc. Understandable. And I can be hired back every year? he thought. Ad infinitum, maybe?

"Yes. What's more . . ." And here the super paused to refill Henry's tumbler with another liberal slashing of Old Grand-Dad straight from the quart, hard on his melted rocks. The super refilled his own glass. ". . . And what's more, if you like the work and we like you, there's always room for bright young men in Washington. You're only a GS-3 now. But someday, maybe twenty years from now, you could be a GS-17." The super, a thoughtful and sensitive man, gazed above Henry's head at the wall beyond, where a bull elk, painted on black velvet, trumpeted his mating call into the Rocky Mountain wilds. "Not that I'd necessarily wish that on any man. But the service does have this policy: upward or out. You'll see."

Gibbs appeared to have forgotten that Henry was already twenty-nine and a half years old. But Henry knew. Where, he wondered, had all those years gone? He'd begun college in—1948? Nine years later he still lacked the M.A. degree, or most of it. And still lacked anything that could be said to resemble a career. Lightcap was one of the few veterans of World War II who never did find full-time work. He also lacked, for the present, a wife. Even a dog. Owned little, in fact, but his '49 Chevy pickup truck, a few apple crates full of books, a tarnished secondhand Haines flute and one shabby leather trunk of shirts, pants, overalls. He'd outgrown his only three-piece suit.

Failure. . . .

But what kind of work did he want? Did he want to be a small-time, independent, hard-scrabbling farmer like Brother Will? No. What Henry really wanted, he wanted to be—a lover. A philosopher. A hunter, warrior and tamer of wild horses. But employment counselors never mentioned such jobs.

"The national park system is expanding," the super went on. 'State park systems also. The American public is demanding more recreational facilities." He belched from deep in the belly, a profound organical carbonated eructation. "We're adding new units to the system every year. Upgrading the monuments to park status. Improving the facilities—new visitor centers, new and better roads, flush toilets in the comfort stations, cement picnic tables, paved nature trails, push-button recorded natural-history lectures. All of which means we'll need more public rangers, more naturalists, and most of all"—belch—"more administrators. Opportunity beckons. The future lies before us."

I don't want to be an administrator, he thought. Why not? Henry Lightcap, you can't be a young man all your life. Why not? It's a logical and chronological impossibility. Says who? I think I *will* be a young man all my life. If you live that long. If I live that long.

The super's wife appeared in the kitchen doorway. Henry politely stood up. The super looked around. "Gibbsie," she said, "you haven't washed the dishes yet."

Gibbsie? thought Henry. Wash the dishes?

The superintendent blushed. "Yes dear, I'll get to them." Embarrassed, he heaved himself from his easy chair. Wobbling somewhat. Put a hand on the fireplace mantel for support. "Get right to it," he said.

"I'm going to bed," the wife said. "Try not to make too much noise when you put away the pans."

The super nodded. The woman shuffled off. This marriage will not last, Henry thought. No more than mine. No matter how hard they work at it. And what's the point of marriage if you have to work at it? Does every fucking thing in our fucking culture have to be a fucking job? This marriage cannot be saved.

And what of it? "I'll help you, Gibbs," he said. He helped himself to more of the bourbon, then followed the boss into the neat little kitchen. The super washed, Henry rinsed and stacked.

"My wife and I have this deal," the super explained. "She cooks, I clean up."

Backwards, said Henry silently; get rid of her. "My wife and I had a similar arrangement," Henry said. The room turned around him for a moment. For a moment he thought he was going to be peculiarly ill, thought he was going to vomit on top of the nice clean dishes in the rinse water. Steady as she goes, partner. He kept it down. "That is, we had what, strictly speaking, you might call an analogous arrangement. That is, she cooked, cleaned, did the laundry, made the bed, paid the bills, and I ate, read the paper and slept on the bed. Symmetry, you'll notice."

"Didn't know you were married, Lightcap."

"I'm not. But I was."

"No kidding. Seriously?"

"Not seriously. But legally. She left a month ago."

"Sorry to hear that. Does she write?"

"I get these documents from deputy sheriffs. Subpoenas and such."

"Don't let it get you down. Every man has to go through three or four wholesome divorces before he finds the right woman. Old story in the Park Service. Remote duty stations. Hazardous work. Marriage is largely a matter of trial and error."

"Or the other way around." Henry dropped a plate on the tiled floor. The plate bounced once and rolled away into the corner. They ignored it. Tupperware. Henry took another hearty gulp from his glass to steady his nerves.

The superintendent did the same. "Well, I hope you have a happy divorce," he said.

"All happy divorces are the same," Henry said. "But unhappy divorces are unhappy each in a different way."

"True. It's an old story in the Park Service. Remote duty stations. Isolation. Hazardous rescue operations. Low pay. But we survive."

"If you live that long."

"Right."

"The important thing, I think," said Henry, "is to avoid succumbing to cynicism—to that weary resignation which passes, in the decadent West, for wisdom and wit."

"Exactly what I always say, Lightcap. Sort of. I like the way you put it."

They returned to the "living" room, full of dead objects: the velvet painting, the head of a bighorn sheep mounted on the wall above the fireplace, the closed and locked spinet piano, the foldout sofa and reclining chairs covered with genuine Leatherette, the shampooed orange shag rug of 100 percent virgin polyester. And so what? thought Henry. So it's cheap, ugly, strictly functional, what of it? We live in a pragmatic socioeconomic system. Charles Peirce, John Dewey, William James got us here. It's tough but it's fair and if you don't like it see the chaplain, get your t.s. card punched. (Eliot? No; tough shit.) They continued their discussion of employment opportunities in the park system and other aspects of life in general until the bottle was empty and no replacement magically appeared.

Taking the hint, Henry rose from his chair—the vinyl clung to the back of his moist shirt, releasing him with a lingering polymeric kiss—and shook hands with Gibbsie, thanking him for the great dinner and the frank exchange of views.

"Nothing, nothing," said the super. "I always like to get to know a new man his first week on the job. Especially an intellectual type like you, Lightcap, we don't get many of them here in Alkali County. Glad to have you aboard."

Henry stumbled forth into the dark. The super followed, kind of, switching on the front porch light but not immediately.

Henry rose to his knees at the foot of the steps.

"You all right?"

"Oh yes sir, yes sir." He stood up fairly straight, brushing the dust and weed seeds from his pants. He peered around doubtfully for his Park Service vehicle, located it, took a bearing. "Thanks again, Gibbs." He lurched toward the pickup truck, climbed in, raced the engine to show that all was well, and proceeded forward in first gear into the night, slowly and carefully. The truck blundered through what felt and sounded like a wall of rocks, climbed beyond and reached the comparative ease of a paved street that led to the road. Henry shifted into higher, finer gears, switched on the headlights and chugged north on the highway. Twenty miles to go before he reached the turnoff, the dirt road that led east for ten miles into the rocks, the desert, the little housetrailer that would be his home for the next six months.

Henry felt he was doing pretty good, considering the alligators that paddled back and forth across the boghole of his brain. And despite the fact that one headlight seemed out of order. Rumbling forward at a safe and sane 55-60 mph, he passed the sign that declared OPEN RANGE. He knew that sign: ten miles to go to the junction. On cue, a cow and calf emerged from the shadows of the junipers on his left and ambled directly into his path.

Henry veered sharply to the right—no chance for a braking stop—and around the cattle, then saw the concrete abutment of a bridge looming ahead. He jerked the truck to his left, moving too fast for stability, and the machine rolled on its side, sliding like a base runner into the cement wall. His bags of groceries, his case of Blatz beer (on sale, cheap) and his body himself hurtled to one side of the cab then the other, upside down. He shut his eyes, felt a rough blow on his shoulder and everything came to a halt.

The wheel remained clutched in his hands. The engine was still running and the one headlight still beaming. He thought of gasoline and fire and turned off the motor. He thought of police, publicity, and switched off the light. All was quiet. A fog of dust floated through the open window above, through the broken windshield before him.

He waited for a time, afraid to move, of discovering that he was dead. But felt no pain, only shock and the taste of disaster: Lightcap—you blew it again. The best job you ever had and you've blown it. Driving while drunk, wrecking a government truck your first week on the job.

When nothing seemed to be happening, he extended his limbs, cautiously—all in working order. No muscles torn, no bones shattered. He heard, in the dark, the trickling of liquids, and felt about his body for open wounds. Hard to locate. Smelled the fragrance of beer, of bourbon, and realized he'd smashed up some of the next two weeks' supply of potables. Better get out of here before the investigation commences. He opened the door on the driver's side, climbed up and out, felt weak, tired, sat down on the gravel under the slowly revolving left front wheel. He rested.

Fucked up royally, old pardner. Never mind. We're nothing but bubbles in the cosmic flow. Detachment, man, that's the thing. For a moment he considered attempting to jack up the truck, righting it, getting the motor started, going home and into bed. Hopeless project. Best salvage what he could, pick up his baggage and beer, his bourbon and bacon, and slink off into the dark, never to be seen again by man, wo-man or dog. Alas, the darkness. Think of Boethius, Henry, and the consolations of philosophy. No help. The poverty of philosophy, actually, when you really need it. There wasn't a problem he couldn't solve right now, when you come right down to it, with a simple annual perpetual grant of about twenty-five thousand dollars from some reputable philanthropic agency. Was that too much to ask?

The stars looked kindly down on Lightcap in his misery. A sick yellow waning moon cast its pallid light upon his inconsequential affairs. The cow and her calf stared at him from the other side of the highway, offering sympathy but no practical assistance. And here came a pair of yellow lights through the dust, following his track. Complications closing in.

Henry roused himself, arose, kicked broken bottles into the ditch, concealing evidence. Futile efforts. Skid marks, broken glass, a curving stain of spilled beer revealed the full extent of his crime. Guilty. Henry sat down again and waited. The car pulled up, stopped. Red gumball light on the roof. The driver emerged wearing a uniform, a gunbelt with gun, a stiff-brimmed Smokey Bear hat.

Pause. "What happened?" asked the superintendent. "Smells like a brewery here."

Only a job, thought Henry. I can always find another one. But a drunk driving charge: this'll cost me a month in the county slammer. "That cow," he said pointing. But the cow had fled.

"You know," the super said, "you drove right through that stone wall in front of my house."

"Sorry sir. It won't happen again."

"Looks like you totaled the truck."

Henry shrugged. They contemplated the wreckage. What the hell, thought Henry, *Vita brevis* and our days are full of trouble. Off in the bleak he heard a coyote cry in self-pity. That coyote sounds like I feel.

"You say it was a cow? Cow crossing the road? Interfering with traffic?"

"Well sir, I ain't sure. But I think—"

"Sure you're sure. It was a cow. This cow jumped in front of you like a rabbit out of a bush. You tried to save its life, I suppose, by swerving around it?"

"Well, sir, there was a little calf—"

"Of course, a poor innocent little calf, following its mother across the highway. You think anyone will believe your story, Lightcap?"

"No sir."

"Of course they'll believe it. I believe it. Headquarters will believe it. Highway Patrol will believe it. Close enough for government work. We'll make out the accident report first thing in the morning, you sign it, I'll sign it, we send it in, the government buys us a new truck. That old Ford was due for replacement anyhow. Now let's clean up this mess and go to bed." The superintendent pulled a broom and a shovel from his patrol car. "You think we can find a few beers in the cab? Not broken, I mean? Christ, it's almost breakfast time."

II

At the end of his first season as a park ranger, in October, when the mule-ear sunflowers, the purple asters and the sore-eye poppies were in full autumnal bloom, he was terminated. Without prejudice. "End of tourist season," said his dismissal form, signed by Superintendent Gibbs Pratt, "recommended for rehire." His employment future was secure, for the moment. He could forget mathematical logic, the general theory of axiology, the meaning of meaning, the methodology of science, the dissertation and the Ph.D. He changed the oil in his Chevy, added antifreeze and oatmeal to the leaky radiator, filled the tank with sixteen gallons of government surplus gasoline and headed east for New York, New York. Why?

Dear Henry,

Please come back. Let's not give it up yet. Let's try it one more time. You'll like it here. We have a rent-free apartment in Uncle Sid's brownstone in Weehawken. [Uncle Sydney the slumlord.] We're only ten minutes by Tubes from the Village.

I've got a gallery on 10th Street. I'll be in a group show in December. I know you hate New York but you also know why I had to come back. Dad's only got a few months to live. Try to understand, Henry. Think of someone besides yourself for a change. If you work on it you can become a warm and giving person. Even you. I'll help. We'll find you a job. Uncle Sid needs somebody to help him collect the rents. You've had six months alone to find yourself. [Find myself? Where to look? Didn't know I was lost.] Also there's one more thing I should tell you. [Oh-oh. . . .] Remember that last night in Albuquerque? In March? When we made love by the gas heater? [No!] Well Henry I have some wonderful beautiful *sacred* news for you. [Catastrophe!] I am pregnant, Henry. Yes I know we used the diaphragm [We?] but there must have been a tiny hole in it. In about six months you are going to become a father. Please come back to *us!*

Love, your Myra

Trapped. His reason, his common sense, his horse sense, his instinct, his emotions instructed him to head south for Tucson, Tubac, the Sea of Cortez. Send Myra enough money for a safe decent abortion in Toronto or wherever available and keep going south till he reached the end of Baja California and the tranquil little city of La Paz—peace!

The sensible solution. But some dark malevolent power from his Calvinist childhood—*duty*—would drag him eastward. How could he quit her now, simply because they had never been able to agree on the simplest things, like where to live (she preferred New York, he hankered after a beach-front lean-to on the coast of Mexico), or how to live (she wanted electricity, plumbing, stability, the full-time job for him with two-week annual vacation, pension plan, medical insurance, a mortgaged home—everything he hated, despised, condemned—while he yearned for woodsmoke and a cabin in the woods), or even why? Or even *why* to live?

Dilemma. Trilemma. Polylemma. Not a difficulty in the world, he recalled, that could not be banished with a simple fifty-thousand-dollar annual grant from some well-endowed charitable institution. If only you were rich! he'd bellowed at her more than once, we wouldn't be in this mess; you're so damned Jewish, why aren't you rich? Don't you bellow at me, she cried. I'll bellow when I want to bellow, he bellowed.

He reached for her. Weeping bitterly, she fell into his arms. They dropped to the mattress on the floor and "made love," as it was said, by the light of the antique unsafe open-burner gas heater in the corner. With music on the record player: the Baroque Wind Ensemble, or was it the Viol Consort, playing something sedate and polyphonic from Henry's (Henry Purcell's) suite for *The Virtuous Wife, or, Good Luck at Last.*

That must have been the fatal night, he thought, driving through a freak snowstorm into Grand Island, Nebraska, for that was the last night he had spent with her. The next day, for no reason that he could remember, she came at him with a beer-can opener in each hand while he was reading a Tolstoy treatise on domestic bliss and the military life. An hour later Henry started off for Utah, alone, followed briefly by a flying copy of *War and Peace*, Modern Library edition, which bounced off the rear of his pickup as he drove away.

Yes, that would have been the night, thought Henry, near the end of March. And then a second thought struck him: that night was six months ago.

Six?

Six.

III

He parked his truck with its New Mexico license tags at the handiest fireplug and walked a half block to the three-story brownstone row house on Hudson Street. Three stories plus a dim dank basement apartment for the building superintendent. The superintendent, in this case, was Jewish: he owned the building.

Henry climbed the stoop, sliding his hands up the polished brass rails, and rapped the brass knocker on the door. Through the frosted glass and lace curtains of the oval window he saw, after a time, a female form present itself in the dimness of the hallway.

A female form? Only in the human race, among the mammalian class, is the form of the female so readily distinctly unmistakably apparent. Henry felt the usual contradictory emotions: a lustful twitching of scrotal hairs in the region of his groin; a chill of fear in his heart.

Myra opened the door. She looked more beautiful than ever, in her ample opulent Oriental way—eyes large and dark and lustrous, the rich mane of curly hair (chrome yellow this year) draped about her head and neck, the twinned bosoms swelling up like bumper guards on an Eldorado. She stared at Henry. "What are you doing here?"

His mouth gaped open. "You asked me to—"

"Shhhhh!" She put a finger to her lips, looked down the hallway behind her. A smell of carbolic acid in the air. The sound of a thin high querulous voice demanding succor. She looked again at Henry. He noticed now that her eyes were ringed with fatigue, her face even more pale than usual. "You'll have to be very quiet," she said. She gave her head a jerk, commanding him to enter.

He followed her into the gloom of the hall and up a broad banistered stairway to the second floor. Myra was wearing the latest from Carnaby Street, a miniskirt and black tights. Among the avantgarde, Myra was always avantest. He ascended dumbly, helplessly, led by the blind but most predacious member of his bodily crew. Even as desire drew him upward, he knew in his soul that he was advancing upon the intersection of gonadal greed and dire predestined calamity.

They entered her apartment. Enormous canvases six feet by ten hung on the walls, their surfaces slathered with great clots of nonobjective paint smeared on like butter with a lavish palette knife. In the corners of the room stood shapeless sculptures of newspaper, cardboard and chickenwire with painted staring faces, glued-together survivors from the holocaust of the Tenth Street Imagination.

She turned toward him, twirling the little skirt. In the black tights she looked like a well-developed pageboy from the court of King Arthur; he felt like a blundering Yankee from Connecticut.

"So," she said, "what do you want?"

Again he was dumbstruck. But rather than fall to quarreling immediately he held out his arms. "My wife," he croaked. If she was pregnant he could see no sign of it yet; she always did have a pleasingly convex belly.

Reluctantly, she let herself be enfolded. Grudgingly, she allowed him to nudge her toward the bed, another blanketed mattress on the floor, where they sank together awkwardly. But before he was permitted to lower her drawers she tried to lift his spirits.

"Be gentle, please. My father is dying downstairs."

Henry muttered condolences with half a heart. He was familiar with this subject. Her father had been dying for the last five years, making a sloppy job of it. It was the *other* subject that Henry wanted to broach—but that, he felt, could best wait for about five more minutes. Whispering regrets in her left ear, he struggled with the inconvenient inconsiderate infuriating tights. The task required two hands and she had his left arm pinned beneath her shoulders.

"You don't mean it," she said. He mumbled, cursing quietly. "He really is this time. He's in an oxygen tent. He's under morphine. He's been in and out of the hospital four times in the last six months."

If these remarks were meant to discourage Henry's lust, they failed. In fact the nearness of the angel of death produced an aphrodisiac effect on him. Lightcap, after all, was a Lightcap—a redneck—an Appalachian hillbilly. With sudden effort he yanked free the accursed tights, exposing his woman to bestial assault.

"Be gentle," she snarled, biting his lower lip, wrapping her thighs around his waist, raking his flanks with her red claws, drawing blood. Three minutes later—both of them still breathing hard, but spent—he brought up the subject:

"Okay Myra, who's the father?"

She smiled, staring up at the ceiling. A plastered ceiling ten feet above, decorated with the twelve signs of the zodiac, and a sun, a moon, a few casual stars.

Henry waited. He laid a hand on her smooth belly. "Are you really pregnant?"

"Three months." She continued to smile her sibylline smile, self-content and satisfied.

He put his ear to her belly and heard, sure enough, the gentle thumping of a tiny fetal heart. "Who's the father?"

"You're the father."

"We've been separated for six months."

"You're my husband. So you'll have to be the father."

Ipso facto, Q.E.D., thusly so, thought Henry. He inverted, reversed, transposed and redacted her syllogism, trying to detect its fatal flaw. "Okay," he said, "but if I might ask, all the same, only out of innocent curiosity you understand, what's the name of the man who did it?"

"Does it really make any difference?"

"Not really. Only—"

"Only you'd like to know so you can take one of those awful guns of yours and go kill him, right Henry?"

Right, he thought. "Oh no," he said.

"You've always wanted an excuse to kill somebody, haven't you? The only way to prove to yourself you're a man, right Henry?"

"Is he an artist?"

"Is who an artist?"

"This son of a bitch who knocked you up."

"Of course he's an artist. A great artist. And a real man. Neither of which you will ever be, Henry."

How many goddamned artists in New York? he thought. About five hundred thousand. Common as cashews at Chock full o' Nuts. Well, he thought, I'll track him down. "You know, Myra, in most states this is grounds for divorce."

She continued to smile at her astrological ceiling. "Grounds for divorce?"

"Infidelity." He could not bring himself to use the word *adultery*. Although either was enough to bring up his own guilt feelings. From their dank Christian root-cellar depths.

As she knew. She laughed. "Henry, I never dreamed I'd hear that word from you. Infidelity . . . what a word."

He was silent for a moment or two. Or three. "But it is grounds."

"Grounds, grounds, coffee grounds." Suddenly she sat up and glared at him. "You can lie there and talk about infidelity? You? And then try to threaten me with this stupid talk about divorce? With my father dying? With me in my third month of pregnancy? You could even think of leaving me now?" The tears began to flow.

"Why don't you marry this artist friend of yours?"

"He's already married," she bawled. "Anyhow I already have a husband."

Namely me, he thought. Henry the cretin. The idiot. *Le fou.* Aloud he said, "How do you think this makes me feel? Here you admit you're going to have a baby—"

"Our baby. It's going to be our baby."

"It's not my baby."

"It will be your baby." She wiped the tears from her cheeks and glared at him again. "Can't you ever grow up? Can't you ever learn to accept responsibility? Is your real name Peter Pan?"

He stared at the ceiling, unable to face the disgust in her eyes. "But damn it, Myra—"

"Don't you love me anymore? You came here just to screw me once and then run? Is that the kind of man you are?"

Henry had never in his life been capable of telling a woman, any woman, that he no longer loved her. He lacked the kindness to be so cruel. "Of course I still love you, but doggone it, Myra. . . ."

She looked at him. Quietly she said, "You left me alone for six months, Henry."

"I know. But—"

"I'm a woman, Henry. A young healthy sensuous woman with real psychosexual needs, Henry."

Silence. Staring intently into his flustered baffled exasperated face, she waited for the appropriate response. It finally came.

"All right Myra, what do you want from me?"

She nodded. Quietly and reasonably she explained his duties to him. "I want you to get a job."

"But I just got laid off. I'm on vacation."

"I mean a real job. Not one of those summertime Smokey Bear jobs. I want you to get a full-time permanent job, here in the city. I want you to settle down and accept the responsibilities of marriage and fatherhood. We'll live in this apartment and the one upstairs. You can help Uncle Sid collect the rents from our tenements on River Street. Those schwartzes and Puerto Ricans are dangerous; he needs a bodyguard. That will give you something to do on weekends."

"What are you going to do?"

"I have my work." She looked with solemn satisfaction at the huge void muddled paintings on the walls, the mute blank-eyed androids slouching in the corners.

She has her work, he thought, and I have my duties. A fair division of labor. What is the perfect robot anyhow but a properly processed human being? a soundly pussywhipped American male? Right. Horns on his head? Think of them as antlers. "So art's the thing?"

"That's right," she said, cheering up rapidly. "And in six months I'm going to be a mother."

"I'm not sure I can go along with this plan."

She smiled brightly, kissed him and drew back to look again at the spacious, gallerylike room. "But you've got to, Henry. We have no alternative. What do you think of those horrible purple drapes on the street windows? We should take them down, put in venetian blinds. Let more light into this room."

IV

Through Myra's Uncle David, a publisher's chief accountant, Henry Lightcap was provided employment as a technical writer with Western Electric. Though neither technical nor a writer, Henry did hold a bachelor's degree. Good enough for corporate work. Along with nineteen other men, young and old, he found himself installed at a desk under fluorescent lights, in a big office on the twenty-second floor of a forty-story tower, editing drafts of training manuals for American military forces stationed in the Arctic.

Since Henry's security clearance would take several weeks, he was assigned the menial chore of editing a nonclassified U.S. government document called *How to Dispose of Human Sewage* [is there any other kind?] *in Permafrost: Preliminary Draft*. A work authored by C. J. Budnik, T. S. Schlunk and B. F. Cudball, FASCE (Fellows, American Society of Civil Engineers). In skimming over this 128-page monograph, the labor of two years by three full-grown men, Henry discovered—through a dense cobweb of subliterate supra-technical jargon complete with maps, charts, graphs, table and organic equations—that Budnik, Schlunk and Cudball had arrived at no final feasible economically solvent solution to the vexing problem of how to dispose of human sewage in permafrost. Various proposals were submitted, outlined, evaluated, rejected: (1) drill boreholes through the permanent ice to a depth of five thousand feet, injecting sewage under pressure into hole casings and then compacting it to a solid state by means of specially devised tamping machines; (2) surface compaction, overland transport by snow tractor and hauler sledges to the nearest maritime port, burial at sea; (3) rocket transport into permanent orbit around Uranus; (4) once-daily transport of human personnel by supersonic jet to restroom facilities at latitudes below or beyond the permafrost zone; (5) special restricted diet for human personnel at military installations, such as, e.g., Triscuit crackers and longhorn (style) cheese; (6) satisfactory conclusion of experimental research toward development and production of a nonlethal antidiuretic colonic bungstopper effective for a minimum three-month period; (7) processing of sewage into recyclable edible matter such as Spam, or "caramel yoghurt" or Cap'n Crunchies or "Viennese sausages," etc.; (8) temporary collection and storage of fecal materials in shallow sewage lagoons until the necessary technology for permanent disposal is developed; and (9) crap in the snow like an Eskimo, let the dogs eat it.

Solution #9, actually, was Henry's own. Leading to an even better idea, which he offered to Karp, the project supervisor.

"What? You wanta what?"

Get on a plane, Mr. Karp, fly to Nome, Point Barrow, Baffin Bay and Ultima Thule, investigate the problem firsthand in the field. Would only take a few weeks, probably; he'd gather the data, fly back with the know-how on file to produce the world's best training manual on Arctic sewage disposal.

Mr. Karp took a drag on his White Owl, puckered his lips to form a nozzle and expelled the smoke in a plume, draping Henry in a blue-gray hood of noxious gases.

"Back to your desk, Lightcap."

"Sir?"

"I mean the answer is no. Your job, Lightcap, is translating these engineers' gobbledygook into readable English, not doing shit research."

Wounded, Henry returned to his desk. Resentful, he sat there for five minutes, then transferred himself to the water cooler by the west-side windows. Paper cup of chlorinated water in hand, he gazed for ten minutes through the murky glass at the Hudson River, the Hoboken waterfront, the heights of Weehawken, the miasmal mists beyond where a red autumn sun was sinking toward Stump Crick West Virginia, Osceola Arkansas, Dalhart Texas, Shiprock New Mexico, Hanksville Utah and the Black Rock Desert of Nevada. His heart ached, his bowels yearned, the salt tears of exile formed in his eyes.

There he stood for about half of the working hours of the next two weeks, not even tasting the bitter water. At the beginning of the third week Mr. Karp descended from his elevation and came to Henry.

"Lightcap."

The young man at the window did not stir.

"I'm talking to you, Lightcap."

No answer.

"Lightcap, I get the feeling you don't really want to be a Western Electric technical writer. I get the feeling, Lightcap, you aren't happy here." A pause. "Am I right, Lightcap?"

No response.

"That's what I thought. So we're letting you go as of the end of this week. If it weren't for your wife's uncle I'd have sent you to the down elevator the minute I laid eyes on you. Where'd you learn to knot a necktie that way?"

Henry did not wait for the end of the week. He left two minutes after the discussion with Mr. Karp. He ricocheted down the twenty-two stairways (faster than waiting for an express elevator) to Ninth Avenue, walked south to the Village giddy with his sense of liberation, paused in the White Horse Tavern for two bourbons and beer in honor of his hero Dylan (the real Dylan), walked on to the Barclay Street Ferry, crossed over the majestic effluent of the Hudson River to Hoboken, idled away some time in the Clam Broth House where he drank four schooners of draft Lowenbräu and ate a platter of steamed clams and then—with a newfound crony from the New York City Welfare Department named Bat Lanahan—took the train to Jersey City for the matinee at Minsky's Burlesque. Lili St. Cyr was in town that week, doing her velvet trapeze act above the heads of Henry, his new friend Bat and three hundred sexual degenerates. Coming next week: Tempest Storm!

But sooner or later he had to confront reality before it confronted him. In the dismal November twilight, through a tenebrous mist of acid rain, over the greasy cobbles of the alleyways, he shambled afoot toward the brownstone apartment house that Mrs. Lightcap called home.

He arrived on a scene of normal Mishkin pandemonium. The old man had relapsed again, been sent by ambulance back to the hospital. Myra's mother Leah, a duck-shaped female of sixty years, sat locked in the bathroom in a coma of despair, while her son Lenny, having just been mugged by a gang of Uncle Sid's tenants—four Puerto Ricans and a Hairless Mexican—lay groaning on the sofa. Myra greeted Henry with the confirmation—hardly news—that he'd been sacked from his job, that she'd been trying to locate him since noon, that she wanted an immediate divorce (hope rose), that she would give him one more chance (then sank), that Uncle David had promised to get Henry a position as chief stock clerk at McGraw-Hill's book warehouse in Hackensack and that her father was dying again while he, Henry, Henry the Schmuck, her so-called "husband," wandered the streets in a state of public drunkenness after spending the last of their money, probably, on some cheap blonde shiksa slut from Boston (she knew his type, she knew his stripe) he'd picked up at MoMA, right? some skinny WASP bitch with tiny tits and no ass, right Henry?

Henry denied everything. Everything, including the obvious. He'd not been fired, he quit. He wasn't drunk, he was only tired. He never went to the MoMA because there was something about Braque, Mondrian, Leger & Co., and Gottlieb, Rothko and Pollock Inc., that inspired him with an animal repugnance. As for Uncle David and his McGraw-Hill, they could shove the whole puke-blue forty-four-story glass-and-tin obelisk up their collective asshole because he, Henry Lightcap, was going to get a new and better job as a social investigator (investigating society) with the NYC Welfare Dept., starting next week, depending on how soon Bat got things lined up.

Who? What? Bat?

Bat Lanahan. My friend Bat. He works there. All I have to do is pass a civil-service test, have a talk with some ward boss, and the job is mine. They're crying for help.

And what's the pay?

Henry paused; he divulged the amount.

What? she screamed. That's half what you get as a technical writer.

But, he explained, as a welfare worker he'd only have to spend two or three days a week in the office. The rest of the time he'd be out in the field, so to speak, investigating, as it were.

Oh God, she moaned, oh God, what's going to become of us. She placed both hands on her belly. It's kicking again, I'm going to have a miscarriage, Daddy's dying, Momma's having a breakdown, my brother's wounded, my husband stabs my back. . . .

And she fled. Downstairs. To where Lenny was screaming at

Mother Leah through the bathroom door. Maw, I'll kick it
down. . . .

Henry crept wearily to bed, lay down and died the little death.
There are days there are nights when that's all a man wants to do:
fall out, turn in, lie down, curl up and die.

V

In February he got a letter from Gibbsie in Utah. His niche was
waiting for him. Report for work April first. One afternoon in mid-
March Henry said goodbye to Bat Lanahan and stumbled out the
door of the White Horse Tavern.

Clouds of steam billowed over the street, bearing a smell of decay.
Henry wandered alone through the dark crowd overflowing the
sidewalks, hearing but indifferent to the whistle of police, the clash
of colliding traffic, the vast roar of the city. He made his way slowly,
on foot, through the canyons of Lower Manhattan to the Barclay
Street terminal of the Erie-Lackawanna. At once he was caught in
converging streams of men in black topcoats and little gray hats
pouring from Wall Street onto the ferry boats.

Newspapers were unfolded; Henry maneuvered through ranks of
the fresh evening same old *Daily News* to the front of the boat. He
looked at the river and the Jersey shore and a faint pinkish glow on
the west symbolizing sunset. He watched the glow fade above the
chemical dumps, toothpaste factories and condemned slaughter-
houses of Jersey City.

Turning and lifting his eyes above the newspapers which everywhere confronted him in place of human faces, he gazed at the old
pinnacled towers of Lower Manhattan, some not quite in plumb,
sagging like tombstones in a jammed, impacted churchyard. The
highest windows caught the setting sun and for a moment blazed as
if filled with fire, a fire soon quenched by the ambiguity of twilight.

The ferry boat thrashed clear of the slip, chugged slantwise across
the Hudson toward Hoboken. The roar of the millions faded away,
the water hissed and slapped at the advancing boat and from the
receding slabs of Vampire City came only echoes—the cry of tugboats, the bray of ships, the scream of gulls.

Henry looked away from the city and down at the water. Floes of ice, sulfur-colored, glided by under the bows of the ferry.

Spring breakup. A thrill of longing coursed through his nerves. He raised his eyes to the red ruin of the sunset and saw, beyond Hoboken, beyond Newark, through a veil of smoke and gas, the slender silver crescent of the new moon, the dim but hopeful beacon of a western star. Courage braced his heart.

It was time to go.

VI

There was a bitter scene. Naturally.

You wretch. You snake. You coward. You schmuck. You goy. You deserter. You traitor. You toad.

He urged her to come with him. They'd manage. There was room for a baby in the ranger's little housetrailer.

Live in that wasteland? Me? With you? With a tiny baby? Thirty miles from the nearest doctor? You think I'm insane?

He'd rent her a room in town.

Rent a room? You mean an apartment? On your seasonal ranger's salary? You cracking up, Henry?

Okay, he'd get a big wall-tent, set it up in one of the unclaimed plats of public domain close to town. Beautiful places: Arsenic Springs or Skull Canyon or Deadhorse Gulch or Rattlesnake Ravine or Death Hollow or Scorpion Ledge or Skeleton Flat or Dungeon Creek or Quicksand Draw or Stinkwater Gap or Alkali Sink— whatever, take your pick, you'd love them all, great motifs for an artist.

You're crazy. You're a fool. And me with my father dying and the baby crying and you can talk like that?

Your father's been dying for five and half years. He's always dying, he'll never be dead.

You scum. You utter shit.

The baby bawled in its bassinet. The fragrance of wet diapers hovered on the air, investing the walls. From downstairs rose the clangor of the patriarch beating with bedpan on the rail of the rented, rickety hospital bed. His hoarse and Demerol-demented howl pierced ceiling, floor and walls: Leah! Leah! I'm again bleedink—!

In and out of ICU, the old man was home again. The boychik

baby had arrived two weeks too soon, was named Samuel after one of Myra's defunct grandfathers and circumcised (despite Henry's horrified protests) by a gray-bearded rabbi with a stone knife. While the child's grandmother, Leah the Sore-Eyed, sat for hours on the toilet, bowels immobilized by six thousand years of matzoh balls and sorrow. And Uncle Sid, aided by Henry packing his piece, collected the rents.

Well, he suggested, she could fly out later. He'd pick her up in Grand Junction, Durango, Mexican Hat, whatever the nearest airport.

How can anybody live on your half-time half-a-year job? Simply. Simply going hungry you mean. Nobody raises a family working six months a year. He could, he thought. They could. And the other six months, he reminded her, would be six months of freedom. Freedom to starve? Freedom to live. He refused to be an industrial serf all his life; half his life was bad enough. We're not going, Henry. I'm going, Myra. Then go, you creep, you worm, you miserable cowardly redneck hillbilly rat, get out of my life. Write to me. Write to you, I'll write to you, you'll get letters from my attorney, I'll write to you.

He looked toward the bassinet. The baby was still crying. He'd kind of miss little Sam. Send pictures, he begged her. I'll come back to visit now and then.

You ever come back here we'll put you in jail, she told him. We'll have a warrant out for your arrest. Uncle Jacob's the best divorce lawyer in New Jersey. You'll be on the wanted list in forty-eight states.

It's nice to be wanted.

Get out.

He left, stumbling down the steps of the front stoop with his patched army duffel bag in one hand and his suncracked wine-stained cardboard footlocker in the other. Into the dark.

Don't forget your *Buddenbrooks*, she called after him. A massive volume from Alfred A. Knopf bounced off his head, dislodging his hat. The door slammed shut. A drizzling rain streamed downward through the urine glow of the streetlamps. He paused to retrieve hat and book and staggered on through the mist. He found the Chevy pickup where he'd left it, halfway down the block with two wheels on the sidewalk and a sodden mass of parking tickets stuffed under the lone windshield wiper. Lightcap the Scofflaw. He loaded his dunnage in the cab, put gear in neutral, found flashlight, unlatched the hood and hotwired the starter. (Myra had flushed the key down the john weeks earlier.) The engine turned over nicely— he did keep it tuned, cleaning the sparkplugs and resetting the points every two thousand miles. Will had taught him that much. He got behind the wheel and headed southwest for the Pulaski Skyway and Route 22. Into the night. Might as well pass through Stump Creek one more time on his way to the deserts of his heart. His mother still loved him. The coondogs liked him. And Brother Will might lend him a couple of twenties.

The divorce decree followed (via Juarez, Mexico) in six weeks, charging extreme mental cruelty, desertion and adultery. Henry brooded and raged and wept for a month, got drunk, signed and returned the papers. Two weeks later her wedding announcement arrived.

13

MOTEL ROOM

Onward. Ever onward.

Heater ain't workin' too good. The dog is shivering and my knees are cold. Got to get down out of these mountains. Huge fat flakes drift like confetti from the gray world above. They gather on the windshield and my worn-out wipers have trouble pushing them aside. Not too fast, at 30 mph, I ease around the curves; the asphalt is slick with wet snow. We cruise without stopping through the hokey resort of Eagle Nest, around the lake, through Ute Park and on to the old frontier town of Cimarron. Oklahoma lies about 130 miles to the east. My goal for the night. We'll camp out there in the grasslands somewhere, among the ghosts of the buffalo and the Kiowa, and tell sad stories—me and the dog—about the death of the patriot chiefs.

But the snow never stops. The wind blows harder as we reach the open plains near Cimarron. An April blizzard coming down from the north. Not unusual. Not on the high plains. Nothing between here and the Arctic Circle but barbed wire, grain towers and railroad tracks. The snow and wind and ice are getting serious. Temperature near freezing and my knuckles on the steering wheel are blue. The night is dark, Solstice is hungry and so am I. Time to seek shelter, make camp. Can't build a fire in this weather though and there aren't any trees out here anyhow. I hate to do it but I do: entering Cimarron I shop around and find a cheap grungy third-class motel: I can't afford it but I rent a room for the night. Twelve bucks. No pool, no coffee shop, no restaurant, no dining salon, but the room has a bed—a bed like a sack for sick bears—and a smelly propane heater in one corner. I turn that thing on, bring in the dog, the grub box, the bedroll, the revolver, the toothbrush (for my tooth). The essentials.

I give the dog her Nizoral, her feed and water, then set a can of baked beans on top of the heater. I light up the Primus camp stove, get out skillet, throw in a pound of bacon, the green chilis, the sliced potato. Your basic workingman's basic grease fix: the bachelor's supper. I'd seen a cafe two blocks down Main Street but by now the wind is howling so hard and the snow blowing so thick I don't feel like venturing out there. Might run into the ghost of Morton Bildad in his cotton robe and bare feet, seated on the sidewalk. Chanting a mantra while his ears and nostrils fill with ice.

The wind blusters at the window. Fine grains of dry snow creep in beneath the hollow core door. The plasterboard walls creak and groan. The room is icy-cold from my knees down; I pull on thermal longjohns for comfort, turn on the TV and try the different channels but the only picture I get is snow, snow, an infinity of snow, an electronic blizzard of pale atoms in space. Democritus verified. Travel advisory time, here and now in the eternal infinite.

My dog sleeps, curled on the dirty carpet before the stinking gas heater. I clean my dishes, light a cigar, ignore the little lurch of pain in my gut and take Gideon's Bible from the lampstand.

Three thousand miles or thereabout yet to go. A thousand leagues of flat land, the mysterious heart of America, spread between me, in this shabby cell in the Kiowa Motel, and the old green hills of home. Should I even go on? I must. But should I?

As others toss coins and consult the I Ching, so do I open Gideon's Good Book, at random, several times if necessary, until I find the auguries I want:

> And all Israel stoned him with stones, and burned him with fire, after they had stoned him with stones . . .

No, that ain't it. I try again:

> And the fourth angel poured out his vial upon the sun; and power was given unto him to scorch men with fire. And men were scorched with great heat, and blasphemed the name of God . . .

Please. Not that. One more time:

Even in laughter the heart is sorrowful; and the end of mirth is heaviness . . .

No! That cannot be! One more, one last, one desperate cast of the book, a final flip of the pages:

I will lift up mine eyes to the hills, from whence cometh my help . . .

Yes. That's what I was looking for. The hills of home. I fade into sleep as the storm moans and mumbles beyond the walls. . . .

I wake to a silent morning, brittle with cold. Lifting the stiff cracked window blind, I look out on downtown Cimarron—an empty street frosted with fresh snow. But the sun is shining and my truck, craftily parked to face the east, basks in the initial rays. Perhaps the motor will start without my building a fire under the block.

Sollie the dog scratches at the door, needing to go out. I open the door, she limps out and squats daintily on the doorstep, pissing holes the color of rust in the snow. Good dog. While I do something similar in the bathroom sink. Must be near freezing in this bleak little room: when I turn the tap nothing comes out but a trickle of blood. No, not blood—old water from a rusty pipe. I try the shower, the plumbing strains, groans, I hear a poltergeist banging on a pipe, but no water emerges. No matter. I had a bath only days before, did I not?, down there in van Hoss's Santa Fe. Seems like a year ago. And why shave anymore? I'll grow a beard like Will.

I call in the dog, shut the door, light up heater and Primus, cook my breakfast: coffee, fried potatoes, sausage, eggs. On a day like this a man needs grease; I mean *grease*. Can't operate the metabolic engines on a frigid morning without a proper lube job. A dog knows that much. Stirring the skillet, I pour off some of the liquid fat onto her Purina chow. She waits a moment for the grease to cool—wise dog—then probes with eager snout into the bowl.

A gentle rapping on my plywood door. Coffee in hand, I turn the knob. The chambermaid stands there, a moonfaced maiden with brown eyes and hair like a raven's wing, blue-black. *Entre usted, chiquita,* I'm about to say, but she only giggles, averts her face and hurries on to the next room, trundling her clean-up wagon at her side.

Check-out time already? I glance about for the notice, see only this reflected image in the mirror on the wall of a long haggard man in pee-stained thermal underwear, limp penis dangling from the opening at the crotch. A shocking sight. And this on a peaceful Sunday morning.

I think of Wallace Stevens. Can't help it. And of our future disembodied life beyond the grave. That beautiful land of pie beyond the sky. Do they wear our colors there? The perfection of the Absolute where all Becoming stops and pure Being, immutable, timeless, unchanging, hangs forever like a ripe peach upon the bough. What else is hanging there, never to rise and throb and ache again?

Breakfast finished, I load our goods back into truck, squirt a jolt of ether into carburetor and fire up the engine. The motor grunts, groans, whinnies like a horse and starts. Good girl. My dog takes her seat, I close the door, we lurch off into the east, into a sea of blazing crystals, bound for Oklahoma.

I glance once at the rearview mirror. The snowy mountains recede in our rear, falling away to the west and south. I am leaving the West and bits of my heart fall behind. Nothing but flat land ahead for a thousand miles. To cheer myself I slip some canned music into the tape deck: Ernest Tubb and his Texas Troubadours. As they say in Lubbock, there's only two kinds of music—country and western.

I'll get along somehow. Have you ever been lonely? When the world has turned you down? I'm walking the floor over you. Driftwood on the river. There's nothing more to say.

A vulture cruises down the sky, one redneck turkey buzzard seeing me off. Lonesome, lonesome, solitary bird. Good sign or bad omen?

I pass an old railway boxcar resting on blocks in the middle of an empty field. SANTA FE ALL THE WAY. Some rancher's improvised granary. Here and there we spy an abandoned farmhouse rotting within a clump of dying Chinese elms, surrounded by a burned-out alfalfa field where derelict tractors rust in the rain and bake in the sun. I cross a branch of the Canadian River. Many a trail drive passed this way only a century ago. I think of freckle-faced boys in gigantic floppy hats, the hats their only shade for many a mile, and the big scarves they wore around the neck, not as ornament but as respirator, pulled up over mouth and nose in the choking dust of the herd.

Slipping around, sings Ernie. I'll always be glad to take you back.

There's a little bit of everything in Texas. Let's say goodbye like we said hello . . .

I follow the vulture toward the east. My V-8 chugs along, hitting on six and burning oil; the pressure has sunk to about 30 psi. Not good. But not yet tragic. If we can make it to Kansas City, to Hannibal and the Mississippi, I'll walk the rest of the way. Only a thousand miles to go from there. If a man can't walk he might as well be dead. Vachel Lindsay walked across the country. So did John Muir and Johnny Appleseed. A pickup truck is fine, a horse is better, but in the end when you come right down to it the noblest mode of locomotion is that by way of the legs, proceeding upright, erect, like a human being, not squatting on the haunches like a frog.

Brave words, brother. With another little jab in the entrails to remind me of mortality. Which will go farther, last longer, me or the truck? I don't know but I expect to find out. The odometer creeps toward its second row of zeros, tenth by tenth. Prufrock measured out his life in coffee spoons, I measure mine by the number of Fords, Chevies and Dodges I've ridden into the ground over the course of my febrile flustered jocund years. Five decades on Planet Earth. Where to next, O Lonesome Traveler?

Master of self-pity, I let the leaky tears dribble untouched through the whisker of my beard. But not without a glance at my dog: she sits with head up at my side, stares with solemn eyes and stoic resignation straight forward through the windshield, watching the asphalt path unreeling toward us. A tall dog and a brave one. A true and salty dog, my Solstice.

We pass the turnoff to places named Yates and Roy. Good sound cow-country names. I can see the leathery faces, the gnarled hands, the coiled ropes and slickhorn saddles and rolled Stetsons and shit-caked boots. Goddamnit, every man should try the cowboy's trade at least once in his life. Like it says on the wall of the men's pissoir in the Dirty Shame Saloon: if you ain't a cowboy you ain't shit.

Approaching Clayton now, only twenty-three miles from the Oklahoma border. Volcanic buttes on the skyline to the north rise up like warts, lavender-hued, through the carpeting of golden grass. Irrigated alfalfa fields near the road. An occasional quarter horse leans against the fence, stretching its neck for a jawful of ditchbank weeds. Cottonwoods down in the arroyo, still naked of leaves. Spring has not yet quite arrived out here in the open.

Entering Clayton, N.M., CO_2 CAPITAL OF THE WORLD, says the first welcoming billboard. Goodbye to the nineteenth century. Sheltered by stucco walls, the lilac bushes are in bloom—each purple plume encircled by its private corona of flies, bees, bumblebees. I see a young apricot tree adorned with flowers and the elms are leafing out.

And then appears an orange-colored geodesic dome—surely the ugliest excuse for a human dwelling ever imagined—and my heart sinks a little. Only a myopic geometer encapsulated in his own brain could have conceived so repellent a structure. Plywood panels of metallic orange tacked to the skeleton of a space-age bug: bleak poverty of the R. Buckminster mathematic soul.

Past the National Guard Armory: light tanks and big trucks of olive-drab rest in ranks inside a cyclone fence topped with barbed wire. Makes me think of Naples, Italy, and the winter of 1945–46. I remember the smell of Cosmoline and the weight of an Army .45 on my hip. While I guarded the gate of the motor pool our C.O. was selling four-by-fours and six-by-sixes through the big hole in the back fence. The Italians may have lost the war—but they robbed us blind in the black market. *Viva Italia*. Anarchy works: the Italians have proved it for a thousand years.

My Carryall rumbles over the railway tracks deeper into downtown Clayton. There's the B&H Feed Supply, Purina Chows, City Drug, the Luna Theater showing *Texas Chainsaw Massacre*, PG, and the Stockman's Bank, a squat smug block of red brick and dingy plaster that looks like it ain't been held up for a long time. Where's Pretty Boy Floyd when we want him? Baby Face Nelson? Jack Dillinger?

North of town I see a pair of small hills: Rabbit Ear Mountain, the early travelers called it, the first topographic feature to meet their eyes as they left Oklahoma headed west toward Santa Fe. Josiah Gregg stopped here for a drink (of water), losing his pistol as he leaned over the horse trough. An unlucky fellow, that Gregg— the Ichabod Klutz of frontier America. Not far east of here he was once pursued by a wildfire for ten miles across the plain. The fire began at his morning camp, making Gregg the only man in American history to be chased by his own campfire.

I do not pause in Clayton. Minutes later we cross the invisible line between New Mexico and Oklahoma and see more Chinese elm, more wooden windmills, more endless shortgrass rangelands. Prairie country—and was there ever so gentle undulant female and sweet a word as *prairie*. French derived from the medieval Latin *prataria*, a meadow.

Meadowlands. I think of Cossacks. Then of Comanches. Then of the pony soldiers in their coats of blue—Negroes, most of them, led by white officers, naturally. Little-known facets of American history. As the first North American cowboys were actually Mexican, so were many of the early American cowboys young blacks—freed slaves and the sons of slaves. The rest were runaway teenagers, poor white trash from east Texas and western Tennessee and central Appalachia. My kind of folk. First took to drinkin', then to card playin', got shot in the bowels and we're dyin' today.

Very deep is the well of the past. Shall we not call it—bottomless? What is our history but a vivid and continuous dream? We skim over the roadway bearing northeast to Kansas, me and my mortal dog, and the infinite dimensions of the recent past—a mere one century—make the brain giddy, the mind reel, the heart to swoon.

Watch that gas pedal, pal. Mind the cops. You can't afford a lockup now.

How true. I slow down. I want to weep. Not for sorrow, not for joy, but for the incomprehensible wonder of our brief lives beneath the oceanic sky. This could never have been a populous land but even here, all about me, lie the unmarked graves of slain Indian warriors, Kiowa, Pawnee and Comanche, their women their children—twenty thousand years of living and dying. And above the natives rests a stratum of trappers, fur traders, buffalo hunters, cavalrymen, drovers, cowboys, sodbusters, more worn-out women and stricken children—the organic mold of thousands of thousands of forgotten human creatures like you, me, him, her, this bank clerk here, that banjo plucker there, those drummers and buglers and music critics yonder . . .

Now now. Best not dwell on it, Lightcap. You'll sink if you do in this sea of grass like the disintegrating plowshares that broke the plain, under a sky of dust, for what purpose, toward what end?

Don't ask. Carry on. Check the gas gauge: ten gallons—half full. Oil pressure: 35 psi. The temp: 140° F. The ammeter: neutral. The tachometer: 1200 rpm. The speedometer: a safe and sane sixty per. Let her roll. We surge through the Rita Blanca National Grassland—badly overgrazed—and into Boise City (empty buildings), on to Keyes through the Okie Panhandle, into the town of Elkhart and the border of Kansas.

I pause for a piss on the roadside ecology of Coors beer cans (this Bud's for you) and plastic Coke bottles and I hear—a meadowlark. My first meadowlark of spring.

Farm country now. Plowed fields touch the shoulder of the highway. Over there is a man on a green tractor pulling a red disk plow through the yellow stubble of his winter wheat. Overhead a blue sky suffused with soft haze. The West is suddenly gone; we're in the Midwest. Breadbasket of America, Russia, Ethiopia and half of Europe. No wonder the trees are gone; little wonder the furrows reach to the edge of the pavement. We're feeding our brothers—friends and enemies—near everywhere. Fraternal goodwill and there's money in it. For a time. Sell now, pay later. The air reeks with the smell of ammonium nitrate. The Missouri and the Mississippi roll toward the Gulf, their waters rich brown with topsoil from what was once upon a time the happiest hunting grounds on Earth.

But the meadowlark don't care and by God neither shall we. I shake it and coil it away, open another can of Bud, hold the door for the return of my dog, close door, press on.

Grain elevators loom in the distance. Ravens pick at the fleshy tidbits of rabbit flattened on the asphalt. Primroses bloom among fields of sorghum, milo, alfalfa, maize. The land lies flat as a pool table. The field of vision shrinks to fifteen miles, with the grain elevators—the farmer's skyscraper, his temple of hope—marking the horizon. Scattered about over the fields are gas wells, the power-driven pumps rocking up and down like iron grasshoppers at prayer. A sign in the shape of a giant sunflower says WELCOME TO KANSAS, MIDWAY USA.

I linger in Elkhart only long enough to buy a Safeway beefsteak, then turn north for six miles on a state road to visit the Cimarron River and what the map labels as Cimarron National Grassland. I feel like celebrating something, I'm not sure what.

The sun goes down, the new moon hangs high. The river seeps down a channel of dry sand lined with groves of cottonwood beginning to leaf out. Cowpaths and dirt-bike trails rove everywhere but not one bovine or human is in sight. I pull off the road and make camp by a sandy wash. I grill my steak over a fire of cottonwood twigs. Poor fuel compared to the mesquite and ironwood of Arizona but it will suffice. The steak is lean, thin and cooks quickly. I am a man of simple tastes.

The song of that mourning dove, for example, down there in the trees, sounds as good to me as Bach's B-minor Mass. Better, in fact. Not so labored, not so laborious, not so massive. There are times when I prefer the music of one kid trying to play "Red River Valley" on his new Marine Band harmonica to the majestic uproar of the Vienna Philharmonic struggling, one more time, through the Mozart Requiem.

That mourning dove. That sad sweet simple call from the grove makes a man want to find the sorry little thing, stroke its wee head, caress its downy breast, murmur soothing words into its ear, wring its scrawny neck. And the dove recalls another day in the woods as well. A different kind of day in another forest two thousand five hundred miles to the east on the side of an older mountain.

I wasn't even there when it happened.

14

1965:
DEATH OF THE OLD MAN

I

The dove called from down by the creek, among the shady willows, when Will left the house to look for Paw. That too was on an April evening.

II

Will returned from the war—his war—Roosevelt's War—in the autumn of 1945. He found the farm a wreck. We'd thought we were doing fine. Will was shocked, enraged, depressed. Rather than live with us he built a cabin in the woods, near the spring under the red oaks. High on the hill.

> Gonna build me a cabin
> On the mountain so high
> That the blackbirds cain't find me
> Nor hear my sad cry . . .

A wreck, he called the farm, a ruin. Strong language for our quiet brother. What bothered him so much? The place still looked good to us.

True, the horses were gone. Paw had sold off the first one, breaking up the team, the same summer that Will joined the Army. He kept one horse for his logging operations—needed old Blue to skid logs down the mountain through the laurel slicks—but when he'd saved enough money to buy a secondhand Ford tractor he sold Blue too. Of course, the children cried—Marcie, Paul, Baby Jim—and Mother went for a long walk the morning the buyers hauled away that big solid old plowhorse.

But Paw could not be moved. He remained as stubborn then as he was the day he sold Bessie—Blue's mate. Remember? We needed the money, Paw said. That horse ate more than he was worth and got sick half the time to boot. Worms, glanders, colic, bots, warbles. Anyhow he was twenty-two years old for Christ's sake. Damn near dead on his feet by noon every day.

Having sold the horses, Paw sold the harness. What good was it now? He sold the bull-tongue plow; you couldn't hitch that thing to a tractor. He sold off all the milk cows but one; we were no longer in the dairy business. The state had put so many sanitary restrictions on dealing in milk that the ordinary farmer could no longer make money at it. Paw plowed up the hayfield with his new used tractor and a gangplow and planted the whole thirty acres in alfalfa. We didn't need the hay anymore, he explained, but you can always sell baled alfalfa. Then he logged off most of the good saw timber—the white oaks, beech, poplar, ash, locust, sassafras, chestnut, red maple—and replanted the devastated hillsides with Scotch fir. Always be a good market for Christmas trees, he said; them fools up in Morgantown and Wheeling and Pittsburgh always will be too damn lazy to get out and cut their own. Easy money.

He spent the war years sawing down trees with his one-man crosscut saw (the chainsaw not yet available), hauling them to his one-man sawmill by Stump Creek, stacking the lumber and retailing it himself. Always a one-man operator, our Paw; he would neither hire help nor work for anyone else.

When he'd cut down all the good trees on the home place he began to buy timber on neighboring farms. He bought the abandoned Waldroop farm for the unpaid back taxes—outbidding the few who came to the sheriff's auction—and made that a base of logging operations for the next decade. And when the strip miners from Westmoreland and Peabody Coal began to move into the country with their Caterpillar tractors, earth movers, dragline power shovels and forty-ton dump trucks, our old man was in there clearing the right-of-way, cutting down the trees and hauling away the logs. Wherever he went he left behind sawdust, slashing, bare stumpage and skid trails. He was not making money—but he was making a living. Paid better, he said, than sidehill farming. And what's more and more important he liked the work. Always did like the smell of sawdust, he said. Always did like to see a big tree fall exactly where he wanted to fell it. Joe Lightcap was one man in Shawnee County who could drive a peg into the ground with a ninety-foot falling tree. He was one logger who never needed a helper, a swamper, a safety lookout. Always loved to eat his lunch deep in the woods where no one could bother him, where the only noise was the sound of a woodpecker hammering on a hollow snag, the chatter of a squirrel, the scream of a hawk, the sweet sad distant call of the mourning dove.

Never did much like stumbling along behind a plow staring at a team of half-ton hind ends, breathing silage-charged horsefarts from the exhaust end of two forty-foot tubes. The farmer, claimed our father, is a slave, a serf, a bondsman, a poor dumb degenerate peasant who plods through life toting a barn, two horses, sixteen half-breed Holsteins and a hundred and twenty acres of red dirt and clay on his back—and it all belongs to the bank anyhow. While the independent logger, he asserted—and thought himself the living proof—is a free man, a citizen, and best of all—a woods man. A *woodsman!*

Will could have humored all that, even gone along for a mile or two. What he could not accept, could not understand, could not forgive, was the raw gash on the north side of our former hayfield. A gash that ruined forty acres and went a hundred feet deep, with spoil banks ranged in windrows fifty feet high before the face of the black coal seam, and stagnant pools of sulfurous water on the floor of the pit—poisoned water with nowhere to go but down into the bedrock and from there into the springs, wells, streams of Stump Creek Valley.

Wasn't my fault, Paw explained. Wasn't me signed that broad-form deed back in 1892. That was your grandpaw done that. Nothin' I could do about it. There was no way in hell we could keep the Peabody Coal Company from a-comin' in when they was ready. How'd we know they was gonna strip that hill? We thought they'd sink a shaft like they used to do. For the War Effort, they said. What was I supposed to do, sit out there with a shotgun and hold off the coal company, their Pinkerton goons, the county sheriff, the state troopers, the National Guard and maybe old Harry S "Shithead" Truman hisself, with half the U.S. Army behind him? Besides, we got a royalty on that coal. Forty cents a ton.

Will said nothing. Not to Paw. To me and Mother he said, It's ruined. He let them ruin one-fourth of the farm. Mother tried to console him. Three-fourths is left, she said. Will shrugged. Someday we'll need that land. He said goodbye to everyone but our old man and disappeared for a month. Next time we heard from him he was married to his old girlfriend Marian Gresak, living in a rented apartment in Shawnee and driving a truck for the lumber company. He went to school evenings, on the G.I. Bill at the Teachers' College, but dropped out after a year. He offered no explanations. On weekends and holidays he and Marian came out to the farm and worked on the cabin up in the woods near the sunken remains of another cabin and the graves—Will had no fear of ghosts—of Doctor Jim and his daughter Cornflower. Inside of ten weeks they completed the board-and-batten walls, shingled the roof and built a porch on the south side. Four weekends later Will finished the fireplace, added a sleeping loft and piped water in from the spring. Their honeymoon cabin, they called it, but seldom stayed there.

For nearly a year Will barely spoke to the old man. For the next ten years he spoke to him only when necessary—at Sunday dinners, holiday assemblies, family reunions, births, graduations, marriages and funerals.

Will and Marian had their first child eight months after the wedding, the second two years later. That was enough, even though Marian was a Roman Catholic. The Pope may be infallible, she explained, but he's never around to help pay the bills.

Will bought Stitler's old auto-repair shop with the aid of a G.I. business loan and supported his family with wrench and screwdriver. "General repair" was his specialty. A greasy line of work but at least he was his own boss. When he felt like going hunting or adding a back porch to the cabin or plowing our cornfield he locked up the shop. Being a mechanic both honest and competent—the only one in the county—he never hurt for lack of customers. They were on the telephone or lined up outside his garage doors every Monday morning.

He could have worked in the woods with Paw, maybe, helped operate that logging business, but he had no desire to form a partnership with our old man. God only knows he'd rather be out among the trees than sliding on a creeper board under the bowels of a broken-down Plymouth—but neither Will nor the old man had any notion of attempting to work together. On anything. They were both too stubborn and independent to even think of reconciliation.

Will kept the farm going in his free time, not for Paw's sake or for Mother's sake either and not even for his own. He did it, I guess (he never explained), for the place itself. To keep it alive, a going concern. Not for monetary profit—he barely broke even—but because he was there, the farm was still there, he had to do it. Who else would?

<h1 style="text-align:center">III</h1>

That April evening when Will left the farmhouse to look for the old man he heard the mourning dove call once, twice, from the willows by the run. And there was nothing unusual about that. But Will noticed the sound, the bird's cry, in a way he had never heard it before. Though he knew that the dove was somewhere among the trees only a hundred yards below the house, the sound of its call seemed to come from a great distance. The sound was clear, as always, but coming to him from a point remote in space, across a strange interval of time. He felt and noted the strangeness of it, at the moment, and then forgot it completely in the hours to come.

Paw often stayed out in the woods until dark but on this day he was expected home by five. As Mother told Will, he had planned to come home early, eat a quick supper and meet two men at his saw-mill for a lumber transaction—somebody driving up from Sutton for a load of two-by-fours. But Joe did not appear. Mother phoned Will, who came at once.

Will had a pretty good idea where the old fool probably was. For a month Joe had been cutting trees on the former Cunningham place, high on the side of Cheat Mountain. Working alone, as always. Without a chain brake on his power saw or a hard hat on his thick head, as usual.

Will drove south past Jefferson Church, past the graveyard, and down the red-dog road along Crooked Creek. He crossed over through the covered bridge—loose planks rumbled under his pickup truck—and took the left lane up the side of the hill. Opening the gate at Cunningham's turnoff he noticed fresh tracks in the mud:

the bald worn tires of the old man's Ford. But only one set of tracks; Paw had entered but not yet left. Will climbed the hill in low gear, over the rocks, forded the stream that ran from what had once been a pasture, now surrendered to the returning blackberry, sumac, dogwood, sapling red maple. He passed the moldering remains of a barn sunk upon its stone foundations and the decayed ruin of a log cabin where only the fireplace and chimney stood intact. Beyond the former homestead the road forked, both branches bearing into the woods. Will stopped his truck, got out to check tracks again.

The soft twilight enfolded him, the lavender glow of evening that would spend two hours in its dying. Far from any highway, the old farm lay enclosed in stillness. Naturally, instinctively, before even glancing at the forks of the road in front of his truck, Will paused to listen.

He hoped for the whine and snarl of chainsaw at work but heard instead only the spring peepers in their rhythmic chant down in the meadow and from the dark woods—after a moment—the silvery lyric of a hermit thrush. That invisible bird.

Will inspected the road. Both forks lay half concealed beneath a rank growth of skunk cabbage and mayapple but on the right, leading up the hill, were the signs of a recent passage—crushed weeds, the drip of oil, tire burns on a patch of bare earth. Will followed, driving upward and deep into the woods until the road dead-ended at a turnaround. There he found the old Ford flatbed half loaded with logs, parked among a circle of slash piles. The driver's door hung open and on the seat was Joe's lunch bucket—the oval-shaped miner's tin—with its lid off, a pack of Bugler tobacco nearby.

Will looked, shut off his engine, got out. He peered into the darkness under the trees. Skid trails led off in various directions. He looked again at the truck. Paw's peavey and cant hook leaned against the side of the bed; underneath was a gasoline can and the empty chainsaw case.

Which way to go? He listened. No sound. Even the hermit thrush, the mourning doves, the tree toads had fallen silent.

Paw, he called, gently. His voice seemed a harsh intrusion on the hush of evening. He waited, hearing no answer. He called again, much louder, bellowing his father's name into the gathering gloom: Joe!

He waited.

This time he heard something, something animal, perhaps human—a sort of low grunt, a growling cough. The sound came from farther up the hill, far off. Will grabbed the peavey by its heavy wooden handle and started up the trail.

He found our father, as he expected, under a down tree, trapped, half crushed, half alive. One glance at the big stump nearby revealed what had happened: a rotten core in the butt of the tree made it split as it fell. Paw had run sidehill, carrying his heavy chainsaw, but not fast enough, not far enough, and the falling tree, doing a "barberchair kickback," had rolled aside and caught him as it crashed to the face of the steep slope. A half dozen widow-makers—dead limbs—lay scattered about; any one could have killed him. But they weren't needed. The tree itself, a ninety-foot poplar, did the job, smashing Joe's body into the earth.

The old man's eyes were open; they focused on Will kneeling over him. Blood leaked from the corner of his mouth. He breathed rapidly but carefully, delicately—each breath a stab of pain. The weight of the split bole lay across his ribs, waist, pelvis.

Goddamnit, Will, he snarls, like a trapped dog, where the hell you been? He was pale as milk, greasy with sweat.

Easy, Paw, easy. Don't talk. Will looked quickly about. He knew he'd have to buck the down tree before he could roll it away from the old man's body. Need the saw, where's that saw? The saw lay ten feet down the slope, broken, its three-foot bar bent like a spoon, the cutting chain dangling free, useless.

Been here since noon, Will. Since noon, goddamnit. Get this tree off me.

Yeah, yeah, Paw. . . . Foolishly, knowing better, Will tried to lift the trunk of the tree. He could not budge it. He took the peavey and attempted to roll the trunk. A useless gesture: the branches, jammed in the ground, made it impossible to roll. He'd have to trim the limbs before he could roll it. Again he looked frantically around through the darkness, trying to spot an ax.

Ax, Paw, ax. Where's your ax?

Seems like all day. Been here all day, Will, waitin' for you. Where in the name of Hell you been?

Shut up, Paw, Will said softly, you shut up now. Save your strength. You got another saw? Where's the ax?

Makes a man so mad he could piss in a milk can.

He spied the ax, a double-bitted timber ax, one blade sunk deep in a stump, the file beside it. Will got up, hurrying, took the ax and lopped branches from the tree, beginning with the first above his father and working up the slope, up the trunk. At each blow he heard the old man grunt with pain. But what else could he do? He thought of running back to the trucks, getting both jacks—but the splintered butt of the down tree offered no purchase.

Halfway up the length of the tree, where the trunk tapered to a two-foot diameter, Will stopped limbing, raised the ax above his shoulder and began to chop through the trunk. Right, left, right, left, he cut a V-shaped notch. He stepped over the trunk and swung from the opposite side, deepening the notch until the cut went clear through. He returned to his father. Paw was still conscious.

How you doin', Paw?

That you, Will? Took you long enough, goddamnit.

Gonna roll this thing off you now, Paw. Don't talk. Take it easy. I'm gonna get you out of here, get you straight to the hospital.

No hospital. Ain't goin' to no goddamn hospital. Take me home, Will. Just take me home, goddamnit, that's all I want, just let me rest awhile.

Sure, Paw. We'll do it.

Will jammed a fallen branch at a right angle against the under-side of what was now a log, not merely a down tree, hooked the peavey into the bark of the log and levered it slowly up onto the branch. As he did so he heard Joe's gasp, then an agonized groan.

Oh goddamnit all, Will. . . .

Paw's body was clear. As gently, mercifully as he could manage, Will pulled the old man from beneath the log. He wiped Joe's face with a bandana, nursing his head in his left arm. Paw looked desperately sick but not dead, not yet. Need a stretcher, thought Will, need a stretcher and another man to help carry it. He was afraid of doing more damage to the old man's insides if he picked him up. Again Will looked around through the darkness of the silent forest, seeking help.

There's nobody here but us.

He looked up into the converging columns of the trees. Through the bare and unleafed branches he saw one star, steadfast, resolute, shining down. You're on your own, Will Lightcap.

Put your arm around my neck, Paw. But Joe made no response.

Will slipped an arm under the shoulders, the other under the knees, and lifted his father from the ground and carried him, like a broken child, down the skid trail through the dark to the head of the road. He was aware of blood, urine, excrement leaking, dripping, from Joe's clothing. Carefully, taking pains, he laid the old man across the bench seat of his pickup truck. He pillowed his head with a folded coat. There was no place else to put him.

Will got in behind the steering wheel, draping his father's lower legs over his lap. He reached for the key in its switch.

Will. . . .

Will hesitated.

That you, Will?

It's me.

The old man's lips moved again but no words came out. Then he said, Forgive. . . .

What? Forgive what?

Forgive. . . .

There's nothing to forgive, Paw. Forget it. Be quiet.

Forgive. . . .

Will paused; he said, I forgive. He started the engine and drove down the road, past the ruins, through the open gate of the old farm and from there to the covered bridge and onto the graveled county road. From there it was fifteen miles over a rough and winding blacktop, riddled with potholes, to the hospital in Shawnee. By the time Will got there, pulling into the emergency entrance, the old man was dead from internal hemorrhages.

IV

Henry flew home from Utah for the funeral. He arrived in time for the church service and the burial.

Will took care of everything else. As soon as he'd obtained a death certificate from the attending physician at the emergency room, he took Joe's broken body—enclosed now in a hospital shroud—out to the truck and drove him home. Meanwhile he had phoned Mother and sent a message to Henry, to our sister Marcie and to the Gatlins.

Will refused, absolutely, to have any dealings with an undertaker. Or a "mortician," as those vultures had begun to call themselves by this time. And Mother backed him up. Though concerned with a proper respect for appearances, she shared her son's contempt for funeral parlors, embalming, hired hearses and commercial mourning procedures. I think maybe you're breakin' some laws, Uncle Jeff told him. Tell the sheriff about it, Will replied. Holyoak did nothing.

That first night Mother sat up with the body and did her weeping. She cried quietly, that is, for about an hour, until some neighbors and relatives began to arrive, then settled down to a stoic acceptance of her duties as widow and hostess. They could all hear, from out in the barn, the noise of Will carpentering a coffin.

Selecting rough, knotty but adequate pine two-by-sixes from Paw's lumber stacks, Will made a rectangular box six and a half feet long, thirty inches wide, two feet deep. He mitered the joints and reinforced the corners with sections of two-by-four and fastened them with screws—no nails, no glue. He screwed on six handles, three to a side. The box looked very large on the barn floor by the light of two kerosene lanterns but our Paw was a large man. Long, anyhow. Will carried the coffin into the parlor—the front room—of the house and set it down on the floor. He and cousin Bill Gatlin laid Joe's stiffening body inside. Even dead, shrunken up by old age and damage, he barely fit. When Mother was ready Will pulled the canvas shroud over the old man's face and head. He packed the body with ice and sawdust from the icehouse and attached the lid of the coffin, screwing it down tight. He let the box and its occupant remain in the house overnight—for Mother's sake—but in the morning, when the sun came up, he stowed the coffin deep inside the cold portal of the coal mine in the hillside above the barn.

Joe would have preferred to be buried in the woods alongside Doctor Jim and Cornflower but on this point Mother insisted on convention. She wanted her husband buried in the graveyard at Jefferson Church, in the plot she had long ago reserved for him and herself, next door to the other Gatlins and Lightcaps.

Joe had never been a member of the congregation. He had often boasted, loudly and aggressively, of his atheistic views: "God," he would say, always putting the name in quotes, is a noise people make when they're too tired to think anymore. Nevertheless, Mother's wishes carried weight in the church community. She was one of the pillars; who else could or would teach Sunday school to the six-year-olds, play both the piano and the organ and rehearse and lead the choir?

Will had no objection to the plan. After stashing the coffin inside the mine, he and Bill Gatlin took a pick, sixpack of beer, shovel and wheelbarrow, drove the three miles to the church and dug the grave. That took till noon. In the afternoon (alone and in secret) Will worked on our old farm wagon, greasing the axle bearings, replacing some missing spokes in the wheels and rebolting the doubletree to the tongue. That wagon was forty years old by then, the wood weathered to the soft silver-gray of the April clouds overhead. In the evening he paid a visit to the Houser brothers, the last farmers in Shawnee County still using work horses.

The funeral service was scheduled for the next day.

Everyone arrived on time, even Henry, except Will Lightcap and our old man himself. We were gathered near the front door of the church, talking with the young new long-haired preacher (Mother's church was one of four he visited every Sunday) and waiting for Will, who was supposed to deliver the guest of honor. The young hippie minister was glancing for the third time at his watch when we heard, from a quarter mile down the dirt road, a grating noise of iron-rimmed wheels on gravel, the creak and rattle of bone-dry wood, the jangle of trace chains, the slap of horsehide on horsehide.

Henry excused himself and left the gathering at the church door to meet Will and the team and wagon. The stiff suit and his high-heel cowboy boots—freshly polished at the Pittsburgh airport—made the short walk uncomfortable but he was grinning when he shook hands with his big brother. He couldn't help it. Will smiled himself, for a moment, but they both assumed solemn faces as they approached the waiting group. In the rear of the wagon, behind the coffin, lay Paw's mangled chainsaw. Will dismounted from the wagon seat. The big draft horses stamped their feet, shook the harness, discharged a pile of green and steamy dung, then stood quietly when Will spoke to them. He tied them, temporarily, to the hemlock by the churchyard gate. Will and Henry and four other men—Bill Gatlin, Uncle Jeff Holyoak, Sam Gatlin and Homer Bishop—carried the coffin into the church and set it on the trestles before the pulpit. Mother placed a bough of flowering dogwood on the coffin. The young Reverend Jonathan Cripps, D.D., delivered his sermon.

I take my text, he began, from the book of Ecclesiastes, chapters one and twelve, verses two and thirteen. He paused and gazed for a moment over his lectern at the widow, at the widow's daughter Marcie, at Will and Henry and other members of the family.

Speaking without notes, in a voice calm and conversational, the minister continued. Vanity of vanities, says the Preacher, all is vanity. Or as we would say these days, Futility, utter futility, the whole thing is futile. I hardly knew the man whose death we have gathered here to mourn. What little I know of him I learned indirectly and by inference, through my brief acquaintance with you people and with Lorraine, his widow. I know that he was a farmer and a logger by trade, a faithful husband to his wife and a steady support for his family. From all report he was a decent honorable man who always did his best in whatever he set out to do. He was also an outspoken man who never hesitated to attack the institutions of our nation when he felt those institutions were betraying traditional American ideals.

Again the young minister halted for a moment. He contemplated the small congregation, a faint smile passing over his face, then went on.

More troubling to us here today was his outlook on our church, our religion. I will not ignore the fact that Mr. Joseph Lightcap was not a member of the church and was not since childhood a practicing Christian. As I think we all know, he made no secret of his hostility to our faith, his rejection of orthodox doctrine, his lack of belief in the Supreme Deity. I will not label him an atheist, however. What man of sense could declare, positively, that there is no God? But we know that he regarded himself as an agnostic, one who doubts the existence of things unseen. . . .

He believed in oak, thought Henry. The golden oak. He believed in board feet and the money tree. But never wore a hard hat—never really believed in the widow-maker.

. . . seems appropriate therefore to consider the meaning of the ancient Preacher's words. For if Joe Lightcap ever read the Old Testament, this must surely have been his favorite book. What could be more apparently agnostic, doubting and skeptical than these words which seem to issue from the heart of despair? Vanity, vanity, all is vanity. The author doubles and redoubles this bitter word, using twice-over a phrase which might be a parody of that other superlative, "holy of holies." Utter futility contrasted with complete holiness. And the terse dismissal: "All is vanity." This whole complicated business of life is brushed aside as a phantom of useless striving and struggle. Or is it? Does this vanity include godliness? And God? Or does the Preacher simply mean everything less than God? Not the whole world—but only the earthly world? Only that which exists under the sun?

Under the sun? thought Henry. I see where he is leading. All is vanity beneath the sun, in this world—but out there, up yonder, in that other world . . . ? Poor old man; they finally got him where he'd have to hear a good Christian sermon whether he wanted to or not.

. . . I think, continued Dr. Cripps, that our author writes from a concealed premise. Ecclesiastes is a work of subtle but Christian apologetics. Its apparent worldliness is dictated by a hidden aim. For does not the writer go on, in verse three, to say "What does man gain by all the toil at which he toils—*under the sun?*" Again I emphasize those last three words. What we have here is a thoroughgoing critique of secularism presented in the guise of radical agnosticism . . .

Henry looked at the dogwood on the coffin. He looked away and through the window where trapped and buzzing flies crawled up and down the glass, seeking escape, and saw outside in the woods a stand of living dogwood in full flower and a mass of budding red maple at the edge of a field—Bill Gatlin's field, plowed but not yet harrowed.

A pang of remembrance pierced his heart. Henry remembered himself at the age of two years, riding on his father's shoulders for the first turn around that field on top of the hill, where the strip mine now began. He remembered his fists clenched in Joe's thick black hair, his bare legs clamped around his father's neck. He had to hold on for dear life because his father had both hands on the plow. In front of the plow, lugging it forward, was the span of horses. The double bridle lines hung looped over the plow handles but Joe seldom had to touch them. They began at the southeast corner of the field near the lane that came up through the woods.

At the end of the first furrow Joe Lightcap laid the plow on its side
and swung the team around. Whoa, he said. He straightened the
plow and turned the moldboard over with his foot, so that the second furrow would be thrown in the opposite direction. The first
few furrows on the lower edge of a field were always thrown uphill—the gathering in—to prevent the gradual buildup, over years,
of a ridge along the fencerow. The team waited.

The boy jogged in place on his father's shoulders, eager to get
moving.

Lightcap spoke to the horses. They squatted for the start of the
pull, massive haunches spread and braced, and leaned into their
collars. The plowshare sank down and in, forging ponderously forward, crunching through rootlets from the trees below the rail fence,
grating between stones, heaving the brown moist earth up, out,
over on the curve of the gleaming moldboard, leaving behind a kerf
that was parallel and true—not to the edge of an imaginary rectan-
gle, but to the first furrow across the fall line of the slope.

Quiet work. The only noise was that of the yielding soil, the strain
of horses and harness leather, the rattle of metal, the questioning
cries of robins in the brush along the fence, where Lightcap always
left a wide belt of weeds, briars and grass. He shared the hill farmer's aversion to a clean and tidy fencerow. He liked a strip of wildness bordering his fields—a home for rabbits and insect-devouring
birds.

Halfway back across the field Joe stopped the team and squatted
down to examine the soil. The boy slid from his shoulders. Joe took
a ball of damp rich dark earth in his huge hand. Look at this,
Henry. He crumbled the soil in his hand. Four earthworms lay in
his palm, slowly coiling and uncoiling their slim pink slick bodies.
Fishin' worms, Henry. He let the worms fall to the ground. You sit
here, son, keep an eye on them worms. I'll take a turn and be right
back.

Henry was not alarmed. So long as he could see his father, lurching off behind the huge shapes of plow and horses, he was not frightened. He loved everything about his father—the coarseness of his
hair, the powerful sweating neck and wide shoulders, the smell of
his cigarette, the sound of his deep soft voice.

Forgetting his father he watched the earthworms crawl into the
dirt. He caught one and ate it, together with the dirt. Saliva and

soil the color of tobacco juice trickled from the corners of his mouth. He ate a second worm.

Henry heard the clash of the locking moldboard. He stood up and struggled over the big clods toward the horses and the man.

They came toward him, gigantic figures towering into the sky, blocking off the sun. They stopped. The horses stared down at the little boy. Green thick saliva drooled from the bridle bits. Vision limited by leather blinders, the horses shook their heads from side to side, trying to get a clear view of the child below. Their shaggy forelegs stood like treetrunks, their mighty feet like boulders in the earth. Sweat glistened on their chests.

The boy tried to find a way around the horses, calling for his father, beginning to be scared.

Joe appeared beside the team, reached down for Henry, swept him up and around, above his head, and placed him once again astride his neck. What's the matter, Henry? Hey? Think we forgot you? His father rolled another cigarette, pasting it to his lower lip and lighting it, then started the horses. The plow handles jerked and twisted in Lightcap's fingers. He tightened his grip and tramped on, rough but steady, over the clods. Henry held to his father's hair. The cool damp earth steamed behind them, vapor rising in the sunlight under the smoky blue of the West Virginia mountains.

Lightcap worked on. At noon by the sun he unhitched the horses and led them down to the water trough—a hollowed-out log—below the spring in the woods. Henry rode Ben, the older steadier horse, holding on to the brass knobs of the collar. Watered, Joe brought the team back to the open field and let them browse on the stubble and weeds. He and little Henry sat on the warm brown grass in a corner of the fence, leaning back against the split rails, and ate fried-egg sandwiches in thick slabs of Lorrie's home-baked bread coated with Lorrie's home-churned butter. They ate small cool knobby apples, tart but sweet, from the bin in the cellar. They ate the fried drumsticks from a pullet named Hoot, who'd strayed too close to the back porch once too often. They each ate a homemade cookie stuffed with stewed raisins. Joe drank the lukewarm coffee from the bottom of the bucket. Little Henry drank chocolate-flavored milk from a half-pint jar. Lightcap rolled himself another Bugler cigarette. Henry chased white cabbage butterflies through the grass. He never caught one. But he always chased them. In the child's eyes they seemed to shimmer like fairies in the April sunlight.

. . . Remember also your Creator in the days of youth, young Reverend Cripps was reciting, before the evil days come, and the years draw nigh when you will say, I have no pleasure in them. . . .

Henry looked at Will. Will stared down at his big rough hands, contemplating his grease-filled fingernails. Beyond Will sat their mother, watching the young preacher. Her eyes, behind their glasses, had a clouded appearance. She would soon be undergoing an operation for cataracts. Her face, touched here and there with the brown spots of aging (too much sun) seemed more birdlike than ever. But she was tough inside, indomitable. Beyond Lorraine sat Sister Marcie, a grown woman now, thirty years old, married and mother of two. She had the dark skin, the beaked nose, the long thick black hair of the Lightcap branch—and the Shawnee strain.

Two of us are missing, Henry thought. Brother Jim in Canada, refusing to serve in the Johnson-Nixon War. And Paul, young Paul, the sweetest gentlest happiest Lightcap who ever lived. Where is Paul? Why, Paul lies nearby, not far at all, only two hundred yards away, down in the earth beside that gaping hole waiting for Paw. Paul has his brass star and his little flag set in its holder, waving over the grass. Home from Korea—Truman's War.

At last we are ready, continued the minister, to look beyond our earthly vanities to God the Creator who made us for Himself. The title Creator is well chosen here, reminding us from earlier passages in Ecclesiastes that He alone sees the pattern of existence whole (chapter three, verse eleven); that His was the workmanship we have spoiled by our devices (chapter seven, verse twenty-nine); and that His creativity is continuous and unresearchable (chapter eleven, verse five). If all is futility under the sun, as even the strongest of us must feel from time to time, as Joseph Lightcap must have felt that last day in the forest, what is there to save us from sinking into despair? Only this: remember thy Creator. Nothing under the sun is ours to keep, least of all life itself. But the spirit returns to God who gave it. And that, my friends, my brothers and sisters, is the end of the matter. Chapter twelve, verse thirteen: Fear God and keep His commandments, for this is the whole duty of man. Let me conclude:

There is a time to mourn, there is also a time to sing and dance. Today we mourn the passing of our brother Joseph, beloved by wife and family. But in those tomorrows yet to come, unless our faith is false, we shall know—beyond the sun—that joy toward which all human longing aims. We shall dance, we shall sing, we shall know the joy of God's love forever, and behold again the faces of those we loved on earth. That is the promise of our belief. For even in this the most bitter, harsh, pessimistic book of the Bible, we find that faith reaffirmed. There is no death, no departure, no tragedy that we cannot overcome by the power of faith. Vanity of vanities, sayeth the Preacher, all is vanity—and the greatest vanity of all is to think that our life on earth is the only life there is.

Here Dr. Cripps paused to gaze once more at the faces and into the eyes of the mourners, and in particular, the eyes of the Lightcap family. Those hard gray cold eyes stared back at him. Only in the eyes of the widow Lorraine and the daughter Marcie could he see a reflection of sympathy, a will to share in his affirmation. They at least were capable of tears.

The young man sighed inwardly, bowed his head, led the prayer. He may have felt, as Henry thought, watching him, that the content of his sermon cut no ice with anyone. No one believed in the referential object of the theopathic rhetoric. The words were meant for ceremony, not meaning. The ritual was the meaning, the only meaning available, to this tiny group of sidehill farmers—grim gaunt red-faced men with bad teeth, wearing stiff black suits, and their lean worn pale women in flowered prints, veils hanging from the brims of little round black hats, wrinkled stockings on varicose calves, feet cramped and aching in their high-heeled Sunday shoes.

Presently the time came to convey Joe Lightcap to his last known permanent address. Will and Henry and the four other pallbearers lifted the crude coffin to their shoulders and bore it out of the church, through the yard, across the dirt road and up the short incline to the graveyard. They passed the Hintons, the Fettermans, the Lingenfelters, the Cotters, the McIntyres, the McElhoes, the McNairs, the Gatlins, the Brandons, the Wades, the Conways, the Taits, the Ginters, the Adamses, and arrived at the site reserved for Lightcaps.

Will passed a rope under each end of the coffin. He and the other men lowered the coffin into the grave. The Reverend Cripps recited the litany for the dead. The widow stepped forward in her turn and dropped a handful of dirt onto the lid of the coffin, making a hollow drumming sound. No one could have likened it to rain falling on a roof. Joe, Lorrie said, as she gazed down at the box, I'll be with you pretty soon. She cried, but quietly, dabbing at her face with a handkerchief. What, join the old man beyond the grave? Not likely. None of us believed that our mother would do anything of the kind; she'd outlive us all.

Marcie followed her mother to the side of the grave, adding her handful of earth. She was crying freely by now and not quietly either. She was the one who really and always loved that cranky, embittered, isolate old man. Dad, Marcie said, half choking on her sobs, I loved you, Dad. You be good now. On that note she nearly giggled, embarrassed by her words. I mean . . . you know what I mean. I mean we'll never forget you. Some of us won't, anyhow. You were a good sweet dad to me. You. . . . Well, anyhow, good-bye for now. She broke away and tottered blindly into her mother's arms.

Henry's turn. He stepped to the edge of the abyss and pulled a harmonica from his suitcoat pocket. He played that largo theme from that Dvorak symphony to which the words *Going home* were inevitably added. Small audience softened to a state of plasmic impressionability, Henry made a speech. He said, My father was a vain stubborn self-centered stiff-necked poker-playing whiskey-drinking gun-toting old son of a—gun. He was a good hunter, a good trapper, a poor farmer and a hotshot but reckless logger. He was hard on himself, on trees, machines and the earth. He never gave his wife the kind of home she wanted or the kind of life she deserved. He was cantankerous, ornery, short-tempered and contentious—probably the most contentious man that ever lived in Shawnee County. He was so contentious he never even realized how contentious he was. He had strong opinions on everything and a neighborly view on almost nothing. He was a hard man to get along with. But I'll say this for him: he was honest. He never cheated anyone. He was gentle with children and animals. He always spoke his mind. And he was a true independent. Independent, like we say, as a hog on ice. I mean he really believed in self-reliance and liberty. He was what some call a hillbilly—but we call a mountaineer. The mountaineer is a free man. Yes, I know, West Virginia was sold to the coal companies and the chemical companies. Most of the people who live in this sad wrinkled-up pancreas-shaped state are serfs and peons these days, helpless dependents on the big corporations. But someday we're going to change all that. West Virginians refused to fight for slavery in 1863; one of these days we're going to fight against slavery. *Montani semper liberii*—*sic*—mountain men will always be free. Our old man believed in that motto. And someday we're going to prove him right. So long, Paw.

Henry picked up a clod of dirt, crumbled it in his fist and cast the earthy crumbs on Joe Lightcap's coffin. Grinning in his guts, grim-faced with satisfaction, he stepped back among the others. No one looked at him.

Will was the last to pay tribute. He stepped forward. He held Paw's big broken forty-pound chainsaw in his hand. A McCulloch original. He looked into the grave for a minute, then dropped the chainsaw on the coffin. It made an awful clatter. He said nothing and turned away.

Well if that don't wake him up, thought Henry, I reckon nothing ever will.

The ceremony was complete. Mother walked away, arm in arm with her sister, Mary Holyoak, and Uncle Jeff and Marcie. The remainder of the mourners—all nine of them—shuffled off. Last to leave was the young minister. He shook hands with Will and Henry. I liked your sermon, he said to Henry; you ought to be a preacher yourself.

I've thought of it, admitted Henry. And I liked your sermon too. Except for that last part—chapter twelve. I always did think chapter twelve must have been stitched on later. Maybe by some tent-maker who was good at patching up holes.

The Reverend Cripps smiled. Why persecutest thou me? It's a matter of interpretation, Mr. Lightcap. I once thought what you think. And then I thought again. He smiled once more, nodded and left, a long-haired short-legged little man on his way to the next Presbyterian outpost in Shawnee County. There were not many.

Will and Henry watched him as he hastened to catch up with the widow and pay his respects to her.

Will said, You gonna let him get away with that, Henry? Ain't you gonna give him an argument?

I was afraid he was waiting for the tip.

Uncle Jeff'll take care of that. That's Holyoak business. He's the banker.

Henry looked at the open grave. Who's going to fill in the hole?

Will began to remove his coat. Me and you. He paused, looked down the hill toward the church and took a pint bottle, half full, from an inside pocket, and unscrewed the cap. Old Forester. He took a pull and handed the bottle, half empty, to Henry.

Henry poured a modest portion on the coffin, then took a deep swig for himself. He wiped his mouth and looked down again at the wrecked chainsaw. Kind of a cheap gesture, Will. Why not the old crosscut saw? Or why not that beautiful two-bitted ax that Paw was always so proud of? Remember how he always said, if he found himself going down the New River in a sinking canoe, the first thing he'd grab would be his ax?

Yeah. Will folded his suitcoat and laid it carefully on the clean grass of Paul's grave. He loosened his necktie and rolled up his shirt-sleeves. He picked up the two spades resting behind the dirt pile and handed one across the open grave to Henry. Yeah. . . .

How come, Will?

How come what? Will spat on his palms and rubbed them together.

How come the chainsaw instead of the ax?

Will put his foot on the top edge of the spade and thrust it deep into the dirt. He levered up a full load and swung it easily into the grave. The dirt boomed on the hollow box below. He paused. Because, he said. Because that ax is a good tool. I already took all the parts I could use out of that there busted chainsaw.

An hour later they climbed in the wagon and drove slowly down the red-dog road toward home. There was no other traffic through the woods. A little rain came down; petals of dogwood and leathery oak leaves lay scattered across the road. Thinking it evening, fooled again, the spring peepers began bleating their hearts out along the creek. Will and Henry rode the wagon into the Lightcap barn, un-hitched the horses and walked them in harness the two miles farther to the Houser farm. When they got back to their own place, still walking, the April twilight had settled in. Marian and Marcie with her husband, Frank, and Lorrie waited for them. Supper was ready.

The remainder of the Joe Lightcap family gathered around the dining room table, laid with a fresh cloth. Mother said a prayer:

O Lord we thank thee
once again. Thou hast taken
another from us but the family
remains. Paul is gone and now
Joe is gone also. And our youngest
lives in exile. But we trust and
hope that he will be returned someday
when the war is over. Meanwhile we take
great joy in the young ones brought into
the world by Will and Marian and Frank
and Marcie. Some are gone, some stay,
and the new lives come. Bless this house forever.
O Lord, we thank thee.

All seated themselves, leaving empty the place at the head of the table. They ate their supper in an amber glow of lamplight and memory. The meal consisted of mashed potatoes and turnips with venison gravy (Henry's favorite dish), venison sausage (Will's favorite, from a buck poached the season before on the side of Cheat Mountain) and string beans and tomatoes from Mother's garden. (Canned the year before.)

Near the end of the meal Lorrie announced that she was renting a small apartment near her brother Jeff's house in Shawnee. She had decided that she was going to enroll as a student at the Shawnee State Teachers' College, study music history, comparative religion, world literature and whatever else caught her interest. Too old? She was only sixty-four. Then to Marian and Will our mother said, I would like you two to live in this house. This place is too big and lonesome for me now. You kept the farm alive all these years; you deserve to live here. Marcie already has a good home. And Henry . . . She looked at him.

Henry grinned back at her. And I'm a westerner.

Yes, she said, you're the westerner.

So it happened. Will and his wife took possession of the farmhouse and with it title to the farm itself—barn, pigpen, sheds, well, springs, implements, pastures, fences, fields and woods—all that remained after our old man had logged off the old-growth timber, planted twenty acres in Christmas trees, left a sawdust pile by the creek, turned the barnyard into a lumberyard, grazed the meadow to death with a herd of black Angus beef cattle and leased one-third of the whole—180 acres minus 60—to the gas company and the coal company. (Union Carbide and U.S. Steel.)

At the age of forty Will finally came into his heritage.

Did he whine much or complain some about the sorry condition of his estate? Not that anyone ever heard. Not Will. Instead he got to work. Down to work.

While young Henry Lightcap went back to the West, put on his ranger suit, adjusted the brim of his big hat, and looked forward to the end of tourist season, only five and a half months away, when he would again be freed from routine and regular hours, eligible to resume collecting unemployment compensation, once more at liberty to reconsider, on a fool-time basis, the ontological significance if any of sublunar existence. Such as it is. If it exists. Precisely the question. And also there was Claire. And Pamela. Also Sandy. And Candy. And Heather and Tammy and Ingrid, Valerie, Vanessa, Kitty and X. Not to mention Waylon Jennings, Willie Nelson, Domenico Zapoli and Johann Sebastian Bach. Or Ludwig Wittgenstein, Arthur Schopenhauer, Diogenes in his doghouse, Heidegger in his Alpine cabin, Montaigne on his tower. And that lonesome juniper tree that lives by itself on a ledge of Jurassic sandstone three thousand feet above the confluence of the Green and Colorado rivers. Under the sun. Under God. God the fodder, God the ghost and God the holy sun. Deep in the space-time manifold.

And also there was Claire.

15

DREAMS

Eastward, onward, I drive through Kansas in the moonlight. (Someone has to do it.) Or more exactly, through the moonlight over Kansas. The moonlight lends a special glamour to the flattest world. Nor do I mean to cast disdain upon our flattest state. No sir, by God, this is where our wheat comes from. Our bread, and more beef, honest unsubsidized taxpaying beef, than in the whole vast mythical sagebrush empires of Montana, Wyoming, Nevada, Utah and Idaho combined. In the Rocky Mountain states ranching is a rich man's hobby but in the midwestern states, in the heart of the heart of America, it's an earnest business carried on by serious folk doing real work for a worthy purpose: food.

Cowboys. Cowboyism. I toss my empty out the window (Kansas needs a bottle bill) and screw the cap off another jug of Blatz. Rolla flits by at my elbow; ten miles of farmland then Hugoton; eleven miles and Moscow; sixteen and Satanta.

Change the subject. The wind shrieks past my ear. Think of death and immortality. I extricate the pill bottle from the mess of junk in the glove box, brace the steering wheel between my knees and shake one small round tab of Dilaudid onto my palm. I pop the pill into my mouth and wash it down with a slug of the cheap rotten beer. A regular Lightcap nightcap these days and not for nothing either. I should have bedded down back there on the banks of the arid Cimarron but the moonlight and the crickets made me nervous. The furies of memory drove me on. Now I'll be forced by the pill to find a campsite within thirty minutes.

Seven miles from Satanta to Sublette. The moon shines down through a decent veil of clouds. The horizon is ringed with the lights of industrial agriculture—yard lights, security lights, flood lights, traffic lights. Each town crouches with empty streets beneath its grain elevators, pale lordly concrete towers lined up between highway and railway.

Oil pressure down. I pause at an all-night gas station for fuel and two quarts of cheap oil. Can't afford it, cashwise—less than $150 in my pocket now—but I've got to nurse the old Dodge along.

The heavy-duty painkiller weighs on my eyelids. For a moment I doze off, then awake with an electric shock of panic to find myself veering into the left lane the wrong lane of this backcountry two-lane highway. I jerk my truck to the right. A forty-ton tractor-trailer rig thunders past on my left, air horn blaring. Cattle truck: the reek of doomed beasts floats on the air. I think of Auschwitz, Belsen, Dachau, Karaganda, Vorkuta, Igarka.

Watch the road, goddamnit. My political nightmares are leading me straight into the ditch. I stick my face out the window for a blast of cold air. That helps, for a minute.

Dirt road off on the right. I stop, reverse, stop, drive into an endless plantation of sorghum and soybeans. The road dead-ends at a water-pumping station. When I shut off my engine I hear the drone of electric motors. This won't do. I return to the highway and continue east into a town named Copeland. Under looming cathedrals of grain I drive through two yellow lights and past the United Brethren Church.

Where there's a church there's the dead. Slowing down, I look for the cemetery, find it and steer down a grassy lane bounded by a fence of steel railings set in concrete posts. I turn a corner and park in the darkness under a tree, another Chinese elm—tree of the prairie.

Time to pill the dog. I give her her Nizoral, a pan of water, a bowl of Purina crunchy granola and spread her rug beneath the rear of my truck. The sky looks clear. The wind has stopped. The graveyard smells newly mown—a sweet odor of timothy hangs in the air. No mercury vapor lights here and no sounds either. No watchman prowling about. In Copeland the dead are allowed to sleep in peace. Bedroll under my arm, I slip through the bars of the fence and spread my sack on cool grass. I lie down among tomb-stones named Houck, Loucke, Starke, Miller, Harrison, Studebaker and Poole. Poole? I look again. Yes, my bedmate for the night is "Thyria Poole, 1872–1963." Goodnight, Thyria. Sweet dreams.

I dream of Claire.

16

1970:

HENRY AT WORK

Yes, it was a good sweet job. Old Gibbsie was a good superintendent. The United States government was a government. Henry
Lightcap had found his niche, his slot, his cranny, his refuge in the
vast vermiculate edifice of the American socioeconomy. And he kept
it too, off and on, for the next fifteen years, working five, six months
a year in various national parks and national forests, through national chaos and international calamity. Brother Will might disap-
prove, thinking such work unworthy of a full-grown man, little
better than welfare, but for Henry Lightcap—a "fool-grown man,"
as he liked to explain, such a part-time occupation made the ideal
vocation. Henry Lightcap needed those half years free. Why? For
what? For the sake of freedom itself, he told his inner critic. Liberty
like virtue is its own reward, the only reward it's likely to get. And
for the sake of simplicity—*la vie philosophique.* Was he, Henry, a
disgrace to the ancient name of Lightcap? Perhaps. But Henry had
conceded, long before the end, that if he couldn't grow up to be
functional at least he could be ornamental—like tits on a motor.
Like ticks on a dog. If not meant to be a wise man he'd settle for
the role of wise guy. Every cobbler to his last? Exactly. Life is a
bitch, his dark companion said—and then you die. Not so! cried
Henry. Life is a glorious shining and splendid adventure—and *then*
you die. Furthermore (there's always that), Henry felt that by contributing nothing to the annual Gross National Product he was
thereby subtracting even less from what was left of the Net National
Heritage. He himself would carry out a private one-man revolution
in the belly of the beast. Freedom begins between the ears. The

Good Life starts where servitude ends. In a nation of sheep one brave man is a majority.

Theory. There was a flaw in the program. The program did not appeal to women, especially married women, especially those married women married to Henry Lightcap. No, screamed Myra (for example), I will not spend my life drifting from park to park, scraping by on unemployment checks, living in a nomadic state. How about Utah, he'd suggested. No! Arizona? Impossible! Alaska? Never! Well, he said, there's Idaho. Why not Siberia? she said; at least then the misery would be permanent. I'll apply, he said. The divorce papers followed soon after.

He liked the job. He even liked the uniform: the green and the gray, the forest green trousers and the cool gray shirts, the fawn-colored Stetson ranger hat, his badge with silver eagle, the arrowhead shoulder patch, the shiny boots and Smith & Wesson .38. He was good for the part and knew it. Henry Lightcap looked as a ranger should look—tall, dark, handsome, not too bright.

He loved the work itself, driving the dusty roads in his dusty new government pickup, patrolling the rocky trails on foot and on horseback, rescuing fat men in distress, answering questions from admiring tourists, and best of all delivering the weekly Campfire Talk—he loved to talk—among a circle of pretty girls, admiring matrons, dozing children, aware of the play of firelight and shadow on his eagle beak nose, his Shawnee cheekbones and his haggard ax-hewn jaw:

"These ancient ontological rocks," he'd explain, "were laid down eons ago in the Sedimentary Era by an aquarian sea that oceanographers call Lake Wittgenstein, after the noted paleontologist of the same name. Opinions differ, of course, as to the exact age of these monumental formations. Deep-time eschatologists such as Dr. Wilhelm Reich of Harvard College (the 'Stanford of the East') believe they were deposited during the shifting of Teutonic Plates in the great Triassic hullabaloo, when the diplodocus, the brontosaurus and the giant trilobite romped like happy children in the primordial sleaze. Others, such as the well-known biblical scholar Archbishop Ussher of Dublin College, Belfast, assert paragorically that the deposition took place a mere 4004 years B.C. during the last Jurassic Period. However—questions? Yes, miss?"

One pale hand had risen, spontaneously, from the lap of a maid with flaxen braids and bright bold blue-gray eyes in a face of heart-troubling ellipsoidal symmetry. Henry had noticed her at once, from the beginning. She sat cross-legged on the sand near the ceremonial fire of juniper, her skirt hiked up far enough to expose a pair of glossy kneecaps to the light. Beyond those knees would be sleek convergent thighs leading—who knows where? Straight into trouble, that's for certain. Smiling, the girl asked her question.

Henry paused, also smiling, and repeated the question for the benefit of those sitting on the far benches. "The young lady's question was, Am I married?" Henry gave the crowd his big toothy loose and goofy grin. "To which I can only reply, in the words of the immortal Benedict Spinoza, 'You better ask my wife.' " (Laughter.) "Seriously, folks, a married philosopher could only be a figure of fun. Right?" (Silence.) "Actually I live alone. Not necessarily by choice. Now where was I?" He continued his lecture on the monoliths, the holes, the bores, the natural and human history of the park, the cactus, the forest, concluding with his standard peroration. "Now I want everybody to have a good time while you're here. If you get lost, report to me at once. Please don't stone the bunny rabbits and if you see a rattlesnake lurking about, hobble the sonofabitch. Don't sit on the cactus; this is a national heritage natural monument and all flora and fauna were placed here for your enjoyment and are protected by law. Take only pictures, leave only Kleenex, goodnight and God bless you all."

The crowd rose, murmuring, and drifted away, flashlights winking on, campers finding their way back to tents, trailers, motorhomes. The girl with the braids remained behind, facing Henry, a sly smile on her rosy face. "Have any Band-Aids?" she asked.

He tried to ignore the spurt of adrenaline to his heart. "What's wrong?"

She showed him a red slash across her bare calf. "This. I guess I backed into something." It was only a scratch; the blood had already clotted and dried.

"That looks serious," Henry said. "Good thing I'm a doctor."

"You're a doctor of malarkey." She was grinning at him. "I never heard such a line of bull as you gave those nice people."

"I improvise a bit."

"A bit? You're outrageous. My father's a professor of geology. If he was here you'd be in deep trouble."

Henry looked around. The fire had died down. They were alone. "What's your name?"

"Claire Mellon. What's yours?" He pointed to the official name tag above his right shirt pocket. "Henry H. Lightcap," she read aloud, leaning close. He smelled the fragrance of apple blossoms. "What's the H. stand for?"

"Holyoak. We're an old Druid family."

"You're a kidder and a wise guy. But that's all right, I like you anyway." She paused. His move. But for the moment he could think of nothing to say. She hesitated, about to turn away. "Guess I'd better go. . . ."

"Wait. . . ." O stay, stay, fair maiden. "Would you like a beer? Something to eat, maybe? We could—we could go to my trailer-house." He gestured into the dark. "Right over there." Anxiety.

"Well . . ." she said. And looked around. They were surrounded by night, a few distant lanterns. The constellations of the desert hung above them like flaming chandeliers. "Actually I don't much like beer. Do you have any white wine?"

I've got Blatz and Schlitz, he thought; chablis with a head on it. "Yes," he lied. "Of course."

"Well . . ." Again she hesitated. "But only for a minute. My mother's waiting for me in our tent. You sure it's okay?"

"Come on." He touched her elbow, led her away from the glow of the embers. He was supposed to drown that fire dead before leaving. But what could burn in this place? The sand? The rock? His blood was burning.

They walked down the winding dirt road toward the little government housetrailer, a half mile off, where Henry lived. She seemed to be leaning toward him, looking up at the stars. He named a few constellations for her but she knew them better than he did. He longed to put his arm around that small firm waist not six inches from his right hand. But dared not. The panicky angels of love panted in his ear. He felt like a teenage acne-cursed gland-enslaved, girl-haunted adolescent. He tried to think of something intelligent, something clever, something engaging to say. Say something, he thought. But what? "Where's your father?"

"My parents are separated. It's pretty awful."

"It's like an amputation," Henry agreed. In more ways than one,

304

he thought; costs you an arm and a leg. However, the limbs grow back. "How old are you?"

"I'm nineteen," she said. "How old are you?"

"Thirty-nine and a half," he lied. He was forty-three.

"I thought so. You have that mature look."

He was disappointed; he thought he looked at least ten years younger. Maybe he should shave off the moustache, chew gum, play a guitar, sing folk songs. Cultivate some pimples.

"I suppose you get awfully lonely out here?"

"Oh—yes and no. Sometimes. How about you?"

"I don't live here. Remember?" She laughed. "You're the one that lives here. I live in Denver."

Love, he thought, I'm in love again. It's horrible.

"Tell me," she asked, "do you think I'm beautiful?"

"What?" The sweat trickled from his armpits.

"Don't be vague."

"Well Jesus Christ. . . ." What's her name? "Jesus Christ, Claire, what kind of question is that? Why do girls always ask that?"

"Because it's hard to be sure. Because it seems to be so important. I'm sick of it."

"You know you're beautiful. Don't you?"

"That's what they say. And I'm supposed to be grateful. Actually I'm sick of it. Sometimes I wish I was fat and ugly, life would be simpler."

Beauty, he thought, is only skin-deep. Ugliness goes all the way through. His mind raced forward, upward, sideways, sprayed out in all directions, a fountain of foolishness. He was painfully aware, as always, of the sheer impossibility of saying exactly what he thought, of saying everything he felt. Candor was impossible but sincerity essential. He compromised, as usual, on the facetious. "Ugliness is only skin-deep. Beauty goes all the way through."

"You are a kidder and a wise guy."

"I was a philosophy major. Well, a second lieutenant. That's why I'm totally confused. Ask me a question, I think of sixteen possible answers, all false. The result is a kind of infantile paralysis."

"I like you anyway. I think I'll major in veterinary medicine."

"You love horses," he said. Should I grab her, he wondered, kiss her right now? Or later? God but it's horrible.

"All girls love horses. I suppose I'll grow out of it. But why philosophy? You look more like one of those country-western music types."

A banjo picker? His vanity was hurt. But he said, in simple honesty, "I wanted to know something about everything."

"Everything?"

"What else is there?"

That made her laugh. And as she laughed he pulled her close and kissed her square on her small neat mouth. She tasted as sweet and warm as she looked. He wanted more but she averted her face and pulled away. "Why'd you do that?"

Why did I do that? Sixteen good sound reasons flashed like neon signs across his brain, none requiring analysis. "It seemed like a good idea. A seminal idea."

She smiled. "Well don't get any ideas."

He was disappointed by the commonplace expression. But reassured by the expression on her face, the sly smile on her lips. She's teasing me and she knows it. And I love it. And she knows it. In what country but America could a girl expect to play a man this way and hope—expect—to get away with it, unpollinated? If she did. Did she? Her mere presence, being here alone with him, was all the invitation a man needed. And if she objected, tried to run away, that would be the most provocative movement of any, triggering in a man—as in a bear—the instinctive reflex of pursuit, capture, ravishment, assault with a friendly weapon. For what could be more provocative to a man than the dorsal view of a female in flight? Origin of The Chase. But how could you explain any of this to any girl, any woman? Well, you didn't have to; they understood it well enough, deep inside, down there in the molten core of the female sexual organism. To be sexually attractive is to be perpetually on guard. A pretty girl lives in a state of constant siege. And how we loved it—the tension, the conflict, the promise of delight. Such were the notions that sped, within seconds, like rush-hour traffic, through the imagination of Henry Lightcap.

But all he said, opening the door to his trailer, was "Come on in." Like the spider to the fly.

She hesitated again, reluctant to proceed through any door, whether in or out. And with good reason. "Don't you have any lights? It's dark in there."

"I'll light a candle."

"No electricity?"

"It's kind of a humble abode. We're twenty miles from the nearest powerline."

"You go in first."

He went in first, fumbled about, found and lit the stub of candle stuck to a saucer on the table. Sound of mice in a scurry of flight. Bending over the low flame, lean face illuminated from below, Lightcap appeared as inviting as Boris Karloff playing Franken-stein's monster. "Come in," he repeated, as the girl remained half in half out the open doorway, feline and cautious as a pussycat. A moth fluttered in above her shining hair and dove headfirst into the flame. Showing off. Passed through and bashed itself against the wall, sticking there, wondering *What the hell happened?*

"I'm not sure I should do this."

"Do what?"

"Come into your—whatever this is. You look like a giant spi-der."

He grinned at her and held open his arms. The effect was ghastly. "Me? Look—two arms, two legs. I'm only half a spider. Come in for godsake and shut the door and sit down."

Slowly she did as invited. After all, she was an American girl; she'd risk a lot for a small adventure. In her nineteen years she had yet to encounter a man she couldn't handle. But she left the door open and sat close to it. Nervous but interested she stared around at the compact interior of the little housetrailer. A machine for liv-ing.

Henry, much more nervous than Miss Mellon, groped through the unlit propane refrigerator, emerging with two cans of beer. He found the magnetic church key, two cone-shaped beer glasses, and sat down at the table opposite his guest.

"What's this?"

"Beer. Blatz beer—it was on sale."

"You said you had wine."

He opened her can with two deft thrusts of the opener—no college education is entirely wasted—and filled her glass, spilling a little as the foam slopped over. "I lied," he confessed. "I never did that before." All generalizations are false.

"I'd prefer chablis."

He filled his own glass. "This is chablis with character. Blatz chablis."

"How plebeian."

"It was on sale—a whole case for $1.98." He tipped his glass against hers. "Skoal!" He gulped down a throatful. Christ, you'd think an old-timer like him, veteran of marriage, divorce, a dozen love affairs, would have more grace. But it was always like this; and I'm operating under terrific pressure, he reminded himself.

She took a sip, made a grimace of distaste. "I really don't like beer."

"I've got some Jim Beam."

"What's that?"

He paused for a moment, touched by her innocence. But innocence is the wickedest of aphrodisiacs. "Well, Beam's a type of Kentucky wine made from corn." Fidgeting about, his knee touched hers beneath the narrow table and he felt a galvanic spark leap between them. My God! His heart swelled, his heartstrings tightened, and as they did his penis rose. Indeed there is, there must be a direct physical linkage between the two organs. But which is the marionette, which the player?

"Beam goes good with Coca-Cola; you'd like that."

"All right, I'll have a Coke."

"As a matter of fact I don't have any."

"You are absolutely the worst liar I ever met."

"You're only nineteen." Good God! he thought, unable to think at all. I'm fucking up royally here. He blathered on, trying to conceal his desperation. He hadn't made love to a woman for—two months. An age. A geological epoch. "Well now tell me all about yourself. You live in Denver? What school are you going to? What's your middle name? Do you like Kurt Vonnegut? Norman Mailer? William Faulkner? Walt Whitman? Play any musical instruments? Which? The violin? Do you like Mozart? Roy Acuff? Bartók? George Jones? Carl Orff? The Sons of the Pioneers? The Champs? The Comets? Bob Dylan? Dylan Thomas?"

She sat there smiling at him, answering his questions more or less, but not letting him get between her and the open door. "Are you serious?" she asked. "Or just crazy?"

Serious? he thought, brain spinning like a flywheel. Testicles connected to the ventricles; ventricles connected to the frontal lobes; frontal lobes connected to the eyeballs. And am I serious? I'm in love, that's what I am, sick with love. And Henry should know, he'd fallen in love thirty-five times in the last twenty-five years. Ever since he came to understand the limitations of masturbation. "Crazy?" he said. "Here I'm yammering like an idiot and you just sit there smiling. Don't let you get in a word edgeways. So why don't you say something, don't let me do all the talking, drink your beer like a good girl and give me a piece of your mind, such as it is, what the hell, I can take it, didn't I make a professional study of detachment, disinterest, the powers of intellectual withdrawal from the mundane and the material? Of course I did. And by the way we still haven't treated that wound of yours, let me see." Getting up again, knocking over his chair, he felt about in the blackness of the cabinet above the sink. "—I think we've got some bandage compresses here, Band-Aids, a hemostat or two, yes, here we are, now let me see that calf again."

Smiling, she turned her leg about, pulled up the hem of her skirt and exposed the injury. Henry went down on one knee and in the guttering light of the dying candle unpeeled a Band-Aid and applied it to the cut. Manfully he resisted the impulse to lick at her knee like a friendly dog. Heroically he fought back the urge to bury his face between her thighs, crawling onward and upward with his tongue for a foot.

"Thank you," she said, withdrawing her limb.

"You're welcome," he said, lurching back into his chair. They stared at each other in sudden embarrassed silence. Now what? "Drink your beer," he suggested. "It's good cheap Blatz."

"I hate Blatz."

There was another short silence. She hates my Blatz, he thought.

Half sighing, she glanced at her wristwatch. "Well, I suppose I ought to go. . . ."

"Oh no, no, wait a minute." O stay, thou art so fair. Jumping up, he fumbled around in the fridge again. "Let me see, maybe there is a Coke in here, a Pepsi or something. You like tomato juice?"

"Only in the morning." She stood up. "I'd better go. My mother will be having a fit. She wants to get off early tomorrow."

He straightened, stared at her. Her words struck hard. She was looking out the open doorway at the spray of stars beyond the silhouette of a phallic pinnacle. "Claire?" She made no reply. "Look, Claire, I have an idea. Let's—make love."

That got her attention. "I'd better go." She stepped toward the doorway. He grabbed her wrist. "Don't," she said, "please." Ashamed, he released her. She stepped outside and stopped, looking up at him. "I'm sorry," she said. "I know I kind of led you on. I just wanted to—see what you were like."

"I'll marry you."

"Oh God," she laughed. "You are crazy. Anyway you're already married. Aren't you?"

"That's neither here nor there." He grinned at her, somewhat relieved, having opened the raincoat and exhibited himself frankly. At least he'd made his overture. "But I'm not. Not anymore."

"Aren't you serious about anything?" But she was smiling. "You'll walk me back to camp, won't you? I'm afraid of rattlesnakes and I don't have a flashlight. Okay?" She gave him her prettiest smile. "You could come and see me in Denver sometime, maybe, if you want to. It's only four hundred fifty miles away. That's nothing for you rangers, right?"

He walked her back to the campground, arm around her waist. They stood face-to-face in the starlight before her mother's tent. Is that you, dear? Yes Mother. It's late. I'll be right in, Mother. Whispering, she gave him a phone number. He gave her a kiss. One final hot clasp of hand and she was gone. Forever, probably.

Henry shuffled homeward through the sand, among the junipers and the prickly pear. Don't let it bother you, he told himself. Girls are like buses; miss one, another will come along in five minutes. And then despised himself for entertaining so cheap and false and vulgar a thought. Not another like her, you fool.

His heart ached, his balls ached, his head ached. Back in the trailer he undressed, masturbated, popped three aspirins, drank a deep slug of Jim Beam and lay down naked on his bunk. Goodnight, Claire, I'll get you in my dreams. But could not sleep. He got up, pulled on socks and a pair of boots, nothing else, and went for a long nude walk into the desert, sucking on another can of Blatz.

He walked and he walked. He watched the Big Dipper swing past midnight. He saw Cassiopeia and Taurus the Bull and the Pleiades and the vast sprawl of Scorpio across the southern horizon. A shower of meteors punched holes through the ozone umbrella. He heard a rattlesnake wagging its tail, like a friendly dog, as he walked past its hiding place under a ledge. Heard a great horned owl call his name: *fool . . . fool . . . fool. . . .* He thought of Claire, Miss Claire Mellon—Honeydew!—and his heart rose and swelled like an unfolding hydrangea. My God I'm in love again.

Not again. Yes, again. The time bomb of romance had been planted and was ticking away. He knew the power of the uncompleted act. She'd be thinking of him. It might take a week, a month, a year, but sooner or later, probably later, she'd be writing to him, care of the National Park Service, Greasepit, Utah. Henry knew, he allowed no doubts and he was right.

He was always right. Only his means were wrong. Always wrong. But if the end don't justify the means, what can?

17

HEART OF THE HEART

I

Eastward, homeward, deep in the heart of Kansas, downhill most all the way.

The old Dodge chugs along like a stout but foundered Belgian plow horse, hitting on five maybe six out of eight. Not bad. Not good. We might be going up hills in reverse by the time we get to eastern Kentucky. My dog's not worried. Solstice she stares straight ahead, gaunt face and hollow eyes solemn, serious but unafraid. Looking death, old debts, billboards and nothingness straight in the eye, steadfast, unblinking. Heart beating within that rack of rib beneath that lusterless coat of hide and hair. Good dog, brave dog, braver than me.

Morning sun in our eyes. Dodge City lies ahead beyond those towers of grain, beneath that yellow eastern haze. Then Kinsley and Larned and Pawnee Rock. Then Great Bend on the bend of the Arkansas River.

Wind in my hair, dust on my sun goggles. Like the dog I ponder the question of annihilation. So easy to grasp the extinction of others, so hard to apply that theorem to oneself. Before I was conceived I was nothing. An eternity of nothing reaching back into nothing forever. Then a glimpse of light, a taste of consciousness, a heart-wrenching spasm of fear and a return to absolute nothing. Out of nothing we come, into nothing we go. The bird that flies from the night into the lighted banquet hall, circles twice around the blazing candles and then flies out—out of the light and back to the darkness. The world is a horrible place, said Bertrand Russell in an interview.

After death, said Schopenhauer on the "Today Show," you will be nothing—and you will be everything. He was interrupted by a station break and four commercials and never had a chance to explain the difference.

Consider the Christian alternative. Life after death in a world beyond time, beyond space. Where there is no time there can be no change, no motion or movement. No space implies no dimension. And yet we would be conscious—of what? Of God, they say, of His Love. We shall bask forever in the Love of God. (Forever is a long time.) Like staring at the sun with hands bound, head in a vise, your eyelids taped open—but in this case without even the hope of blindness or the salvation of shrieking insanity.

Suppose what survives bodily death is the disembodied soul—an ethereal consciousness lacking flesh, limbs, sense organs. Now imagine a living brain removed by clever surgeons from its familiar housing in the skull. Imagine this living, functioning, conscious brain afloat in a tray of sustaining liquids, racked among others in a laboratory incubator, thought flashing through the billions of neural synapses like sheet lightning in a gray cloudbank—mind aware of itself—imagine this brain without connection to eyes, ears, nose, tongue, touch, but awake and thinking, reworking over and over again its finite storage batteries of memory—for memory is all it has. Isolated, cut off from contact with any world but its internal self, this blind brain this floating bodiless consciousness would have no present, no future, and nothing to hope for but a lucky accident: a power failure, a clumsy move by a lab assistant that dashes the containing tray to the floor, the explosion of an overcharged electrode inserted deep in the cerebrum. But even this dim hope could be based on nothing but surmise; for the detached and living brain would have no means, no way whatsoever, to investigate and determine the nature of its horrifying predicament. What nightmares then might come half so hideous as its actual and immediate and inescapable situation?

The man-made world is a horrible place. Most of it. But not a tithe so horrible as the existence imagined for us beyond the grave. Given such conjectures, old-fashioned death—the decomposition of the body and the obliteration of consciousness—begins to assume a comforting aspect. A deep sleep in cool darkness among the cold stones, the grains of soil, the earthworms, the probing tendrils of the roots of trees. Don't sound so bad. But never to awake? *Never?* Even so—better that than the Hell of Christian Heaven, the torture chamber of spiritualist immortality. Picture a culture in which suicide is not only forbidden but effectively, scientifically prevented—and then we recognize the reassuring options of the anarchic slum we inhabit. Ours may be a horrible world; it is not the most horrible of all possible worlds. Cheerful thought: at once I feel much better.

Entering Dodge. Near the outskirts we pass through a few acres of natural unplowed unimproved prairie, one remnant of that sea of grass which formerly stretched from the Mississippi to the base of the Rocky Mountains. The open range. Where the buffalo roamed, where the deer and the antelope played for twenty thousand years. And then up from Texas came the mass herds of stinking shambling fly-specked dung-smeared bawling bellowing bulge-eyed cattle. Followed by cowboys, beef ranchers, barbed wire, cross fencing, locked gates, private property, whores, bores and real-estate developers.

Dodge City still looks more western than eastern but not by much. Where the East begins. Transition zone. Sign for NU OLD STUFF—an antique store. Another offers KANSAS OXYGEN (welding supplies). WAREHOUSE CARPET SALE. GAS & GO—GAS, BEER, DIESEL, GAMES! COOPER MUFFLER SERVICE. GOFF MOTORS LIKE NEW USED CARS. GOODWILL PRE-OWNED CARS. DILLON'S DOUBLE COUPON FOOD MARKET. BOB'S CAFÉ—HOME COOKED MEALS. MALCO GAS, REG 1.09. RIVER MOTEL—on the banks of the trickling Arkansas River. More gigantic grain elevators. The road to Boot Hill.

We leave the plastic highway strip and enter old town, downtown, the decayed and dying core of Dodge City. Two- and three-story buildings of red brick with square false fronts. An empty department store For Rent, Sale or Lease. Pawnshops full of unredeemed and burgled goods. The Santa Fe depot—locked and boarded up. A century-old hotel now a flophouse where abandoned cowpunchers sit staring at a TV set in the lobby, waiting for their Old Age Survivor's Insurance checks. Departing historic Front Street, three blocks long, we return to 1980, rumbling on rough asphalt past huge tractor and farm implement emporia, through another gauntlet of Big Boy, A&W, Kentucky Fried, Dairy Queen, Whiting Bros gas stations, Honest John used-car lots and Crazy Bill truck stops and into the suburbs—a half-mile-long feedlot in which

314

imprisoned Herefords, Charolais and black Angus beefburgers, on the hoof and more or less alive, standing room only, mill about under the sun on a carpet of mud, urine and manure. Past the Liquid Carbonics Corporation—fertilizer. Androgynous ammonia. Carbon dioxide. Fertilizer tanks stand parked in rows of four-wheel rubber-tire caissons. This is not farm country but an agricultural factory where not only the soil, air and water but living animals themselves, kine and swine, mammals like us, mothers with emotions similar to ours—love, lust, fear—are treated as raw raw-material for packaged meats. Enough to make a man a bloody vegetarian if he lets his mind dwell on it. Best not to dwell on it. Think of death not life next time you stuff your chops with veal, sirloin, ham, bratwurst. . . . I tremble for us Christians if there is a Christian god.

Me and my dog. We think this way sometimes.

I pet her bony shoulder. She twitches her tail. I twist the top from a jug of Big Mouth beer and sluice the stumps of my tonsils. I check the view in the rearview mirror, empty the bottle and let it hang for a moment from one finger on the outside of the door. Dispose of with care. It dangles in the cool wind, it whistles, carefully it falls, a splash of green glass brightens the pavement.

Time to clear out of Dodge.

Onward onward into the wind and the sun and Kinsley, Kansas—midpoint USA. Halfway, says a billboard, between New York and San Francisco. New York: 1,561 miles. San Francisco: 1,561 miles. We're getting there. Getting where? There. Somewhere.

I pause at the city park to give the dog a roll in the grass and a drink of water from her bowl. She laps it up with a tongue the color of salmon eggs, an unwholesome pallid pink. I give her another pill in a bite-size ball of longhorn cheese. She won't take the pill straight and probably has good reason.

I lift hood of truck, pull dipstick from crankcase. A quart low already. I punch two holes with a screwdriver in the top of a can of Yellow Front's 40-weight nondetergent economy brand ("For Motorists With Oil Consumption Problems") and pour contents into thirsty filler pipe. The oil gurgles out of sight, the engine's hot head smokes and gasps and sighs, the radiator drips a few drops of green diluted coolant on the gravel. Check fanbelt: taut but not tight. Jiggle clamps on battery terminals: corroded but firm. Inspect fuel filter: looks clear. Screw down air filter a couple of turns. Reset distributor cap, pull and resnap cable to sparkplug heads, four on each side. Nothing wrong with this old rig—318 cubic inches of failing power—that a simple ring-and-piston job wouldn't help. Will could rebuild this motor in two or three working days. All I got to do is get it to Stump Crick for the overhaul before it burns out, blows up, seizes tight or throws a rod.

A chilly west wind boosts us on. Under a hazy yellow sky we steam through Garfield, Larned and Pawnee Rock, outposts on the original Santa Fe Trail. Flat plains lie on either side, relieved only by the continuous growth of alder and cottonwood that marks the course of the Arkansas River, if it is a river anymore. There by Pawnee Rock, sole natural landmark in this segment of the long route west, the Indians dallied between buffalo hunts, jerking meat (etc.), and sallied forth from time to time to harass travelers on the Trail. A danger point on the central plain. Pike, Doniphan, Webb and Gregg mention this place in their journals. Kit Carson, in 1826, made a bid for fame here, shooting his own mule while standing guard for a wagon caravan. He was a green scout in those days, only seventeen years old. He mistook the mule, he explained, for two Pawnees in mufti.

Not much left of Pawnee Rock today. Most of it removed by local road builders. In fact from the highway you can't even see it. So much for historic monuments.

Approaching Great Bend. Gas and oil territory. Black iron pumps rise and bob at scattered gas wells in the fields. I pass a shop called Mountain Iron & Supply. *Mountain*—the word, the simple easy bisyllabic denotative, sends a little pang of nostalgia through my central nervous system: homesick—I am sick for home.

Wherever whatever that may be.

Great Bend Drive-In Movie Theater: an imposing edifice of six Corinthian columns with bell-shaped capitals feigning support of a towering façade of painted aluminum. Black letters on the white marquee announce the current attraction: FOR SALE 12 ACRES. Death of another passion pit. No more necking, no more heavy petting in the cockpit of Dad's LTD.

Again, as in Dodge City, we pass through the nineteenth-century heart of town, vivid with the beauty of mellow brick, serene with the dignity of elm trees and broad shaded sidewalks. But the storefronts are vacant, the drug stores closed, their tile floors and soda fountains under dust. I pass the county courthouse and a grassy park with iron-wheeled artillery piece, its trails down and spread among dandelions, violets, buttercups. Two old men in pearl gray Stetsons sit on a green iron bench. One whittles on a stick of wood. The other coughs and spits. A mottled mutt with dragging ears slinks behind them. The clock on the courthouse dome speculates on the time of day and guesses wrong—four hours slow or eight hours fast and ninety years behind.

The compass on my dashboard trembles, does a forty-five-degree turn as we leave Great Bend and head due east for Ellinwood, Little River, Strong City, Emporia, Homewood, LeLoup, Gardner, Lenexa and Kansas City.

Temp 180°. Oil pressure 30 psi. Tach 1900 rpm. Ammeter neutral. Fuel one-half. Speedometer 65 mph. Odometer (1)98944.6. Altimeter 1800′. Cab temp 75°. Compass E. Stewart-Warner gauges, all too honest.

Reaching out, I stroke old dying Sollie. Thinking back, I fondle memories growing always younger. . . .

18

1940-70:

THE LOST YEARS

Me and those girls, those girls. . . .

There was Candy, sweet as her name. She loved to make love in
a tent. There's something extra sexy about a tent, she explained. A
tent makes me feel like a harem girl, hot for the camel's hump. She
draped my red bandana over the lamp. Puts the right glow on naked
bods, she said, makes them look warm and fruity and full of fun.

Les girls. . . .

Joy Galore (as she called herself) writhing like a python beyond
the footlights, the crazed cocaine glitter in her seagreen eyes. She
stared at herself with love, with adoration, with envy, in the mirror
behind the bottles of the backbar. The nipples of her splendid
breasts covered with little pink pasties. Stick 'em on peel 'em off,
she said, that's the law. She wore a black G-string beneath a fringed
miniskirt, a lacy black garter around one thigh, a bracelet high on
one arm and a silver chain around each ankle. What else? Yes, a
thimble-size zircon set in the navel of her plump blond belly. And
a tattooed butterfly on her rump. Her skin was the color of clover-
bloom honey and so soft to the touch you could scarcely feel it, so
kissed, caressed and lufa-rubbed smooth it seemed to lack the quality of friction; his fingers glided over and upon it like oil upon butter, meeting no resistance until socketed deep in the succulent
quivering core of her apex. I want it all, she said, all of it now and
I don't mean that I mean this. She had no talent for patience. He
loved her madly urgently desperately, Henry did, every Friday
night for hours, until the day she thundered off to California on the
buddyseat of a Harley Hog, arms wrapped around the waist of a

318

bisexual thug in black horsehide, her sweet knees clasping his flanks. She departed Henry with four hundred of his dollars in her purse but left him for keepsake a flimsy bit of black nylon and a note, a billet-doux, a sweet letter saying

Dere Henry your a nice man but a dumb jerk and I might come back someday but you got to learn to dance man you move like a wooden Indian love & kisses from your one & only

J. G.

Candy on the other hand was reliable, faithful in her fashion, always overbooked but available when properly bribed. An outdoors girl, she loved him in his ranger suit. Leave the Smokey Bear hat on, she said, but take off your socks please. They made love on the rocks at Grandview Point on the verge of a fifteen-hundred-foot vertical drop-off. A light rain was falling when she ran nude as a dryad, wearing nothing but sandals, among the junipers and pinyon pine at Anticline Overlook. Catch me, she hollered, catch me, as Henry lunged forward in mock pursuit. She laughed, springing away, he stopped and waited behind a tree until she came circling back like a rabbit, the prey in search of her predator. They rolled in the bunch grass and sand until Ranger Henry, always the gallant, brought her to a fixed position atop his long body. A pissant or two explored the sweating crevice of his buttocks. They always did. He ignored them until Candy, working hard in semiprivate delirium, came off like a firecracker—Henry meanwhile doing his best to recall the won-lost records compiled by Elroy Face, Vernon Law and Bob Friend of the 1960 Pittsburgh Pirates.

Good Lord but he wanted them all. Not all there were but—all the ones he wanted. Was that not fair?

What about—what *was* her name? Jill? Judy? Trudy? Ruby? Dixie? Trixie? The one he met at a party in Tucson the night the police ran amuck in Chicago. WELCOME TO PRAGUE, said a hand-painted poster in the gallery. WE LOVE MAYOR DALEY, said a flock of union-printed placards waved in the eyes of the TV cameras by a regiment of garbage collectors, aldermen, firemen, policemen, relatives and relations. Henry was drinking mescal, eyeing the worm in the bottom of the bottle, wishing he owned a machine gun. Then he met this chick and told her about his lonely post at a Forest

Service Fire Lookout high on Bumblebee Peak in the Atascosa Range. She was lovely, cold, distant if mildly curious. He told her about the ten miles of rocky road, the bull in the pasture at the foot of the trail, the six-mile horse path up three thousand feet to the peak, the rattlesnakes and Gila monsters, the bark scorpions, the yellowjackets, the kissing bugs in the rocks. How interesting, she said, drifting away to refill her drink. Come up and see me sometime, he called as she faded beyond his ken. She glanced back at him once, shrugged, disappeared. Delayed fuse? Until two weeks later, sleeping on his bunk through an evening thunderstorm, he was awakened by a gentle tapping, a persistent rapping, on his cabin door. Yes, her name was Jill. She shivered in her rain-soaked blouse and jeans. He built a fire in the stove. She pulled a bottle of wine from her daypack and stayed for seven nights and days. Her home was in Washington, her father a senator's chief aide. Henry never saw her again. But remembrance kept him warm for weeks.

How long could a man nourish himself on reminiscence alone? Henry sometimes feared that he was condemned to learn the answer.

He had other memories of Bumblebee Peak. He remembered the night he walked those six uphill miles after learning that another drugged and brain-retreaded crackpot had pulled a gun on another Kennedy. On to Chicago! shouted the jubilant Robert. Minutes later he was a goner, shot down in a Los Angeles hotel. Henry wept when he heard the news on his pickup radio and he wept for two hours more as he trudged up the mountain. Weeping, he climbed the stony trail with thirty pounds of booze and grub in the pack on his back, and wept for Robert Kennedy and Jack Kennedy, for Medgar Evers and Malcolm X and Ché Guevara, for the latest defeat in the hopeless attempt to stop a useless one-sided dishonorable war. He wept for himself, he wept for his country, he wept for the death of democracy. Long time dying, never fully born.

O Freunde! nix such tones!

He thought of Loralee. How about that Loralee kid now, that Loralee Croissant as he called her—the real name was something like Kressbacher or Krumpacker—who showed up one rare day in June, a year or two before—or was it after?—the Bumblebee affair. Henry worked as a river ranger that summer, pulling his hitch at a place called Lonely Dell on the banks of the Colorado River near

320

the throat of Marble Gorge. She was from San Francisco, going down the river with a boating party of fifteen others, mostly men. He squeezed her lifejacket, checking for leaks, and slipped her a piece of paper with his name and mailing address as she climbed in her swimsuit over the silver-gray tubes into the wallowing rubber raft. Others helped her aboard. The boatman leaned back on his oars. The girl the boat the boatmen disappeared. But again he felt he had planted a little time bomb in a sensitive female heart. Three months later, in October near the end of his season, a letter of pastel blue arrived from San Francisco. Two weeks later he was walking the steep incline of Diamond Street between rows of white blue-trimmed happy houses when he saw the red-gold banner stretched between two second-story windows:

WELCOME, HENRY LIGHTCAP

He knocked on the door and she let him in. She was alone, cooking her specialty, *lasagna con amore*. She wore a minidress of the period, showing off short rounded tanned legs. Her chestnut hair hung straight and loose to the small of her back. Her eyes were dark, large, bright with play, augmented by a set of interesting crinkles at the outer corner of each. She was twenty-four years old, divorced twice, fond of the male animal and its principal member.

Henry needed a bath. (He usually did.) She ran hot water—adding shampoo—in a deep Victorian tub six feet long, its leonine feet painted gold with red toenails. She ran to the kitchen as he slid into the steaming and sudsy bath, then returned three minutes later, licking her lips, to scrub his back, massage his scalp and minister to his urgent erection. He took her and she took him in right there in the tub, Miss Yin and Mr. Yang in symbiotic synchromesh, splashing water all over the tiles, making one hell of a mess. Then came the lasagna (Loralee made her own pasta) and hot garlic bread and a bottle of Chianti and they were at it again like dogs forty minutes later, right there on the dining room rug, the woman on all fours as Lightcap, moaning like a hound, mounted from the rear. They collapsed. They half recovered. They went for a walk around the neighborhood. Peace signs and rainbow flags hung from windows. The flag of freedom, Loralee explained—symbol of sexual liberty. They returned to Diamond Street licking on cones of ice cream,

321

vanilla for her, wild cherry for him. Back in the house she showed
him her collection of R. Crumb Comix and before he knew what
he was doing he was sunk again, eight inches deep in Loralee on
the purple velour of the parlor sofa. Her roommates came in, two
boys, a girl, greeted the pair on the couch with smiles and aplomb,
with a peach, with a bunch of grapes, and scampered upstairs to
their rooms.

Why are you so good to me?

Don't ask, she said.

Exhausted, he sank back on the couch, the woman in his arms,
and drifted down the river.

On the river. He lay in a leaky rowboat, motionless, drifting with
the current down a wide bold river the color of brass. Above hung
a fierce sun. Eyes shaded by the wide brim of a straw hat, he re-
packed his corncob pipe with Bull Durham from the pouch in his
shirt pocket, struck a kitchen match on his teeth and relit the pipe.
A puff of blue smoke strayed over the swirling silt-loaded water.
The boat turned idly in the stream, pivoted off the end of a sand-
bar—oars dragging—and glided on. Small birds slipped through the
thicket of willow on either shore. Behind the fringe of green a wall
of sandstone five hundred feet high curved around the bend ahead.
The wall was sheer, slick, unscalable, smooth and pink as the face
of a sliced ham. He passed a nameless side canyon, a deep fissure in
the monolithic rock where acid green cottonwoods trembled in the
sunlight and a clear stream poured down a stairway of rosy polished
overhanging ledges. He pressed a wad of oily cheese on the end of
a fishhook, dropped a line over the side and waited for the first tug
of channel catfish. For twelve days and one hundred and sixty miles
of river he found nothing but primeval wildness, passed neither boat
nor home nor any sign of man but the rusty boilers of a gold dredge
half buried in the river bottom, a zigzag trace of toeholds and fin-
gerholds—Moki steps—leading up and over a dome of bare rock to
the ruins of a village of mortared stone high in an alcove on the
south-facing wall of a cliff. Miles away stood purple mesas and beyond the mesas blue mountains dappled with snow.

Down the river. Over the sea. He remembered a ship passing east
by the rock called Gibraltar. And the ship passing north by the red
cliffs and blue grottoes of Capri. And the ship as it entered the Bay

of Naples, dark Vesuvio smoking against the sky. He remembered a girl named Brunetta who lived (with a dozen others) in a pastel-orange villa in a town called Amalfi. He remembered Napoli, the odor of burned olive oil, the trained expert whine of the child-beggars, the clashing gears of his motorcycle, the cry of the fish vendors, the smell and the texture of fried squid, the taste of cheese and tomato sauce on a circular crust of pizza hot from the tiled oven. And the red lamps on the rear of the one-horse carriages that patrolled the Via Roma at evening, the golden chandeliers of the San Carlo Opera, the pink shoes and pale tights and ruffled gauze tutus of the ballerinas. He remembered the rats that fled in hordes down the cobbled alleyways in the heart of the city late at night, his buddy Ken Wolfe at the wheel of the open Jeep, the windshield flat on the hood, the kick of the Colt .45 in his hand. My turn my turn, cried Wolfe, you drive now.

On with the river, endless river. He thought of the dank dark medieval quad of Edinburgh University on a dark dank misty day in September. Prince's Street and the floodlit castle on the rock. The bloodthrilling bloodthirsty skirl of the bagpipes. He remembered a tawny mountain rising into clouds and a warning placard that read HERE LIE THE BONES OF DENNIS HUGHES / WHO CLIMBED BEN NEVIS IN TENNIS SHOES. He remembered a scowling poet named Hugh Mc-Diarmid buttoned up in tweed and the flock of students around him, roaring with love. The Isle of Skye, as beautiful as its name. Bleak Inverness, cold Aberdeen, and a street in Edinburgh called Eden Lane that led into a bourgeois slum of identical red brick cottages, each with its plot of soot-black grass enclosed by a black iron picket fence. All doors closed tight, windows curtained, the street empty.

A channel crossing, gray Paris in its negligee of winter rain, a queer hotel on the Left Bank, the echoing caverns of the railway stations and the long journey south by rail to the sunlight and warmth and evil glamour of Franco Spain. He remembered that border crossing at Irún and the harsh masculine bellow of official Spanish voices blaring out of loudspeakers; he felt at once, after a week in Paris, that he had returned to a man's country and dropped backward through time to the century before.

He remembered the mountains of Austria, the descent on skis from the Arlberg that lasted half a day. He remembered the boat to Bergen and the hills of Norway covered in snow and an early spring in Stockholm, splendid city of lakes and parks, and the student festival at Uppsala, the streets overrun by lanky drunken boys pursuing the most beautiful most golden girls in the world. In all eyes but their own. He remembered the return to Edinburgh and the news that he had failed every course. Easily.

So—Henry wandered south on bicycle to Cornwall, loafed for a week in the town of Bude, met a barmaid with perfect breasts and sweaty armpits and the violet-blue eyes of a Technicolor movie actress, walked her to the beach wrestled her into the sand pledged his eternal love and one week later walked up the gangplank through the gangway (tourist class) of the *Queen Elizabeth* and steamed at once for New York City where he met, mated and married one Myra Mishkin, artist. A marriage that lasted, off and on but more off than on, for years and years. How many? Who's counting?

Down the river. Down and down the lazy river, the mud-colored meandering lonesome river. El Río Bravo, the Green, the Dirty Devil, the Colorado. The Big Sandy. Crooked Creek. Stump Crick. He remembered the clouds in the sky, the wind on the hill as he rode on a high-built wagonload of timothy grass down the lane to the barn. He clutched at the handle of a pitchfork plunged deep in the hay, saving himself from a long slide to the ground, while Brother Will drove the team. Sunlight flashed on the brass knobs of the horsecollars, the doubletree jangled, the traces rattled, the hames jingled, the ironbound wooden wheels creaked and groaned as Will hauled back on the brake. They came to the ford where he stopped to let the horses drink, then lashed them hard for the haul uphill to the barn. The horses grunted, farted, haunches spread and straining as their iron-shod hooves struck sparks on the stone, and the wagon lurched forward, rolled through the muddied water—schools of minnows streaming up-current—and rocked through the mud and upward through pasture grass on the two bare ruts of the lane. He remembered the thunder of the team's great feet when they cleared the entrance ramp and clattered onto the planks of the barn floor. And the choking dust that rose in clouds under the roof as he and Will pitched the loose dry sweet hay into the loft. And afterward the retreat to the springhouse in the side of the hill where steel milkcans beaded with dew stood in the flow of cold water down a cement trough, and they dipped a tin dipper in the water—he and his brother—and rinsed the jaggers from their parched throats and slaked their bottomless thirst.

Him and Will. Me and my brother.

19

KANSAS TO MISSOURI

On through rural Kansas, out of the high plains into the Midwest. The air is different here—no longer dry and thin, but soft, thick, humid, balmy with April. Lilacs in bloom, a sinful gorgeous purple. Dogwoods flowering here and there. Old gray farmhouses empty of life returning to earth within a protecting quadrangle of neglected woods, while round about, on all sides, back and forth, gigantic tractors with eight wheels and air-conditioned operator's cabs pull gangplows and seed drills through the black soil. Sluggish little streams wind over the flat terrain. Surprise!—a great blue heron flaps across the highway. There must be a lake or pond nearby. A good omen, that bird, appearing to me now.

We stop for a while, a piss for me, a bowl of water for my dog, at a place named Cow Creek. Coronado also paused here, in 1541, before giving up his search for the Seven Golden Cities of Cíbola and turning back toward Texas, New Spain and Old Mexico. Coronado recognized the potential of the Kansas plains, a region, he said, "capable of producing all the products of Spain." He had his mounted soldiers with him, baking in their tin suits, and a priest named Juan de Padilla. Padilla returned to Cow Creek—then known as Quivira—a year later to christianize the Indians. As if they weren't dangerous enough already. In return they martyrized him, thus pleasing both men and God. A monument to Padilla stands here, a twenty-foot white cross of cast concrete. "Jesus Christ, Victor" says the Latin symbol at the crux of the cross, commemorating the victory of faith and sacrifice and the delights of Christendom in the geographical center of the New World. Erected by the Knights of Columbus in 1950.

Cast a cold eye on life, on death. Motorist, pass by. We pass by, me and my dog, forging on into the leafy renascence of spring, the deep end of Kansas, the dense human drama of the American Midwest. But where are they, the people? I drive through a gentle time-eroded town called Marion and see rows of empty stores and boarded-up hotels. Main Street. One car and not a man, woman or child on the sidewalks. Is it Sunday? I stop for lunch in the Marion City Park, taking a table by the side of a barely moving stream called Cottonwood Creek. The afternoon seems perfect: soft vague clouds drift on a pale sky, the air is mellow with the fragrance of green grass and dandelions, a cluster of midges and a few dragonflies play above the creek. But there's nobody in the park except a couple of mothers with children and one teenage boy on a two-cycle motorbike. Where are the men? Where are the good male citizens of Marion, Kansas, on this sweet April day in the year of our Lord, *Anno Domini* 1980? I see neither hide nor hair of the rascals. Can they all be encysted in their stuffy fetid tract houses watching the National Lobotomy Machine? Or puttering about in golf carts over insipid greens in pursuit of little white balls? Fondling their niblicks, their spoons, their mashies and putters?

Approaching Emporia. Civilization once again. We dive beneath an overpass called Graphic Arts Road, passing a turnoff to Industrial Street, bypassing original Emporia neat and clean. Good old William Allen White would hardly recognize his hometown now. I latch on to the tail draft of a forty-ton Mayflower moving van and let it suck me like a bug through the near-continuous development—gas stations, boxfood joints, suburban box homes, condominiums, truck stops, shopping centers, redlight greenlight intersections, office buildings of pink cement and dark glass, assembly plants with walls of slump block and no windows at all, block-long warehouses and storage depots of bolted-together sheet metal—that walls in the four-lane superhighway from Emporia to Kansas City.

It don't take long. Before sunset I'm one unit in the mass of wheeled helots streaming on elevated roadways between the towers of K.C. We cross the Big Muddy on a bridge so high and broad I scarcely notice the ancient river meandering below; we enter the state of Missouri.

Down a secondary blacktop route I drive through a series of small towns—Mosby, Richmond, Hardin, Norborne—until I find a dead-end dirt road leading through puddles to the swamps and woods along the north side of the Missouri River. The track ends in two miles at the ruin of a vine-covered swaybacked barn. Nobody here. Not even a KEEP OUT THIS MEANS YOU sign. Looks like Lightcap territory. I steer the truck under an unpruned apple tree and shut off the works.

We sit there in the dark for a while, me and Solstice, hearing the toads chanting in the trees, the bullfrogs grunting in the bog, a whippoorwill singing deep in the woods, one lone screech owl muttering in the haunted barn. Our kind of place. Everything's here but the fireflies—too early in spring for them. A couple of bluish security lights glare through the mist but they are a good half-mile away. I hear a dog yapping at the drift of our scent but his alarm sounds tentative, detached, and within minutes dies off altogether.

I get out and open the back of the truck. No need for a fire. The night is warm and I can see well enough by the stars to fill Sollie's bowl with chow and open a can of beans for myself. The dog munches at her supper and goes nosing off in the dark to see what's doing in this neighborhood. I light the Primus, warm the beans and eat if you call that eating. Not much appetite on my part anyhow. The gnawing bite in my guts seems worse this evening. I take a pill—old friend Dilaudid. I open my bedroll on the bed of the truck and lie down, my head out on the back where I can keep an eye on the stars. Drove most of the way across Kansas today and another sixty miles into Missouri. I am tired. I am more than forty-nine and a half years old. I am mortal as sin.

Claire!

20

1971-77:

HENRY IN LOVE—AN INTERLUDE

I

I am a scoundrel, he reflected, dialing the sacred number. This girl's young enough to be my daughter. So what? Let's make the most of it.

"Yes?" inquired a gentle voice on the other end of the line. She sounded sweet enough to eat with a spoon.

"Claire? This is Henry." He felt the first drops of sweat begin to trickle from his armpits, the first involuntary twitching in his groin.

"Henry? Henry who?"

He hesitated. "Is this Claire? Claire Mellon?"

"No, this is Grace Mellon. Just a moment, please."

Long pause. Must be her sister. Henry waited, gripped in terror. How to begin? Would she even remember? She must have got his letters. Letters she never answered. Must have read them. But then what? What then?

A second voice vibrated in his ear, a voice sweeter, younger, even more delicious than the first. "Hello, Henry."

"Claire. It's me."

"Yes, Henry, it's you."

"Henry the Ranger. Remember?"

"Henry the Ranger. Yes, I remember."

"I'm in Denver, Claire. Only ten blocks away. I want to see you."

"That's sweet of you, Henry. But we're going to a concert. We have to leave in a few minutes."

"Oh." He stopped. Now what? "Well—I'll go with you. I'll buy the tickets."

She laughed. An angel's laugh, it seemed to him. "But Henry, I'm in the orchestra."

"In the orchestra?"

"String section. Second violin."

"Oh." What now. "Well—I'll come and watch."

"You're not supposed to watch, Henry, you're supposed to listen. Both, rather. But yes, do come. Meet me at the reception afterward."

His heart swelled with relief. She does remember me. Joyously he said, "I'll bring my harmonica. And my Jew's harp. And my Paiute foreskin fertility dance drum."

"What?"

"Dogskin." Giddy with sudden happiness, he barely heard her instructions. But he found the place, the concert hall—after a quick stop at a gas station to bathe, change shirt, whip on necktie and jacket—and bought a cheap seat high in the peanut gallery, among the music students. He noticed a few of them adjusting opera glasses. The orchestra had not yet come onstage. Henry hurried out to his truck and returned with his 7 × 50 U.S. government official forest ranger binoculars. The tympani leaped to his eyes. The harp stood five feet before him. He could read the lettering of the open score on the conductor's podium: *Leonore* Overture no. 2. Henry was so excited he could barely restrain himself from turning to the young people around him and announcing in bold frank supercharged tones that he, Henry Holyoak Lightcap, was boldly frankly candidly in love with a girl, with a violinist, with the whole string section, with the entire Denver Fucking Symphony Orchestra, with Leonore too and Ludwig Whatshisname. . . .

He waited, waited.

The members of the orchestra began to file in—first the percussionists (how he envied the man at the great copper bowls of the kettledrums) then the brass then the woodwinds then finally the string folk: the bass viols, the violincellos, the violas, the violins—including yes, yes, there she was a slender figure holding her dainty instrument (and later mine, hoped Henry) in one hand, plucking up the long skirt of her formal blue-black velvet gown, trimmed at neck and sleeve with snowy lace, as she picked her way on slick black glossy pointy shoes among assorted elbows, cellos, legs and feet toward her chair. Henry stood up, the better to see her—and as he did so a number of others around him also stood, following his lead, assuming the advent of an important personage onstage— and waved at Claire. Already tuning her fiddle, however, she failed to notice Henry, failed even to look up. Henry sat down, disappointed. Those around him sat down. He remembered the giant field glasses hanging from his neck. He raised the eyepieces to his eyes, adjusted the focus and grazed with greedy looks upon the radiance of her flowing butter-colored hair (no braids tonight), the rosy luster of her cheeks, the bare glowing flesh of neck, bosom, arms . . .

Entered the concertmeister and took his place. A man with a pickled face and a nut-brown oboe sounded his nasaline keynote. The other players took up the note, converged upon consonance, groped closer and closer until the entire Denver Symphony Orchestra was braying forth one sustained and mighty A. (Often the highlight of an entire concert.) Satisfied, the first violinist nodded his sleek rodentine Central European head. The musicians fell into silence.

Pause.

Then applause, beginning with a tentative few, catching on with more, bursting out from the entire hall as the members of the orchestra rose to their feet and the conductor marched onstage. Smiling, the maestro—a brusque fellow named Fritz—bowed once to the audience, turned briskly to his reseated orchestra, faced the music, uplifted his baton . . .

Now what?

Two hours of bliss, by the clock. An eternal moment, in Henry's soul.

The question of temporal sequence hardly entered into the matter. With Henry H. Lightcap the dance of love began as a mad impulse followed, in due course, by leisurely regret. Events in between proceeded by quantum jumps, often without traversing the intervening space, sometimes jogging through time in reverse. Each particle indeterminate and unpredictable but the aggregate bound tighter than a bull's asshole in flytime to the iron laws of probability. As Henry would have phrased it, composing his footnote to Plato.

He found the reception, smuggling himself in when challenged by affecting a Continental accent. Smiling, shrugging, spreading his hands—"Mein Hinklish"—an apologetic grimace—"iss how you say?"—tapping his skull, "Not zee best he could be, eh? Je ne c'est pas, non?" He drew a faded card from his jacket pocket, allowing the usher a brief glimpse: "H. Holyoak Lightcap, M.A.; Special Project Consultant."

Working his way politely but firmly through the jostling mass of bald heads, black coats, lacquered hairdos and velvet gowns, he established himself at the vantage point of the punch bowl. He sloshed a champagne glass through the punch, avoiding the fruit, and looked about. Over a bobbing bubbling cumulus of svelte heads he looked for the golden radiant one he sought. And found her, after a moment, trapped within a tight circle of all-male music lovers. Lecherous swine. Henry dipped a second glass into the bowl—the server busy with a queue on the other side of the table—and forged a path through the murmuring mob toward Claire. *Light* was her name, bright star of his soul. The cuffs of his shirt were wet but little he cared about that. Little he knew.

She smiled at his earnest approach, his uncombed head and padded shoulders rising above the crowd, his unsteady hands holding aloft two glasses of punch. He held one toward her, providing her with a pretext for escaping her admirers. My God she's beautiful, thought Henry. The thought left him speechless. Him, Lightcap, speechless.

"Well here you are," she said. He nodded; they touched glasses. "Where's your Smokey Bear suit?" He grinned and nodded, unable to take his eyes from her face, hair, the bare neck and shoulders. Take your eyes off my face for godsake, he imagined her thinking, unable for the moment to imagine what else he could do. "I was hoping you'd be wearing the big hat," she went on.

"Crowded in here."

"It's supposed to be crowded. This is a reception. Our first concert of the season."

"I didn't know you were—so good."

"I'm only a fiddle player. Second fiddle. Besides there's a lot you don't know about me."

"I know. Let's get out of here."

"Don't you want to meet my mother?" A smiling woman stood beside them, looking at her daughter, then up at Henry. She too was beautiful, more beautiful than her daughter: taller, elegantly slender, refulgently blond, with the patrician nose and dramatic cheekbones of an actress.

"Not really," Henry said.

The woman laughed and elevated her little gloved mitt toward his lips. "But now you must."

Blushing, he took the hand in his huge paw, looked down at the thing, squeezed it gently, bent and kissed the fingers.

"Such a gallant ranger. I am Mrs. Mellon. My name is Grace."

Claire said, "Now aren't you sorry? Wouldn't you rather have a date with my mother?"

Slowly, with difficulty, Henry herded his wits together. "You're both beautiful. Let's all three get out of here."

"That's better," the mother said. "Let's do that."

Shit, said Henry. Silently.

"Soon as I make my goodbyes," said Claire, moving off. He watched her exchange a smiling kiss with the concertmaster, then bounce on to the drummers, the trumpeters, the little men with the slide trombones. Swine, all of them.

"Claire loves people," the mother explained. "She's the most popular girl in the orchestra." Taking Henry by the elbow, she began guiding him toward the nearest exit. "We'll wait for her outside."

Under the portico, in the cool October air, she took a lengthy cigarette from a gold case in her handbag. She paused. Henry produced a wooden kitchen match from his pocket, ignited it with his thumbnail and lit Mrs. Mellon's cigarette.

"Thank you." She puffed and inhaled and expelled. "That was clever. What else can you do?"

Silently, Henry produced a second match, tautened his right trouser leg by lifting his right knee and struck the match on the seat of his forest green twill ranger pants.

"Dear me. . . ."

He produced a third match and struck it on his teeth. They both stared at the yellow flame.

"You *are* a clever young man. And how young are you, Mr. Lightcap, if I may ask."

About forty-four, he explained.

"About forty-four. Good. You don't look a day over forty. My age." For a moment she mused over the ironies of life. "Claire's new young man. And I understand that you work as—a park ranger?"

Only in the summer.

"Only in the summer? Good. And in the winter . . . ?"

He rested.

"I see. Marvelous. What a marvelous way to set one's course through life. You have a family, Mr. Lightcap?"

He mentioned the Lightcaps of Stump Creek, West Virginia.

"Really? West Virginia? Why we're practically neighbors. My people live in the Old Dominion."

East Virginia?

She laughed. She had a fine grave well-modulated laugh. Highly musical. "And your wife, Mr. Lightcap?"

No wife, he said. Been divorced for many years.

"And her family?"

Henry mentioned the Mishkins of New Rochelle, later Weehawken.

Mishkin, he explained, was a well-known slumlord family in the waterfront district of that urban-surburban North Jersey complex. Or perplex, as they say.

She peered at her smoking cigarette. "I see. . . ."

Claire came bustling up with her violin case, cashmere shawl upon her shoulders. The three walked under the trees, around the corner of the music hall, to a parking lot. Mrs. Mellon unlocked the door of a substantial gray motorcar of recent European extraction. She took the cased violin from Henry's hands, stowed it on the passenger's seat and kissed her daughter on the cheek. "Don't forget, dear, you have classes in the morning."

"I'll be home in an hour, Mother."

"It's eleven already."

"I know that, Mother."

"And you, Mr. Lightcap—" She gave him a thin ironic smile. "I do hope that we meet again someday—perhaps in another of America's splendid national parks or forests."

Henry agreed. For a moment, holding the car door open and observing her form as she eased gracefully into the driver's seat, he imagined the lady spread-eagled on an Indian blanket, nude beneath a canopy of whispering pines as he, Ranger Lightcap, performed his manly duty. Having Grace under pressure.

They watched her drive away.

"Did she give you a hard time?"

"Your mother is a concerned woman."

"She's a prig and a snob but I love her anyway. Let's walk."

They walked through the park near the concert hall. They shared the banalities of tentative love. Whom did she love most? Mozart, she said, and after Mozart, Stravinsky. I don't like either of those guys much, he admitted. I can tell, she said, but if you ever want to be a gentleman you must learn to admire them both. What about Minnie Pearl? he inquired. Minnie's all right in her way, she said, but for real country give me Conway Twitty and Loretta Lynn. They're good, he agreed, but I like Dmitri better. Shostakovich? she asked. No, he said, Kabalevsky. Oh bland, she said, bland as tapioca, oh Henry you must be kidding. I'm kidding, he said.

He slipped an arm around her waist. She leaned toward him. Thigh against thigh, they walked beneath the well-groomed elms. Her moving hip, beneath his hand, felt like warm black velvet. I love this dress you're wearing. It is rather sexy, isn't it?; but all the women in the orchestra were wearing black; you must have noticed. Can't say I did. What a liar you are. Come with me, he said. Where? Anywhere. (Oh my God, Claire, anywhere, he thought, anywhere.) Can't you be more specific, Henry? South, he suggested; let's go down to Tampico, lay on the beach all winter long. Can't, she said.

That was that.

They walked in silence for a while, under the trees, around and around in a meandering loop before the muted glow of the concert hall. Beyond, illuminated by hidden floodlights, the dome of the state capitol shone against the night sky.

You're wondering why I came here? Not at all, she said, not at all. How come you never answered my letters? I apologize; I didn't really think you were serious. Those others? Other men write me letters. Do you think I'm serious now? Yes, right now I think you're serious. What does that mean? It means that I think you're serious right now. You're right. It's a now thing. What does that mean? What else could it mean, Henry?

He stopped at the side of a sycamore, leaned his back against the smooth bole of the trunk and drew the girl gently into his arms. She looked up at him, no longer smiling. He kissed her.

Why did you do that?

That's what you said last time. He kissed her again, seriously. She responded by putting both her hands on the back of his head and pulling down, pressing herself against him, arching her body like a bow.

Let's go somewhere, he suggested. Make love.

Love?

Get this agony over with.

Oh no, Henry, I can't do that. Please don't ask me to do that. One hour together and then I don't see you again for—how long? Six months? A year? Ever?

I could stick around for a few days. We could go camping in the mountains. The aspens are turning gold now. The sunflowers are in full bloom—and the purple asters and the globe mallow. It's beautiful up there, Claire. Cattle gone. Bull elk bugling in the high meadows. Brown trout jumping in the lakes.

She smiled up at him, her eyes misty with pain. No, I can't do it. That would make it even worse for me. I'd be miserable all winter long, thinking about it. Missing you.

It's a now thing, he said.

It's too much of a now thing.

He walked her home, a mile over the sidewalks under the trees through shadowy residential streets. She lived with her mother— father gone—in a fine old brick-and-stucco house, three stories high, behind a wall, in a well-groomed neighborhood of fine old grave Victorian houses. She turned a key in the gate, they said goodbye and kissed once more. She entered and closed the gate, they touched hands through the iron bars, she withdrew. Henry watched her walk to the deep porch of the house, unlock and enter the front door, disappear.

Henry walked back to his pickup truck through the Denver night. At two o'clock in the morning, too restless and agitated for sleep, he started the engine and headed home. Whatever that was. Weehawken? No more. Stump Creek? Not really. Albuquerque, El Culito, San Francisco, Edinburgh, Naples, London, Paris, Madrid? Those days were gone. Back to the park in Utah? That season was over.

He realized with a shock of horror that he was at liberty to go anywhere he wished. Nobody cared where he went.

336

II

He wanted her so much. For so long. He desired her so intensely over such a length of time that the longing became a malaise, a sickness. *Desire*—the word itself, in its very sound, with its dying fall of suspiration, resembled the enchanted misery of his fever. A fever in the blood, fever in the mind, fever of soul.

He tried to telephone her from a town called McCook in Nebraska, two hundred miles east of Denver. Stump Creek was a week behind him when he called the magic number and reached only her mother.

I'm afraid she's not here, Mr. Lightcap. No she's not. I said she's not. She's in Rhode Island now, visiting her grandmother. Spring break, you know. Where in Rhode Island? Does it really matter, Mr. Lightcap? Where are you, if I may ask? On your way to Utah, I suppose? That "seasonal" job, as you call it? I said she's with her grandmother now. In Newport. No, I think I'd rather not divulge the address. There's a quality of *enthusiasm* in you, Mr. Lightcap, that suggests madness. I think you're a dangerous man, Mr. Lightcap, and frankly would prefer that you not see my daughter, frankly. Yes, frankly. I know you appreciate frankness. We have something in common then, don't we? I'm sure that she'll write to you from time to time, if she wishes. I've no control over that. But I will not encourage your interest in her. She sees various young men, you know. Young men, I said. Men her own age. Do you have difficulty hearing me? Your right ear? From what? Guns, you say? Gunnery? Mr. Lightcap, this information does not surprise me in the least, indeed it confirms my worst fears and suspicions. Thank you, sir. Thank you, Mr. Lightcap. Goodbye now. I said goodbye.

Thinking that the mother might be lying, he tried again when he reached the city, slunk about the Mellon house for two days and nights hoping for a glimpse of Claire; she did not appear. He called the secretary of the Symphony Association and learned only that the concert season was over and that Miss Mellon, like other members of the orchestra, had been furloughed for the spring and summer. He visited the music department at the University of Colorado in Boulder but found nobody there except a departmental assistant who refused to reveal any information whatsoever about any stu-

dent. Henry left a message for her sealed in a departmental envelope:

Claire—
   Come.
                        —Henry

III

That didn't work.

IV

He wrote her letters, long rambling humorous and pathologic letters, often in blank verse, sometimes in rhyme, from his sun-cooked
outpost in the Utah desert. Sent her pictures of himself in ranger
suit, Smokey Bear hat, smug smirk, with views beyond of a rearing
phallic monument silhouetted against the pure indigo of desert sky.
Sent her sketches in his own hand of Navajo hogans, buckboard
wagons, tired saddlehorses, sick cowboys vomiting in the horse
trough. Sent her a sprig of sagebrush, a corsage of juniper, a mountain lupine wreathed in maidenhair fern. She acknowledged his
gifts—some of them—with cryptic notes, highly delayed, that
promised nothing.

Finally she agreed to meet him for a day, on his day off, at the
town of Glenwood Springs in western Colorado, a midway point
between Denver and Moab, Utah. She would not stay overnight
with him, no she would not. Would not or could not? Both. She
would arrive on the westbound morning train—Denver, Western &
Rio Grande—and depart on the eastbound evening train. She owned
no car of her own and preferred not to borrow one from her mother.

Wear that black velvet dress, he begged her on the telephone,
with the lacy trim. Henry don't be silly, she replied. . . .

At five o'clock, official quitting time, on the day before the tryst,
Henry retired to his plywood ranger hut among the juniper trees,
stripped off his sweat-soaked uniform, and took a shower. Not in
the little trailerhouse, a cramped bug-infested sweatbox with apol-

ogetic plumbing, but out back on the rock, in the sun, with two buckets of water, one soapy one clear. He bathed in the soapy bucket and poured the contents of the other over his shaggy head. Shivering with cold goosebumps, at a temperature of 102° F, as a fiery breeze swept down from the rosy, infernal cliffs. The humidity was 6 percent.

He dressed in his sportiest Dacron slacks and loudest Hawaiian shirt, filled his canvas waterbag and hung it on the front bumper of his pickup, loaded buckets, bedroll and cooking gear in bed of truck, tossed in a rag satchel with clean shirt and underwear, toothbrush and razor and comb, locked up his trailer and bolted off like a rabbit for the highway, ten miles away by sand and stone. He paused in Moab for oil, gasoline and beer, then headed northeast up the river road through the gorge past Nigger Bill Canyon, La Sal Creek, Castle Valley, Professor Valley, Onion Creek, Fisher Towers. Flaming with joy, fear, intolerable anticipation, he rumbled—engine faltering—over the Colorado River on the half-century-old one-lane Dewey Bridge. Stopped to fill a bucket and add water to his leaky radiator. Scalding his fingers in the steam. Draped a wet rag over the carburetor to soothe the vapor lock. And waited, walking irritably back and forth in the shade of the cottonwood trees on the riverbank, switching impatiently at the heads of dried cheatgrass with his agave walking stick. Returned to his vehicle, added a quart of reprocessed oil and slammed down the hood, securing it to the grille with the leather latigo that hung from the hood ornament.

Henry drove on, passed the mouth of the Dolores (Sorrows) River, forded a stream that came down from the Roan Cliffs on the north, and entered the ghost slum of Cisco. From there it was but a mile to the paved highway—US 6-50—and an easy roll over the lonely lovely desert to the riverside Mormon towns of Mack, Loma, Fruita and Grand Junction. Only ninety-one miles to Glenwood Springs. And seven-thirty P.M.: only fifteen hours before her scheduled arrival.

Air cooling, engine cooling, sun well down behind him, he motored on through Palisade, De Beque, Rulison, Rifle, Antlers and Silt, following the river as the highway did, and entered the fine old resort town of Glenwood Springs. An odor of therapeutic sulfur floated from the baths and through the streets. Henry made sure, first of all, that he could find the railway station and passenger depot. Not hard. The railroad, like the highway, paralleled the river. Anything of any importance in Glenwood Springs ran along the river. He found another clock. He had thirteen hours to wait but at least he was here. Not there. He walked about the streets still flustered a bit from the six cans of beer he'd absorbed during the drive up from Moab but taking care not to attract the eye of the city police. This would be the wrong night to spend in a drunk tank.

Checked a clock in a jewelry store, another in a hotel lobby, a third in a supermarket. Twelve hours to go. He bought a can of sweet corn, some hamburger, an onion, a tomato, a jar of mustard and a package of sesame rolls and drove up into the hills north of town, into White River National Forest, parked his truck facing downhill, cooked his supper over a scrub-oak fire and made camp for the night.

He decided not to eat the onion. He brushed and flossed his teeth, had a long walk in the woods, took a shortcut coming back and got lost for two hours. Near midnight he slid into his sack and tried to sleep. Sleep came hard. About four in the morning, judging by the stance of the Big Dipper, he dozed off, dreaming of a symphony orchestra with one vital violinist missing.

A bird coughed. A daddy longlegs walked across his face. He rolled on his side and saw the bright green leaves on an aspen tree trembling before the morning light. A mountain bluebird swooped like an arc of electricity from the aspen into the shaggy dark arms of a spruce. He heard the sound of mountain water.

A worm fence four aspen poles high, looking fifty years old, zigged and zagged across one corner of the meadow. He thought of West Virginia. For a moment. He looked at the smooth white bark of the aspens and read the names of the sheepherders dead and gone— Garcia, Vargas, Barrutti—and the vague heart-shaped growth-expanded symbols of youthful love, enclosing the initials of brave lads and dark-eyed lasses long forgotten. His heart swelled with joy. Yes, he would bring her here for the day. They'd picnic in the shade at the edge of the trees, they'd drink from the mountain brook, they'd walk up that soft brown lane that led into the depths of the aspen groves, he'd carve her name and his own

inside a heart for all the world to see.

My God! He shivered alert, dashed through the goldenrod, morning glory, dockweed and locoweed to the window of his pickup. A two-dollar Westclox pocket watch hung on the dashboard, suspended by a leather thong from the choke rod. The hands on the watch read ten after ten. Impossible. Horror and panic flashed through his nerves: the train was due at ten-thirty. He grabbed the watch, held it to his ear: no sound. He shook it, banged it on the roof of the cab. The thing began to tick then stopped again, dead. He hurled it over the trees, out of sight.

Glancing again at the sun for reassurance, he skinned on a pair of Levi's blue jeans. No underwear for Henry. Then remembered the baggy slacks with the drape shape and the reat pleats at the waistband—only fifteen years old. His Eisenhower pants, 100 percent virgin Dacron. His wino pants. His dress-up pants. He peeled off the tight jeans and stepped into the slacks and tried to see himself in the side mirror of the truck. Wrong. This would not do. He dropped the slacks, balled them up and stuffed them down a badger hole. Again he pulled on the Levi's jeans—old and faded and not very clean but at least they fit. Then reevaluated what he had long ignored, that the crotch was frayed to a frazzle. If he sat with legs spread his scrotum could be seen, leaking out like some obscure form of marine polyp.

He looked at the badger hole. Decisions. He dug up the slacks, shook off the dirt, considered and reconsidered. Meanwhile the sun was rising, soaring like the fire of his hopes well into early morning. That Amtrak train would already be coming down the grade from Loveland Pass, bearing in its Vista-Vu dome car the bonniest colleen in the Golden West.

Haste! He counted his money: twenty-one dollars. (No credit card.) Enough to buy a pair of decent pants at Sears or J. C. Penney maybe, but what about the feast he planned for her, the imported Danish cheese, the Prague pilsener, the Swedish flatbread,

341

the grapes, the Italian salami, a pair of filet mignons (mignones? mignoneaux? mignoni?) with bacon and mushrooms or else some lamb, marinated in a garlic lemon wine sauce, skewered with peppers and onions and tomatoes on a spit and broiled over the fire and—and of course the wine, two bottles of a fine Bordeaux perhaps, one red one white, one served at forest temperature the other chilled in ice *pourquoi non?*

He rehearsed the plan, rolling down the mountain toward Glenwood Springs, where he arrived to find that the time of day, Rocky Mountain Daylight Saving Time, was 6:04 A.M. He drove to the railway station anyhow, double-checking, but found the passenger depot locked. Peering through the dusty glass of the windows he read the chalked writing on the blackboard inside, the schedule of arrivals. Ten-thirty, said the board.

He had time for a cup of coffee. He located a cowboy and truckers' café, ordered coffee, flapjacks and pigmeat. Might need the strength later. For what? Who could say? For a rescue operation, perhaps: pretty Claire treed by a bear or frozen with fear on a crag of rock or swept by chance down a raging torrent toward a thundering waterfall, who knows? Henry the Ranger would be prepared.

He left the café. Seven o'clock. Three and a half hours yet to go. He walked around the block five times, drove to the biggest food store in town, parked, waited. Made notes in his diary. Played a few tunes on his harmonica, wondering which might most impress a professional musician. None, probably. He bought a copy of the morning newspaper and read the same old news. Nothing new. Same rotten war dragging on and on, same scoundrels still in office, same derailed freight trains and overturned truck-tankers spreading chlorine gases, flammable fluids, alarums, confusion and terror. What else is new?

Finally the supermarket was opened. Henry entered, first customer of the day, and pushed his cart up and down the quiet aisles. He found most of the items on his list. When the cashier at the check-out counter added things up, Henry had only enough money left for gasoline to return to Moab and his job.

Poverty. Lacking an icebox, he buried the perishables inside his sleeping bag, insulating them from the sun, and drove once again to the railroad station. The passengers' waiting room was open. He entered, looked at the clock on the wall above the ticket windows then at the schedule board. The westbound train would be twenty minutes late. Fifty minutes yet to go. He went into the men's room with his satchel in hand, peeled off his sweaty shirt and bathed himself from the waist up with soap and cold water. He dried himself with paper towels, took out his razor and shaved his bristling jaw, his blue-gray chin and upper lip. Trimmed his eyebrows. With thumb and forefinger plucked a few hairs from his nostrils. He ran a hand through his black hair, finding it greasy again; just another greaseball hillbilly. He shampooed his hair for the second time in less than twenty-four hours and slicked it down with a comb, then fingerwaved his standing pompadour. He brushed his teeth and deodorized his hairy armpits.

Now what?

The pants. He took the slacks from the satchel and held them up to the window. They were so thin at the seat the light shone through. And completely wrinkled—Dacron or not—smeared with damp earth, smelling of roots, rocks, rat turds and badger dung. Unsuitable for the occasion. He would have to wear what he was wearing, the little boy blue jeans with the peekaboo crotch. He stuffed the slacks into a garbage can, thought for a moment, pulled the blue bandana from his hip pocket and lined the inside of the Levi's crotch. The effect was curious but would pass. He put on a fresh white shirt, his finest, and snapped shut the pearly buttons one by one. Looking himself over in the mirror, forcing a grin, tilting his head first right then left, he found little to admire but hoped that little would suffice. He took his spare bandana, a red one, from the satchel and knotted it loosely about his throat. Nice. But it seemed an affectation—with the clean shirt, the lean jeans, the high-heeled pointy-toe boots on his feet, he looked too much like a dude-ranch cowboy. Perhaps she preferred the urban existential type, the subbohemian *verité*, a touch of defiant squalor from the student ghetto. Retrieve the Dacron slacks once more?

No! Enough of the waffling. Train's a-coming, boy. Henry joined the crowd outside on the loading docks and watched the train come around the bend uptrack, headlight glaring, power units puffing smoke. A trickle of sweat crept down his ribs. The engines grumbled past, champing steel, smelling of burning oil and hot iron, air brakes hissing. The tall bilevel blue-and-silver passenger cars glided along

343

the platform, slowed, stopped. The conductor's assistant in his brass buttons and suit of navy blue swung down from the gangway holding the steel step-box in hand.

Henry looked for Claire's rosy face, bright eyes, golden head of hair but the tinted windows allowed no positive identification. He saw a few hands waving and waved his own in return. He watched as the first passenger descended the steps—a blue-haired lady in a print dress, followed by a pink-cheeked gentleman wearing a Panama hat. Two little boys in suits got off and rushed into the arms of a waiting mother. Three more elderly couples descended, then a pretty girl with red hair; Henry envied the young man who stepped quickly forward to hug, kiss and take her away—but she was nothing, a drab and a dormouse compared to his Claire, his Honeydew, his radiant ripe and unplucked Mellon.

He waited. He watched. But no one else came out. The conductor was already attending to the tickets of five passengers about to board. Moments later the engine whistled once, twice, thrice, the heavy wheels began to turn. Next stop Thompson Springs, Utah. The Amtrak rumbled off, rattled away and dwindled out of sight, airhorns wailing through the valley. . . .

Slowly, carefully, Henry sat down on a bench, his bag between his feet. He was alone on the platform. He licked his dry lips, felt the shocked slow thumping of his heart. Something like a paralyzing drug spread through his nervous system. He felt dazed, cold, hollow. He felt empty and useless and worthless. He stared at the vacant tracks of the railway, at the trees of the park along the river, at the spas and hotels on the other side and saw nothing. Nothing at all.

He sat there for some time—five minutes? fifteen?—then bestirred himself, picked up his bag and walked on numb legs and nerveless feet into the waiting room. He shuffled to the clerk's window and inquired after a message for Henry H. Lightcap.

The clerk looked. There was nothing.

Henry shuffled outside into the hearty sunlight. He saw dozens of happy people moving about, couples arm in arm, young lovers snuggled close on the front seat of automobiles. He raised his eyes to the dark conifers and pale green aspens crowding the mountainsides, to the gray scree of the peaks, to the snowfields and the first thick clouds forming out of nothing, *ex nihilo,* on the skyline. Stunned, he waited another hour, then drove slowly out of town.

He was ten miles west before he remembered to shift from second into third, twenty miles farther before he remembered the beer and the two bottles of wine, one red one white, wrapped in his bedroll.

Somewhere along the river road to Moab, under the beaked gods and visored goddesses of Fisher Towers, he turned aside up a rocky ravine, plowed firmly into the boughs of a juniper tree and stalled. Little blue-green berries rained down on cab and hood of truck. Henry kicked open the door to let his legs hang out, stretched lengthwise on the bench seat, pillowed his head on his forearm and subsided into the nirvana of unconsciouness.

V

On the afternoon of the following day he checked in at Park Headquarters for mail. Among the letters, bills and junk in his box he found a memo.

> Lightcap: Some female named Claire phoned long-distance yesterday to say she could not keep her date. Asked us to relay the message. We called you on the radio but you were already gone. Hope everything turned out all right.
>
> —Gibbs

VI

He found other diversions.

But the pain lingered for weeks, months, years. He did not write to her again until her letter came, a week after his happy journey to Glenwood Springs and back.

> Dear Henry,
>
> Sorry I couldn't make it to the Springs last week. Had a fight with my mother that day—she still wants me to go to Smith, just because she went there. What kind of logic is that? Then I found out there was no return train on the same day. It seemed

better to forget the whole thing. Maybe some other time. I trust that you received my phone message in time. Do write to me now and then, when you feel like it. I love your letters. You are the most desperately romantic man I have ever known, and if I believed half of what you write I'd be a little worried about your mental health. (Just kidding, Henry.) I appreciate your feelings about me but—you must try to remember that I don't feel ready to enter into a serious relationship—let alone an "affair"—with any man as of yet. Maybe next year. But you are the funniest one I know and really I do like you a lot. Best regards from your friend,

Claire

He studied and analyzed that letter for days trying to find solace in its careless text. "Do write to me . . ." He liked that. But "now and then"? What good was that? ". . . When you feel like it"? A casual dismissal. But then she writes "I love your letters." I *love* your letters. How far is that from saying I love *you?* Well—about a mile. Two miles. Am I indeed "desperately romantic"? Perhaps I frighten her with my ardor. Must cultivate an attitude of ironic nonchalance. Worries about my mental health. That's all right, so do I. Perfectly reasonable. Appreciates my feelings but not ready for a serious relationship? What kind of ship does she want? She "likes me a lot." Jejune phrase. No nourishment there. "Your friend . . ." Friend? She dares call herself my friend? After this?

He waited as long as he could before writing to her again. Kept her dangling in agonized suspense for five days—nearly a week. Then wrote her a jaunty note eleven pages long, full of lies. The principal lie was one of omission: he said nothing of his trip to Glenwood Springs. He wrote about the red sands of the desert, the pattern of tracks a dung beetle makes on a dune, the arcs of the wild ricegrass in the wind. He related his more symbolic dreams, hinting of erotic splendors. Described a flash flood pouring like gravy down a chasm in the cliffs. Etc. Inquired politely after the health of Mrs. Mellon, wishing in his heart the woman would get herself flattened by a steamroller while crossing the street to buy a quart of milk, leaving behind only a caricature of the female form stamped on a patch of asphalt paving. Then perhaps, bereft, Claire would come to him in the night, tears streaming down her lovely cheeks, seeking in his arms the warmth of human love. Et cetera.

While waiting for a response to his letter, Ranger Henry journeyed after duty hours to the town of Moab, where he consorted with such old friends as Felicia Hastings, Bliss Quickly and Candy Cotten. Good sweet ladies fresh from the battlefields of divorce and ruptured rapture, ready for fresh adventures.

But his mind was fixed on Claire Mellon. He waited and after two weeks, his letter still unanswered, he decided to give her a ring on the national telephone system. He stacked quarters dimes nickels on the shelf of the public phone in Woody's Bar, dialed the operator and waited.

Your number, sir? The number I'm calling? The number you're calling from. He read the number. And the number you wish to call? He gave that number. A pause. That will be two dollars and eighty-five cents, please. He deposited the coins. Thank you.

He waited, heard the phone begin to ring in the Grace T. Mellon residence. The phone rang and waited, rang and waited, one phone ringing in an empty home. No one answers, sir. Okay operator, I'll try later. Thank you.

He hung up. He waited for his money to come jingling into the return slot. Nothing happened. He pushed the coin-return button. Nothing happened. He hammered on the phone with his fist. Useless. He poked his little finger up the slot, feeling for a wad of cotton. The cotton was there but when he removed it no money followed. He dialed the operator and got a busy signal. Tried again. Still busy. He bought another glass of beer at the bar and returned to the phone booth. It was occupied. He sat down nearby, staring at the man inside the booth, pointedly waiting. The man ignored him. Henry went outside to a public phone on the street, one of the new economical installations shielded from rain and wind by nothing but a little plastic hood. Yelping teenagers in eight-cylinder Camaros with four-barrel jets and overhead cams, gigantic trailer trucks hauling uranium ore to the mill, bearded bandits on snarling Kawasaki motorcycles—all raced by on the street, six feet from where he crouched with his head inside the tiny quasi phone booth designed evidently for midgets and Filipinos. After a while he obtained an operator's ear—one finger in his own—and explained his problem. The unrefunded two dollars and eighty-five cents. She needed to know both numbers again, the one called, the one called from. He asked her to hold on, dashed into the bar. The inside booth was still occupied. He tried to peer through the glass to read the number on the telephone. Could not be done. The man inside the booth scowled at Henry, revealing yellow fangs and molars full of lead. Henry backed off, ordered another beer, waited. Finally he got a second chance at the inside booth. He dialed the operator again and asked for the return of his two dollars and eighty-five cents. The operator asked for Henry's name and address.

Address? he said. I'm in Woody's Bar.

We'll have to mail you the money, she explained.

He asked her, in that case, to give him credit and he would simply repeat the call to Denver. Do you have a Mountain Bell credit card? No I do not have a Mountain Bell credit card, that's not what I meant, he explained, what I meant was that you give me credit for the money that this telephone—this goddamned telephone machine right here in Woody's Bar—stole from me about fifteen minutes ago. Sorry, sir, she explained, no credit calls without a credit card. Then all right, mail me the fucking goddamned money. It's a violation of federal law to use obscenities over the telephone, the operator said.

Listen, ma'am, Henry said, you take that two dollars and eighty-five cents and you go to the bank and get it changed for two hundred and eighty-five bright new copper pennies and you go home with them pennies and get a wooden mallet and you lie down on the floor and wrap your legs around your ears—are you listening to me, operator?

All he heard was a busy signal. The FBI would be flying into Moab within hours armed with arrest warrants and automatic shotguns. He dialed the operator, tied a bandana over his mouth and said that he wished to place a collect call. By and by the Mellon telephone began to ring. Presently he heard the drawling voice of Mother Mellon:

Ah yes . . . ?

Collect call from Robert Redford for Claire Mullins, the operator said, will you accept?

The name is Mellon. Not Mullins.

For Claire Mellon. Will you accept?

From whom, please?

From Robert Redford.

I'm afraid we don't know any Mr. Redford.

The actor, Henry burst in, Robert Redford the noted film actor. It's about Miss Mellon's audition. We have some good news for her. She—

Will you accept the call, please? the operator repeated.

No, said Mrs. Mellon. Decidedly not.

Henry brooded over his beer. He found a dime in his pocket and called Bliss Quickly. Later, near midnight, he drove the thirty miles of sand and stone, flushing nighthawks from the road, that led to his lonely hut among the erect and impotent phalli of the hoodoo desert.

He lit his Aladdin lamp and began a letter. "Dear darling Claire," he wrote, "If I cannot see you again I will surely die. . . ."

VII

Surely die? What a redundancy is death. He wrote that he would come to visit in early October, at the end of his working season at the park. She wrote back, after a time, that she was leaving for New England in early September. To a town called Northampton Mass. To a school named Smith, entering as a junior. Why? Because of its proximity to Boston, she said, and the world of music. She wished Henry the best of everything (except herself) and hoped that he would continue to "drop her a line" now and then when the "mood took him." She planned to spend the following summer at Tanglewood. Goodbye. Claire.

He patrolled his back roads and walked his foot trails. He searched for lost little boys, helped fear-frozen rock climbers down from cliffs and shepherded fat bull snakes and faded pygmy rattlesnakes out of the garbage dump. He listened to his old battery-powered Hallicrafter radio late at night, receiving strange signals from Quebec, Ciudad Juárez, Radio Havana, Lubbock Texas, and a police station in Ethel Oregon. Where the town-limit signs read ENTERING ETHEL.

Well then, he considered, if she was going to be that way he'd make a dash for Denver on his next two days off. Only 350 miles from Moab—an easy seven-hour drive. If his pickup would run. Since it was down he'd take the Greyhound, catch the eastbound at ten P.M., arrive in Denver at eight A.M., walk to Claire's house, spend the day and evening with her, catch the two A.M. bus back to Junction, be home by suppertime. Simplicity enclosing *felicitas.* Embracing *claritas.* He hoped. He concluded, after further consideration, that his reentry into Denver had best be stealthy, unannounced. The surprise visit entailed severe risks but the more formal and courteous approach lent itself to a formal and courteous rejection. On one pretext or another she could make herself unavailable. The pattern was becoming plain, even to a fool as blinded by desire as Lightcap. As the moth is drawn to the candle he was determined to plunge into pain, to drown his anxiety, misery and uncertainty in despair. It seemed a reasonable, commonsensical solution.

Canvas satchel in hand, he boarded the bus. Old women with anxious eyes, grim faces, prim knees, filled the supervisory seats in front, assisting the driver in his duties. Henry stumbled to the rear, found adjoining vacant seats, staked his claim to both. He sat in the dark sipping from a square bottle of Jim Beam bourbon, eating peanuts from a sack.

The whiskey purled in his brain. The bus rolled softly eastward into the dark. He tried not to think of Claire by focusing his thoughts on Joy, on Jill, on Loralee, on Whatshername, on Candy, on Bliss. Useless.

He switched on the little overhead reading light, opened a book and began to read the Navajo Creation Myth, a guaranteed soporific.

The First World, Ni'hodilqil, was black as black wool. It had four corners and over these appeared four clouds. These four clouds contained within themselves the elements of the First World. They were a black cloud, a white cloud, a blue cloud and a red cloud. . . .

He dozed. He read. He read and dozed. He dreamed a dream that meandered on in various directions but mostly four and involved a man disguised as a badger, a badger disguised as a woman, a woman disguised as a man and an ear of corn on the cob, actually White Shell Girl who becomes the Moon and Yellow Corn Boy who becomes the Sun but the entire scheme is wrecked when Coyote-Who-Was-Formed-In-Water steals a blue turquoise charm that belongs to Water Buffalo's Babies which makes the Great Yei, Hasjelti, very angry. . . .

He was awakened by lights in the bus station at Grand Junction, Colorado, and the hiss and grunt of air brakes. He got off the bus to pee, entered the men's pissoir and read the wisdom on the wall:

Why dont Jesus walk on water anymore?
Because his feet leak.

(We need more Jews like Jesus.)

If all college girls was laid end to end—
I wouldn't be surprized.

(All Honkies must die.)

The blue-and-silver bus rolled eastward into night. Henry drank his bourbon, emptied the bottle and slept. Uneasily. In fits. Dreaming bad, lengthy and complex dreams that faded, when he woke, back into the addled cells from which they'd come. Buses roused his latent claustrophobia. But he was a poor boy, couldn't afford air flights or even Amtrak. He rode the bus and dreamed his suffocating dreams.

The red dawn found them grinding over Shrine Pass east of Vail, 11,050 feet above sea level. Blue snowfields on either side. Sick from the booze but too stubborn to puke it up, Henry steeled his stomach for grim gray grimy hours ahead. The bus rumbled down the grade, pistons braking against gravity, as they headed on for Dillon, Silver Plume, Lawson, Golden and Denver City. Henry sank into a queasy coma, one dead soldier upright between his thighs, and floated forth onto another lake of complicated nightmares.

He dreamed. He endured. He hoped. He groped toward consciousness out of the anesthesia of alcohol and discovered himself, Henry Lightcap, sitting on a stool in a steel stall with his pants down around his ankles. Canvas satchel on the cement deck. He read the writing on the inside of the stall door.

Here I sit all brokenhearted
Paid a nickel to shit and only farted

He washed his hangover face at the washbasin, shaved the blue stubble from his jaws, shampooed and combed his hair and put on once again his best and cleanest shirt. Feeling slightly better, roughly human, he found the bus station coffee shop and treated himself to a mug of steaming, translucent-black coffee and one stale but greasy doughnut.

Where are we? he asked the waitress.

God only knows, she said. More coffee?

Thanks.

You look awful, she added. She was a bigboned middleaged squareshouldered woman with plucked eyebrows and purple lips. A chin mole with bristles added the only decorative touch to her square and honest face. What's wrong with you?

I'm in love, Henry explained. That explains it; you look like I do. I'm in love with you. You are sick. What's your name? Read my tag; see?—June. What's yours? Henry. Well Henry, if I was you I'd go find a nice park bench and get some sleep. Looks that bad, huh? You'll get over it.

He left her a dollar tip and wandered outside into the gray and concrete boulevards of Denver. The brown air reeked with exhaust gases. Didn't really know where he was. Went back into the bus depot, found a phonebook and looked for a map of the city.

The clock on the wall said nine-thirty. He checked his satchel in a locker and headed north past the U.S. mint and the state capitol, then east along Colfax Avenue toward the city park, the museums, the opera house, the prep schools, the elm-shaded streets of her neighborhood.

What exactly would he do when he arrived? How would she receive this unexpected pleasure? And suppose—suppose she were not even at home?

He stepped up the pace.

Mountain clouds hung above the Mile-Hi City, casting transient shadows across the glassy façades of The Bank of Denver, The Federal Savings & Trust, The All-America Building, The Brown Palace, The Hilton Tower. A light rain began to fall but that was all right with Henry, it added drama to his pain and cooled the air.

He stopped for a few minutes in the park to recomb his wet hair—he wore no hat today—and to rebrush his teeth at a drinking fountain. He was feeling better. The brisk walk had restored his confidence. He glanced at his visage in the window of a parked automobile and it seemed presentable. Well, passable. The rain stopped. He marched north again, the last mile beyond the music hall, and came to the wall on the corner, the gate, the handsome square and bourgeois house. Lilacs and hollyhocks in bloom.

Now what, Lightcap?

He tried the gate. It was unlocked. He opened it and followed the curving flagstone walk to the portico, climbed two broad stone steps and found himself standing before the door. He hesitated. He listened. He heard music within, the duet of piano and violin, a phrase broken off and repeated and broken again, followed by sweet laughter, the tenor tones of a man's voice and more laughter. Unwelcome sounds to Henry's ear. One hand on the bronze knocker, he still hesitated. He heard the music resume, violin and piano in sibilant concord and he recognized the piece: filthy Mozart, the Sonata in F Major, Köchel 376. Parlor music.

Rain began to fall again.

Who was the scoundrel in there with her? A lover—or only a friend? A friend or only a teacher? Or both? All three? He waited, stiff with anxiety, heart chilled with fear. Rainwater trickled from his hair, down his face and neck. He realized more fully than before the depth of his folly in coming here uninvited, unannounced. He was a fool. He was a lunatic. A pathetic fool, a pitiable lunatic.

The music continued, halted, repeated itself, went on. Henry lowered the heavy knocker silently and stole away on tippytoe, down the walk, out the gate and around the corner before any eye detected him.

One block away he halted once more. In painful thought. He had to see her. That much was clear. He would not travel seven hundred miles by stinking Greyhound without even a glimpse of the girl he loved.

He returned to a point from which he could see the front of Claire's home, the wall, the gate. Perhaps the man inside would soon leave. There were a number of cars parked along the street, all new, enamel gleaming under the renewed descent of rain. Perhaps one of them belonged to Claire's visitor. No doubt he'd soon be departing.

Henry leaned against the trunk of an elm, turned up the collar of his shirt and lit a cigar, assuming a pose of casual and innocent introspection. An automobile passed, tires hissing on the wet asphalt. And then another. But no pedestrians, not one, appeared on the sidewalks. Henry began to feel conspicuous. He longed for the relative anonymity of hat and umbrella. He noticed curtains stirring in a front window of a nearby square three-storied house of brick, important-looking. He left his post under the leaky shelter of the tree and walked up the sidewalk past Claire's house, on the opposite side of the street. He walked two blocks, glancing back from time to time, then returned and resumed his place under the dripping tree. He waited.

After a while a police car came around the corner and stopped beside the tree. The two men in blue stared at Henry; he stared at them. Neither got out of the car. The driver beckoned Henry close with two significant twitches of a thick forefinger. He wore three chevrons on his sleeve.

Yessir?

Let's see some I.D. The policemen stared intently at Henry as he pulled out his wallet and fished his Utah driver's license—illustrated—from its once-clear now-grizzled plastic case. He gave it to the driver. The driver studied it. His partner watched Henry, a short-barreled riot gun held upright between his knees.

The rain poured gently but steadily on Henry's head.

What's your date of birth, Henry? the driver asked. He told them. Where do you live, Henry? Moab, Utah. Says here your address is P.O. Box 69, Moab, Utah; you live in a mailbox? No sir; I get my mail there. Where's your car, Henry? He explained. All right, you came by bus. The driver returned his license. What are you doing here? Henry hesitated. I'm waiting to see a friend. Waiting to see a friend. Why here? Kind of wet, wouldn't you say? She was gonna meet me here. She a little late? Again he hesitated. Henry Lightcap wore no wristwatch. Neither wristwatch nor underwear. I'm not sure, he said; I guess so. You guess so. Funny place to meet. Where's she live? Sir? Your lady friend; where's her house? Henry made a vague gesture up the street, pointing with thumb and chin. His hair and shirt were now soaked with rain. He shivered. The police sergeant opened his door, getting out. Turn around, he said to Henry. Sir? Turn your back to me; lean against the car; spread your legs. Henry did as ordered. The policeman searched him quickly, running his hands up and down Henry's body from armpits to boots.

354

He removed the jackknife from Henry's pocket. You always carry a knife, Henry? Yes sir. Doesn't everybody? But that was the wrong remark. He felt steel cuffs clamped on his wrists. Get in the car. What? Get in the car. The driver opened the rear door. Henry crouched low and eased himself into the back seat. At least he was out of the rain. The driver slammed the door shut. The door lacked an inside handle, as did the opposite door. Henry found himself separated from the two men in front by a black mesh of heavy-duty steel. He could hardly see their faces.

Now Henry, the driver said, where's this lady friend live?

He hesitated again. Both of the cops looked like reasonable, intelligent men. Surely he could explain everything easily enough—but how?—maybe even get a free ride back to the bus station. Well, he said, she lives up the block. I think.

Up the block you think. The driver twisted in his seat, looking back at Henry. Both men watched him. Maybe I'd better explain your situation, Henry. There's been a dozen rapes and robberies in this part of town in the last six months. The driver paused.

Henry said nothing.

That mean anything to you, Henry? Henry said, I never heard of a woman getting raped in broad daylight. On a public street. I have, the driver said. He looked at Henry. I'd like to believe your story, Henry. But it's not a good one. Now show us where this friend lives or we're taking you to city hall. What's the charge? Oh we'll hold you for a while, put you in the lineup, see what the victims have to say. We'll think of something. Henry shivered. Guilt rose up to match the sick dread in his stomach. All right, the driver said, putting the car into drive and moving forward, I didn't believe you anyhow.

Straight ahead, Henry said. What? Straight ahead. She lives in that place on the corner. Right or left? On the right. The car stopped before the Mellon residence. Light rain pattered on the roof of the car, on the sidewalk, on the trees. This it, Henry? He looked down at his lap, his groin—source of his troubles—shook his wet, shaggy hair, tried to raise his hands. He groaned. What's that? Yes, he moaned. But for godsake . . . Both policemen got out of the car. The one with the shotgun opened the door by the sidewalk. Out of the car, he muttered. Move.

Henry bent low, crawled out, straightened up. He shuffled between the two policemen as they advanced through the open gate and up the flagstone walk toward the house—a gaunt soaked scarecrow between a pair of uniformed gladiators. As the three tramped up the steps of the porch he heard the music from inside the house— K. 376 still, andante movement—come to a sudden stop. A murmur of voices. Before the police sergeant could push the doorbell button the front door was opened from within. Opened wide.

Mrs. Mellon stood in the doorway. Behind her, near a baby grand piano, stood Claire with her violin and bow. At her side—chin on her shoulder—stood a fair young man of medium height (short) with pink cheeks and a blond mustache; he wore a blue blazer, a tie, a white shirt with button-down collar. His left arm lay about Claire's slender waist, his small white graceful hand resting lightly but protectively, with possessive assurance, on the warm curve of her hip. He smiled, affecting disdainful amusement but staring all the same. Claire looked pale, beautiful, alarmed, amazed.

Politely the sergeant tipped his black-visored cap to the lady of the house. He tightened his grip on Henry Lightcap's upper arm. Madame, he said, we found this—this fellow here—lurking under a tree down the street. He looked at Henry, then back at Mrs. Mellon. He claims he knows you. Care to identify him?

Mrs. Mellon looked at Henry, at the police sergeant, at the manacled prisoner and his keepers. A glitter appeared in her distinguished eyes. Her mouth formed a small satisfied smile, revealing in the chink between her lips the firm set of her whitened whetted central incisors, the points of her canines.

Claire took a deep breath.

VIII

They were married ten months later. The modest ceremony took place at Point Imperial on the north rim of the Grand Canyon, on a peninsula of limestone overlooking Marble Gorge, Saddle Mountain, Cape Solitude, the mouth of the Little Colorado River, the Vermillion Cliffs, the Echo Cliffs, Coconino County, the Navajo Reservation, the Painted Desert, Navajo Mountain, the San Francisco Peaks, one-sixth of Arizona and various other features of geological, historical, morphological and ethnographic interest. Eight thousand eight hundred and three feet above sea level. At evening, under the new moon.

Claire's idea.

Presiding was an Episcopalian priest flown all the way from Denver, along with Mrs. Mellon and friend and friends of the bride, in a chartered Learjet. A solemn comely bearded man, Father Cheswick spoke with a slight lisp, concluding his every other sentence with the phrase *et thetera* or alternately *and soo* [*sic*] *forth*. He liked cigars with his champagne.

He was Mrs. Mellon's idea.

The bride and groom were attended by two uniformed park rangers (one a female), three big ugly river guides from Lee's Ferry and six members of the North Rim fire-fighting crew wearing their yellow hard hats and orange fire-resistant shirts. (Two females.) A pumper unit mounted on a government Dodge three-quarter-ton four-by-four stood by, available for action in case, as the boys said, the nuptial embraces became overheated.

Music for the occasion was supplied by Slim Randles and The Dusty Chaps, an amateur jug band of cooks, dishwashers and mule wranglers from the North Rim Lodge. The band performed a honkytonk version of Wagner's "Wedding March," a medley of tunes by Johnny Cash, Phil Ochs, Johnny Paycheck, Marty Robbins, Willie Nelson, Ernest Tubb, Kinky Friedman, Hank Williams, Bob Wills ("still the King") and Claude "Curly" Debussy (*Claire de Lune*).

Henry's idea.

The groom wore formal attire, a traditional gangster suit of blue serge with mighty padded shoulders, rented for the occasion from McCabe's Funeral Home, Kanab, Utah. Since the pants were six inches too short for his legs he tucked the cuffs into the top of his machine-tooled dude boots and looked fairly presentable.

The bride wore virgin white, a filmy diaphanous ankle-length multilayered froth of lace, gauze, vapor, satin and soo forth, with a coronet of silverleaf lupine, scarlet gilia and white campion at rest on the crown of her yellow hair. Like the groom (but as only he knew) she wore no undies. Excepting, in her case, the requested black lace garter high on the left thigh. She carried a bouquet of mountain wild flowers matching the coronet. When she tossed the bouquet to her maids an errant gust of wind carried it over the edge of the cliff. One of the river guides leaped after it, caught it in midair and disappeared. The band played on—Ernie Ford's "Tennessee Waltz"—without missing a beat. Mrs. Mellon's sister fainted. Father Cheswick looked concerned, hiked up his gown and pulled a sterling-silver flask from his hip pocket. The firefighters danced with the ladies from Denver. One of the rangers tossed a coil of purple Perlon line over the rimrock and hoisted up the gnarly, scratched but grinning river guide, the bride's bouquet still clutched in his bloody right hand.

The bride's mother smiled at Henry when they danced but the glint in her eyes was not the light of love. Nor of charity.

The sun went down. The music got louder. Violet-green swallows jetted through the air. The music got faster. The bride and groom slipped off through the dusk to Henry's pickup truck, fell into the cab and sank from view. Henry sat up a minute later with a moist nose and the torn garter clenched in his teeth. The bride rearranged her skirts, Henry stepped on the starter and nothing happened. Laughter burst from the nearby shrubbery. Henry rolled out cursing, waddled awkwardly to the front of his truck, uncinched the hood and looked inside. He reattached a battery cable, got back in the cab, started the engine, geared down and engaged clutch. Nothing happened. He gunned the motor to a furious roar—wheels spinning—but the truck did not move. He slid out, found the rear axle chained to a tree. More laughter. He unhooked the chain, returned to the wheel, shifted into low, raced the engine and popped the clutch. The rear wheels spun and fishtailed in the dirt, blasting the nearby scrub oak with a spray of heavy shot. Somebody yelled. The wheels dug in, found hard ground, the truck leaped forward like a prod-stung bull and vanished into the timber, dragging a ten-foot tail of beer cans.

They spent their wedding night in a grove of aspens a quarter mile from Henry's fire lookout cabin. He had left his truck parked at the door. They made love immediately and then lay awake for a time, still connected, still one flesh, smiling up at the stars and listening to the uproar of gunfire, bongo drums, bugles, coyote howls and drunken song from the clearing around the cabin. Still *in situ* he felt himself swelling within her. She felt it too.

Henry—what're you doing? Who, me? No, him. That hain't me, Honeydew, that's Gawd Hisself entering into you: all ten inches of sacred cock. Ten inches my foot, you blasphemer. It's all I got, but there's more to come; it's the thought that counts. It's the diameter that fulfills. You mean the circumference. Don't be a pedant; if you're the Holy Ghost I'm the Virgin Mary. Not now you're not. Oh Henry, Henry, oh my God Henry I love you. . . .

The leaves of the quaking aspens twinkled above them. A golden meteor soared eastward across the Pleiades. The new moon went down in the western sky and the sounds of the shivaree began to fade.

Nine thousand five hundred feet and ten inches above sea level.

IX

They spent the remainder of that summer at the fire lookout on North Rim. The regulation ninety days of passion came and passed and even so he continued to marvel in her, to dote upon her, to adore each detail of her flesh and hair and mind and character. They quarreled about nothing, now and then, when the isolation of the place cast a pall of melancholy over her spirit but resolved each quarrel in a warm solution of sexual salts, weeping, laughter, plenty of wine and long walks through the woods.

Mornings she worked on her Mozart sonatas and Bach partitas, sawing away on her fiddle inside the board-and batten-shack, sitting on a rickety chair before her music stand, turning pages. While Henry in his open-aired lookout ninety feet above closed his book or put down his binoculars and listened, found himself leaking tears over the perfection of Mozart and struck into awe by the vast echoing unanswerable vision of the grand Bach chaconne.

In the afternoon Claire straddled her ten-speed Peugeot and bicycled fourteen miles in a couple of hours to her evening job at the lodge, where she worked as hostess in the restaurant. Henry would meet her at the end of her shift, spend half her tips on drinks at the bar with buddies from the fire crew and their girlfriends. Half tipsy then they loaded her bike in his pickup—their bike, their pickup— and motored easily, idly through the woods and past the open meadows where deer grazed in the moonlight and up the dirt lane under the aspens to their cabin and tower on the highest point of the entire Kaibab Plateau. The air would be chill by then but a fire was set in the stove: Henry lit the fire and by its light undressed her (tired poor working girl) inch by inch and rolled her on her belly and putting his large hairy hands to practical use massaged her neck and ears, her shoulders, her shoulder blades and back, the small of the back above the twin dimples at the base of her spine, her rounded, full and lightly suntanned rump, her thighs calves ankles feet toes—and then, and then he made the return journey up her legs but always hesitated, paused near the midpoint of his pilgrimage to bite each plump buttock once, not too gently, and to roll her over again or perhaps to simply slide upon her as she was, belly down, and spread her legs with his knees, take the nape of her neck in his teeth, grasp her breasts in each hand, whisper sweet vile proposals in her ear before inserting himself to perform his duly obligated lawfully approved formally licensed divinely consecrated conjugal duty. She murmured in reaction, half asleep, then less asleep began to whimper like a child, like a girl, like a roused and dangerous woman until she had squeezed from that curious innerspace probe of his the last full measure of devotion. After which, sprawled and tangled limb on limb, they slept and snored innocent as babes in the wood. This sort of thing went on and on for weeks, months, years, shocking the great horned owls of the forest, the starnosed moles beneath the cabin floor, the giant fur-winged Luna moths that gathered outside the window screens.

On rainy days he came down from his tower. If the air was cold and she wanted to continue practice he built a fire for her. This often led to the usual collusion:

Come on. I can't. Come on; two more times; you can do it. Henry, I can't. We'll set a new world's record. Most multiple multiple-orgasm by WASP wench in lookout cabin in Southwest USA since Frieda Von Richthofen Lawrence diddled Mabel Dodge Luhan in the men's room in the Taos Inn. I'm tired; you're disgusting. Think about what we're doing; feel that? I feel it. Then come again. I can't. You can.

She could. Afterward, in the rain, they wandered through the spruce and fir picking morels, puffballs, chanterelles, wild onions, wild currants and strawberries, lamb's quarter, pokeweed greens. She believed in a diet of fresh and raw vegetables. He preferred pigmeat, poached venison, potatoes, gravy and beer. They compromised by trying everything, culinary and sexual, that seemed mutually appealing.

Mrs. Lightcap had no desire to return to Smith College in September. One year in that place, she explained, was enough. Henry felt grateful. The prospect of eight months in a town named Northampton in a state of New England had filled him with claustrophobic angst, though he'd kept mostly silent about it.

Thoreau liked it there, she said. Thoreau was a creepy little pederast. That's a lie. He liked to take young boys on huckleberry parties; and I mean take. You have the lowest, filthiest mind; you're worse than any pederast; Thoreau was a flutist and a wilderness lover; he should be a hero of yours. He did have an elegant prose style. He still does. But his poems are mediocre even for a Harvard man. That's true; get out your flute, Henry. This one? That one.

He uncased his old beaten secondhand Haines. Claire placed on the music stand some Bach gigues, gavottes and bourrées which she had transcribed for him. He attempted the first.

Too many flats, he complained. I made it as simple as I could; anyhow the notes are not your problem. What's my problem? You have a good tone; you have clear phrasing, decent timbre, adequate fingering; but—. Yes? This is Bach, not some Irish folk tune; not a cowboy song. What do you mean? I mean that it has to be played with metrical precision; you're not counting, Henry; you don't seem to have any sense of measure; how could you ever play with other musicians? Well, I never tried; I'm a soloist. But this is J. S. Bach, soloist or not. Well, I'm Henry H. Lightcap and I don't care who knows it. Sweetheart, we're aware of that. But you don't have to be so aggressive about it. It suggests a certain quality about you which, well, is not your best.

Claire was smiling at him as she said it, her hand on his knee. He looked away, out the open doorway of the cabin, and felt, for a moment, a sickly sadness trickle through his nerves. He waited for his inward anger to subside and said, I know what you mean.

Of course you do.

I've suffered from it all my life.

We all do. She watched him with her gray-blue eyes, her gaze level and sympathetic, her lips parted in a tentative smile.

What the French call *ressentiment*, he said. Is there such a word? A kind of sick resentment of anything—excellent. Beyond my reach. Superior. Incomprehensible. Like quadratic fucking equations. Fucking symbolic logic. Like fucking Benedict Spinoza. Like—many things.

Oh Henry. . . .

But: I accept my limitations, he proclaimed. Proudly.

She smiled at that. By God you'd better.

And they collapsed together in a fit of laughter. To merge in heat.

Instead of New England they squandered the autumn in a tour of the hidden Southwest. He showed her his secret places, his treasured canyons, holy rivers, sacred mountains. Sleeping on a mattress in the bed of the pickup truck, they camped for a week by a cold bright creek in the San Miguel Mountains eating brook trout for breakfast, Claire's stir-fried rice and vegetables for supper, each other for lunch. When the sun was shining. When a second motor vehicle came groaning up the dirt track and parked only half a mile below, Henry loaded his backpack with tent, fly rod, grub, sleepingbag etc.—"and soo forth," as she said—and led her by deer path five miles farther and three thousand feet higher to a nameless small lake at timberline. He set up the tent and caught a mess of native browns. They stayed there for five days and on the fifth climbed the craggy peak above the lake, embraced in the wind at 14,211 feet above sea level, glissaded down a snowfield, inspected the ruins of an abandoned gold mine and returned to camp. Next morning they descended to the truck through the first blizzard of the mountain fall.

He took her next to the high desert, to the canyonlands of southern Utah and northern Arizona. Down in the canyons at the side of pools the leaves of the cottonwoods were beginning to change from acid-green to pale yellow. The shade beneath the trees had a greengold tone, reflected by the water. The canyon walls appeared rosy red at dawn, buff brown at noon, pink and lavender and purple through the continuum of evening and twilight. He parked the truck under the trees by a waterfall with plunge pool big enough for swimming. They played in the water nude as fish and made love in the hot sun on a limestone ledge slick as marble. He pointed out the ancient pictographs and petroglyphs on the rock wall above; she found new ones that he had overlooked. They filled their pockets with raisins and venison jerky and hiked for five miles up the canyon, wading the water and found more pictures on the canyon walls, a dwelling of mud and stone in an inaccessible alcove in the cliff and a natural arch sculptured by erosion through a sandstone fin. The fin was twenty feet wide, a hundred high. The moon of evening floated on the ellipsoid patch of sky inside the arch: like a blue eye with white iris and pupil mounted in the socket of a rose-colored skull. One mourning dove chanted in the distance.

Are there more of those in here?

Natural arches? This is the biggest.

This place should be a national park.

He put a finger to his lips and looked around. The walls have ears.

And eyes. She smiled. Are we being selfish?

You're damn right. Let them others find this place like we did. By looking for it. By dreaming of it.

They lingered in the canyons for two weeks, exploring pockets and corners in a maze of wonders. They slept under the stars, swam in the pools beneath waterfalls, climbed the strange monoliths.

Henry, I'm frightened.

Why?

Because I'm so happy; I've never been so happy in my life; it's frightening.

He held her in his arms, stroked her flowing hair, caressed the supple rondure of her breasts, arms, hips. He said nothing. He understood her fear and had no answer for it.

They camped for three days and nights on a point of naked stone two thousand five hundred feet above the Colorado River. The place had no name on the maps. Henry broke a bottle of wine on the rock and christened it Cape Claire. They were eighty miles by burro path, jeep trail and dirt track from the nearest county highway—a gravel-surfaced road connecting a place called Pipe Spring (pop. 10) to a place called Wolf Hole (pop. 0). They watched five small pretty boats—dories—pass beneath them on the river, pitching and yawing through whitewater rapids, bound for the stagnant cesspool of Lake Mead sixty miles downstream. They saw bighorn sheep scrambling from ledge to ledge on the cliffs below, on the crags above. Golden eagles, red-tailed hawks, black vultures and raucous blueblack ravens circled in the air above and below. Lean stalks of agave grew by the side of sandy basins in the stone, seedpods rattling in the wind. A squall of rain passed through one night transforming each basin into a shallow tiger's eye of water. They refilled their water cans cup by cup. The sun emerged from a range of clouds, the wind blew and by evening the pools were dry. They walked in twilight on a path through a silent village of basaltic boulders set on pedestals of mudstone. A coiled and excited rattlesnake challenged their advance. Henry squatted on his heels, spoke to the snake, stroked the underside of its neck with his stick until the snake became quiet, then lifted it draped on the stick to the side of the trail and set it safely down. They walked on, climbed a ridge, circled back to camp and watched the red sun sink beneath a quilted ceiling of clouds, a grand excessive baroque display of color and fire that overspread the entire sky for an hour and lingered in the west for three hours more.

They worked their way off Cape Claire, driving the unreliable two-wheel-drive pickup down stony ravines and across sand-filled washes and onto the deep-rutted jeep trail that meandered in various directions around numerous obstacles but kept bearing north. Henry stopped frequently to get out his shovel and bevel off cutbanks, remove rocks and circle ahead on foot in search of the route when it disappeared on acres of bare hardpan. They found a shortcut through the Grand Wash Cliffs, camped under the Virgin Mountains and by noon of the second day reached a town named Mesquite and the paved highway that led to Las Vegas. By late afternoon they were lying together in a tub of hot soapy water in a room on the tenth floor of the Mint Hotel. They stayed there for two nights, saw Woody Allen at Caesar's Palace, ate the bargain meals at the Stardust, admired the Las Vegas architecture, won seventy dollars at the blackjack tables in the Fremont Casino and left town quickly.

I don't like this, she said.

Why not?

We're too lucky.

Don't worry, said Henry. We deserve it.

They drove the pickup, refueled, retuned and repaired, across the basins and over the ranges of the Amargosa Desert, the Grapevine Mountains, Death Valley, the Panamint Range, Saline Valley, Eureka Valley, the Inyo Mountains and down into Lone Pine on the eastern slope of the Sierra Nevadas, left their signatures in the hikers' register on the summit of Mount Whitney (14,494 feet above sea level), drove south to Mojave, Santa Monica, Laguna Beach, Oceanside, dipped their feet and immersed their bodies together in the green waves and white surf of the western sea. Unable to afford a hotel room, they drove eastward to the crest of the Vallecito Mountains and made camp on a high good place from which they could see west to the Pacific, east to Arizona. They counted their money. Four dollars and two cents.

We're broke, she said, delighted by the novelty of the sensation.

You want to go back to Denver?

And live with Mother? You're kidding of course. No thanks. Anywhere but there. Let's go someplace different.

Different from what?

Different from Denver.

They drove east next day across the desert, past the Salton Sea, the Chocolate Mountains, the Sand Hills, across the Colorado through Yuma and deep into the Sonoran Desert, refueling at Gila Bend, Fan Belt Capital of southern Arizona, soon after dark. Claire disapproved, as Henry knew she would, but finally agreed out of necessity to stand guard while Henry dipped his siphon hose into the tank of a city car behind City Hall. They drove on to Tucson that night and camped in the saguaro forest west of the city. Tucson, they decided, would do for the winter. In the morning Claire found a job as a waitress at the Arizona Inn near the University; she placed an ad in the school paper offering tutorial instruction in music theory, history, piano, flute and violin. Henry stood in line for two hours at the State Department of Employment Security, downtown, made formal application for a position as professor of philosophy, park ranger, fire lookout or social worker, and filed a claim against Utah and the National Park Service for unemployment compensation. Such gall, such brass, such insolence—but was he not "entitled," by custom and by law? He was. But he knew what his old man would have said about such beggary and he dared not even imagine what his brother Will would think. The economic honeymoon was over.

To soothe his conscience and appease Claire, Henry took a part-time job (for a time) as *plongeur* or pearl diver in the kitchen of Mother Hooper's Café, a dark den for transients, winos, welfare recipients and other derelicts such as himself. Within two weeks he and Claire had accrued enough cash and credit to rent a three-room "studio" apartment in the student ghetto of the University. They took the mattress from the bed of the pickup, beat the dust out of it, laid it on their parlor floor. They bought four gallons of latex enamel and repainted the walls. They improvised bookcases, repaired a salvaged sofa, reglued a pair of chairs, equipped the kitchen with toaster and new table from the Goodwill store and bullied the landlord into fixing the plumbing. Claire rented an upright piano, had it tuned and trundled into the apartment. She picked volunteer snapdragons from the weedy yards in the neighborhood and set them in beer cans and jelly jars on top of the piano, in the kitchen, in the bath. When her students (some of them boys) began to appear, one by one, Henry would sneak off surly to the University library for study or to the bar downtown known as the Dirty Shame Saloon where he began to acquire a circle of cronies, possibly friends, with names like Lacey, Harrington, Richard "Rick" Arriaga and Daniel K. "Decay" Hooligan. The isolate honeymoon was over.

The basic honeymoon was over but Claire and Henry remained lovers nonetheless. He loved her for her brisk energy, her calm courage, her cheerful determination to make a functional marriage of this bizarre connection with an elderly academic bum and liberated libertine like Henry H. Lightcap. What was the point of him? He posed the question often enough himself:

What are you going to do with your life, Henry?

My life? *Do* with my life? Why should I *do* anything with my life? I live my life. Or—is it mine? Or am I merely the temporal instrument of my life? A reed in the wind, a seed passing through the bowels of a cactus wren, a swirl of dust rising from an alkaline playa in the heart of the Black Rock Desert, a ripple of motion across the surface of a pond, an ephemeral downward shift of sand on the slipface of a dune? Eh? Speak, O vocalissimus.

Claire never charged him with idleness. But there was a kind of wonder in her eyes sometimes when she asked him, How can you spend so much time reading books?

He smiled. I'd rather be on a horse. Then we'll get you a horse. We'll need a one-horse ranch to keep it on. We'll get you a ranch. Sure. A wedding gift from your mother, I suppose. Henry remembered the gleam of hatred in Mrs. Mellon's eyes when she'd embraced him, smiling, after the modest ceremony at Point Imperial.

My mother would do anything for us if I asked her; but I don't intend to ask her. Good, said Henry; I'm sure glad to hear that. But I will come into a trust fund when I'm twenty-five. We won't need it, he said. ("Come into"? he thought.) It's not much; about twenty thousand a year. (Henry's heart skipped a beat. That was twice what he'd ever earned in a single year.) But we could buy a piece of land somewhere, build a house on it. Make a home, raise a garden, keep a pair of horses if you wish.

And a pair of children, I suppose?

Yes.

All right. But I'm not living on your money. I'm a working man. I believe in working for my bread—six months a year. That's the way we're going to live. In honest poverty. Voluntary simplicity, like Thoreau said. The pederast? Yeah—him.

X

They would settle for the time being on Tucson, Arizona, a resort town for trust funders and rednecks both, with a symphony orchestra for ambitious violinists. In January Claire enrolled at the University, beginning her senior year as a student of higher leaning. Henry complained when he discovered that she had borrowed money from her mother in order to pay the high tuition fees required of nonresidents.

Nonresident? he said; we live here.

We have to live here for a year to qualify as residents.

Lie.

I'd rather not, Henry; and you've still got Utah plates on that truck of yours.

Well, goddamnit I'm your husband; I pay the bills around here, not your mother.

Then you'd better get a job, earn some money.

All right, I'll earn some money. While she was at school he disassembled, cleaned and reassembled his revolver and his deer rifle and went off into the desert with D. K. Hooligan for target practice. Borrowing his friend's ear protectors, he fired five rounds out of six into a beer can at fifty feet with the .357 and seven out of seven at a hundred feet with the .30-.30. Satisfied, Hooligan hired him for a one-night job at a nameless dirt airstrip on the Papago Indian Reservation fifty miles southwest of Tucson. The plane came in at twilight from the south, circled twice, put down and taxied to a stop. The pilot did not shut off the motor. There was an exchange of light signals between the airplane and Hooligan. Hooligan put away his flashlight, unchained the huge wallet from the hip pocket of his jeans and walked to the side of the plane, under the wing. Henry waited fifty feet away under the branches of a mesquite tree, rifle in his hands, revolver in his belt. He watched the door of the plane open, heard a quiet exchange of words, saw a dozen squarish bundles in white sacking tumble out, saw Hooligan pay and shake hands with the man inside. The engine roared, the pilot released the brakes, the airplane rolled then raced down the remainder of the strip, bouncing over bursage and panic grass and took off, wings waggling, into the flamboyant Papago sunset.

Henry and D. K. loaded the odd-size bales of what looked and felt like alfalfa into Hooligan's van and started off for Tucson.

Friends of yours? Henry asked.

We've been doing business for a while.

Why'd you need me?

Hooligan smiled his rich and satisfied smile. That's the kind of business it is, he said. Friendly but not too friendly.

They knew I was there? Under the tree?

You bet. That's the first thing I told them. About my friend Dogmeat the Green Beret. They could see you. They trust my judgment.

Three hours later they reached the Dirty Shame. Hooligan paid Henry five hundred dollars in cash for the evening's work and bought them each a drink. Arriaga and Lacey appeared and joined them for a second round. Sometime after midnight Hooligan drove Henry to his apartment house. Henry entered to find Claire sitting up in her nightgown, wide awake, waiting for him. She said nothing as he stood the rifle in the corner, sat down beside her on the rehabilitated sofa and slipped an arm around her bare shoulders.

I'm home, Honeydew. She said nothing. He felt his sheepish, guilty grin slipping away. I've been working, he said. Earning money. Dinero. Moola. Frogskins. She said nothing. He pulled a wad of bills from his pocket, placed it in her palm and folded her fingers over it. Give that to your mother, he said.

She looked at the four century notes, the three or four twenties, the fives and ones. She crushed the bills into a ball and put them in the big ceramic ashtray on the apple-box coffee table before them. Two of Henry's cigar butts rested in the ashtray, together with matchbooks labeled Pandora's Box and the Dirty Shame.

Say something, he demanded.

She struck a match and applied the clear yellow flame to the crinkled pile of paper money. The finely engraved, labor-ennobled, leathery-textured legal tender began to burn, slow but willing. Henry watched.

I risked my life for that money.

She made no immediate reply except to strike a second match and encourage the fire. She said, I know what Hooligan's business is. You don't have to tell me.

They watched the flames creep over the noble faces of Washington, Lincoln, Jackson, Franklin.

It's only marijuana, he pleaded. No proof yet it does anybody any harm. Good placebo anyhow. He pulled a plastic Baggie from his jacket. Brought a sample home for you. For you, Honeydew. You like the stuff don't you? Seems like I see you smoke it now and then.

She said nothing. They watched the flames continue their patient consumption of his earnings.

That's more than I get in four weeks of unemployment compensation, he complained. Finally she looked at him. Henry, are you really as stupid as you pretend? How stupid is that? You really don't understand what I'm angry about? I guess not. You don't like Hooligan? The stink of burning money passed his nose, floated on. Is that it? I don't care about Hooligan, I care about you. You mean—? Keep trying. You mean that if something happens to me, if I got killed so to speak, you'd never speak to me again?

She lifted her arms and hung her interlocked hands around his red skinny vulturine neck. From a distance of six inches she peered into his eyes: soft gray-blue the color of smoked sapphire peering into squinty bloodshot gooseberry green. Looking very serious, she touched his lips with her lips. She licked the lobe of his left ear with her tongue, veiling his face with the fall of her hair. Her pink-tipped breasts within the filmy stuff of her gown pressed upon his white chest.

She said, Take a shower Henry and brush your teeth and come to bed. I'll explain everything to you in terms that you can understand.

XI

Through the winter he filed his applications. In March the offers began to arrive: seasonal ranger jobs at Arches, Isle Royale, Grand

Canyon, Gila Wilderness, Glen Canyon; fire lookouts at North Rim, Glacier Park, Tonto National Forest. . . . Nixon still in office, the war yet smoldering on, prosperity burgeoning, Henry Lightcap the permanent part-time career anarchist enjoyed a wide choice of attractive low-paying untenured futureless upwardly immobile temporary jobs. The only kind he wanted. The only type he thought he needed.

In April he made his selection and on May Day (Law Day in the US, Workers' Day in the SU, Fertility Day in pagan Europe, Homecoming Day in Henry's heart) he started work as a five-month fire lookout on a mountaintop near Globe, Arizona, one hundred miles by road from Tucson. He might have preferred other places but by this choice he remained within easy driving distance of his young wife, who had three weeks of school remaining in May and would return to school in early September. They would sublet the apartment through the summer.

In mid-June they celebrated their first conjugal anniversary with caviar (red), champagne, wild flowers and commemorative love on the lookout's chair (mounted on insulators) inside the cabin of the fire lookout tower. Love at timberline again, seven thousand nine hundred ninety-two feet above sea level.

That same day, in the evening by a ceremonial fire on a rim of rock overlooking five separate mountain ranges, the canyons of the Salt River and a *gran finale* of a sunset beyond Four Peaks and the Superstitions, Claire informed Henry that she wanted a baby. That she wanted to become a mother. That she was out of b.c. pills and ready to begin ovulating most any time. Like right now.

Anatomy is destiny, agreed Henry, but what about your musical career? Lightning crackled nearby—the smell of ozone blended with his wife's Shalimar by Guerlain Inc., New York. His choice, not hers.

Fuck my musical career, she said, leaning toward him in the firelight. Her eyes shone like a tiger's eyes. No, blue-gray but fiery, like the eyes of an ocelot. Fuck me.

Goodness gracious. Such language from my child bride. Honeydew Mellon, I'm shocked, really.

Thunder rumbled through the woods.

Shut up and kiss me you fool. She sprawled upon him, flattening him to the stone. Her tongue probed his mouth, her knees clutched him by the rib cage. Defenseless, overwhelmed, he lay on his back with his pants down, his prick up and one hand hanging idly, helpless, over the edge of a fifty-foot drop-off straight down to a nest of timber rattlers sleeping in a bed of stiletto-bladed yuccas. Raindrops splashed on his face, dribbled through his hair, soaked the shirt on Claire's slender back and ran in rivulets down the sweet cleft perfection of her bottom, trickling from there onto his balls. The rain increased but failed to quench or even dampen the fire of their reciprocating lust. They came when they came—her phrase—like overlapping fumaroles spouting molten magma in the night. His image. Coiled together they lay in the falling rain, drenched, besotted, gasping for air, searching for their scattered wits.

We done it that time, he said.

We did it. I could feel it. Now we're really in the animal soup.

Henry pulled up his jeans as he struggled from beneath her relaxed weight. It's raining, he mentioned, tugging her to her feet. Hand in hand they ran for the lookout cabin. Ribbons of pink lightning skittered across the black sky—an insane scribbling, a blind demented fury. They laughed and slammed the door, stripped off their soaked clothes and tumbled into bed and slept for ten hours. Blue light flashed and vanished beyond the windowpanes. Thunder echoed thunderblast as the rain came down in advancing then retreating waves.

Henry dreamed of woodsmoke. He awoke at sunrise to see two pine snags flaring like torches a mile below. Naked as a jaybird he switched on the forest radio to report the fires while Claire, wearing nothing but her pink ruffled apron, made coffee, folded an omelet of eggs, peppers and tomatoes in the skillet and quartered two fat oranges into eight golden sections. Facing each other across the tiny foldout table they drank the coffee, ate the omelet, sucked on the oranges and strove but failed to contain their idiotic smiles. Henry stuck a section of orange over his gums and offered her his patent golden grin.

Henry, Henry. . . .

He removed the orange. I know, he said.

I can't bear it. I'm so happy I want to weep.

I know, he said. Me too—happy as a dead pig in the sunshine, like Grandma always said.

I think I'm going to cry.

Me too.

They wept for a while together then wandered off through a mist of fog and the tang of smoke to hunt for mushrooms.

XII

In August she announced that she was pregnant. I'm preggers, she said, the rabbit never lies.

That night on the rimrock? When it rained? That was the night. I hope it's twins, he said. Might as well have an instant family, get this thing going whole hog. How nicely you put it. He embraced and kissed her, letting his hands slip down to her haunches. How nice it is to put. You're so vulgar. Henry H. Lightcap here. Man of the people. Voice of the common man. *L'homme sensual,* as the Frogs say. That's not quite the way the French pronounce it. What can you expect from a Frog?

Mildly panicked, he worried about money. She reminded him that she would receive an income of her own in only a few more years. That was some comfort but small consolation to Henry: assuaged his fear but provoked his pride.

Your money is your money, he said. I'll support my family myself. Somehow. (Furthermore, he thought, there's something tainted about trust fund money.)

I see, she said. What's yours is mine but what's mine is mine?

That's right. (Would have to talk to her about that. That matter of unearned income. Someday.)

That's not right, that's a double standard. Well goddamnit you're a woman I'm a man. There's your double standard, built into biology. I've got a million years of mammalian tradition behind me. Some of us don't accept that kind of thinking anymore. I've read about it. I've read Beauvoir and Friedan too and that long-nosed goon-eyed harpy Virginia Woolf. Those lilies of the valley. A room of their own? They should each have a cell in a nunnery. On Lesbos Island.

You can be so cruel. There's a mean streak in you, Henry. That's one of the things I don't like about you. Only one? What else? Oh— the way you blow your nose on the ground then wipe your hand on a tree. Can't you use a handkerchief? Did you ever hear of Kleenex? What else? Come on, let's hear it. Peeing in the bathroom washbasin. You'd rather see me piss in the kitchen sink? Why can't you use the toilet like everyone else? Because the damn things are built for Puerto Ricans, that's why. If I piss in the toilet bowl I splash piss all over the wall. Try sitting down. I'm a man. An American. Only Hindus squat to piss, for christsake. Hindus and women. Anyhow I usually piss off the back porch, you know that. It's unnatural to piss indoors. Unsanitary.

I give up. Suppose the baby is born deformed or something? What are you talking about? You heard me; what should we do? Suppose it's a Mongoloid idiot? You mean Down's Syndrome? I mean Mongoloid idiot; what should we do?

She stared at him. Tears welled up in her eyes. Henry, please, don't even think such a thing.

Well. . . . Ashamed of himself, he tried to hug her to him. She turned away. Just thought . . . he said. But he wasn't thinking very well.

Visitors appeared from time to time. Claire's friends from the music department at the University—a violist, a cello player, another violinist. With Claire and her fiddle they played a Haydn quartet and a Mozart quartet among the noble columns of a grove of Ponderosa pines. Henry on duty in the fire lookout heard the music ascending past his tower and thought of Vienna, the Hapsburgs, elegant salons lit by a thousand candles, ladies in powdered wigs and hoopskirts, gentlemen in pigtails and satin knee britches, the silent stream of servants flowing from kitchen to salon and back, the greasy slaveys in the scullery, the ragged prisoners in the dungeons, chains on the wall, torches burning in the darkness of an inquisitorial chamber, the sweating ogre in the black leather hood . . .

Mozart. Papa Haydn. Them good old rococo times. Or as it should be spelled, he thought, R*o*C*o*C*oo.

Without torturers like Igor, explained Le Duc de Camembert (a soft dense mellow fellow) to Le Duc d'Angoisse-Frisson, there could be no gentlemen like us. *Ipsissima verba.* The very words.

But Henry had a sick imagination, obsessed with history. Aloft in his tower too long he'd been reading too much Gibbon, Mommsen, Acton, Toynbee, Becker, Wells, Braudel, Prescott, Beard, Wittfogel. . . . Torture, massacre, slavery, peonage and serfdom, rank and caste and hierarchy, the nightmare unfolding for five six seven thousand years or ever since the first Pharaoh hissed, uncoiled and rose like a hooded cobra from the slime of the Nile and our hydraulic tyranny began its self-perpetuating growth.

Sometimes he heard voices:

It is not enough to understand the world of man. The point is to change it. He looked around. Who said that?

Dr. Harrington arrived one day, accompanied by Lacey and Arriaga and their wives. There was a picnic on the rim at evening and a liberal flow of wine, beer, Pepsi-Cola. From white-haired Keaton Lacey, a gentleman bowman and gunner, Henry learned that one of their favorite Arizona game ranges would soon be closed to hunting.

How come?

Lacey explained: An outfit called Lovers of Fur Bearers has received a big bequest from some millionaire animal sentimentalist in California. They bought out the cow ranch at the mouth of Turkey Creek Canyon. That means they control access to about ten-by-ten miles of state land and federal land. Sixty-four thousand acres. They're gonna make it what they call a wildlife preserve. Closed to hunting.

That'll make a lot of people very unhappy.

It makes me unhappy.

Those critter freaks are going to need a gamekeeper.

They sure are. About a dozen gamekeepers. Well-armed gamekeepers. Drunk and ignorant suicidal gamekeepers.

Sounds like work for you, Lacey. You and Hooligan.

We're not that drunk and ignorant.

Henry drove into town on his next day off and applied for the position himself. He would soon be a family man, needing steady employment. He was interviewed by Mr. Joseph S. Harlow, III, stockbroker by trade, who occupied an office suite on the top floor of the Pioneer Building in downtown Tucson, only two blocks in fact from the green spittoons, rancid air, creaky floorboards and eroded slate pool tables of the Dirty Shame Saloon. But what an abysm yawned between.

Mr. Harlow, gray-haired and square-headed, peered at Henry over spectacles lowered to the tip of his nose. Feet on desk, he clipped the tip from a Macanudo, passed a lighter to Henry, brushed copies of *Forbes* magazine, the *Wall Street Journal*, *Audubon* mag-

azine and the *Sierra Club Bulletin* to the side. Henry lit his cigar—
a huge fat gentleman's smoke of a quality to which he was not,
actually, fully accustomed.

Any background in law enforcement, Mr. Lightcap?

Henry mentioned his year and a half with the Military Police in
Italy, his six months with the Border Patrol in Big Bend, Texas, his
seven or eight intermittent years as a park ranger in Utah, Arizona,
Montana, Florida.

Six months with the Border Patrol?

Yessir.

Why only six months?

I didn't really like the work.

You're a liberal, I suppose?

No sir, I'm a bigot. It was shooting those damn Mex cows with
the hoof-and-mouth disease that got me down. Can't stand the noise
a hollow-point bullet makes when it hits a living body.

A brief pause.

Married? Yessir; twice. Divorced? Yep; once. Childen? None on
the streets; one in the oven.

Pause. Lightcap and Harlow puffed on their great rich turdlike
cigars, blowing ragged clouds of smoke at the ceiling. Portofino fog.

Are you a Harvard man, Mr. Lightcap?

Me?

You're wearing a Harvard tie.

I am? Henry looked down and lifted the crimson pennon, like the
parboiled tongue of a cow, that dangled from his collar. He gazed
at the thing in wonder. A gift from my mother-in-law, he explained. The Snag. No sir, as a matter of fact I went to school in
New Mexico.

Familiar with horses?

Yes. But not too familiar.

Good. We understand each other. Most of the Turkey Creek preserve can be patrolled by jeep but some will require a horse. Ex-
tremely rugged terrain. You'd have eight or nine horses in your care,
about forty miles of fencing to keep up, three windmills, two alfalfa
fields and a small citrus orchard to look after. From time to time
you'd be expected to give the grand dames of our organization a
tour of the premises—and they'd be very disappointed, I might add,
if our caretaker failed to produce a few live deer, javelina, coati-

mundi, a bobcat or two. Keep that in mind. But of course the difficult part of the job involves public relations with the local citizenry. Have you ever confronted a group of drunken pig hunters, Mr. Lightcap, on the opening day of javelina season?

No sir.

Demanding access over private property to public lands?

No.

How do you think you would handle such a situation?

Henry paused for thought. Thought seemed appropriate here. Inwardly he decided, I'd have Lacey with his steel crossbow and Hooligan with a light machine gun enfilading from the shrubbery. Aloud he said, I'd treat them with tact and delicacy, sir, but politely forbid access.

Suppose they offered violence?

I would honor the offer.

A pause. Harlow considered that remark, savoring its facetious ambiguity, then said, This could be dangerous work, Mr. Lightcap, at least for the first few years or until our legal rights are respected.

Yessir. Well, it sounds like interesting work to me. I'm ready to try something different.

You sure?

You only live once.

True; a comforting thought. A pause. Now as to emolument, Mr. Lightcap, we could offer something in the neighborhood of, say, twelve thousand per annum?

Henry looked thoughtfully at his cigar.

Plus expenses, of course: fuel for vehicles and horses, fencing and equipment repair. Living quarters provided, including utility bills. Not a bad deal. The organization has a group medical-insurance plan and a pension plan. I'm sure our wildlife caretaker would be included in both.

What kind of pension? A widow's pension?

Disability, retirement or death. Whichever comes first.

I'd need a little extra help during hunting season.

Certainly. That would come under annual operating expenses.

Henry paused for reflection while Harlow continued his study of Henry's physiognomy. I'll take the job, Henry said.

Mr. Harlow lowered his feet from the desk and rose gracefully from his chair. He extended his right hand. Goodbye, Mr. Lightcap. We're not taking employment applications yet actually, not formally I mean, but if you will leave your name and address with my secretary out front . . .

Yessir. They shook. Henry departed, satisfied. He felt he had made his point.

He was correct. In early September came the letter on official Lovers of Fur Bearers stationery offering Henry H. Lightcap, Esq., the position of "wildlife warden" at the newly established Emily Ives Bancroft Sanctuary for Fur-Bearing Quadrupeds. Prompt reply requested. Signed, Caroline Currier Mills, Executive Director, Washington, D.C. Among the trustees listed on the letterhead was Joseph S. Harlow, III, Tucson, Arizona.

What about fur-bearing bipeds? asked Claire. Such as Mother.

Good point. As a matter of fact the javelina is not a fur-bearing beast. Hairy yes, piglike yes, but not furry.

Like yourself?

Yeah—like me.

XIII

The first thing Henry did was hire a part-time assistant. Twelve thousand dollars a year—one thousand a month, two hundred and fifty a week! plus expenses!—was twice any salary he had ever earned before in his life. It seemed to him easy, then, only natural, to share part of such bounty, such booty, with his friend Lacey, a Vietnam veteran with hunter's eyes, the panther's caution, a 50 percent (mental) disability allowance from the VA and a sound wholesome distrust of the human race. He didn't need the work, Lacey agreed, but he could use the money. His Ford 250 needed a new engine.

Claire disapproved of these procedures. You shouldn't do this without consulting Harlow, she said. He may not like it. And I don't trust that man Lacey. He's crazier than Hooligan.

They're war vets, honey. You've got to make allowances.

I don't care for self-pity. Those two may have suffered. No doubt they witnessed some terrible things. But—

Yeah, like seeing their best buddies torn open by mortar shells. Like seeing children roasted in napalm.

Henry, I can't bear that kind of talk.

I'm sorry. He enfolded her in his arms and drew her close. Here's the beauty of hiring Lacey, he said, murmuring in her ear. With that bandit installed out at Turkey Creek I can spend more time here in town with you. You and our incipient child. Due when?

She liked that. Due in February.

Henry and Lacey went to look at their new home in the country, 120 miles from Tucson. Eighty miles of pavement and forty miles of ranch road—dust, mud, sand, rock. Both were familiar with the road and neither distressed nor surprised by the leaky-roofed puncheon-floored urine-smelling log cabin that served as main ranch house or by the weed-grown garden, the unpruned orchard, the pastures rank with prickly pear, mesquite, cheatgrass and tumbleweed. Cow country.

Not bad, said Lacey, not half bad. It's all bad. How much you say those Fur Bearers paid for this weed ranch?

About three hundred thousand. Down. You don't have to live in the house.

I don't intend to.

They checked out the rolling stock, a tractor, a cattle truck, the four-by-four Chevy pickup. All three needed work but they would function.

And the outbuildings: the workshop-smithy looked usable. A ton of baled alfalfa was stacked in the hayshed. The tack room contained three repairable roping saddles and the cannibalized remains of a dozen medieval rigs with rat-chewed leather that must have seen their best days on the Goodnight-Butterworth Trail. Okay, sighed Henry, let's have a look at the horses.

He led the way into the pasture. Lacey—a city man—followed at a distance, keeping to the outside of the pole fence. The horses stood watching in a group from the far end by the creek but when they noticed the bucket of grain in Henry's hand first one then the rest came sauntering up. He studied their approach with appraising eyes. Neglected-looking cow horses, a mixed breed, shaggy in their winter coats.

What do you think? asks Lacey.

Cannery meat, replies Henry. But he liked the look of the tall bay mare coming in front. She had the deep barrel, square straight-legged gait, black feet, wide and shapely ears that he liked. She'll do, thought Henry, and when the horse came close, snuffling at the grain, and he got a good look into her big dark kindly eyes free of white and set wide apart—like his own—he was convinced. He let the bay have at the bucket for a moment, as the other horses crowded around, and felt the withers and stroked the short back and well-muscled rump. As he talked to her attentive ears, he felt and heard at the same time a hot heavy liquid drumming on the toe and instep of his right boot.

That other horse is pissing on your shoes, called Lacey.

This was a gelding sorrel even bigger than the bay, with dark skin for a sorrel, which Henry approved of, and long stout legs, but he noticed at once the white ring of rolling eyeball and a rough knobby appearance about the head, as if some wetback cowboy had been training the sorrel with a section of lead pipe. Your name is Hook, thought Henry, and if it isn't it should be, and I don't think we'll get along too good.

The rest were a mixture of fair to bad, like low-class citizens anywhere: a pretty palomino mare with sloping pasterns and too round a chest; a hopeless ewe-necked hammerheaded gelded wreck of a gray; a small sluggish bay mare with a ganted yearling colt that looked as if it had found a near-fatal patch of locoweed; a fair buckskin, a reasonable part-Appaloosa roan and a friendly little pinto pony that a growing child could probably ride.

Off by itself, in its eyes an expression of ironic, calculating suspicion, watching Henry carefully, stood a brown mule with a dark stripe down its back. Nothing better than a good mule, thought Henry, and nothing worse than a spoiled one. A good mule, like a human being, can be worked for thirty years. They can be that dumb. And a bad one has a kick like a rattlesnake's strike. And will wait thirty years for a chance to show it.

What about 'em? Lacey asked again.

What do I think? Henry glanced once more at the mare with foal and at the aging gray. Well as you can see there's three don't belong here. They'd be happier inside tin cans. But at least we ain't stuck with no rib-short dish-faced dingy-brained A-rabs.

They pitched a ten-by-six wall tent under the nearby sycamores of Turkey Creek. Here Lacey would make his residence through the coming month while refurbishing the cabin for winter. Here he would live with his woman friend—but which one?—while guarding the gate that barred the road that led into Turkey Creek Canyon and the wild uplands beyond.

Henry stayed with Lacey for three days and nights. He helped him restore the plumbing in the ranch house, hook up propane tanks to the kitchen, repair the windmill and get the generator going. On the second day he bridled and saddled the bay and herded the old gray, the sick mare and her sickly colt into the canyon and up the jeep trail that led onto the plateau above. There was water up there, in the draws and stockponds, and plenty of forage to keep the animals alive until mortality caught up with them—disease, old age, a mountain lion—whatever came first. He returned down canyon to Lacey, who was working on the four-wheel-drive pickup.

Next day, satisfied with the sound of the pickup's motor, they toured the entire ranch. In a fold of the mountain eight miles southwest they found a line cabin in good shape: roof intact, windows complete, the door hanging straight on its hinges. Inside was a cast-iron cookstove (like my mother's, thought Henry), table, chairs, a pair of steel cots. A mesquite-log corral stood behind the cabin, enclosing a flowing spring lined with watercress. Near the spring they found sign of deer, javelina, bighorn sheep, black bear, coyote, bobcat.

Henry left next morning with a list of needed tools, supplies, automotive parts and reading material. Lacey had forgotten to bring his Louis L'Amour books and his *Soldier of Fortune* magazines. But not his rifle, his shotgun, his sidearms, his crossbow, his recurved bow, his compound bow or his case of military cutlery.

Feeling that the Emily Ives Bancroft Sanctuary for Fur-Bearing Quadrupeds lay under good hands, Henry Lightcap drove back to Tucson. He found his wife barefoot and knocked up, spraddle-legged on a chair, reading another Bach invention on her violin. She looked strong, rosy, smug with pleasure and pride—pregnancy became her. He stroked her hair, touched her ears, caressed her neck, withers, back, croup. Good conformation. She stirred with satisfaction, lowering her bow. He checked the eyes: her eyes seemed darker, bluer, softer than before; they looked upon him—him, Lightcap, hillbilly redneck pseudointellectual—with kindness, with a deep steady unlimited love that melted the gristled cockles of his bewildered heart. He crawled before her on the floor, lifted the loose dress she wore and kissed her glossy knees, the warmth of her inner thighs, the pink labia beneath the delicate golden curls of her mons veneris. Claire put down her instrument and reached for his. She read no more that day.

XIV

The bear hunters and lion hunters with their packs of dogs gave Henry a little trouble in October. But they were few and sober. They laughed at Henry when he explained the new policy at Turkey Creek: hunters welcome but no motorized transport allowed. Shoot your bear, he said, kill your lion, but you'll have to pack it out on your shoulders. Or rent his mule, Daphne, for $250 a day. The men grinned, fingering their whiskers, spat on the ground, looked at the neatly dressed unarmed clean-shaven Lightcap and then at those shady characters, Hooligan and Lacey, lounging under the syca-mores near the tent, playing two-hand stud.

You got yourself a tough job, buddy.

Henry smiled: I get paid pretty good.

They turned back to their pickup trucks. We'll see you again, buddy, said the last to depart.

Have a nice day.

In November the deerslayers began to appear, pale-faced chiro-practors, warehouse clerks, computer tapers from Tucson and Phoe-nix. Arriving at evening on day before opening, they'd been driving for many miles and they tended to reek, as sport hunters do, of Wild Turkey, Old Grandad and too much Jack Daniel's. The first group left peaceably, pausing only at the sanctuary entrance a mile down the road to shoot up the sanctuary entrance sign. A second group put on a show of resolve. Six men in a caravan of three new pickup campers, each truck towing a jeep, they were not about to be turned away. They'd been here before, the spokesman explained to Henry, many times, and the former owner had never denied them use of the canyon road. His tone was testy, his eyelid jumping with ner-vous tics.

New ownership, explained Henry, new rules: no motor vehicles allowed on what always was and still is a private road. He indicated the old wooden hang-gate across the dirt lane, the rusted, bullet-riddled but still legible NO TRESPASSING sign. Entrance by permission only, he explained.

We don't want to hunt on your private land, the man said—a short bulky fellow with fat mustache and restless eyes. We just want access to the state land above the canyon. We request permission to use your jerkass road.

Sorry, explained Henry, but my orders are no motor vehicles allowed.

The hunter aimed his rifle—a 30.06 with scope—at the wildlife warden's belly. We demand permission, he explained. The five men with him smiled, holding their rifles at the ready. Whiskey fumes hung in waves above their heads. Keaton Lacey came out of the tent wearing his quick-draw holster tied to his thigh. Henry glanced at him, held up one hand, shook his head. To the hunters he said, In that case, gentlemen, permission granted. He opened the gate.

Henry and Lacey watched the caravan of trucks and jeeps—one jeep with a ripped bikini top, the others with no tops at all—roll through and disappear into the twilight under the sycamores. When the noise of their low-gear driving faded out, Lacey said, Why'd you do that?

I was afraid you'd shoot somebody.

Why not? said Lacey. The way they was bunched up I could've fatally maimed all six with maybe three, four shots.

That's what I mean.

So we're gonna let those bastards get away with threatening you with a deadly weapon?

I guess so. You have any better ideas?

Lacey thought. For about a moment. How'd you like that brand-new Ford 250?

Where's the Hooligan? Henry said.

He went to town. He should be back anytime.

All right, soon as he gets here we'll go up on the mesa.

Hooligan returned near midnight. Henry and Lacey left at once in the four-wheel-drive ranch pickup, following the deer hunters. In the bed of the truck they carried a block and tackle with frame, Lacey's large and comprehensive box of tools and a canvas tarpaulin. They discussed the plan as they drove along the creek, under the ghostly trees and up the narrow cliff road.

When they reached the rim of the canyon Lacey shut off his lights and drove by starlight. After a while they saw the glow of a fire a mile ahead near the first windmill. Lacey pulled into a grove of scrub oak. In the dark, under the canopy of dry fluttering leathery leaves, they laid out bedrolls and slept until an hour before dawn.

Waking, Lacey stayed with the truck. Henry walked forward until he reached a lookout point above the hunters' camp. As expected they were stirring about, despite heavy-duty hangovers, fixing breakfast by lantern light on their Coleman stoves. Henry waited and watched, binoculars dangling from his neck. Finally the hunters were ready. Two to a jeep and loaded for game, they motored off to the south, taking the trail road that led to Flat Top Mountain, six miles away. Henry climbed the windmill, gave the all-clear signal to Lacey—a circular sweep with his flashlight. The glow of the rising sun began to touch the horizon with color.

Henry stayed aloft on the windmill tower, keeping watch, as Lacey drove up and went to work at once under the hood of the Ford 250. Within thirty minutes he had the radiator out, all hoses and wiring disconnected, the frame blocked up with steel jackstands, the rear wheels chocked and the block and tackle rigged above the motor.

Henry looked down, saw Lacey slide on his back under the front of the truck, wrenches in hand. He thought of the grease, the dust, the mud, and raised his eyes to the horizon. The morning sun beamed forth beneath a gold-vermilion ceiling of cirrocumulus clouds. Another mackerel sky in Christian America.

He heard the clank of metal below, the noise of driveshaft being pulled from transmission box, the clank of exhaust pipe freed from manifold, looked down and saw Lacey emerging, saw him stand and tug on chains and hoist the great Ford V-8 powerplant—390 cubic inches—up from its black cavity in the Ford's bosom. The engine hung within the tackle frame, swaying slightly, dripping oil, while Lacey jacked up bumper, removed stands, lowered front end to normal position, chained the ranch Chevrolet to rear of trespassing Ford and dragged it six feet backward, out from beneath the hanging motor.

Henry climbed down the windmill as Lacey backed the ranch truck under the hoisted engine. Finishing his work, Lacey covered it with the canvas tarp while Henry tidied up, closing the hood on the hunter's Ford, wiping off grease stains, polishing the chrome trim. Again Lacey drove their ranch truck behind the Ford and pushed the Ford into precisely the position it had occupied before, concealing the oily mess on the ground.

They drove home in time for lunch. Skipping the meal this time Lacey announced that he'd be performing an engine transplant—not his first—within the next twenty-four hours. Thank that donor for me, he said, and motored off to Tucson in the loaded pickup. The hunters came down from the hill that evening in heavy rain with four dead bucks but driving only two pickup campers instead of the original three.

Henry demanded an explanation for the missing vehicle before he would let them out the gate. The owner of the donor Ford, sitting rigid, soaked and cold behind the wheel of his open jeep, looked grim. His red nose leaked. His eyelid twitched. He chewed on his dripping mustache.

You're behind this, he said to Henry. Open that gate.

You're the one pointed the rifle at me, Henry said. I'd recognize you anywhere. Like in a court of law for instance.

Open that gate.

Smiling, Henry opened the gate. I'll be back, the man said, wiping his wet mustache. Rain dripping down his neck.

He never came back. Probably declared the truck stolen, collected a claim against his insurance company. Lacey waited a month, then towed the gutless Ford under some trees and stripped it down to nothing but frame and cab. He even sold the doors, the windshield, the fenders, the hood, the leaf springs, the coil springs, the floor mats. He removed the wool-upholstered bench seat and used it for a sofa outside his tent, where it soon acquired the fine sun-bleached silver-gray patina of maturity.

Much later they discovered the remains of the sick mare and her colt, shot dead by persons unknown, rotting in a ravine west of the windmill.

XV

Henry Lightcap found himself summoned from time to time to the corner office on the fourteenth floor of the Pioneer Building. Joseph S. Harlow, III, seemed ever affable, the cigars first-rate, the Scotch, with a brand name seen by Henry only on backbars and in magazine advertisements, freely offered. Mr. Harlow called Henry Henry and insisted in turn on being addressed as Joe. Nevertheless, despite his democratic show, there remained an obtuse angle to the relationship that irked and puzzled Lightcap. He was easily irked. Slow of wit, he was easily puzzled, but finally figured things out one afternoon.

Henry delivered his reports, oral and written, and handed over the monthly accounting of expenses. Harlow seemed pleased with the first and barely glanced at the second, nodding with approval. Henry finished his drink and took a final puff on the fat cigar in his thumb and fingers. He was eager to leave. He'd not set eyes on Claire for three days and two nights. She was now great with child, an egg with legs, ripe as a golden honeydew melon.

Harlow said, One thing I'd better tell you now, Henry.

What's that, Joe?

You won't like it, Henry.

Then don't tell me, Joe.

Harlow smiled. We're going to have to restock the place with cattle.

No!

I said you wouldn't like it. But we have to do it. If we don't we lose the grazing permits. We lose our leases.

Can't do that, Joe. The Emily Ives Bancroft Sanctuary is going to be an elk farm, not another goddamned stinking cow ranch.

I don't like it either, Henry. But we're going to do it. It appears that both the state and the federals have the same policy on grazing permits—use them or lose them.

That's the beef ranchers' policy. Anyhow we are using them. We've got mule deer, whitetail deer, coatimundi, black bear, coyote, javelina, badger, gray fox, ringtail coat, kit fox, raccoon, gopher, ground squirrel, packrat, desert turtle, bighorn, bobcat, mountain lion, maybe a jaguar, and if we can get the goddamned Fish & Game to move we'll have elk and even some grizzly on the place.

Harlow gazed at Henry, still smiling. I know, Henry, I know. But we have no choice. Wildlife doesn't qualify as livestock.

Fight those swine. Sue the bastards. You've got a law firm around here somewhere. Henry looked under the desk, into the corners of the room, through the floor.

Yes, Henry, two floors down.

That Collude, Obfuscate, Shyster & Pettifog group.

Yes. They're good. But we're not using them. We're going to buy cattle and you and your little helpers—that Lacey? that O'Hooligan? Henry, where do you find such people?—are going to haul them out to Turkey Creek and turn them loose.

I won't do it.

But first you're going to put in more cross fencing.

There's too many cross fences already. I won't do it.

Not right away, of course. But in March and April, when the javelina season is over and the pig hunters return to their ratholes.

Can't do it, Joe.

Furthermore the board has decided that the sanctuary must begin to pay its own way. No one thinks your salary is high or your operating expenses unreasonable. But the income from the bequest is not going to be enough to pay all expenses plus meet annual mortgage payments. Or so it appears. Raising cattle will help.

Raising cattle defeats the purpose. Cows piss in the water holes, shit in the streams, grow flies, eat up the forage, tramp down seedlings, ruin damn near everything. I won't do it.

But Henry—you're working for us.

No, I'm working for the wildlife.

No, you're working for us. We hired you, Henry, remember? You're what is called an employee, Henry.

An employee?

Yes, Henry. You are an employee. I am the employer. The board makes policy, I carry it out, you do the fieldwork.

I refuse to be an employee.

Then you resign?

I refuse to be forced out. Henry stared through the window at the gathering twilight, the brass and violet sky, the fading profile of the mountains. That wildlife preserve is like home to me, Joe. I belong there. That place needs me. You can't fire me, I won't resign, and I won't turn it over to a herd of ugly stupid stinking spongy bawling bellowing shambling shit-smeared fly-covered disease-spreading lop-eared dewlapped splayfooted inbred degenerate bovine brutes.

Well phrased, Henry. Harlow's voice remained as placid as before, his tone amused and tolerant. I appreciate your crescendos. But it's futile. You understand? We can always replace you. Easily, I'd imagine. Harlow gazed, like Henry, out the wide corner window, enjoying the diminuendos of the light. I'd advise you to consider the matter carefully.

Henry stood up. *You* consider; I'm leaving.

Leaving the job?

Leaving this fucking air-conditioned fucking soundproofed glassy-walled claustrophobical six-sided overpriced high-rise stalinoidal administrative fucking prison cell.

Not so good, not so good, you're weakening, Harlow said as Henry Lightcap strode from the room, attempting but failing to slam the door behind him. The door closed with an institutional-strength hydraulic braking device that prohibited slamming. Hydraulic tyranny, *hic et ubique.*

XVI

Henry stared at the ceiling, his arm around Claire's bare shoulders. They lay in their master bed, the mattress on the floor, and listened to a recording of Glenn Gould playing the *Goldberg Variations.* Intended to be soporific for an insomniac nobleman, the thirty transsubstantiations of an enigmatic theme had been keeping spirits bright and intellects entertained for 230 years.

What's that? he asked.

The *Goldberg Variations.*

Best Jewish music I ever heard.

Gould's first recording was better. The one he made back in the fifties. This new one's self-indulgent. He's playing with himself.

Play with me.

She turned toward him, stroking the black hairs on his white narrow pigeon-breasted chest, the wiry curls on his sunken loins. You're so skinny, Henry. How am I ever going to fatten you up?

Go two inches farther down.

You're so subtle. Her exploring fingers descended to his private parts. She fondled the delicate balls, the limp languid connecting rod. No response from the sensitive plant.

Not much life in the old sexual organism tonight. Am I getting too pregnant for you?

Henry placed a hand on her swollen belly, her dimple of an umbilicus. He thought he could feel tremors of the life within. Never, he said. When's this thing due now?

About six more weeks. Maybe seven. She waited; he made no answer. Are you worried, Henry?

What about?

About the baby? You think it's going to tie you down too much? Restrict your freedom?

Freedom's just another word. He stared up through candlelight at the old-time water stains on the plaster, the hairline crack that seemed to be growing a little, week by week, inch by inch, toward the defunct light fixture bolted to the middle of the ceiling.

You're thinking about something. Tell me.

A pause. From the street outside came the noise of a barking motorcycle, sparks flying, as it backfired to a halt at the intersection. Four or five fenced-in chained-up psychotic Beware Dogs barked in reaction, idiots to an idiot. Thyroid cases.

He lied to her: Pig season starts in two weeks. I'm going to have to spend at least ten days out at Turkey Creek. Can't let Lacey and the Hooligan face those pig hunters alone. They'll kill somebody.

That's what you're worried about?

The music came to its end, the record player click-clacked to a predetermined stop.

Yes, he said.

I'm going with you.

No you're not. In your eighth month? Absolutely not. No.

Yes. It won't hurt me. We'll be careful. I want to see that line cabin at the spring, that Oak Springs you call it, the place you say is so beautiful. I want one more wilderness honeymoon with my husband before I become a professional mother. I need one more final vacation, Henry.

Out of the question, he explained.

XVII

Henry and Claire stayed in the ranch house for the first three days of javelina season. While his wife knitted booties and caps and a sweater for a miniature humanoid, Henry guarded the gate. Backed up by the reasonably sober Lacey and the fairly straight Hooligan he faced down the sportsmen, the drunk and the ignorant, the shit-faced the red-eyed the mean. A surly crew, the pig hunters spat on the ground toward Henry's feet, wrinkled their brows in dense concentration upon his words and spat again. Carbines and rifles cradled in their arms, jeep and truck motors idling behind them, vapors rising in the gelid air. A cold rain fell along Turkey Creek, blackening the sycamore leaves that covered the ground, swelling the fluted columns of the giant saguaro cactus on the bench above. Beyond the cactus forest, over the cliff walls of rosy-red andesite, blue-gray basalt, anyone with eyes could see the gleam of snow at the four-thousand-foot line on the slopes of Flat Top. Winter up there. Late autumn down here.

The pig hunters came, they growled, grunted, threatened, looked hurt and menacing and went away, tailpipes smoking. Five minutes down the rocky road and the report of handguns, the violent discharge of rifles, echoed through the canyon. The entrance sign at the cattle guard took on the sievelike aspect, more holes than substance, of Swiss cheese or Scholastic metaphysics—as Henry pointed out when the six of them, he and Claire and Hooligan and Lacey and their two young women friends, strolled down the road at evening for relaxation and laughter.

WELCOME TO THE
EMILY IVES BANCROFT
SANCTUARY FOR FUR-BEARING
QUADRUPEDS
(No Firearms Allowed)

How big is a javelina? Claire asked, from the depths of the downy hood on her down jacket.

I've seen 'em get up to fifty pounds, Hooligan said.

That's the size of a medium-small dog.

Yeah except that little pig can tear up a Doberman, a pit bull, a Rhodesian ridgeback, any dog there is.

Do the hunters eat them?

Oh some eat what there is to eat. Javelina's mostly hoof and bone, bristle and gristle. Some people like to roast the head, eat the brains. Hooligan grinned. That's the tastiest part of javelina. I like the tongue myself. There ain't much else.

Then why kill them?

Why? Hooligan paused, looked helplessly at Lacey, at Henry, at the other two girls. Why? Help me, somebody. He opened a round tin from the hip pocket of his jeans and packed a wad of snuff between gum and cheek. Tell her something, Keaton.

Lacey smiled at Claire. Thirty years old, he had a mane of snowy white hair. He was broad, blue-eyed, square-jawed, handsome as a store-window mannequin. He sucked on the joint of marijuana between his lips, passed it to his girlfriend. For the sport, Claire, what else? The little beasts are fast, hard to find, hard to hit. The pig hunters shoot them for the sport.

Disgusting, Claire said.

Lacey looked cross. You wouldn't understand, he said. Only a hunter can understand hunting.

It's a spiritual thing, Henry explained. *Le sport.*

I can understand hunting for food, said Claire, but I do not understand hunting for sport. It seems to me there's a big difference.

There is and there ain't, said Hooligan, grinning.

It's a thing men do, Lacey growled.

And you have to be a man to understand men. Is that right, Keaton?

That's right.

Disgusting, said Claire.

On the third day they were left in peace. No hunters appeared. The rain stopped and the sun came out. The word is getting around, Hooligan said. Unless they're sneaking in the back way, said Henry, around the mountain and past Oak Springs. Let's go, Claire said.

No. The road's too rough for you now.

I want to see that place. It might be my last chance for a long time.

Out of the question, Henry said. Absolutely.

Claire smiled. Absolutely?

Absolutely.

On the morning of the fourth day Henry loaded bedrolls, first-aid kit and a week's supply of food in the bed of the ranch pickup and headed up Turkey Creek under the leafless sycamores. He forded the winding stream, muddy from the rains, a dozen times in four miles and reached the foot of the steep switchbacks where the road climbed out of the canyon. He got out and locked the front hubs, got back in and shifted into four-wheel drive, low gear low range and started up the staircase of stone ledges that led to the mesa rim above. The engine whined, the cab rocked from side to side, pitching like a boat though he drove as slowly and carefully as he could. Really do need new shocks on this old wreck, he thought, just like Lacey says. He reached the top, opened the wire gate and drove through, stopped and closed the gate. The old gray gelding stood nearby, watching, hoping. Henry drove on for another five miles and turned left at the fork near the windmill. He looked at the pocket watch swinging back and forth on the dashboard: nine miles in forty-five minutes. He drove west and south along the base of Flat Top Mountain, climbing slowly. There were plates of ice on the puddles in the road but the snow was gone at this elevation, sublimated by the sun. He drove on, slowly, carefully, easing over the rocks, ruts, bumps, painfully aware of the passenger at his side. The road traversed a talus slope, loose stone above and below reposing uneasily at an angle of fifty degrees. He rolled a few rocks from the track and drove ahead, cleared the slope, reached a bench of level land overgrown with a pygmy forest of juniper, pinyon pine, agave, manzanita, hackberry. The road wound across the base of the bench, following the contour line, and entered a wide ravine in the next fold of the mountain. They came to the bare sycamores along the little run, then the horse corral and the cabin itself half hidden under the grove of Arizona white oaks. Henry drove the truck to the cabin porch, stopped, shut off the motor. He looked at Claire.

Are you all right?

She smiled, though her face seemed tense and white. I'm fine, she said.

You sure?

That road is a little rough.

He checked the time. Almost two hours to get here. We should not have done this, he said. I should not have brought you up here. This was a crazy stupid thing to do.

It's beautiful here. I love it. I wouldn't have missed this for anything.

You stay here till I get a fire going. Sick with dread, he pushed open the cabin door and kindled a fire in the iron cookstove. Flame rumbled up the pipe. He closed the damper and went outside. Claire had disobeyed him, left the truck and climbed the point of rock above the spring. Golden hair streaming in the wind, she faced the sun and the west, gazing across the olive benchlands and purple canyons toward the valley, the dim outline of the Superstition Range, the poisonous haze of Phoenix a hundred miles away.

Get down from there. Where's your coat?

Beautiful, she said, it's absolutely splendid here.

Get down.

Oh Henry be quiet. I'm not an invalid. I'm not sick. I'm only pregnant for godsake. The most natural thing in the world. Stop fussing over me so much. She gazed about for another minute, smiling with pleasure, and began to climb down from the sandstone slabs, moving heavily, awkwardly. She was wearing one of Henry's flannel shirts, size extra-large, which hung over her distended abdomen like a smock. Stop staring at me, I'll be right down.

She slipped. He sprang forward to catch her but she caught herself before falling, hands around the bole of a young oak. On her knees, she looked at him, grinned, pulled herself up, took his extended hand and came down over the damp grass to the cabin.

Stupid, he muttered, stupid, I should never have brought you here.

Stop fussing. She clung to his neck, kissed him on nose and grizzled cheek and mouth. I'm hungry. Get out the wine, I'll get dinner started.

He glanced at the sun, half concealed behind a shoal of accumulating clouds. A stiff breeze blew from the northwest. Dinner? he said. It's only about three o'clock.

What does that have to do with anything? I'm hungry. It's winter. It'll be dark soon. I hate to cook in the dark. Hate to eat in the dark. Hate to make love in the dark.

He led her inside, restoked the fire, lit the kerosene lamp on the table. The cabin did seem small and gloomy with the door shut and windows only on the north and east. He opened two bottles of wine—one red, one white—and carried in the grub box and the bedroll, a bucketful of fresh water from the spring and an armload of split juniper and oak. The fragrance of good wood graced the chill air of the cabin.

Claire held a pan up to the weak light, looking for mouse droppings, dead silverfish, retired spiders. Satisfied, she put the pan on the stove and began to slice onions. Henry embraced her from behind, burying his face in her hair, kissed her neck, her earlobe. Be back in ten minutes, he whispered. Stay inside or I'll kill you. She was singing as he left.

With ax, gloves and fencing pliers he walked the path beyond the cabin to the boundary line. He saw the tread marks of a light motorcycle in the mud. The fence was down. He walked farther to a thicket of scrub oak on the uphill side, cut down a dozen small trees—every third one—and left them lying in a brushy tangle across the trail. He returned to the fenceline, stretched and spliced the four strands of barbed wire. The metal placard hanging from the top strand—WILDLIFE SANCTUARY, NO FIREARMS OR MOTORIZED VEHICLES PERMITTED—was shot full of bullet holes. Like the others. Henry returned to the cabin, the glow of lamplight in the window, the woodsmoke streaming flat out southeastward from the top of the chimney. His ears felt cold. As he opened the door he smelled the welcoming aroma of sautéed onions, steamed brown rice, baked chicken, fried vegetables. Her specialty: his favorite dish.

Claire was sitting on the near cot, glass of white wine in hand. You need a double bed in this hut, she said; I don't sleep alone anymore.

Me neither, he said.

Did you ever?

Henry felt the reflexive smirk forming on his face and suppressed it. That was long ago, he said. Long ago and far away. He thought she looked flushed, her eyes cloudy—but that would be from the cooking. Or the wine. He pushed the second cot against the first, both against the wall, unrolled the first-class zip-together sleeping bags and joined them as one.

Is that what you call a two-man bag, Henry?

Nope. It's a Claire-and-Henry bag.

What are you, a sexist? some kind of homophobe?

Yep.

Good. I'm glad. She poured him a glass of the red wine. They touched glasses. Here's to Junior.

Here's to Shorty.

They drank. He placed a hand on her belly. What are we gonna call this critter anyhow? He put his mouth to her belly. Hey you in there: what's your name, kid? He put his cold ear down, listening for the answer.

If it's a boy we call it Paul after your little brother. Right? And if it's a girl—? Any new ideas?

The only girl's name I can ever think of is Claire.

Oh you're such a sappy fellow. And such a liar. All those wenches and witches you used to to know, all those Comforts and Joys and Jills and Valeries and Kathys and Candys and Susans and Serenas and Sibyls and Myrtles and Mary Anns . . .

Never heard of them. Supper ready?

Do you realize we've been married for a year and a half now, Henry? Or is it two and a half? You realize that, Henry?

It's been a long time.

And we're still in love? Do you realize that?

I know, he said, it's ridiculous. I can't understand it myself. And he slipped to his knees before her, wrapped his arms and locked his hands around her hips, shut his eyes and sank his face in her lap. He thought he was going to weep. And she ran her free hand through his thatch of black greasy hair, sipped more wine and stared out the north window at the red light in the sky, the remote and undiscovered mountains, the trees swaying in the wind.

He heard a little scream. He opened his eyes and heard the wail of wind, the loose sheet of metal rattling on the roof. The room was pitch-dark, the night black and starless beyond the window glass. He heard the scream again, cut short, smothered, and reached toward Claire. The lining of the sleeping bag was wet beneath her, the bottom of her nightshirt soaked with a sticky liquid. He sat up suddenly. She was staring at him, her face pale in the darkness.

Claire!

The bag broke.

What?

The bag. The water sac. I'm getting contractions.

He scrambled from the bed, found his flashlight, struck a match and lit the kerosene lamp. Claire was looking wide-eyed at the roof-beams, hands on her belly, knees up, waiting for the next wave of pain. The fire was nearly dead in the stove, the air chilly, but he saw sweat on her forehead. You think it's coming?

Feels like it. Oh Henry, oh my God Henry, it feels like it. I think so. What should we do?

Easy. Take it easy. Let's be calm. He looked wildly about the cabin, searching for something. What? He didn't know. Build up the fire, get some water heated? What for? Or get her at once into the truck, head for the ranch headquarters two three hours away in the dark, race for Tucson and the hospital another four or five hours beyond the ranch? Labor, her first baby: how long would it take? No first-aid course he'd ever dozed through had taught him the most elementary of procedures: the home delivery of a child. A premature child? What did that involve?

He knelt by the bed, wiped her forehead and upper lip with his bandana. She stared upward, eyes wide open, anticipating pain. Look, he said, relax now. Rest between the contractions. I'll go out and get the truck warmed up.

It's too soon, she whispered. Too soon. It's a month early. The baby will die.

No it won't. You're okay, nothing to worry about. Hang tight there, I'll be right back. He pulled on his jacket and hustled out into the cold wind. Darkness. He felt sleet or snow stinging his face. He stumbled toward the black bulk of the truck, found the driver's door, got in, started the engine. He put the transmission in neutral, set the hand throttle, turned on heater and blower, hurried back into the cabin. Claire lay as before, waiting. He put one arm under her shoulders, outside of the sleeping bag, and the other under her legs. He meant to carry her, bag and all, to the truck.

Wait, she said.

We better get going.

No, wait. It's coming. And she stiffened, groaned, bit her lower lip and reached for Henry's neck, clinging to him for what seemed like long slow minutes but was probably no more than a few seconds. Should time these things, he knew, but he'd forgotten to bring the watch in from the truck. Then he realized that Claire had a watch on her wrist and that she was checking it.

Thirty seconds, she said, that one lasted thirty seconds. And it's four minutes since the last one. Henry, it's coming now. The baby is coming.

No, listen, this is your first baby, it's gotta take at least six hours, ten hours. (I think—he thought.) We better go. We have time to get to a hospital. We could go to Safford. A lot closer than Tucson.

I'm afraid to ride down that awful road again.

Honey, my Honeydew, we have to do it.

Let me see your flashlight. He gave her the light. She switched it on, lifted the cover of the sleeping bag and looked down at the pinkish fluids between her legs. He looked too. The membrane has ruptured, she said. It's coming.

Yes, he agreed. (But what membrane is that? he wondered.) Then we better get on the road.

No Henry, wait. She looked at her watch. She seemed calmer now, at least for the moment. She looked at him and he saw thought and planning behind the glaze of fear in her eyes. I don't want to ride in that truck now. Not over that awful road. I'm afraid something terrible will happen. I'll have the baby right here. This is better. You can help me.

They stared at each other, amazed, daring, frightened.

Damn it Claire, how could I do this to you?

Don't talk that way. I wanted to come. I bullied you into it. And stop gaping at me. It's cold. Build a fire.

She squeezed shut her eyes, gritted her teeth, began to moan. He wadded his bandana into a tight roll and pushed it between her lips. Bite on this, honey. She took it and reached for him. They clung to each other as the wave of contractions came and passed.

Sweating again, she opened her eyes and read her wristwatch. Thirty-five seconds.

All right, he said. Take it easy now. Save your strength. You're gonna have to do some heavy pushing pretty soon. Gently he disengaged her hands, opened the firebox of the stove, thrust in sticks of kindling on top of the red coals. Heard the pickup's motor rumbling outside. Can't let that thing run out of gas. He went out, aware of snow streaming past his eyes, shut off the engine. If only we had radio contact, he thought; we need some Motorolas on this place. But what good would that be in this situation? Have Lacey and Hooligan bring their lady friends up here? What could they do that Henry could not do? Neither was a medic of any kind; Lacey's girl Christine worked as a go-go dancer—what else?—in some sleaze pit called the Blue Note that Henry himself was not unacquainted with. And the other, Anne, peddled dope for a living. And also danced. Nice girls—but not mothers. Not yet. Not exactly motherly types.

Into the cabin again. He closed the door against the pressure of the wind, taking care not to slam it. Claire gave him a weak smile. He added fuel to the stove, pulled aside a stove lid and set the dishpan, half filled with clear rinse water, over the flames in the opening. The water bucket was empty. He grabbed bucket and flashlight and rushed out to the spout of water from the log trough below the spring. Filled the bucket as streaks of the old cowardice rose to the surface of his consciousness: What am I doing here? How'd I get in this mess? Me, Henry, Henry Holyoak Lightcap, born to be a raider on horseback from the steppes, a relentless hunter stalking a wounded hairy mammoth through alder jungles under the blue-green wall of a glacier, a professor of existentialist metaphysics illuminating the essence of Being and Nothingness in a lecture hall—SRO—packed with five hundred breathless awestruck adoring students . . .

The wind whistled past his ears, the dead but clinging leaves of the oaks fluttered with the noise of a thousand whipped flags in the darkness that surrounded him. He heard another scream.

She lay curved like a bow in the disorder of the bedclothes, back arched, neck arched, biting on the red plug between her teeth. He grasped her shoulders, pressed his face against her neck, held on.

Look, she gasped, take a look.

He didn't want to. There seemed too much slime and gore down there already; he did not want to look on the center of her suffering. But he looked and saw the blood, the running sweat in the crease between abdomen and thighs, the strangely exfolded vaginal opening. As another contraction and expansion convulsed her uterus he saw something exotic, alien, foreign in there seeking outlet, a pale crown of skin the size of a half dollar, with black hairs, that appeared for a moment then disappeared. He waited for it to show again but the contractions eased away.

Did you see it?

Yes. Yes. I saw something.

She grinned—not smiled—at him through a film of tears and sweat. It's the baby. I can feel it. The cervix is dilated. All the way. It's coming out. Should I start pushing next time? She was panting, panting, as she talked.

He wiped the perspiration from her face. Labor, he thought, no wonder they call it labor. This slim slight bloated-up little girl is working harder than I ever worked in my life. Should she push? Good God I don't know. It seems much too soon. Hours too soon. Weeks too soon.

Does it hurt too much? he said.

I can take it. Clutching at his hand, she bit playfully on the thick part of his thumb. If you help I can take anything.

We've got Demerol. Demerol tabs in the first-aid kit.

No, no, not that. Oh no that might hurt the baby. I'd be afraid of that. Anyhow—this time she managed a smile not a grimace—somebody has to tell you what to do.

Henry pretended to smile. He thought he was smiling but could not be sure. He dabbed at the sweat on her upper lip and kissed her. She glanced at her watch and reached for his neck. Here we go again, she groaned. The contractions began. Should I push? she cried, should I push? She was overexcited yet already half exhausted.

Do what feels right, whatever feels right. He embraced her shoulders, back, and tried to absorb the pain with her.

The pains came and she labored. They receded and she rested. An hour passed and a second. Henry kept the fire going, the water warm in dishpan and bucket. He added kerosene to the lamp. With paper towels he cleaned as best he could his wife's vaginal area—between the attacks of pain—and removed the trickle of excrement that she'd expelled, helplessly, during the last contraction.

Poor Henry, she said, stroking his bowed head, poor Henry, I'm so sorry. . . .

Bullshit, he said, don't you feel sorry for nobody. You rest now.

He scrubbed his hands with soap and hot water, returned to Claire's side, waited, held her, waited . . .

He was dozing when her scream brought him once again tensely awake. With both hands she clutched the steel bar at the head of the bed. Her knees were up, splayed far apart. Sweat shone on her face, her eyes bulged, rolled, her mouth was strained wide open as if for a mighty yell. She did not yell. She champed down on the red rag balled in her teeth, gasping for breath. Henry, it's coming, it's coming, I know it's coming.

Gripping her arm, he looked again and saw the top of a small pink head, smeared with ooze, wedged like a grapefruit in the vagina. The flesh around the jammed head seemed horribly distended, dangerously taut, about to burst or tear. He remembered something—the *episiotomy*—and pulled out his pocketknife, thought better of that, opened the first-aid box, found the snakebite kit. Inside the rubber suction cup was a narrow razor blade fitted with a two-inch plastic handle. He struck a match, sterilized the blade, bent close to his woman's straining body. I can't do this, he thought, I cannot do this. But he did it. With a hand made steady by adrenaline, or wonder, or by necessity and terror, he made a short incision through the margins of the vulva toward the anus. A little blood began to flow but Claire seemed not to feel the cut.

Help me. Help me. Henry, help me.

He dropped the blade and put his hands on her belly, adding pressure, reinforcing the contraction. The head emerged, facing down toward the floor, turning a little to the left. Push, Claire, push, he urged, push it out. He attempted to grasp the baby's head with his fingers but could get no purchase on that slippery half-emerging half-retracting thing. Should raise Claire up, he thought, help her squat or crouch, let gravity give us some help here. Too late for that idea. Push, he urged, push, in rhythm with her straining muscles, and the head came fully out, rotating further, followed by the tiny shoulders cauled in the bloodstained silver suit of a space traveler. He held the creature in both hands and drew it forth, trailing its twisted bluish blood-filled lifeline. A gush of multicolored fluids followed, streaming onto the bed. Claire yelled—in agony or relief he could not tell—and the baby yelled in response, very much alive.

Now what? Yes: tie the cord. He pulled a shoelace from Claire's tennis shoes, waited a moment, and tied off the umbilicus close to the baby's belly. He glanced up at Claire's face. Eyes shut, she panted like a runner at the end of a marathon, huffing, sweating. Henry made a second tie in the thick slippery cord, opened his knife and cut the cord between the two ties. Not too different from a calf, he thought. He carried the baby to the stove, held it in one hand and with a lukewarm cloth rinsed off the slime and blood. Claire opened her eyes, looked for him and her baby, found them and stared in wonder. Is it all right? she asked.

Henry turned to the bed and offered the red bawling wrinkled monkeylike thing to its mother. She's a girl, he said, and she is perfect. Claire began to cry. She took the baby in her arms and hugged it to her breast, rocking it back and forth.

We did it, she cried.

Henry knelt at the mother's bottom end to complete his job. He dabbed a little alcohol on the wounded vagina, chilling the flesh by rapid evaporation—the only anesthetic he could think of—and sutured the cut with fine needle and thread. Claire whimpered from the pain but held on, cuddling her baby.

Next, Henry pushed tenderly on Claire's belly, in time with her renewed contractions, pressing out the placenta that streamed, like a purple amoeba with many pseudopodia, upon the newspaper he'd spread beneath her buttocks. Should fry it up, have her eat that stuff, he thought; a cow or mother coyote would. Supposed to be good for you—very nourishing. He gathered the mess in the newspaper and deposited it outside the door where it would soon stabilize like gelatin under the pelting sleet. He looked at Claire. Mother and child seemed both to be sleeping. He stepped outside, closed the door and stood in the wind, feeling the icy sleet beat on his face. There were no stars visible in any direction. He looked up at the black sky. You up there, he said, monster of the universe, I have defeated you again. But back in the cabin he discovered that Claire was still bleeding. And not from his petty surgery but from deep inside. This time he gathered her up, with baby and covers, ignoring her protests, and bundled her into the pickup truck.

He drove slowly, in low gear and four-wheel-drive, out of the fold of the mountain, over the bench and across the mile-wide slope of scree. Claire sat beside him leaning against his shoulder. Half asleep, she held her sleeping baby in her arms. She seemed exhausted. Her face looked dead white. She was still bleeding from the birth canal. Nothing he did could stanch the small but steady flow. Perhaps he had failed to squeeze out the entire placenta. Perhaps something else was wrong.

Fallen rocks lay tumbled across the road. Henry stopped, leaving his headlights on, rolled the rocks over the edge. He drove on, straddling other rocks, and reached the east side of the slope. He drove through the pygmy forest on the flank of the mountain, churning through pools of ice and liquid mud. They passed the windmill, barely visible in the windy dark. The truck fishtailed in the clay on the surface of the mesa but got through and reached firm wheeling on the stony road that led to the rim. When he came to the wire gate Henry did not halt but drove through it, breaking the loop of rope on the end post and bearing the strands of barbwire to the ground. The old gray horse, still waiting, a dim form in the night, followed through the opening.

Henry geared down into compound low, low range, and began the steep descent of the one-lane switchback trail to the canyon floor a thousand feet below. The jolting of the truck over the ledges awoke Claire. Where are we? she mumbled.

It's all right, honey, we're on the way.

She nodded, closed her eyes and sagged against his side once more. The baby stirred in her arms, only its face showing from the mass of down-stuffed nylon.

He steered the truck over slides of gravel and mud that had sloughed from the bank above and poured across the road. The mud appeared frozen on the surface but he felt the rear wheels skid sideways, the rear end shifting toward the side of the road. He gunned the engine, trying to rush the pickup through before the rear slipped over the edge. Too late. They were going over.

Henry was on the outer side; he lunged across Claire and baby, half opened the door on her right, tried to push her out. Out! he shouted, get out! Half asleep, she did not understand. The pickup tilted toward the sky, at the same time sliding off the verge. Claire screamed. Henry wrapped his arms around her and held tight as the truck heeled completely over, crashed on the boulders below and rolled again. And again. The doors sprang open. The lights exploded. The cab of the truck filled with dust. Henry glimpsed dim stars wheeling above, saw a startled bird flash past, heard the shattering of glass, the smash of branches in a tree. A starburst flared behind his eyes, his world went black. . . .

Falling rain streamed on his head. He heard the sound of wailing going on and on, on and on, as it must have sounded through eternity. He tasted something warm and salty on his lips. He opened his eyes, unwilling, and saw the pickup truck hanging above, upside down, wrapped around the trunk of a pinyon pine. The roots of the pine, loosened by the impact, rose clear of the yellow clay. The near door of the truck hung on one hinge. The glass of the window seemed covered with frost, a filigree of shatter lines. A slender bare arm dangled from the open doorframe. Threads of bright blood ran braided down the white skin, pooled at the tight gold band of a wristwatch and overflowed onto the palm and through the partly curled fingers. The sound of wailing continued, muted by the falling rain but persistent, tireless, demanding.

It seemed to Henry that his head was split from ear to jaw. He tried to lift himself to his knees. He found that one leg would not function and looking down saw the crooked bulge in his thighbone, the dark stain soaking through the pantleg of his jeans. He felt pain but the pain seemed far away. He crawled on one leg and his arms to the truck and looked at Claire inside. Her body was crushed between the buckled-in dashboard and the crumpled roof of the cab. Bits of glass glittered in her hair. Blood covered half her face, her throat, her clothing. Rain drummed on metal. The baby had disappeared.

Claire's eyes were open and Henry thought that she was looking for him. He crawled closer until he could reach and grasp her dangling hand. It still seemed warm though he felt no pulse of blood in her palm. He thought she was smiling.

Is that you, Henry?

Yes, he said.

It's snowing again.

Yes.

Is my baby all right?

Sure is, honey, She's fine.

I hear her crying.

She's all right, sweetheart.

You're sure?

Yes, Claire.

Why is it snowing all the time?

It's winter, Honeydew. Wintertime.

Are we almost home?

Yes.

You sure?

Almost there, honey.

Well I hope so. I sure am tired of nothing but snow all the time.

She was right. He saw the snow too, a thickening veil of white pure falling gentle snow that drifted closer then farther then closer again between his eyes and Claire's smiling face. He heard the wailing through the snow but that too, like the pain, seemed far away. He knew that he would need help but Lacey and Hooligan should arrive soon. He could almost hear their voices now, the sound of their big booted feet stumbling down the slope of rocks, clashing through the broken glass.

XVIII

Grace Mellon, his mother-in-law, Grace Whateveritwas Mellon stood beside the hospital bed, holding his baby in her arms, and said, I knew you'd do something like that. The hatred in her eyes shone clearly now, untempered by the ironical disdain that Henry had grown accustomed to and even learned to respect, in a way, knowing that she was not entirely wrong. You crazy reckless scheming cur, she said in her admirably low and even-tempered voice (a comely thing in woman), I knew you'd find a way to kill her sooner or later.

Grace paused; she spoke so calmly, smoothly, that the nurse standing at the door seemed to notice nothing out of order. Grace continued, her eyes fixed on his with murderous intensity: But you couldn't wait. You outwitted yourself, Mr. Lightcap. You'll not get one cent of her inheritance. Not one cent. You jumped the gun. You killed her too soon. You couldn't wait.

He made no attempt to answer. The woman was out of her mind—temporarily insane, he guessed. She'd had Claire buried in some family plot in Denver, against his wishes, and she took the baby too. His little girl. Had her christened Claire, also over his protest, and built a living wall of lawyers between him and his daughter. When Henry limped from the University Hospital two months later and got to Denver he found the woman gone—to England, her lawyer said—and his baby gone with her. The lawyer explained that Grace had legal custody of his daughter, by court order, on grounds that Henry was incompetent, of low moral character, mentally unstable and financially insolvent. The order could be appealed, of course, and possibly reversed in due time, if he was prepared to take the matter up with the appropriate "authorities." Said he'd be happy to recommend good legalistical assistance for

him if he wanted it. Henry said he'd be back. But he was never
able to gain custody of the girl or even obtain clear rights of visi-
tation. Grace Mellon never returned to Denver. The most he ever
got from his kid—Henry called her Ellie, after her middle name,
Ellsworth—were holiday report cards from a town in Rhode Island
identified as Newport, a place in Virginia known as The Plains.

They were right about one thing. He was financially insolvent.
Insoluble, in fact. No, they were right about it all. After Denver,
rather than return to Turkey Creek—unbearable thought—he drove
slowly over the mountains through a blizzard to the western slope
of Colorado and into the bleak wastelands of Utah. Late March.
Sent no word to Harlow, to Lacey, Hooligan or the Lovers of Fur
Bearers. Near the little town of Green River, Utah, he parked on
the highway bridge and watched the brown waters of the river
called Green flowing beneath, bearing a few yellowish cakes of ice,
an uprooted tree, the occasional dead cow. Henry borrowed a fiberglass canoe from a riverman he knew, left his pickup outside the
friend's warehouse, paddled onto the stream, floated away. On his
knees in the stern of the canoe, his hospital cane beside him.

He was gone for a month.

He drifted down the river, built little fires at evening, tried to
eat. He drifted between the high walls of Labyrinth Canyon and
Stillwater Canyon, under the White Rim and the spires of the Maze
and could find no beauty in the land he had once loved more than
any other. He drifted through the confluence with the Colorado
River, in the center of everything and nothing, and could hardly
lift his eyes to see. He camped for days, perhaps weeks, on a beach
near the head of Cataract Canyon, the roar of white water a constant in his ears. He meant to drown himself in those falls and rapids
but hunger began to return. He shot a deer, kept the meat in shade,
watched the moon pass in its phases over the walls of the canyon,
hobbled one day to the rim and saw the snow-covered mountains
east, southeast, southwest and north, shining under the spring sun.

Those mountains. That river. That land and his friends and this
absurd garment of irritation, aspiration, intuition, irrational reason, inconsolable memories that he wore as symbol of life. Death
would be better, sweeter, simpler. But death like anybody else must
wait his turn.

Down that wilderness river alone for thirty days in a canoe

through a world frozen in stone. Ravens squawked at him from the rimrock. Hummingbirds throbbed before the scarlet monkeyflower of gardens hanging from seeps a hundred feet above the river. Winding tributary canyons like the corridors of a labyrinth led away from the river into the bowels of the plateau, gorges in the seamless stone that were so deep, so narrow that for hundreds of yards he could not see the sky. He followed one to where it narrowed to a pinch so thin he dared not wedge his body through. He returned to his canoe and floated down the river and made his camp and a great horned owl hooted softly through the night and in the blue light of dawn deer walked over the sandbars to the water. He fried catfish for breakfast, made coffee and loaded the boat, untied the bowline from a willow and shoved off into the current. The sun oozed over the eastern rim, a squat bulge of plasmic fire so bright it lacked any definition of color. He soaked his hat and shirt in the silty water at his side, put both back on and drifted downstream. . . .

He lived alone in a board-and-batten cabin at 9,500 feet above sea level, in a forest of spruce, fir and quaking aspen. Each morning he climbed the steps of a ninety-foot steel tower into the cab on top, entering through a trapdoor in the floor, switched on the Forest Service radio, leaned against an Osborne Firefinder and gazed through open windows looking for smoke. He could see for ninety miles in any direction, clear to the blue-gray mountains that circled the horizon. He did his work in that place for two long spring and summer seasons and the same work in similar places for another five. He heard the hermit thrush calling from the darkness under the trees. A redtail hawk screamed across the nearest meadow and one lone silent yellowbeaked rednecked turkey vulture soared in the sky a thousand feet above. Kinfolk.

He lived alone in various cities after the women left (slamming doors) and walked the streets by himself and sat at tables by the window in underclass cafés, drinking hot thin black coffee out of thick stained mugs. He walked half the length of Manhattan, from Ninety-second Street to the Battery, seven times. He walked from the edge of Albuquerque over a ten-mile stretch of mesa, through prickly pear and staghorn cholla, and up to the crest of the Sandia Mountains, once. He walked twice across the Cabeza Prieta Desert of Arizona, along the Mexican border, 120 miles of gravel, sand, volcanic cinder, with forty pounds of food, water and a gun in the pack on his back. He descended into the Grand Canyon of the Colorado by one trail, five thousand feet down, and emerged by another, six thousand feet up, five weeks later.

The flowing river. He lived for three seasons in a plywood housetrailer in a hoodoo land of voodoo stone—pillars, pinnacles, arches, windows, balanced rocks, eighty-foot phallic erections—patrolled the trails by foot, the dirt roads by pickup truck, and at evening cooked his supper over an open fire outside the trailer, watching the creeping lights of automobiles on the paved highway twenty miles beyond his private sea of dunes. He lived in one room in a crumbling adobe fort on a desert plateau where the Rio Grande makes its big bend into Chihuahua and Coahuila. Behind him stood the Chisos Mountains like the crenellated ramparts one mile high of an abandoned, forgotten city. In the corral beside his adobe hut he kept two saddlehorses, each with the U.S. brand on its left hip. He worked for a winter in the Everglades, patrolling at night the empty highway between Long Pine Key and Flamingo, herding alligators out of the restrooms at the Park Visitor Center, staking out poachers at the side of snake-infested mosquito-clouded sloughs. He lived and worked for an eight-month season in Death Valley, driving a school bus by day and at night still-hunting girls in the bar of the Furnace Creek Inn. He worked as a backcountry ranger in the Gila Wilderness, Glacier Park, the Superstition Wilderness, Canyonlands Park, and again in the mile-deep trench below the Funeral Range and the Panamint Mountains—Death Valley.

Not always alone. The girls came, the women left, old friends arrived for a visit and stayed for a week, two weeks, three. But half the time he lived by himself in the luxury of his aloneness, in the rich tragic romance of solitude. Rising in the morning before the sun he found himself again at one with nobody but himself. Ate lunch in total silence in a clearing in the cactus forest, in the aspen forest, in a formation of mudstone hobgoblins. Walked alone at evening down a sandy road toward a flamboyant sunset he never reached, turned and returned through the dark waving a long stick across his path to brush the rattlesnakes aside. Played cowboy tunes and hillbilly folk songs on his flute from the catwalk of a fire tower: the forest repeated each clear-cut phrase. Fed the chipmunks for entertainment. Trained the docile mule deer to lick at his salt block under a board platform in a sycamore tree. Sat by the fire in twenty different cast-iron stoves on rainy days, on snowy mornings, through blizzard afternoons, through howling storms at night, to read the complete (or incomplete) works of B. Traven, Jack London, Marcel Proust, Thomas Mann, Leo Tolstoy, Raymond Chandler, James M. Cain, Henry Thoreau, Walt Whitman, Arthur Rimbaud, Ferdinand Céline, Robert Burns, Manuel Azuela, Knut Hamsun, Arthur Schopenhauer, Henri Bergson, Lewis Mumford, Michel de Montaigne, Will Shakespeare and Bertolt Brecht, Titus Lucretius and J.-P. Sartre, struggled through the suffocating entrails of James, Dante, Sophocles, Plato, Melville, Hardy, Dostoyevsky and others, many others, too many others, and what did all that laborious reading gain him?

Couldn't say.

He remembered best not the development of character or the unraveling of plot or the structure of an argument—philosophy is an art form, not a science—but simply the quality of the author's mind. That part remained and by that standard alone he finally judged his author and either threw the book aside or read it through and searched out more by the same writer.

And that drive also, the mania to know and understand, it too waned somewhat with the passing of years, until he found himself again alone, far out on the rim of some awful desolation of forest or desert with a red sun descending in a blood-soaked carnage of clouds toward the apocalypse of night, jags of lightning overhead, thunder crashing, nothing in his hands but a wedge-shaped maul and a chunk of stovewood set upright on a stump waiting for the splitting blow. Raising his weapon high, he stared at the flames in the west, remembered the first or last woman he had won and lost, thought of the corpus mysticum he would never embrace, the home by the river he could not find, and howled—*howled* at the sky:

You up there—God.

This is me, Henry.

Henry Holyoak Fucking Lightcap the First.

And I challenge you, oh God—

J'appelle de ta rigueur—

Speak to me or strike me dead!

He waited. (No clear reply.) *You* die then! he bellowed, and swung from high above his shoulders—while thunder rumbled—slashing down with all his strength, cleaving the aspen billet in two with a single mighty blow, and sank the head of the maul so deep in the green fir stump he had to pry it loose next day with a log chain and a high-lift truck jack.

He hugged his solitude to his heart, regretting (much later) not one hour of the pain and loneliness or the long days dreamed away in a stupor of meditation. He could not imagine a single moment he would choose to alter, for better or worse, and when the long cycle came round again—as Nietzsche and Heraclitus and hosts of squatting Hindus said it must—he was prepared to repeat each detail every nuance all the cheapest gags of the entire performance verbatim.

Wearisome prospect. But it was his. But was it true?

On that river, lonesome river, mudbrown golden western river searching for its snotgreen foamcapped western sea.

Thinking: *Claire Claire Claire my Honeydew, if I don't find thee again I will surely die. . . .*

He did not die. He never went back to Turkey Creek Canyon, he never again worked for the wildlife sanctuary, but he did not die. Not yet. Men die, worms eat them, but not for love. He found instead, walking toward him with her father, through the twilight of a Tucson Arizona evening, another girl too young fair slim and beautiful for so weak and foolish a rogue as Henry H. Lightcap—

Dad, she said, as they passed him by with only a glance, let's get out of here.

Sure, Elaine, the father said, why not?

Street fairs attract so many—you know—nothing but bums.

True, the father said. Bums and bandits.

21

TO THE MISSISSIPPI

Routine and repetition is the secret of survival. I wake, I reclose my eyes—must I face reality again so soon?—and attempt to sleep, to dream, for another five minutes more. But I cannot, the light is breaking through the trees, the dog is mumbling at my feet, the noise of early motor traffic comes toward me from the highway two miles north.

Routine: arise, piss, pull on pants—always the left leg first, then the right. If I attempt even as an experiment to reverse that sequence I find my legs, arms, nerves and thoughts getting hopelessly muddled. Button or zip fly, buckle belt, stuff in shirttail. Feed and water dog. Light up camp stove, place pot of water on to boil, make cup of tea. Dunk in a few doughnuts, cookies, Fig Newtons, whatever available. Take bamboo stick or agave staff or blackthorn shillelagh and go for a little walk, no more than a couple of miles, return and fry the bacon, galvanize the eggs, prepare my grease fix for the day. No wonder my stomach feels so queer. No wonder that gnawing nagging agenbiting crab deep in my guts won't go away. The swine. The son of a whore. The sneaking puke-faced stalk-eyed side-scuttling slime-covered worm-hearted spawn of a cast-off two-bit three-legged hairless Mexican dumpster-diving dog. And so on.

On to Hannibal, by christ. We steam out from swamp and woods, me and my Dodge and my worthless mongrel, and hit the asphalt trail again. Past the Pisgah Baptist Church—DO WE HAVE GOOD NEWS FOR YOU!—and into fields of glowing iridescent windswept April grass where lonesome nags, forgotten by their masters, stand hock-deep in Heaven and stare with twitching ears, dark winsome eyes, at a man and a dog rolling by in a gray plus rust-colored 1962 Dodge Carryall truck. Empty canvas waterbag flapping on the grille. Duct tape peeling from the parking-light frames. Oil smoke venting from the exhaust connections and a trail of water dribbling from the dangling tailpipe. Muffler split and braying like a jackass.

We follow the Missouri River as far as a town called Brunswick. There the river turns southeast toward St. Louis; we head on east and east northeast toward Keytesville, Huntsville, Paris, Monroe City, Wither's Mill and—Hannibal.

Spring advances to meet me: the trees leafed out, the dandelions set to seed, the smell of damp raw earth from plowed fields, the distant puttering noise of tractors when I stop beside the road to take a leak, to make a peanut butter sandwich, to pick a sprig of dogwood and some wild irises for the water-filled beer bottle at rest in my dashboard beer-bottle holder. I open a fresh bottle of Budweiser, ignoring the twitch of anguish in my pancreatic gland, drink hearty and drive on.

Solstice the dog stares straight ahead, watching the road while I watch the passage of rural Missouri. She looks bad, bleary-eyed and melancholy. I know she's clear of ticks but she could have worms. Will have to make inspection next time she takes a shit. Unpleasant duty but I'd rather look at hers than mine.

We roll through the towns, the franchise strips, the Sonic Happy Eating and Radio Shacks and Pizza Huts and Serve-Ur-Self Gas and Good Will Pre-Used Cars and the candidly usurious glass-boxy banks with no pretense at anything but money. As usual the most stately and dignified house in town has become a "Funeral Home." Smells of formaldehyde and greasepaint follow us down the red brick street. Everything that's beautiful decays from neglect; the cheap false synthetic transitory structures inspired by greed spread along the highways like mustard weed, like poison ivy, like the creeping kudzu vine. The vampires of real estate, the leeches of finance, the tapeworms of profit, have fastened themselves to the body of my nation like a host from Hell. No wonder the land, the towns and villages, the old homes and farms and so many of the people wear that worn-out used-up blood-sucked bled-white look. Ill fares the land. The aliens are here. The body snatchers have arrived.

We reach Hannibal in midafternoon. Once through the gauntlet of commerce that leads to the original town, as everywhere else, I find myself within the familiar necrosis of the center. I park my truck on the waterfront by a gaudily painted steamboat with fake stern wheel—the *Mark Twain* of course—and take a schooner of draft Bud at the nearby B & G Bar. Not a tourist joint: this dark damp dingy dump reeks of piss and beer, tobacco smoke and sweat and rotting duckboards behind the bar. A row of old men in khaki work clothes straddle wooden stools, peering and jabbering at one another from beneath the bills of St. Louis Cardinal baseball caps. Two fat women in holey sweaters, beer-stained dresses, stockings rolled to varicose ankles, screech at one another by the shuffleboard table. Unemployed hoodlums in black T-shirts lurk in the back room shooting pool. The TV set winks and blinks above the far end of the bar: nobody watches the thing and its plaintive bleats sink beneath the general clamor. From an opposite and apposite corner booms the roar of a vibrant jukebox—Merle Haggard singing "Jailhouse Blues." Good man, Haggard. Good song, that "Jailhouse Blues." Like they say in Muleshoe, Texas, there's only two kinds of music—country and late Bartók.

A good bar, the B & G. A Henry Lightcap kind of bar. Buzzing finely, chromatically from three more brimming schooners, I wander the streets for a while, looking into the windows of the Becky Thatcher Bookstore and contributing my dollar for a visit to the Sam Clemens Museum. Here I see the expected first editions, the photographs, Sam's cap and gown from Oxford, the Norman Rockwell paintings of top scenes from the stories, the author's riverboat pilot's certificate, the towering "Orchestrelle" machine. I drop my quarter in the slot and set off a jerky medley of 1890s dance hall tunes. But somehow I find no shade of the great old man himself in this place. Not in this room, not in this building, not in this town.

I leave and walk the streets till evening, treat myself to a catfish supper at the Missouri Territory Restaurant, a grand echoing hall of stone that was formerly Hannibal's main post office. The meal is good, the atmosphere baronial—but where are the people?

I walk back to the waterfront, feed my dog, take her for a short walk with a rope for leash. Darkness settles in, the cool night of April, the endless twilight of the humid lands. We return to truck and drive south, out of town and under the stony bluffs that line the river on the west. Tom Sawyer's cave is up in there but I haven't the heart to search for it this evening. I'm now on the Great River

Road and the compulsive pull of homeward suction keeps me bound to the asphalt for another twenty, thirty miles. Finally we pull off the highway onto the kind of narrow winding dirt road that looks good to me, friendly, comfortable, hospitable, leading into dark woods and the smell of leaves and mud, the music of tree frogs, mosquitoes, screech owls, the feel of rain on the air. My sense of safety and relative well-being is always strengthened by the sight of forest, hills, rocky dells, valleys, undammed and meandering watercourses.

A place for rest, for sleep. . . .

Morning comes, once again. One more time at least. We perform our ritual, the dog and I, and carry on through the fogs on the riverbank and into the villages of Calumet, Elsberry, Foley and Winfield. At Winfield I turn east and wait near Lock & Dam #25 for the ferryboat across the Mississippi to the state and condition of Illinois. From there to New Harmony and Louisville. Kentucky today! West Virginia tomorrow! Rest and peace, simplicity and order thereafter. Such is the master plan.

The ferry comes, I drive aboard. No other vehicle appears. The ferryman in his little offdeck cabin pulls the throttle and the ferry churns toward the shore of Illinois, three hundred yards away. A pretty red-haired girl, the assistant ferryman, comes to me and takes my two-dollar fare. I take her picture with my Kodak Instamatic and ask her why she's not in school today. Playing hooky? She has freckles, green eyes, bountiful breasts, small waist, a round compact heart-shaped bottom like an inverted valentine. Yes, my type.

"I'm twenty years old," she says. "Ain't gotta go to school no more."

"What's your name?" Always was my type.

"Anna-May McElroy. What's yourn?" From her lovely lips the word comes forth as "urine."

"My name is Henry Lightcap and I'm in love." Always will be. "Do you like this job?"

"It's boring. All we do all summer is go back and cross and back and cross. Who y'all in love with?"

"I'm in love with you." Why do my girlfriends all look alike? Because they all look like the type I like.

She eyes me briefly. "You need a shave."

"Always do. Come with me. Come with me and be my love."

She smiles and looks across the golden sun-glinting waters of the great river. The wooded banks of Illinois float toward us. "My gee," she says, "if you only knowed, mister, how often you men say that. Seems like ever day I hear them say that."

"I believe it, honey. You look 'em over and you make your choice when you feel like it. Don't let nobody like me sweet-talk somebody like you."

The landing board of the ferry grates onto the graveled ramp. The girl unlinks the chain, smiling at me but thinking of somebody else and who can blame her. "I'll send you a picture," I say as I climb in my truck. "Winfield, Missouri, right? Lock and Dam Number Twenty-five?" I drive away into the woods and cornfields.

Will I ever see Anna-May again? No. Will anyone ever see Anna-May again? Not me. Will she ever again exist? Who knows. These are the questions that drift across my mind as I bear south and east for Alton, Granite City, East St. Louis. The memory of sweet flame-haired Anna-May will haunt me forever for at least a day or two. Roused a flicker of the old Lightcap there. I might be old I might be sick but I ain't dead. Not yet I reckon.

We pause by a grove of trees to contemplate pigs in a pasture, robins in the grass, a redheaded woodpecker drumming on a hollow snag. Crows, blackbirds, cardinals busy in the foreground. The pigs are black-and-white Berkshires, the kind I raised and loved when I was a boy. Inside a board fence weathered to silver-gray, they romp like happy kids, rooting up the clover, snuffling for acorns under the red oaks, cheerful clever little beasts. Never knew a pig as stupid as a sheep, as goofy as a horse, as mean as a dog. Or as greedy as a man. Furthermore they're good to eat.

Bunch of milk cows yonder. Holsteins—they look strangely clean, long-legged and elegant after my years of seeing nothing but the squat stumbling shit-smeared Hereford beef cattle of the West. A rooster crows near the barn. Two-story white farmhouse nearby, shaded by maple trees. Lilacs blooming at the door. A black cat scampers from barn to house, pursued halfway by the rooster. Bees murmur in the flowering dogwood. Poison ivy sweats in the ditch. The pang of April pierces my heart. I think of the mourning dove that calls from the forest on the side of Noisy Mountain, across the valley from Stump Crick, when the sun begins to burn away the mists of daybreak.

We cross the Illinois River on another ferry—no Anna-May here—and bear southeast past the Mark Twain National Wildlife Refuge (a crane rises up and sinks down beyond the screen of trees) and the Père Marquette State Park. I stop in the little town of Grafton for coffee and a doughnut. The café is full of cigarette smoke, shouts from the kitchen, the soft talk and gentle laughter of a dozen men in bib overalls and visored caps fueling up for the day's work, packing down scrambled eggs, hashbrown potatoes, grits and biscuits and redeye gravy, pink ham and red bacon and brown sausage. Getting ready for a day in the mill, they gulp down the hot black coffee, slap backs, roughhouse around. A huge man over six feet tall and 250 pounds heavy sits in the center of the group, red-faced, smiling. Naturally everybody calls him Tiny. An old skinny gent with gappy grin gets up to leave, pushes Tiny's cap down over his face, squeezes his shoulder and lurches to the cash register.

I follow the road along the Mississippi, refueled and oiled (burning a quart every fifty miles now, I don't care for that), and enter at once the industrial wonderland of the St. Louis megalopolis—heavy-duty freight train, smokestack and warehouse territory. Barges of steel a block long move upriver loaded with coal and scrap iron, dragged through the filthy water by tugboats with three-story superstructures. Oil refineries appear, catalytic cracking plants, a thicket of pipes and stacks with flare-off fires brighter than the sunlight. Nostril-prickling smells float on the air, sly and sinister. Factory buildings of rusty red sheet metal, their windows broken, stand next to foundries and blast furnaces with brick chimneys sixty eighty a hundred feet high. Near each clanging workshop is a settling pond, a tailings dump, a slime pit filled with oily sludge, toxic solvents, pathogenic chemicals, black tars and industrial vomit roiled together in a marbled arabesque of brilliant, unforeseeable colors.

We roll along in the sewer of traffic, walled in by giant freight trucks, Fruehauf mudguards in front and Mack radiator grilles with bulldog figurehead looming over my rear. I recall the inscription on the wall back in the pissoir of that Grafton café: "There's two things awful over-rated: teenage pussy and Mack trucks." True, true—and suppose this mad environment went on forever?

I leave the highway and the industrial madhouse, turn off for rest in a state park on the shore of the river. Sollie and I get out, piss on the leaves, read the words on the base of a monument by the parking lot:

Near this site, at the confluence of the Missouri and Mississippi Rivers, Meriwether Lewis and William Clark spent the winter of 1803–1804, preparing for their journey to the Pacific Coast. President Jefferson had commissioned them to explore the newly acquired Louisiana Territory. They called their winter quarters Camp Dubois and their party of 44 men the Corps of Discovery. On May 14, 1804, the Corps of Discovery left Camp Dubois, ascended the Missouri River to its source, and crossed the Great Divide, reaching the Pacific on November 7, 1805. They returned to Illinois on September 23, 1806, having concluded one of the most dramatic and significant episodes in American history.

When Clark and Lewis came for the first time in sight of the western sea, Clark wrote in his journal, "Ocian [sic] in view. O, the joy!" A poor speller but a man of heart.

Me and the dog munch on some lunch, peanuts and beer for me, Purina's crunchy granola and E. St. Louis tap water for her. Around us extends this park of mud, weeds, garbage. A few sickly trees gather the soot and acids from the sky. From beyond that meager screen of life comes the unrelenting clamor of the highway, the city, the modern industrial state. Except for one old black man casting a line into the river, the dog and I are the only visitors at Camp Dubois at this landfill in time. What would Lewis say? what would Clark feel? if they could revisit their old campground now. What would they think, for example, of those wistful puffs of steam that rise from behind that black slagheap of burned muck and blistered metal looming above the trees in the southeast quadrant?

Ocian in view O joy?

Onward into the industrial jungles. Weaving through a tangle of intersecting freeways, I steer by blind luck onto the correct ramp and find myself rolling southeastward minutes later into the sylvan monotony of agrarian Illinois. Nothing in my foreground but cement and cute little green trees, while coming and going, rumbling toward me and howling past, roars the continuous caravan of tractor-trailers, the world of Mack and Kenilworth and White and Peterbilt.

Should not be cluttering up this here Interstate. Asking for trouble. But I am weary of this flat land, this ironed-out countryside, and long to see the fuzzy conical hills of east Kentucky, the long blue smoky ridges of West Virginia, the hills of home. Therefore I take the fast road, the quicker to get through.

Besides I don't feel good. Don't feel right at all. If I weren't intent on making two more hundred miles today I'd pop a Demerol tab right now. Or Dilaudid. But that can wait. Must wait.

What about Will? There's the question. Will he be glad to see me? Coming down on old Will one more time, bringing along my train of troubles to unload on his back, why should he care about Elaine? How can he grieve for Claire, whom he never even met? Whose fault but mine that my daughter Ellie's in Rhode Island? Or maybe East Virginia? Where can he find the tears to mourn the loss of Myra Mishkin, nonobjective abstractionist? He's certainly not going to sympathize with the loss of my job at the Tucson Welfare Department or my permanently foundered career opportunities with the United States Federal Fucking Government. Can't hardly burden him with something new, can I? Him and Marian they got troubles enough of their own, what with Pittsburgh and Morgantown and Wheeling moving down from the north and the tentacles of Charleston and Huntington creeping in from the west. Beleaguered, besieged, beset, they're lucky they've survived as long as they have.

And here comes I.

With my little secret.

22

1975:

FORT LIGHTCAP, WEST VIRGINIA

They walked the entire boundary line one Sunday afternoon in November. Indian summer, with maple leaves crackling underfoot and the harvest moon due to rise at sundown. Will showed Henry his six-rail worm fence, newly erected. Couldn't afford barbwire, he explained, and anyhow these split blackjack pines was cheaper. In fact Will earned a part of his income now splitting rails and building ornamental fences for the suburbanites' new homes outside of Shawnee. He was, he boasted, the last rail-splitter in Appalachia.

Henry carried a shotgun, Will an old single-shot .22. Watching for cottontails. Never too late for fence-row chicken. No dogs with them; Will's son Joe had taken the beagles away for the day, off on a hunting trip of his own down along Crooked Creek. He'd also taken Will's twelve-gauge double-barreled LC Smith. Not that Will minded. He could get as many rabbits with a .22 and without dogs as the boy could with shotgun and with dogs.

And he proved it quickly. Holding up one hand, he stopped Henry and pointed with the rifle at something concealed in the brown bunchgrass at the base of the fence. Henry looked, looked hard, could not see it.

One little bright brown eye, Will said. See him?

Henry stared, concentrated, shook his head. Will raised his boy's rifle, aimed, cracked off a shot. The rabbit took one hop forward—already dead—and collapsed, neatly perforated through the brain. Will gutted the little beast and tucked him away inside the game pocket of an old canvas hunting coat that looked familiar to Henry. It was the same coat their father had worn through the forties and fifties. The hunting license inside the celluloid case on the back was dated 1952.

They walked on, up the hill toward the woods. They jumped a second rabbit; Henry flung the shotgun to his shoulder, fired and missed.

Thought you was supposed to be some kind of game warden, Will said. You shoot like one of them sportsmen types from Pittsburgh.

Well shit, says Henry. Well fuck. Well christ out west we don't waste ammo on rabbits. We hunt *big* game out there. I mean elk. Mule deer. Moose. Antelope. Black bear. Bison. Slow elk.

Slow what?

Beef cow.

Will smiled. They entered the woods, following Will's new fence. Henry noticed the red and white PRIVATE PROPERTY KEEP OUT NO HUNTING signs tacked up on fence and trees. Yeah, Will explained, had to do that now. Too many strangers around these days. Kids with rifles. Grown men in little jeeps. People he didn't know, had never even seen before, coming around, climbing fences, blasting away at anything that moved, in season and out. Didn't know where the hell they all came from but there seemed to be more of them every year.

Country's growing, Will. You're out of date.

It can't last.

Don't be too sure. When we were kids the teachers taught us that the population of America was 120 million. Remember? As if that figure was meant to be permanent, absolute, like the mileage from Stump Crick to California.

Well ain't it?

Now it's 230 million. In other words, Will old fart, the population of our country has nearly doubled in only forty years. And it's growing faster. We're in trouble.

I noticed things was getting kind of crowded. Like the rabbits is worse some years than others. Had a plague of grasshoppers last year. But it don't last—they come and they go.

That's so. But it takes time.

The brothers walked through the golden shade of the trees—red oak, white oak, poplar, beech, sassafras, Osage orange, red maple, black walnut, butternut, shagbark hickory. All hardwoods, all young, a third- or fourth-growth Appalachian forest. The best crop

418

this country could grow, said Will, was trees. Trees and game. That's what this hill country was meant for: hardwood trees, deer, bear, turkey, honeybees and wild hogs. And maybe just enough corn to feed some pigs. Someday these trees of ours will be worth a million dollars, Henry.

Ours?

That's right. Ours. Lightcaps'. When we get these 120 acres all growing hardwoods we'll be the richest family in Shawnee County. You wait and see.

How long do we have to wait?

Will smiled again. About a hundred years. Little Joe's grandkids will get the benefit.

They followed the old wagon road up through the woods. They paused at the graves of their grandmother and great-grandfather, Cornflower and Doctor Jim. Will had cleared away the running blackberry vines and poison ivy, restored the ancient monuments and rerouted the lettering.

We should've buried the old man here too, Will.

Naw, I don't think so.

Why not?

This is still Shawnee territory. Us Lightcaps ain't been around long enough to lay claim to it.

Henry stared at his older brother. Four inches shorter, thirty pounds heavier, two years older, black-bearded and baldheaded, Will seemed like a different man, a new man, in his middle middle age. Not nearly so dumb and stupid as Henry remembered him. Heavier, thicker, slow, stiff, rednecked and wrinkled like jerky around the eyes but—different. Possibly wiser.

Will, sometimes you talk like a philosopher.

Brother Will shifted his chew from one cheek to the other, spat a stream of brown juice to the ground. He grinned at Henry. Kind of work I do, Henry, I got a lot of time to think. Not like you with all your technical intellectual type jobs.

Will the farmer had practically given up farming. He kept a pair of mules for his logging operations and raised enough hay to feed the team through the winter. Each year he raised two pigs for slaughter, butchered them himself, ground his own sausage, cured and hickory-smoked his own hams. His wife, Marian, kept a vegetable garden, a sweet-corn patch for roasting ears and a small flock of hens. They still tapped the sugar maples every March, distilling enough fancy-grade pancake syrup to trade in town for a year's supply of medical care, dentistry, wholesale auto parts, kerosene, underwear, overalls, shoes or shoe repair, movies or books, whatever needed or available. The underground economy. Marian drove the local school bus and sometimes worked as a teacher's aide—when they needed cash. We got more time than money, she'd explain. Will heated his house with coal, which he obtained himself, in the traditional Lightcap fashion, from the C&O Railroad, and with wood. He kept the telephone as a business necessity but had long ago stopped paying power-company bills. Just never found no need for that electric stuff, he explained. For toilet facilities they used the outhouse most of the time, a chamberpot down in the basement by the coal furnace in the bitterest days of winter. Saves time and trouble, Will pointed out: I'd have to work a whole year to get a regular bathroom installed in the house and then a month every year after that to pay the plumber. With my thundermug system I put in five minutes a day about ninety days a year—what's that add up to?—and it don't cost me a cent. We borrowed the pisspot from Charlie Holyoak's attic twenty years ago. When the wife wants a bath I light up the butane under the water heater, let it burn for half an hour, shut it off and fill the tub by gravity flow. Marian enjoys lying around in a tub of hot water, so what the hell, might as well take advantage of this here modern high technology while it's still cheap. It won't last, you know.

How do you get the water into the kitchen?

Gravity flow. From the springhouse.

So why the hell not have a regular toilet?

Well because then the goddamn county building code would make me pay for a goddamn septic tank and leach field, that's why, cost me another year's work in the garage and muck up the garden besides. Don't need it.

Therefore Will had abandoned farming. With the children grown up and gone there was no need for a milk cow. He'd have stopped bothering with hogs too except that you could not get decent bacon, sausage or properly cured hams at the supermarket or any place else. He no longer raised cash crops such as cereals, maize and cattle-feed because the midwestern agrofactories had long ago cornered that market. Will refused to specialize in any line of work full time at any trade. His auto-repair and welding shop, in the village of Stump Creek, was open for business only by appointment. Like our father he spent more time in the woods—where he was happiest—than in the shop or on the farm or in the house. Unlike Henry, he was only a moderate drinker, mainly with his poker-playing friends on Friday nights. He attended church every Sunday morning but more for the neighbors and the gossip than the Gospel.

Where does God live, Will Lightcap?

Him? Well I'll tell you, brother. See that old tamarack snag on the north side of Noisy Mountain? That's where.

How do you know that?

Well, that's my guess. What's yours?

Will and Henry walked through the woods, through the shadows, approaching the amber-golden evening light that shone across the meadow beyond. They came to the spring and cabin. They took the pint Mason jar from its stub on the maple tree, dipped it into the cold clear water and drank. They drank again. They stepped into the cabin that Will had built nearly thirty years before. All was intact, in good order, neat, clean, smelling of pine tars and wood-smoke. The windows were open, allowing the autumn air to move through the single room. The cot was made up with fresh sheets and a quilt, the floor swept, a load of kindling, pine cones, and split beech logs filled the woodbox by the stove, and the mousetrap under the cupboard held one fresh dead mouse. Will removed the mouse and reset the trap, baiting it with bacon grease.

Mother's coming out? Henry said.

Oh sure, she'll be out tonight. For supper. But Marian cleaned this place up for you.

How's Mother doing, Will?

She's fine. You'll see. Getting a little older, all gray on the head, but not stooped over and just as busy as ever.

What's she do?

She keeps busy. The church and going to college. Takes a bunch of courses. Like "women studies," whatever the hell that is. And then there's that Meals on Wheels volunteer job.

Meals on Wheels?

That's what they call it. She drives around town, delivers hot meals to old bats and ancient farts too sick to cook for themselves anymore.

Old folks, eh? Henry smiled. But she's over seventy herself.

That's right.

They left the cabin, taking their guns, and walked up the hill, through the fringe of the trees and across the hayfield to the crest. From there they looked eastward across ridge after wooded ridge toward the soft blue haze of the Allegheny and Shenandoah mountains, the backbone of Appalachia.

A pall of smoke hung across the sky. Looks like the world's on fire, Henry said.

There's a good fire a-goin' on Cheat Mountain.

Who set it?

Will smiled. Hard to tell. There's a lot of boys around here need the work. It'll do the woods good anyhow, burn out the underbrush and laurel, grow some feed for the deer. You read history, Henry. Didn't the Indians always start a lot of fires?

What's that mess down there? Henry pointed into the valley below, past the recontoured slope of the strip mine toward a vast cleared area beyond. The yellow bulldozers and earthmovers were at rest now, for the weekend, but it was plain their work was not completed. What the hell are they up to? Isn't that Ginter Hollow?

Will smiled again. You been away too long, Henry. The Ginters are in real-estate development these days. They live in town and spend their winters in Florida. What we're a-lookin' at down there is what they call Sylvan Dell Lake. Dam up the crick, make a little lake, clear off the woods, sell five-acre homesites. Might even be a golf course down there someday. God knows what they're up to and I don't want to know. Might make me sick in the stomach.

They walked along the ridgetop, following the boundary line. Will complained about the always rising property tax: since he lived by barter the government was coming at him in another way, rezoning the land—against his wishes—as potential development property. The fact that the farm was close to the boundary of a national forest made it, in the eyes of the land sharks, a valuable piece of real estate. Every urban dweller, it seemed, now hankered for a weekend home, a vacation home, a hideaway near a national forest or national park or national seashore. The new four-lane superhighways slashed through the hills made access to the farthest coves of Appalachia easy and quick.

You better sell out and come west, Henry said, before they run right over you.

From what I hear, says Will, it's no better out there.

Well, we're thirty years behind the East. That means thirty years of hope.

Hope for what?

Henry shuffled through the brown weeds along the fence, staring ahead, watching for rabbit. Hope for what? he echoed. Well—hope that something big will happen. Earthquakes, maybe, with volcanic eruptions here and there. A fast, efficient and painless plague. Desertification. A return of the Ice Age. I don't know, Will. But something better happen soon.

Something happened right here. Will pointed to a gap in the fence, the split rails knocked aside by the forcible entry of some kind of machine. The tracks were plain to see: wide knobby-treaded tires, three of them, that entered the field and circled and left again through the same gap.

What the hell is this? Will said in exasperation. *Three* wheels? Some kind of oversize goddamn tricycle? With a goddamn motor?

It's what they call an ATV, said Henry. Where you been, Will? ATV: all-terrain vehicle.

All-terrain vermin, if you ask me.

They repaired the break in the fence, Will grumbling, then followed a deer path into the woods. The trail led past a salt block sculptured into softly rounded form by delicate velveteen tongues. Henry paused, looking at Will. Will pointed upward, grinning, and Henry saw a ladder of railroad spikes leading up the trunk of a poplar to a small platform of planks lashed to a pair of parallel limbs.

Deer never look up, Will said.

I know that and so does any game warden. So now you've sunk to poaching venison.

Tastes better that way. Anyhow—Will led on, following the heart-shaped hoofprints—it's our property.

Yeah, but Fish & Game claims the wildlife.

They heard the sound of shooting below, over the brow of the hill. The crack of a rifle: one, two, three shots.

Come on, Will said. He hurried down the trail. Henry checked the load in his shotgun and followed. They could hear a high keen screaming in the distance, as of a child. Will began to run and Henry had to hustle to keep pace with him. The orange of the sun winked through the screen of passing trees. He heard another shot. They passed a second break in the fence, Will not stopping, and saw again the tracks of the three-wheeled machine plowing through the brush, grass and dead leaves, churning up the earth.

They came abruptly to a clearing in the woods and there it was, the red gleaming miniature tractor with three grotesquely bloated rubber tires, a plastic-covered saddle big enough for two and on the fuel tank the name *Honda*. Two teenage boys in jackets and billed caps stared at them. One boy held a rifle in his hand and a dead marsh hawk by the legs, its breast a bloody mess of flesh and feathers. Overhead a second hawk soared in circles, the mate screaming again and again in outraged useless protest. Hawks like eagles mate for life.

The boys looked frightened when Will tramped toward them, his rifle cradled in one arm. He smiled his broad, reassuring smile, showing big teeth inside the black beard, but the little red glint of anger in his eyes lacked charm. Henry stopped at a strategic distance, twenty feet off.

Hello boys, Will said, what do you got there, a hawk? Pretty good shooting. Let me see that thing.

The boy with the hawk started to hand it over.

No, I don't mean that, Will said, I mean your gun. I want to see your gun. The boy hesitated; Will snatched it from his grasp. The boys glanced at each other. They looked like brothers or even twins—each about eighteen or nineteen years old, with sallow complexions, eyes set close together above long damp noses, the pink flush of acne showing through their adolescent whiskers. But they were well-fed heavy-limbed hulking louts, fully grown from the feet to the neck.

Will laid down his .22 and checked out the boy's rifle. Pretty nice, he said, a brand-new lever-action Winchester, what do you know? You get this at Sears Roebuck? Huh? Or Monkey Ward's? Hey?

No answer. The boys stared at Will, then at Henry with his shotgun a few yards beyond. Will jacked the remaining cartridges out of the boy's rifle, made sure the firing chamber was empty and reversed his grip, holding the rifle by the end of its barrel. Where you boys from? he said, looking around.

Clarksburg, one of them muttered.

Clarksburg? You come sixty miles to shoot a hawk? On that three-wheeled contraption? He stepped toward a young hickory.

We got a pickup too, the boy said. We're just having fun.

Will smashed the rifle across the trunk of the tree. The boys froze. Will offered the broken-backed ruin to its owner, shoving it into his face. The boy cowered back. Take it, Will said, it's yours, ain't it? Take it and get the hell out. Go home. Don't never come back here.

Holding the broken rifle, the boy and his mate slouched toward the Honda ATV. They climbed on the double saddle, started the engine and rumbled away, leaving behind the elephant tracks and a blue smudge of exhaust gases. From a safe distance, out of sight, came the inevitable yelping of insults.

Should of bashed up their goddamn machine for them too, Will muttered. Got half a mind to do it yet. We could cut them off down in Ginter Hollow.

Henry put a hand on his brother's thick forearm. You punished them enough.

The hell I did. That hawk is worth a thousand trashy punks like them.

Now now, that's no way to feel. You know what they say in more advanced circles.

What's that?

All men are brothers.

Bullshit.

That's what they say in more advanced circles.

Those punks ain't men. They never will be.

They're the new breed, Will. Not exactly men, not exactly women, but something in between they call "guys."

I've heard of them. Will looked at the light dying beyond the trees, listened to the fading whine of the three-wheeler. There was no other sound but the faint and intermittent screaming in the sky— that lonely cry soaring higher, farther away, toward the western sun. In Europe by this time of day there'd be a tolling of church bells across the fields reminding the faithful of the Annunciation. Angelus time. But this was Stump Crick, Shawnee County, West

Virginia, Appalachia, in our United States of North America. The brothers looked at the torn and mortal marsh hawk lying in the weeds, its blood already drying, the first exploratory black ants coming near. Fifty feet up in the dead branches of a nearby snag was a tangled thicket of twigs the size of a bushel basket: the hawks' perennial home, with streaks of white lime on nest and branch and limb.

All right, goddamnit, Will said. He grinned at Henry. Don't stand there like a stump. Let's go back to the house, see if we can get the women to cook this rabbit for supper. He patted the bulge in his game pocket.

They marched off through the trees, through the gold and purple evening toward the wagon road, the cornfield, the ungrazed pasture, the bright stream meandering in bights and bends across the bottom, the lightning-blasted but still living shagbark hickory beside the stream, the vacant hogpen, the black creosoted barn with its weathered legend barely legible—CHEW MAIL POUCH TREAT YOURSELF TO THE BEST—and past the barn, the corncrib, the workshop and smithy, the icehouse, the wagonshed, the little whitewashed privy surrounded by sunflowers and hollyhocks gone to seed, the stone springhouse above, the giant and ancient sugar maple tree with auto tire dangling by one rope to the main branch, and came at last to the farmhouse itself, the two-story peaked-roof gray gothic frame dwelling with attic above and basement below that had sheltered the Lightcap family, or what remained of it, for sixty-five years. Home, you might say. And as the brothers walked toward it, they saw the glow of lamps through the curtained downstairs windows, woodsmoke rising from the kitchen stovepipe, and the brilliant flare of sunset on the glass of the attic window. Welcome. . . .

Henry paused, hearing the brittle clash of splitting wood, the blows of an ax. Their father!

Will tramped on but Henry stopped, dazzled and dismayed by the sensation of eternal return. Had he not seen all of this before, heard that sound a hundred times, a thousand times, twenty thirty forty years ago? He looked again and saw that the stocky fellow cleaving wood near the cellar door was not the old man, not his father, but young Joe, Will's grown-up but youngest son, returned at evening from his hunt along Crooked Creek. And yet they were very much alike, the vanished father, the present grandson. Almost the same. And the dogs that came running and barking toward Will, delirious with delight, were they not the same hounds that Henry and Will had hunted for rabbit with back in the forties, in the thirties? They were; they were not. They were a new generation. They were the same.

23

INTO THE SHADE

I

Now. Now is dogmatically now. Each moment I am reincarnated into another self, myself, the same reluctant predictable self. My belly aches from the pinch of a crab's claw and the engine is loping—PSI:24—losing power mile by mile. Next truck stop we must buy a case of cheap fifty-weight high sulfur oil, keep that weary motor alive. Five hundred miles yet to go. I believe. I guess. I hope. Only ten hours driving if all goes well. If we don't have to grind up the hills of Kentucky in reverse. (My most powerful gear ratio.)

Southern Illinois finally lies behind. Solstice the dog permits herself a sigh of relief. We cross the Wabash River into the fine rich bountiful state of Indiana and through the town of New Harmony. One of Robert Owen's nineteenth-century experiments, a community for celibate and commonweal living. The founders called themselves Rappites, after their leader the Reverend George Rapp. They were farmers—what else? The men and women lived in separate houses, forbidden to mingle. Recruitment of new members failed to replace defunct virgins, the experiment collapsed, the communal property became private property. But they tried, those Owenites and Rappites, from 1814 until 1825 before surrendering to biology and reality. You can't change human nature without mutilating human beings.

Onward, eastward toward Louisville, through the gloomy green of Hoosier National Forest. A forest with farms however, former grain farms now given over to beef ranching—and why not? Pastoralize the country, I say. There are more beef cattle in little Indiana than in the whole sagebrush empire of Idaho, Wyoming, Nevada and Utah combined. This is where the grass grows. Here is where the people live.

I pause in Carefree Indiana for gas and oil, adding sixteen gallons of regular to the fuel tank and three quarts of lowgrade to the crankcase. That should help I hope. Eventually we'll be driven to adding sawdust, rolled oats, Bull Durham tobacco—anything to maintain piston pressure.

I walk to the cashier's box in the center of the fuel-pump islands— this is another self-serve station—and push my credit card through the opening in the bulletproof Plexiglas wall. The bat-eared wire-haired rat-faced woman inside checks the number of my card against the numbers near the bottom of a long list on her wall. I smell trouble. Sure enough, she frowns and says,

"You'll have to surrender this card, sir." I can hear the *schadenfreude* in her voice: she's caught a malefactor, a cheat, a swindler.

Feigning cold outrage, I thrust my hand through the speakhole. "Give me that card."

"No sir. You'll have to pay cash."

"I'll call the police."

"So will I."

A file of three men stand behind me, waiting, listening with interest to this dialogue. Too late for MasterGun®. I consider, reconsider, and say, "What's wrong with my card?" But I can guess.

"The number's on the default list."

Of course it is. And whose fault is that? I'm inclined to argue with her, to inflame this bitch's bleeding ulcer, ratchet up her hypertension, grease her slide into a well-deserved grave—but pause. Have charity, man. Be kind. Give the lady a break. She too is caught in the techno-industrial stress & pressure lab, like two hundred million others. Enduring her slavery by trying to ignore it. Pay up and get out.

"What do I owe?"

She glances at the digits of electronic red on her digital-display console. Megatrend country.

"Sixteen dollars and thirty-two cents."

I pay and walk back to my truck, still a free man anyhow. I count my money. About forty honky pesos left. May have to get out the "leetle robber hose," my Hispanic credit card, or never see Stump Crick again. Or else walk.

I drive away from the hateful gas station, park in the gloom under some trees in a roadside garbage dump—the same roadside dump that extends along a thousand coordinates from San Diego Cal to Caribou Maine, from Coral Gables Florida to Cape Flattery Wash—and feed and water the dog, give her the pill, let her nose among the trash piles and do her squat and pee. And then, feeling the old bite in the entrails I rummage through my pharmaceuticals from aspirin to Zomac, choose Demerol over Dilaudid this time, and dose myself. Nothing less can ease the pang now. It's nearly bedtime anyhow, a gaudy sunset shaping up in the west, and when I ease onto Interstate 64 I feel once more at ease in the world. This world, such as it is. The time is short, the distance far, but I must see Will and the green green grass of home one more time. I slip into the vacuum drag behind a forty-ton Bekins moving van. Into the night at seventy mph. A decent pace. In thirty minutes we're entering the suburbs of a big city as the full moon rises beyond the Ohio River and the Belle of Louisville. We roll into the valley, bridge the river in a torrent of mad motors, pass beneath glittering towers of babylonic splendor, hanging gardens of electricity, and debouch minutes later like riffraff from a whirlpool into the open bluegrass country beyond.

Mild qualms of regret. Would have liked to visit the factory where Louisville Sluggers are made—I think of heroes: Ted Williams, Roger Maris, Roberto Clemente, Henry Aaron—and dogleg south for a leisurely tour of the Barton Museum of Whiskey History; God knows I owe that place some homage—but I don't. Caught in the mainstream of eastbound traffic, hypnotized by flaring lights and the scream of the wind past my elbow, towed along by the racing caravans of monster tractor-trailer rigs, I let the machine master my impulses.

Until weariness overcomes me, the bliss of dozing followed a moment later by the shock of alarm as I awake to find my Dodge edging toward the shoulder of the highway. Frightened, chastened, I turn right at the next exit, wander down a blacktop road between white fences, find a lane into a copse of trees and bed down for the night. The moon glares on frosty stubble. Nightbirds croak. The giant trucks driven by sleepless maniacs on Dexedrine keep roaring past, all night long, down the asphalt trail to Hell . . .

II

North-central Kentucky. Through Simpsonville, Shelbyville, Veachland and Bridgeport. Past billboards proclaiming JESUS DIED FOR YOUR SINS. Ain't that the truth. They don't make Jews like Jesus anymore. Into the valley of the Kentucky River and through the old frontier town of Frankfort by another maze of freeways. There's the gray Roman dome of the capitol building. Rust-red factories with idle smokestacks stand by the river. Hard times for somebody. For everybody. Rising out of the bowl we find the graveyards on top of the hills. Daniel Boone lies buried here. Surveyor, settler, legislator, sheriff, trailblazer, warrior against both the Indians and the British. At one time he claimed possession of 100,000 Kentucky acres—all for himself. Could not maintain the claim, kept moving farther west every time he saw smoke from a neighbor's chimney. Good idea.

Into the manorlands. Long-legged thoroughbreds range the bluegrass pastures. Black Angus on the hillsides. White board fences and walls of fieldstone line curving driveways of gray gravel leading to three-story red brick châteaux with stone doorframes and Corinthian columns. The pride and pleasures of the rich—I hope they enjoy them while they can, the swine.

Bourbon County: through Georgetown, Newtown, Centreville and Paris—the narrow crowded one-way streets of Paris. The first hillbilly town—a rough and wary look on every face. Through North Middletown, Sideview, Mount Sterling, Camargo and Jeffersonville. Funny little conical hills begin to appear through the haze of afternoon. Pointy hills each topped with a ragged fringe of black pine, red maple, dogwood, wild cherry. The foothills of Appalachia at last. Now we're getting somewhere. I refill the gas tank, add two more quarts of heavyweight oil and chug onward into the low-class hinterlands. Twenty dollars in my britches, a crazy crackpot wonder in my heart, the clenching talons at my gut.

The road becomes narrow and crooked, ascending past black barns, tobacco sheds, housetrailers, junkyards and tarpaper shanties into the hills. A chicken scuttles across the road, squawking under my wheels. Missed—and a good thing too. This is shotgun country, redneck territory, hillbilly heaven. A lounging sullen homicidal primitive in every doorway. My people.

Each backyard sports a clothesline strung with the honest tattered garments of the poor. Why are poor folks always doing so much laundry? Because they have so many children. And why do they have so many children? Because they are poor. Because they are ignorant. Because they are sex-crazed. Because they just don't give a damn.

Damn truck lurching up the grade, engine sputtering, oil pressure down to 21. What happened to this steel horse of mine anyhow? Did I blow a gasket racing across southern Illinois? Should stop and pull the sparkplugs, gauge the gaps, clean the points—but that won't help the oil pressure. Fact is the piston rings are going. I've known it, felt it, for a thousand miles. There's something fundamentally wrong, an organic disorder, deep in the entrails of my laboring machine.

Never mind. We soldier on.

We soldier on by Gawd. Too late to pause for technical refreshment now. Too late the phalarope. Too late to rethink, regroup, rephrase the great endeavor. Myra my Mishkin where are you now? Where's my Elaine? Where's my Ellsworth? Where's my Claire? . . .

Seized by compulsion I stop at the village up ahead—a quaint rural slum called Ezel—you'll find one every three four miles now—locate a phone and dial a familiar Manhattan number. She won't be there, of course, or she won't answer or I'll get the answering machine or she'll refuse to take my call but no harm in trying. Will ease my conscience anyhow.

The phone rings three times, is picked up, I hear that harsh sweet Yiddish snarl again: "Yes, Mishkin-Miller here."

Mishkin-*Miller?* She's married another goy?

"Collect call," the operator says, "for Myra Mishkin from—" The operator hesitates.

"Yes yes," says Myra, "collect from whom please?"

"—collect from Robert Redford will you accept?"

"Not him again."

"Will you accept?"

"Okay, put him on. I accept. Hello, Bob."

"Hello, Myra."

"Where are you this time, Henry?"

"I'm in Ezel Kentucky bound for Stump Crick West Virginia."

"Sounds like the place for you."

"Who's this Miller interloper? I thought your name was Mishkin hyphen Weasel or something like that. What happened to poor old Weasel?"

"The name was Weisel, you shithead. We made it final two years ago. On friendly terms. I see him now and then. I'm Mrs. Mishkin hyphen Miller now."

"You didn't marry another goy?"

"Miller is a fine old Jewish name."

"Of course."

"You WASPs are on the way out, Henry. An idea whose time was always premature. What do you want?"

"How are you, Myra?"

"I thought you'd never ask. I'm fine. I'm having a one-woman show at the Y.M.H.A. this fall. Had my face lifted last fall. Dyed my hair purple. How's your liver?"

"How's your father? How's Sam?"

"Dad's back in the hospital again. As if you ever gave a damn. The doctors give him one more month. And Sam's my handsome darling. What do you want? I have work to do."

"Just wanted to say hello, Myra."

"So?"

"Hello and goodbye. *Ave atque vale*, as they say."

"Such melodrama. And that's all? Good."

"Still love you, Myra, you know. Sort of. In my peculiar twisted fashion."

"Fuck you."

"Should I interpret that as a cry for help?"

"You never helped anybody, Henry. You never loved anybody but yourself. I pity you and I hope you end up in an oxygen tent like my father, because maybe then you'd become a human being. Goodbye, Henry."

"Goodbye, Myra."

I wait for her to hang up her phone. But she doesn't. I hear her breathing—or maybe sobbing—five hundred miles away (by airline) on the Upper West Side of Manhattan Island. Forgot to ask about her mother—Leah—that poor crushed subterranean wraith. I smell chicken soup. Matzoh balls. Sewer gas. The story of her life. A frightening thought that probably half the American population has never seen sunlight on a pasture stream, never heard a rooster crow, never smelled the tang of skunk on an autumn night at the edge of the big dark woods. Not even on the Tee Vee.

"Christ, Myra. . . ." She fails to reply. "Leave that guy. Take his money, meet me in Pittsburgh, we'll fly to L.A., Fiji, Sydney, Perth, sit on the beach at the western end of the civilized world and watch the sun go down over Africa. Where it all began." No answer. "What do you say, kid?"

"It's too late, Henry."

"It's never too late."

"It's too late. You'll understand someday. Goodbye." She hangs up.

The storekeeper stares at me from behind his meat display case. He has a bald head like Brother Will and a red skinny turkey neck like my father would have developed if he'd only been quick enough to dodge that last widow-maker. I buy a pound of longhorn cheese and a box of soda crackers—no beer in sight, this is a dry county in the heart of Baptist country. Back to the Babble land. There's a big picture of the Reverend Jerry Falwell smiling at me from above the canned goods. The old man hands over my change.

"Got any beer?" I ask him.

He looks at the cap on my head. My cap says NRA. With eagle and crossed long rifles. His cap says Westmoreland Coal Co. No illustrations. He says, "How come you got Arizona plates on your truck?"

"That's where I'm from."

"Where you headed?"

"Shawnee West Virginia."

"Never heard of it."

"Nobody there ever heard of Ezel Kentucky."

He looks me over once more, glances out the front window and says, "What kind you want?"

"Six bottles of Iron City Pilsener."

He opens a door to his rear and returns with a six-pack of Old Milwaukee in cans. A lager, so-called, and one of America's worst beers. Old Milkweed. That's all he has. I pay and leave.

434

I know I shouldn't drink this stuff anymore but we're approaching Big Sandy River and the West Virginia line, seventy miles away, and I aim to force myself into a celebratory mood. And I mean force. If it won't come voluntarily then I'll force it. Anything for a laugh, as the trapeze artist said when he dropped his partner.

Opening the first can, I enter the village of Mize. Any relation to Johnny Mize, I wonder, one-time first baseman for the New York Giants? The second can brings me to Grassy Creek and Index, the third to Elkfork, Crockett, Moon and Relief. The road becomes ever more narrow, winding, crude, as we snake upward deeper into the hills. The road has no shoulder. The creek below is sulfur yellow. The hillsides left and right are scarred with the lifeless trenches of unreclaimed strip mines.

Two cans left. I don't feel so good. We chug through Redbush, Flat Gap, Keaton and Martha, tailpipe smoking. The people around here have a sullen, peaked appearance. They live in frame shanties covered with rust-brown asphalt shingles. Each little hovel has its pile of coal in the backyard, an overturned automobile in the front-yard and a nest of yellow curs and/or tick-ridden hounds under the front porch. That porch wherefrom the master of the house, at night, before retiring, discharges upon dust and dogs below a golden arching stream—often tinged with blood—from a coal miner's bladder, a truck driver's kidneys.

I open the fifth can and gear down into low, grinding up a grotesquely steep hill toward the blue of evening. A huge coal truck, exhaust pipes smoking, looms against the sky, topping the summit, and rumbles down the grade toward me. I pull to the right as far as I can, brushing the branches of the trees. Not far enough or else I've miscalculated for the coal truck, rushing past, clips my left-hand rearview mirror, knocks it loose. I pull to the top of the hill and park across a dirt side road. My mirror dangles by one broken strut. The coal truck vanishes below, snorting into Martha, diesel smoke spreading above the green. I finish off the fifth can of beer, then double up, clutching my stomach. I've got to vomit, defecate, both at once. I stagger into the elderberry bushes, tramping over the customary carpet of crumpled tin, broken glass, rotten plastic, and kneel with my head against the trunk of a tree. A gush of pink and green fluids pours from my throat, out my mouth and nostrils— Christ I must be dying already—and leaves me gasping for breath, eyes stinging with tears. And then the other end demands attention. Barely in time I lower my pants as an explosive outburst shakes my bowels. Sweat pours down my face. When the eruption seems completed I clean myself as best I can with handfuls of moss from the base of the tree, with a damp and soggy swatch of yellow newspaper from the garbage nearby. Compelled by habit I glance at the paper before putting it to my rear: some old-time movie actor, it appears, has been exhumed from Forest Lawn—rouged cheeks, redyed pomaded hair, Lucite teeth, duct-taped jaws, formaldehyde and all—brought back from the living dead—to run for national office of some kind. The caption blurs before my eyes, the paper disappears, I find myself vomiting again.

The spasms pass. I lie facedown on dead leaves, on tiny gentian violets, on a bed of crushed mayapple stems, and wait. I hear traffic climbing up the hill. I roll aside and haul my pants up to my hips and lie on my back, staring through a thin April canopy of leaves toward a vague, clouded sky. Don't feel too bad at the moment, in this position. Half dead but half alive. Cars and another heavy truck roll by. I am left unnoticed, or disregarded, and for that kindness I am grateful. I close my eyes and doze off for a moment—to be awakened by flies crawling on my lips, probing my nose, investigating items of interest on my chin and neck. I open my eyes to find one shit-eating blue-green bottle fly perched on my right hand, rubbing its dainty forepaws together like a pawnbroker computing the profit he'll make on your pitiful collateral—your last handgun, your only camera, your final binoculars, your ultimate brass trumpet in its case of purple velveteen.

I sit up and wipe my mouth and chin with my faithful red bandana. Over there not three feet away is a pile of something dreadful, a black pudding of excrement. Whose? Whose indeed? And why black? In the name of Jesus, Mary and God, why that tarry black? But I know very well what that grim complexion means. The color black is not a color at all but the absence of color, the withdrawal of every color, the extinction of light, the perfection of darkness. And so on. I dig dirt from between the exposed roots of the nearest tree and spread the dirt over my dropping. No one should ever have to look upon such loathsome efflux as that. My vomit I ignore; some dog from the neighborhood will come by soon to make a meal of it—yes, and he'll no doubt root up the other as well.

436

After a long while I grab ahold the tree I'm sitting against, pull myself to my feet and tread slowly, carefully, back to my truck. The nausea has passed, the bowels seem emptied for the time, but that sharp cramp in my middle stomach stabs as deep as ever. Time for Dr. Morpheus. Dr. Laudanum. Dr. Feelgood. I get out my pill cache and pop a Demerol. Then, what the hell, I'm a sick son of a bitch today, I pop a Dilaudid. Let the two of them get together down in there and mess around; maybe they'll come up with a new formula for chemotherapeutic happiness.

There's one can of Old Milkweed left but it looks wrong. I kick it, with its empty plastic collar, out the open door and lie down across the front seat, closing my eyes. I hear my dog outside, snuffling about in the weeds and refuse, searching for that bone she buried here, ages ago, in a far-off former life. I listen to her wheezing breath, her limping gait and speculate: which goes first? The dog, the truck or me? Lightcap old buddy you simple shit you knot-headed pisscutter you sure fucked up royally this time.

The light is fading, my eyelids sinking. I sit up, shaking myself awake, and slide behind the wheel. We're pledged to be sleeping in West Virginia tonight. That's for a fact. Only twenty-five miles to Big Sandy and the border. Let's get out of these hard-luck hills. I call the dog, start the engine, ease over the pass and drive down into the woods on the other side. Two more hamlets and into farther woods. Dark in here. I brush the cobwebs from my eyes. The pang in the gut seems farther away, unpleasant but lending itself to varied interpretations. Lights glare in my eyes as another coal truck passes. My broken mirror flaps in the wind. An owl swoops across the road, through my headlight beams, from darkness into darkness. Sollie the dog stares straight ahead, watching the road, while I note the dusty green of the passing trees, the depth of the night within the forest, the flight of dark birds here, there, everywhere. Very strange.

But then—what's this? A constellation of lights ahead and I've reached a town called Louisa and U.S. Highway 23.

Dumbly, humbly, I follow the main current north along the Big Sandy, cross the river in the glare and stink from a fire-belching smoke-pumping petrochemical plant and roll eastward into West Virginia. A solemn exultation charges my heart as we race down the four-lane highway toward Charleston. Hang in there, ride the draft from the freight trucks till we reach the hills and woods again. From Charleston it's only seventy-five miles—by country road—to Shawnee County, Shawnee Town, Stump Crick and Lightcap Hollow.

We cross the Kanawha, broad beautiful river heading northwest toward the great Ohio. Tugboats and barges glide on the water. Yes, I always wanted to be a tugboat captain tugging a barge full of traprock downriver from Hometown West Virginia to Triumph Louisiana. Now I guess I never will.

Rain streaks the windshield and I set the worn blades to sweeping back and forth. No moon tonight. Black clouds illuminated from below by the blaze of Charleston—the sky resembles a rumpled mattress full of bedbugs and urine stains. Coming home. I feel pretty good, despite signals of distress from some remote internal organ.

We sweep through Charleston in a shifting maze of lights, every wall every rooftop shining from the rain. Down into the cup of the hills and up the other side, northeast, where my engine labors, labors hard, and I gear down into second then first to keep her chuffing up the long grade. A hundred cars and trucks blast by on my left, horns blaring. Should I shift into granny gear, my compound low? Am I going to have to turn around and back up this here mountain?

No, we make it, sort of, with radiator boiling, and wheel down the far side and take the next exit east at Big Chimney, finding the poor boy's road into the hills again. Kind of groggy at the wheel here and I've got the notion the definite notion I should pull off soon and take about a twenty-four-hour nap. I pass more shacks, shanties and trailerhouse slums, junked automobiles, trucks with the hood up, dogs creeping through the rain. I note a revival in progress at The Temple of the Burning Bush Primitive Baptist Church. I hear the faithful shouting as I steam past, see the dark shapes dancing before a fountain of candles. Should stop. Should go back. Should join them, lay on hands, purge the last of my evil demons. But I don't.

I turn right at somebody's pigyard, find a muddy dirt road under the trees that leads over a wooden bridge, around a hill past two abandoned barns and into another forest. I drive through a tunnel of trees following the dim beams of my headlights, of my intelligence, of my hopes, into deeper darkness. Rain blears my windshield, rattles on the roof, pummels the puddles on the road ahead.

The road bends around the black ruin of a cabin and dips into what looks like a ford across the wide stream before me. I can see at a glance that the water is not more than a foot deep. I step on the gas, we drop off a cutbank and plunge into the water with a belly-whopping crash. The engine goes dead. The headlights wane to a yellow glow then die to nothing. We've shorted out. My truck shudders to a halt in the middle of the creek. Steam rises from the radiator.

What now? I sit there in the dark, my old sick dog beside me, and wonder what if anything I should do. I attempt to restart the engine but nothing reacts. Apparently the whole electrical system has been stricken lifeless by that one big cold splash of muddy water. I think of the tape, electrical, friction, duct, that I've wound and rewound through the years about so much of the wiring under the hood, and for what? It's no laughing matter but I laugh.

The rain patters on the metal roof, a pleasant and soothing noise. I roll down the window at my side and listen to the suck and gurgle of the creek as it rushes beneath the frame of my truck. From the woods on either side of the water—out of the dark—comes the surging chant of fifty thousand tree frogs, the song of springtime in Appalachia, of sexual love in the night, frantic with joy. I smile and slide deeper into the seat, feeling warm, comfortable and tired, very tired. Those difficult snaky miles through the mountains among children, chickens and dogs, between cabins set so close to the road their doorsteps adjoin the asphalt, have left me weary. And that drastic purging of belly and bowels near the trash dump on the hill sapped my vitals to the core. I feel a great peace in my head, a blank oblivion in the lower regions, an overwhelming desire for rest in everything. I close my eyes. I am going to end this day, this chapter in my life, in sleep. Blessed sleep. . .

Sinking into a coma of bliss, I hear the whining of a dog, the faintest of mosquito cries. But the sound persists, comes closer, louder. Clumsy feet step on my arm, stomach, pass over, return. A hot dry muzzle pokes me in the nose.

I open my slow heavy eyes. Looking out the window I can see only falling rain, no lights, no stars. I shove the whining dog from my lap and sink back into unconsciousness. But the dog tramps over me again, back and forth, and again I open my eyes. Now I become aware of the gentle rocking of the truck, from side to side, like a cradle in the stream. A sweet and lulling motion. But the noise of the water is stronger than before, much louder, rushing against the door panel on the upstream side.

A little red nerve of alarm penetrates my sluggish brains. Better move. I turn the key in the switch, step on the starter. No response. Sloshing about, I realize that my feet are underwater, that the well of the cab is flooded.

I pull the flashlight off the dash. At least it works and by its slender beam my eyes confirm what my flesh has felt: we're sinking. Or the river is rising. Or both.

Time for some careful, patient thought. I switch off the light and think, well, what the hell, let the water rise, we'll float away with it, stay warm and comfortable on the seat of the truck and float down this creek to the Kanawha, down the Kanawha to the Ohio, down the Ohio to that Old Man River, down the Mississippi to the Gulf of Mexico, float out on the great blue sea like a beer can from a sewer pipe and greet the morning with upraised arms, a shout of joy, a chorus of eternal exaltation—

Welcome back my son, says a voice like God's trombone, beaming down from Heaven as we sink, me and my Dodge Carryall, my dog, my crackers and cheese, my bedroll, ax, toolbox, Buck knife, firearms, loading kit, spare tire and empty flapping canvas water-bag, into the realm of the great white shark.

—and why not? Hart Crane did it why not us?

But Sollie the dog has another opinion, won't let me be. "All right," I growl, "all right, let's get out of here," and again I try to start the motor, knowing it's futile, and it is, and then attempt to open the driver's door. I cannot do it; the power of the stream is too much. I clap my hat on my head, take the .357 from the glove-box and tuck it in my belt, grab flashlight and open the door on the downstream side. This too is difficult, with a vortex or hydraulic keeper forming below, but not impossible.

We stumble out, my light on the swirling black waters, where I find myself crotch-deep in the flood. The dog, paddling desperately, head high, drifts away. I lunge and catch her by the collar. We struggle toward the shore, a jungle of shrubs leaning over the stream.

The current startles me with its strength. But we reach the bank and drag ourselves up the mud into the thicket.

We lie there, breathing hard. The pain in my guts seems stronger. Drugs wearing off. I am wet, cold, miserable, sick as a dog with the flux. Need warmth, love, shelter. I rest for a minute, then rouse myself. Taking flashlight only, I sink into the water and struggle toward my swaying truck, a dark mass of metallurgic matter in the night. I reach the back door, open it to find my bedroll and duffel bag and other items half-floating in a foot of water. My good hunting rifle in its sheepskin case lies under the surface, wrapped in a heavy tarpaulin tied with rope. I load my arms with all I can carry. The water is up to my waist. The truck begins to roll, heaving over me. I abandon duffel bag and flounder to the bank, clutch at a living bush and haul myself onto the semisolid earth. The stream sucks at my feet, tugging at my boots, pulling me back. I wriggle farther into the brush and rest.

The rain falls steadily on my head. The dog laps tenderly at my face, then backs off a step to barf on the leaves. That dog is nearly as sick as I am. Got to try and get a fire going.

I rise to my knees, gather my belongings, stand up and force a path through the riparian jungle into the forest beyond. I shine my light around for some glimpse of barn or shed or hut or pigsty; nothing available. Only the narrow rutted water-streaming dirt road leading up the hillside under the trees. What's up that way? Probably nothing but another strip mine—towering spoil banks of yellow clay above a trench full of stagnant sludge. West Virginia, country home. Taking the canvas tarp, I rig a rainfly between two locust trees, back to the wind, pull a branch from a dead tamarack, break it into little pieces on the trunk of the snag, unfold pocketknife and whittle some shavings under the rainfly. No good. As I discover the next moment, the matches in my shirt pocket are soaked, useless.

I think of my hero Jack London. To build a fire. What would he do now? Drink himself to death? Take an overdose of Demerol? Good idea. And then I realize, to my horror, that my pills, my Band-Aids, my entire medical kit is in the truck. Inside that listing foundered worthless wreck of a Dodge now half submerged and slipping inch by inch downstream in the center of the flood. Shall I venture in one more time, stumble through the waves again to rescue that metal First-Aid box in the so-called "glove" compartment? My sheath knife, my wallet with expired operator's license, my last few dollars . . . Hesitating, I shine my light over the roiling stream toward the Dodge. The creek pours through the open window on the driver's side, out the open door on the other. Too late. Even as I watch the truck rolls again, wallowing onto its back to accommodate the weight of the water. The four wheels turn slowly above the waves, dripping and gleaming in the beam of my flashlight.

This is getting absurd. Even serious. And I don't feel so good myself. I sense the coming of another internal purge. I back away from the rising creek, crouch under the poor shelter of the rainfly, cuddle close to my dying dog and wait for the message to come down, my private, personalized, gold-embossed passport to mortality, Everyman's visa to the ancient chaos of the sun.

What sun?

24

JUDGMENT DAY

His internal trouble seemed to begin, or rather to reveal itself, on that pleasant night in March about a month before Elaine departed, slamming the door, cracking the plaster, never to return.

Henry had gone straight from his desk at the welfare office to the Dirty Shame, driven by inner necessity. He was on his third bourbon and beer when Rick Arriaga showed up, then Doc Harrington, then the Hooligan. Such glittering company made going home superfluous. Together they took their supper of sauerkraut and sausages, scalloped potatoes and black bread and a pitcher apiece of Heineken's dark and Heineken's light. A moderate but satisfying meal. Followed by cigars and a snifter of cognac, two of each for Henry. After the waitress cleared away the dishes they settled down to some serious drinking.

With good cause. All but Arriaga were suffering from female disorders. Henry's wife threatening to leave, carrying on with her secret cybernetic lover; Harrington's wife outraged by Harrington's unseemly friends and frequent absences; and Hooligan plagued by a trio of jealous mistresses, all of whom danced at the same strip joint. Arriaga alone claimed to be happily married but was in difficulty with his boss, Father Castelli, for having sent too many teenage clients to the Planned Parenthood Association for maternal counseling. Like Henry Lightcap, young Arriaga was in the love-thy-neighbor and do-unto-others business: he worked for the county hospital. Handsome, energetic, intelligent, a student of law, a master of social work, Richard "Rick" Arriaga had political ambitions but was off to a bad start, among bad influences, in a bad world.

Harrington raised his glass: Here's to our wives and sweethearts.

May they never meet, said Henry.

They drank. Soon after, Doc Harrington stole away, sneaking home to his wife. He said. The other three remained. They discussed the mysterious disappearance of Keaton Lacey down in Mexico—but many were disappearing there these days. Hooligan started to talk of the good old times at Turkey Creek Canyon and the wildlife sanctuary, but Henry changed that subject. Arriaga was next to leave: had to read a book to his three-year-old, he explained. Her bedtime coming soon and they were halfway through *The Adventures of Speedy Gonzales*. My little Ellie is now five, thought Henry. I want her back. Or is it six? Anyway I want her. I ain't much but she's all I got.

He and Hooligan remained at the bar for another hour, drinking slowly but steadily. When Henry began to reel from the barstool Hooligan helped him out the door and into his van. The dealer's van. The pander wagon. Henry did not want to go home. He'd made phone calls an hour before, thirty minutes before, and knew what awaited him there: a dark and empty house with only Bach or Beethoven or Billie Holliday for love.

We'll go to my place, said the Hooligan. The girls are working tonight. You can sleep in Gloria's bed. Or Sunshine's. Or Velvet's, take your pick. They won't be back till who knows.

What's it like being a pimp?

It's hard, it's hard. Nothing but heartache and worry, that's my life. Busy busy busy all week long.

Henry collapsed on somebody's bed and closed his eyes. He felt a strange unpleasant pressure in his upper abdomen. Nausea in his stomach. He rolled on his back and found that the pain went all the way through. He tried lying on his left side then the right side but neither position was tolerable. He tried kneeling. No good. He sat up in the dim light of the room, duly alarmed, and discovered he was about to vomit. No time to search for the bathroom; he was in a strange house, a strange world, in a strange condition. There was only the window by the bed, a streetlight outside. He stuck his head through the window, failing to notice the pane of glass, and caring less, and threw up a quart of green, yellow and lavender goulash onto the bare dirt and bright shards below. Blood dripped from his skull. Badly shaken, he pushed off and plucked out the

444

fragments of glass from the bottom of the window frame, rested his chin on the knuckles of his hands and stared into the street. He felt ghastly.

Two dogs went by walking their transients toward the railway yard. The young bearded men in greasy rags, packs on their shoulders, muttered to each other as the dogs led them on through the dim light of calamity toward their terminal fate in the darkness. Henry heard them, heard the words, recognized the general import.

Fucker said get outa here I said who wants to stay.

What'd he say?

He never said nothin'. I busted him in the mouth with the brass knucks and walked out. He never even whimpered. Teeth all over the floor. What could he say?

The light snapped on behind Henry. He heard Hooligan speak: You all right, Henry?

Slowly he turned his head, saw his buddy standing in the doorway with a pistol in each hand. Hooligan the gun nut. I'm okay, Henry said.

Okay hell—you're bleeding all over your face; what happened?

Nothing. Just sick.

Hooligan came close. You look blue as a skinned rabbit. He dropped the guns on the bed, grasped Henry by the wrist. You're cold and clammy, man. What's wrong with you?

Hangover.

Hangover hell you're dying man. Come on. Hooligan put an arm under Henry's arms and tried to lift him to a standing position. Henry writhed in pain, his body straining toward a fetal position. The powerful Hooligan lifted Henry in both his arms and carried him out of the room. Henry gasped, suppressing a howl of agony. Hooligan got him out of the house, into the van and drove to the emergency room of the nearest hospital. There Henry crouched on his knees on a bench, sweating, groaning, while Hooligan and the admissions clerk performed a quick biopsy on Henry's wallet. Fortunately for Henry he was currently a state employee (public welfare caseworker) and carried a card that identified him as a member in good standing of a group medical insurance scheme (Blue Cross of Arizona).

Henry was laid on a hard bed inside walls painted a gleaming white, among mysterious devices of stainless steel and brushed aluminum, under a light both brilliant and soft. In the red haze of trauma he felt clean hairy pale medical hands palpating his belly and abdomen. Somebody drew down his pants. He sensed the needle sinking into one buttock, his own, felt the injection of a hard icy drug as firm hands compressed the plunger on a hypodermic syringe. Despite near total absorption in his private world of pain he retained presence of mind sufficient to make interested inquiry. What's the dope, doc?

Pain reliever, the voice said. Relax, it'll work faster.

Sodium pentothal? Percodan? Morphine? WD-40? STP?

A derivative. Relax, you're going to sleep in about one minute.

STP? Rubber cement? Nostalgia? Weltschmerz? Existential angst?

He felt himself being wheeled through marble halls, down corridors of bliss where smiling faces floated toward him, expanded, swept by with supersonic speed. Mad molecules of color flew overhead. Thank you, he thought, reality at last. I am about to meet my maker in Maw's Home Kitchen. He bathed in a luxuriant warmth, deliriously content. . . .

Coming back. Stiff bed. Half naked under a starchy sheet. He turned his eyes away from swords of light as hands not his own tinkered with the blinds, then returned to stroke his brow, his hair. Soft hands.

How do you feel, Henry?

I'm okay. He considered the interior of his body. Something like a cuttlefish stirred about in his entrails, seeking an exit. Feel like hell but I'll be okay.

Had a little drinking binge the other night, didn't you?

That's right, Elaine. And where were you? I phoned five times, he lied, exaggerating.

I was out, she said. Visiting a friend.

Pause. That friend. What to say? he wondered. What difference does it make? he concluded.

Hooligan and Dr. Andrew Harrington came in. They greeted Elaine, sat on the broad windowsill near the bed and smiled at Henry. He grinned back. What's wrong with me, Andy? he said to Harrington.

Acute pancreatitis, probably.

What do you mean, probably?

You have the classic symptoms. But they'll run you through a few tests, make certain.

I hope you're not my doctor.

Harrington smiled. Not a chance. Just a visitor. But you're getting the best gastroenterologist in the city.

What's that?

Internal medicine.

What's his name?

His name is McNeil, said Harrington, and he comes from Harvard. Dr. Hugh McNeil.

No bullshit, Henry said. Tell me about this acute pancreatic crap.

Pancreatitis. Means you'll have to stay in bed for a while. And no more alcohol, ever.

Thank God, said Elaine.

This is serious, agreed Henry. He looked at the needle taped to his wrist, the I.V. tube, the inverted bottle of glucose hanging from its portable rack. Nearly empty.

Attendants came and went. One pricked Henry's fingertip for a drop of bright red blood. Another inserted a syringe into a vein on the inside of his elbow and drew out a few cubic centimeters of dark purple blood. A nurse entered and changed the empty I.V. for a full one. Henry studied the upended bottle, the transparent plastic line, watching for air bubbles. He knew that if one air bubble—one single tiny bubble—entered his bloodstream and reached the heart he was a goner. Kaput. There were quite a few bubbles in the tube. He waited for Harrington to notice. Harrington was supposed to be an M.D., though only a bone specialist.

What's wrong, Henry?

There's bubbles in this I.V. tube.

There're bubbles in your head. They won't hurt you. Be glad there's not a couple of fish swimming around in that bottle. And Harrington told them of his former days as resident intern in a hospital in Chicago. Of the chief surgeon making his rounds in the intensive-care unit. Of the man's lack of humor.

You actually put goldfish in the I.V. bottles? Elaine asked.

Only with terminal cases.

I don't think that's very funny either. And what about the goldfish?

They died. Martyrs to the full rigors of Western medicine.

McNeil entered, a short stout forty-year-old man in a too-tight plaid sportcoat. The coat had two vents in the rear, Henry noticed. That meant something important but he could not remember what it was, having not read *Esquire* magazine or *Gentlemen's Quarterly* for many years. It meant I.V. League, maybe? McNeil had a red plump face with broken veins on the nose, brown hair combed flat, tired blue eyes, a small weary shy smile with yellow teeth. He shook hands with Harrington and Henry's other visitors, then sat down on the edge of the bed and looked at the patient.

You look frightful, Mr. Lightcap.

I don't feel as bad as I look.

Thank heaven for that. Been drinking a bit lately?

Not lately. But I was yesterday.

McNeil smiled. He touched his nose. Smirnoff's Disease. He placed a large pale hand on Henry's abdomen. What do you think's wrong with you? He probed and squeezed, testing the tone and distension of those slime-covered organs under the skin—liver, pancreas, spleen, gall bladder, duodenum, stomach, intestines. Any ideas?

Acute pancreatitis, Henry said. That's my guess.

Good guess. But we'll see. Dr. McNeil leaned forward and spread Henry's eyelids, taking a close look at each bloodshot green eye.

Nothing wrong with my eyes, Henry said. I got good eyes.

Yes you do. Bit of jaundice in the sclerae. McNeil sat back. There's a curious theory floating about these days that we can diagnose an internal illness by patterns of disturbance in the iris of the eyes. Iridiology, they call it.

What do you see in my eyes?

McNeil hesitated. Skepticism, he said.

Sounds life-threatening.

Well, don't be too sure of that. Might be the healthiest of attitudes in the long run. Also the short run. McNeil stood up. Very well, Mr. Lightcap. I'll get you out of here in a few days. Give you some rest, medication, routine testing first. See you tomorrow. He shook Henry's hand, grinned weakly at the others, hurried out of the room. A busy man. Many sick people in hospitals.

Skepticism, Elaine said. I don't think that's a very hopeful philosophy for a medical doctor.

He's a Scot, Harrington said, they're that way. A blunt empiric race, those Caledonians.

448

Henry asked about the tests. Harrington explained: X rays, liver biopsy, CAT scan, maybe a sonic probe, probably endoscopy and colonoscopy, the usual battery of invasive procedures. Plus blood tests, urinalysis, stool inspection, of course.

Don't like the sound of any of it.

All virtually painless. You'll be so doped up and blissed out you won't give a damn what they do. It's for your own good, try to remember that. Been drinking any mountain water lately?

Every chance I get.

You might have giardia, you fool. Some kind of bug in your bowels. Amoebic dysentery. They'll look at the simplest things first.

Simplest? Simplest compared to what?

Harrington paused. Compared to what? Well, compared to other possibilities. Like gallstones, for example. Gallstones can cause an angry pancreas. And vice versa.

You're speculating, Andrew.

That's right. That's why you've got to take the tests.

Henry took the tests. After two days' rest under the enchantment of the "derivative," he drank a barium milkshake, was rolled onto another gurney by two husky homosexuals in white suits and carted through the corridor into an elevator that sank, sank, like his heart, opening into further corridors of trauma and anxiety. His gay aides, laughing and joking all the way, steered him past thick leaden doors and placed his vulnerable meat on a steel altar beneath a massive death-ray apparatus. He was turned this way, that way, bent, straightened, inverted, between each descent of the insolent silent blank blue-black eye of the machine, its idiot genius searching for Henry's more sensitive ganglia, the entryway best suited for administering the most prolonged and exquisite, least endurable but not unendurable agony. He could hear no sound but the voice of the torture research technician coming through the wall—take a deep breath . . . hold it—and a sinister buzzing noise as a burst of ionizing radiation streamed through his defenseless body. He felt his tissues disintegrate, dissolving to a swarm of primitive power-greedy cells.

After the X rays he met the CAT scanner. Computer tomography. Laid on a cold motorized slab, he was inserted like bread into an oven, like a corpse into a furnace, into the body-size opening of a device that looked to Henry's eyes like the dryer in a Laundromat.

He expected to be revolved, revolutionized, spun round and round like a load of clean damp underwear. He was not. Something in the machine rotated instead. He observed particles of dust or rust or bone slipping from a crevice in the steel and drifting to the floor. He looked for the maker's label, the metal tag riveted to the scanner's enameled hood. Maytag, it said. Or was it Frigidaire? Whoever whatever cobbled the thing together, he felt himself electronically vivisected slide by slice, a forked length of old baloney in a magical guillotine. Painless, certainly, but harmless? He wondered.

Dr. McNeil and a nurse came into Henry's room next day. The nurse carried a tray of boiled hardware—gleaming Inquisition tools. McNeil explained the purpose of a liver biopsy; against his better judgment Henry consented. The doctor injected a local anesthetic and slipped a needle between the sick man's lower ribs. Henry heard the puncture, felt the brief sting of pain, nothing more. Grinning, McNeil showed Henry a fragment of raw pink-and-blue flesh in the tip of the forceps. Looks good enough to eat, he said; but we'll check it under a microscope. Henry shrugged. He felt weary of it all. The smell of his own breath frightened him. My breath stinketh, he thought. There's a creature dying inside of me. When the doctor and nurse departed he turned his face to the window, seeing silver clouds towering without movement in a cobalt sky, and he wept for a while, quietly, privately, furtively, feeling sorry for himself.

There were other tests, less mechanical, more chemical, or sonic, like the ultrasonograph, then a twenty-four-hour pause in the proceedings. After the pause the X ray and CAT scan examinations were repeated. Exactly as before. With method, precision and no variation.

Why the hell do I have to go through this garbage again? Henry grumbled, feeling fear. Why twice?

I don't know, the technician said, a pretty girl in tight white uniform who switched her hips adroitly aside when Henry's wandering hands came groping close. Sometimes they do that. The radiologist wants another look, I guess.

What?

Take a deep breath . . . hold it. . . .

After the second set of tests there was a second pause in the pro-

ceedings. On the following day, in the morning, McNeil entered
Henry's room. Worried but calm, Henry sat on the edge of his bed
clipping fingernails with a toenail clipper. He was bathed, dressed,
ready to go home. Or somewhere. Wherever. The doctor, a friend
by this time, smiled at him, a smile even more shy, more timid,
than before. His eyes looked furtive, wet, hurt. Henry felt a chill
numbness rise—like hemlock—from groin through heart to his
throat. I knew it, he thought. I knew it.

Well, Henry.

Well, Hugh.

We're in trouble, Henry.

We?

Mostly you.

Okay. What is it?

Follow me. McNeil walked out of the room and down the hall,
entering a small office where oversize X-ray photographs hung before a fluorescent panel. Henry shuffled after. He felt weak in the
knees. Like a cigar? the doctor said, opening a cedarwood box on
his desk.

Not really.

Me neither. McNeil closed the box and snapped a toggle switch
on the side of the light panel. He pulled a silver pencil from his coat
pocket and indicated something on the X-ray picture. Notice that?

Henry saw a vague darkish blob, like dust in a star cloud, among
a medley of incomprehensible shapes in the ghostly cage of somebody's ribs. He noted a name—Lightcap, Henry H.—on the margin
of the photo. I see a dark blur, he said. What is it?

It appears to be a tumorous mass on the pancreas gland. An advanced cancer, in other words.

No kidding? Henry sat back on the edge of the doctor's desk. Well
I'll be doggoned. He paused, swallowed, and said, What should I
do about it, Hugh?

McNeil stared at the picture, then out his window, then at Henry,
licked his lips and stared out the window again. Same old blue
Arizona sky. Same vapor trails. Same dark mountains bristling on
the horizon. If I were you, he said. Pause. There's nothing to be
done, Henry. If it's really a pancreatic cancer—and that's what it
looks like—your chances of survival are zero. Oh, we could operate,

take heroic measures, remove the pancreas, maybe the biliary duct as well, implant a stent. But you wouldn't live any longer and you'd be spending your remaining months in a hospital bed.

No kidding. Months. Henry felt like laughing. But he didn't. His nerves seemed frozen. So it's a matter of months. How many would you say?

Six to nine. A year if you're lucky.

Six months to a year. That's no misdemeanor, Doc, that's a felony. That's a goddamned bloody felony, Dr. McNeil.

It is indeed. McNeil continued to stare out the window.

Henry thought of a joke. At least I won't have to floss my teeth anymore.

No you won't.

What about radiation? Chemotherapy? Aspirin? Wholesome natural raw fruits and cereals? Sit-ups?

Not applicable in this case. We don't know what to do about this kind of cancer, Henry.

What do the other doctors say?

I've consulted two radiologists, two oncologists and another gastroenterologist. They've seen the pictures, the results of the tests, our interpretations agree.

And all the instruments agree.

They agree. McNeil looked at Henry, trying to smile. But it's only science, you know. An inferential chain of reasoning. Not immediately verifiable—unless we cut you open—but a high probability quotient. What we know is that we know nothing with absolute certainty.

Henry's eyes were drawn to the window. To the outside, the free air, the open sky. After a moment he said, I suppose it's going to hurt some.

Yes it will. But there's one thing I can do for you. I'm going to prescribe the entire cabinet of analgesics. You're going to get them all, Henry. I'm going to give you Demerol, Percodan, Diluadid, Dolophine and methadone—all good oral pain-killers. And you'll get relief for nausea, diarrhea, insomnia, depression, vertigo.

But what about fear? thought Henry. What about terror? What about despair?

McNeil was already busy scribbling on a pad. Don't you sell this stuff on the street. Use it. This will keep you going for the next few

months. And when things get extreme—well, there's always morphine.

When things get extreme, Henry said, I'll take care of things myself.

I understand. We'll see. You might change your mind later. They
usually do.

What about a Bromley cocktail?

Brompton cocktail? Sorry, not legal here. Heroin. Morphine's just
as powerful.

Again Henry gazed out the window. A swirl of little pale birds,
like confetti, like a net of lace, exfoliated from the sky and draped
themselves upon an Aleppo pine. Water sprinklers jetted in explosive circles, drenching the hospital lawns. Just plain folks walked
about. The world continued, bland and blasé, while catastrophe
opened beneath the one who cared.

One thing, Henry said, don't tell Elaine about this. Or anyone
else. I don't want anyone to know. Not even Andy. I mean Harrington. Let them think I had pancreatitis.

McNeil folded the sheaf of prescriptions and tucked them into
Henry's shirt pocket. You still have pancreatitis. No more alcohol.
And you should tell your wife. You're going to need all the love and
support you can get.

I don't want it on these terms.

McNeil lifted his shoulders in a provisional shrug, embarrassed,
and wrote a number on a card. Secret home phone number, he said.
Call whenever you wish. If my wife says I'm not in give her your
name.

Thank you, Hugh. Guess I'll go now.

McNeil put his hand on the telephone. Need a taxi?

No thanks. Elaine's meeting me outside.

That was a lie. Henry planned to walk home. It was only five
miles from the hospital to his house. He planned to do his weeping
on the way, in the desert. He held out a hand to the doctor. Thanks
for everything. McNeil's eyes were brimming with tears. Oh hell,
Hugh, I can manage this business. I know what has to be done. I've
been planning on this kind of thing all my life. I guess I did about
everything I ever wanted to do. I'll go make a large deposit in a
bank, a sperm bank I mean, for the girls, Elaine too when she wants
it, and that's really—damn it, Hugh, it's all right—that's really

about all I have to do. Visit old Will again, shoot the dog, that about wraps it up. No problem. No sweat. No big deal, McNeil. What the fuck—I'm fifty-three years old, that's plenty, that's more than Jack London or Chekhov had or Henry Thoreau not to mention a whole herd of poets and Mahler and Mozart and Schubert and almost as much as Beethoven and all of them other old buddies of mine so what the hell, Hugh, blow your nose and shake hands and let me get the hell out of here.

McNeil blew his nose as suggested. But holding Henry's right hand, he gently pushed him back down on the edge of the desk. I want to look at your eyes one more time, he explained. Hold still. He parted the lids of Henry's small squinty eyes—left eye, right eye—peering intently into each for what seemed to Henry like a full minute. Then he backed off. He put his hands in his pockets and looked out the window.

What's wrong? said Henry. What'd you see?

The doctor smiled a crooked little smile. I think I see hope in your eyes. Not much but some.

Pause. What's wrong with a little hope? Henry paused again. For Christ's sake, he added for emphasis.

Wrong attitude.

Wrong attitude? What do you mean, wrong attitude? First you tell me I've got a cancer in my fucking pancreas gland, now you tell me I've got the wrong attitude in my fucking eyes? Is that fair? I ask you. Stop staring out the window and talk to me.

Silence. Jesus, thought Henry, talk to me, where'd that phrase come from? I sound like my wife. Like every wife I ever had. Say something, he said aloud to Dr. McNeil. And I don't want any bed-pan manners, please.

Henry had risen from the desk, thumbs hooked in pockets, and now stood leaning over the doctor, glaring down at him. Condemned, he had the doomed man's freedom to cast aside all deference, to bully his betters if he wished.

McNeil, eyes still a bit red and moist, smiled up at Henry. He reached out his hands, squeezing Henry's sloped narrow bony shoulders. What I want to see in your eyes, he explained, is not hope but—something else.

Something else?

Like faith. Faith, Henry. You follow me?

Faith in what?

The doctor paused. The doctor smiled. His turn for a joke. Skepticism, he said. He repeated the word, whispering: Skepticism.

Henry stared at McNeil. Henry bit on his lower lip, trying to understand. His brain felt numb like his limbs and nerves. He managed to come up with a weak warped grin—a twist of the upper lip to one side, exposing yellowish fangs, that more resembled a snarl than a grin. I'll work on it, he said; I will, Hugh. You're a big help. Goodbye, Doc.

They hugged each other, grinning through their tears. Henry walked away.

25

OCIAN IN VIEW

I

The rain drips on my tarpaulin all night long. Twice I am forced to crawl from my sack, once to defecate on the innocent soaked leaves outside the shelter, once to vomit. I'd have preferred to do both jobs at once but the timing could not be properly arranged. Solstice the dog merely watches, not moving, no help at all. Or is she even watching? That glaze on the eyeballs—maybe she's already defunct.

No sun appears with the hangover dawn but that's all right, you can't expect everything all the time. Not in the misty hills of West Virginia in the early spring of April. Ice crackles on my sleeping bag as I creep, like a worm from its sac, out into the pseudolight of another quasi day. A stiff frost glows on the rigid panicles of grass. Yes indeed it's true—April is the coolest month.

The first thing I think of is fire, hot forbidden coffee and the wet matches in my damp shirt pocket. I verify: yes, matches still damp. Could make a fire drill—if I could find any dry wood. But I've got neither coffee nor pot anyhow. Or to phrase it positively, if we had a pot we could make some coffee if we had any coffee.

I rise to my knees and stay there awhile, not so much in prayer as in self-analysis. The head aches, of course, and my hollow stomach feels like it's been strip-mined by a Mitsubishi bulldozer. Then salted with arsenic. The bite, the secret little bite, remains, though it seems a shade easier at the moment. The upper abdomen is bloated with serous fluid—ascites, no doubt, as McNeil had promised. Swollen spleen, necrotic pancreas, rotten attitude, that's my condition and to hell with it. What I need are some pills, capsules, horse spansules, spiritual suppositories. The hell with it.

But I can't refrain from rising, staggering to the bank of the creek and looking downstream for my truck. The water level has gone down a foot or two and there it is, the old Dodge, on its side and coated with mud, half submerged at a point fifty feet beyond where I'd last seen it.

I look at that wreck like Robinson Crusoe at his ruined ship. Perhaps there's something out there I can salvage. The pills, maybe, in the waterproof first-aid kit. My wallet with my last ten bucks, I.D. and pictures. Sollie's Nizoral and crunchy granola. My signal flares, ammo cans, loading kit, grub box with its canned goods, sprouting potatoes, dried noodles, a warm coat, books, record albums, tow chain, Come-Along, Hi-Lift jack. Absurd. Everything is soaked, saturated with silt, worthless. Forget your *things*. Life is too short for *things*. I remember an old song, never more fitting than now:

> Oh if I had the wings of an angel
> High over these prison walls I'd fly;
> I would fly to the arms of my sweetheart
> And there I'd be willing to die . . .

Yes. Nevertheless, I derig the rainfly, take rope and bushwhack through the brush on the bank to a muskrat slide about ten feet upstream from the truck. Although the flood is receding, the swollen creek looks much too big and violent for swimming. And me lacking the strength to crawl from a bathtub. I hitch one end of the line to a stout tree, tie the other in a bowline knot around my chest and slip into the water. The current sweeps me toward the truck. I clutch at the doorframe on the passenger's side of the cab—the door itself hanging by one hinge—and grope beneath the muddy water for the glove compartment. Bad news: it's open, my wallet is gone and everything else that was in there. But jammed in the wiring under the dashboard I find the metal box containing my precious analgesics. Our God is a just God and being just he may even just exist, who can say. I set the box on the upturned side of the truck and feel around in the slime for other treasures. I find a few sodden rags, a rusted wrench, my channel-lock pliers, nothing more. No billfold, no paper money, no sealed matches, not even my ax. The back door of the truck, like the side door, is open to the flood. God is just? Well now, he saved my medicine but carried off everything else. He is not so much just as a comedian, a joker, a wise guy. And nobody loves a wise guy.

Back on shore I take stock of my assets, my situation, my prospect. Desperate but not serious. My good old reliable .444 Marlin lies in its sheepskin case, presumably okay. I'm afraid to look. The two-shot Derringer, of course, the shotgun, the .32 special lie under the muck somewhere inside my sunken truck. Did I really bring so many firearms all the way from Tucson? And if so why? Not to mention the .357 Magnum, safe in its holster inside my bedroll. What was I doing with all that iron? Plus the old carbine I sold to Don Williams back in Gallup. I'm no gun nut. If I support the National Rifle Association it's only because I favor the second amendment. Not because I like guns. I don't like guns. Guns frighten me.

I pack the remaining two—the revolver and the rifle—inside the heavy canvas tarpaulin. Where to stow it? Up in a tree? Some kid will spot it or some black bear climb up and tear my package apart. Bury it under the leaves or in the dirt? The varmints—smelling salt—will dig it up. Finally I hang the roll to a bent-over sapling in the densest part of the thicket, out of reach of bear. That should keep till me and Will get back here, in a day or two. At the last minute, overcome by sentiment, I pull the .357 from the bundle and stash it in my belt. Dangerous to carry a concealed weapon; even more dangerous, even provocative, to carry it openly and legally; but most dangerous, in a modern civilized nation, to carry no weapon at all. Any fool knows that and if I ain't a fool what am I doing here?

Now what? I stuff rope, sleeping bag and medical kit inside the duffel bag—all that I hope to carry—and stumble through the wet woods to the road. I mean the dirt road, the parallel tire tracks with a centerline of grass and skunk cabbage, that leads up the hill on my right.

The hill is difficult for me, gravity dragging at my heels, but I trudge along, upward onward homeward, only sixty miles or thereabouts to go. One mourning dove croons from a distance, as they always do, calling through the rain.

Hey hoo . . . hoo hoo. . . .

My dog follows close, eyes dull, head hanging, tail drooping.

Would be an act of mercy, I suppose, to end her misery at once, quick and simply, with this heavy metal head-blaster in my belt. But is that what Solstice herself would choose?

Let her come as far as she can. We pass a tumbledown barn, a fallingdown cabin, a rickety board fence that once enclosed a hog pasture. Nobody's been home for years. Apple trees unpruned for a decade hang ragged limbs to the ground. A bunch of Black Angus beef cattle range on the hillside below the encroaching forest. Somebody's homestead, abandoned or sold for taxes, has become a part of some urban syndicate's tax shelter.

We pass a living farm. White clapboard house with smoking chimney, barking dog chained to a kennel, car in the driveway, woman and children staring from the kitchen door. I see a telephone line linking this house with Sutton, Stump Creek, Morgantown, London, Tokyo, and am tempted to stop, ask for permission to use the household phone, call Will.

But I walk on. I know that I must be a fearsome sight with my red eyes and sunken cheeks, whiskery jaws and mud-coated outfit. The duffel bag slung on my shoulder makes me look like a bum and the fat revolver in my belt, barely concealed by shirt and jacket, gives me away for sure as a dangerous criminal.

That's my excuse. It's a good one. But something deeper in my soul prefers to keep on walking. To keep Will waiting. To see if I can make it a few miles farther on my own. Why? Why is always a good question. Why not? is my inward answer. A foolish answer but it's mine.

Now I have to worry about police, sheriff's deputies and state troopers. That woman back there in the farmhouse may be the paranoid type, like me. And with equally good reason. Got to keep the eyes skinned for approaching metal, the ears open for sound of tires and motor. I feel eyes watching my back.

But nothing yet disturbs the gentle strum of rain on road, the tramp-tramp-tramp of my soggy boots, the delicate pitterpatter of four dogfeet at my heels. I shift the bag to the other shoulder, readjust the uncomfortable but comforting gun in my belt, its muzzle aimed at my groin, and tramp on past a cornstubble field, a silent Massy-Ferguson hitched to a rusty disk plow, a park of noble white oaks beyond a meandering pasture stream. A lovely farm. A marginal farm, sustained by faith not economics. The owner probably makes his basic living in a chemical plant, a coal mine, a power station.

The road slants downhill through the trees, joins a two-lane asphalt road in the valley between the high ridges. Here the trees are leafing out—the old familiar pale green of linwood and gum, sycamore and sassafras and locust. It looks like home. And there, beyond a fenced-in pasture containing a few long-legged milk cows, on the far side of an ocher-colored creek, is a railway.

The sight does my heart good. Two gleaming tracks on gray ties laid on a bed of black cinders winding under the trees northeast toward Shawnee and Stump Creek. Toward Honey Hollow and home.

Sound of wheels on the asphalt road. I slink aside into the dogwood, squat down with my duffel bag and wait. A car passes, whizzing down the road. A second appears, slowing to turn up the dirt road that I've been walking. No insignia on the door panel but a whiptail radio antenna rises from the trunk lid and the man at the wheel wears a tight gray shirt with badge and shoulder patch. The law has been called. And me innocent as a babe. Innocent of any crimes but poverty, vagrancy, concealed weapon, possession of hard drugs and absolutely no identification. No money in my pockets, no I.D. on my person—imagine what the local *rurales* would make of that. Refer them to Will Lightcap? Who's he? they'd say. Never heard of him. Will lives in a different valley, a different county, fifty sixty miles away.

No, I'd best stay off the roads from here on. Minimize human contact. I can see myself getting backed into a corner, feeling trapped, all too easily pulling this heavy instrument of murder from my belt. What would I have to lose?

The rain drizzles down, a gray mist filling the valley. I look for a bridge across that creek, a road to the railroad. Waiting, looking, feeling internal troubles stirring about, I open my kit and swallow one nausea tab. Make it two. Followed, after a moment's hesitation—got to try to keep alert—by one tiny Demerol.

Now, before we float and wobble into dreamland, got to find a way across yonder crick. I stare up and down the valley, searching. Two cars, a pickup truck, go by. Then a caravan of four giant coal trucks races past, beating hell out of the blacktop.

In each direction I see fenced-in pasture fields, ragged woods, broken-back barns beside canted old two-story farmhouses with that familiar vacant look. Keeping to the brush above the road, I head up-valley toward the nearest group of farm buildings. A dirt lane leads between fields toward a flat wooden bridge over the creek. I watch another pair of automobiles pass, then slide down the mud-bank, jog across the asphalt and slip like a fox down the narrow sideroad. Safe; I stagger forward into the mist.

A sleek automobile sneaks up behind me, pulls alongside and halts. The whiptail quivers. The man in the tight gray shirt studies my eyes.

I lower my bag to the mud. My jacket is buttoned over the gun but I'm conscious of the bulge beneath—like a man with a badly swollen spleen. The splenetic type.

He stares. I wait. End of the road for Lightcap. (They'll never take me alive, I think, half believing it.)

"How you doing, buddy?"

Buddy—that means comrade, companion, fellow soldier. Honorary brother. But of course he doesn't mean it. Wouldn't know the meaning. "Just a-walkin' along," I reply.

He considers my answer, looking me over carefully. His face is fat, rosy, smug, with little pink-blue porcine eyes. Greasy slicked-back hair and a pencil-thin mustache on his upper lip. Red ears, a double chin, and a hog's belly squeezed beneath the steering wheel. Another inbred degenerate hillbilly. Marginal I.Q. and the morality of a Ku Klux Klansman. God knows I know his type. The backwoods cop. A native redneck bully with a gun on his hip and an automatic shotgun in the rack behind his left shoulder. He looks to be about my age. But I must look older.

"Where you headed?"

"Shawnee."

"You got a long walk. Folks there?"

"Yep."

"Why don't you phone them?"

An intelligent question. I pause and say, "I'd rather walk."

He seems to understand. He jerks a thumb over his shoulder. "The road's behind you."

"I'm gonna walk the railroad. It's shorter."

He considers my words, watching me. "You look too sick to walk. What you got in that duffel bag?"

"A bedroll and some medicine."

"Any food?"

"Sure. I have food."

He eyes me with disbelief. "You look like you ain't had a square meal in a week. Your dog looks better than you do. You have any money?"

"I've got a few bucks."

He stares at me. A weak embarrassed smile appears on his face. "You're lying, buddy. Here—" He opens the metal lunchbucket beside him on the seat, takes out two sandwiches wrapped in wax paper, a greenish banana and a tiny round fruit pie encased in clear plastic. "You eat this," he says, pushing the stuff at me through his open window. I hesitate. "Go on, take it."

I take it. "Thanks."

He grins. "Don't thank me, thank my old lady." He shifts his patrol car into reverse—no space for a one-eighty on this road—half turns in his seat, looking out the rear window, and roars back to the paved road, wheels throwing mud.

The dog and I sit down on the bridge over the creek. I give Sollie the sandwiches: meat loaf with mayo and lettuce clapped inside sliced Wonder Bread. Nausea: I have no appetite but force myself to eat the gluey little pie; maybe the sugar will boost me on. We save the banana for future use, get up and start down the railroad.

The rain has stopped, a pale sun glows dim on the western sky above this deep and narrow Appalachian valley. We trudge onward, tie after tie, every step a small victory.

Pleasant final dreams. I dream as I walk. The air seems warmer now. I smell the fragrance of warm creosote, of damp trillium, Juneberry and ground ivy blooming on the ditchbanks. I hear the trickle of running water in the ditch, gurgling out of the culverts. I pass an upright concrete post beside the tracks, the letter W engraved upon its head. Whistle sign—road crossing around that next bend. I walk and dream as I walk of Wilma Fetterman climbing the school-bus steps. Of Donna Shoemaker turning cartwheels. Of the first two-base hit I got off Tony Kovalchick and of Red Ginter's last home run. I remember Mary and the backseat of the Hudson Terraplane. I remember Sally Buterbaugh who worked as a maid in the Shawnee Hotel the summer I was bellhop there, the perfume of her little room on the top floor, the way she looked as she lay on her bed wearing only a satin slip and lacy bra: *Come on in, Henry. Close the door, Henry.*

A locomotive whistles behind me. I stumble into the ditch dragging the duffel bag. A short freight thunders past, horn blaring, trailing a hot wind, black smoke, dancing leaves. A brakeman sits at the side window of a yellow caboose. Without a glance my way he tosses out a cigarette package. I pick it up: two Camel cigarettes and a book of matches stuck inside the cellophane wrapper. Bless the man. I must be nearing home. Even the brakemen, even the sheriff's deputies, are being generous as giants.

I give one cigarette to Solstice, the other to myself. Beggars' democracy. She swallows hers in one gulp, I strike a match and smoke mine. I'd prefer a cigar. Cautiously I save the matches, sealing them inside the foil of the empty pack. We come to a road crossing. I pause.

There's a little town to the west less than a mile away. I see a white church steeple with clock, a paved road with traffic, the bright red-and-yellow signs of a Shell gasoline station. I smell woodsmoke and think of Stump Creek, Will's house, the sweet suggestion of suppertime. There will be a public telephone over there, if not at the gas station then at the general store. Could hide my bag here, saunter into the village like a regular freeborn American citizen, learn the name of the place, make that one simple phone call. Collect, naturally. Sit down on the churchyard fence and wait. Will, he'd come. He'd take the call and he'd come. What choice would he have? I ain't heavy I'm his brother, the poor unlucky slob. Stump Creek cannot be more than a two- or three-hour drive from here.

I stash the duffel bag in the elderberry bushes and walk toward the town. We come to a bridge over the creek. I lean on the rail and gaze down at the rushing, muddy waters. I remember McKinley Morganfield. Got my mojo workin', he would sing.

My dog sits beside me, watching the flood below, waiting. The creek is flowing north. Joyous, exultant, spring-flood waters streaming toward the Buckhannon River, the mighty Monongahela. Who was Buckhannon? I don't know but with a name like that he must have been a distinguished man. And Mononga-hela, now there's a name to scare the deerskin britches off Buck Buckhannon himself.

Mononga, Shawnee chieftain, warrior, deerslayer, husband of twenty squaws, father of Tecumseh, ally of King George, his lodge festooned with many a black-, brown-, yellow- and red-haired scalp.

The dog waits. We ponder the racing waters. The sun has dropped behind the western ridge. A yellow glow clarifies the texture of the forest crowning the crest line. It's about four P.M. in Tucson now; the paloverdes are turning golden with flowers; scorpions rustle over the sand; the inferno of desert summer lies only a few weeks off.

About that phone call. I look again at the little town strung along the county road, rooftops and steeple showing above the trees. Some of those unhooded mercury-vapor yardlights, activated automatically by sundown, have begun to glare through the twilight. For five hundred thousand years the human race survived without those things; now they're everywhere, from Point Barrow to Tierra del Fuego. The brighter the lights the greater the fear. The peace of sunset, evening star, moonrise and starlight, of fireflies and soft lamps has become one more privilege of the rich.

Shall we make that telephone call?

I debate the matter in my head, hands on the bridge rail, knowing full well that I've already decided. The water rushes beneath. If we had a canoe, a johnboat, a Boston whaler, even a little rubber raft . . . I shift my feet. The dog waits, watching me.

"Let's go, Sollie."

We return to the iron road, the railroad, picking up my duffel on the way. This bag gets heavier by the mile. Maybe tomorrow, I think, opening the medical kit, I'll hang this thing too on a sapling deep in the forest. I swallow a Dilaudid (derived from laudanum derived from opium) this time, not feeling too good. What I really need is a drink of water. And an intravenous dinner. I'm dehydrated from that bout of puking and diarrhea last night. Nausea, most discouraging of emotions, keeps haunting my stomach. I'll probably lose the deputy's chemical pie before evening becomes night. I swallow more Phenergan tablets for the nausea, dip my hands in the running ditch beside the tracks and drink as much of the cold iron-flavored water as I can keep down.

Hoist the duffel bag to shoulder. Crank nose, belly, petcock and toes to the northeast. Push left foot forward. Place weight on left foot. Push right foot forward. Weight on right. Each step an arrested fall, an averted accident, a postponed disaster. The inconvenient interval between the ties does not help. I shift to the cinders on the shoulder of the roadbed but that too makes awkward walking: the cinders are loose, rough, uneven beneath my foot. But even so it's better than walking the highway where grease-slick steel sharks screech past your elbow every two-three minutes. The railroad these days is what the American country road used to be: a quiet lane winding through the forest, following the riverside and contours of the hills—not gashing through them. Nobody bothers you on the railway, nobody watches, nobody worries about your business there.

The Appalachian twilight deepens about me. The hoot owl calls again from the dripping woods. Frogs clank in the bogs along the creek, tree toads chant among the willows. The sky above resembles a blanket of purple wool. Not a star in sight. More rain a-comin' for sure. Got to find shelter soon. The railway bridges the creek ahead but a railway bridge makes a leaky roof.

The railroad passes behind a coal-mining town. I see the rows of company houses lining the single street, each two-story box weathered to matching shades of gray and rust. Autos, pickup trucks, motorcycles stand parallel to the housefronts. Vapor lights burn blue-white in the gloaming, mimicking the blue glow of TV in the windows.

Kids are yelling on the sidewalks—not many. I smell burned olive oil, refried grease, smoking garbage. On a field between town and coal-loading tipple lies the ghost of a baseball diamond: open bleachers, a backstop cage of chickenwire, the dugouts behind each baseline, the bare infield black with coal dust, a gray-green outfield with cindery warning track and board fence advertising CHURCH'S AUTO REPAIR, BOGGS' FUNERAL HOME, HIRES' ROOT BEER, SUTTON'S FORD, GRESAK'S TAVERN, IRON CITY PILSENER, PEPSI-COLA BOTTLING CO., HINTON'S HARDWARE . . .

Sky leaking again. The track winds out of town past the riprap of junked cars shoring up the banks of the creek, through another swamp, past a strip mine and quarry, into the comforting dark of the woods again. But the trees are leaking too. Raindrops trickle from the beak of my cap. And then I spot a covered bridge spanning the creek. I go on, descend a weedy bank, crawl through a barbed wire fence and drag myself and bedroll beneath the sheltering stone abutment of the bridge.

Even in the dark I can see that others have camped here before me: the stone is black from the smoke of campfires. I drop my bag, scrape a hole in the dirt and build a tiny fire of beer-bottle labels and sassafras twigs. Small fire in a hole, deep under base of bridge, means less chance of being observed. I warm my hands at the fire, unroll the sleeping bag on the dirt, tug off my wet warped boots and slide socks-first into the sack.

The bleak but consoling rain falls on the shingled roof of the bridge, drips through the planking of the roadway, slides down spiderwebs and crossbeams, spatters drop by drop into craters in the mud and dust.

II

The dog lies prone between the rails, stretched out on cinder and tie, unwilling to move.

I talk to her, command her, bark at her, lift her to her feet and drag her a few steps forward—nothing works. She subsides once more to her belly, closing her eyes. Flies buzz about her ears and nose.

Again I pull the revolver from my belt, thumb back the hammer, place the muzzle to her forehead. I shut my eyes and begin to squeeze the trigger.

Again I fail. Can't quite do it.

"Goddamnit dog, what do you want from me?"

No response. Sollie lies in the filtered sunshine, wheezing slowly, eyes leaking a yellow matter, ribs gaunt beneath her dull and useless hide.

Don't feel too good myself. More pills less relief with each passing day. At least I've got enough bullets in the gun for both of us and that's some consolation.

Damn worthless stinking ugly mongrel mutt. . . .

Insults don't help. She won't move. Cursing, I drag the duffel bag containing my bedroll down the slope of the roadbed and into the woods. I take out the green banana, my supply of pills and capsules and hang the bag to another bent-over birch. How will I find this when we return? If we return. I don't know and I don't care.

Back on the tracks I pick up my dying dog—she smells like buzzard meat already—and hold her in my arms like a baby. She's nothing but bone and skin, light as a puppy. I put her down, take off my jacket and make a neat hobo's bindle of my remaining supplies: the loaded .357, the packet of medicines, the banana, tying everything in a tight ball with the jacket's sleeves. I push the end of my walking stick through the knot and balance the bindle on my shoulder. The bindle stiff is ready.

Now the dog. I pick her up under my left arm. The smell is sickening. We step forward. Left foot, right foot, hay foot, straw foot. Ten feet, twenty feet, forty feet, eighty . . .

Can't take the smell. Can't handle the double load. I'm breathing hard already. If I'm not careful I'm gonna throw up again and there's nothing in my stomach but tatters of liver, biliary duct, pancreas, gall bladder. Nor any strength left in either arm. I let the dog drop. She flops to the cinders without complaint.

I sit on the rail and talk to Sollie, saying goodbye. I review our years together, the good times and the bad, and apologize for leaving her now. She consents, too tired to care anymore. I drag her to the ditch on the left, where water runs over the dead leaves and mud. Here she can drink if she wants it. Before the vultures come, the black bear or the bobcat, whatever it may be—neighborhood dogs most likely—that finally terminates her canine existence. Would be the merciful thing, the decent humane thing, to put one of my hollow-point .357s through her brain. But I've tried that. I lack the courage to be so kind.

I climb the embankment, pick up my stick and bundle, stagger on. The railway curves before me. At the far end of the turn I look back. Solstice still lies in the ditch, nose down, limp as the dead.

I walk on, no longer a we, searching my heart for a sense of regret. Hard to locate. That dog is better off than I am, damn her lousy mangy flea-bit tick-sucked worm-riddled fungoid carcass, let her die in peace. *Pax vobiscum.*

I stop. Now that I'm free of that deadweight dog maybe I should go back for my bedroll? No. Too far. The idea of retracing my steps for even a hundred feet seems too wearisome and tragic even for thought. Let it hang.

But I turn back. Sure enough, as I've half expected, that dog has crawled from the ditch back up on the railway and is dragging herself along from sleeper to sleeper, spike to spike, nose fastened to my spoor. I walk past her without a word. She halts, watching.

I retrieve my duffel bag and return to the dog between the rails, pack her into the bag and lurch on down the track. Stupid, I know, but maybe she'll suffocate in there, die quietly, quickly. Then I'll dump her in the ditch for good. For eternity. Life is a dog and then you die? No no, life is a joyous dance through daffodils beneath cerulean blue skies. And then? Then what? I forget. I forget what happens next.

III

Night comes sifting through the trees, the clouds, the sweet sad music of April in the woods. Looks like rain again and we're glad to take shelter in a tarpaper shack at the side of a shutdown strip mine. I let the dog out of the bag and she curls up on the boards behind a potbellied stove. Might build a fire in that thing before the night is over. There's a chill in the wind suggesting sleet. Even snow. Would not be the first time I've seen a snowstorm in April in these Allegheny Mountains.

I sit against the wall for a time, then untie my bundle and take out my precious pills, two for the nausea and two for the pain. That should get me through till midnight. I put on the jacket and rest. Getting dark. I force myself to rise and step outside until I find some dead sticks, old boards, a few chunks of soft coal. I peel the *Playboy* pictures from the wall and set a fire in the stove, ready for the match.

Feeling slightly better, I sit on the doorstep and stare across the railroad to the lights of a fair-size town on the far side of the creek. Where am I? What town is that? And do I care?

I believe I've been walking for two full days now. Maybe three. Let's see: first night under the covered bridge abutment. Second night inside the cab of that burned-out dragline rig above the tracks. Hail came down that night. Third night here. Three days. If I walked say fifteen miles each day I'm nearly home. Maybe I've done better, walked farther.

What is that town beyond the river? Could that be—Shawnee? I'm not sure. I slide into my bag and wait for the Demerol to do its work. When it does I sleep.

Late in the night I rise, free of all pain, all melancholy, put on jacket and cap and step outside, closing the door on my comatose

468

dog. A dark, starless night. Stick in hand, revolver in my belt, I walk down the muddy road to the tracks and the river, cross over by a familiar iron truss bridge and enter the town.

Lamps burn above an empty street paved in red brick, warm and mellow. Not a soul in sight. It must be very late. There is no traffic nor any vehicles parked at the curb.

Yes, I know this street. I've seen these elm and maple trees before, those square frame houses painted white, these small shops close to the sidewalk. Of course. I stop in front of Marla's Beauty Salon and read the labels in her display window:

ZS Zoto's Texture Care
Ion Hair Spray
Thermal Styling Lotion
Gentle Surgi-Cream
Nucleic "A" Body Plus Styling Mousse
Nexus Humectress: A Polymerized Electrolytic
    Moisture Potion for the Hair
Triple Lanolin Aloe Vera Lotion

Nothing new there. Same as before. I was amazed by those names when I was a boy. I walk on, cut across an intersection—no traffic light—and stop in front of Elliot's Cut-Rate Drug Store. Lights burn inside but nobody sits at the stools along the marbletop soda fountain or in the high-backed cream-colored wooden booths lining the wall. As always, two green milkshake mixers stand at the far end of the back counter and the gorgeous oversize illustrations of strawberry sundaes, banana splits, root-beer floats, chocolate sodas hang on the wall. But where are the pretty girls I used to love—Betsy, Donna, Wilma, Sybil, Helen, Mary?

I cross the Old Turnpike Road and walk over the cool grass of Courthouse Park. By streetlight I read the remembered names on the Revolutionary War Monument:

Boggs	Gatlin
Dobbins	Holyoak
Fisher	Shields

And on the World War I monument:

Adams	Hunter
Boggs	Keith

Bishop	Knight
Buckner	Lightcap
Carr	Martin
Criss	Singleton
Fetterman III	Tait
Fisher	Tanner
Gatlin	Taylor
Ginter	Weaver
Goley	White
Hacker	Woods
Hamric	Young

We don't commemorate the Civil War around these parts. Too many families on the wrong side. As for the names of those who died in World War II and the Korean War and the Vietnam War—they are too many to remember, too many to weep for. Paul Lightcap alone was far too many, too much.

I read the bronze plaque on the granite obelisk that rises between two rust-green field artillery pieces (Spanish-American War):

Shawnee, West Virginia. County seat of Shawnee County. Named for former prevalence of indigenous tribesmen. Founded and settled by Jeremiah & Benjamin Shields in 1784, both later killed by Indians. Town burned by Confederate troops in 1861. Birthplace of Henry H. Lightcap.

Not strictly true of course. I went to high school here but I was actually born on the farm in Honey Hollow near Stump Creek eight miles to the northeast. I stroll around the domed courthouse building, looking at the enclosed walkway two stories up that leads—like a bridge of sighs—from the county courtroom to the county jail. Dim lights glow behind the barred windows but no shadows move across them. Not tonight. Lights burn in the police station below, the steel entrance door stands wide open but there's nobody inside, neither prisoners nor police. The clock on the wall behind the booking desk says two forty-five. The police parking lot is empty.

Returning to Main Street—devoid as before of any traffic, any life—I walk past Waxler's Department Store, the Dairy Dell (another ice cream parlor), the Criterion Movie Theater (showing a double feature Saturday matinee tomorrow: Buck Jones in *Guns on the Pecos* and Ken Maynard in *Outlaw Creek*). I'd be interested but I've seen those picture shows twice each already. They're good but not as good as Hopalong Cassidy. Next door beyond the theater is the cement stairway leading down to Nick's Shoeshine Parlor and Pool Hall. Light slants from the open doorway; I hear the crash of cueball breaking a rack. Who could be playing pool this time of night? The courthouse clock reads three ten. One car waits in the alley, the only automobile I've seen in the entire town—a 1935 Hudson Terraplane with foxtail on the aerial and a classy necker's knob of red agate clamped to the steering wheel. I descend the greasy steps of the pool hall and look inside: nobody there but Will and our little brother Paul shooting a game of eight ball. Paul chalks his stick; he looks pale and skinny as always but gives me a friendly smile. I nod; we watch Will sink three in a row then miss an easy corner shot. He straightens up, gives me a wink and backs into the shadows beyond the hooded table light. I see his big hand reach for the chalk hanging by a string from the ceiling. Paul bends at the rail, cuestick sliding slowly back and forth between forefinger and thumb of his right hand as he takes aim on the four ball. He's a lefty. A southpaw. No wonder he's always had trouble. I say nothing, give them both a wave and climb the steps to the street. I know where Will hides the extra key to his car, taped inside the chrome-plated grille. But the Terraplane is gone.

Very well, I'll walk. I take the shortcut out of town, the cinder road past the flaming coke ovens at Blacklick, then the dirt lane over the hill at Gatlin's farm. This brings me to Jefferson Church, lit up like a theater despite the lateness of the hour. I stop for a glance through the open double doors and see Mother in there, who else, pumping on the broad pedals of the organ. I know that tune: "Bringing in the Sheaves." She's alone, except for Marcie and Baby Jim arranging flowers at the rail before the pulpit. Must be something special happening tomorrow. Easter, could be. Smell of violets and iris. I wave at them but no one notices. I leap off the porch of the church, spring over the hedge at the corner, and glide through the dark, without effort, past Trimble's and Fetterman's up the red-slag road, under the nave of sugar maple trees that leads to our place. I overtake my father on the way: he's tramping home with his ax in his right hand, the limber shining crosscut saw over his left shoulder. He whistles a march tune. He laughs as I pass him, calling my name—Henry? that you Henry?—and keeps on whistling as he walks. I know as he fades behind me that I will not see him again.

I never reach the house. A baby wails among the trees below the road, down in the dark of the woods, the sound of an infant baby that is hurt, alone, frightened, a dreadful dirge a terrifying cry prolonged forever. I pause, peering into the dark, straining to perceive a child's form in the chaos of shattered space and night.

Something huge, black, grasping, looming above the trees, blotting out the few dim stars, shambles toward me from the forest. Watching that shadow come I feel gathering within me the power of an ancient rage, the strength of a never-forgiving hate. I draw the gun from my belt, tighten my grip on my stick and advance with joy, in an ecstasy of anger, to meet the shapeless thing as it reaches forth to embrace me.

Henry, it says, Henry my friend my very best friend, where have you been? I've been looking for you everywhere. . . .

26

COMING HOME

He walked the railway mile by mile. Stick and bindle over right shoulder, dragging the duffel bag with his left hand. The bag bumped over the ties, lumpy and inert, stinking to heaven. One Gulf-Coast Appalachian vulture soared above, quartering downwind, patient but hopeful, hopeful but proud. There are no strangers here, only friends we haven't met.

He wore the beak of his cap pulled low to the right, shading his eyes. After four days and nights of mostly rain the sun was shining.

A coal train thundered toward him, air horns bellowing. He stepped aside off the roadbed hauling the duffel bag, and waited. The train swept by in a blast of iron and sparks and swirling gray coal dust, followed by the silence, the amazing sudden grace. The robins began to bleat again. The man shambled back to the roadbed and shuffled on, northeast by east, into the morning sun.

The railway wound through another half-deserted village. He passed the backside of the Sovereign Grace Baptist Church. Slab-wood shanties lined the road, each with swing on front porch, washing machine on back porch, and the remnants of Detroit automobiles in yard and alley. Barefoot children stared at the tramp. He looked sick but tall and hairy, thin but strange. Pregnant women watched him shuffle by, their eyes soft and curious. He was nearly beyond the village when two little boys came running after him, a pair of snot-nosed towheaded brothers in bleached-out overalls. The older boy held a small package wrapped in a page of the Shawnee *Morning Gazette*.

"Hey mister," the boy called, "wait up a minute."

The man stopped, looking at the boys. Their mother watched from the next-to-last shack in the town. The taller boy offered the little package. "Here mister."

He took it, unwrapped it. Inside was a hard boiled egg and two sandwiches of clean white Holsum bread and bright yellow USDA surplus commodity cheese.

"Thank you, boys. Much obliged." They stared up at him, shifting their bare feet on the warm cinders, flexing their ankles. "You tell your maw I am much obliged."

"Whatcha got in the big bag, mister?"

He looked down at the slack, half-filled duffel bag. "Christ if I know," he mumbled. "I forget." The boys seemed disappointed. "But look here," the man said. He fumbled through the pockets of his filthy jeans, found his jackknife, a few coins and three small polished stones. He gave two stones to the older boy and one to the younger. "Chert," he said. "Agatized rainbow. See the colors? Genuine petrified wood from the Painted Desert, Arizona. Give one to your mama. Okay?"

The older boy nodded, turned and ran off. The little brother gaped at his stone for a moment, then scampered after him.

The man sat on a rail and cracked the egg. He peeled the shell and slowly ate the bluish-white albumen, the firm orange-tinted yolk. The egg stayed down. He considered the two cheese sandwiches. They looked less palatable. He shoved one inside the opening of the duffel bag—Have a sandwich, kid—and raised the other to his mouth. The cheese had a dyed appearance, the pale bread was smeared with mayonnaise. Not much nutriment, he thought, even for a hungry hobo. Chewing carefully, he noticed the colored illustration, torn from a magazine, that lay on the sheet of newspaper. He picked it up. The picture showed a court jester in cap and bells contemplating a doughnut. A poem served as explanatory caption:

> As you travel on through life, brother
> Whatever be your goal;
> Keep your eye upon the doughnut,
> And not upon the hole.

By God, he thought. By God there's wisdom, of a sort, in them simple lines. Fuck Plato. Epictetus also. He looked back down the converging rails toward the hamlet in the hills, the peaked-roof shacks and clotheslines and floating haze of woodsmoke, the glints of glass and aluminum and plastic scattered about on roadway, yard and hillside. He saw the form of a woman, short but large, leaning with folded arms against the jamb of an open door. He waved, blew her a kiss. No response. Wrong woman. Where is that open door?

He ate half the sandwich, rewrapped the remainder in the sheet of newspaper—*that* might come in handy—and stowed the package in his bindle. He got up from his rail, not easily, helping himself with the stick. He tossed another salute toward his observers and resumed his march up the tracks, dragging the duffel bag over the square-cornered sleepers.

Warm today. Humid. The sun beamed down through a fleece of drifting clouds. The man paused to remove his greasy flannel shirt, tying it around his waist by the arms. He tramped on. His long-sleeved thermal undershirt, originally white, was now a blended gray of sweat, dust, grease, floodwater, sulfur and coal smoke. The smell surrounded him like an aura, real but transparent, visible to enlightened eyes. April magic.

He tramped on.

He was aware of birdsong. He heard the robins, certainly, but also the mating calls of woodthrush, crow, woodpecker, marsh hawk, bobwhite, bobolink, phoebe, red-winged blackbird, cardinal and dove. And the unknown bird that nests in cast-off empty engine blocks.

The trees, some beginning to leaf out, others still in bud, lined his way. The dogwood and red maple were in full flower; the fragrance of the dogwood reminded him of orange blossoms, of cliff rose, of a certain perfume in a golden vial on the dressing table of a long-gone princess. The red maple made him think of blooming redbud in the canyons of the Rainbow Trail, under Navajo Mountain, out there in the enchanted wilderness of stone.

The man was tempted to sing. He did sing. His voice seemed weak, harsh, a dismal croak even in his own ears but he sang.

> Eyes like the morning star
> Lips like the rose
> Claire she was a pretty girl
> Lord almighty knows . . .

He passed another village a half mile on his left, two rows of white houses shaded by trees, united by a blacktop road. A lazy winding creek flowed through a bog of stumps, bending around the outfield of a forgotten baseball park. Mustard weed spread its yellow glow from deep left across center to far right; traces of the infield lay under a lake of rusty floodwater two inches deep. Junked cars rusted within a jungle of blackberry vines and dead goldenrod where home base and the backstop must once have been. The man hardly glanced at the ruins. He trudged heavily on, sack bumping over the ties, and did not rest again until he reached the place where the railway bridged a stream and side road leading up into a small hollow between the hills.

The valley appeared, from his point of view, to be filled with trees, a mass of silent transpiring forest budding into a promise of green. The narrow road was unpaved, ungraded, no more than parallel tire tracks beaten down on red slag. Fresh green grass—with dandelions—grew in the dirt between the tracks. The little stream flowed clear and bright, dropping over ledges of bedrock sandstone.

He noted the hobo signs carved by knifeblade in the wooden stringers of the bridge, decades old but still legible. The plain "X" meant handout available at nearest house; the "X" underlined signified dogs but friendly dogs. The pointing finger with thumb erect indicated direction—up the road beside the stream.

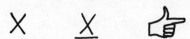

The man sat on the edge of the bridge for a long time, watching the road and the stream and the woods. Finally he stirred himself and started down the embankment toward the trees. He stumbled in the loose cinders, fell, rolled twice but never let go of bindlestick or duffel bag. He reached bottom, got to his feet, slapped dust from his clothes and staggered a short distance up the road. When the farmhouse appeared, beyond the archway of maple trees, he stopped. An old pickup truck stood parked on the ramp of the barn. Smoke rose from the house chimney, floating toward him. A dog began to bark. He gazed up the road at the farm, hesitating, then labored to his right over a split-rail fence into the woods.

He abandoned the duffel bag at the fence, weary of it at last, and limped through the shade of the trees, his boots making no sound in the damp leaves. One heel missing. He crossed the stream and angled upward on the farther hillside until he came to a weed-grown wagon track. He followed it toward the crest of the hill.

Below, far behind, the slumped duffel bag lay inside the fence. The buzzard floated on the thermal currents a thousand feet overhead, patient but not indifferent. The duffel bag waited below, becoming animated after a time, twitching in the sunlight. New folds and rumples formed themselves in the gray-green fabric, the mouth of the bag was enlarged from within and the black dog crept out. Nose in the weeds and leaves, she picked up the man's trail and crawled into the woods, ears flopping, tail drooping, eyes nearly sealed by rheum.

Henry squatted by the spring, laboring for breath, sick in the stomach again, unclear in the head. No more goddamn hills, he thought. Hain't gonna climb no more goddamn hills today. He lifted the jar from the stub branch, dipped it in the water, drank. That water's as good as ever. He popped four pills, Lomotil and Dilaudid, and washed them down with another draft of the oak-root-flavored water. Below stood the board-and-batten cabin. Beyond, through the tall trunks of the oaks, he could see the farmhouse, the barn, the array of smaller buildings. The coon dogs barked under the back porch, noses in the air. Will came out the kitchen door with a coffee mug in hand, hushed the dogs and looked around, up and down the road, across the pasture and over the hillside. After a moment he went back into the kitchen. Henry stayed as he was, on his heels, breathing hard, sheltered and concealed by the sumac and willow surrounding the spring and by the screen of trees.

The sun stood three o'clock high on its southerly arc. Henry leaned back against the trunk of a tree, stretched out his legs, put on his jacket—cool in the shade—and waited, watching the life of the farm.

Saw the chickens scratching in their run. The dogs scratching their fleas under the porch. Will's two mules, the gray and the buckskin, rubbed their backsides on the pasture fence. There were no other animals on the place anymore but housecats, weasels and raccoons. And why wasn't Will out in the woods today? Or up at the shop in Stump Creek? Must be Sunday. The day felt like a Sunday.

Smoke rose steadily from the kitchen chimney: Marian was probably baking a cake or a chicken or both—maybe a roast of poached venison. Company coming? Will emerged again from the kitchen door, a rag rug draped over one arm; he hung the rug over the pumpstand railing and started whacking at it with a broom. The long winter's dust billowed up and drifted away. Will Lightcap—beating on a rug. Henry smiled at the sight. That Women's Liberation has penetrated even to Shawnee County. But Will he always was an easy mark for a woman's touch, a woman's gentle words.

Marian came out of the kitchen carrying what looked, from Henry's vantage point, like a wooden bucket. After a moment he recognized it as the hand-cranked ice cream mixer. She carried it into the cold crypt of the springhouse, returning with a white pitcher. He noticed that she was wearing what appeared to be a new dress, turquoise blue with a yellow sash around the waist. Her dark hair was down, shining, her head up to the sky. She was fat, she was middle-aged, she was happy, she was beautiful.

Will carried his rug into the house and came out with a second rug. He looked heavier than Henry remembered, a little slower, and the sunlight glistened on his bald pate, but he swung the broom against the rug with a lusty wallop. Each blow was followed—after a time—by a double echo from the wooded hills. The crows complained about the noise, rising from the trees along the cornpatch, circling and descending again.

Will returned to the house. Spring cleaning? Not on a Sunday. A plume of black smoke rose from the main chimney. That would be Will firing up the furnace in the basement, pouring a can of kerosene on kindling and coal. Cool inside the house, of course, especially in the front rooms away from the kitchen. Maybe Will's getting ready to take a bath—like Henry he always needed one. Especially on a Sunday. Particularly if they're expecting visitors.

The mourning dove called again from somewhere deep in the forest on the ridge to the east, off toward Cheat Mountain and that Spruce Knob five thousand feet above sea level. That same old lonely dove that Henry first heard more than half a century ago when he was a baby on a blanket in the April grass, his mother nearby hanging up the wet sweet-smelling sheets and diapers. The first birdsong he ever learned to recognize and never learned to separate from distance, from the darkness under the trees, from the brooding stillness of the hills.

Up on the mountain, thought Henry. That's where he'd go. Up in the national forest. Move into one of them falling-down cabins. No blackbird's gonna find him up there. No, nor hear his sad cry. He waited, watching the house, the Lightcaps' worthless comical obsolete farm, the drift of smoke. As he watched the black dog crept close and licked the salt from his hand. He stroked the hard bony overheated head. Ain't that right, old dog?

A small automobile rolled up the red-slag road and stopped in front of the house. A man and woman got out, followed by two children. Henry knew that slender woman in the jeans, the big straw bonnet: our little sister Marcie. With her second husband, Frank. Back from California for good. Thank God she got rid of the other, that clown Whatshisname, the no-good philandering insurance-peddling jerk. The man and woman approached the front door of the house, passing out of Henry's sight, but he heard shouts of greeting, saw the two kids—your niece and nephew, Uncle Henry—run across the lawn to the tire swing dangling from the sugar maple tree.

Henry watched. Happy people. Those are happy people down there. I can't do it, he thought. Not to them. I cannot I will not do it.

Another car pulled in from down the road, parked near the giant maple. Another couple climbed out, Will's youngest son, Joe, and his wife, Kathy. Then their child, the little girl, Nancy. The back door of the car remained open and after a moment one more person extricated herself from the cramped steel shell. She stood up, holding a package in her hands, and stepped briskly across the grass toward the kitchen door. Her customary entrance. She was a tiny woman with gray hair and glasses, wearing a sweater and loose slacks. She carried herself erect; though close to eighty there was no stoop to her shoulders, no old woman's hump in her back. She stopped once to kick a football out of her way. Will's dog greeted her with acclaim.

Lord, thought Henry, that woman is meant to live forever. She will too. He felt a surge of blood-pride rise from his heart.

The men came out of the house—Will, Joe, Frank. Walking to the end of the yard, they picked up the horseshoes at the near peg. Will held a smoking cigar clamped in his teeth; like Henry he had his weakness. He said something to the other two men, walked to his pickup truck on the barn ramp and drove away. Needs more beer? Young Joe and Marcie's husband began pitching the horseshoes. Henry heard the clang of iron on iron, followed by echoes.

They don't need me down there. One thing none of them need is my pack of terminal troubles. I will not lay that sorry load on those good people, kinfolk though they be. The one decent thing I can do is let them all alone.

Henry watched and waited, preparing to leave. He heard a motor grinding uphill on the far side of the ridge behind him, then fading off. Long shadows spread northeastward from the farmhouse, the maple tree, the barn, the wagon shed, the corncrib, the pigpen, the lone hickory in the meadow by the run. The mules waited near the stable door, expecting their evening feed. That late sun slanted through the trees, amber shafts of light bearing a suspension of dust, vapor, white cabbage butterflies and yellow monarchs.

He heard the music of a piano. That's Mother, he thought; Marcie had a harder rougher style. He heard a motorcycle coming up the road, looked and saw the one headlight burning. He recognized the motor's throaty roar. That's no Jap crap; that's a Harley-Davidson. Maybe those Nips do make better machines but they never made a Harley. The concept is too subtle for the Oriental mind. The motorcycle wheeled slowly toward the house, engine throttled down, muttering. Stopped at the door; a tall slim fellow in leather jacket lifted one leg and slid off the saddle, stretched himself, stood looking about. He wore no helmet; his coal-black hair fell like a mane to his shoulders. That's Jim by God, that's got to be Jim. He's back. Our no-good punk kid brother, back from exile, back from Canada at last. He would not serve. He would not submit. That's our little Jim all right. Again Henry felt the hot blood of family glory spreading through his veins. What do you Lightcaps think you are? Why we're Lightcaps, that's what we are, what more do we need?

Watching the house, seeing the lights come on through the curtained windows, Henry smiled with pleasure. He felt sick, he felt hollow as a dead sycamore, he felt mortal as the dog beside him, and he didn't care. He fumbled in his kit for the pills. Take another drink this here spring water, swallow my medicine, go down find that damn bag, go off deep in the woods to sleep. Head for Spruce Knob tomorrow. Looks like a clear night. Ain't that Jupiter I see a-shining over yonder?

The dog growled; Henry turned onto one knee. He braced his stick against the ground and pushed himself to his feet. He trembled, legs shaky, and steadied himself with a hand against the tree at his side. He saw a man in the shadows about thirty feet up the hill. A man with a shotgun cradled in one arm. Saw the bald head, the potbelly, the red coal of the cigar. The wide and bearded grin.

The two men stared at each other for a long moment before the older one spoke: "Okay Henry, enough fooling around. We been expecting you for weeks. For years. Come on down to the house now. Supper's almost ready."

Henry felt a great bewildered joy rising in his heart; fifty-three years—maybe that was enough after all. But what he said was, "I don't think I can stay, Will."

The other cast his cigar into the damp leaves. "Nobody said you had to stay, you damn fool." Will stepped toward him, broad smile on his face, holding out his right hand. "And nobody ever said you had to leave neither."

A Postlude

Roaring westward at evening, top down, red sun of Texas burning in their eyes. Smoke of El Paso—city on fire—smeared across a yellow sky. Barbed wire. Windrows of dead tumbleweed piled on the fence. Scrub cattle with splintered horns, fly-covered hides, broken hooves, range over the rocky desert, munching on cactus, on the dried seedpods of thorny mesquite. Newspapers yellow with lies, bleached by the sun, flap like startled fowl with ragged wings across the asphalt road. Welcome to the West.

Welcome to the West! he'll shout in the wind, grinning his vulpine grin, teeth hanging out, and hug her tighter to his side, his gaunt ribs, his beating swelling joyous heart. By God we're gonna get there, Ellsworth, we're a-gonna make it yet, I tell you, there's no way they can stop us now.

The child will gaze ahead in wonder, her dark eyes shining in fear and excitement, long black hair whipped wildly by the stream of air pouring in mad invisible vortices over the windshield, around their shoulders, across and through the baggage—suitcases, duffel bags, stuffed bears, bedrolls, books, boxes, sacks full of food— jammed in a fury of haste within the well and upon the backseat of their open, boat-shaped, rollicking automobile.

Self-propelled. The open boat on the desert sea. A fat faded near-antique almost-classic but wrinkled motorcar, of dubious value, doubtful make, uncertain age but clearly a piece of iron. Detroit iron. A fringe of mud hangs from the fenders. Hubcaps missing. One savage portside sideswipe scar from headlight to tail fin reveals the cancer of rust beneath the veneer of baked-on bleached-out once purple-hued enamel. A repaint job. Hillbilly overhaul. The pimp-sized convertible, the rednecked dreamboat. Choice of any honest country boy with big feet, a limber cock, a lank frame too long in the torso.

He'll lift his eyes from the girl to the road to the rearview mirror and its image: blue-black highway tapering off into the eastern dark. An empty highway at the moment: no red glare or blinking blue of police, no menacing array of tractor-trailer rig, nothing and nobody whatsoever following. At the moment. But the wicked flee pursued or not.

Once we get there, he'll say, speaking hoarsely but loudly above the rush of wind, we'll hide this junkyard wreck under the willows down by the crick for a year or so, give it some rest till Grandma cools down, let them pistons get some rest, we'll ride the horses into town, you and me, yessir and we'll eat good too I tell you.

Where do you mean, Daddy? What horses?

Most anywhere, honey, anywhere. Anywhere west of the Rio Grandee. There's Cherry Creek under Aztec Mountain. There's Bisbee, good sensible hippie town, we're welcome there. Maybe Mexican Hat up in Utah. Over there under the cottonwoods along that old Green River south of Ruby Ranch. Honey, I know a hundred places. Lone Pine in the Owens Valley. Or why not Big Pine or Independence? There's Arcata on the coast. And just a little ways beyond sets that big island down below. Brisbane's a good city. You might like Alice Springs. Or what the hell, go all the way to Eighty Mile Beach, the Hamersley Mountains, the Black Swan River, watch the sun go down over the bloody Indian Ocean toward bleeding bloody Africa where our troubles all began. Look in my eyes, Ellie, tell me—

He'll check the road once more, let up on the gas pedal, lean toward her, smiling, and stare straight into her big solemn hazel-brown eyes with his red iron-flecked squinting happy eyes and say, What do you see, Ellie?

She will look hard, concentrating, thinking.

Hey? What do you see?

Dad? Well . . . you're crazy as a bedbug.

Yeah yeah sure, but what else? He'll glance at the highway again, no traffic in sight, nothing ahead but the fiery glow of the city, the glare of the descending sun, the dust, the smoke, and return his gaze to his daughter. What do you see, sweetheart? Look me in the eyeballs ball to ball and tell me what you see.

I see a crazy cuckoo Daddy.

What else?

Her nose is sunburned, starting to peel, her lips chapped, but she will crack a tiny smile. A growing smile, matching his. I see . . . lights. Little lights jumping around.

Dancing. He'll check the road again, the car slowing, wheels grating on the tin cans and gravel of the shoulder, and look once more into the girl's eyes. What color?

She'll laugh. Red.

Right. And what does red mean?

She will laugh again. Same as always: full speed ahead.

Right, he will yell, you got it. He'll pull her small body firmly to his side, steer back onto the pavement, press the pedal to the floor.

The big brute motor will grumble like a lion, old, tired, hesitating, then catch fire and roar, eight-hearted in its block of iron, driving onward, westward always, into the sun. . . .